T0043305

Classic Tales
of Mystery

Word Cloud Classics
San Diego

Canterbury Classics

An imprint of Printers Row Publishing Group

10350 Barnes Canyon Road, Suite 100, San Diego, CA 92121

www.canterburyclassicsbooks.com • mail@canterburyclassicsbooks.com

© 2019 Canterbury Classics

All rights reserved. No part of this publication may be reproduced, distributed, or transmitted in any form or by any means, including photocopying, recording, or other electronic or mechanical methods, without the prior written permission of the publisher, except in the case of brief quotations embodied in critical reviews and certain other noncommercial uses permitted by copyright law.

Printers Row Publishing Group is a division of Readerlink Distribution Services, LLC. Canterbury Classics and Word Cloud Classics are registered trademarks of Readerlink Distribution Services, LLC.

Correspondence concerning the content of this book should be addressed to Canterbury Classics, Editorial Department, at the above address.

Publisher: Peter Norton • Associate Publisher: Ana Parker
Senior Developmental Editor: April Graham Farr
Editor: Dan Mansfield • Editorial Team: Traci Douglas
Senior Product Manager: Kathryn C. Dalby
Production Team: Jonathan Lopes, Rusty von Dyl

Cover and endpaper designer: Catherine Courtenaye

Library of Congress Cataloging-in-Publication Data

Title: Classic tales of mystery.
Description: San Diego : Word Cloud Classics, [2019] | Summary: "Classic Tales of Mystery contains eight famous stories from well-known authors, including Agatha Christie, Arthur Conan Doyle, and G. K. Chesterton. Each story presents the reader with a puzzle that can be solved only through logic and deduction, a hallmark of classic detective tales. Famous sleuths-including Hercule Poirot and Sherlock Holmes-have unique personalities that endear them to readers across the world, which has allowed them to maintain their superstar status to the present day"-- Provided by publisher.
Identifiers: LCCN 2019027050 (print) | LCCN 2019027051 (ebook) | ISBN 9781645171539 (paperback) | ISBN 9781645171829 (ebook)
Subjects: LCSH: Detective and mystery stories.
Classification: LCC PN6071.D45 C54 2019 (print) | LCC PN6071.D45 (ebook) | DDC 808.83/872--dc23
LC record available at https://lccn.loc.gov/2019027050
LC ebook record available at https://lccn.loc.gov/2019027051

PRINTED IN CHINA
23 22 21 20 19 1 2 3 4 5

Editor's Note: These works have been published in their original form to preserve the authors' intent and style.

CONTENTS

The Murder on the Links

Agatha Christie

1. A Fellow Traveller

I believe that a well-known anecdote exists to the effect that a young writer, determined to make the commencement of his story forcible and original enough to catch and rivet the attention of the most blasé of editors, penned the following sentence:

"'Hell!' said the Duchess."

Strangely enough, this tale of mine opens in much the same fashion. Only the lady who gave utterance to the exclamation was not a Duchess!

It was a day in early June. I had been transacting some business in Paris and was returning by the morning service to London where I was still sharing rooms with my old friend, the Belgian ex-detective, Hercule Poirot.

The Calais express was singularly empty—in fact, my own compartment held only one other traveller. I had made a somewhat hurried departure from the hotel and was busy assuring myself that I had duly collected all my traps when the train started. Up till then I had hardly noticed my companion, but I was now violently recalled to the fact of her existence. Jumping up from her seat, she let down the window and stuck her head out, withdrawing it a moment later with the brief and forcible ejaculation "Hell!"

Now I am old-fashioned. A woman, I consider, should be womanly. I have no patience with the modern neurotic girl who jazzes from morning to night, smokes like a chimney, and uses language which would make a Billingsgate fishwoman blush!

I looked up now, frowning slightly, into a pretty, impudent face, surmounted by a rakish little red hat. A thick cluster of black curls hid each ear. I judged that she was little more than seventeen, but her face was covered with powder, and her lips were quite impossibly scarlet.

Nothing abashed, she returned my glance, and executed an expressive grimace.

"Dear me, we've shocked the kind gentleman!" she observed to an imaginary audience. "I apologize for my language! Most unladylike, and all that, but Oh, Lord, there's reason enough for it! Do you know I've lost my only sister?"

"Really?" I said politely. "How unfortunate."

"He disapproves!" remarked the lady. "He disapproves utterly—of me, and my sister—which last is unfair, because he hasn't seen her!"

I opened my mouth, but she forestalled me.

"Say no more! Nobody loves me! I shall go into the garden and eat worms! Boohoo! I am crushed!"

She buried herself behind a large comic French paper. In a minute or two I saw her eyes stealthily peeping at me over the top. In spite of myself I could not help smiling, and in a minute she had tossed the paper aside, and had burst into a merry peal of laughter.

"I knew you weren't such a mutt as you looked," she cried.

Her laughter was so infectious that I could not help joining in, though I hardly cared for the word "mutt." The girl was certainly all that I most disliked, but that was no reason why I should make myself ridiculous by my attitude. I prepared to unbend. After all, she was decidedly pretty . . .

"There! Now we're friends!" declared the minx. "Say you're sorry about my sister—"

"I am desolated!"

"That's a good boy!"

"Let me finish. I was going to add that, although I am desolated, I can manage to put up with her absence very well." I made a little bow.

But this most unaccountable of damsels frowned and shook her head.

"Cut it out. I prefer the 'dignified disapproval' stunt. Oh, your face! 'Not one of us,' it said. And you were right there—though, mind you, it's pretty hard to tell nowadays. It's not every one who can distinguish between a demi and a duchess. There now, I believe I've shocked you again! You've been dug out of the backwoods, you have. Not that I mind that. We could do with a few more of your sort. I just hate a fellow who gets fresh. It makes me mad."

She shook her head vigorously.

"What are you like when you're mad?" I inquired with a smile.

"A regular little devil! Don't care what I say, or what I do, either! I nearly did a chap in once. Yes, really. He'd have deserved it too. Italian blood I've got. I shall get into trouble one of these days."

"Well," I begged, "don't get mad with me."

"I shan't. I like you—did the first moment I set eyes on you. But you looked so disapproving that I never thought we should make friends."

"Well, we have. Tell me something about yourself."

"I'm an actress. No—not the kind you're thinking of, lunching at the Savoy covered with jewellery, and with their photograph in every paper saying how much they love Madame So and So's face cream. I've been on the boards since I was a kid of six—tumbling."

"I beg your pardon," I said puzzled.

"Haven't you seen child acrobats?"

"Oh, I understand."

"I'm American born, but I've spent most of my life in England. We got a new show now—"

"We?"

"My sister and I. Sort of song and dance, and a bit of patter, and a dash of the old business thrown in. It's quite a new idea, and it hits them every time. There's to be money in it—"

My new acquaintance leaned forward, and discoursed volubly, a great many of her terms being quite unintelligible to me. Yet I found myself evincing an increasing interest in her. She seemed such a curious mixture of child and woman. Though perfectly worldly-wise, and able, as she expressed it, to take care of herself, there was yet something curiously ingenuous in her single-minded attitude towards life, and her whole-hearted determination to "make good." This glimpse of a world unknown to me was not without its charm, and I enjoyed seeing her vivid little face light up as she talked.

We passed through Amiens. The name awakened many memories. My companion seemed to have an intuitive knowledge of what was in my mind.

"Thinking of the War?"

I nodded.

"You were through it, I suppose?"

"Pretty well. I was wounded once, and after the Somme they invalided me out altogether. I had a half fledged Army job for a bit. I'm a sort of private secretary now to an M. P."

"My! That's brainy!"

"No, it isn't. There's really awfully little to do. Usually a couple of hours every day sees me through. It's dull work too. In fact, I don't know what I should do if I hadn't got something to fall back upon."

"Don't say you collect bugs!"

"No. I share rooms with a very interesting man. He's a Belgian—an ex-detective. He's set up as a private detective in London, and he's doing extraordinarily well. He's really a very marvellous little man. Time and again he has proved to be right where the official police have failed."

My companion listened with widening eyes.

"Isn't that interesting, now? I just adore crime. I go to all the mysteries on the movies. And when there's a murder on I just devour the papers."

"Do you remember the Styles Case?" I asked.

"Let me see, was that the old lady who was poisoned? Somewhere down in Essex?"

I nodded.

"That was Poirot's first big case. Undoubtedly, but for him, the murderer would have escaped scot-free. It was a most wonderful bit of detective work."

Warming to my subject, I ran over the heads of the affair, working up to the triumphant and unexpected denouement. The girl listened spellbound. In fact, we were so absorbed that the train drew into Calais station before we realized it.

"My goodness gracious me!" cried my companion. "Where's my powder-puff?"

She proceeded to bedaub her face liberally, and then applied a stick of lip salve to her lips, observing the effect in a small pocket glass, and betraying not the faintest sign of self-consciousness.

"I say," I hesitated. "I dare say it's cheek on my part, but why do all that sort of thing?"

The girl paused in her operations, and stared at me with undisguised surprise.

"It isn't as though you weren't so pretty that you can afford to do without it," I said stammeringly.

"My dear boy! I've got to do it. All the girls do. Think I want to look like a little frump up from the country?" She took one last look in the mirror, smiled approval, and put it and her vanity-box away in her bag. "That's better. Keeping up appearances is a bit of a fag, I grant, but if a girl respects herself it's up to her not to let herself get slack."

To this essentially moral sentiment, I had no reply. A point of view makes a great difference.

I secured a couple of porters, and we alighted on the platform. My companion held out her hand.

"Good-bye, and I'll mind my language better in future."

"Oh, but surely you'll let me look after you on the boat?"

"Mayn't be on the boat. I've got to see whether that sister of mine got aboard after all anywhere. But thanks all the same."

"Oh, but we're going to meet again, surely? I—" I hesitated. "I want to meet your sister."

We both laughed.

"That's real nice of you. I'll tell her what you say. But I don't fancy we'll meet again. You've been very good to me on the journey, especially after I cheeked you as I did. But what your face expressed first thing is quite true. I'm not your kind. And that brings trouble—*I* know that well enough . . ."

Her face changed. For the moment all the light-hearted gaiety died out of it. It looked angry—revengeful . . .

"So good-bye," she finished, in a lighter tone.

"Aren't you even going to tell me your name?" I cried, as she turned away.

She looked over her shoulder. A dimple appeared in each cheek. She was like a lovely picture by Greuze.

"Cinderella," she said, and laughed.

But little did I think when and how I should see Cinderella again.

2. An Appeal for Help

It was five minutes past nine when I entered our joint sitting-room for breakfast on the following morning.

My friend Poirot, exact to the minute as usual, was just tapping the shell of his second egg.

He beamed upon me as I entered.

"You have slept well, yes? You have recovered from the crossing so terrible? It is a marvel, almost you are exact this morning. *Pardon*, but your tie is not symmetrical. Permit that I rearrange him."

Elsewhere, I have described Hercule Poirot. An extraordinary little man! Height, five feet four inches, egg-shaped head carried a little to one side, eyes that shone green when he was excited, stiff military moustache, air of dignity immense! He was neat and dandified in appearance. For neatness of any kind, he had an absolute passion. To see an ornament set crooked, or a speck of dust, or a slight disarray in one's attire, was torture to the little man until he could ease his feelings by remedying the matter. "Order" and "Method" were his gods. He had a certain disdain for tangible evidence, such as footprints and cigarette ash, and would maintain that, taken by themselves, they would never enable a detective to solve a problem. Then he would tap his egg-shaped head with absurd complacency, and remark with great satisfaction: "The true work, it is done from *within. The little grey cells*—remember always the little grey cells, *mon ami*!"

I slipped into my seat, and remarked idly, in answer to Poirot's greeting, that an hour's sea passage from Calais to Dover could hardly be dignified by the epithet "terrible."

Poirot waved his egg-spoon in vigorous refutation of my remark.

"*Du tout*! If for an hour one experiences sensations and emotions of the most terrible, one has lived many hours! Does not one of your English poets say that time is counted, not by hours, but by heart-beats?"

"I fancy Browning was referring to something more romantic than sea sickness, though."

"Because he was an Englishman, an Islander to whom *la Manche* was nothing. Oh, you English! With *nous autres* it is different. Figure to yourself that a lady of my acquaintance at the beginning of the war fled to Ostend. There she had a terrible crisis of the nerves. Impossible to escape further except by crossing the sea! And she had a horror—*mais une horreur*!—of the sea! What was she to do? Daily *les Boches* were drawing nearer. Imagine to yourself the terrible situation!"

"What did she do?" I inquired curiously.

"Fortunately her husband was *homme pratique*. He was also very calm, the crises of the nerves, they affected him not. *Il l'a emportée simplement*! Naturally when she reached England she was prostrate, but she still breathed."

Poirot shook his head seriously. I composed my face as best I could.

Suddenly he stiffened and pointed a dramatic finger at the toast rack.

"Ah, par exemple, c'est trop fort!" he cried.

"What is it?"

"This piece of toast. You remark him not?" He whipped the offender out of the rack, and held it up for me to examine.

"Is it square? No. Is it a triangle? Again no. Is it even round? No. Is it of any shape remotely pleasing to the eye? What symmetry have we here? None."

"It's cut from a cottage loaf," I explained soothingly.

Poirot threw me a withering glance.

"What an intelligence has my friend Hastings!" he exclaimed sarcastically. "Comprehend you not that I have forbidden such a loaf—a loaf haphazard and shapeless, that no baker should permit himself to bake!"

I endeavoured to distract his mind.

"Anything interesting come by the post?"

Poirot shook his head with a dissatisfied air.

"I have not yet examined my letters, but nothing of interest arrives nowadays. The great criminals, the criminals of method, they do not exist. The cases I have been employed upon lately were *banal* to the last degree. In verity I am reduced to recovering lost lap-dogs for fashionable ladies! The last problem that presented any interest was that intricate little affair of the Yardly diamond, and that was—how many months ago, my friend?"

He shook his head despondently, and I roared with laughter.

"Cheer up, Poirot, the luck will change. Open your letters. For all you know, there may be a great case looming on the horizon."

Poirot smiled, and taking up the neat little letter opener with which he opened his correspondence he slit the tops of the several envelopes that lay by his plate.

"A bill. Another bill. It is that I grow extravagant in my old age. Aha! a note from Japp."

"Yes?" pricked up my ears. The Scotland Yard Inspector had more than once introduced us to an interesting case.

"He merely thanks me (in his fashion) for a little point in the Aberystwyth Case on which I was able to set him right. I am delighted to have been of service to him."

"How does he thank you?" I asked curiously, for I knew my Japp.

"He is kind enough to say that I am a wonderful sport for my age, and that he was glad to have had the chance of letting me in on the case."

This was so typical of Japp, that I could not forbear a chuckle. Poirot continued to read his correspondence placidly.

"A suggestion that I should give a lecture to our local Boy Scouts. The Countess of Forfanock will be obliged if I will call and see her. Another lap-dog without doubt! And now for the last. Ah—"

I looked up, quick to notice the change of tone. Poirot was reading attentively. In a minute he tossed the sheet over to me.

"This is out of the ordinary, *mon ami*. Read for yourself."

The letter was written on a foreign type of paper, in a bold characteristic hand:

> *Villa Geneviève*
> *Merlinville-sur-Mer*
> *France*

DEAR SIR,

I am in need of the services of a detective and, for reasons which I will give you later, do not wish to call in the official police. I have heard of you from several quarters, and all reports go to show that you are not only a man of decided ability, but one who also knows how to be discreet. I do not wish to trust details to the post, but, on account of a secret I possess, I go in daily fear of my life. I am convinced that the danger is imminent, and therefore I beg that you will lose no time in crossing to France. I will send a car to meet you at Calais, if you will wire me when you are arriving. I shall be obliged if you will drop all cases you have on hand, and devote yourself solely to my interests. I am prepared to pay any compensation necessary. I shall probably need your services for a considerable period of time, as it may be necessary for you to go out to Santiago, where I spent several years of my life. I shall be content for you to name your own fee.

Assuring you once more that the matter is *urgent*,

Yours faithfully,

P. T. Renauld

Below the signature was a hastily scrawled line, almost illegible:

For God's sake, come!

I handed the letter back with quickened pulses.

"At last!" I said. "Here is something distinctly out of the ordinary."

"Yes, indeed," said Poirot meditatively.

"You will go of course," I continued.

Poirot nodded. He was thinking deeply. Finally he seemed to make up his mind, and glanced up at the clock. His face was very grave.

"See you, my friend, there is no time to lose. The Continental express leaves Victoria at 11 o'clock. Do not agitate yourself. There is plenty of time. We can allow ten minutes for discussion. You accompany me, *n'est-ce pas?*"

"Well—"

"You told me yourself that your employer needed you not for the next few weeks."

"Oh, that's all right. But this Mr. Renauld hints strongly that his business is private."

"Ta-ta-ta. I will manage M. Renauld. By the way, I seem to know the name?"

"There's a well-known South American millionaire fellow. His name's Renauld. I don't know whether it could be the same."

"But without doubt. That explains the mention of Santiago. Santiago is in Chile, and Chile it is in South America! Ah, but we progress finely."

"Dear me, Poirot," I said, my excitement rising, "I smell some goodly shekels in this. If we succeed, we shall make our fortunes!"

"Do not be too sure of that, my friend. A rich man and his money are not so easily parted. Me, I have seen a well-known millionaire turn out a tramful of people to seek for a dropped halfpenny."

I acknowledged the wisdom of this.

"In any case," continued Poirot, "it is not the money which attracts me here. Certainly it will be pleasant to have *carte blanche* in our investigations; one can be sure that way of wasting no time, but it is something a little bizarre in this problem which arouses my interest. You remarked the postscript? How did it strike you?"

I considered.

"Clearly he wrote the letter keeping himself well in hand, but at the end his self-control snapped and, on the impulse of the moment, he scrawled those four desperate words."

But my friend shook his head energetically.

"You are in error. See you not that while the ink of the signature is nearly black, that of the postscript is quite pale?"

"Well?" I said puzzled.

13

"*Mon Dieu, mon ami*, but use your little grey cells! Is it not obvious? M. Renauld wrote his letter. Without blotting it, he reread it carefully. Then, not on impulse, but deliberately, he added those last words, and blotted the sheet."

"But why?"

"*Parbleu*! so that it should produce the effect upon me that it has upon you."

"What?"

"*Mais, oui*—to make sure of my coming! He reread the letter and was dissatisfied. It was not strong enough!"

He paused, and then added softly, his eyes shining with that green light that always betokened inward excitement: "And so, *mon ami*, since that postscript was added, not on impulse, but soberly, in cold blood, the urgency is very great, and we must reach him as soon as possible."

"Merlinville," I murmured thoughtfully. "I've heard of it, I think."

Poirot nodded.

"It is a quiet little place—but chic! It lies about midway between Bolougne and Calais. It is rapidly becoming the fashion. Rich English people who wish to be quiet are taking it up. M. Renauld has a house in England, I suppose?"

"Yes, in Rutland Gate, as far as I remember. Also a big place in the country, somewhere in Hertfordshire. But I really know very little about him, he doesn't do much in a social way. I believe he has large South American interests in the City, and has spent most of his life out in Chile and the Argentine."

"Well, we shall hear all details from the man himself. Come, let us pack. A small suit-case each, and then a taxi to Victoria."

"And the Countess?" I inquired with a smile.

"Ah! *je m'en fiche*! Her case was certainly not interesting."

"Why so sure of that?"

"Because in that case she would have come, not written. A woman cannot wait—always remember that, Hastings."

Eleven o'clock saw our departure from Victoria on our way to Dover. Before starting Poirot had despatched a telegram to Mr. Renauld giving the time of our arrival at Calais. "I'm surprised you haven't invested in a few bottles of some sea sick remedy, Poirot," I observed maliciously, as I recalled our conversation at breakfast.

My friend, who was anxiously scanning the weather, turned a reproachful face upon me.

"Is it that you have forgotten the method most excellent of Laverguier? His system, I practise it always. One balances oneself, if you remember, turning the head from left to right, breathing in and out, counting six between each breath."

"H'm," I demurred. "You'll be rather tired of balancing yourself and counting six by the time you get to Santiago, or Buenos Aires, or wherever it is you land."

"*Quelle idée*! You do not figure to yourself that I shall go to Santiago?"

"Mr. Renauld suggests it in his letter."

"He did not know the methods of Hercule Poirot. I do not run to and fro, making journeys, and agitating myself. My work is done from within—*here*—" he tapped his forehead significantly.

As usual, this remark roused my argumentative faculty.

"It's all very well, Poirot, but I think you are falling into the habit of despising certain things too much. A finger-print has led sometimes to the arrest and conviction of a murderer."

"And has, without doubt, hanged more than one innocent man," remarked Poirot dryly.

"But surely the study of finger-prints and footprints, cigarette ash, different kinds of mud, and other clues that comprise the minute observation of details—all these are of vital importance?"

"But certainly. I have never said otherwise. The trained observer, the expert, without doubt he is useful! But the others, the Hercules Poirots, they are above the experts! To them the experts bring the facts, their business is the method of the crime, its logical deduction, the proper sequence and order of the facts; above all, the true psychology of the case. You have hunted the fox, yes?"

"I have hunted a bit, now and again," I said, rather bewildered by this abrupt change of subject. "Why?"

"*Eh bien*, this hunting of the fox, you need the dogs, no?"

"Hounds," I corrected gently. "Yes, of course."

"But yet," Poirot wagged his finger at me. "You did not descend from your horse and run along the ground smelling with your nose and uttering loud Ow Ows?"

In spite of myself I laughed immoderately. Poirot nodded in a satisfied manner.

"So. You leave the work of the d——— hounds to the hounds. Yet you demand that I, Hercule Poirot, should make myself ridiculous by lying down (possibly on damp grass) to study hypothetical footprints, and should scoop up cigarette ash when I do not know one kind from the other. Remember the Plymouth Express mystery. The good Japp departed to make a survey of the railway line. When he returned, I, without having moved from my apartments, was able to tell him exactly what he had found."

"So you are of the opinion that Japp wasted his time."

"Not at all, since his evidence confirmed my theory. But *I* should have wasted my time if *I* had gone. It is the same with so called 'experts.' Remember the handwriting testimony in the Cavendish Case. One counsel's questioning brings out testimony as to the resemblances, the defence brings evidence to show dissimilarity. All the language is very technical. And the result? What we all knew in the first place. The writing was very like that of John Cavendish. And the psychological mind is faced with the question 'Why?' Because it was actually his? Or because some one wished us to think it was his? I answered that question, *mon ami*, and answered it correctly."

And Poirot, having effectually silenced, if not convinced me, leaned back with a satisfied air.

On the boat, I knew better than to disturb my friend's solitude. The weather was gorgeous, and the sea as smooth as the proverbial mill-pond, so I was hardly surprised to hear that Laverguier's method had once more justified itself when a smiling Poirot joined me on disembarking at Calais. A disappointment was in store for us, as no car had been sent to meet us, but Poirot put this down to his telegram having been delayed in transit.

"Since it is *carte blanche*, we will hire a car," he said cheerfully. And a few minutes later saw us creaking and jolting along, in the most ramshackle of automobiles that ever plied for hire, in the direction of Merlinville.

My spirits were at their highest.

"What gorgeous air!" I exclaimed. "This promises to be a delightful trip."

"For you, yes. For me, I have work to do, remember, at our journey's end."

"Bah!" I said cheerfully. "You will discover all, ensure this Mr. Renauld's safety, run the would-be assassins to earth, and all will finish in a blaze of glory."

"You are sanguine, my friend."

"Yes, I feel absolutely assured of success. Are you not the one and only Hercule Poirot?"

But my little friend did not rise to the bait. He was observing me gravely.

"You are what the Scotch people call 'fey,' Hastings. It presages disaster."

"Nonsense. At any rate, you do not share my feelings."

"No, but I am afraid."

"Afraid of what?"

"I do not know. But I have a premonition—a *je ne sais quoi*!"

He spoke so gravely, that I was impressed in spite of myself.

"I have a feeling," he said slowly, "that this is going to be a big affair—a long, troublesome problem that will not be easy to work out."

I would have questioned him further, but we were just coming into the little town of Merlinville, and we slowed up to inquire the way to the Villa Geneviève.

"Straight on, monsieur, through the town. The Villa Geneviève is about half a mile the other side. You cannot miss it. A big Villa, overlooking the sea."

We thanked our informant, and drove on, leaving the town behind. A fork in the road brought us to a second halt. A peasant was trudging towards us, and we waited for him to come up to us in order to ask the way again. There was a tiny Villa standing right by the road, but it was too small and dilapidated to be the one we wanted. As we waited, the gate of it swung open and a girl came out.

The peasant was passing us now, and the driver leaned forward from his seat and asked for direction.

"The Villa Geneviève? Just a few steps up this road to the right, monsieur. You could see it if it were not for the curve."

The chauffeur thanked him, and started the car again. My eyes were fascinated by the girl who still stood, with one hand on the gate, watching us. I am an admirer of beauty, and here was one whom nobody could have passed without remark. Very tall, with the proportions of a young goddess, her uncovered golden head gleaming in the sunlight, I swore to myself that she was one of the most beautiful girls I had ever seen. As we swung up the rough road, I turned my head to look after her.

"By Jove, Poirot," I exclaimed, "did you see that young goddess."

Poirot raised his eyebrows.

"*Ça commence!*" he murmured. "Already you have seen a goddess!"

"But, hang it all, wasn't she?"

"Possibly. I did not remark the fact."

"Surely you noticed her?"

"*Mon ami*, two people rarely see the same thing. You, for instance, saw a goddess. I—" he hesitated.

"Yes?"

"I saw only a girl with anxious eyes," said Poirot gravely.

But at that moment we drew up at a big green gate, and, simultaneously, we both uttered an exclamation. Before it stood an imposing *sergent de ville*. He held up his hand to bar our way.

"You cannot pass, monsieurs."

"But we wish to see Mr. Renauld," I cried. "We have an appointment. This is his Villa, isn't it?"

"Yes, monsieur, but—"

Poirot leaned forward.

"But what?"

"M. Renauld was murdered this morning."

3. *At the Villa Geneviève*

In a moment Poirot had leapt from the car, his eyes blazing with excitement. He caught the man by the shoulder.

"What is that you say? Murdered? When? How?"

The *sergent de ville* drew himself up.

"I cannot answer any questions, monsieur."

"True. I comprehend." Poirot reflected for a minute. "The Commissary of Police, he is without doubt within?"

"Yes, monsieur."

Poirot took out a card, and scribbled a few words on it.

"*Voilà!* Will you have the goodness to see that this card is sent in to the commissary at once?"

The man took it and, turning his head over his shoulder, whistled. In a few seconds a comrade joined him and was handed Poirot's message. There was a wait of some minutes, and then a short stout man with a huge moustache came bustling down to the gate. The *sergent de ville* saluted and stood aside.

"My dear M. Poirot," cried the new-comer, "I am delighted to see you. Your arrival is most opportune."

Poirot's face had lighted up.

"M. Bex! This is indeed a pleasure." He turned to me. "This is an English friend of mine, Captain Hastings—M. Lucien Bex."

The commissary and I bowed to each other ceremoniously, then M. Bex turned once more to Poirot.

"*Mon vieux*, I have not seen you since 1909, that time in Ostend. I heard that you had left the Force?"

"So I have. I run a private business in London."

"And you say you have information to give which may assist us?"

"Possibly you know it already. You were aware that I had been sent for?"

"No. By whom?"

"The dead man. It seems he knew an attempt was going to be made on his life. Unfortunately he sent for me too late."

"*Sacré tonnerre!*" ejaculated the Frenchman. "So he foresaw his own murder? That upsets our theories considerably! But come inside."

He held the gate open, and we commenced walking towards the house. M. Bex continued to talk:

"The examining magistrate, M. Hautet, must hear of this at once. He has just finished examining the scene of the crime and is about to begin his interrogations. A charming man. You will like him. Most sympathetic. Original in his methods, but an excellent judge."

"When was the crime committed?" asked Poirot.

"The body was discovered this morning about nine o'clock. Madame Renauld's evidence, and that of the doctors goes to show that the death must have occurred about 2 a.m. But enter, I pray of you."

We had arrived at the steps which led up to the front door of the Villa. In the hall another *sergent de ville* was sitting. He rose at sight of the commissary.

"Where is M. Hautet now?" inquired the latter.

"In the *salon*, monsieur."

M. Bex opened a door to the left of the hall, and we passed in. M. Hautet and his clerk were sitting at a big round table. They looked up as we entered. The commissary introduced us, and explained our presence.

M. Hautet, the Juge d'Instruction, was a tall, gaunt man, with piercing dark eyes, and a neatly cut grey beard, which he had a habit of caressing as he talked. Standing by the mantelpiece was an elderly man, with slightly stooping shoulders, who was introduced to us as Dr. Durand.

"Most extraordinary," remarked M. Hautet, as the commissary finished speaking. "You have the letter here, monsieur?"

Poirot handed it to him, and the magistrate read it.

"H'm. He speaks of a secret. What a pity he was not more explicit. We are much indebted to you, M. Poirot. I hope you will do us the honour of assisting us in our investigations. Or are you obliged to return to London?"

"M. le juge, I propose to remain. I did not arrive in time to prevent my client's death, but I feel myself bound in honour to discover the assassin."

The magistrate bowed.

"These sentiments do you honour. Also, without doubt, Madame Renauld will wish to retain your services. We are expecting M. Giraud from the Sûreté in Paris any moment, and I am sure that you and he will be able to give each other mutual assistance in your investigations. In the meantime, I hope that you will do me the honour to be present at my interrogations, and I need hardly say that if there is any assistance you require it is at your disposal."

"I thank you, monsieur. You will comprehend that at present I am completely in the dark. I know nothing whatever."

M. Hautet nodded to the commissary, and the latter took up the tale:

"This morning, the old servant Françoise, on descending to start her work, found the front door ajar. Feeling a momentary alarm as to burglars, she looked into the dining-room, but seeing the silver was safe she thought no more about it, concluding that her master had, without doubt, risen early, and gone for a stroll."

"Pardon, monsieur, for interrupting, but was that a common practice of his?"

"No, it was not, but old Françoise has the common idea as regards the English—that they are mad, and liable to do the most unaccountable things at any moment! Going to call her mistress as usual, a younger maid, Léonie, was horrified to discover her gagged and bound, and almost at the same moment news was brought that M. Renauld's body had been discovered, stone dead, stabbed in the back."

"Where?"

"That is one of the most extraordinary features of the case. M. Poirot, the body was lying, face downwards, *in an open grave.*"

"What?"

"Yes. The pit was freshly dug—just a few yards outside the boundary of the Villa grounds."

"And he had been dead—how long?"

Dr. Durand answered this.

"I examined the body this morning at ten o'clock. Death must have taken place at least seven, and possibly ten hours previously."

"H'm, that fixes it at between midnight and 3 a.m."

"Exactly, and Madame Renauld's evidence places it at after 2 a.m. which narrows the field still further. Death must have been instantaneous, and naturally could not have been self-inflicted."

Poirot nodded, and the commissary resumed:

"Madame Renauld was hastily freed from the cords that bound her by the horrified servants. She was in a terrible condition of weakness, almost unconscious from the pain of her bonds. It appears that two masked men entered the bedroom, gagged and bound her, whilst forcibly abducting her husband. This we know at second hand from the servants. On hearing the tragic news, she fell at once into an alarming state of agitation. On arrival, Dr. Durand immediately prescribed a sedative, and we have not yet been able to question her. But without doubt she will awake more calm, and be equal to bearing the strain of the interrogation."

The commissary paused.

"And the inmates of the house, monsieur?"

"There is old Françoise, the housekeeper, she lived for many years with the former owners of the Villa Geneviève. Then there are two young girls, sisters, Denise and Léonie Oulard. Their home is in Merlinville, and they come of the most respectable parents. Then there is the chauffeur whom M. Renauld brought over from England with him, but he is away on a holiday. Finally there are Madame Renauld and her son, M. Jack Renauld. He, too, is away from home at present."

Poirot bowed his head. M. Hautet spoke:

"Marchaud!"

The *sergent de ville* appeared.

"Bring in the woman Françoise."

The man saluted, and disappeared. In a moment or two, he returned, escorting the frightened Françoise.

"Your name is Françoise Arrichet?"

"Yes, monsieur."

"You have been a long time in service at the Villa Geneviève?"

"Eleven years with Madame la Vicomtesse. Then when she sold the Villa this spring, I consented to remain on with the English milor'. Never did I imagine—"

The magistrate cut her short.

"Without doubt, without doubt. Now, Françoise, in this matter of the front door, whose business was it to fasten it at night?"

"Mine, monsieur. Always I saw to it myself."

"And last night?"

"I fastened it as usual."

"You are sure of that?"

"I swear it by the blessed saints, monsieur."

23

"What time would that be?"

"The same time as usual, half-past ten, monsieur."

"What about the rest of the household, had they gone up to bed?"

"Madame had retired some time before. Denise and Léonie went up with me. Monsieur was still in his study."

"Then, if any one unfastened the door afterwards, it must have been M. Renauld himself?"

Françoise shrugged her broad shoulders.

"What should he do that for? With robbers and assassins passing every minute! A nice idea! Monsieur was not an imbecile. It is not as though he had had to let *cette dame* out—"

The magistrate interrupted sharply:

"*Cette dame*? What lady do you mean?"

"Why, the lady who came to see him."

"Had a lady been to see him that evening?"

"But yes, monsieur—and many other evenings as well."

"Who was she? Did you know her?"

A rather cunning look spread over the woman's face. "How should I know who it was?" she grumbled. "I did not let her in last night."

"Aha!" roared the examining magistrate, bringing his hand down with a bang on the table. "You would trifle with the police, would you? I demand that you tell me at once the name of this woman who came to visit M. Renauld in the evenings."

"The police—the police," grumbled Françoise. "Never did I think that I should be mixed up with the police. But I know well enough who she was. It was Madame Daubreuil."

The commissary uttered an exclamation, and leaned forward as though in utter astonishment.

"Madame Daubreuil—from the Villa Marguerite just down the road?"

"That is what I said, monsieur. Oh, she is a pretty one, *cellela*!" The old woman tossed her head scornfully.

"Madame Daubreuil," murmured the commissary. "Impossible."

"*Voilà*," grumbled Françoise. "That is all you get for telling the truth."

"Not at all," said the examining magistrate soothingly. "We were surprised, that is all. Madame Daubreuil then, and Monsieur Renauld, they were—" he paused delicately. "Eh? It was that without doubt?"

"How should I know? But what will you? Monsieur, he was *milord anglais—très riche*—and Madame Daubreuil, she was poor, that one—and *très chic* for all that she lives so quietly with her daughter. Not a doubt of it, she has had her history! She is no longer young, but *ma foi*! I who speak to you have seen the men's heads turn after her as she goes down the street. Besides lately, she has had more money to spend—all the town knows it. The little economies, they are at an end." And Françoise shook her head with an air of unalterable certainty.

M. Hautet stroked his beard reflectively.

"And Madame Renauld?" he asked at length. "How did she take this—friendship."

Françoise shrugged her shoulders.

"She was always most amiable—most polite. One would say that she suspected nothing. But all the same, is it not so, the heart suffers, monsieur? Day by day, I have watched Madame grow paler and thinner. She was not the same woman who arrived here a month ago. Monsieur, too, has changed. He also has had his worries. One could see that he was on the brink of a crisis of the nerves. And who could wonder, with an affair conducted such a fashion? No reticence, no discretion. *Style anglais*, without doubt!"

I bounded indignantly in my seat, but the examining magistrate was continuing his questions, undistracted by side issues.

"You say that M. Renauld had not to let Madame Daubreuil out? Had she left, then?"

"Yes, monsieur. I heard them come out of the study and go to the door. Monsieur said good night, and shut the door after her."

"What time was that?"

"About twenty-five minutes after ten, monsieur."

"Do you know when M. Renauld went to bed?"

"I heard him come up about ten minutes after we did. The stair creaks so that one hears every one who goes up and down."

"And that is all? You heard no sound of disturbance during the night?"

"Nothing whatever, monsieur."

"Which of the servants came down the first in the morning?"

"I did, monsieur. At once I saw the door swinging open."

"What about the other downstairs windows, were they all fastened?"

"Every one of them. There was nothing suspicious or out of place anywhere."

"Good, Françoise, you can go."

The old woman shuffled towards the door. On the threshold she looked back.

"I will tell you one thing, monsieur. That Madame Daubreuil she is a bad one! Oh, yes, one woman knows about another. She is a bad one, remember that." And, shaking her head sagely, Françoise left the room.

"Léonie Oulard," called the magistrate.

Léonie appeared dissolved in tears, and inclined to be hysterical. M. Hautet dealt with her adroitly. Her evidence was mainly concerned with the discovery of her mistress gagged and bound, of which she gave rather an exaggerated account. She, like Françoise, had heard nothing during the night.

Her sister, Denise, succeeded her. She agreed that her master had changed greatly of late.

"Every day he became more and more morose. He ate less. He was always depressed." But Denise had her own theory. "Without doubt it was the Mafia he had on his track! Two masked men—who else could it be? A terrible society that!"

"It is, of course, possible," said the magistrate smoothly. "Now, my girl, was it you who admitted Madame Daubreuil to the house last night?"

"Not *last* night, monsieur, the night before."

"But Françoise has just told us that Madame Daubreuil was here last night?"

"No, monsieur. A lady *did* come to see M. Renauld last night, but it was not Madame Daubreuil."

Surprised, the magistrate insisted, but the girl held firm. She knew Madame Daubreuil perfectly by sight. This lady was dark also, but shorter, and much younger. Nothing could shake her statement.

"Had you ever seen this lady before?"

"Never, monsieur." And then the girl added diffidently: "But I think she was English."

"English?"

"Yes, monsieur. She asked for M. Renauld in quite good French, but the accent—one can always tell it, *n'est-ce pas*? Besides when they came out of the study they were speaking in English."

"Did you hear what they said? Could you understand it, I mean?"

"Me, I speak the English very well," said Denise with pride. "The lady was speaking too fast for me to catch what she said, but I heard Monsieur's last words as he opened the door for her." She paused, and then repeated carefully and laboriously:

"'Yeas—yeas—butt for Gaud's saike go nauw!'"

"Yes, yes, but for God's sake go now!" repeated the magistrate.

He dismissed Denise and, after a moment or two for consideration, recalled Françoise. To her he propounded the question as to whether she had not made a mistake in fixing the night of Madame Daubreuil's visit. Françoise, however, proved unexpectedly obstinate. It was last night that Madame Daubreuil had come. Without a doubt it was she. Denise wished to make herself interesting, *voilà tout*! So she had cooked up this fine tale about a strange lady. Airing her knowledge of English too!

Probably Monsieur had never spoken that sentence in English at all, and even if he had, it proved nothing, for Madame Daubreuil spoke English perfectly, and generally used that language when talking to M. and Madame Renauld. "You see, M. Jack, the son of Monsieur, was usually here, and he spoke the French very badly."

The magistrate did not insist. Instead he inquired about the chauffeur, and learned that only yesterday, M. Renauld had declared that he was not likely to use the car, and that Masters might just as well take a holiday.

A perplexed frown was beginning to gather between Poirot's eyes.

"What is it?" I whispered.

He shook his head impatiently, and asked a question:

"Pardon, M. Bex, but without doubt M. Renauld could drive the car himself?"

The commissary looked over at Françoise, and the old woman replied promptly:

"No, Monsieur did not drive himself."

Poirot's frown deepened.

"I wish you would tell me what is worrying you," I said impatiently.

"See you not? In his letter M. Renauld speaks of sending the car for me to Calais."

"Perhaps he meant a hired car," I suggested.

"Doubtless that is so. But why hire a car when you have one of your own. Why choose yesterday to send away the chauffeur on a holiday—suddenly, at a moment's notice? Was it that for some reason he wanted him out of the way before we arrived?"

4. The Letter Signed "Bella"

Françoise had left the room. The magistrate was drumming thoughtfully on the table.

"M. Bex," he said at length, "here we have directly conflicting testimony. Which are we to believe, Françoise or Denise?"

"Denise," said the commissary decidedly. "It was she who let the visitor in. Françoise is old and obstinate, and has evidently taken a dislike to Madame Daubreuil. Besides, our own knowledge tends to show that Renauld was entangled with another woman."

"*Tiens*!" cried M. Hautet. "We have forgotten to inform M. Poirot of that." He searched amongst the papers on the table, and finally handed the one he was in search of to my friend. "This letter, M. Poirot, we found in the pocket of the dead man's overcoat."

Poirot took it and unfolded it. It was somewhat worn and crumbled, and was written in English in a rather unformed hand:

MY DEAREST ONE:

Why have you not written for so long? You do love me still, don't you? Your letters lately have been so different, cold and strange, and now this long silence. It makes me afraid. If you were to stop loving me! But that's impossible—what a silly kid I am—always imagining things! But if you *did* stop loving me, I don't know what I should do—kill myself perhaps! I couldn't live without you. Sometimes I fancy another woman is coming between us. Let her look out, that's all—and you too! I'd as soon kill you as let her have you! I mean it.

But there, I'm writing high-flown nonsense. You love me, and I love you—yes, love you, love you, love you!

Your own adoring

BELLA

There was no address or date. Poirot handed it back with a grave face.

"And the assumption is, M. le juge—?"

The examining magistrate shrugged his shoulders.

"Obviously M. Renauld was entangled with this Englishwoman—Bella. He comes over here, meets Madame Daubreuil, and starts an intrigue with her. He cools off to the other, and she instantly suspects something. This letter contains a distinct threat. M. Poirot, at first sight the case seemed simplicity itself. Jealousy! The fact that M. Renauld was stabbed in the back seemed to point distinctly to its being a woman's crime."

Poirot nodded.

"The stab in the back, yes—but not the grave! That was laborious work, hard work—no woman dug that grave, monsieur. That was a man's doing."

The commissary exclaimed excitedly: "Yes, yes, you are right. We did not think of that."

"As I said," continued M. Hautet, "at first sight the case seemed simple, but the masked men, and the letter you received from M. Renauld complicate matters. Here we seem to have an entirely different set of circumstances, with no relationship between the two. As regards the letter written to yourself, do you think it is possible that it referred in any way to this 'Bella,' and her threats?"

Poirot shook his head.

"Hardly. A man like M. Renauld, who has led an adventurous life in out-of-the-way places, would not be likely to ask for protection against a woman."

The examining magistrate nodded his head emphatically.

"My view exactly. Then we must look for the explanation of the letter—"

"In Santiago," finished the commissary. "I shall cable without delay to the police in that city, requesting full details of the murdered man's life out there, his love affairs, his business transactions, his friendships, and any enmities he may have incurred. It will be strange if, after that, we do not hold a clue to his mysterious murder."

The commissary looked round for approval.

"Excellent," said Poirot appreciatively.

"His wife, too, may be able to give us a pointer," added the magistrate.

"You have found no other letters from this Bella amongst M. Renauld's effects?" asked Poirot.

"No. Of course one of our first proceedings was to search through his private papers in the study. We found nothing of interest, however. All seemed square and above-board. The only thing at all out of the ordinary was his will. Here it is."

Poirot ran through the document.

"So. A legacy of a thousand pounds to Mr. Stonor—who is he, by the way?"

"M. Renauld's secretary. He remained in England, but was over here once or twice for a week-end."

"And everything else left unconditionally to his beloved wife, Eloise. Simply drawn up, but perfectly legal. Witnessed by the two servants, Denise and Françoise. Nothing so very unusual about that." He handed it back.

"Perhaps," began Bex, "you did not notice—"

"The date?" twinkled Poirot. "But yes, I noticed it. A fortnight ago. Possibly it marks his first intimation of danger. Many rich men die intestate through never considering the likelihood of their demise. But it is dangerous to draw conclusions prematurely. It points, however, to his having a real liking and fondness for his wife, in spite of his amorous intrigues."

"Yes," said M. Hautet doubtfully. "But it is possibly a little unfair on his son, since it leaves him entirely dependent on his mother. If she were to marry again, and her second husband obtained an ascendancy over her, this boy might never touch a penny of his father's money."

Poirot shrugged his shoulders.

"Man is a vain animal. M. Renauld figured to himself, without doubt, that his widow would never marry again. As to the son, it may have been a wise precaution to leave the money in his mother's hands. The sons of rich men are proverbially wild."

"It may be as you say. Now, M. Poirot, you would without doubt like to visit the scene of the crime. I am sorry that the body has been removed, but of course photographs have been taken from every conceivable angle, and will be at your disposal as soon as they are available."

"I thank you, monsieur, for all your courtesy."

The commissary rose.

"Come with me, monsieurs."

He opened the door, and bowed ceremoniously to Poirot to precede him. Poirot, with equal politeness, drew back and bowed to the commissary.

"Monsieur."

"Monsieur."

At last they got out into the hall.

"That room there, it is the study, *hein*?" asked Poirot suddenly, nodding towards the door opposite.

"Yes. You would like to see it?" He threw the door open as he spoke, and we entered.

The room which M. Renauld had chosen for his own particular use was small, but furnished with great taste and comfort. A businesslike writing desk, with many pigeon holes, stood in the window. Two large leather-covered armchairs faced the fireplace, and between them was a round table covered with the latest books and magazines. Bookshelves lined two of the walls, and at the end of the room opposite the window there was a handsome oak sideboard with a tantalus on top. The curtains and *portière* were of a soft dull green, and the carpet matched them in tone.

Poirot stood a moment talking in the room, then he stepped forward, passed his hand lightly over the backs of the leather chairs, picked up a magazine from the table, and drew a finger gingerly over the surface of the oak sideboard. His face expressed complete approval.

"No dust?" I asked, with a smile.

He beamed on me, appreciative of my knowledge of his peculiarities.

"Not a particle, *mon ami*! And for once, perhaps, it is a pity."

His sharp, birdlike eyes darted here and there.

"Ah!" he remarked suddenly, with an intonation of relief. "The hearth-rug is crooked," and he bent down to straighten it.

Suddenly he uttered an exclamation and rose. In his hand he held a small fragment of paper.

"In France, as in England," he remarked, "the domestics omit to sweep under the mats!"

Bex took the fragment from him, and I came closer to examine it.

"You recognize it—eh, Hastings?"

I shook my head, puzzled—and yet that particular shade of pink paper was very familiar.

The commissary's mental processes were quicker than mine.

"A fragment of a cheque," he exclaimed.

The piece of paper was roughly about two inches square. On it was written in ink the word "Duveen."

"*Bien*," said Bex. "This cheque was payable to, or drawn by, one named Duveen."

"The former, I fancy," said Poirot, "for, if I am not mistaken, the handwriting is that of M. Renauld."

That was soon established, by comparing it with a memorandum from the desk.

"Dear me," murmured the commissary, with a crestfallen air, "I really cannot imagine how I came to overlook this."

Poirot laughed.

"The moral of that is, always look under the mats! My friend Hastings here will tell you that anything in the least crooked is a torment to me. As soon as I saw that the hearth-rug was out of the straight, I said to myself: '*Tiens*! The leg of the chair caught it in being pushed back. Possibly there may be something beneath it which the good Françoise overlooked.'"

"Françoise?"

"Or Denise, or Léonie. Whoever did this room. Since there is no dust, the room *must* have been done this morning. I reconstruct the incident like this. Yesterday, possibly last night, M. Renauld drew a cheque to the order of some one named Duveen. Afterwards it was torn up, and scattered on the floor. This morning—" But M. Bex was already pulling impatiently at the bell.

Françoise answered it. Yes, there had been a lot of pieces of paper on the floor. What had she done with them? Put them in the kitchen stove of course! What else?

With a gesture of despair, Bex dismissed her. Then, his face lightening, he ran to the desk. In a minute he was hunting through the dead man's cheque book. Then he repeated his former gesture. The last counterfoil was blank.

"Courage!" cried Poirot, clapping him on the back. "Without doubt, Madame Renauld will be able to tell us all about this mysterious person named Duveen."

The commissary's face cleared. "That is true. Let us proceed."

As we turned to leave the room, Poirot remarked casually: "It was here that M. Renauld received his guest last night, eh?"

"It was—but how did you know?"

"By *this*. I found it on the back of the leather chair."

And he held up between his finger and thumb a long black hair—a woman's hair!

M. Bex took us out by the back of the house to where there was a small shed leaning against the house. He produced a key from his pocket and unlocked it.

"The body is here. We moved it from the scene of the crime just before you arrived, as the photographers had done with it."

He opened the door and we passed in. The murdered man lay on the ground, with a sheet over him. M. Bex dexterously whipped off the covering. Renauld was a man of medium height, slender and lithe in figure. He looked about fifty years of age, and his dark hair was plentifully streaked with grey. He was clean shaven with a long thin nose, and eyes set rather close together, and his skin was deeply bronzed, as that of a man who had spent most of his life beneath tropical skies. His lips were drawn back from his teeth and an expression of absolute amazement and terror was stamped on the livid features.

"One can see by his face that he was stabbed in the back," remarked Poirot.

Very gently, he turned the dead man over. There, between the shoulder-blades, staining the light fawn overcoat, was a round dark patch. In the middle of it there was a slit in the cloth. Poirot examined it narrowly.

"Have you any idea with what weapon the crime was committed?"

"It was left in the wound." The commissary reached down a large glass jar. In it was a small object that looked to me more like a paper-knife than anything else. It had a black handle, and a narrow shining blade. The whole thing was not more than ten inches long. Poirot tested the discoloured point gingerly with his finger tip.

"*Ma foi*! but it is sharp! A nice easy little tool for murder!"

"Unfortunately, we could find no trace of fingerprints on it," remarked Bex regretfully. "The murderer must have worn gloves."

"Of course he did," said Poirot contemptuously. "Even in Santiago they know enough for that. The veriest amateur of an English Mees knows it—thanks to the publicity the Bertillon system has been given in the Press. All the same, it interests me very much that there were no finger-prints. It is so amazingly simple to leave the finger-prints of some one else! And then the police are happy." He shook his head. "I very much fear our criminal is not a man of method—either that or he was pressed for time. But we shall see."

He let the body fall back into its original position.

"He wore only underclothes under his overcoat, I see," he remarked.

"Yes, the examining magistrate thinks that is rather a curious point."

At this minute there was a tap on the door which Bex had closed after him. He strode forward and opened it. Françoise was there. She endeavoured to peep in with ghoulish curiosity.

"Well, what is it?" demanded Bex impatiently.

"Madame. She sends a message that she is much recovered, and is quite ready to receive the examining magistrate."

"Good," said M. Bex briskly. "Tell M. Hautet and say that we will come at once."

Poirot lingered a moment, looking back towards the body. I thought for a moment that he was going to apostrophize it, to declare aloud his determination never to rest till he had discovered the murderer. But when he spoke, it was tamely and awkwardly, and his comment was ludicrously inappropriate to the solemnity of the moment.

"He wore his overcoat very long," he said constrainedly.

5. Mrs. Renauld's Story

We found M. Hautet awaiting us in the hall, and we all proceeded upstairs together, Françoise marching ahead to show us the way. Poirot went up in a zigzag fashion which puzzled me, until he whispered with a grimace:

"No wonder the servants heard M. Renauld mounting the stairs; not a board of them but creaks fit to wake the dead!"

At the head of the staircase, a small passage branched off.

"The servants' quarters," explained Bex.

We continued along a corridor, and Françoise tapped on the last door to the right of it.

A faint voice bade us enter, and we passed into a large sunny apartment looking out towards the sea, which showed blue and sparkling about a quarter of a mile distant.

On a couch, propped up with cushions, and attended by Dr. Durand, lay a tall, striking-looking woman. She was middle-aged, and her once dark hair was now almost entirely silvered, but the intense vitality and strength of her personality would have made itself felt anywhere. You knew at once that you were in the presence of what the French call "*une maitresse femme.*"

She greeted us with a dignified inclination of the head.

"Pray be seated, messieurs."

We took chairs, and the magistrate's clerk established himself at a round table.

"I hope, madame," began M. Hautet, "that it will not distress you unduly to relate to us what occurred last night?"

"Not at all, monsieur. I know the value of time, if these scoundrelly assassins are to be caught and punished."

"Very well, madame. It will fatigue you less, I think, if I ask you questions and you confine yourself to answering them. At what time did you go to bed last night?"

"At half-past nine, monsieur. I was tired."

"And your husband?"

"About an hour later, I fancy."

"Did he seem disturbed—upset in any way?"

"No, not more than usual."

"What happened then?"

"We slept. I was awakened by a hand being pressed over my mouth. I tried to scream out, but the hand prevented me. There were two men in the room. They were both masked."

"Can you describe them at all, madame?"

"One was very tall, and had a long black beard, the other was short and stout. His beard was reddish. They both wore hats pulled down over their eyes."

"H'm," said the magistrate thoughtfully, "too much beard, I fear."

"You mean they were false?"

"Yes, madame. But continue your story."

"It was the short man who was holding me. He forced a gag into my mouth, and then bound me with rope hand and foot. The other man was standing over my husband. He had caught up my little dagger paper-knife from the dressing-table and was holding it with the point just over his heart. When the short man had finished with me, he joined the other, and they forced my husband to get up and accompany them into the dressing-room next door. I was nearly fainting with terror, nevertheless I listened desperately.

"They were speaking in too low a tone for me to hear what they said. But I recognized the language, a bastard Spanish such as is spoken in some parts of South America. They seemed to be demanding something from my husband, and presently they grew angry, and their voices rose a little. I think the tall man was speaking. 'You know what we want!' he said. '*The secret*! Where is it?' I do not know what my husband answered, but the other replied fiercely: 'You lie! We know you have it. Where are your keys?'

"Then I heard sounds of drawers being pulled out. There is a safe on the wall of my husband's dressing-room in which he always keeps a fairly large amount of ready money. Léonie tells me this has been rifled and the money taken, but evidently what they were looking for was not there, for presently I heard the tall man, with an oath, command my husband to dress himself. Soon after that, I think some noise in the house must have disturbed them, for they hustled my husband out into my room only half dressed."

"*Pardon*," interrupted Poirot, "but is there then no other egress from the dressing-room?"

"No, monsieur, there is only the communicating door into my room. They hurried my husband through, the short man in front, and the tall man behind him with the dagger still in his hand. Paul tried to break away to come to me. I saw his agonized eyes. He turned to his captors. 'I must speak to her,' he said. Then, coming to the side of the bed, 'It is all right, Eloise,' he said. 'Do not be afraid. I shall return before morning.' But, although he tried to make his voice confident, I could see the terror in his eyes. Then they hustled him out of the door, the tall man saying: 'One sound—and you are a dead man, remember.'

"After that," continued Mrs. Renauld, "I must have fainted. The next thing I recollect is Léonie rubbing my wrists, and giving me brandy."

"Madame Renauld," said the magistrate, "had you any idea what it was for which the assassins were searching?"

"None whatever, monsieur."

"Had you any knowledge that your husband feared something?"

"Yes. I had seen the change in him."

"How long ago was that?"

Mrs. Renauld reflected.

"Ten days perhaps."

"Not longer?"

"Possibly. I only noticed it then."

"Did you question your husband at all as to the cause?"

"Once. He put me off evasively. Nevertheless, I was convinced that he was suffering some terrible anxiety. However, since he evidently wished to conceal the fact from me, I tried to pretend that I had noticed nothing."

"Were you aware that he had called in the services of a detective?"

"A detective?" exclaimed Mrs. Renauld, very much surprised.

"Yes, this gentleman—M. Hercule Poirot." Poirot bowed. "He arrived today in response to a summons from your husband." And taking the letter written by M. Renauld from his pocket he handed it to the lady.

She read it with apparently genuine astonishment.

"I had no idea of this. Evidently he was fully cognizant of the danger."

"Now, madame, I will beg of you to be frank with me. Is there any incident in your husband's past life in South America which might throw light on his murder?"

Mrs. Renauld reflected deeply, but at last shook her head.

"I can think of none. Certainly my husband had many enemies, people he had got the better of in some way or another, but I can think of no one distinctive case. I do not say there is no such incident—only that I am not aware of it."

The examining magistrate stroked his beard disconsolately.

"And you can fix the time of this outrage?"

"Yes, I distinctly remember hearing the clock on the mantelpiece strike two." She nodded towards an eight-day travelling clock in a leather case which stood in the centre of the chimney-piece.

Poirot rose from his seat, scrutinized the clock carefully, and nodded, satisfied.

"And here too," exclaimed M. Bex, "is a wrist watch, knocked off the dressing-table by the assassins, without doubt, and smashed to atoms. Little did they know it would testify against them."

Gently he picked away the fragments of broken glass. Suddenly his face changed to one of utter stupefaction.

"*Mon Dieu!*" he ejaculated.

"What is it?"

"The hands of the watch point to seven o'clock!"

"What?" cried the examining magistrate, astonished.

But Poirot, deft as ever, took the broken trinket from the startled commissary, and held it to his ear. Then he smiled.

"The glass is broken, yes, but the watch itself is still going."

The explanation of the mystery was greeted with a relieved smile. But the magistrate bethought him of another point.

"But surely it is not seven o'clock now?"

"No," said Poirot gently, "it is a few minutes after five. Possibly the watch gains, is that so, madame?"

Mrs. Renauld was frowning perplexedly.

"It does gain," she admitted, "but I've never known it to gain quite so much as that."

With a gesture of impatience, the magistrate left the matter of the watch and proceeded with his interrogatory.

"Madame, the front door was found ajar. It seems almost certain that the murderers entered that way, yet it has not been forced at all. Can you suggest any explanation?"

"Possibly my husband went out for a stroll the last thing, and forgot to latch it when he came in."

"Is that a likely thing to happen?"

"Very. My husband was the most absent-minded of men."

There was a slight frown on her brow as she spoke, as though this trait in the dead man's character had at times vexed her.

"There is one inference I think we might draw," remarked the commissary suddenly. "Since the men insisted on M. Renauld dressing himself, it looks as though the place they were taking him to, the place where 'the secret' was concealed, lay some distance away."

The magistrate nodded.

"Yes, far, and yet not too far, since he spoke of being back by morning."

"What time does the last train leave the station of Merlinville?" asked Poirot.

"Eleven-fifty one way, and 12:17 the other, but it is more probable that they had a motor waiting."

"Of course," agreed Poirot, looking somewhat crestfallen.

"Indeed, that might be one way of tracing them," continued the magistrate, brightening. "A motor containing two foreigners is quite likely to have been noticed. That is an excellent point, M. Bex."

He smiled to himself, and then, becoming grave once more, he said to Mrs. Renauld:

"There is another question. Do you know any one of the name of 'Duveen'?"

"Duveen?" Mrs. Renauld repeated, thoughtfully. "No, for the moment, I cannot say I do."

"You have never heard your husband mention any one of that name?"

"Never."

"Do you know any one whose Christian name is Bella?"

He watched Mrs. Renauld narrowly as he spoke, seeking to surprise any signs of anger or consciousness, but she merely shook her head in quite a natural manner. He continued his questions.

"Are you aware that your husband had a visitor last night?"

Now he saw the red mount slightly in her cheeks, but she replied composedly.

"No, who was that?"

"A lady."

"Indeed?"

But for the moment the magistrate was content to say no more. It seemed unlikely that Madame Daubreuil had any connection with the crime, and he was anxious not to upset Mrs. Renauld more than necessary.

He made a sign to the commissary, and the latter replied with a nod. Then rising, he went across the room, and returned with the glass jar we had seen in the outhouse in his hand. From this, he took the dagger.

"Madame," he said gently, "do you recognize this?"

She gave a little cry.

"Yes, that is my little dagger." Then—she saw the stained point, and she drew back, her eyes widening with horror. "Is that—blood?"

"Yes, madame. Your husband was killed with this weapon." He removed it hastily from sight. "You are quite sure about its being the one that was on your dressing-table last night?"

"Oh, yes. It was a present from my son. He was in the Air

Force during the War. He gave his age as older than it was." There was a touch of the proud mother in her voice. "This was made from a streamline aeroplane wire, and was given to me by my son as a souvenir of the War."

"I see, madame. That brings us to another matter. Your son, where is he now? It is necessary that he should be telegraphed to without delay."

"Jack? He is on his way to Buenos Aires."

"What?"

"Yes. My husband telegraphed to him yesterday. He had sent him on business to Paris, but yesterday he discovered that it would be necessary for him to proceed without delay to South America. There was a boat leaving Cherbourg for Buenos Aires last night, and he wired him to catch it."

"Have you any knowledge of what the business in Buenos Aires was?"

"No, monsieur, I know nothing of its nature, but Buenos Aires is not my son's final destination. He was going overland from there to Santiago."

And, in unison, the magistrate and the commissary exclaimed:

"Santiago! Again Santiago!"

It was at this moment, when we were all stunned by the mention of that word, that Poirot approached Mrs. Renauld. He had been standing by the window like a man lost in a dream, and I doubt if he had fully taken in what had passed. He paused by the lady's side with a bow.

"*Pardon*, madame, but may I examine your wrists."

Though slightly surprised at the request, Mrs. Renauld held them out to him. Round each of them was a cruel red mark where the cords had bitten into the flesh. As he examined them, I fancied that a momentary flicker of excitement I had seen in his eyes disappeared.

"They must cause you great pain," he said, and once more he looked puzzled.

But the magistrate was speaking excitedly.

"Young M. Renauld must be communicated with at once by wireless. It is vital that we should know anything he can tell us about this trip to Santiago." He hesitated. "I hoped he might have been near at hand, so that we could have saved you pain, madame." He paused.

"You mean," she said in a low voice, "the identification of my husband's body?"

The magistrate bowed his head.

"I am a strong woman, monsieur. I can bear all that is required of me. I am ready—now."

"Oh, tomorrow will be quite soon enough, I assure you—"

"I prefer to get it over," she said in a low tone, a spasm of pain crossing her face. "If you will be so good as to give me your arm, Doctor?"

The doctor hastened forward, a cloak was thrown over Mrs. Renauld's shoulders, and a slow procession went down the stairs. M. Bex hurried on ahead to open the door of the shed. In a minute or two Mrs. Renauld appeared in the doorway. She was very pale, but resolute. Behind her, M. Hautet was clacking commiserations and apologies like an animated hen.

She raised her hand to her face.

"A moment, messieurs, while I steel myself."

She took her hand away and looked down at the dead man. Then the marvellous self-control which had upheld her so far deserted her.

"Paul!" she cried. "Husband! Oh, God!" And pitching forward she fell unconscious to the ground.

Instantly Poirot was beside her, he raised the lid of her eye, felt her pulse. When he had satisfied himself that she had really fainted, he drew aside. He caught me by the arm.

"I am an imbecile, my friend! If ever there was love and grief in a woman's voice, I heard it then. My little idea was all wrong. *Eh bien*! I must start again!"

6. The Scene of the Crime

B etween them, the doctor and M. Hautet carried the unconscious woman into the house. The commissary looked after them, shaking his head.

"*Pauvre femme*," he murmured to himself. "The shock was too much for her. Well, well, we can do nothing. Now, M. Poirot, shall we visit the place where the crime was committed?"

"If you please, M. Bex."

We passed through the house, and out by the front door. Poirot had looked up at the staircase in passing, and shook his head in a dissatisfied manner.

"It is to me incredible that the servants heard nothing. The creaking of that staircase, with *three* people descending it, would awaken the dead!"

"It was the middle of the night, remember. They were sound asleep by then."

But Poirot continued to shake his head as though not fully accepting the explanation. On the sweep of the drive, he paused, looking up at the house.

"What moved them in the first place to try if the front door were open? It was a most unlikely thing that it should be. It was far more probable that they should at once try to force a window."

"But all the windows on the ground floor are barred with iron shutters," objected the commissary.

Poirot pointed to a window on the first floor.

"That is the window of the bedroom we have just come from, is it not? And see—there is a tree by which it would be the easiest thing in the world to mount."

"Possibly," admitted the other. "But they could not have done so without leaving footprints in the flower-bed."

I saw the justice of his words. There were two large oval

45

flower-beds planted with scarlet geraniums, one each side of the steps leading up to the front door. The tree in question had its roots actually at the back of the bed itself, and it would have been impossible to reach it without stepping on the bed.

"You see," continued the commissary, "owing to the dry weather no prints would show on the drive or paths; but, on the soft mould of the flower-bed, it would have been a very different affair."

Poirot went close to the bed and studied it attentively. As Bex had said, the mould was perfectly smooth. There was not an indentation on it anywhere.

Poirot nodded, as though convinced, and we turned away, but he suddenly darted off and began examining the other flower-bed.

"M. Bex!" he called. "See here. Here are plenty of traces for you."

The commissary joined him—and smiled.

"My dear M. Poirot, those are without doubt the footprints of the gardener's large hobnailed boots. In any case, it would have no importance, since this side we have no tree, and consequently no means of gaining access to the upper story."

"True," said Poirot, evidently crestfallen. "So you think these footprints are of no importance?"

"Not the least in the world."

Then, to my utter astonishment, Poirot pronounced these words:

"I do not agree with you. I have a little idea that these footprints are the most important things we have seen yet."

M. Bex said nothing, merely shrugged his shoulders. He was far too courteous to utter his real opinion.

"Shall we proceed?" he asked instead.

"Certainly. I can investigate this matter of the footprints later," said Poirot cheerfully.

Instead of following the drive down to the gate, M. Bex

turned up a path that branched off at right angles. It led, up a slight incline, round to the right of the house, and was bordered on either side by a kind of shrubbery. Suddenly it emerged into a little clearing from which one obtained a view of the sea. A seat had been placed here, and not far from it was a rather ramshackle shed. A few steps further on, a neat line of small bushes marked the boundary of the Villa grounds. M. Bex pushed his way through these and we found ourselves on a wide stretch of open downs. I looked round, and saw something that filled me with astonishment.

"Why, this is a golf course," I cried.

Bex nodded.

"The limits are not completed yet," he explained. "It is hoped to be able to open them sometime next month. It was some of the men working on them who discovered the body early this morning."

I gave a gasp. A little to my left, where for the moment I had overlooked it, was a long narrow pit, and by it, face downwards, was the body of a man! For a moment, my heart gave a terrible leap, and I had a wild fancy that the tragedy had been duplicated. But the commissary dispelled my illusion by moving forward with a sharp exclamation of annoyance:

"What have my police been about? They had strict orders to allow no one near the place without proper credentials!"

The man on the ground turned his head over his shoulder.

"But I have proper credentials," he remarked, and rose slowly to his feet.

"My dear M. Giraud," cried the commissary. "I had no idea that you had arrived, even. The examining magistrate has been awaiting you with the utmost impatience."

As he spoke, I was scanning the new-comer with the keenest curiosity. The famous detective from the Paris Sûreté was familiar to me by name, and I was extremely interested to see him in the flesh. He was very tall, perhaps about thirty years of age, with auburn hair and moustache, and a military carriage. There was a trace of arrogance in his manner which showed that he was fully alive to his own importance. Bex introduced us, presenting Poirot as a colleague. A flicker of interest came into the detective's eye.

"I know you by name, M. Poirot," he said. "You cut quite a figure in the old days, didn't you? But methods are very different now."

"Crimes, though, are very much the same," remarked Poirot gently.

I saw at once that Giraud was prepared to be hostile. He resented the other being associated with him, and I felt that if he came across any clue of importance he would be more than likely to keep it to himself.

"The examining magistrate—" began Bex again. But Giraud interrupted him rudely:

"A fig for the examining magistrate! The light is the important thing. For all practical purposes it will be gone in another half-hour or so. I know all about the case, and the people at the house will do very well until tomorrow, but, if we're going to find a clue to the murderers, here is the spot we shall find it. Is it your police who have been trampling all over the place? I thought they knew better nowadays."

"Assuredly they do. The marks you complain of were made by the workmen who discovered the body."

The other grunted disgustedly.

"I can see the tracks where the three of them came through the hedge—but they were cunning. You can just recognize the centre footmarks as those of M. Renauld, but those on either side have been carefully obliterated. Not that there would really be much to see anyway on this hard ground, but they weren't taking any chances."

"The external sign," said Poirot. "That is what you seek, eh?"

The other detective stared.

"Of course."

A very faint smile came to Poirot's lips. He seemed about to speak, but checked himself. He bent down to where a spade was lying.

"That's what the grave was dug with, right enough," said Giraud. "But you'll get nothing from it. It was Renauld's own spade, and the man who used it wore gloves. Here they are." He gesticulated with his foot to where two soiled earth-stained gloves were lying. "And they're Renauld's too—or at least his gardener's. I tell you, the men who planned out this crime were taking no chances. The man was stabbed with his own dagger, and would have been buried with his own spade. They counted on leaving no traces! But I'll beat them. There's always *something*! And I mean to find it."

But Poirot was now apparently interested in something else, a short discoloured piece of lead-piping which lay beside the spade. He touched it delicately with his finger.

"And does this, too, belong to the murdered man?" he asked, and I thought I detected a subtle flavour of irony in the question.

Giraud shrugged his shoulders to indicate that he neither knew nor cared.

"May have been lying around here for weeks. Anyway, it doesn't interest me."

"I, on the contrary, find it very interesting," said Poirot sweetly.

I guessed that he was merely bent on annoying the Paris detective and, if so, he succeeded. The other turned away rudely, remarking that he had no time to waste, and bending down he resumed his minute search of the ground.

Meanwhile Poirot, as though struck by a sudden idea, stepped back over the boundary, and tried the door of the little shed.

"That's locked," said Giraud over his shoulder. "But it's only a place where the gardener keeps his rubbish. The spade didn't come from there, but from the toolshed up by the house."

"Marvellous," murmured M. Bex, to me ecstatically. "He has been here but half an hour, and he already knows everything!

49

What a man! Undoubtedly Giraud is the greatest detective alive today."

Although I disliked the detective heartily, I nevertheless was secretly impressed. Efficiency seemed to radiate from the man. I could not help feeling that, so far, Poirot had not greatly distinguished himself, and it vexed me. He seemed to be directing his attention to all sorts of silly, puerile points that had nothing to do with the case. Indeed, at this juncture, he suddenly asked:

"M. Bex, tell me, I pray you, the meaning of this whitewashed line that extends all round the grave. Is it a device of the police?"

"No, M. Poirot, it is an affair of the golf course. It shows that there is here to be a 'bunkair,' as you call it."

"A bunkair?" Poirot turned to me. "That is the irregular hole filled with sand and a bank at one side, is it not?"

I concurred.

"You do not play the golf, M. Poirot?" inquired Bex.

"I? Never! What a game!" He became excited. "Figure to yourself, each hole it is of a different length. The obstacles, they are not arranged mathematically. Even the greens are frequently up one side! There is only one pleasing thing—the how do you call them?—tee boxes! They, at least, are symmetrical."

I could not refrain from a laugh at the way the game appeared to Poirot, and my little friend smiled at me affectionately, bearing no malice. Then he asked:

"But M. Renauld, without doubt he played the golf?"

"Yes, he was a keen golfer. It's mainly owing to him, and to his large subscriptions, that this work is being carried forward. He even had a say in the designing of it."

Poirot nodded thoughtfully.

Then he remarked:

"It was not a very good choice they made—of a spot to bury the body? When the men began to dig up the ground, all would have been discovered."

"Exactly," cried Giraud triumphantly. "And that *proves* that they were strangers to the place. It's an excellent piece of indirect evidence."

"Yes," said Poirot doubtfully. "No one who knew would bury a body there—unless—unless—they *wanted* it to be discovered. And that is clearly absurd, is it not?"

Giraud did not even trouble to reply.

"Yes," said Poirot, in a somewhat dissatisfied voice. "Yes—undoubtedly—absurd!"

7. The Mysterious Madame Daubreuil

As we retraced our steps to the house, M. Bex excused himself for leaving us, explaining that he must immediately acquaint the examining magistrate with the fact of Giraud's arrival. Giraud himself had been obviously delighted when Poirot declared that he had seen all he wanted. The last thing we observed, as we left the spot, was Giraud, crawling about on all fours, with a thoroughness in his search that I could not but admire. Poirot guessed my thoughts, for as soon as we were alone he remarked ironically:

"At last you have seen the detective you admire—the human foxhound! Is it not so, my friend?"

"At any rate, he's *doing* something," I said, with asperity. "If there's anything to find, he'll find it. Now you—"

"*Eh bien!* I also have found something! A piece of lead-piping."

"Nonsense, Poirot. You know very well that's got nothing to do with it. I meant *little* things—traces that may lead us infallibly to the murderers."

"*Mon ami*, a clue of two feet long is every bit as valuable as one measuring two millimetres! But it is the romantic idea that all important clues must be infinitesimal! As to the piece of lead-piping having nothing to do with the crime, you say that because Giraud told you so. No"—as I was about to interpose a question—"we will say no more. Leave Giraud to his search, and me to my ideas. The case seems straightforward enough— and yet—and yet, *mon ami*, I am not satisfied! And do you know why? Because of the wrist watch that is two hours fast. And then there are several curious little points that do not seem to fit in. For instance, if the object of the murderers was revenge, why did they not stab Renauld in his sleep and have done with it?"

"They wanted the 'secret,'" I reminded him.

Poirot brushed a speck of dust from his sleeve with a dissatisfied air.

"Well, where is this 'secret'? Presumably some distance away, since they wish him to dress himself. Yet he is found murdered close at hand, almost within ear-shot of the house. Then again, it is pure chance that a weapon such as the dagger should be lying about casually, ready to hand."

He paused frowning, and then went on:

"Why did the servants hear nothing? Were they drugged? Was there an accomplice and did that accomplice see to it that the front door should remain open? I wonder if—"

He stopped abruptly. We had reached the drive in front of the house. Suddenly he turned to me.

"My friend, I am about to surprise you—to please you! I have taken your reproaches to heart! We will examine some footprints!"

"Where?"

"In that right-hand bed yonder. M. Bex says that they are the footmarks of the gardener. Let us see if that is so. See, he approaches with his wheelbarrow."

Indeed an elderly man was just crossing the drive with a barrowful of seedlings. Poirot called to him, and he set down the barrow and came hobbling towards us.

"You are going to ask him for one of his boots to compare with the footmarks?" I asked breathlessly. My faith in Poirot revived a little. Since he said the footprints in this right-hand bed were important, presumably they *were*.

"Exactly," said Poirot.

"But won't he think it very odd?"

"He will not think about it at all."

We could say no more, for the old man had joined us.

"You want me for something, monsieur?"

"Yes. You have been gardener here a long time, haven't you?"

"Twenty-four years, monsieur."

"And your name is—?"

"Auguste, monsieur."

"I was admiring these magnificent geraniums. They are truly superb. They have been planted long?"

"Some time, monsieur. But of course, to keep the beds looking smart, one must keep bedding out a few new plants, and remove those that are over, besides keeping the old blooms well picked off."

"You put in some new plants yesterday, didn't you? Those in the middle there, and in the other bed also?"

"Monsieur has a sharp eye. It takes always a day or so for them to 'pick up.' Yes, I put ten new plants in each bed last night. As Monsieur doubtless knows, one should not put in plants when the sun is hot."

Auguste was charmed with Poirot's interest, and was quite inclined to be garrulous.

"That is a splendid specimen there," said Poirot, pointing. "Might I perhaps have a cutting of it?"

"But certainly, monsieur." The old fellow stepped into the bed, and carefully took a slip from the plant Poirot had admired.

Poirot was profuse in his thanks, and Auguste departed to his barrow.

"You see?" said Poirot with a smile, as he bent over the bed to examine the indentation of the gardener's hobnailed boot. "It is quite simple."

"I did not realize—"

"That the foot would be inside the boot? You do not use

your excellent mental capacities sufficiently. Well, what of the footmark?"

I examined the bed carefully.

"All the footmarks in the bed were made by the same boot," I said at length after a careful study.

"You think so? *Eh bien*, I agree with you," said Poirot.

He seemed quite uninterested, and as though he were thinking of something else.

"At any rate," I remarked, "you will have one bee less in your bonnet now."

"*Mon Dieu*! But what an idiom! What does it mean?"

"What I meant was that now you will give up your interest in these footmarks."

But to my surprise Poirot shook his head.

"No, no, *mon ami*. At last I am on the right track. I am still in the dark, but, as I hinted just now to M. Bex, these footmarks are the most important and interesting things in the case! That poor Giraud—I should not be surprised if he took no notice of them whatever."

At that moment, the front door opened, and M. Hautet and the commissary came down the steps.

"Ah, M. Poirot, we were coming to look for you," said the magistrate. "It is getting late, but I wish to pay a visit to Madame Daubreuil. Without doubt she will be very much upset by M. Renauld's death, and we may be fortunate enough to get a clue from her. The secret that he did not confide to his wife, it is possible that he may have told it to the woman whose love held him enslaved. We know where our Samsons are weak, don't we?"

I admired the picturesqueness of M. Hautet's language. I suspected that the examining magistrate was by now thoroughly enjoying his part in the mysterious drama.

"Is M. Giraud not going to accompany us?" asked Poirot.

"M. Giraud has shown clearly that he prefers to conduct the case in his own way," said M. Hautet dryly. One could see easily enough that Giraud's cavalier treatment of the examining magistrate had not prejudiced the latter in his favour. We said no more, but fell into line. Poirot walked with the examining magistrate, and the commissary and I followed a few paces behind.

"There is no doubt that Françoise's story is substantially correct," he remarked to me in a confidential tone. "I have been telephoning headquarters. It seems that three times in the last six weeks—that is to say since the arrival of M. Renauld at Merlinville—Madame Daubreuil has paid a large sum in notes into her banking account. Altogether the sum totals two hundred thousand francs!"

"Dear me," I said, considering, "that must be something like four thousand pounds!"

"Precisely. Yes, there can be no doubt that he was absolutely infatuated. But it remains to be seen whether he confided his secret to her. The examining magistrate is hopeful, but I hardly share his views."

During this conversation we were walking down the lane towards the fork in the road where our car had halted earlier in the afternoon, and in another moment I realized that the Villa Marguerite, the home of the mysterious Madame Daubreuil, was the small house from which the beautiful girl had emerged.

"She has lived here for many years," said the commissary, nodding his head towards the house. "Very quietly, very unobtrusively. She seems to have no friends or relations other than the acquaintances she has made in Merlinville. She never refers to the past, nor to her husband. One does not even know if he is alive or dead. There is a mystery about her, you comprehend." I nodded, my interest growing.

"And—the daughter?" I ventured.

"A truly beautiful young girl—modest, devout, all that she should be. One pities her, for, though she may know nothing of the past, a man who wants to ask her hand in marriage must necessarily inform himself, and then—" The commissary shrugged his shoulders cynically.

"But it would not be her fault!" I cried, with rising indignation.

"No. But what will you? A man is particular about his wife's antecedents."

I was prevented from further argument by our arrival at the door. M. Hautet rang the bell. A few minutes elapsed, and then we heard a footfall within, and the door was opened. On the threshold stood my young goddess of that afternoon. When she saw us, the colour left her cheeks, leaving her deathly white, and her eyes widened with apprehension. There was no doubt about it, she was afraid!

"Mademoiselle Daubreuil," said M. Hautet, sweeping off his hat, "we regret infinitely to disturb you, but the exigencies of the Law—you comprehend? My compliments to Madame your mother, and will she have the goodness to grant me a few moments' interview."

For a moment the girl stood motionless. Her left hand was pressed to her side, as though to still the sudden unconquerable agitation of her heart. But she mastered herself, and said in a low voice:

"I will go and see. Please come inside."

She entered a room on the left of the hall, and we heard the low murmur of her voice. And then another voice, much the same in timbre, but with a slightly harder inflection behind its mellow roundness said:

"But certainly. Ask them to enter."

In another minute we were face to face with the mysterious Madame Daubreuil.

She was not nearly so tall as her daughter, and the rounded curves of her figure had all the grace of full maturity. Her hair, again unlike her daughter's, was dark, and parted in the middle in the madonna style. Her eyes, half hidden by the drooping lids, were blue. There was a dimple in the round chin, and the half parted lips seemed always to hover on the verge of a mysterious smile. There was something almost exaggeratedly feminine about her, at once yielding and seductive. Though very well preserved, she was certainly no longer young, but her charm was of the quality which is independent of age.

Standing there, in her black dress with the fresh white collar and cuffs, her hands clasped together, she looked subtly appealing and helpless.

"You wished to see me, monsieur?" she asked.

"Yes, madame." M. Hautet cleared his throat. "I am investigating the death of M. Renauld. You have heard of it, no doubt?"

She bowed her head without speaking. Her expression did not change.

"We came to ask you whether you can—er—throw any light upon the circumstances surrounding it?"

"I?" The surprise of her tone was excellent.

"Yes, madame. It would, perhaps, be better if we could speak to you alone." He looked meaningly in the direction of the girl.

Madame Daubreuil turned to her.

"Marthe, dear—"

But the girl shook her head.

"No, *maman*, I will not go. I am not a child. I am twenty-two. I shall not go."

Madame Daubreuil turned back to the examining magistrate.

"You see, monsieur."

"I should prefer not to speak before Mademoiselle Daubreuil."

"As my daughter says, she is not a child."

For a moment the magistrate hesitated, baffled.

"Very well, madame," he said at last. "Have it your own way. We have reason to believe that you were in the habit of visiting the dead man at his Villa in the evenings. Is that so?"

The colour rose in the lady's pale cheeks, but she replied quietly:

"I deny your right to ask me such a question!"

"Madame, we are investigating a murder."

"Well, what of it? I had nothing to do with the murder."

"Madame, we do not say that for a moment. But you knew the dead man well. Did he ever confide in you as to any danger that threatened him?"

"Never."

"Did he ever mention his life in Santiago, and any enemies he may have made there?"

"No."

"Then you can give us no help at all?"

"I fear not. I really do not see why you should come to me. Cannot his wife tell you what you want to know?" Her voice held a slender inflection of irony.

"Madame Renauld has told us all she can."

"Ah!" said Madame Daubreuil. "I wonder—"

"You wonder what, madame?"

"Nothing."

The examining magistrate looked at her. He was aware that he was fighting a duel, and that he had no mean antagonist.

"You persist in your statement that M. Renauld confided nothing in you?"

"Why should you think it likely that he should confide in me?"

"Because, madame," said M. Hautet, with calculated brutality. "A man tells to his mistress what he does not always tell to his wife."

"Ah!" she sprang forward. Her eyes flashed fire. "Monsieur, you insult me! And before my daughter! I can tell you nothing. Have the goodness to leave my house!"

The honours undoubtedly rested with the lady. We left the Villa Marguerite like a shamefaced pack of schoolboys. The magistrate muttered angry ejaculations to himself. Poirot seemed lost in thought. Suddenly he came out of his reverie with a start, and inquired of M. Hautet if there was a good hotel near at hand.

"There is a small place, the Hotel des Bains, on this side of town. A few hundred yards down the road. It will be handy for your investigations. We shall see you in the morning then, I presume?"

"Yes, I thank you, M. Hautet."

With mutual civilities, we parted company, Poirot and I going towards Merlinville, and the others returning to the Villa Geneviève.

"The French police system is very marvellous," said Poirot, looking after them. "The information they possess about every one's life, down to the most commonplace detail, is extraordinary. Though he has only been here a little over six weeks, they are perfectly well acquainted with M. Renauld's tastes and pursuits, and at a moment's notice they can produce information as to Madame Daubreuil's banking account, and the sums that have lately been paid in! Undoubtedly the *dossier* is a great institution. But what is that?" He turned sharply.

A figure was running hatless, down the road after us. It was Marthe Daubreuil.

"I beg your pardon," she cried breathlessly, as she reached us. "I—I should not do this, I know. You must not tell my mother. But is it true, what the people say, that M. Renauld called in a detective before he died, and—and that you are he?"

"Yes, mademoiselle," said Poirot gently. "It is quite true. But how did you learn it?"

"Françoise told our Amélie," explained Marthe, with a blush.

Poirot made a grimace.

"The secrecy, it is impossible in an affair of this kind! Not that it matters. Well, mademoiselle, what is it you want to know?"

The girl hesitated. She seemed longing, yet fearing, to speak. At last, almost in a whisper, she asked:

"Is—any one suspected?"

Poirot eyed her keenly.

Then he replied evasively:

"Suspicion is in the air at present, mademoiselle."

"Yes, I know—but—any one in particular?"

"Why do you want to know?"

The girl seemed frightened by the question. All at once Poirot's words about her earlier in the day recurred to me. The "girl with the anxious eyes!"

"M. Renauld was always very kind to me," she replied at last. "It is natural that I should be interested."

"I see," said Poirot. "Well, mademoiselle, suspicion at present is hovering round two persons."

"Two?"

I could have sworn there was a note of surprise and relief in her voice.

"Their names are unknown, but they are presumed to be Chileans from Santiago. And now, mademoiselle, you see what comes of being young and beautiful! I have betrayed professional secrets for you!"

The girl laughed merrily, and then, rather shyly, she thanked him.

"I must run back now. *Maman* will miss me."

And she turned and ran back up the road, looking like a modern Atalanta. I stared after her.

"*Mon ami*," said Poirot, in his gentle ironical voice, "is it that we are to remain planted here all night—just because you have seen a beautiful young woman, and your head is in a whirl?"

I laughed and apologized.

"But she *is* beautiful, Poirot. Any one might be excused for being bowled over by her."

Poirot groaned.

"*Mon Dieu*! But it is that you have the susceptible heart!"

"Poirot," I said, "do you remember after the Styles Case when—"

"When you were in love with two charming women at once, and neither of them were for you? Yes, I remember."

"You consoled me by saying that perhaps some day we should hunt together again, and that then—"

"*Eh bien?*"

"Well, we are hunting together again, and—" I paused, and laughed rather self-consciously.

But to my surprise Poirot shook his head very earnestly.

"Ah, *mon ami*, do not set your heart on Marthe Daubreuil. She is not for you, that one! Take it from Papa Poirot!"

"Why," I cried, "the commissary assured me that she was as good as she is beautiful! A perfect angel!"

"Some of the greatest criminals I have known had the faces of angels," remarked Poirot cheerfully. "A malformation of the grey cells may coincide quite easily with the face of a madonna."

"Poirot," I cried, horrified, "you cannot mean that you suspect an innocent child like this!"

"Ta-ta-ta! Do not excite yourself! I have not said that I suspected her. But you must admit that her anxiety to know about the case is somewhat unusual."

"For once, I see further than you do," I said. "Her anxiety is not for herself—but for her mother."

"My friend," said Poirot, "as usual, you see nothing at all. Madame Daubreuil is very well able to look after herself without her daughter worrying about her. I admit I was teasing you just now, but all the same I repeat what I said before. Do not set your heart on that girl. She is not for you! I, Hercule Poirot, know it. *Sacré!* if only I could remember where I had seen that face!"

"What face?" I asked, surprised. "The daughter's?"

"No. The mother's."

Noting my surprise, he nodded emphatically.

"But yes—it is as I tell you. It was a long time ago, when I was still with the Police in Belgium. I have never actually seen the woman before, but I have seen her picture—and in connection with some case. I rather fancy—"

"Yes?"

"I may be mistaken, but I rather fancy that it was a murder case!"

8. An Unexpected Meeting

We were up at the Villa betimes next morning. The man on guard at the gate did not bar our way this time. Instead, he respectfully saluted us, and we passed on to the house. The maid Léonie was just coming down the stairs, and seemed not averse to the prospect of a little conversation.

Poirot inquired after the health of Mrs. Renauld.

Léonie shook her head.

"She is terribly upset, *la pauvre dame*! She will eat nothing—but nothing! And she is as pale as a ghost. It is heartrending to see her. Ah, *par exemple*, it is not I who would grieve like that for a man who had deceived me with another woman!"

Poirot nodded sympathetically.

"What you say is very just, but what will you? The heart of a woman who loves will forgive many blows. Still, undoubtedly there must have been many scenes of recrimination between them in the last few months?"

Again Léonie shook her head.

"Never, monsieur. Never have I heard Madame utter a word of protest—of reproach, even! She had the temper and disposition of an angel—quite different to Monsieur."

"Monsieur Renauld had not the temper of an angel?"

"Far from it. When he enraged himself, the whole house knew of it. The day that he quarrelled with M. Jack—*ma foi*! they might have been heard in the market place, they shouted so loud!"

"Indeed," said Poirot. "And when did this quarrel take place?"

"Oh! it was just before M. Jack went to Paris. Almost he

missed his train. He came out of the library, and caught up his bag which he had left in the hall. The automobile, it was being repaired, and he had to run for the station. I was dusting the salon, and I saw him pass, and his face was white—white—with two burning spots of red. Ah, but he was angry!"

Léonie was enjoying her narrative thoroughly.

"And the dispute, what was it about?"

"Ah, that I do not know," confessed Léonie. "It is true that they shouted, but their voices were so loud and high, and they spoke so fast, that only one well acquainted with English could have comprehended. But Monsieur, he was like a thundercloud all day! Impossible to please him!"

The sound of a door shutting upstairs cut short Léonie's loquacity.

"And Françoise who awaits me!" she exclaimed, awakening to a tardy remembrance of her duties. "That old one, she always scolds."

"One moment, mademoiselle. The examining magistrate, where is he?"

"They have gone out to look at the automobile in the garage. Monsieur the commissary had some idea that it might have been used on the night of the murder."

"*Quelle idée*," murmured Poirot, as the girl disappeared.

"You will go out and join them?"

"No, I shall await their return in the *salon*. It is cool there on this hot morning."

This placid way of taking things did not quite commend itself to me.

"If you don't mind—" I said, and hesitated.

"Not in the least. You wish to investigate on your own account, eh?"

"Well, I'd rather like to have a look at Giraud, if he's anywhere about, and see what he's up to."

"The human foxhound," murmured Poirot, as he leaned back

in a comfortable chair, and closed his eyes. "By all means, my friend. Au revoir."

I strolled out of the front door. It was certainly hot. I turned up the path we had taken the day before. I had a mind to study the scene of the crime myself. I did not go directly to the spot, however, but turned aside into the bushes, so as to come out on the links some hundred yards or so further to the right. If Giraud were still on the spot, I wanted to observe his methods before he knew of my presence. But the shrubbery here was much denser, and I had quite a struggle to force my way through. When I emerged at last on the course, it was quite unexpectedly and with such vigour that I cannoned heavily into a young lady who had been standing with her back to the plantation.

She not unnaturally gave a suppressed shriek, but I, too, uttered an exclamation of surprise. For it was my friend of the train, Cinderella!

The surprise was mutual.

"You," we both exclaimed simultaneously.

The young lady recovered herself first.

"My only Aunt!" she exclaimed. "What are you doing here?"

"For the matter of that, what are you?" I retorted.

"When last I saw *you*, the day before yesterday, you were trotting home to England like a good little boy. Have they given you a season ticket to and fro, on the strength of your M.P.?"

I ignored the end of the speech.

"When last I saw you," I said, "you were trotting home with your sister, like a good little girl. By the way, how is your sister?"

A flash of white teeth rewarded me.

"How kind of you to ask! My sister is well, I thank you."

"She is here with you?"

"She remained in town," said the minx with dignity.

"I don't believe you've got a sister," I laughed. "If you have, her name is Harris!"

"Do you remember mine?" she asked, with a smile.

"Cinderella. But you're going to tell me the real one now, aren't you?"

She shook her head with a wicked look.

"Not even why you're here?"

"Oh, *that*! I suppose you've heard of members of my profession 'resting.'"

"At expensive French watering-places?"

"Dirt cheap if you know where to go."

I eyed her keenly.

"Still, you'd no intention of coming here when I met you two days ago?"

"We all have our disappointments," said Miss Cinderella sententiously. "There now, I've told you quite as much as is good for you. Little boys should not be inquisitive. You've not yet told me what you're doing here? Got the M.P. in tow, I suppose, doing the gay boy on the beach."

I shook my head. "Guess again. You remember my telling you that my great friend was a detective?"

"Yes?"

"And perhaps you've heard about this crime—at the Villa Geneviève—?"

She stared at me. Her breast heaved, and her eyes grew wide and round.

"You don't mean—that you're in on *that*?"

I nodded. There was no doubt that I had scored heavily. Her emotion, as she regarded me, was only too evident. For some few seconds, she remained silent, staring at me. Then she nodded her head emphatically.

"Well, if that doesn't beat the band! Tote me round. I want to see all the horrors."

"What do you mean?"

"What I say. Bless the boy, didn't I tell you I doted on crimes? What do you think I'm imperilling my ankles for in high-heeled shoes over this stubble? I've been nosing round for hours. Tried the front way in, but that old stick-in-the-mud of a French gendarme wasn't taking any. I guess Helen of Troy, and Cleopatra, and Mary, Queen of Scots, rolled in one wouldn't cut ice with him! It's a real piece of luck happening on you this way. Come on, show me all the sights."

"But look here—wait a minute—I can't. Nobody's allowed in. They're awfully strict."

"Aren't you and your friend the big bugs?"

I was loath to relinquish my position of importance.

"Why are you so keen?" I asked weakly. "And what is it you want to see."

"Oh, everything! The place where it happened, and the weapon, and the body, and any finger-prints or interesting things like that. I've never had a chance of being right in on a murder like this before. It'll last me all my life?"

I turned away, sickened. What were women coming to nowadays? The girl's ghoulish excitement nauseated me. I had read of the mobs of women who besieged the law courts when some wretched man was being tried for his life on the capital charge. I had sometimes wondered who these women were. Now I knew. They were of the likeness of Cinderella, young, yet obsessed with a yearning for morbid excitement, for sensation at any price, without regard to any decency or good feeling. The vividness of the girl's beauty had attracted me in spite of myself, yet at heart I retained my first impression of disapproval and dislike. I thought of my mother, long since dead. What would she have said of this strange modern product of girlhood? The pretty face with the paint and powder, and the ghoulish mind behind!

"Come off your high horse," said the lady suddenly. "And don't give yourself airs. When you got called to this job, did you put your nose in the air and say it was a nasty business, and you wouldn't be mixed up in it?"

"No, but—"

"If you'd been here on a holiday, wouldn't you be nosing round just the same as I am? Of course you would."

"I'm a man. You're a woman."

"Your idea of a woman is some one who gets on a chair and shrieks if she sees a mouse. That's all prehistoric. But you *will* show me round, won't you? You see, it might make a big difference to me."

"In what way?"

"They're keeping all the reporters out. I might make a big scoop with one of the papers. You don't know how much they pay for a bit of inside stuff."

I hesitated. She slipped a small soft hand into mine.

"*Please*—there's a dear."

I capitulated. Secretly, I knew that I should rather enjoy the part of showman. After all, the moral attitude displayed by the girl was none of my business. I was a little nervous as to what the examining magistrate might say, but I reassured myself by the reflection that no harm could possibly be done.

We repaired first to the spot where the body had been discovered. A man was on guard there, who saluted respectfully, knowing me by sight, and raised no question as to my companion. Presumably he regarded her as vouched for by me. I explained to Cinderella just how the discovery had been made, and she listened attentively, sometimes putting an intelligent question. Then we turned our steps in the direction of the Villa. I proceeded rather cautiously, for, truth to tell, I was not at all anxious to meet any one. I took the girl through the shrubbery round to the back of the house where the small shed was. I recollected that yesterday evening, after relocking the door, M. Bex had left the key with the *sergent de ville* Marchaud, "in case M. Giraud should require it while we are upstairs." I thought it quite likely that the Sûreté detective, after using it, had returned it to Marchaud again. Leaving the girl out of sight in the shrubbery,

I entered the house. Marchaud was on duty outside the door of the *salon*. From within came the murmur of voices.

"Monsieur desires Hautet? He is within. He is again interrogating Françoise."

"No," I said hastily, "I don't want him. But I should very much like the key of the shed outside if it is not against regulations."

"But certainly, monsieur." He produced it. "Here it is. M. le juge gave orders that all facilities were to be placed at your disposal. You will return it to me when you have finished out there, that is all."

"Of course."

I felt a thrill of satisfaction as I realized that in Marchaud's eyes, at least, I ranked equally in importance with Poirot. The girl was waiting for me. She gave an exclamation of delight as she saw the key in my hand.

"You've got it then?"

"Of course," I said coolly. "All the same, you know, what I'm doing is highly irregular."

"You've been a perfect duck, and I shan't forget it. Come along. They can't see us from the house, can they?"

"Wait a minute." I arrested her eager advance. "I won't stop you if you really wish to go in. But do you? You've seen the grave, and the grounds, and you've heard all the details of the affair. Isn't that enough for you? This is going to be gruesome, you know, and— unpleasant."

She looked at me for a moment with an expression that I could not quite fathom. Then she laughed.

"Me for the horrors," she said. "Come along."

In silence we arrived at the door of the shed. I opened it and we passed in. I walked over to the body, and gently pulled down the sheet as M. Bex had done the preceding afternoon. A little gasping sound escaped from the girl's lips, and I turned and looked at her. There was horror on her face now, and those debonair high spirits of hers were quenched utterly. She had not chosen to listen to my advice, and she was punished now for her disregard of it. I felt singularly merciless towards her. She should go through with it now. I turned the corpse gently over.

"You see," I said, "he was stabbed in the back."

Her voice was almost soundless.

"With what?"

I nodded towards the glass jar.

"That dagger."

Suddenly the girl reeled, and then sank down in a heap. I sprang to her assistance.

"You are faint. Come out of here. It has been too much for you."

"Water," she murmured. "Quick. Water . . ."

I left her, and rushed into the house. Fortunately none of the servants were about, and I was able to secure a glass of water unobserved and add a few drops of brandy from a pocket flask. In a few minutes I was back again. The girl was lying as I had left her, but a few sips of the brandy and water revived her in a marvellous manner.

"Take me out of here—oh, quickly, quickly!" she cried, shuddering.

Supporting her with my arm I led her out into the air, and she pulled the door to behind her. Then she drew a deep breath.

"That's better. Oh, it was horrible! Why did you ever let me go in?"

I felt this to be so feminine that I could not forbear a smile. Secretly, I was not dissatisfied with her collapse. It proved that she was not quite so callous as I had thought her. After all she was little more than a child, and her curiosity had probably been of the unthinking order.

"I did my best to stop you, you know," I said gently.

"I suppose you did. Well, good-bye."

"Look here, you can't start off like that—all alone. You're not fit for it. I insist on accompanying you back to Merlinville."

"Nonsense. I'm quite all right now."

"Supposing you felt faint again? No, I shall come with you."

But this she combated with a good deal of energy. In the end, however, I prevailed so far as to be allowed to accompany her to the outskirts of the town. We retraced our steps over our former route, passing the grave again, and making a detour on to the road. Where the first straggling line of shops began, she stopped and held out her hand.

"Good-bye, and thank you ever so much for coming with me."

"Are you sure you're all right now?"

"Quite, thanks. I hope you won't get into any trouble over showing me things?"

I disclaimed the idea lightly.

"Well, good-bye."

"Au revoir," I corrected. "If you're staying here, we shall meet again."

She flashed a smile at me.

"That's so. Au revoir, then."

"Wait a second, you haven't told me your address?"

"Oh, I'm staying at the Hôtel du Phare. It's a little place, but quite good. Come and look me up tomorrow."

"I will," I said, with perhaps rather unnecessary *empressement.*

I watched her out of sight, then turned and retraced my steps to the Villa. I remembered that I had not relocked the door of the shed. Fortunately no one had noticed the oversight, and turning the key I removed it and returned it to the *sergent de ville.* And, as I did so, it came upon me suddenly that though Cinderella had given me her address I still did not know her name.

9. M. Giraud Finds Some Clues

In the *salon* I found the examining magistrate busily interrogating the old gardener, Auguste. Poirot and the commissary, who were both present, greeted me respectively with a smile and a polite bow. I slipped quietly into a seat. M. Hautet was painstaking and meticulous in the extreme, but did not succeed in eliciting anything of importance.

The gardening gloves Auguste admitted to be his. He wore them when handling a certain species of primula plant which was poisonous to some people. He could not say when he had worn them last. Certainly he had not missed them. Where were they kept? Sometimes in one place, sometimes in another. The spade was usually to be found in the small tool shed. Was it locked? Of course it was locked. Where was the key kept? *Parbleu*, it was in the door of course! There was nothing of value to steal. Who would have expected a party of bandits, of assassins? Such things did not happen in Madame la Vicomtesse's time. M. Hautet signifying that he had finished with him, the old man withdrew, grumbling to the last. Remembering Poirot's unaccountable insistence on the footprints in the flower beds, I scrutinized him narrowly as he gave his evidence. Either he had nothing to do with the crime or he was a consummate actor. Suddenly, just as he was going out of the door, an idea struck me. "*Pardon* M. Hautet," I cried, "but will you permit me to ask him one question?"

"But certainly, monsieur."

Thus encouraged, I turned to Auguste.

"Where do you keep your boots?"

"*Sac à papier!*" growled the old man. "On my feet. Where else?"

"But when you go to bed at night?"

"Under my bed."

"But who cleans them?"

"Nobody. Why should they be cleaned? Is it that I promenade myself on the front like a young man? On Sunday I wear the Sunday boots, *bien entendu*, but otherwise—!" he shrugged his shoulders.

I shook my head, discouraged.

"Well, well," said the magistrate. "We do not advance very much. Undoubtedly we are held up until we get the return cable from Santiago. Has any one seen Giraud? In verity that one lacks politeness! I have a very good mind to send for him and—"

"You will not have to send far, M. le juge."

The quiet voice startled us. Giraud was standing outside looking in through the open window.

He leaped lightly into the room, and advanced to the table.

"Here I am, M. le juge, at your service. Accept my excuses for not presenting myself sooner."

"Not at all. Not at all," said the magistrate, rather confused.

"Of course I am only a detective," continued the other. "I know nothing of interrogatories. Were I conducting one, I should be inclined to do so without an open window. Any one standing outside can so easily hear all that passes . . . But no matter."

M. Hautet flushed angrily. There was evidently going to be no love lost between the examining magistrate and the detective in charge of the case. They had fallen foul of each other at the start. Perhaps in any event it would have been much the same. To Giraud, all examining magistrates were fools, and to M. Hautet who took himself seriously, the casual manner of the Paris detective could not fail to give offence.

"*Eh bien*, M. Giraud," said the magistrate rather sharply. "Without doubt you have been employing your time to a marvel? You have the names of the assassins for us, have you not? And also the precise spot where they find themselves now?"

Unmoved by this irony, Giraud replied:

"I know at least where they have come from."

"*Comment?*"

Giraud took two small objects from his pocket and laid them down on the table. We crowded round. The objects were very simple ones: the stub of a cigarette, and an unlighted match. The detective wheeled round on Poirot.

"What do you see there?" he asked.

There was something almost brutal in his tone. It made my cheeks flush. But Poirot remained unmoved. He shrugged his shoulders.

"A cigarette end, and a match."

"And what does that tell you?"

Poirot spread out his hands.

"It tells me—nothing."

"Ah!" said Giraud, in a satisfied voice. "You haven't made a study of these things. That's not an ordinary match—not in this country at least. It's common enough in South America. Luckily it's unlighted. I mightn't have recognized it otherwise. Evidently one of the men threw away his cigarette end, and lit another, spilling one match out of the box as he did so."

"And the other match?" asked Poirot.

"Which match?"

"The one he *did* light his cigarette with. You have found that also?"

"No."

"Perhaps you didn't search very thoroughly."

"Not search thoroughly—" For a moment it seemed as though the detective were going to break out angrily, but with an effort he controlled himself. "I see you love a joke, M. Poirot. But in any case, match or no match, the cigarette end would be sufficient. It is a South American cigarette with liquorice pectoral paper."

Poirot bowed. The commissary spoke:

"The cigarette end and match might have belonged to M. Renauld. Remember, it is only two years since he returned from South America."

73

"No," replied the other confidently. "I have already searched among the effects of M. Renauld. The cigarettes he smoked and the matches he used are quite different."

"You do not think it odd," asked Poirot, "that these strangers should come unprovided with a weapon, with gloves, with a spade, and that they should so conveniently find all these things?"

Giraud smiled in a rather superior manner.

"Undoubtedly it is strange. Indeed, without the theory that I hold, it would be inexplicable."

"Aha!" said M. Hautet. "An accomplice. An accomplice within the house!"

"Or outside it," said Giraud with a peculiar smile.

"But some one must have admitted them? We cannot allow that, by an unparalleled piece of good fortune, they found the door ajar for them to walk in?"

"*D'accord*, M. le juge. The door was opened for them, but it could just as easily be opened from outside—by some one who possessed a key."

"But who did possess a key?"

Giraud shrugged his shoulders.

"As for that, no one who possesses one is going to admit the fact if they can help it. But several people *might* have had one. M. Jack Renauld, the son, for instance. It is true that he is on his way to South America, but he might have lost the key or had it stolen from him. Then there is the gardener—he has been here many years. One of the younger servants may have a lover. It is easy to take an impression of a key and have one cut. There are many possibilities. Then there is another person who, I should judge, is exceedingly likely to have such a thing in her keeping."

"Who is that?"

"Madame Daubreuil," said the detective dryly.

"Eh, eh!" said the magistrate, his face falling a little, "so you have heard about that, have you?"

"I hear everything," said Giraud imperturbably.

"There is one thing I could swear you have not heard," said M. Hautet, delighted to be able to show superior knowledge, and without more ado, he retailed the story of the mysterious visitor the night before. He also touched on the cheque made out to "Duveen," and finally handed Giraud the letter signed "Bella."

Giraud listened in silence, studied the letter attentively, and then handed it back.

"All very interesting, M. le juge. But my theory remains unaffected."

"And your theory is?"

"For the moment I prefer not to say. Remember, I am only just beginning my investigations."

"Tell me one thing, M. Giraud," said Poirot suddenly. "Your theory allows for the door being opened. It does not explain why it was *left* open. When they departed, would it not have been natural for them to close it behind them? If a *sergent de ville* had chanced to come up to the house, as is sometimes done to see that all is well, they might have been discovered and overtaken almost at once."

"Bah! They forgot it. A mistake, I grant you."

Then, to my surprise, Poirot uttered almost the same words as he had uttered to Bex the previous evening:

"*I do not agree with you.* The door being left open was the result of either design or necessity, and any theory that does not admit that fact is bound to prove vain."

We all regarded the little man with a good deal of astonishment. The confession of ignorance drawn from him over the match end had, I thought, been bound to humiliate him, but here he was self-satisfied as ever, laying down the law to the great Giraud without a tremor.

The detective twisted his moustache, eyeing my friend in a somewhat bantering fashion.

"You don't agree with me, eh? Well, what strikes you particularly about the case. Let's hear your views."

"One thing presents itself to me as being significant. Tell me, M. Giraud, does nothing strike you as familiar about this case? Is there nothing it reminds you of?"

"Familiar? Reminds me of? I can't say off-hand. I don't think so, though."

"You are wrong," said Poirot quietly. "A crime almost precisely similar has been committed before."

"When? And where?"

"Ah, that, unfortunately, I cannot for the moment remember—but I shall do so. I had hoped you might be able to assist me."

Giraud snorted incredulously.

"There have been many affairs of masked men! I cannot remember the details of them all. These crimes all resemble each other more or less."

"There is such a thing as the individual touch." Poirot suddenly assumed his lecturing manner, and addressed us collectively. "I am speaking to you now of the psychology of crime. M. Giraud knows quite well that each criminal has his particular method, and that the police, when called in to investigate—say a case of burglary—can often make a shrewd guess at the offender, simply by the peculiar method he has employed. (Japp would tell you the same, Hastings.) Man is an unoriginal animal. Unoriginal within the law in his daily respectable life, equally unoriginal outside the law. If a man commits a crime, any other crime he commits will resemble it closely. The English murderer who disposed of his wives in succession by drowning them in their baths was a case in point. Had he varied his methods, he might have escaped detection to this day. But he obeyed the common dictates of human nature, arguing that what had once succeeded would succeed again, and he paid the penalty of his lack of originality."

"And the point of all this?" sneered Giraud.

"That when you have two crimes precisely similar in design and execution, you find the same brain behind them both. I am looking for that brain, M. Giraud—and I shall find it. Here we have a true clue—a psychological clue. You may know all about cigarettes and match ends, M. Giraud, but I, Hercule Poirot, know the mind of man!" And the ridiculous little fellow tapped his forehead with emphasis.

Giraud remained singularly unimpressed.

"For your guidance," continued Poirot, "I will also advise you of one fact which might fail to be brought to your notice. The wrist watch of Madame Renauld, on the day following the tragedy, had gained two hours. It might interest you to examine it."

Giraud stared.

"Perhaps it was in the habit of gaining?"

"As a matter of fact, I am told it did."

"*Eh bien*, then!"

"All the same, two hours is a good deal," said Poirot softly. "Then there is the matter of the footprints in the flower-bed."

He nodded his head towards the open window. Giraud took two eager strides, and looked out.

"This bed here?"

"Yes."

"But I see no footprints?"

"No," said Poirot, straightening a little pile of books on a table. "There are none."

For a moment an almost murderous rage obscured Giraud's face. He took two strides towards his tormentor, but at that moment the *salon* door was opened, and Marchaud announced.

"M. Stonor, the secretary, has just arrived from England. May he enter?"

10. Gabriel Stonor

The man who entered the room was a striking figure. Very tall, with a well-knit athletic frame, and a deeply bronzed face and neck, he dominated the assembly. Even Giraud seemed anaemic beside him. When I knew him better I realized that Gabriel Stonor was quite an unusual personality. English by birth, he had knocked about all over the world. He had shot big game in Africa, travelled in Korea, ranched in California, and traded in the South Sea Islands. He had been secretary to a New York railway magnate, and had spent a year encamped in the desert with a friendly tribe of Arabs.

His unerring eye picked out M. Hautet.

"The examining magistrate in charge of the case? Pleased to meet you, M. le juge. This is a terrible business. How's Mrs. Renauld? Is she bearing up fairly well? It must have been an awful shock to her."

"Terrible, terrible," said M. Hautet. "Permit me to introduce M. Bex—our commissary of police, M. Giraud of the Sûreté. This gentleman is M. Hercule Poirot. M. Renauld sent for him, but he arrived too late to do anything to avert the tragedy. A friend of M. Poirot's, Captain Hastings."

Stonor looked at Poirot with some interest.

"Sent for you, did he?"

"You did not know, then, that M. Renauld contemplated calling in a detective?" interposed M. Bex.

"No, I didn't. But it doesn't surprise me a bit."

"Why?"

"Because the old man was rattled! I don't know what it was all about. He didn't confide in me. We weren't on those terms. But rattled he was—and badly!"

"H'm!" said M. Hautet. "But you have no notion of the cause?"

"That's what I said, sir."

"You will pardon me, M. Stonor, but we must begin with a few formalities. Your name?"

"Gabriel Stonor."

"How long ago was it that you became secretary to M. Renauld?"

"About two years ago, when he first arrived from South America. I met him through a mutual friend, and he offered me the post. A thundering good boss he was too."

"Did he talk to you much about his life in South America?"

"Yes, a good bit."

"Do you know if he was ever in Santiago?"

"Several times, I believe."

"He never mentioned any special incident that occurred there—anything that might have provoked some vendetta against him?"

"Never."

"Did he speak of any secret that he had acquired whilst sojourning there?"

"No."

"Did he ever say anything at all about a secret?"

"Not that I can remember. But, for all that, there *was* a mystery about him. I've never heard him speak of his boyhood for instance, or of any incident prior to his arrival in South America. He was a French-Canadian by birth, I believe, but I've never heard him speak of his life in Canada. He could shut up like a clam if he liked."

"So, as far as you know, he had no enemies, and you can give us no clue as to any secret to obtain possession of which he might have been murdered?"

"That's so."

"M. Stonor, have you ever heard the name of Duveen in connection with M. Renauld?"

"Duveen. Duveen." He tried the name over thoughtfully. "I don't think I have. And yet it seems familiar."

"Do you know a lady, a friend of M. Renauld's whose Christian name is Bella?"

Again Mr. Stonor shook his head.

"Bella Duveen? Is that the full name? It's curious! I'm sure I know it. But for the moment I can't remember in what connection."

The magistrate coughed.

"You understand, M. Stonor—the case is like this. *There must be no reservations.* You might, perhaps, through a feeling of consideration for Madame Renauld—for whom, I gather, you have a great esteem and affection, you might—*enfin!*" said M. Hautet getting rather tied up in his sentence, "there must absolutely be no reservations."

Stonor stared at him, a dawning light of comprehension in his eyes.

"I don't quite get you," he said gently. "Where does Mrs. Renauld come in? I've an immense respect and affection for that lady; she's a very wonderful and unusual type, but I don't quite see how my reservations, or otherwise, could affect her?"

"Not if this Bella Duveen should prove to have been something more than a friend to her husband?"

"Ah!" said Stonor. "I get you now. But I'll bet my bottom dollar that you're wrong. The old man never so much as looked at a petticoat. He just adored his own wife. They were the most devoted couple I know."

M. Hautet shook his head gently.

"M. Stonor, we hold absolute proof—a love letter written by this Bella to M. Renauld, accusing him of having tired of her. Moreover, we have further proof that, at the time of his death, he was carrying on an intrigue with a Frenchwoman, a Madame Daubreuil, who rents the adjoining Villa. And this is the man who, according to you, never looked at a petticoat!"

The secretary's eyes narrowed.

"Hold on, M. le juge. You're barking up the wrong tree. I knew

Paul Renauld. What you've just been saying is utterly impossible. There's some other explanation."

The magistrate shrugged his shoulders.

"What other explanation could there be?"

"What leads you to think it was a love affair?"

"Madame Daubreuil was in the habit of visiting him here in the evenings. Also, since M. Renauld came to the Villa Geneviève, Madame Daubreuil has paid large sums of money into the bank in notes. In all, the amount totals four thousand pounds of your English money."

"I guess that's right," said Stonor quietly. "I transmitted him those sums at his request. But it wasn't an intrigue."

"Eh! *mon Dieu*! What else could it be?"

"*Blackmail*," said Stonor sharply, bringing down his hand with a slam on the table. "That's what it was."

"Ah! Voilà une idée!" cried the magistrate, shaken in spite of himself.

"Blackmail," repeated Stonor. "The old man was being bled—and at a good rate too. Four thousand in a couple of months. Whew! I told you just now there was a mystery about Renauld. Evidently this Madame Daubreuil knew enough of it to put the screws on."

"It is possible," the commissary cried excitedly. "Decidedly, it is possible."

"Possible?" roared Stonor. "It's certain! Tell me, have you asked Mrs. Renauld about this love affair stunt of yours?"

"No, monsieur. We did not wish to occasion her any distress if it could reasonably be avoided."

"Distress? Why, she'd laugh in your face. I tell you, she and Renauld were a couple in a hundred."

"Ah, that reminds me of another point," said M. Hautet. "Did M. Renauld take you into his confidence at all as to the dispositions of his will?"

"I know all about it—took it to the lawyer for him after he'd drawn it out. I can give you the name of his solicitors if you want to see it. They've got it there. Quite simple. Half in trust to his wife for her lifetime, the other half to his son. A few legacies. I rather think he left me a thousand."

"When was this will drawn up?"

"Oh, about a year and a half ago."

"Would it surprise you very much, M. Stonor, to hear that M. Renauld had made another will, less than a fortnight ago?"

Stonor was obviously very much surprised.

"I'd no idea of it. What's it like?"

"The whole of his vast fortune is left unreservedly to his wife. There is no mention of his son."

Mr. Stonor gave vent to a prolonged whistle.

"I call that rather rough on the lad. His mother adores him, of course, but to the world at large it looks rather like a want of confidence on his father's part. It will be rather galling to his pride. Still, it all goes to prove what I told you, that Renauld and his wife were on first rate terms."

"Quite so, quite so," said M. Hautet. "It is possible we shall have to revise our ideas on several points. We have, of course, cabled to Santiago, and are expecting a reply from there any minute. In all possibility, everything will then be perfectly clear and straightforward. On the other hand, if your suggestion of blackmail is true, Madame Daubreuil ought to be able to give us valuable information."

Poirot interjected a remark:

"M. Stonor, the English chauffeur, Masters, had he been long with M. Renauld?"

"Over a year?"

"Have you any idea whether he has ever been in South America?"

"I'm quite sure he hasn't. Before coming to Mr. Renauld, he had been for many years with some people in Gloucestershire whom I know well."

"In fact, you can answer for him as being above suspicion?"

"Absolutely."

Poirot seemed somewhat crestfallen.

Meanwhile the magistrate had summoned Marchaud.

"My compliments to Madame Renauld, and I should be glad to speak to her for a few minutes. Beg her not to disturb herself. I will wait upon her upstairs."

Marchaud saluted and disappeared.

We waited some minutes, and then, to our surprise, the door opened, and Mrs. Renauld, deathly pale in her heavy mourning, entered the room.

M. Hautet brought forward a chair, uttering vigorous protestations, and she thanked him with a smile. Stonor was holding one hand of hers in his with an eloquent sympathy. Words evidently failed him. Mrs. Renauld turned to M. Hautet.

"You wished to ask me something, M. le juge."

"With your permission, madame. I understand your husband was a French-Canadian by birth. Can you tell me anything of his youth, or upbringing?"

She shook her head.

"My husband was always very reticent about himself, monsieur. He came from the North West, I know, but I fancy that he had an unhappy childhood, for he never cared to speak of that time. Our life was lived entirely in the present and the future."

"Was there any mystery in his past life?"

Mrs. Renauld smiled a little, and shook her head.

"Nothing so romantic, I am sure, M. le juge."

M. Hautet also smiled.

"True, we must not permit ourselves to get melodramatic. There is one thing more—" he hesitated.

Stonor broke in impetuously:

"They've got an extraordinary idea into their heads Mrs. Renauld. They actually fancy that Mr. Renauld was carrying on an intrigue with a Madame Daubreuil who, it seems, lives next door."

The scarlet colour flamed into Mrs. Renauld's cheeks. She flung her head up, then bit her lip, her face quivering. Stonor stood looking at her in astonishment, but M. Bex leaned forward and said gently: "We regret to cause you pain, madame, but have you any reason to believe that Madame Daubreuil was your husband's mistress?"

With a sob of anguish, Mrs. Renauld buried her face in her hands. Her shoulders heaved convulsively. At last she lifted her head, and said brokenly:

"She may have been."

Never, in all my life, have I seen anything to equal the blank amazement on Stonor's face. He was thoroughly taken aback.

11. Jack Renauld

What the next development of the conversation would have been, I cannot say, for at that moment the door was thrown violently open, and a tall young man strode into the room.

Just for a moment I had the uncanny sensation that the dead man had come to life again. Then I realized that this dark head was untouched with grey, and that, in point of fact, it was a mere boy who now burst in among us with so little ceremony. He went straight to Mrs. Renauld with an impetuosity that took no heed of the presence of others.

"Mother!"

"Jack!" With a cry she folded him in her arms. "My dearest! But what brings you here? You were to sail on the *Anzora* from Cherbourg two days ago?" Then, suddenly recalling to herself the presence of others, she turned with a certain dignity, "My son, messieurs."

"Aha!" said M. Hautet, acknowledging the young man's bow. "So you did not sail on the *Anzora*?"

"No, monsieur. As I was about to explain, the *Anzora* was

detained twenty-four hours through engine trouble. I should have sailed last night instead of the night before, but, happening to buy an evening paper, I saw in it an account of the—the awful tragedy that had befallen us—" His voice broke and the tears came into his eyes. "My poor father—my poor, poor, father."

Staring at him like one in a dream, Mrs. Renauld repeated: "So you did not sail?" And then, with a gesture of infinite weariness, she murmured as though to herself, "After all, it does not matter—now."

"Sit down, M. Renauld, I beg of you," said M. Hautet, indicating a chair. "My sympathy for you is profound. It must have been a terrible shock to you to learn the news as you did. However, it is most fortunate that you were prevented from sailing. I am in hopes that you may be able to give us just the information we need to clear up this mystery."

"I am at your disposal, M. le juge. Ask me any questions you please."

"To begin with, I understand that this journey was being undertaken at your father's request?"

"Quite so, M. le juge. I received a telegram bidding me to proceed without delay to Buenos Aires, and from thence via the Andes to Valparaiso and on to Santiago."

"Ah. And the object of this journey?"

"I have no idea, M. le juge."

"What?"

"No. See, here is the telegram."

The magistrate took it and read it aloud.

"'Proceed immediately Cherbourg embark *Anzora* sailing tonight Buenos Aires. Ultimate destination Santiago. Further instructions will await you Buenos Aires. Do not fail. Matter is of utmost importance. Renauld.' And there had been no previous correspondence on the matter?"

Jack Renauld shook his head.

"That is the only intimation of any kind. I knew, of course, that my father, having lived so long out there, had necessarily many interests in South America. But he had never mooted any suggestion of sending me out."

"You have, of course, been a good deal in South America, M. Renauld?"

"I was there as a child. But I was educated in England, and spent most of my holidays in that country, so I really know far less of South America than might be supposed. You see, the war broke out when I was seventeen."

"You served in the English Flying Corps, did you not?"

"Yes, M. le juge."

M. Hautet nodded his head, and proceeded with his inquiries along the, by now, well-known lines. In response, Jack Renauld declared definitely that he knew nothing of any enmity his father might have incurred in the city of Santiago, or elsewhere in the South American continent, that he had noticed no change in his father's manner of late, and that he had never heard him refer to a secret. He had regarded the mission to South America as connected with business interests.

As M. Hautet paused for a minute, the quiet voice of Giraud broke in.

"I should like to put a few questions on my own account, M. le juge."

"By all means, M. Giraud, if you wish," said the magistrate coldly.

Giraud edged his chair a little nearer to the table.

"Were you on good terms with your father, M. Renauld?"

"Certainly I was," returned the lad haughtily.

"You assert that positively?"

"Yes."

"No little disputes, eh?"

Jack shrugged his shoulders. "Every one may have a difference of opinion now and then."

"Quite so, quite so. But if any one were to assert that you had a violent quarrel with your father on the eve of your departure for Paris, that person, without doubt, would be lying?"

I could not but admire the ingenuity of Giraud. His boast "I know everything" had been no idle one. Jack Renauld was clearly disconcerted by the question.

"We—we did have an argument," he admitted.

"Ah, an argument! In the course of that argument did you use this phrase: 'When you are dead, I can do as I please?'"

"I may have done," muttered the other. "I don't know."

"In response to that, did your father say: 'But I am not dead yet!' To which you responded: 'I wish you were!'"

The boy made no answer. His hands fiddled nervously with the things on the table in front of him.

"I must request an answer, please, M. Renauld," said Giraud sharply.

With an angry exclamation, the boy swept a heavy paper-knife on to the floor.

"What does it matter? You might as well know. Yes, I did quarrel with my father. I dare say I said all those things—I was so angry I cannot even remember what I said! I was furious—I could almost have killed him at that moment—there, make the most of that!" He leant back in his chair, flushed and defiant.

Giraud smiled, then, moving his chair back a little, said:

"That is all. You would, without doubt, prefer to continue the interrogatory, M. le juge."

"Ah, yes, exactly," said M. Hautet. "And what was the subject of your quarrel?"

"I decline to state."

M. Hautet sat up in his chair.

"M. Renauld, it is not permitted to trifle with the law!" he thundered. "What was the subject of the quarrel?"

Young Renauld remained silent, his boyish face sullen and overcast. But another voice spoke, imperturbable and calm, the voice of Hercule Poirot.

"I will inform you, if you like, M. le juge."

"You know?"

"Certainly I know. The subject of the quarrel was Mademoiselle Marthe Daubreuil."

Renauld sprang round, startled. The magistrate leaned forward.

"Is this so, monsieur."

Jack Renauld bowed his head.

"Yes," he admitted. "I love Mademoiselle Daubreuil, and I wish to marry her. When I informed my father of the fact, he flew at once into a violent rage. Naturally I could not stand hearing the girl I loved insulted, and I, too, lost my temper."

M. Hautet looked across at Mrs. Renauld.

"You were aware of this—attachment, madame."

"I feared it," she replied simply.

"Mother," cried the boy. "You too! Marthe is as good as she is beautiful. What can you have against her?"

"I have nothing against Mademoiselle Daubreuil in any way. But I should prefer you to marry an Englishwoman, or if a Frenchwoman not one who has a mother of doubtful antecedents!"

Her rancour against the older woman showed plainly in her voice, and I could well understand that it must have been a bitter blow to her when her only son showed signs of falling in love with the daughter of her rival.

Mrs. Renauld continued, addressing the magistrate:

"I ought, perhaps, to have spoken to my husband on the subject, but I hoped that it was only a boy and girl flirtation which would blow over all the quicker if no notice was taken of it. I blame myself now for my silence, but my husband, as I told you, had seemed so anxious and care-worn, different altogether from his normal self, that I was chiefly concerned not to give him any additional worry."

M. Hautet nodded.

"When you informed your father of your intentions towards Mademoiselle Daubreuil," he resumed, "he was surprised?"

"He seemed completely taken aback. Then he ordered me peremptorily to dismiss any such idea from my mind. He would never give his consent to such a marriage. Nettled, I demanded what he had against Mademoiselle Daubreuil. To that he could give no satisfactory reply, but spoke in slighting terms of the mystery surrounding the lives of the mother and daughter. I answered that I was marrying Marthe, and not her antecedents, but he shouted me down with a peremptory refusal to discuss the matter in any way. The whole thing must be given up. The injustice and high-handedness of it all maddened me—especially since he himself always seemed to go out of his way to be attentive to the Daubreuils and was always suggesting that they should be asked to the house. I lost my head, and we quarrelled in earnest. My father reminded me that I was entirely dependent on him, and it must have been in answer to that that I made the remark about doing as I pleased after his death—"

Poirot interrupted with a quick question.

"You were aware, then, of the terms of your father's will?"

"I knew that he had left half his fortune to me, the other half in trust for my mother to come to me at her death," replied the lad.

"Proceed with your story," said the magistrate.

"After that we shouted at each other in sheer rage, until I suddenly realized that I was in danger of missing my train to Paris. I had to run for the station, still in a white heat of fury. However, once well away, I calmed down. I wrote to Marthe, telling her what had happened, and her reply soothed me still further. She pointed out to me that we had only to be steadfast, and any opposition was bound to give way at last. Our affection for each other must be tried and proved, and when my parents realized that it was no light infatuation on my part they would doubtless relent towards us. Of course, to her, I had not dwelt on my father's principal objection to the match. I soon saw that I should do my cause no good by violence. My father wrote me several letters to Paris, affectionate in tone, and which did not refer to our disagreement or its cause, and I replied in the same strain."

"You can produce those letters, eh?" said Giraud.

"I did not keep them."

"No matter," said the detective.

Renauld looked at him for a moment, but the magistrate was continuing his questions.

"To pass to another matter, are you acquainted with the name of Duveen, M. Renauld?"

"Duveen?" said Jack. "Duveen?" He leant forward, and slowly picked up the paper-knife he had swept from the table. As he lifted his head, his eyes met the watching ones of Giraud. "Duveen? No, I can't say I am."

"Will you read this letter, M. Renauld? And tell me if you have any idea as to who the person was who addressed it to your father?"

Jack Renauld took the letter, and read it through, the colour mounting in his face as he did so.

"Addressed to my father?" The emotion and indignation in his tones were evident.

"Yes. We found it in the pocket of his coat."

"Does—" He hesitated, throwing the merest fraction of a glance towards his mother. The magistrate understood.

"As yet—no. Can you give us any clue as to the writer?"

"I have no idea whatsoever."

M. Hautet sighed.

"A most mysterious case. Ah, well, I suppose we can now rule out the letter altogether. What do you think, M. Giraud? It does not seem to lead us anywhere."

"It certainly does not," agreed the detective with emphasis.

"And yet," sighed the magistrate, "it promised at the beginning to be such a beautiful and simple case!" He caught Mrs. Renauld's eye, and blushed in immediate confusion. "Ah, yes," he coughed, turning over the papers on the table. "Let me see, where were we? Oh, the weapon. I fear this may give you pain, M. Renauld. I understand it was a present from you to your mother. Very sad—very distressing—"

Jack Renauld leaned forward. His face, which had flushed during the perusal of the letter, was now deadly white.

"Do you mean——that it was with an aeroplane wire paper cutter that my father was—was killed? But it's impossible! A little thing like that!"

"Alas, M. Renauld, it is only too true! An ideal little tool, I fear. Sharp and easy to handle."

"Where is it? Can I see it? Is it still in the—the body?"

"Oh, no, it had been removed. You would like to see it? To make sure? It would be as well, perhaps, though madame has already identified it. Still—M. Bex, might I trouble you?"

"Certainly, M. le juge. I will fetch it immediately."

"Would it not be better to take M. Renauld to the shed?" suggested Giraud smoothly. "Without doubt he would wish to see his father's body."

The boy made a shivering gesture of negation, and the magistrate, always disposed to cross Giraud whenever possible, replied.

"But no—not at present. M. Bex will be so kind as to bring it to us here."

The commissary left the room. Stonor crossed to Jack, and wrung him by the hand. Poirot had risen and was adjusting a pair of candlesticks that struck his trained eye as being a shade askew. The magistrate was reading the mysterious love-letter through a last time, clinging desperately to his first theory of jealousy and a stab in the back.

Suddenly the door burst open and the commissary rushed in. "M. le juge! M. le juge!"

"But yes. What is it?"

"The dagger! It is gone!"

"*Comment*—gone?"

"Vanished. Disappeared. The glass jar that contained it is empty!"

"What?" I cried. "Impossible. Why, only this morning I saw—" The words died on my tongue.

But the attention of the entire room was diverted to me.

"What is that you say?" cried the commissary. "This morning?"

"I saw it there this morning," I said slowly. "About an hour and a half ago, to be accurate."

"You went to the shed, then? How did you get the key?"

"I asked the *sergent de ville* for it."

"And you went there? Why?"

I hesitated, but in the end I decided that the only thing to do was to make a clean breast of it.

"M. le juge," I said. "I have committed a grave fault, for which I must crave your indulgence."

"*Eh bien*! Proceed, monsieur."

"The fact of the matter is," I said, wishing myself anywhere else than where I was, "that I met a young lady, an acquaintance of mine. She displayed a great desire to see everything that was to be seen, and I—well, in short, I took the key to show her the body."

"Ah, *par exemple*," cried the magistrate indignantly. "But it is a grave fault you have committed there, Captain Hastings. It is altogether most irregular. You should not have permitted yourself this folly."

"I know," I said meekly. "Nothing that you can say could be too severe, M. le juge."

"You did not invite this lady to come here?"

"Certainly not. I met her quite by accident. She is an English lady who happens to be staying in Merlinville, though I was not aware of that until my unexpected meeting with her."

"Well, well," said the magistrate, softening. "It was most irregular, but the lady is without doubt young and beautiful, *n'est-ce pas*? What it is to be young! *O jeunesse, jeunesse!*" And he sighed sentimentally.

But the commissary, less romantic, and more practical, took up the tale:

"But did not you reclose and lock the door when you departed."

"That's just it," I said slowly. "That's what I blame myself for so terribly. My friend was upset at the sight. She nearly fainted. I got her some brandy and water, and afterwards insisted on accompanying her back to town. In the excitement, I forgot to relock the door. I only did so when I got back to the Villa."

"Then for twenty minutes at least—" said the commissary slowly. He stopped.

"Exactly," I said.

"Twenty minutes," mused the commissary.

"It is deplorable," said M. Hautet, his sternness of manner returning. "Without precedent."

Suddenly another voice spoke.

"You find it deplorable, M. le juge?" asked Giraud.

"Certainly I do."

"*Eh bien*! I find it admirable!" said the other imperturbably.

This unexpected ally quite bewildered me.

"Admirable, M. Giraud?" asked the magistrate, studying him cautiously out of the corner of his eye.

"Precisely."

"And why?"

"Because we know now that the assassin, or an accomplice of the assassin, has been near the Villa only an hour ago. It will be strange if, with that knowledge, we do not shortly lay hands upon him." There was a note of menace in his voice. He continued: "He risked a good deal to gain possession of that dagger. Perhaps he feared that finger-prints might be discovered on it."

Poirot turned to Bex.

"You said there were none?"

Giraud shrugged his shoulders.

"Perhaps he could not be sure."

Poirot looked at him.

"You are wrong, M. Giraud. The assassin wore gloves. So he must have been sure."

"I do not say it was the assassin himself. It may have been an accomplice who was not aware of that fact."

"*Ils sont mal renseignés, les accomplices!*" muttered Poirot, but he said no more.

The magistrate's clerk was gathering up the papers on the table. M. Hautet addressed us:

"Our work here is finished. Perhaps, M. Renauld, you will listen whilst your evidence is read over to you. I have purposely kept all the proceedings as informal as possible. I have been called original in my methods, but I maintain that there is much to be said for originality. The case is now in the clever hands of the renowned M. Giraud. He will without doubt distinguish himself. Indeed, I wonder that he has not already laid his hands upon the murderers! Madame, again let me assure you of my heartfelt sympathy. Messieurs, I wish you all good day." And, accompanied by his clerk and the commissary, he took his departure.

Poirot tugged out that large turnip of a watch of his, and observed the time.

"Let us return to the hotel for lunch, my friend," he said. "And you shall recount to me in full the indiscretions of this morning. No one is observing us. We need make no adieux."

We went quietly out of the room. The examining magistrate had just driven off in his car. I was going down the steps when Poirot's voice arrested me:

"One little moment, my friend." Dexterously, he whipped out his yard measure, and proceeded, quite solemnly, to measure an overcoat hanging in the hall from the collar to the hem. I had not seen it hanging there before, and guessed that it belonged to either Mr. Stonor, or Jack Renauld.

Then, with a little satisfied grunt, Poirot returned the measure to his pocket, and followed me out into the open air.

12. Poirot Elucidates Certain Points

Why did you measure that overcoat?" I asked, with some curiosity, as we walked down the hot white road at a leisurely pace.

"*Parbleu!* to see how long it was," replied my friend imperturbably.

I was vexed. Poirot's incurable habit of making a mystery out of nothing never failed to irritate me. I relapsed into silence, and followed a train of thought of my own. Although I had not noticed them specially at the time, certain words Mrs. Renauld had addressed to her son now recurred to me, fraught with a new significance. "So you did not sail?" she had said, and then had added: "*After all, it does not matter—now.*"

What had she meant by that? The words were enigmatical—significant. Was it possible that she knew more than we supposed? She had denied all knowledge of the mysterious mission with which her husband was to have entrusted his son. But was she really less ignorant than she pretended? Could she enlighten us if she chose, and was her silence part of a carefully thought out and preconceived plan?

The more I thought about it, the more I was convinced that I was right. Mrs. Renauld knew more than she chose to tell. In her surprise at seeing her son, she had momentarily betrayed herself. I felt convinced that she knew, if not the assassins, at least the motive for the assassination. But some very powerful considerations must keep her silent.

"You think profoundly, my friend," remarked Poirot, breaking in upon my reflections. "What is it that intrigues you so?"

I told him, sure of my ground, though feeling expectant that he would ridicule my suspicions. But to my surprise he nodded thoughtfully.

"You are quite right, Hastings. From the beginning I have been sure that she was keeping something back. At first I suspected her, if not of inspiring, at least of conniving at the crime."

"You suspected *her*?" I cried.

"But certainly! She benefits enormously—in fact, by this new will, she is the only person to benefit. So, from the start, she was singled out for attention. You may have noticed that I took an early opportunity of examining her wrists. I wished to see whether there was any possibility that she had gagged and bound herself. *Eh bien*, I saw at once that there was no fake, the cords had actually been drawn so tight as to cut into the flesh. That ruled out the possibility of her having committed the crime single-handed. But it was still possible for her to have connived at it, or to have been the instigator with an accomplice. Moreover, the story, as she told it, was singularly familiar to me—the masked men that she could not recognize, the mention of 'the secret'—I had heard, or read, all these things before. Another little detail confirmed my belief that she was not speaking the truth. *The wrist watch, Hastings, the wrist watch!*"

Again that wrist watch! Poirot was eyeing me curiously.

"You see, *mon ami*? You comprehend?"

"No," I replied with some ill humour. "I neither see nor comprehend. You make all these confounded mysteries, and it's useless asking you to explain. You always like keeping everything up your sleeve to the last minute."

"Do not enrage yourself, my friend," said Poirot with a smile. "I will explain if you wish. But not a word to Giraud, *c'est entendu*? He treats me as an old one of no importance! *We shall see*! In common fairness I gave him a hint. If he does not choose to act upon it, that is his own lookout."

I assured Poirot that he could rely upon my discretion.

"*C'est bien!* Let us then employ our little grey cells. Tell me, my friend, at what time, according to you, did the tragedy take place?"

"Why, at two o'clock or thereabouts," I said, astonished. "You remember, Mrs. Renauld told us that she heard the clock strike while the men were in the room."

"Exactly, and on the strength of that, you, the examining magistrate, Bex, and every one else, accept the time without further question. But I, Hercule Poirot, say that Madame Renauld lied. *The crime took place at least two hours earlier.*"

"But the doctors—"

"They declared, after examination of the body, that death had taken place between ten and seven hours previously. *Mon ami*, for some reason, it was imperative that the crime should seem to have taken place later than it actually did. You have read of a smashed watch or clock recording the exact hour of a crime? So that the time should not rest on Mrs. Renauld's testimony alone, some one moved on the hands of that wrist watch to two o'clock, and then dashed it violently to the ground. But, as is often the case, they defeated their own object. The glass was smashed, but the mechanism of the watch was uninjured. It was a most disastrous manoeuvre on their part, for it at once drew my attention to two points—first, that Madame Renauld was lying: secondly, that there must be some vital reason for the postponement of the time."

"But what reason could there be?"

"Ah, that is the question! There we have the whole mystery. As yet, I cannot explain it. There is only one idea that presents itself to me as having a possible connection."

"And that is?"

"The last train left Merlinville at seventeen minutes past twelve."

I followed it out slowly.

"So that, the crime apparently taking place some two hours later, any one leaving by that train would have an unimpeachable alibi!"

"Perfect, Hastings! You have it!"

I sprang up.

"But we must inquire at the station. Surely they cannot have failed to notice two foreigners who left by that train! We must go there at once!"

"You think so, Hastings?"

"Of course. Let us go there now."

Poirot restrained my ardour with a light touch upon the arm.

"Go by all means if you wish, *mon ami*—but if you go, I should not ask for particulars of two foreigners."

I stared, and he said rather impatiently:

"Là, là, you do not believe all that rigmarole, do you? The masked men and all the rest of *cette histoire-là*!"

His words took me so much aback that I hardly knew how to respond. He went on serenely:

"You heard me say to Giraud, did you not, that all the details of this crime were familiar to me? *Eh bien*, that presupposes one of two things, either the brain that planned the first crime also planned this one, or else an account read of a *cause célèbre* unconsciously remained in our assassin's memory and prompted the details. I shall be able to pronounce definitely on that after—" he broke off.

I was revolving sundry matters in my mind.

"But Mr. Renauld's letter? It distinctly mentions a secret and Santiago?"

"Undoubtedly there was a secret in M. Renauld's life—there can be no doubt of that. On the other hand, the word Santiago, to my mind, is a red herring, dragged continually across the track to put us off the scent. It is possible that it was used in the same way on M. Renauld, to keep him from directing his suspicions into a quarter nearer at hand. Oh, be assured, Hastings, the danger that threatened him was not in Santiago, it was near at hand, in France."

He spoke so gravely, and with such assurance, that I could not fail to be convinced. But I essayed one final objection:

"And the match and cigarette end found near the body? What of them."

A light of pure enjoyment lit up Poirot's face.

"Planted! Deliberately planted there for Giraud or one of his tribe to find! Ah, he is smart, Giraud, he can do his tricks! So can a good retriever dog. He comes in so pleased with himself. For hours he has crawled on his stomach. 'See what I have found,' he says. And then again to me: 'What do you see here?' Me, I answer, with profound and deep truth, 'Nothing.' And Giraud, the great Giraud, he laughs, he thinks to himself, 'Oh, that he is imbecile, this old one!' *But we shall see . . .*"

But my mind had reverted to the main facts.

"Then all this story of the masked men—?"

"Is false."

"What really happened?"

Poirot shrugged his shoulders.

"One person could tell us—Madame Renauld. But she will not speak. Threats and entreaties would not move her. A remarkable woman that, Hastings. I recognized as soon as I saw her that I had to deal with a woman of unusual character. At first, as I told you, I was inclined to suspect her of being concerned in the crime. Afterwards I altered my opinion."

"What made you do that?"

"Her spontaneous and genuine grief at the sight of her husband's body. I could swear that the agony in that cry of hers was genuine."

"Yes," I said thoughtfully, "one cannot mistake these things."

"I beg your pardon, my friend—one can always be mistaken. Regard a great actress, does not her acting of grief carry you away and impress you with its reality? No, however strong my own impression and belief, I needed other evidence before I allowed myself to be satisfied. The great criminal can be a great actor. I base my certainty in this case, not upon my own impression, but upon the undeniable fact that Mrs. Renauld actually fainted. I turned up her eyelids and felt her pulse. There was no deception—the swoon was genuine. Therefore I was satisfied that her anguish was real and not assumed. Besides, a small additional point not without interest, it was unnecessary for Mrs. Renauld to exhibit unrestrained grief. She had had one paroxysm on learning of her husband's death, and there would be no need for her to simulate another such a violent one on beholding his body. No, Mrs. Renauld was not her husband's murderess. But why has she lied? She lied about the wrist watch, she lied about the masked men—she lied about a third thing. Tell me, Hastings, what is your explanation of the open door?"

"Well," I said, rather embarrassed, "I suppose it was an oversight. They forgot to shut it."

Poirot shook his head, and sighed.

"That is the explanation of Giraud. It does not satisfy me. There is a meaning behind that open door which for a moment I cannot fathom."

"I have an idea," I cried suddenly.

"*A la bonne heure*! Let us hear it."

"Listen. We are agreed that Mrs. Renauld's story is a fabrication. Is it not possible, then, that Mr. Renauld left the house to keep an appointment—possibly with the murderer—leaving the front door open for his return. But he did not return, and the next morning he is found, stabbed in the back."

"An admirable theory, Hastings, but for two facts which you have characteristically overlooked. In the first place, who gagged and bound Madame Renauld? And why on earth should they return to the house to do so? In the second place, no man on earth would go out to keep an appointment wearing his underclothes and an overcoat. There are circumstances in which a man might wear pajamas and an overcoat—but the other, never!"

"True," I said, rather crest-fallen.

"No," continued Poirot, "we must look elsewhere for a solution of the open door mystery. One thing I am fairly sure of—they did not leave through the door. They left by the window."

"What?"

"Precisely."

"But there were no footmarks in the flower bed underneath."

"No—*and there ought to have been*. Listen, Hastings. The gardener, Auguste, as you heard him say, planted both those beds the preceding afternoon. In the one there are plentiful impressions of his big hobnailed boots—in the other, *none*! You see? Some one had passed that way, some one who, to obliterate their footprints, smoothed over the surface of the bed with a rake."

"Where did they get a rake?"

"Where they got the spade and the gardening gloves," said Poirot impatiently. "There is no difficulty about that."

"What makes you think that they left that way, though? Surely it is more probable that they entered by the window, and left by the door."

"That is possible of course. Yet I have a strong idea that they left by the window."

"I think you are wrong."

"Perhaps, *mon ami*."

I mused, thinking over the new field of conjecture that Poirot's deductions had opened up to me. I recalled my wonder at his cryptic allusions to the flower bed and the wrist watch. His remarks had seemed so meaningless at the moment and now, for the first time, I realized how remarkably, from a few slight incidents, he had unravelled much of the mystery that surrounded the case. I paid a belated homage to my friend. As though he read my thoughts, he nodded sagely.

"Method, you comprehend! Method! Arrange your facts. Arrange your ideas. And if some little fact will not fit in—do not reject it but consider it closely. Though its significance escapes you, be sure that it is significant."

"In the meantime," I said, considering, "although we know a great deal more than we did, we are no nearer to solving the mystery of who killed Mr. Renauld."

"No," said Poirot cheerfully. "In fact we are a great deal further off."

The fact seemed to afford him such peculiar satisfaction that I gazed at him in wonder. He met my eye and smiled.

"But yes, it is better so. Before, there was at all events a clear theory as to how and by whose hands he met his death. Now that is all gone. We are in darkness. A hundred conflicting points confuse and worry us. That is well. That is excellent. Out of confusion comes forth order. But if you find order to start with, if a crime seems simple and above-board, *eh bien, méfiez vous*! It is, how do you say it?—*cooked*! The great criminal is simple—but very few criminals *are* great. In trying to cover up their tracks, they invariably betray themselves. Ah, *mon ami*, I would that some day I could meet a really great criminal—one who commits his crime, and then—does nothing! Even I, Hercule Poirot, might fail to catch such a one."

But I had not followed his words. A light had burst upon me.

"Poirot! Mrs. Renauld! I see it now. She must be shielding somebody."

From the quietness with which Poirot received my remark, I could see that the idea had already occurred to him.

"Yes," he said thoughtfully. "Shielding some one—or screening some one. One of the two."

I saw very little difference between the two words, but I developed my theme with a good deal of earnestness. Poirot maintained a strictly non-committal attitude, repeating:

"It may be—yes, it may be. But as yet I do not know! There is something very deep underneath all this. You will see. Something very deep."

Then, as we entered our hotel, he enjoined silence on me with a gesture.

13. The Girl with the Anxious Eyes

We lunched with an excellent appetite. I understood well enough that Poirot did not wish to discuss the tragedy where we could so easily be overheard. But, as is usual when one topic fills the mind to the exclusion of everything else, no other subject of interest seemed to present itself. For a while we ate in silence, and then Poirot observed maliciously:

"*Eh bien*! And your indiscretions! You recount them not?"

I felt myself blushing.

"Oh, you mean this morning?" I endeavoured to adopt a tone of absolute nonchalance.

But I was no match for Poirot. In a very few minutes he had extracted the whole story from me, his eyes twinkling as he did so.

"*Tiens*! A story of the most romantic. What is her name, this charming young lady?"

I had to confess that I did not know.

"Still more romantic! The first *rencontre* in the train from Paris, the second here. Journeys end in lovers' meetings, is not that the saying?"

"Don't be an ass, Poirot."

"Yesterday it was Mademoiselle Daubreuil, today it is Mademoiselle—Cinderella! Decidedly you have the heart of a Turk, Hastings! You should establish a harem!"

"It's all very well to rag me. Mademoiselle Daubreuil is a very beautiful girl, and I do admire her immensely—I don't mind admitting it. The other's nothing—don't suppose I shall ever see her again. She was quite amusing to talk to just for a railway journey, but she's not the kind of girl I should ever get keen on."

"Why?"

"Well—it sounds snobbish perhaps—but she's not a lady, not in any sense of the word."

Poirot nodded thoughtfully. There was less raillery in his voice as he asked:

"You believe, then, in birth and breeding?"

"I may be old-fashioned, but I certainly don't believe in marrying out of one's class. It never answers."

"I agree with you, *mon ami*. Ninety-nine times out of a hundred, it is as you say. But there is always the hundredth time! Still, that does not arise, as you do not propose to see the lady again."

His last words were almost a question, and I was aware of the sharpness with which he darted a glance at me. And before my eyes, writ large in letters of fire, I saw the words "Hôtel du Phare," and I heard again her voice saying "Come and look me up" and my own answering with *empressement*: "I will."

Well, what of it? I had meant to go at the time. But since then, I had had time to reflect. I did not like the girl. Thinking it over in cold blood, I came definitely to the conclusion that I disliked her intensely. I had got hauled over the coals for foolishly gratifying her morbid curiosity, and I had not the least wish to see her again.

I answered Poirot lightly enough.

"She asked me to look her up, but of course I shan't."

"Why 'of course'?"

"Well—I don't want to."

"I see." He studied me attentively for some minutes. "Yes. I see very well. And you are wise. Stick to what you have said."

"That seems to be your invariable advice," I remarked, rather piqued.

"Ah, my friend, have faith in Papa Poirot. Some day, if you permit, I will arrange you a marriage of great suitability."

"Thank you," I said laughing, "but the prospect leaves me cold."

Poirot sighed and shook his head.

"*Les Anglais!*" he murmured. "No method—absolutely none whatever. They leave all to chance!" He frowned, and altered the position of the salt cellar.

"Mademoiselle Cinderella is staying at the Hôtel d'Angleterre you told me, did you not?"

"No. Hôtel du Phare."

"True, I forgot."

A moment's misgiving shot across my mind. Surely I had never mentioned any hotel to Poirot. I looked across at him, and felt reassured. He was cutting his bread into neat little squares, completely absorbed in his task. He must have fancied I had told him where the girl was staying.

We had coffee outside facing the sea. Poirot smoked one of his tiny cigarettes, and then drew his watch from his pocket.

"The train to Paris leaves at 2:25," he observed. "I should be starting."

"Paris?" I cried.

"That is what I said, *mon ami*."

"You are going to Paris? But why?"

He replied very seriously.

"To look for the murderer of M. Renauld."

"You think he is in Paris?"

"I am quite certain that he is not. Nevertheless, it is there that I must look for him. You do not understand, but I will explain it all to you in good time. Believe me, this journey to Paris is necessary. I shall not be away long. In all probability I shall return tomorrow. I do not propose that you should accompany me. Remain here and keep an eye on Giraud. Also cultivate the society of M. Renauld *fils*. And thirdly, if you wish, endeavour to cut him out with Mademoiselle Marthe. But I fear you will not have great success."

I did not quite relish the last remark.

"That reminds me," I said. "I meant to ask you how you knew about those two?"

"*Mon ami* —I know human nature. Throw together a boy young Renauld and a beautiful girl like Mademoiselle Marthe, and the result is almost inevitable. Then, the quarrel! It was money or a woman and, remembering Léonie's description of the lad's anger, I decided on the latter. So I made my guess—and I was right."

"And that was why you warned me against setting my heart on the lady? You already suspected that she loved young Renauld?"

Poirot smiled.

"At any rate—*I saw that she had anxious eyes*. That is how always think of Mademoiselle Daubreuil *as the girl with the anxious eyes* . . ."

His voice was so grave that it impressed me uncomfortably.

"What do you mean by that, Poirot?"

"I fancy, my friend, that we shall see before very long. But I must start."

"You've oceans of time."

"Perhaps—perhaps. But I like plenty of leisure at the station. I do not wish to rush, to hurry, to excite myself."

"At all events," I said, rising, "I will come and see you off."

"You will do nothing of the sort. I forbid it."

He was so peremptory that I stared at him in surprise. He nodded emphatically.

"I mean it, *mon ami*. Au revoir! You permit that I embrace you? Ah, no, I forget that it is not the English custom. Une poignee de main, alors."

I felt rather at a loose end after Poirot had left me. I strolled down the beach, and watched the bathers, without feeling energetic enough to join them. I rather fancied that Cinderella might be disporting herself amongst them in some wonderful costume, but I saw no signs of her. I strolled aimlessly along the sands towards the further end of the town. It occurred to me that, after all, it would only be decent feeling on my part to inquire after the girl. And it would save trouble in the end. The matter would then be finished with. There would be no need for me to trouble about her any further. But, if I did not go at all, she might quite possibly come and look me up at the Villa. And that would be annoying in every way. Decidedly it would be better to pay a short call, in the course of which I could make it quite clear that I could do nothing further for her in my capacity of showman.

Accordingly I left the beach, and walked inland. I soon found the Hôtel du Phare, a very unpretentious building. It was annoying in the extreme not to know the lady's name and, to save my dignity, I decided to stroll inside and look around. Probably I should find her in the lounge. Merlinville was a small place, you left your hotel to go to the beach, and you left the beach to return to the hotel. There were no other attractions. There was a Casino being built, but it was not yet completed.

I had walked the length of the beach without seeing her, therefore she must be in the hotel. I went in. Several people were sitting in the tiny lounge, but my quarry was not amongst them. I looked into some other rooms, but there was no sign of her. I waited for some time, till my impatience got the better of me. I took the concierge aside, and slipped five francs into his hand.

"I wish to see a lady who is staying here. A young English lady, small and dark. I am not sure of her name."

The man shook his head, and seemed to be suppressing a grin.

"There is no such lady as you describe staying here."

"She is American possibly," I suggested. These fellows are so stupid.

But the man continued to shake his head.

"No, monsieur. There are only six or seven English and American ladies altogether, and they are all much older than the lady you are seeking. It is not here that you will find her, monsieur."

He was so positive that I felt doubts.

"But the lady told me she was staying here."

"Monsieur must have made a mistake—or it is more likely the lady did, since there has been another gentleman here inquiring for her."

"What is that you say?" I cried, surprised.

"But yes, monsieur. A gentleman who described her just as you have done."

"What was he like?"

"He was a small gentleman, well dressed, very neat, very spotless, the moustache very stiff, the head of a peculiar shape, and the eyes green."

Poirot! So that was why he refused to let me accompany him to the station. The impertinence of it! I would thank him not to meddle in my concerns. Did he fancy I needed a nurse to look after me? Thanking the man, I departed, somewhat at a loss, and still much incensed with my meddlesome friend. I regretted that he was, for the moment, out of reach. I should have enjoyed telling him what I thought of his unwarranted interference. Had I not distinctly told him that I had no intention of seeing the girl? Decidedly, one's friends can be too zealous!

But where was the lady? I set aside my wrath, and tried to puzzle it out. Evidently, through inadvertence, she had named the wrong hotel. Then another thought struck me. Was it inadvertence? Or had she deliberately withheld her name and given me the wrong address? The more I thought about it, the more I felt convinced that this last surmise of mine was right. For some reason or other she did not wish to let the acquaintance ripen into friendship. And though half an hour earlier this had been precisely my own view, I did not enjoy having the tables turned upon me. The whole affair was profoundly unsatisfactory, and I went up to the Villa Geneviève in a condition of distinct ill humour. I did not go to the house, but went up the path to the little bench by the shed, and sat there moodily enough.

I was distracted from my thoughts by the sound of voices close at hand. In a second or two I realized that they came, not from the garden I was in, but from the adjoining garden of the Villa Marguerite, and that they were approaching rapidly. A girl's voice was speaking, a voice that I recognized as that of the beautiful Marthe.

"*Chéri*," she was saying, "is it really true? Are all our troubles over."

"You know it, Marthe," Jack Renauld replied. "Nothing can part us now, beloved. The last obstacle to our union is removed. Nothing can take you from me."

"Nothing?" the girl murmured. "Oh, Jack, Jack—I am afraid."

I had moved to depart, realizing that I was quite unintentionally eavesdropping. As I rose to my feet, I caught sight of them through a gap in the hedge. They stood together facing me, the man's arm round the girl, his eyes looking into hers. They were a splendid looking couple, the dark, well-knit boy, and the fair young goddess. They seemed made for each other as they stood there, happy in spite of the terrible tragedy that overshadowed their young lives.

But the girl's face was troubled, and Jack Renauld seemed to recognize it, as he held her closer to him and asked:

"But what are you afraid of, darling? What is there to fear—now?"

And then I saw the look in her eyes, the look Poirot had spoken of, as she murmured, so that I almost guessed at the words.

"I am afraid—for *you* . . ."

I did not hear young Renauld's answer, for my attention was distracted by an unusual appearance a little further down the hedge. There appeared to be a brown bush there, which seemed odd, to say the least of it, so early in the summer. I stepped along to investigate, but, at my advance, the brown bush withdrew itself precipitately, and faced me with a finger to its lips. It was Giraud.

Enjoining caution, he led the way round the shed until we were out of ear-shot.

"What were you doing there?" I asked.

"Exactly what you were doing—listening."

"But I was not there on purpose!"

"Ah!" said Giraud. "I was."

As always, I admired the man whilst disliking him. He looked me up and down with a sort of contemptuous disfavour.

"You didn't help matters by butting in. I might have heard something useful in a minute. What have you done with your old fossil?"

"M. Poirot has gone to Paris," I replied coldly.

"And I can tell you, M. Giraud, that he is anything but an old fossil. He has solved many cases that have completely baffled the English police."

"Bah! The English police!" Giraud snapped his fingers disdainfully. "They must be on a level with our examining magistrates. So he has gone to Paris, has he? Well, a good thing. The longer he stays there, the better. But what does he think he will find there?"

I thought I read in the question a tinge of uneasiness. I drew myself up.

"That I am not at liberty to say," I said quietly.

Giraud subjected me to a piercing stare.

"He has probably enough sense not to tell *you*," he remarked rudely. "Good afternoon. I'm busy." And with that, he turned on his heel, and left me without ceremony.

Matters seemed at a standstill at the Villa Geneviève. Giraud evidently did not desire my company and, from what I had seen, it seemed fairly certain that Jack Renauld did not either.

I went back to the town, had an enjoyable bath and returned to the hotel. I turned in early, wondering whether the following day would bring forth anything of interest.

I was wholly unprepared for what it did bring forth. I was eating my *petit déjeuner* in the dining-room, when the waiter, who had been talking to someone outside, came back in obvious excitement. He hesitated for a minute, fidgeting with his napkin, and then burst out:

"Monsieur will pardon me, but he is connected, is he not, with the affair at the Villa Geneviève?'

"Yes," I said eagerly. "Why?"

"Monsieur has not heard the news, though?"

"What news?"

"That there has been another murder there last night!"

"*What*?"

Leaving my breakfast, I caught up my hat and ran as fast as I could. Another murder—and Poirot away! What fatality. But who had been murdered?

I dashed in at the gate. A group of the servants was in the drive, talking and gesticulating. I caught hold of Françoise.

"What has happened?"

"Oh, monsieur! monsieur! Another death! It is terrible. There is a curse upon the house. But yes, I say it, a curse! They should send for M. le curé to bring some holy water. Never will I sleep another night under that roof. It might be my turn, who knows?"

She crossed herself.

"Yes," I cried, "but who has been killed?"

"Do I know—me? A man—a stranger. They found him up there—in the shed—not a hundred yards from where they found poor Monsieur. And that is not all. He is stabbed—stabbed to the heart *with the same dagger*!"

14. The Second Body

Waiting for no more, I turned and ran up the path to the shed. The two men on guard there stood aside to let me pass and, filled with excitement, I entered.

The light was dim, the place was a mere rough wooden erection to keep old pots and tools in. I had entered impetuously, but on the threshold I checked myself, fascinated by the spectacle before me.

Giraud was on his hands and knees, a pocket torch in his hand with which he was examining every inch of the ground. He looked up with a frown at my entrance, then his face relaxed a little in a sort of good-humoured contempt.

"Ah, *c'est l'Anglais!* Enter then. Let us see what you can make of this affair."

Rather stung by his tone, I stooped my head, and passed in.

"There he is," said Giraud, flashing his torch to the far corner.

I stepped across.

The dead man lay straight upon his back. He was of medium height, swarthy of complexion, and possibly about fifty years of age. He was neatly dressed in a dark blue suit, well cut and probably made by an expensive tailor, but not new. His face was terribly convulsed, and on his left side, just over the heart, the hilt of a dagger stood up, black and shining. I recognized it. It was the same dagger I had seen reposing in the glass jar the preceding morning!

"I'm expecting the doctor any minute," explained Giraud. "Although we hardly need him. There's no doubt what the man died of. He was stabbed to the heart, and death must have been pretty well instantaneous."

"When was it done? Last night?"

Giraud shook his head.

"Hardly. I don't lay down the law on medical evidence, but the man's been dead well over twelve hours. When do you say you last saw that dagger?"

"About ten o'clock yesterday morning."

"Then I should be inclined to fix the crime as being done not long after that."

"But people were passing and repassing this shed continually."

Giraud laughed disagreeably.

"You progress to a marvel! Who told you he was killed in this shed?"

"Well—" I felt flustered. "I—I assumed it."

"Oh, what a fine detective! Look at him, *mon petit*—does a man stabbed to the heart fall like that—neatly with his feet together, and his arms to his side? No. Again does a man lie down on his back and permit himself to be stabbed without raising a hand to defend himself? It is absurd, is it not? But see here—and here—" He flashed the torch along the ground. I saw curious irregular marks in the soft dirt. "He was dragged here after he was dead. Half dragged, half carried by two people. Their tracks do not show on the hard ground outside, and here they have been careful to obliterate them—but one of the two was a woman, my young friend."

"A woman?"

"Yes."

"But if the tracks are obliterated, how do you know?"

"Because, blurred as they are, the prints of the woman's shoe are unmistakable. Also, by *this*—" And, leaning forward, he drew something from the handle of the dagger and held it up for me to see. It was a woman's long black hair—similar to the one Poirot had taken from the arm-chair in the library.

With a slightly ironic smile he wound it round the dagger again.

"We will leave things as they are as much as possible," he explained. "It pleases the examining magistrate. *Eh bien*, do you notice anything else?"

I was forced to shake my head.

"Look at his hands."

I did. The nails were broken and discoloured, and the skin was hard. It hardly enlightened me as much as I should have liked it to have done. I looked up at Giraud.

"They are not the hands of a gentleman," he said, answering my look. "On the contrary his clothes are those of a well-to-do man. That is curious, is it not?"

"Very curious," I agreed.

"And none of his clothing is marked. What do we learn from that? This man was trying to pass himself off as other than he was. He was masquerading. Why? Did he fear something? Was he trying to escape by disguising himself? As yet we do not know, but one thing we do know—he was as anxious to conceal his identity as we are to discover it."

He looked down at the body again.

"As before there are no finger-prints on the handle of the dagger. The murderer again wore gloves."

"You think, then, that the murderer was the same in both cases?" I asked eagerly.

Giraud became inscrutable.

"Never mind what I think. We shall see. Marchaud!"

The *sergent de ville* appeared at the doorway.

"Monsieur?"

"Why is Madame Renauld not here? I sent for her a quarter of an hour ago?"

"She is coming up the path now, monsieur, and her son with her."

"Good. I only want one at a time, though."

Marchaud saluted and disappeared again. A moment later he reappeared with Mrs. Renauld.

"Here is Madame."

Giraud came forward with a curt bow.

"This way, madame." He led her across, and then, standing suddenly aside. "Here is the man. Do you know him?"

And as he spoke, his eyes, gimlet-like, bored into her face, seeking to read her mind, noting every indication of her manner.

But Mrs. Renauld remained perfectly calm—too calm, I felt. She looked down at the corpse almost without interest, certainly without any sign of agitation or recognition.

"No," she said. "I have never seen him in my life. He is quite a stranger to me."

"You are sure?"

"Quite sure."

"You do not recognize in him one of your assailants, for instance?"

"No," she seemed to hesitate, as though struck by the idea. "No, I do not think so. Of course they wore beards—false ones the examining magistrate thought, but still—no." Now she seemed to make her mind up definitely. "I am sure neither of the two was this man."

"Very well, madame. That is all, then."

She stepped out with head erect, the sun flashing on the silver threads in her hair. Jack Renauld succeeded her. He, too, failed to identify the man, in a completely natural manner.

Giraud merely grunted. Whether he was pleased or chagrined I could not tell. He merely called to Marchaud:

"You have got the other there?"

"Yes, monsieur."

"Bring her in then."

"The other" was Madame Daubreuil. She came indignantly, protesting with vehemence.

"I object, monsieur! This is an outrage! What have I to do with all this?"

"Madame," said Giraud brutally, "I am investigating not one murder, but two murders! For all I know you may have committed them both."

"How dare you?" she cried. "How dare you insult me by such a wild accusation! It is infamous."

"Infamous, is it? What about this?" Stooping, he again detached the hair, and held it up. "Do you see this, madame?" He advanced towards her. "You permit that I see whether it matches?"

With a cry she started backwards, white to the lips.

"It is false—I swear it. I know nothing of the crime—of either crime. Any one who says I do lies! Ah! *mon Dieu*, what shall I do?"

"Calm yourself, madame," said Giraud coldly. "No one has accused you as yet. But you will do well to answer my questions without more ado."

"Anything you wish, monsieur."

"Look at the dead man. Have you ever seen him before?"

Drawing nearer, a little of the colour creeping back to her face, Madame Daubreuil looked down at the victim with a certain amount of interest and curiosity. Then she shook her head.

"I do not know him."

It seemed impossible to doubt her, the words came so naturally. Giraud dismissed her with a nod of the head.

"You are letting her go?" I asked in a low voice. "Is that wise? Surely that black hair is from her head."

"I do not need teaching my business," said Giraud dryly. "She is under surveillance. I have no wish to arrest her as yet."

Then, frowning, he gazed down at the body.

"Should you say that was a Spanish type at all?" he asked suddenly.

I considered the face carefully.

"No," I said at last. "I should put him down as a Frenchman most decidedly."

Giraud gave a grunt of dissatisfaction.

"Same here."

He stood there for a moment, then with an imperative gesture he waved me aside, and once more, on hands and knees, he continued his search of the floor of the shed. He was marvellous. Nothing escaped him. Inch by inch he went over the floor, turning over pots, examining old sacks. He pounced on a bundle by the door, but it proved to be only a ragged coat and trousers, and he flung it down again with a snarl. Two pairs of old gloves interested him, but in the end he shook his head and laid them aside. Then he went back to the pots, methodically turning them over one by one. In the end, he rose to his feet, and shook his head thoughtfully. He seemed baffled and perplexed. I think he had forgotten my presence.

But, at that moment, a stir and bustle was heard outside, and our old friend, the examining magistrate, accompanied by his clerk and M. Bex, with the doctor behind him, came bustling in.

"But this is extraordinary, Mr. Giraud," cried M. Hautet. "Another crime! Ah, we have not got to the bottom of this case. There is some deep mystery here. But who is the victim this time?"

"That is just what nobody can tell us, M. le juge. He has not been identified."

"Where is the body?" asked the doctor.

Giraud moved aside a little.

"There in the corner. He has been stabbed to the heart, as you see. And with the dagger that was stolen yesterday morning. I fancy that the murder followed hard upon the theft—but that is for you to say. You can handle the dagger freely—there are no finger-prints on it."

The doctor knelt down by the dead man, and Giraud turned to the examining magistrate.

"A pretty little problem, is it not? But I shall solve it."

"And so no one can identify him," mused the magistrate. "Could it possibly be one of the assassins? They may have fallen out among themselves."

Giraud shook his head.

"The man is a Frenchman—I would take my oath of that—"

But at that moment they were interrupted by the doctor who was sitting back on his heels with a perplexed expression.

"You say he was killed yesterday morning?"

"I fix it by the theft of the dagger," explained Giraud. "He may, of course, have been killed later in the day."

"Later in the day? Fiddlesticks! This man has been dead at least forty-eight hours, and probably longer."

We stared at each other in blank amazement.

15. A Photograph

The doctor's words were so surprising that we were all momentarily taken aback. Here was a man stabbed with a dagger which we knew to have been stolen only twenty-four hours previously, and yet Dr. Durand asserted positively that he had been dead at least forty-eight hours! The whole thing was fantastic to the last extreme.

We were still recovering from the surprise of the doctor's announcement, when a telegram was brought to me. It had been sent up from the hotel to the Villa. I tore it open. It was from Poirot, and announced his return by the train arriving at Merlinville at 12:28.

I looked at my watch and saw that I had just time to get comfortably to the station and meet him there. I felt that it was of the utmost importance that he should know at once of the new and startling developments in the case.

Evidently, I reflected, Poirot had had no difficulty in finding what he wanted in Paris. The quickness of his return proved that. Very few hours had sufficed. I wondered how he would take the exciting news I had to impart.

The train was some minutes late, and I strolled aimlessly up and down the platform, until it occurred to me that I might pass the time by asking a few questions as to who had left Merlinville by the last train on the evening of the tragedy.

I approached the chief porter, an intelligent looking man, and had little difficulty in persuading him to enter upon the subject. It was a disgrace to the Police, he hotly affirmed, that such brigands of assassins should be allowed to go about unpunished. I hinted that there was some possibility they might have left by the midnight train, but he negatived the idea decidedly. He would have noticed two foreigners—he was sure of it. Only about twenty people had left by the train, and he could not have failed to observe them.

I do not know what put the idea into my head—possibly it was the deep anxiety underlying Marthe Daubreuil's tones—but I asked suddenly:

"Young M. Renauld—he did not leave by that train, did he?"

"Ah, no, monsieur. To arrive and start off again within half an hour, it would not be amusing, that!"

I stared at the man, the significance of his words almost escaping me. Then I saw . . .

"You mean," I said, my heart beating a little, "that M. Jack Renauld arrived at Merlinville that evening?"

"But yes, monsieur. By the last train arriving the other way, the 11:40."

My brain whirled. That, then, was the reason of Marthe's poignant anxiety. Jack Renauld had been in Merlinville on the night of the crime! But why had he not said so? Why, on the contrary, had he led us to believe that he had remained in Cherbourg? Remembering his frank boyish countenance, I could hardly bring myself to believe that he had any connection with the crime. Yet why this silence on his part about so vital a matter? One thing was certain, Marthe had known all along. Hence her anxiety, and her eager questioning of Poirot to know whether anyone were suspected.

My cogitations were interrupted by the arrival of the train, and in another moment I was greeting Poirot. The little man was radiant. He beamed and vociferated and, forgetting my English reluctance, embraced me warmly on the platform.

"*Mon cher ami*, I have succeeded—but succeeded to a marvel!"

"Indeed? I'm delighted to hear it. Have you heard the latest here?"

"How would you that I should hear anything? There have been some developments, eh? The brave Giraud, he has made an arrest? Or even arrests perhaps? Ah, but I will make him look foolish, that one! But where are you taking me, my friend? Do we not go to the hotel? It is necessary that I attend to my moustaches—they are deplorably limp from the heat of travelling. Also, without doubt, there is dust on my coat. And my tie, that I must rearrange."

I cut short his remonstrances.

"My dear Poirot—never mind all that. We must go to the Villa at once. *There has been another murder!*"

I have frequently been disappointed when fancying that I was giving news of importance to my friend. Either he has known it already or he has dismissed it as irrelevant to the main issue—and in the latter case events have usually proved him justified. But this time I could not complain of missing my effect. Never have I seen a man so flabbergasted. His jaw dropped. All the jauntiness went out of his bearing. He stared at me open-mouthed.

"What is that you say? Another murder? Ah, then, I am all wrong. I have failed. Giraud may mock himself at me—he will have reason!"

"You did not expect it, then?"

"I? Not the least in the world. It demolishes my theory—it ruins everything—it—ah, no!" He stopped dead, thumping himself on the chest. "It is impossible. I *cannot* be wrong! The facts, taken methodically and in their proper order admit of only one explanation. I must be right! I *am* right!"

"But then—"

He interrupted me.

"Wait, my friend. I must be right, therefore this new murder is impossible unless—unless—oh, wait, I implore you. Say no word—"

He was silent for a moment or two, then, resuming his normal manner, he said in a quiet assured voice: "The victim is a man of middle-age. His body was found in the locked shed near the scene of the crime and had been dead at least forty-eight hours. And it is most probable that he was stabbed in a similar manner to M. Renauld, though not necessarily in the back."

It was my turn to gape—and gape I did. In all my knowledge of Poirot he had never done anything so amazing as this. And, almost inevitably, a doubt crossed my mind.

"Poirot," I cried, "you're pulling my leg. You've heard all about it already."

He turned his earnest gaze upon me reproachfully.

"Would I do such a thing? I assure you that I have heard nothing whatsoever. Did you not observe the shock your news was to me?"

"But how on earth could you know all that?"

"I was right then? But I knew it. The little grey cells, my friend, the little grey cells! They told me. Thus, and in no other way, could there have been a second death. Now tell me all. If we go round to the left here, we can take a short cut across the golf links which will bring us to the back of the Villa Geneviève much more quickly."

As we walked, taking the way he had indicated, I recounted all I knew. Poirot listened attentively.

"The dagger was in the wound, you say? That is curious. You are sure it was the same one?"

"Absolutely certain. That's what make it so impossible."

"Nothing is impossible. There may have been two daggers."

I raised my eyebrows.

"Surely that is in the highest degree unlikely? It would be a most extraordinary coincidence."

"You speak as usual, without reflection, Hastings. In some

cases two identical weapons *would* be highly improbable. But not here. This particular weapon was a war souvenir which was made to Jack Renauld's orders. It is really highly unlikely, when you come to think of it, that he should have had only one made. Very probably he would have another for his own use."

"But nobody has mentioned such a thing," I objected.

A hint of the lecturer crept into Poirot's tone. "My friend, in working upon a case, one does not take into account only the things that are 'mentioned.' There is no reason to mention many things which may be important. Equally, there is often an excellent reason for *not* mentioning them. You can take your choice of the two motives."

I was silent, impressed in spite of myself. Another few minutes brought us to the famous shed. We found all our friends there and, after an interchange of polite amenities, Poirot began his task.

Having watched Giraud at work, I was keenly interested. Poirot bestowed but a cursory glance on the surroundings. The only thing he examined was the ragged coat and trousers by the door. A disdainful smile rose to Giraud's lips, and, as though noting it, Poirot flung the bundle down again.

"Old clothes of the gardener's?" he queried.

"Exactly," said Giraud.

Poirot knelt down by the body. His fingers were rapid but methodical. He examined the texture of the clothes, and satisfied himself that there were no marks on them. The boots he subjected to special care, also the dirty and broken finger-nails. Whilst examining the latter he threw a quick question at Giraud.

"You saw these?"

"Yes, I saw them," replied the other. His face remained inscrutable.

Suddenly Poirot stiffened.

"Dr. Durand!"

"Yes?" The doctor came forward.

"There is foam on the lips. You observed it?"

"I didn't notice it, I must admit."

"But you observe it now?"

"Oh, certainly."

Poirot again shot a question at Giraud.

"You noticed it without doubt?"

The other did not reply. Poirot proceeded. The dagger had been withdrawn from the wound. It reposed in a glass jar by the side of the body. Poirot examined it, then he studied the wound closely. When he looked up, his eyes were excited, and shone with the green light I knew so well.

"It is a strange wound, this! It has not bled. There is no stain on the clothes. The blade of the dagger is slightly discoloured, that is all. What do you think, M. le docteur?"

"I can only say that it is most abnormal."

"It is not abnormal at all. It is most simple. The man was stabbed *after he was dead*." And, stilling the clamour of voices that arose with a wave of his hand, Poirot turned to Giraud and added, "M. Giraud agrees with me, do you not, monsieur?"

Whatever Giraud's real belief, he accepted the position without moving a muscle. Calmly and almost scornfully he replied:

"Certainly I agree."

The murmur of surprise and interest broke out again.

"But what an idea!" cried M. Hautet. "To stab a man after he is dead! Barbaric! Unheard of! Some unappeasable hate, perhaps."

"No, M. le juge," said Poirot. "I should fancy it was done quite cold-bloodedly—to create an impression."

"What impression?"

"The impression it nearly did create," returned Poirot oracularly.

M. Bex had been thinking.

"How, then, was the man killed?"

"He was not killed. He died. He died, M. le juge, if I am not much mistaken, of an epileptic fit!"

This statement of Poirot's again aroused considerable excitement. Dr. Durand knelt down again, and made a searching examination. At last he rose to his feet.

"Well, M. le docteur?"

"M. Poirot, I am inclined to believe that you are correct in your assertion. I was misled to begin with. The incontrovertible fact that the man had been stabbed distracted my attention from any other indications."

Poirot was the hero of the hour. The examining magistrate was profuse in compliments. Poirot responded gracefully, and then excused himself on the pretext that neither he nor I had yet lunched, and that he wished to repair the ravages of the journey. As we were about to leave the shed, Giraud approached us.

"One more thing, M. Poirot," he said, in his suave mocking voice. "We found this coiled round the handle of the dagger. A woman's hair."

"Ah!" said Poirot. "A woman's hair? What woman's, I wonder?"

"I wonder also," said Giraud. Then, with a bow, he left us.

"He was insistent, the good Giraud," said Poirot thoughtfully, as we walked towards the hotel. "I wonder in what direction he hopes to mislead me? A woman's hair—h'm!"

We lunched heartily, but I found Poirot somewhat distrait and inattentive. Afterwards we went up to our sitting-room and there I begged him to tell me something of his mysterious journey to Paris.

"Willingly, my friend. I went to Paris to find *this*."

He took from his pocket a small faded newspaper cutting. It was the reproduction of a woman's photograph. He handed it to me. I uttered an exclamation.

"You recognize it, my friend?"

I nodded. Although the photo obviously dated from very many years back, and the hair was dressed in a different style, the likeness was unmistakable.

"Madame Daubreuil!" I exclaimed.

Poirot shook his head with a smile.

"Not quite correct, my friend. She did not call herself by that name in those days. That is a picture of the notorious Madame Beroldy!"

Madame Beroldy! In a flash the whole thing came back to me. The murder trial that had evoked such world-wide interest.

The Beroldy Case.

16. The Beroldy Case

S ome twenty years or so before the opening of the present story, Monsieur Arnold Beroldy, a native of Lyons, arrived in Paris accompanied by his pretty wife and their little daughter, a mere babe. Monsieur Beroldy was a junior partner in a firm of wine merchants, a stout middle-aged man, fond of the good things of life, devoted to his charming wife, and altogether unremarkable in every way. The firm in which Monsieur Beroldy was a partner was a small one, and although doing well, it did not yield a large income to the junior partner. The Beroldys had a small apartment and lived in a very modest fashion to begin with.

But unremarkable though Monsieur Beroldy might be, his wife was plentifully gilded with the brush of Romance. Young and good looking, and gifted withal with a singular charm of manner, Madame Beroldy at once created a stir in the quarter, especially when it began to be whispered that some interesting mystery surrounded her birth. It was rumoured that she was the illegitimate daughter of a Russian Grand Duke. Others asserted that it was an Austrian Archduke, and that the union was legal, though morganatic. But all stories agreed upon one point, that Jeanne Beroldy was the centre of an interesting mystery. Questioned by the curious, Madame Beroldy did not deny these rumours. On the other hand she let it be clearly understood that, though her "lips" were "sealed," all these stories had a foundation in fact. To intimate friends she unburdened herself further, spoke of political intrigues, of "papers," of obscure dangers that threatened her. There was also much talk of Crown jewels that were to be sold secretly, with herself acting as the go-between.

Amongst the friends and acquaintances of the Beroldys was a young lawyer, Georges Conneau. It was soon evident that the fascinating Jeanne had completely enslaved his heart. Madame Beroldy encouraged the young man in a discreet fashion, but being always careful to affirm her complete devotion to her middle-aged husband. Nevertheless, many spiteful persons did not hesitate to declare that young Conneau was her lover—and not the only one!

When the Beroldys had been in Paris about three months, another personage came upon the scene. This was Mr. Hiram P. Trapp, a native of the United States, and extremely wealthy. Introduced to the charming and mysterious Madame Beroldy, he fell a prompt victim to her fascinations. His admiration was obvious, though strictly respectful.

About this time, Madame Beroldy became more outspoken in her confidences. To several friends, she declared herself greatly worried on her husband's behalf. She explained that he had been drawn into several schemes of a political nature, and also referred to some important papers that had been entrusted to him for safekeeping and which concerned a "secret" of far reaching European importance. They had been entrusted to his custody to throw pursuers off the track, but Madame Beroldy was nervous, having recognized several important members of the Revolutionary Circle in Paris.

On the 28th day of November, the blow fell. The woman who came daily to clean and cook for the Beroldys was surprised to find the door of the apartment standing wide open. Hearing faint moans issuing from the bedroom, she went in. A terrible sight met her eyes. Madame Beroldy lay on the floor, bound hand and foot, uttering feeble moans, having managed to free her mouth from a gag. On the bed was Monsieur Beroldy, lying in a pool of blood, with a knife driven through his heart.

Madame Beroldy's story was clear enough. Suddenly awakened from sleep, she had discerned two masked men bending over her. Stifling her cries, they had bound and gagged her. They had then demanded of Monsieur Beroldy the famous "secret."

But the intrepid wine merchant refused point-blank to accede to their request. Angered by his refusal, one of the men incontinently stabbed him through the heart. With the dead man's keys, they had opened the safe in the corner, and had carried away with them a mass of papers. Both men were heavily bearded, and had worn masks, but Madame Beroldy declared positively that they were Russians.

The affair created an immense sensation. It was referred to variously as "the Nihilist Atrocity," "Revolutionaries in Paris," and the "Russian Mystery." Time went on, and the mysterious bearded men were never traced. And then, just as public interest was beginning to die down, a startling development occurred. Madame Beroldy was arrested and charged with the murder of her husband.

The trial, when it came on, aroused widespread interest. The youth and beauty of the accused, and her mysterious history, were sufficient to make of it a cause célèbre. People ranged themselves wildly for or against the prisoner. But her partisans received several severe checks to their enthusiasm. The romantic past of Madame Beroldy, her royal blood, and the mysterious intrigues in which she had her being were shown to be mere fantasies of the imagination.

It was proved beyond doubt that Jeanne Beroldy's parents were a highly respectable and prosaic couple, fruit merchants, who lived on the outskirts of Lyons. The Russian Grand Duke, the court intrigues, and the political schemes—all the stories current were traced back to—the lady herself! From her brain had emanated these ingenious myths, and she was proved to have raised a considerable sum of money from various credulous persons by her fiction of the "Crown jewels"—the jewels in question being found to be mere paste imitations. Remorselessly the whole story of her life was laid bare. The motive for the murder was found in Mr. Hiram P. Trapp. Mr. Trapp did his best, but relentlessly and agilely cross-questioned he was forced to admit that he loved the lady, and that, had she been free, he would have asked her to be his wife. The fact that the relations between them were admittedly platonic strengthened the case against the accused. Debarred from becoming his mistress by the simple honourable nature of the man, Jeanne Beroldy had conceived the monstrous project of ridding herself of her elderly undistinguished husband, and becoming the wife of the rich American.

Throughout, Madame Beroldy confronted her accusers with complete sang froid and self possession. Her story never varied. She continued to declare strenuously that she was of royal birth, and that she had been substituted for the daughter of the fruit seller at an early age. Absurd and completely unsubstantiated as these statements were, a great number of people believed implicitly in their truth.

But the prosecution was implacable. It denounced the masked "Russians" as a myth, and asserted that the crime had been committed by Madame Beroldy and her lover, Georges Conneau. A warrant was issued for the arrest of the latter, but he had wisely disappeared. Evidence showed that the bonds which secured Madame Beroldy were so loose that she could easily have freed herself.

And then, towards the close of the trial, a letter, posted in Paris, was sent to the Public Prosecutor. It was from Georges Conneau and, without revealing his whereabouts, it contained a full confession of the crime. He declared that he had indeed struck the fatal blow at Madame Beroldy's instigation. The crime had been planned between them. Believing that her husband ill-treated her, and maddened by his own passion for her, a passion which he believed her to return, he had planned the crime and struck the fatal blow that should free the woman he loved from a hateful bondage. Now, for the first time, he learnt of Mr. Hiram P. Trapp, and realized that the woman he loved had betrayed him! Not for his sake did she wish to be free—but in order to marry the wealthy American. She had used him as a cat's-paw, and now, in his jealous rage, he turned and denounced her, declaring that throughout he had acted at her instigation.

And then Madame Beroldy proved herself the remarkable woman she undoubtedly was. Without hesitation, she dropped her previous defence, and admitted that the "Russians" were a pure invention on her part. The real murderer was Georges Conneau. Maddened by passion, he had committed the crime, vowing that if she did not keep silence he would enact a terrible vengeance from her. Terrified by his threats, she had consented—also fearing it likely that if she told the truth she might be accused of conniving at the crime. But she had steadfastly refused to have anything more to do with her husband's murderer, and it was in revenge for this attitude on her part that he had written this letter accusing her. She swore solemnly that she had had nothing to do with the planning of the crime, that she had awoke on that memorable night to find Georges Conneau standing over her, the blood-stained knife in his hand.

It was a touch and go affair. Madame Beroldy's story was hardly credible. But this woman, whose fairy tales of royal intrigues had been so easily accepted, had the supreme art of making herself believed. Her address to the jury was a masterpiece. The tears streaming down her face, she spoke of her child, of her woman's honour—of her desire to keep her reputation untarnished for the child's sake. She admitted that, Georges Conneau having been her lover, she might perhaps be held morally responsible for the crime—but, before God, nothing more! She knew that she had committed a grave fault in not denouncing Conneau to the law, but she declared in a broken voice that that was a thing no woman could have done . . . She had loved him! Could she let her hand be the one to send him to the guillotine? She had been guilty of much, but she was innocent of the terrible crime imputed to her.

However that may have been, her eloquence and personality won the day. Madame Beroldy, amidst a scene of unparalleled excitement, was acquitted. Despite the utmost endeavours of the police, Georges Conneau was never traced. As for Madame Beroldy, nothing more was heard of her. Taking the child with her, she left Paris to begin a new life.

17. We Make Further Investigations

I have set down the Beroldy case in full. Of course all the details did not present themselves to my memory as I have recounted them here. Nevertheless, I recalled the case fairly accurately. It had attracted a great deal of interest at the time, and had been fully reported by the English papers, so that it did not need much effort of memory on my part to recollect the salient details.

Just for the moment, in my excitement, it seemed to clear up the whole matter. I admit that I am impulsive, and Poirot deplores my custom of jumping to conclusions, but I think I had some excuse in this instance. The remarkable way in which this discovery justified Poirot's point of view struck me at once.

"Poirot," I said, "I congratulate you. I see everything now."

"If that is indeed the truth, *I* congratulate *you, mon ami*. For as a rule you are not famous for seeing—eh, is it not so?"

I felt a little annoyed.

"Come now, don't rub it in. You've been so confoundedly

mysterious all along with your hints and your insignificant details that any one might fail to see what you were driving at."

Poirot lit one of his little cigarettes with his usual precision. Then he looked up.

"And since you see everything now, *mon ami*, what exactly is it that you see?"

"Why, that it was Madame Daubreuil—Beroldy, who murdered Mr. Renauld. The similarity of the two cases proves that beyond a doubt."

"Then you consider that Madame Beroldy was wrongly acquitted? That in actual fact she was guilty of connivance in her husband's murder?"

I opened my eyes wide.

"But of course! Don't you?"

Poirot walked to the end of the room, absentmindedly straightened a chair, and then said thoughtfully.

"Yes, that is my opinion. But there is no 'of course' about it, my friend. Technically speaking, Madame Beroldy is innocent."

"Of that crime, perhaps. But not of this."

Poirot sat down again, and regarded me, his thoughtful air more marked than ever.

"So it is definitely your opinion, Hastings, that Madame Daubreuil murdered M. Renauld?"

"Yes."

"Why?"

He shot the question at me with such suddenness that I was taken aback.

"Why?" I stammered. "Why? Oh, because—" I came to a stop.

Poirot nodded his head at me.

"You see, you come to a stumbling-block at once. Why should Madame Daubreuil (I shall call her that for clearness sake) murder M. Renauld? We can find no shadow of a motive. She does not benefit by his death; considered as either mistress or blackmailer she stands to lose. You cannot have a murder without a motive. The first crime was different, there we had a rich lover waiting to step into her husband's shoes."

"Money is not the only motive for murder," I objected.

"True," agreed Poirot placidly. "There are two others, the *crime passionnel* is one. And there is the third rare motive, murder for an idea which implies some form of mental derangement on the part of the murderer. Homicidal mania, and religious fanaticism belong to that class. We can rule it out here."

"But what about the *crime passionnel*? Can you rule that out? If Madame Daubreuil was Renauld's mistress, if she found that his affection was cooling, or if her jealousy was aroused in any way, might she not have struck him down in a moment of anger?"

Poirot shook his head.

"If—I say *if*, you note—Madame Daubreuil was Renauld's mistress, he had not had time to tire of her. And in any case you mistake her character. She is a woman who can simulate great emotional stress. She is a magnificent actress. But, looked at dispassionately, her life disproves her appearance. Throughout, if we examine it, she had been cold-blooded and calculating in her motives and actions. It was not to link her life with that of her young lover that she connived at her husband's murder. The rich American, for whom she probably did not care a button, was her objective. If she committed a crime, she would always do so for gain. Here there was no gain. Besides, how do you account for the digging of the grave? That was a man's work."

"She might have had an accomplice," I suggested, unwilling to relinquish my belief.

"I pass to another objection. You have spoken of the similarity between the two crimes. Wherein does that lie, my friend?"

I stared at him in astonishment.

"Why, Poirot, it was you who remarked on that! The story of the masked men, the 'secret,' the papers!"

Poirot smiled a little.

"Do not be so indignant, I beg of you. I repudiate nothing. The similarity of the two stories links the two cases together inevitably. But reflect now on something very curious. It is not Madame Daubreuil who tells us this tale—if it were all would indeed be plain sailing—it is Madame Renauld. Is she then in league with the other?"

"I can't believe that," I said slowly. "If it is so, she must be the most consummate actress the world has ever known."

"Ta-ta-ta," said Poirot impatiently. "Again you have the sentiment, and not the logic! If it is necessary for a criminal to be a consummate actress, then by all means assume her to be one. But is it necessary? I do not believe Madame Renauld to be in league with Madame Daubreuil for several reasons, some of which I have already enumerated to you. The others are self-evident. Therefore, that possibility eliminated, we draw very near to the truth which is, as always, very curious and interesting."

"Poirot," I cried, "what more do you know?"

"*Mon ami*, you must make your own deductions. You have 'access to the facts!' Concentrate your grey cells. Reason—not like Giraud—but like Hercule Poirot."

"But are you *sure*?"

"My friend, in many ways I have been an imbecile. But at last I see clearly."

"You know everything?"

"I have discovered what M. Renauld sent for me to discover."

"And you know the murderer?"

"I know one murderer."

"What do you mean?"

"We talk a little at cross-purposes. There are here not one crime, but two. The first I have solved, the second—*eh bien*, I will confess, I am not sure!"

"But, Poirot, I thought you said the man in the shed had died a natural death?"

"Ta-ta-ta." Poirot made his favourite ejaculation of impatience.

"Still you do not understand. One may have a crime without a murderer, but for two crimes it is essential to have two bodies."

His remark struck me as so peculiarly lacking in lucidity that I looked at him in some anxiety. But he appeared perfectly normal. Suddenly he rose and strolled to the window.

"Here he is," he observed.

"Who?"

"M. Jack Renauld. I sent a note up to the Villa to ask him to come here."

That changed the course of my ideas, and I asked Poirot if he knew that Jack Renauld had been in Merlinville on the night of the crime. I had hoped to catch my astute little friend napping, but as usual, he was omniscient. He, too, had inquired at the station.

"And without doubt we are not original in the idea, Hastings. The excellent Giraud, he also has probably made his inquiries."

"You don't think—" I said, and then stopped. "Ah, no, it would be too horrible!"

Poirot looked inquiringly at me, but I said no more. It had just occurred to me that though there were seven women directly or indirectly connected with the case—Mrs. Renauld, Madame Daubreuil and her daughter, the mysterious visitor, and the three servants—there was, with the exception of old Auguste who could hardly count, only one man—Jack Renauld. *And a man must have dug a grave . . .*

I had no time to develop further the appalling idea that had occurred to me, for Jack Renauld was ushered into the room.

Poirot greeted him in a business-like manner.

"Take a seat, monsieur. I regret infinitely to derange you, but you will perhaps understand that the atmosphere of the Villa is not too congenial to me. M. Giraud and I do not see eye to eye about everything. His politeness to me has not been striking and you will comprehend that I do not intend any little discoveries I may make to benefit him in any way."

"Exactly, M. Poirot," said the lad. "That fellow Giraud is an ill-conditioned brute, and I'd be delighted to see someone score at his expense."

"Then I may ask a little favour of you?"

"Certainly."

"I will ask you to go to the railway station and take a train to the next station along the line, Abbalac. Ask there at the cloak-room whether two foreigners deposited a valise there on the night of the murder. It is a small station, and they are almost certain to remember. Will you do this?"

"Of course I will," said the boy, mystified, though ready for the task.

"I and my friend, you comprehend, have business elsewhere," explained Poirot. "There is a train in a quarter of an hour, and I will ask you not to return to the Villa, as I have no wish for Giraud to get an inkling of your errand."

"Very well, I will go straight to the station."

He rose to his feet. Poirot's voice stopped him.

"One moment, M. Renauld, there is one little matter that puzzles me. Why did you not mention to M. Hautet this morning that you were in Merlinville on the night of the crime?"

Jack Renauld's face went crimson. With an effort he controlled himself.

"You have made a mistake. I was in Cherbourg, as I told the examining magistrate this morning."

Poirot looked at him, his eyes narrowed, cat-like, until they only showed a gleam of green.

"Then it is a singular mistake that I have made there—for it is shared by the station staff. They say you arrived by the 11:40 train."

For a moment Jack Renauld hesitated, then he made up his mind.

"And if I did? I suppose you do not mean to accuse me of participating in my father's murder?" He asked the question haughtily, his head thrown back.

"I should like an explanation of the reason that brought you here."

"That is simple enough. I came to see my fiancée, Mademoiselle Daubreuil. I was on the eve of a long voyage, uncertain as to when I should return. I wished to see her before I went, to assure her of my unchanging devotion."

"And you did see her?" Poirot's eyes never left the other's face.

There was an appreciable pause before Renauld replied. Then he said:

"Yes."

"And afterwards?"

"I found I had missed the last train. I walked to St. Beauvais where I knocked up a garage and got a car to take me back to Cherbourg."

"St. Beauvais? That is fifteen kilometres. A long walk, M. Renauld."

"I—I felt like walking."

Poirot bowed his head as a sign that he accepted the explanation. Jack Renauld took up his hat and cane and departed. In a trice Poirot jumped to his feet.

"Quick, Hastings. We will go after him."

Keeping a discreet distance behind our quarry, we followed him through the streets of Merlinville. But when Poirot saw that he took the turning to the station, he checked himself.

"All is well. He has taken the bait. He will go to Abbalac, and will inquire for the mythical valise left by the mythical foreigners. Yes, *mon ami*, all that was a little invention of my own."

"You wanted him out of the way!" I exclaimed.

"Your penetration is amazing, Hastings! Now, if you please, we will go up to the Villa Geneviève."

18. Giraud Acts

By the way, Poirot," I said, as we walked along the hot white road, "I've got a bone to pick with you. I dare say you meant well, but really it was no business of yours to go mouching round to the Hôtel du Phare without letting me know."

Poirot shot a quick sidelong glance at me.

"And how did you know I had been there?" he inquired.

Much to my annoyance I felt the colour rising in my cheeks.

"I happened to look in in passing," I explained with as much dignity as I could muster.

I rather feared Poirot's banter, but to my relief, and somewhat to my surprise, he only shook his head with a rather unusual gravity.

"If I have offended your susceptibilities in any way, I demand pardon of you. You will understand better soon. But, believe me, I have striven to concentrate all my energies on the case."

"Oh, it's all right," I said, mollified by the apology. "I know it's only that you have my interests at heart. But I can take care of myself all right."

Poirot seemed to be about to say something further, but checked himself.

Arrived at the Villa, Poirot led the way up to the shed where the second body had been discovered. He did not, however, go in, but paused by the bench which I have mentioned before as being set some few yards away from it. After contemplating it for a moment or two, he paced carefully from it to the hedge which marked the boundary between the Villa Geneviève and the Villa Marguerite. Then he paced back again, nodding his head as he did so. Returning again to the hedge, he parted the bushes with his hands.

"With good fortune," he remarked to me over his shoulder, "Mademoiselle Marthe may find herself in the garden. I desire to speak to her and would prefer not to call formally at the Villa Marguerite. Ah, all is well, there she is. Pst, mademoiselle! Pst! *Un moment, s'il vous plaît.*"

I joined him at the moment that Marthe Daubreuil, looking slightly startled, came running up to the hedge at his call.

"A little word with you, mademoiselle, if it is permitted?"

"Certainly, Monsieur Poirot."

Despite her acquiescence, her eyes looked troubled and afraid.

"Mademoiselle, do you remember running after me on the road the day that I came to your house with the examining magistrate? You asked me if any one were suspected of the crime."

"And you told me two Chileans." Her voice sounded rather breathless, and her left hand stole to her breast.

"Will you ask me the same question again, mademoiselle?"

"What do you mean?"

"This. If you were to ask me that question again, I should give you a different answer. Some one is suspected—but not a Chilian."

"Who?" The word came faintly between her parted lips.

"M. Jack Renauld."

"What?" It was a cry. "Jack? Impossible. Who dares to suspect him?"

"Giraud."

"Giraud!" The girl's face was ashy. "I am afraid of that man. He is cruel. He will——he will——" She broke off. There was courage gathering in her face, and determination. I realized in that moment that she was a fighter. Poirot, too, watched her intently.

"You know, of course, that he was here on the night of the murder?" he asked.

"Yes," she replied mechanically. "He told me."

"It was unwise to have tried to conceal the fact," ventured Poirot.

"Yes, yes," she replied impatiently. "But we cannot waste time on regrets. We must find something to save him. He is innocent, of course, but that will not help him with a man like Giraud who has his reputation to think of. He must arrest some one, and that some one will be Jack."

"The facts will tell against him," said Poirot. "You realize that?"

She faced him squarely, and used the words I had heard her say in her mother's drawing-room.

"I am not a child, monsieur. I can be brave and look facts in the face. He is innocent, and we must save him."

She spoke with a kind of desperate energy, then was silent, frowning as she thought.

"Mademoiselle," said Poirot observing her keenly, "is there not something that you are keeping back that you could tell us?"

She nodded perplexedly.

"Yes, there is something, but I hardly know whether you will believe it—it seems so absurd."

"At any rate, tell us, mademoiselle."

"It is this. M. Giraud sent for me, as an afterthought, to see if I could identify the man in there." She signed with her head towards the shed. "I could not. At least I could not at the moment. But since I have been thinking—"

"Well?"

"It seems so queer, and yet I am almost sure. I will tell you. On the morning of the day M. Renauld was murdered, I was walking in the garden here, when I heard a sound of men's voices quarrelling. I pushed aside the bushes and looked through. One of the men was M. Renauld and the other was a tramp, a dreadful-looking creature in filthy rags. He was alternately whining and threatening. I gathered he was asking for money, but at that moment *maman* called me from the house, and I had to go. That is all, only—I am almost sure that the tramp and the dead man in the shed are one and the same."

Poirot uttered an exclamation.

"But why did you not say so at the time, mademoiselle?"

"Because at first it only struck me that the face was vaguely familiar in some way. The man was differently dressed, and apparently belonged to a superior station in life. But tell me, Monsieur Poirot, is it not possible that this tramp might have attacked and killed M. Renauld, and taken his clothes and money?"

"It is an idea, mademoiselle," said Poirot slowly. "It leaves a lot unexplained, but it is certainly an idea. I will think of it."

A voice called from the house.

"*Maman*," whispered Marthe, "I must go." And she slipped away through the trees.

"Come," said Poirot, and taking my arm, turned in the direction of the Villa.

"What do you really think?" I asked, in some curiosity. "Was that story true, or did the girl make it up in order to divert suspicion from her lover?"

"It is a curious tale," said Poirot, "but I believe it to be the absolute truth. Unwittingly, Mademoiselle Marthe told us the truth on another point—and incidentally gave Jack Renauld the lie. Did you notice his hesitation when I asked him if he saw Marthe Daubreuil on the night of the crime? He paused and then said 'Yes.' I suspected that he was lying. It was necessary for me to see Mademoiselle Marthe before he could put her on her guard. Three little words gave me the information I wanted. When I asked her if she knew that Jack Renauld was here that night, she answered 'He *told* me.' Now, Hastings, what was Jack Renauld doing here on that eventful evening, and if he did not see Mademoiselle Marthe whom did he see?"

"Surely, Poirot," I cried, aghast, "you cannot believe that a boy like that would murder his own father."

"*Mon ami*," said Poirot, "you continue to be of a sentimentality unbelievable! I have seen mothers who murdered their little children for the sake of the insurance money! After that, one can believe anything."

"And the motive?"

"Money of course. Remember that Jack Renauld thought that he would come in to half his father's fortune at the latter's death."

"But the tramp. Where does he come in?"

Poirot shrugged his shoulders.

"Giraud would say that he was an accomplice—an apache who helped young Renauld to commit the crime, and who was conveniently put out of the way afterwards."

"But the hair round the dagger? The woman's hair?"

"Ah," said Poirot, smiling broadly. "That is the cream of Giraud's little jest. According to him, it is not a woman's hair at all. Remember that the youths of today wear their hair brushed straight back from the forehead with pomade or hairwash to make it lie flat. Consequently some of the hairs are of considerable length."

"And you believe that too?"

"No," said Poirot with a curious smile. "For I know it to be the hair of a woman—and more, which woman!"

"Madame Daubreuil," I announced positively.

"Perhaps," said Poirot, regarding me quizzically.

But I refused to allow myself to get annoyed.

"What are we going to do now?" I asked, as we entered the hall of the Villa Geneviève.

"I wish to make a search amongst the effects of M. Jack Renauld. That is why I had to get him out of the way for a few hours."

"But will not Giraud have searched already?" I asked doubtfully.

"Of course. He builds a case, as a beaver builds a dam, with a fatiguing industry. But he will not have looked for the things that I am seeking—in all probability he would not have seen their importance if they stared him in the face. Let us begin."

Neatly and methodically, Poirot opened each drawer in turn, examined the contents, and returned them exactly to their places. It was a singularly dull and uninteresting proceeding. Poirot waded on through collars, pajamas and socks. A purring noise outside drew me to the window. Instantly I became galvanized into life.

"Poirot!" I cried. "A car has just driven up. Giraud is in it, and Jack Renauld, and two gendarmes."

"*Sacré tonnerre!*" growled Poirot. "That animal of a Giraud, could he not wait? I shall not be able to replace the things in this last drawer with the proper method. Let us be quick."

Unceremoniously he tumbled out the things on the floor, mostly ties and handkerchiefs. Suddenly with a cry of triumph Poirot pounced on something, a small square cardboard, evidently a photograph. Thrusting it into his pocket, he returned the things pell-mell to the drawer, and seizing me by the arm dragged me out of the room and down the stairs. In the hall stood Giraud, contemplating his prisoner.

"Good afternoon, M. Giraud," said Poirot. "What have we here?"

Giraud nodded his head towards Jack.

"He was trying to make a getaway, but I was too sharp for him. He is under arrest for the murder of his father, M. Paul Renauld."

Poirot wheeled to confront the boy who leaned limply against the door, his face ashy pale.

"What do you say to that, *jeune homme*?"

Jack Renauld stared at him stonily.

"Nothing," he said.

19. I Use My Grey Cells

I was dumbfounded. Up to the last, I had not been able bring myself to believe Jack Renauld guilty. I had expected a ringing proclamation of his innocence when Poirot challenged him. But now, watching him as he stood, white and limp against the wall, and hearing the damning admission fall from his lips, I doubted no longer.

But Poirot had turned to Giraud.

"What are your grounds for arresting him?"

"Do you expect me to give them to you?"

"As a matter of courtesy, yes."

Giraud looked at him doubtfully. He was torn between a desire to refuse rudely and the pleasure of triumphing over his adversary.

"You think I have made a mistake, I suppose?" he sneered.

"It would not surprise me," replied Poirot, with a soupçon of malice.

Giraud's face took on a deeper tinge of red.

"*Eh bien*, come in here. You shall judge for yourself." He flung open the door of the *salon*, and we passed in, leaving Jack Renauld in the care of the two other men.

"Now, M. Poirot," said Giraud laying his hat on the table, and speaking with the utmost sarcasm, "I will treat you to a little lecture on detective work. I will show you how we moderns work."

"*Bien!*" said Poirot, composing himself to listen. "I will show you how admirably the Old Guard can listen," and he leaned back and closed his eyes, opening them for a moment to remark. "Do not fear that I shall sleep. I will attend most carefully."

"Of course," began Giraud, "I soon saw through all that Chilean tomfoolery. Two men were in it—but they were not mysterious foreigners! All that was a blind."

"Very creditable so far, my dear Giraud," murmured Poirot. "Especially after that clever trick of theirs with the match and cigarette end."

Giraud glared, but continued:

"A man must have been connected with the case, in order to dig the grave. There is no man who actually benefits by the crime, but there was a man who *thought* he would benefit. I heard of Jack Renauld's quarrel with his father, and of the threats that he had used. The motive was established. Now as to means. Jack Renauld was in Merlinville that night. He concealed the fact—which turned suspicion into certainty. Then we found a second victim—*stabbed with the same dagger*. We know when that dagger was stolen. Captain Hastings here can fix the time. Jack Renauld, arriving from Cherbourg, was the only person who could have taken it. I have accounted for all the other members of the household."

Poirot interrupted:

"You are wrong. There is one other person who could have taken the dagger."

"You refer to M. Stonor? He arrived at the front door, in an automobile which had brought him straight from Calais. Ah, believe me, I have looked into everything. M. Jack Renauld arrived by train. An hour elapsed between his arrival, and the moment he presented himself at the house. Without doubt, he saw Captain Hastings and his companion leave the shed, slipped in himself and took the dagger, stabbed his accomplice in the shed—"

"Who was already dead!"

Giraud shrugged his shoulders.

"Possibly he did not observe that. He may have judged him to be sleeping. Without doubt they had a rendezvous. In any case he knew this apparent second murder would greatly complicate the case. It did."

"But it could not deceive M. Giraud," murmured Poirot.

"You mock yourself at me. But I will give you one last irrefutable proof. Madame Renauld's story was false—a fabrication from beginning to end. We believe Madame Renauld to have loved her husband—*yet she lied to shield his murderer*. For whom will a woman lie? Sometimes for herself, usually for the man she loves, *always* for her children. That is the last—the irrefutable proof. You can not get round it."

Giraud paused, flushed and triumphant. Poirot regarded him steadily.

"That is my case," said Giraud. "What have you to say to it?"

"Only that there is one thing you have failed to take into account."

"What is that?"

"Jack Renauld was presumably acquainted with the planning out of the golf course. He knew that the body would be discovered almost at once, when they started to dig the bunker."

Giraud laughed out loud.

"But it is idiotic what you say there! He wanted the body to be found! Until it was found, he could not presume death, and would have been unable to enter into his inheritance."

I saw a quick flash of green in Poirot's eyes as he rose to his feet.

"Then why bury it?" he asked softly. "Reflect, Giraud. Since it was to Jack Renauld's advantage that the body should be found without delay, *why dig a grave at all?*"

Giraud did not reply. The question found him unprepared. He shrugged his shoulders as though to intimate that it was of no importance.

Poirot moved towards the door. I followed him.

"There is one more thing that you have failed to take into account," he said over his shoulder.

"What is that?"

"The piece of lead piping," said Poirot, and left the room.

Jack Renauld still stood in the hall, with a white dumb face, but as we came out of the *salon*, he looked up sharply. At the same moment there was the sound of a footfall on the staircase. Mrs. Renauld was descending it. At the sight of her son, standing between the two myrmidons of the law, she stopped as though petrified.

"Jack," she faltered. "Jack, what is this?"

He looked up at her, his face set.

"They have arrested me, mother."

"What?"

She uttered a piercing cry, and before any one could get to her swayed and fell heavily. We both ran to her and lifted her up. In a minute Poirot stood up again.

"She has cut her head badly, on the corner of the stairs. I fancy there is a slight concussion also. If Giraud wants a statement from her, he will have to wait. She will probably be unconscious for at least a week."

Denise and Françoise had run to their mistress, and leaving her in their charge Poirot left the house. He walked with his head bent down, frowning thoughtfully at the ground. For some time I did not speak, but at last I ventured to put a question to him.

"Do you believe then, in spite of all appearances to the contrary, that Jack Renauld may not be guilty?"

Poirot did not answer at once, but after a long wait he said gravely:

"I do not know, Hastings. There is just a chance of it. Of course Giraud is all wrong—wrong from beginning to end. If Jack Renauld is guilty, it is in spite of Giraud's arguments, not *because* of them. And the gravest indictment against him is known only to me."

"What is that?" I asked, impressed.

"If you would use your grey cells, and see the whole case clearly as I do, you too would perceive it, my friend."

This was what I called one of Poirot's irritating answers. He went on, without waiting for me to speak.

"Let us walk this way to the sea. We will sit on that little mound there, overlooking the beach, and review the case. You shall know all that I know, but I would prefer that you should come at the truth by your own efforts—not by my leading you by the hand."

We established ourselves on the grassy knoll as Poirot had suggested, looking out to sea. From farther along the sand, the cries of the bathers reached us faintly. The sea was of the palest blue, and the halcyon calm reminded me of the day we had arrived at Merlinville, my own good spirits, and Poirot's suggestion that I was "fey." What a long time seemed to have elapsed since then. And in reality it was only three days!

"Think, my friend," said Poirot's voice encouragingly. "Arrange your ideas. Be methodical. Be orderly. There is the secret of success."

I endeavoured to obey him, casting my mind back over all the details of the case. And reluctantly it seemed to me that the only clear and possible solution was that of Giraud—which Poirot despised. I reflected anew. If there was daylight anywhere it was in the direction of Madame Daubreuil. Giraud was ignorant of her connection with the Beroldy Case. Poirot had declared the Beroldy Case to be all important. It was there I must seek. I was on the right track now. And suddenly I started as an idea of bewildering luminosity shot into my brain. Trembling I built up my hypothesis.

"You have a little idea, I see, *mon ami*! Capital. We progress."

I sat up, and lit a pipe.

"Poirot," I said, "it seems to me we have been strangely remiss. I say we—although I dare say *I* would be nearer the mark. But you must pay the penalty of your determined secrecy. So I say again we have been strangely remiss. There is some one we have forgotten."

"And who is that?" inquired Poirot, with twinkling eyes.

"Georges Conneau!"

20. An Amazing Statement

The next moment Poirot embraced me warmly. "*Enfin*! You have arrived. And all by yourself. It is superb! Continue your reasoning. You are right. Decidedly we have done wrong to forget Georges Conneau."

I was so flattered by the little man's approval that I could hardly continue. But at last I collected my thoughts and went on.

"Georges Conneau disappeared twenty years ago, but we have no reason to believe that he is dead."

"*Aucunement*," agreed Poirot. "Proceed."

"Therefore we will assume that he is alive."

"Exactly."

"Or that he was alive until recently."

"*De mieux en mieux!*"

"We will presume," I continued, my enthusiasm rising, "that he has fallen on evil days. He has become a criminal, an apache, a tramp—a what you will. He chances to come to Merlinville. There he finds the woman he has never ceased to love."

"Eh eh! The sentimentality," warned Poirot.

"Where one hates one also loves," I quoted or misquoted. "At any rate he finds her there, living under an assumed name. But she has a new lover, the Englishman, Renauld. Georges Conneau, the memory of old wrongs rising in him, quarrels with this Renauld. He lies in wait for him as he comes to visit his mistress, and stabs him in the back. Then, terrified at what he has done, he starts to dig a grave. I imagine it likely that Madame Daubreuil comes out to look for her lover. She and Conneau have a terrible scene. He drags her into the shed, and there suddenly falls down in an epileptic fit. Now supposing Jack Renauld to appear. Madame Daubreuil tells him all, points out to him the dreadful consequences to her daughter if this scandal of the past is revived. His father's murderer is dead—let them do their best to hush it up. Jack Renauld consents—goes to the house and has an interview with his mother, winning her over to his point of view. Primed with the story that Madame Daubreuil has suggested to him, she permits herself to be gagged and bound. There, Poirot, what do you think of that?" I leaned back, flushed with the pride of successful reconstruction.

Poirot looked at me thoughtfully.

"I think that you should write for the Kinema, *mon ami*," he remarked at last.

"You mean—?"

"It would make a good film, the story that you have recounted to me there—but it bears no sort of resemblance to everyday life."

"I admit that I haven't gone into all the details, but—"

"You have gone further—you have ignored them magnificently. What about the way the two men were dressed? Do you suggest that after stabbing his victim, Conneau removed his suit of clothes, donned it himself, and replaced the dagger?"

"I don't see that that matters," I objected rather huffily. "He may have obtained clothes and money from Madame Daubreuil by threats earlier in the day."

"By threats—eh? You seriously advance that supposition?"

"Certainly. He could have threatened to reveal her identity to the Renaulds, which would probably have put an end to all hopes of her daughter's marriage."

"You are wrong, Hastings. He could not blackmail her, for she had the whip hand. Georges Conneau, remember, is still wanted for murder. A word from her and he is in danger of the guillotine."

I was forced, rather reluctantly, to admit the truth of this.

"*Your* theory," I remarked acidly, "is doubtless correct as to all the details?"

"My theory is the truth," said Poirot quietly. "And the truth is necessarily correct. In your theory you made a fundamental error. You permitted your imagination to lead you astray with midnight assignations and passionate love scenes. But in investigating crime we must take our stand upon the commonplace. Shall I demonstrate my methods to you?"

"Oh, by all means let us have a demonstration!"

Poirot sat very upright and began, wagging his forefinger emphatically to emphasize his points.

"I will start as you started from the basic fact of Georges

Conneau. Now the story told by Madame Beroldy in court as to the 'Russians' was admittedly a fabrication. If she was innocent of connivance in the crime, it was concocted by her, and by her only as she stated. If, on the other hand, she was not innocent, it might have been invented by either her or Georges Conneau.

"Now is this case we are investigating, we meet the same tale. As I pointed out to you, the facts render it very unlikely that Madame Daubreuil inspired it. So we turn to the hypothesis that the story had its origin in the brain of Georges Conneau. Very good. Georges Conneau, therefore, planned the crime with Madame Renauld as his accomplice. She is in the limelight, and behind her is a shadowy figure whose alias is unknown to us.

"Now let us go carefully over the Renauld Case from the beginning, setting down each significant point in its chronological order. You have a notebook and pencil? Good. Now what is the earliest point to note down?"

"The letter to you?"

"That was the first we knew of it, but it is not the proper beginning of the case. The first point of any significance, I should say, is the change that came over M. Renauld shortly after arriving in Merlinville, and which is attested to by several witnesses. We have also to consider his friendship with Madame Daubreuil, and the large sums of money paid over to her. From thence we can come directly to the 23rd May."

Poirot paused, cleared his throat, and signed to me to write.

"*23rd May.* M. Renauld quarrels with his son over latter's wish to marry Marthe Daubreuil. Son leaves for Paris.

"*24th May.* M. Renauld alters his will, leaving entire control of his fortune in his wife's hands.

"*7th June.* Quarrel with tramp in garden, witnessed by Marthe Daubreuil.

"Letter written to M. Hercule Poirot, imploring assistance.

"Telegram sent to Jack Renauld, bidding him proceed by the *Anzora* to Buenos Aires.

"Chauffeur, Masters, sent off on a holiday.

"Visit of a lady, that evening. As he is seeing her out, his words are 'Yes, yes—but for God's sake go now . . .'"

Poirot paused.

"There, Hastings, take each of those facts one by one, consider them carefully by themselves and in relation to the whole, and see if you do not get new light on the matter."

I endeavoured conscientiously to do as he had said. After a moment or two, I said rather doubtfully:

"As to the first points, the question seems to be whether we adopt the theory of blackmail, or of an infatuation for this woman."

"Blackmail, decidedly. You heard what Stonor said as to his character and habits."

"Mrs. Renauld did not confirm his view," I argued.

"We have already seen that Madame Renauld's testimony cannot be relied upon in any way. We must trust to Stonor on that point."

"Still, if Renauld had an affair with a woman called Bella, there seems no inherent improbability in his having another with Madame Daubreuil."

"None whatever, I grant you, Hastings. But did he?"

"The letter, Poirot. You forget the letter."

"No, I do not forget. But what makes you think that letter was written to M. Renauld?"

"Why it was found in his pocket and—and—"

"And that is all!" cut in Poirot. "There was no mention of any name to show to whom the letter was addressed. We assumed it was to the dead man because it was in the pocket of his overcoat. Now, *mon ami*, something about that overcoat struck me as unusual. I measured it, and made the remark that he wore his overcoat very long. That remark should have given you to think."

"I thought you were just saying it for the sake of saying something," I confessed.

"Ah, *quelle idée*! Later you observed me measuring the overcoat of M. Jack Renauld. *Eh bien*, M. Jack Renauld wears his overcoat very short. Put those two facts together with a third, namely that M. Jack Renauld flung out of the house in a hurry on his departure for Paris, and tell me what you make of it!"

"I see," I said slowly, as the meaning of Poirot's remarks bore in upon me. "That letter was written to Jack Renauld—not to his father. He caught up the wrong overcoat in his haste and agitation."

Poirot nodded.

"*Précisement*! We can return to this point later. For the moment let us content ourselves with accepting the letter as having nothing to do with M. Renauld *père*, and pass to the next chronological event."

"May 23rd," I read, "M. Renauld quarrels with his son over latter's wish to marry Marthe Daubreuil. Son leaves for Paris. I don't see anything much to remark upon there, and the altering of the will the following day seems straightforward enough. It was the direct result of the quarrel."

"We agree, *mon ami*—at least as to the cause. But what exact motive underlay this procedure of M. Renauld's?"

I opened my eyes in surprise.

"Anger against his son of course."

"Yet he wrote him affectionate letters to Paris?"

"So Jack Renauld says, but he cannot produce them."

"Well, let us pass from that."

"Now we come to the day of the tragedy. You have placed the events of the morning in a certain order. Have you any justification for that?"

"I have ascertained that the letter to me was posted at the same time as the telegram was despatched. Masters was informed he could take a holiday shortly afterwards. In my opinion the quarrel with the tramp took place anterior to these happenings."

"I do not see that you can fix that definitely—unless you question Mademoiselle Dabreuil again."

"There is no need. I am sure of it. And if you do not see that, you see nothing, Hastings!"

I looked at him for a moment.

"Of course! I am an idiot. If the tramp was Georges Conneau, it was after the stormy interview with him that Mr. Renauld apprehended danger. He sent away the chauffeur, Masters, whom he suspected of being in the other's pay, he wired to his son, and sent for you."

A faint smile crossed Poirot's lips.

"You do not think it strange that he should use exactly the same expressions in his letter as Madame Renauld used later in her story? If the mention of Santiago was a blind, why should Renauld speak of it, and—what is more—send his son there?"

"It is puzzling, I admit, but perhaps we shall find some explanation later. We come now to the evening, and the visit of the mysterious lady. I confess that that fairly baffles me, unless it was Madame Daubreuil, as Françoise all along maintained."

Poirot shook his head.

"My friend, my friend, where are your wits wandering? Remember the fragment of cheque, and the fact that the name Bella Duveen was faintly familiar to Stonor, and I think we may take it for granted that Bella Duveen is the full name of Jack's unknown correspondent, and that it was she who came to the Villa Geneviève that night. Whether she intended to see Jack, or whether she meant all along to appeal to his father we cannot be certain, but I think we may assume that this is what occurred. She produced her claim upon Jack, probably showed letters that he had written her, and the older man tried to buy her off by writing a cheque. This she indignantly tore up. The terms of her letter are those of a woman genuinely in love, and she would probably deeply resent being offered money. In the end he got rid of her, and here the words that he used are significant."

"'Yes, yes, but for God's sake go now,'" I repeated. "They seem to me a little vehement, perhaps, that is all."

"That is enough. He was desperately anxious for the girl to go. Why? Not only because the interview was unpleasant. No, it was the time that was slipping by, and for some reason time was precious."

"Why should it be?" I asked, bewildered.

"That is what we ask ourselves. Why should it be? But later we have the incident of the wrist watch—which again shows us that time plays a very important part in the crime. We are now fast approaching the actual drama. It is half-past ten when Bella Duveen leaves, and by the evidence of the wrist watch we know that the crime was committed, or at any rate that it was staged, before twelve o'clock. We have reviewed all the events anterior to the murder, there remains only one unplaced. By the doctor's evidence, the tramp, when found, had been dead at least forty-eight hours—with a possible margin of twenty-four hours more. Now, with no other facts to help me than those we have discussed, I place the death as having occurred on the morning of June 7th."

I stared at him, stupefied.

"But how? Why? How can you possibly know?"

"Because only in that way can the sequence of events be logically explained. *Mon ami*, I have taken you step by step along the way. Do you not now see what is so glaringly plain?"

"My dear Poirot, I can't see anything glaring about it. I did think I was beginning to see my way before, but I'm now hopelessly fogged."

Poirot looked at me sadly, and shook his head. "*Mon Dieu*! But it is *triste*! A good intelligence—and so deplorably lacking in method. There is an exercise most excellent for the development of the little grey cells. I will impart it to you—"

"For Heaven's sake, not now! You really are the most irritating of fellows, Poirot. For goodness' sake, get on and tell me who killed M. Renauld."

"That is just what I am not sure of as yet."

"But you said it was glaringly clear?"

"We talk at cross-purposes, my friend. Remember, it is two crimes we are investigating—for which, as I pointed out to you, we have the necessary two bodies. There, there, *ne vous impatientez pas*! I explain all. To begin with, we apply our psychology. We find three points at which M. Renauld displays a distinct change of view and action—three psychological points therefore. The first occurs immediately after arriving in Merlinville, the second after quarrelling with his son on a certain subject, the third on the morning of June 7th. Now for the three causes. We can attribute No. 1 to meeting Madame Daubreuil. No. 2 is indirectly connected with her since it concerns a marriage between M. Renauld's son and her daughter. But the cause of No. 3 is hidden from us. We have to deduce it. Now, *mon ami*, let me ask you a question; who do we believe to have planned this crime?"

"Georges Conneau," I said doubtfully, eyeing Poirot warily.

"Exactly. Now Giraud laid it down as an axiom that a woman lies to save herself, the man she loves, and her child. Since we are satisfied that was Georges Conneau who dictated the lie to her, and as Georges Conneau is not Jack Renauld, follows that the third case is put out of court. And, still attributing the crime to Georges Conneau, the first is equally so. So we are forced to the second—that Madame Renauld lied for the sake of the man she loved—or in other words, for the sake of Georges Conneau. You agree to that."

"Yes," I admitted. "It seems logical enough."

"*Bien*! Madame Renauld loves Georges Conneau. Who, then, is Georges Conneau?"

"The tramp."

"Have we any evidence to show that Madame Renauld loved the tramp?"

"No, but—"

"Very well then. Do not cling to theories where facts no longer support them. Ask yourself instead who Madame Renauld *did* love."

I shook my head perplexed.

"*Mais, oui*, you know perfectly. Who did Madame Renauld love so dearly that when she saw his dead body, she fell down in a swoon?"

I stared dumbfounded.

"Her husband?" I gasped.

Poirot nodded.

"Her husband—or Georges Conneau, whichever you like to call him."

I rallied myself.

"But it's impossible."

"How 'impossible?' Did we not agree just now that Madame Daubreuil was in a position to blackmail Georges Conneau?"

"Yes, but—"

"And did she not very effectively blackmail M. Renauld?"

"That may be true enough, but—"

"And is it not a fact that we know nothing of M. Renauld's youth and upbringing? That he springs suddenly into existence as a French-Canadian exactly twenty-two years ago?"

"All that is so," I said more firmly, "but you seem to me to be overlooking one salient point."

"What is it, my friend?"

"Why, we have admitted Georges Conneau planned the crime. That brings us to the ridiculous statement that he planned his own murder!"

"*Eh bien, mon ami,*" said Poirot placidly, "that is just what he did do!"

21. Hercule Poirot on the Case

In a measured voice, Poirot began his exposition.

"It seems strange to you, *mon ami*, that a man should plan his own death? So strange, that you prefer to reject the truth as fantastic, and to revert to a story that is in reality ten times more impossible. Yes, M. Renauld planned his own death, but there is one detail that perhaps escapes you—he did not intend to die."

I shook my head, bewildered.

"But no, it is all most simple really," said Poirot kindly. "For the crime that M. Renauld proposed a murderer was not necessary, as I told you, but a body was. Let us reconstruct, seeing events this time from a different angle.

"Georges Conneau flies from justice—to Canada. There, under an assumed name he marries, and finally acquires a vast fortune in South America. But there is a nostalgia upon him for his own country. Twenty years have elapsed, he is considerably changed in appearance, besides being a man of such eminence that no one is likely to connect him with a fugitive from justice many years ago. He deems it quite safe to return. He takes up his headquarters in England, but intends to spend the summers in France. And ill fortune, that obscure justice which shapes men's ends, and will not allow them to evade the consequences of their acts, takes him to Merlinville. There, in the whole of France, is the one person who is capable of recognizing him. It is, of course, a gold mine to Madame Daubreuil, and a gold mine of which she is not slow to take advantage. He is helpless, absolutely in her power. And she bleeds him heavily.

"And then the inevitable happens. Jack Renauld falls in love with the beautiful girl he sees almost daily, and wishes to marry her. That rouses his father. At all costs, he will prevent his son marrying the daughter of this evil woman. Jack Renauld knows nothing of his father's past, but Madame Renauld knows everything. She is a woman of great force of character, and passionately devoted to her husband. They take counsel together. Renauld sees only one way of escape—death. He must appear to die, in reality escaping to another country where he will start again under an assumed name, and where Madame Renauld, having played the widow's part for a while, can join him. It is essential that she should have control of the money, so he alters his will. How they meant to manage the body business originally, I do not know—possibly an art student's skeleton—and a fire or something of the kind, but long before their plans have matured an event occurs which plays into their hands. A rough tramp, violent and abusive, finds his way into the garden. There is a struggle, M. Renauld seeks to eject him, and suddenly the tramp, an epileptic, falls down in a fit. He is dead. M. Renauld calls his wife. Together they drag him into the shed—as we know, the event had occurred just outside—and they realize the marvellous opportunity that has been vouchsafed them. The man bears no resemblance to M. Renauld, but he is middle-aged, of a usual French type. That is sufficient.

"I rather fancy that they sat on the bench up there, out of earshot from the house, discussing matters. Their plan was quickly made. The identification must rest solely on Madame Renauld's evidence. Jack Renauld and the chauffeur (who had been with his master two years) must be got out of the way. It was unlikely that the French women servants would go near the body, and in any case Renauld intended to take measures to deceive any one not likely to appreciate details. Masters was sent off, a telegram despatched to Jack, Buenos Aires being selected to give credence to the story that Renauld had decided upon. Having heard of me, as a rather obscure elderly detective, he wrote his appeal for help, knowing that when I arrived, the production of the letter would have a profound effect upon the examining magistrate—which, of course, it did.

"They dressed the body of the tramp in a suit of M. Renauld's and left his ragged coat and trousers by the door of the shed, not daring to take them into the house. And then, to give credence to the tale Madame Renauld was to tell, they drove the aeroplane dagger through his heart. That night, M. Renauld will first bind and gag his wife, and then, taking a spade, will dig a grave in that particular spot of ground where he knows a—how do you call it? bunkair?—is to be made. It is essential that the body should be found—Madame Daubreuil must have no suspicions. On the other hand, if a little time elapses, any dangers as to identity will be greatly lessened. Then, M. Renauld will don the tramp's rags, and shuffle off to the station, where he will leave, unnoticed, by the 12:10 train. Since the crime will be supposed to have taken place two hours later, no suspicion can possibly attach to him.

"You see now his annoyance at the inopportune visit of the girl Bella. Every moment of delay is fatal to his plans. He gets rid of her as soon as he can, however. Then, to work! He leaves the front door slightly ajar to create the impression that the assassins left that way. He binds and gags Madame Renauld, correcting his mistake of twenty-two years ago, when the looseness of the bonds caused suspicion to fall upon his accomplice, but leaving her primed with essentially the same story as he had invented before, proving the unconscious recoil of the mind against originality. The night is chilly, and he slips on an overcoat over his underclothing, intending to cast it into the grave with the dead man. He goes out by the window, smoothing over the flower bed carefully, and thereby furnishing the most positive evidence against himself. He goes out on to the lonely golf links, and he digs—and then—"

"Yes?"

"And then," said Poirot gravely, "the justice that he has so long eluded overtakes him. An unknown hand stabs him in the back . . . Now, Hastings, you understand what I mean when I talk of *two* crimes. The first crime, the crime that M. Renauld, in his arrogance, asked us to investigate (ah, but he made a famous mistake there! He misjudged Hercule Poirot!) is solved. But behind it lies a deeper riddle. And to solve that will be difficult—since the criminal in his wisdom, has been content to avail himself of the devices prepared by M. Renauld. It has been a particularly perplexing and baffling mystery to solve. A young hand, like Giraud, who does not place any reliance on the psychology, is almost certain to fail."

"You're marvellous, Poirot," I said, with admiration. "Absolutely marvellous. No one on earth but you could have done it!"

I think my praise pleased him. For once in his life, he looked almost embarrassed.

"Ah, then you no longer despise poor old Papa Poirot? You shift your allegiance back from the human foxhound?"

His term for Giraud never failed to make me smile.

"Rather. You've scored over him handsomely."

"That poor Giraud," said Poirot, trying unsuccessfully to look modest. "Without doubt it is not all stupidity. He has had *la mauvaise chance* once or twice. That dark hair coiled round the dagger, for instance. To say the least, it was misleading."

"To tell you the truth, Poirot," I said slowly, "even now I don't quite see—whose hair was it?"

"Madame Renauld's of course. That is where *la mauvaise chance* came in. Her hair, dark originally, is almost completely silvered. It might just as easily have been a grey hair—and then, by no conceivable effort could Giraud have persuaded himself it came from the head of Jack Renauld! But it is all of a piece. Always the facts must be twisted to fit the theory! Did not Giraud find the traces of two persons, a man and a woman, in the shed? And how does that fit in with his reconstruction of the case? I will tell you—it does not fit in, and so we shall hear no more of them! I ask you, is that a methodical way of working? The great Giraud! The great Giraud is nothing but a toy balloon—swollen with its own importance. But I, Hercule

Poirot, whom he despises, will be the little pin that pricks the big balloon—*comme ça*!" And he made an expressive gesture. Then, calming down, he resumed:

"Without doubt, when Madame Renauld recovers, she will speak. The possibility of her son being accused of the murder never occurred to her. How should it, when she believed him safely at sea on board the *Anzora*? Ah! *voilà une femme*, Hastings! What force, what self-command! She only made one slip. On his unexpected return: 'It does not matter—*now*.' And no one noticed—no one realized the significance of those words. What a terrible part she has had to play, poor woman. Imagine the shock when she goes to identify the body and, instead of what she expects, sees the actual lifeless form of the husband she has believed miles away by now. No wonder she fainted! But since then, despite her grief and her despair, how resolutely she has played her part, and how the anguish of it must wring her. She cannot say a word to set us on the track of the real murderers. For her son's sake, no one must know that Paul Renauld was Georges Conneau, the criminal. Final and most bitter blow, she has admitted publicly that Madame Daubreuil was her husband's mistress—for a hint of blackmail might be fatal to her secret. How cleverly she dealt with the examining magistrate when he asked her if there was any mystery in her husband's past life. 'Nothing so romantic, I am sure, M. le juge.' It was perfect, the indulgent tone, the *soupçon* of sad mockery. At once M. Hautet felt himself foolish and melodramatic. Yes, she is a great woman! If she loved a criminal, she loved him royally!"

Poirot lost himself in contemplation.

"One thing more, Poirot, what about the piece of lead piping?"

"You do not see? To disfigure the victim's face so that it would be unrecognizable. It was that which first set me on the right track. And that imbecile of a Giraud, swarming all over it to look for match ends! Did I not tell you that a clue of two feet long was quite as good as a clue of two inches?"

"Well, Giraud will sing small now," I observed hastily, to lead the conversation away from my own shortcomings.

"As I said before, will he? If he has arrived at the right person by the wrong method, he will not permit that to worry him."

"But surely—" I paused as I saw the new trend of things.

"You see, Hastings, we must now start again. Who killed M. Renauld? Someone who was near the villa just before twelve o'clock that night, someone who would benefit by his death—the description fits Jack Renauld only too well. The crime need not have been premeditated. And then the dagger!"

I started, I had not realized that point.

"Of course," I said. "The second dagger we found in the tramp was Mrs. Renauld's. There *were* two, then."

"Certainly, and, since they were duplicates, it stands to reason that Jack Renauld was the owner. But that would not trouble me so much. In fact I have a little idea as to that. No, the worst indictment against him is again psychological—heredity, *mon ami*, heredity! Like father, like son—Jack Renauld, when all is said or done, is the son of Georges Conneau."

His tone was grave and earnest, and I was impressed in spite of myself.

"What is your little idea that you mentioned just now?" I asked.

For answer, Poirot consulted his turnip-faced watch, and then asked:

"What time is the afternoon boat from Calais?"

"About five, I believe."

"That will do very well. We shall just have time."

"You are going to England?"

"Yes, my friend."

"Why?"

"To find a possible—witness."

"Who?"

With a rather peculiar smile upon his face, Poirot replied:

"Miss Bella Duveen."

"But how will you find her—what do you know about her?"

"I know nothing about her—but I can guess a good deal. We may take it for granted that her name *is* Bella Duveen, and since that name was faintly familiar to M. Stonor, though evidently not in connection with the Renauld family, it is probable that she is on the stage. Jack Renauld was a young man with plenty of money, and twenty years of age. The stage is sure to have been the home of his first love. It tallies, too, with M. Renauld's attempt to placate her with a cheque. I think I shall find her all right—especially with the help of *this*."

And he brought out the photograph I had seen him take from Jack Renauld's drawer. "With love from Bella," was scrawled across the corner, but it was not that which held my eyes fascinated. The likeness was not first rate—but for all that it was unmistakable to me. I felt a cold sinking, as though some unutterable calamity had befallen me.

It was the face of Cinderella.

22. I Find Love

For a moment or two I sat as though frozen, the photograph still in my hand. Then, summoning all my courage to appear unmoved, I handed it back. At the same time, I stole a quick glance at Poirot. Had he noticed anything? But to my relief he did not seem to be observing me. Anything unusual in my manner had certainly escaped him.

He rose briskly to his feet.

"We have no time to lose. We must make our departure with all despatch. All is well—the sea it will be calm!"

In the bustle of departure, I had no time for thinking, but once on board the boat, secure from Poirot's observation (he, as usual, was "practising the method most excellent of Laverguier") I pulled myself together, and attacked the facts dispassionately.

How much did Poirot know? Was he aware that my acquaintance of the train and Bella Duveen were one and the same? Why had he gone to the Hôtel du Phare? On my behalf as I had believed? Or had I only fatuously thought so, and was this visit undertaken with a deeper and more sinister purpose?

But in any case, why was he bent on finding this girl? Did he suspect her of having seen Jack Renauld commit the crime? Or did he suspect—but that was impossible! The girl had no grudge against the elder Renauld, no possible motive for wishing his death. What had brought her back to the scene of the murder? I went over the facts carefully. She must have left the train at Calais where I parted from her that day. No wonder I had been unable to find her on the boat. If she had dined in Calais, and then taken a train out to Merlinville, she would have arrived at the Villa Geneviève just about the time that Françoise said. What had she done when she left the house just after ten? Presumably either gone to an hotel, or returned to Calais. And then? The crime had been committed on Tuesday night. On Thursday morning, she was once more in Merlinville. Had she ever left France at all? I doubted it very much. What kept her there—the hope of seeing Jack Renauld? I had told her (as at the time we believed) that he was on the high seas *en route* to Buenos Aires. Possibly she was aware that the *Anzora* had not sailed. But to know that she must have seen Jack. Was that what Poirot was after? Had Jack Renauld, returning to see Marthe Daubreuil, come face to face instead with Bella Duveen, the girl he had heartlessly thrown over?

I began to see daylight. If that were indeed the case, it might furnish Jack with the alibi he needed. Yet under those circumstances his silence seemed difficult to explain. Why could he not have spoken out boldly? Did he fear for this former entanglement of his to come to the ears of Marthe Daubreuil? I shook my head, dissatisfied. The thing had been harmless enough, a foolish boy-and-girl affair, and I reflected cynically that the son of a millionaire was not likely to be thrown over by a penniless French girl, who moreover loved him devotedly, without a much graver cause.

Altogether I found the affair puzzling and unsatisfactory. I disliked intensely being associated with Poirot in hunting this girl down, but I could not see any way of avoiding it, without revealing everything to him, and this, for some reason, I was loath to do.

Poirot reappeared brisk and smiling at Dover, and our journey to London was uneventful. It was past nine o'clock when we arrived, and I supposed that we should return straight away to our rooms and do nothing till the morning. But Poirot had other plans.

"We must lose no time, *mon ami*. The news of the arrest will not be in the English papers until the day after tomorrow, but still we must lose no time."

I did not quite follow his reasoning, but I merely asked how he proposed to find the girl.

"You remember Joseph Aarons, the theatrical agent? No? I assisted him in a little matter of a Japanese wrestler. A pretty little problem, I must recount it to you one day. He, without doubt, will be able to put us in the way of finding out what we want to know."

It took us some time to run Mr. Aarons to earth, and it was after midnight when we finally managed it. He greeted Poirot with every evidence of warmth, and professed himself ready to be of service to us in any way.

"There's not much about the profession I don't know," he said, beaming genially.

"*Eh bien*, M. Aarons, I desire to find a young girl called Bella Duveen."

"Bella Duveen. I know the name, but for the moment I can't place it. What's her line?"

"That I do not know—but here is her photograph."

Mr. Aarons studied it for a moment, then his face lighted.

"Got it!" He slapped his thigh. "The Dulcibella Kids, by the Lord!"

"The Dulcibella Kids?"

"That's it. They're sisters. Acrobats, dancers and singers. Give quite a good little turn. They're in the provinces somewhere, I believe—if they're not resting. They've been on in Paris for the last two or three weeks."

"Can you find out for me exactly where they are?"

"Easy as a bird. You go home, and I'll send you round the dope in the morning."

With this promise we took leave of him. He was as good as his word. About eleven o'clock the following day, a scribbled note reached us.

"The Dulcibella Sisters are on at the Palace in Coventry. Good luck to you."

Without more ado, we started for Coventry. Poirot made no inquiries at the theatre, but contented himself with booking stalls for the variety performance that evening.

The show was wearisome beyond words—or perhaps it was only my mood that made it seem so. Japanese families balanced themselves precariously, would-be fashionable men, in greenish evening dress and exquisitely slicked hair, reeled off society patter and danced marvellously, stout prima donnas sang at the top of the human register, a comic comedian endeavoured to be Mr. George Robey and failed signally.

At last the number went up which announced the Dulcibella Kids. My heart beat sickeningly. There she was—there they both were, the pair of them, one flaxen haired, one dark, matching as to size, with short fluffy skirts and immense Buster Brown bows. They looked a pair of extremely piquant children. They began to sing. Their voices were fresh and true, rather thin and music-hally, but attractive.

It was quite a pretty little turn. They danced neatly, and did some clever little acrobatic feats. The words of their songs were crisp and catchy. When the curtain fell, there was a full meed of applause. Evidently the Dulcibella Kids were a success.

Suddenly I felt that I could remain no longer. I must get out into the air. I suggested leaving to Poirot.

"Go by all means, *mon ami*. I amuse myself, and will stay to the end. I will rejoin you later."

It was only a few steps from the theatre to the hotel. I went up to the sitting-room, ordered a whisky and soda, and sat drinking it, staring meditatively into the empty grate. I heard the door open, and turned my head, thinking it was Poirot. Then I jumped to my feet. It was Cinderella who stood in the doorway. She spoke haltingly, her breath coming in little gasps.

"I saw you in front. You and your friend. When you got up to go, I was waiting outside and followed you. Why are you here—in Coventry? What were you doing there to-night? Is the man who was with you the—the detective?"

She stood there, the cloak she had wrapped round her stage dress slipping from her shoulders. I saw the whiteness of her cheeks under the rouge, and heard the terror in her voice. And in that moment I understood everything—understood why Poirot was seeking her, and what she feared, and understood at last my own heart . . .

"Yes," I said gently.

"Is he looking for—me?" she half whispered.

Then, as I did not answer for a moment, she slipped down by the big chair, and burst into violent, bitter weeping.

I knelt down by her, holding her in my arms, and smoothing the hair back from her face.

"Don't cry, child, don't cry, for God's sake. You're safe here. I'll take care of you. Don't cry, darling. Don't cry. I know—I know everything."

"Oh, but you don't!"

"I think I do." And after a moment, as her sobs grew quieter, I asked: "It was you who took the dagger, wasn't it?"

"Yes."

"That was why you wanted me to show you round? And why you pretended to faint?"

Again she nodded. It was a strange thought to come to me at the moment, but it shot into my mind that I was glad her motive was what it had been—rather than the idle and morbid curiosity I had accused her of at the time. How gallantly she had played her part that day, inwardly racked with fear and trepidation as she must have been. Poor little soul, bearing the burden of a moment's impetuous action.

"Why did you take the dagger?" I asked presently.

She replied as simply as a child:

"I was afraid there might be finger-marks on it."

"But didn't you remember that you had worn gloves?"

She shook her head as though bewildered, and then said slowly:

"Are you going to give me up to—to the Police?"

"Good God! no."

Her eyes sought mine long and earnestly, and then she asked in a little quiet voice that sounded afraid of itself:

"Why not?"

It seemed a strange place and a strange time for a declaration of love—and God knows, in all my imagining, I had never pictured love coming to me in such a guise. But I answered simply and naturally enough:

"Because I love you, Cinderella."

She bent her head down, as though ashamed, and muttered in a broken voice:

"You can't—you can't—not if you knew—" And then, as though rallying herself, she faced me squarely, and asked:

"What do you know, then?"

"I know that you came to see Mr. Renauld that night. He offered you a cheque and you tore it up indignantly. Then you left the house—" I paused.

"Go on—what next?"

"I don't know whether you knew that Jack Renauld would be coming that night, or whether you just waited about on the chance of seeing him, but you did wait about. Perhaps you were just miserable, and walked aimlessly—but at any rate just before twelve you were still near there, and you saw a man on the golf links—"

Again I paused. I had leapt to the truth in a flash as she entered the room, but now the picture rose before me even more convincingly. I saw vividly the peculiar pattern of the overcoat on the dead body of Mr. Renauld, and I remembered the amazing likeness that had startled me into believing for one instant that the dead man had risen from the dead when his son burst into our conclave in the *salon*.

"Go on," repeated the girl steadily.

"I fancy his back was to you—but you recognized him, or thought you recognized him. The gait and the carriage were familiar to you, and the pattern of his overcoat." I paused. "You told me in the train on the way from Paris that you had Italian blood in your veins, and that you had nearly got into trouble once with it. You used a threat in one of your letters to Jack Renauld. When you saw him there, your anger and jealousy drove you mad—and you struck! I don't believe for a minute that you meant to kill him. But you did kill him, Cinderella."

She had flung up her hands to cover her face, and in a choked voice she said:

"You're right . . . you're right . . . I can see it all as you tell it." Then she turned on me almost savagely. "And you love me? Knowing what you do, how can you love me?"

"I don't know," I said a little wearily. "I think love is like that—a thing one cannot help. I have tried, I know—ever since the first day I met you. And love has been too strong for me."

And then suddenly, when I least expected it, she broke down again, casting herself down on the floor and sobbing wildly.

"Oh, I can't!" she cried. "I don't know what to do. I don't know which way to turn. Oh, pity me, pity me, someone, and tell me what to do!"

Again I knelt by her, soothing her as best I could.

"Don't be afraid of me, Bella. For God's sake don't be afraid of me. I love you, that's true—but I don't want anything in return. Only let me help you. Love him still if you have to, but let me help you, as he can't."

It was as though she had been turned to stone by my words. She raised her head from her hands and stared at me.

"You think that?" she whispered. "You think that I love Jack Renauld?"

Then, half laughing, half crying, she flung her arms passionately round my neck, and pressed her sweet wet face to mine.

"Not as I love you," she whispered. "Never as I love you!"

Her lips brushed my cheek, and then, seeking my mouth, kissed me again and again with a sweetness and fire beyond belief. The wildness of it—and the wonder, I shall not forget—no, not as long as I live!

It was a sound in the doorway that made us look up. Poirot was standing there looking at us.

I did not hesitate. With a bound I reached him and pinioned his arms to his sides.

"Quick," I said to the girl. "Get out of here. As fast as you can. I'll hold him."

With one look at me, she fled out of the room past us. I held Poirot in a grip of iron.

"*Mon ami*," observed the latter mildly, "you do this sort of thing very well. The strong man holds me in his grasp and I am helpless as a child. But all this is uncomfortable and slightly ridiculous. Let us sit down and be calm."

"You won't pursue her?"

"*Mon Dieu!* no. Am I Giraud? Release me, my friend."

Keeping a suspicious eye upon him, for I paid Poirot

the compliment of knowing that I was no match for him in astuteness, I relaxed my grip, and he sank into an armchair, feeling his arms tenderly.

"It is that you have the strength of a bull when you are roused, Hastings! *Eh bien*, and do you think you have behaved well to your old friend? I show you the girl's photograph and you recognize it, but you never say a word."

"There was no need if you knew that I recognized it," I said rather bitterly. So Poirot had known all along! I had not deceived him for an instant.

"Ta-ta! You did not know that I knew that. And tonight you help the girl to escape when we have found her with so much trouble! *Eh bien*! it comes to this—are you going to work with me or against me, Hastings?"

For a moment or two I did not answer. To break with my old friend gave me great pain. Yet I must definitely range myself against him. Would he ever forgive me, I wondered? He had been strangely calm so far, but I knew him to possess marvellous self-command.

"Poirot," I said, "I'm sorry. I admit I've behaved badly to you over this. But sometimes one has no choice. And in future I must take my own line."

Poirot nodded his head several times.

"I understand," he said. The mocking light had quite died out of his eyes, and he spoke with a sincerity and kindness that surprised me. "It is that, my friend, is it not? It is love that has come—not as you imagined it, all cock-a-hoop with fine feathers, but sadly, with bleeding feet. Well, well—I warned you. When I realized that this girl must have taken the dagger, I warned you. Perhaps you remember. But already it was too late. But, tell me, how much do you know?"

I met his eyes squarely.

"Nothing that you could tell me would be any surprise to me, Poirot. Understand that. But in case you think of resuming your search for Miss Duveen, I should like you to know one thing clearly. If you have any idea that she was concerned in the crime, or was the mysterious lady who called upon Mr. Renauld that night, you are wrong. I travelled home from France with her that day, and parted from her at Victoria that evening so that it is clearly impossible for her to have been in Merlinville."

"Ah!" Poirot looked at me thoughtfully. "And you would swear to that in a court of law?"

"Most certainly I would."

Poirot rose and bowed.

"*Mon ami*! *Vive l'amour*! It can perform miracles. It is decidedly ingenious what you have thought of there. It defeats even Hercule Poirot!"

23. Difficulties Ahead

After a moment of stress, such as I have just described, reaction is bound to set in. I retired to rest that night on a note of triumph, but I awoke to realize that I was by no means out of the wood. True, I could see no flaw in the alibi I had so suddenly conceived. I had but to stick to my story, and I failed to see how Bella could be convicted in face of it. It was not as though there was any old friendship between us that could be raked up, and which might lead them to suspect that I was committing perjury. It could be proved that in actual fact I had only seen the girl on three occasions. No, I was still satisfied with my idea—had not even Poirot admitted that it defeated him?

But there I felt the need of treading warily. All very well for my little friend to admit himself momentarily nonplussed. I had far too much respect for his abilities to conceive of him as being content to remain in that position. I had a very humble opinion of my wits when it came to matching them against his. Poirot would not take defeat lying down. Somehow or other, he would endeavour to turn the tables on me, and that in the way, and at the moment, when I least expected it.

We met at breakfast the following morning as though nothing had happened. Poirot's good temper was imperturbable, yet I thought I detected a film of reserve in his manner which was new. After breakfast, I announced my intention of going out for a stroll. A malicious gleam shot through Poirot's eyes.

"If it is information you seek, you need not be at the pains of deranging yourself. I can tell you all you wish to know. The Dulcibella Sisters have cancelled their contract, and have left Coventry for an unknown destination."

"Is that really so, Poirot?"

"You can take it from me, Hastings. I made inquiries the first thing this morning. After all, what else did you expect?"

True enough, nothing else could be expected under the circumstances. Cinderella had profited by the slight start I had been able to assure her, and would certainly not lose a moment in removing herself from the reach of the pursuer. It was what I had intended and planned. Nevertheless, I was aware of being plunged into a network of fresh difficulties.

I had absolutely no means of communicating with the girl, and it was vital that she should know the line of defence that had occurred to me, and which I was prepared to carry out. Of course it was possible that she might try to send word to me in some way or another, but I hardly thought it likely. She would know the risk she ran of a message being intercepted by Poirot, thus setting him on her track once more. Clearly her only course was to disappear utterly for the time being.

But, in the meantime, what was Poirot doing? I studied him attentively. He was wearing his most innocent air, and staring meditatively into the far distance. He looked altogether too placid and supine to give me reassurance. I had learned, with Poirot, that the less dangerous he looked, the more dangerous he was. His quiescence alarmed me. Observing a troubled quality in my glance, he smiled benignantly.

"You are puzzled, Hastings? You ask yourself why I do not launch myself in pursuit?"

"Well—something of the kind."

"It is what you would do, were you in my place. I understand that. But I am not of those who enjoy rushing up and down a country seeking a needle in a haystack, as you English say. No— let Mademoiselle Bella Duveen go. Without doubt, I shall be able to find her when the time comes. Until then, I am content to wait."

I stared at him doubtfully. Was he seeking to mislead me? I had an irritating feeling that, even now, he was master of the situation. My sense of superiority was gradually waning. I had contrived the girl's escape, and evolved a brilliant scheme for saving her from the consequences of her rash act—but I could not rest easy in my mind. Poirot's perfect calm awakened a thousand apprehensions.

"I suppose, Poirot," I said rather diffidently, "I mustn't ask what your plans are? I've forfeited the right."

"But not at all. There is no secret about them. We return to France without delay."

"*We?*"

"Precisely—'*we*'! You know very well that you cannot afford to let Papa Poirot out of your sight. Eh, is it not so, my friend? But remain in England by all means if you wish—"

I shook my head. He had hit the nail on the head. I could not afford to let him out of my sight. Although I could not expect his confidence after what had happened, I could still check his actions. The only danger to Bella lay with him. Giraud and the French police were indifferent to her existence. At all costs I must keep near Poirot.

Poirot observed me attentively as these reflections passed through my mind, and gave a nod of satisfaction.

"I am right, am I not? And as you are quite capable of trying to follow me, disguised with some absurdity such as a false beard—which every one would perceive, *bien entendu*—I much prefer that we should voyage together. It would annoy me greatly that any one should mock themselves at you."

"Very well, then. But it's only fair to warn you—"

"I know—I know all. You are my enemy! Be my enemy then. It does not worry me at all."

"So long as it's all fair and above-board, I don't mind."

"You have to the full the English passion for 'fair play'! Now your scruples are satisfied, let us depart immediately. There is no time to be lost. Our stay in England has been short but sufficient. I know—what I wanted to know."

The tone was light, but I read a veiled menace into the words.

"Still—" I began, and stopped.

"Still—as you say! Without doubt you are satisfied with the part you are playing. Me, I preoccupy myself with Jack Renauld."

Jack Renauld! The words gave me a start. I had completely forgotten that aspect of the case. Jack Renauld, in prison, with the shadow of the guillotine looming over him! I saw the part I was playing in a more sinister light. I could save Bella—yes, but in doing so I ran the risk of sending an innocent man to his death.

I pushed the thought from me with horror. It could not be. He would be acquitted. Certainly he would be acquitted! But the cold fear came back. Suppose he were not? What then? Could I have it on my conscience—horrible thought! Would it come to that in the end? A decision. Bella or Jack Renauld? The promptings of my heart were to save the girl I loved at any cost to myself. But, if the cost were to another, the problem was altered.

What would the girl herself say? I remembered that no word of Jack Renauld's arrest had passed my lips. As yet she was in total ignorance of the fact that her former lover was in prison charged with a hideous crime which he had not committed. When she knew, how would she act? Would she permit her life to be saved at the expense of his? Certainly she must do nothing rash. Jack Renauld might, and probably would, be acquitted without any intervention on her part. If so, good. But if he was not . . . That was the terrible, the unanswerable problem. I fancied that she ran no risk of the extreme penalty. The circumstances of the crime were quite different in her case. She could plead jealousy and extreme provocation, and her youth and beauty would go for much. The fact that by a tragic mistake it was old Mr. Renauld, and not his son, who paid the penalty would not alter the motive of the crime. But in any case, however lenient the sentence of the Court, it must mean a long term of imprisonment.

No, Bella must be protected. And, at the same time, Jack Renauld must be saved. How this was to be accomplished I did not see clearly. But I pinned my faith to Poirot. He knew. Come what might, he would manage to save an innocent man. He must find some pretext other than the real one. It might be difficult, but he would manage it somehow. And with Bella unsuspected, and Jack Renauld acquitted, all would end satisfactorily.

So I told myself repeatedly, but at the bottom of my heart there still remained a cold fear.

24. *"Save Him!"*

We crossed from England by the evening boat, and the following morning saw us in Saint-Omer, whither Jack Renauld had been taken. Poirot lost no time in visiting M. Hautet. As he did not seem disposed to make any objections to my accompanying him, I bore him company.

After various formalities and preliminaries, we were conducted to the examining magistrate's room. He greeted us cordially.

"I was told that you had returned to England, M. Poirot. I am glad to find that such is not the case."

"It is true that I went there, M. le juge, but it was only for a flying visit. A side issue, but one that I fancied might repay investigation."

"And it did—eh?"

Poirot shrugged his shoulders. M. Hautet nodded, sighing.

"We must resign ourselves, I fear. That animal Giraud, his manners are abominable, but he is undoubtedly clever! Not much chance of that one making a mistake."

"You think not, M. le juge?"

It was the examining magistrate's turn to shrug his shoulders.

"*Eh bien*, speaking frankly—in confidence, *c'est entendu*—can you come to any other conclusion?"

"Frankly, M. le juge, there seem to me to be many points that are obscure."

"Such as—?"

But Poirot was not to be drawn.

"I have not yet tabulated them," he remarked. "It was a general reflection that I was making. I liked the young man, and should be sorry to believe him guilty of such a hideous crime. By the way, what has he to say for himself on the matter?"

The magistrate frowned.

"I cannot understand him. He seems incapable of putting up any sort of defence. It has been most difficult to get him to answer questions. He contents himself with a general denial, and beyond that takes refuge in a most obstinate silence. I am interrogating him again tomorrow; perhaps you would like to be present?"

We accepted the invitation with *empressement*.

"A distressing case," said the magistrate with a sigh. "My sympathy for Madame Renauld is profound."

"How is Madame Renauld?"

"She has not yet recovered consciousness. It is merciful in a way, poor woman, she is being spared much. The doctors say that there is no danger, but that when she comes to herself she must be kept as quiet as possible. It was, I understand, quite as much the shock as the fall which caused her present state. It would be terrible if her brain became unhinged; but I should not wonder at all—no, really, not at all."

M. Hautet leaned back, shaking his head, with a sort of mournful enjoyment, as he envisaged the gloomy prospect.

He roused himself at length, and observed with a start.

"That reminds me. I have here a letter for you, M. Poirot. Let me see, where did I put it?"

He proceeded to rummage amongst his papers. At last he found the missive, and handed it to Poirot.

"It was sent under cover to me in order that I might forward it to you," he explained. "But as you left no address I could not do so."

Poirot studied the letter curiously. It was addressed in a long, sloping, foreign hand, and the writing was decidedly a woman's. Poirot did not open it. Instead he put it in his pocket and rose to his feet.

"*À demain* then, M. le juge. Many thanks for your courtesy and amiability."

"But not at all. I am always at your service. These young detectives of the school of Giraud, they are all alike—rude, sneering fellows. They do not realize that an examining magistrate of my—er—experience is bound to have a certain discernment, a certain—*flair. Enfin*! the politeness of the old school is infinitely more to my taste. Therefore, my dear friend, command me in any way you will. We know a thing or two, you and I—eh?"

And laughing heartily, enchanted with himself and with us, M. Hautet bade us adieu. I am sorry to have to record that Poirot's first remark to me as we traversed the corridor was:

"A famous old imbecile, that one! Of a stupidity to make pity!"

We were just leaving the building when we came face to face with Giraud, looking more dandified than ever, and thoroughly pleased with himself.

"Aha! M. Poirot," he cried airily. "You have returned from England then?"

"As you see," said Poirot.

"The end of the case is not far off now, I fancy."

"I agree with you, M. Giraud."

Poirot spoke in a subdued tone. His crestfallen manner seemed to delight the other.

"Of all the milk-and-water criminals! Not an idea of defending himself. It is extraordinary!"

"So extraordinary that it gives one to think, does it not?" suggested Poirot mildly.

But Giraud was not even listening. He twirled his cane amicably.

"Well, good day, M. Poirot. I am glad you're satisfied of young Renauld's guilt at last."

"*Pardon*! But I am not in the least satisfied. Jack Renauld is innocent."

Giraud stared for a moment—then burst out laughing, tapping his head significantly with the brief remark: "*Toqué*!"

Poirot drew himself up. A dangerous light showed in his eyes.

"M. Giraud, throughout the case your manner to me has been deliberately insulting! You need teaching a lesson. I am prepared to wager you 500 francs that I find the murderer of M. Renauld before you do. Is it agreed?"

Giraud stared helplessly at him, and murmured again: "*Toqué*!"

"Come now," urged Poirot, "is it agreed?"

"I have no wish to take your money from you."

"Make your mind easy—you will not!"

"Oh, well then, I agree! You speak of my manner to you being insulting. *Eh bien*, once or twice, *your* manner has annoyed *me*."

"I am enchanted to hear it," said Poirot. "Good morning, M. Giraud. Come, Hastings."

I said no word as we walked along the street. My heart was

heavy. Poirot had displayed his intentions only too plainly. I doubted more than ever my powers of saving Bella from the consequences of her act. This unlucky encounter with Giraud had roused Poirot and put him on his mettle.

Suddenly I felt a hand laid on my shoulder, and turned to face Gabriel Stonor. We stopped and greeted him, and he proposed strolling with us back to our hotel.

"And what are you doing here, M. Stonor?" inquired Poirot.

"One must stand by one's friends," replied the other dryly. "Especially when they are unjustly accused."

"Then you do not believe that Jack Renauld committed the crime?" I asked eagerly.

"Certainly I don't. I know the lad. I admit that there have been one or two things in this business that have staggered me completely, but none the less, in spite of his fool way of taking it, I'll never believe that Jack Renauld is a murderer."

My heart warmed to the secretary. His words seemed to lift a secret weight from my heart.

"I have no doubt that many people feel as you do," I exclaimed. "There is really absurdly little evidence against him. I should say that there was no doubt of his acquittal—no doubt whatever."

But Stonor hardly responded as I could have wished.

"I'd give a lot to think as you do," he said gravely. He turned to Poirot. "What's your opinion, monsieur?"

"I think that things look very black against him," said Poirot quietly.

"You believe him guilty?" said Stonor sharply.

"No. But I think he will find it hard to prove his innocence."

"He's behaving so damned queerly," muttered Stonor. "Of course I realize that there's a lot more in this affair than meets the eye. Giraud's not wise to that because he's an outsider, but the whole thing has been damned odd. As to that, least said soonest mended. If Mrs. Renauld wants to hush anything up, I'll take my cue from her. It's her show, and I've too much respect for her judgment to shove my oar in, but I can't get behind this attitude of Jack's. Any one would think he *wanted* to be thought guilty."

"But it's absurd," I cried, bursting in. "For one thing, the dagger—" I paused, uncertain as to how much Poirot would wish me to reveal. I continued, choosing my words carefully, "We know that the dagger could not have been in Jack Renauld's possession that evening. Mrs. Renauld knows that."

"True," said Stonor. "When she recovers, she will doubtless say all this and more. Well, I must be leaving you."

"One moment." Poirot's hand arrested his departure. "Can you arrange for word to be sent to me at once should Madame Renauld recover consciousness?"

"Certainly. That's easily done."

"That point about the dagger is good, Poirot," I urged as we went upstairs. "I couldn't speak very plainly before Stonor."

"That was quite right of you. We might as well keep the knowledge to ourselves as long as we can. As to the dagger, your point hardly helps Jack Renauld. You remember that I was absent for an hour this morning, before we started from London?"

"Yes?"

"Well, I was employed in trying to find the firm Jack Renauld employed to convert his souvenirs. It was not very difficult. *Eh bien*, Hastings, they made to his order not *two* paper-knives, but *three*."

"So that—?"

"So that, after giving one to his mother, and one to Bella Duveen, there was a third which he doubtless retained for his own use. No, Hastings, I fear the dagger question will not help us to save him from the guillotine."

"It won't come to that," I cried, stung.

Poirot shook his head uncertainly.

"You will save him," I cried positively.

Poirot glanced at me dryly.

"Have you not rendered it impossible, *mon ami*?"

"Some other way," I muttered.

"Ah! *Sapristi*! But it is miracles you ask from me. No—say no more. Let us instead see what is in this letter."

And he drew out the envelope from his breast pocket.

His face contracted as he read, then he handed the one flimsy sheet to me.

"There are other women in the world who suffer, Hastings."

The writing was blurred and the note had evidently been written in great agitation:

> DEAR M. POIROT:
> If you get this, I beg of you to come to my aid. I have no one to turn to, and at all costs Jack must be saved. I implore of you on my knees to help us.
>
> MARTHE DAUBREUIL

I handed it back, moved.

"You will go?"

"At once. We will command an auto."

Half an hour later saw us at the Villa Marguerite. Marthe was at the door to meet us, and led Poirot in, clinging with both hands to one of his.

"Ah, you have come—it is good of you. I have been in despair, not knowing what to do. They will not let me go to see him in prison even. I suffer horribly, I am nearly mad. Is it true what they say, that he does not deny the crime? But that is madness. It is impossible that he should have done it! Never for one minute will I believe it."

"Neither do I believe it, mademoiselle," said Poirot gently.

"But then why does he not speak? I do not understand."

"Perhaps because he is screening some one," suggested Poirot, watching her.

Marthe frowned.

"Screening some one? Do you mean his mother? Ah, from

the beginning I have suspected her. Who inherits all that vast fortune? She does. It is easy to wear widow's weeds and play the hypocrite. And they say that when he was arrested she fell down—like *that.*" She made a dramatic gesture. "And without doubt, M. Stonor, the secretary, he helped her. They are thick as thieves, those two. It is true she is older than he—but what do men care—if a woman is rich!"

There was a hint of bitterness in her tone.

"Stonor was in England," I put in.

"He says so—but who knows?"

"Mademoiselle," said Poirot quietly, "if we are to work together, you and I, we must have things clear. First, I will ask you a question."

"Yes, monsieur?"

"Are you aware of your mother's real name?"

Marthe looked at him for a minute, then, letting her head fall forward on her arms, she burst into tears.

"There, there," said Poirot, patting her on the shoulder. "Calm yourself, *petite*, I see that you know. Now a second question, did you know who M. Renauld was?"

"M. Renauld," she raised her head from her hands and gazed at him wonderingly.

"Ah, I see you do not know that. Now listen to me carefully."

Step by step, he went over the case, much as he had done to me on the day of our departure for England. Marthe listened spellbound. When he had finished, she drew a long breath.

"But you are wonderful—magnificent! You are the greatest detective in the world."

With a swift gesture she slipped off her chair and knelt before him with an abandonment that was wholly French.

"Save him, monsieur," she cried. "I love him so. Oh, save him, save him—save him!"

25. An Unexpected Dénouement

We were present the following morning at the examination of Jack Renauld. Short as the time had been, I was shocked at the change that had taken place in the young prisoner. His cheeks had fallen in, there were deep black circles round his eyes, and he looked haggard and distraught, as one who had wooed sleep in vain for several nights. He betrayed no emotion at seeing us.

The prisoner and his counsel, Maître Grosíer, were accommodated with chairs. A formidable guard with resplendent sabre stood before the door. The patient *greffier* sat at his desk. The examination began.

"Renauld," began the magistrate, "do you deny that you were in Merlinville on the night of the crime?"

Jack did not reply at once, then he said with a hesitancy of manner which was piteous:

"I—I—told you that I was in Cherbourg."

Maître Grosíer frowned and sighed. I realized at once that Jack Renauld was obstinately bent on conducting his own case as he wished, to the despair of his legal representative.

The magistrate turned sharply.

"Send in the station witnesses."

In a moment or two the door opened to admit a man whom I recognized as being a porter at Merlinville station.

"You were on duty on the night of June 7th?"

"Yes, monsieur."

"You witnessed the arrival of the 11:40 train?"

"Yes, monsieur."

"Look at the prisoner. Do you recognize him as having been one of the passengers to alight?"

"Yes, Monsieur le juge."

"There is no possibility of your being mistaken?"

"No, monsieur. I knew M. Jack Renauld well."

"Nor of your being mistaken as to the date?"

"No, monsieur. Because it was the following morning, June 8th, that we heard of the murder."

Another railway official was brought in, and confirmed the first one's evidence. The magistrate looked at Jack Renauld.

"These men have identified you positively. What have you to say?"

Jack shrugged his shoulders.

"Nothing."

M. Hautet exchanged a glance with the *greffier*, as the scratching of the latter's pen recorded the answer.

"Renauld," continued the magistrate, "do you recognize this?"

He took something from the table by his side, and held it out to the prisoner. I shuddered as I recognized the aeroplane dagger.

"Pardon," cried Maître Grosíer. "I demand to speak to my client before he answers that question."

But Jack Renauld had no consideration for the feelings of the wretched Grosíer. He waved him aside, and replied quietly:

"Certainly I recognize it. It is a present given by me to my mother, as a souvenir of the war."

"Is there, as far as you know, any duplicate of that dagger in existence?"

Again Maître Grosíer burst out, and again Jack overrode him.

"Not that I know of. The setting was my own design."

Even the magistrate almost gasped at the boldness of the reply. It did, in very truth, seem as though Jack was rushing on his fate. I realized, of course, the vital necessity he was under of concealing, for Bella's sake, the fact that there was a duplicate dagger in the case. So long as there was supposed to be only one weapon, no suspicion was likely to attach to the girl who had had the second paper-knife in her possession. He was valiantly shielding the woman he had once loved—but at what a cost to himself! I began to realize the magnitude of the task I had so lightly set Poirot. It would not be easy to secure the acquittal of Jack Renauld, by anything short of the truth.

M. Hautet spoke again, with a peculiarly biting inflection:

"Madame Renauld told us that this dagger was on her dressing table on the night of the crime. But Madame Renauld is a mother! It will doubtless astonish you, Renauld, but I consider it highly likely that Madame Renauld was mistaken, and that, by inadvertence perhaps, you had taken it with you to Paris. Doubtless you will contradict me——"

I saw the lad's handcuffed hands clench themselves. The perspiration stood out in beads upon his brow, as with a supreme effort he interrupted M. Hautet in a hoarse voice:

"I shall not contradict you. It is possible."

It was a stupefying moment. Maître Grosíer rose to his feet, protesting:

"My client has undergone a considerable nervous strain. I should wish it put on record that I do not consider him answerable for what he says."

The magistrate quelled him angrily. For a moment a doubt seemed to arise in his own mind. Jack Renauld had almost overdone his part. He leaned forward, and gazed at the prisoner searchingly.

"Do you fully understand, Renauld, that on the answers you have given me I shall have no alternative but to commit you for trial?"

Jack's pale face flushed. He looked steadily back.

"M. Hautet, I swear that I did not kill my father."

But the magistrate's brief moment of doubt was over. He laughed a short, unpleasant laugh.

"Without doubt, without doubt—they are always innocent, our prisoners! By your own mouth you are condemned. You can offer no defence, no alibi—only a mere assertion which would not deceive a babe!—that you are not guilty. You killed your father, Renauld— cruel and cowardly murder—for the sake of money which you believed would come to you at his death. Your mother was an accessory after the fact. Doubtless, in view of the fact that she acted as a mother, the courts will extend an indulgence to her that they will not accord to you. And rightly so! Your crime was a horrible one—to be held in abhorrence by gods and men!" M. Hautet was enjoying himself, working up his period, steeped in the solemnity of the moment, and his own role as representative of justice. "You killed—and you must pay the consequences of your action. I speak to you, not as a man, but as Justice, eternal Justice, which—"

M. Hautet was interrupted—to his intense annoyance. The door was pushed open.

"M. le juge, M. le juge," stammered the attendant, "there is a lady who says—who says—"

"Who says what?" cried the justly incensed magistrate. "This is highly irregular. I forbid it—I absolutely forbid it."

But a slender figure pushed the stammering gendarme aside. Dressed all in black, with a long veil that hid her face, she advanced into the room.

My heart gave a sickening throb. She had come then! All my efforts were in vain. Yet I could not but admire the courage that had led her to take this step so unfalteringly.

She raised her veil—and I gasped. For, though as like her as two peas, this girl was not Cinderella! On the other hand, now that I saw her without the fair wig she had worn on the stage, I recognized her as the girl of the photograph in Jack Renauld's room.

"You are the Juge d'Instruction, M. Hautet?" she queried.

"Yes, but I forbid—"

"My name is Bella Duveen. I wish to give myself up for the murder of Mr. Renauld."

26. I Receive a Letter

MY FRIEND:
You will know all when you get this. Nothing that
I can say will move Bella. She has gone out to give
herself up. I am tired out with struggling.

You will know now that I deceived you, that where
you gave me trust I repaid you with lies. It will seem,
perhaps, indefensible to you, but I should like, before
I go out of your life for ever, to show you just how
it all came about. If I knew that you forgave me, it
would make life easier for me. It wasn't for myself I
did it—that's the only thing I can put forward to say
for myself.

I'll begin from the day I met you in the boat train
from Paris. I was uneasy then about Bella. She was just
desperate about Jack Renauld, she'd have lain down
on the ground for him to walk on, and when he began
to change, and to stop writing so often, she began
getting in a state. She got it into her head that he was
keen on another girl—and of course, as it turned out
afterwards, she was quite right there. She'd made up
her mind to go to their Villa at Merlinville, and try and
see Jack. She knew I was against it, and tried to give
me the slip. I found she was not on the train at Calais,
and determined I would not go on to England without
her. I'd an uneasy feeling that something awful was
going to happen if I couldn't prevent it.

I met the next train from Paris. She was on it, and
set upon going out then and there to Merlinville. I
argued with her for all I was worth, but it wasn't any
good. She was all strung up and set upon having her
own way. Well, I washed my hands of it. I'd done all I

could! It was getting late. I went to an hotel, and Bella started for Merlinville. I still couldn't shake off my feeling of what the books call "impending disaster."

The next day came—but no Bella. She'd made a date with me to meet at the hotel, but she didn't keep it. No sign of her all day. I got more and more anxious. Then came an evening paper with the news.

It was awful! I couldn't be sure, of course—but I was terribly afraid. I figured it out that Bella had met Papa Renauld and told him about her and Jack, and that he'd insulted her or something like that. We've both got terribly quick tempers.

Then all the masked foreigner business came out, and I began to feel more at ease. But it still worried me that Bella hadn't kept her date with me.

By the next morning, I was so rattled that I'd just got to go and see what I could. First thing, I ran up against you. You know all that . . . When I saw the dead man, looking so like Jack, and wearing Jack's fancy overcoat, I knew! And there was the identical paper-knife—wicked little thing!—that Jack had given Bella! Ten to one it had her finger-marks on it. I can't hope to explain to you the sort of helpless horror of that moment. I only saw one thing clearly—I must get hold of that dagger, and get right away with it before they found out it was gone. I pretended to faint, and whilst you were away getting water I took the thing and hid it away in my dress.

I told you that I was staying at the Hôtel du Phare, but of course really I made a beeline back to Calais, and then on to England by the first boat. When we were in mid-Channel, I dropped that little devil of a dagger into the sea. Then I felt I could breathe again.

Bella was at our digs in London. She looked like

nothing on God's earth. I told her what I'd done, and that she was pretty safe for the time being. She stared at me, and then began laughing . . . laughing . . . laughing . . . it was horrible to hear her! I felt that the best thing to do was to keep busy. She'd go mad if she had time to brood on what she'd done. Luckily we got an engagement at once.

And then, I saw you and your friend, watching us that night . . . I was frantic. You must suspect, or you wouldn't have tracked us down. I had to know the worst, so I followed you. I was desperate. And then, before I'd had time to say anything, I tumbled to it that it was *me* you suspected, not Bella! Or at least that you thought I *was* Bella since I'd stolen the dagger.

I wish, honey, that you could see back into my mind at that moment . . . you'd forgive me, perhaps . . . I was so frightened, and muddled, and desperate . . . All I could get clearly was that you would try and save me. I didn't know whether you'd be willing to save her . . . I thought very likely not—it wasn't the same thing! And I couldn't risk it! Bella's my twin—I'd got to do the best for her. So I went on lying . . . I felt mean—I feel mean still . . . That's all—enough too, you'll say, I expect. I ought to have trusted you . . . If I had—

As soon as the news was in the paper that Jack Renauld had been arrested, it was all up. Bella wouldn't even wait to see how things went . . .

I'm very tired . . . I can't write any more . . .

She had begun to sign herself CINDERELLA, but had crossed that out and written instead "DULCIE DUVEEN."

It was an ill-written, blurred epistle but I have kept it to this day.

Poirot was with me when I read it. The sheets fell from my hand, and I looked across at him.

"Did you know all the time that it was—the other?"

"Yes, my friend."

"Why did you not tell me?"

"To begin with, I could hardly believe it conceivable that you could make such a mistake. You had seen the photograph. The sisters are very alike, but by no means incapable of distinguishment."

"But the fair hair?"

"A wig, worn for the sake of a piquant contrast on the stage. Is it conceivable that with twins one should be fair and one dark?"

"Why didn't you tell me that night at the hotel in Coventry?"

"You were rather high-handed in your methods, *mon ami*," said Poirot dryly. "You did not give me a chance."

"But afterwards?"

"Ah, afterwards! Well, to begin with, I was hurt at your want of faith in me. And then, I wanted to see whether your—feelings would stand the test of time. In fact, whether it was love, or a flash in the pan, with you. I should not have left you long in your error."

I nodded. His tone was too affectionate for me to bear resentment. I looked down on the sheets of the letter. Suddenly I picked them up from the floor, and pushed them across to him.

"Read that," I said. "I'd like you to."

He read it through in silence, then he looked up at me.

"What is it that worries you, Hastings."

This was quite a new mood in Poirot. His mocking manner seemed laid quite aside. I was able to say what I wanted without too much difficulty.

"She doesn't say—she doesn't say—well, not whether she cares for me or not!"

Poirot turned back the pages.

"I think you are mistaken, Hastings."

"Where?" I cried, leaning forward eagerly.

Poirot smiled.

"She tells you that in every line of the letter, *mon ami*."

"But where am I to find her? There's no address on the letter. There's a French stamp, that's all."

"Excite yourself not! Leave it to Papa Poirot. I can find her for you as soon as I have five little minutes!"

27. Jack Renauld's Story

"Congratulations, M. Jack," said Poirot, wringing the lad warmly by the hand.

Young Renauld had come to us as soon as he was liberated—before starting for Merlinville to rejoin Marthe and his mother. Stonor accompanied him. His heartiness was in strong contrast to the lad's wan looks. It was plain that the boy was on the verge of a nervous breakdown. Although delivered from the immediate peril that was hanging over him, the circumstances of his release were too painful to let him feel full relief. He smiled mournfully at Poirot, and said in a low voice:

"I went through it to protect her, and now it's all no use!"

"You could hardly expect the girl to accept the price of your life," remarked Stonor dryly. "She was bound to come forward when she saw you heading straight for the guillotine."

"*Eh ma foi*! and you were heading for it too!" added Poirot, with a slight twinkle. "You would have had Maître Grosíer's death from rage on your conscience if you had gone on."

"He was a well meaning ass, I suppose," said Jack. "But he worried me horribly. You see, I couldn't very well take him into my confidence. But, my God! what's going to happen about Bella?"

"If I were you," said Poirot frankly, "I should not distress myself unduly. The French Courts are very lenient to youth and beauty, and the *crime passionnel*. A clever lawyer will make out a great case of extenuating circumstances. It will not be pleasant for you—"

"I don't care about that. You see, M. Poirot, in a way I *do* feel guilty of my father's murder. But for me, and my entanglement with this girl, he would be alive and well today. And then my cursed carelessness in taking away the wrong overcoat. I can't help feeling responsible for his death. It will haunt me for ever!"

"No, no," I said soothingly.

"Of course it's horrible to me to think that Bella killed my father," resumed Jack, "but I'd treated her shamefully. After I met Marthe, and realized I'd made a mistake, I ought to have written and told her so honestly. But I was so terrified of a row, and of its coming to Marthe's ears, and her thinking there was more in it than there ever had been, that—well, I was a coward, and went on hoping the thing would die down of itself. I just drifted, in fact—not realizing that I was driving the poor kid desperate. If she'd really knifed me, as she meant to, I should have got no more than my deserts. And the way she's come forward now is downright plucky. I'd have stood the racket, you know—up to the end."

He was silent for a moment or two, and then burst out on another tack:

"What gets me is why the Governor should be wandering about in underclothes and my overcoat at that time of night. I suppose he'd just given the foreign johnnies the slip, and my mother must have made a mistake about its being 2 o'clock when they came. Or—or, it wasn't all a frame up, was it? I mean, my mother didn't think—couldn't think—that—that it was *me*?"

Poirot reassured him quickly.

"No, no, M. Jack. Have no fears on that score. As for the rest, I will explain it to you one of these days. It is rather curious. But will you recount to us exactly what did occur on that terrible evening?"

"There's very little to tell. I came from Cherbourg, as I told you, in order to see Marthe before going to the other end of the world. The train was late, and I decided to take the short cut across the golf links. I could easily get into the grounds of the Villa Marguerite from there. I had nearly reached the place when—"

He paused and swallowed.

"Yes?"

"I heard a terrible cry. It wasn't loud—a sort of choke and gasp—but it frightened me. For a moment I stood rooted to the spot. Then I came round the corner of a bush. There was moonlight. I saw the grave, and a figure lying face downwards, with a dagger sticking in the back. And then—and then—I looked up and saw *her*. She was looking at me as though she saw a ghost—it's what she must have thought me at first—all expression seemed frozen out of her face by horror. And then she gave a cry, and turned and ran."

He stopped, trying to master his emotion.

"And afterwards?" asked Poirot gently.

"I really don't know. I stayed there for a time, dazed. And then I realized I'd better get away as fast as I could. It didn't occur to me that they would suspect me, but I was afraid of being called upon to give evidence against her. I walked to St. Beauvais as I told you, and got a car from there back to Cherbourg."

A knock came at the door, and a page entered with a telegram which he delivered to Stonor. He tore it open. Then he got up from his seat.

"Mrs. Renauld has regained consciousness," he said.

"Ah!" Poirot sprang to his feet. "Let us all go to Merlinville at once!"

A hurried departure was made forthwith. Stonor, at Jack's instance, agreed to stay behind and do all that could be done for Bella Duveen. Poirot, Jack Renauld and I set off in the Renauld car.

The run took just over forty minutes. As we approached the doorway of the Villa Marguerite, Jack Renauld shot a questioning glance at Poirot.

"How would it be if you went on first—to break the news to my mother that I am free—"

"While you break it in person to Mademoiselle Marthe, eh?" finished Poirot, with a twinkle. "But yes, by all means, I was about to propose such an arrangement myself."

Jack Renauld did not wait for more. Stopping the car, he swung himself out, and ran up the path to the front door. We went on in the car to the Villa Geneviève.

"Poirot," I said, "do you remember how we arrived here that first day? And were met by the news of M. Renauld's murder?"

"Ah! yes, truly. Not so long ago, either. But what a lot of things have happened since then—especially for you, *mon ami*!"

"Poirot, what have you done about finding Bel—I mean Dulcie?"

"Calm yourself, Hastings. I arrange everything."

"You're being a precious long time about it," I grumbled.

Poirot changed the subject.

"Then the beginning, now the end," he moralized, as we rang the bell. "And, considered as a case, the end is profoundly unsatisfactory."

"Yes, indeed," I sighed.

"You are regarding it from the sentimental standpoint, Hastings. That was not my meaning. We will hope that Mademoiselle Bella will be dealt with leniently, and after all Jack Renauld cannot marry both the girls. I spoke from a professional standpoint. This is not a crime well ordered and regular, such as a detective delights in. The *mise en scène* designed by Georges Conneau, that indeed is perfect, but the *dénouement*—ah, no! A man killed by accident in a girl's fit of anger—ah, indeed, what order or method is there in that?"

And in the midst of a fit of laughter on my part at Poirot's peculiarities, the door was opened by Françoise.

Poirot explained that he must see Mrs. Renauld at once, and the old woman conducted him upstairs. I remained in the *salon*.

It was some time before Poirot reappeared. He was looking unusually grave.

"*Vous voilà*, Hastings! *Sacré tonnerre*, but there are squalls ahead!"

"What do you mean?" I cried.

"I would hardly have credited it," said Poirot thoughtfully, "but women are very unexpected."

"Here are Jack and Marthe Daubreuil," I exclaimed, looking out of the window.

Poirot bounded out of the room, and met the young couple on the steps outside.

"Do not enter. It is better not. Your mother is very upset."

"I know, I know," said Jack Renauld. "I must go up to her at once."

"But no, I tell you. It is better not."

"But Marthe and I—"

"In any case, do not take Mademoiselle with you. Mount, if you must, but you would be wise to be guided by me."

A voice on the stairs behind made us all start.

"I thank you for your good offices, M. Poirot, but I will make my own wishes clear."

We stared in astonishment. Descending the stairs, leaning upon Léonie's arm, was Mrs. Renauld, her head still bandaged. The French girl was weeping, and imploring her mistress to return to bed.

"Madame will kill herself. It is contrary to all the doctor's orders!"

But Mrs. Renauld came on.

"Mother," cried Jack, starting forward. But with a gesture she drove him back.

"I am no mother of yours! You are no son of mine! From this day and hour I renounce you."

"Mother," cried the lad, stupefied.

For a moment she seemed to waver, to falter before the anguish in his voice. Poirot made a mediating gesture, but instantly she regained command of herself.

"Your father's blood is on your head. You are morally guilty of his death. You thwarted and defied him over this girl, and by your heartless treatment of another girl, you brought about his death. Go out from my house. Tomorrow I intend to take such steps as shall make it certain that you shall never touch a penny of his money. Make your way in the world as best you can with the help of the girl who is the daughter of your father's bitterest enemy!"

And slowly, painfully, she retraced her way upstairs.

We were all dumbfounded—totally unprepared for such a demonstration. Jack Renauld, worn out with all he had already gone through, swayed and nearly fell. Poirot and I went quickly to his assistance.

"He is overdone," murmured Poirot to Marthe. "Where can we take him?"

"But home! To the Villa Marguerite. We will nurse him, my mother and I. My poor Jack!"

We got the lad to the Villa, where he dropped limply on to a chair in a semi-dazed condition. Poirot felt his head and hands.

"He has fever. The long strain begins to tell. And now this shock on top of it. Get him to bed, and Hastings and I will summon a doctor."

A doctor was soon procured. After examining the patient, he gave it as his opinion that it was simply a case of nerve strain. With perfect rest and quiet, the lad might be almost restored by the next day, but, if excited, there was a chance of brain fever. It would be advisable for some one to sit up all night with him.

Finally, having done all we could, we left him in the charge of Marthe and her mother, and set out for the town. It was past our usual hour of dining, and we were both famished. The first restaurant we came to assuaged the pangs of hunger with an excellent *omelette*, and an equally excellent *entrecôte* to follow.

"And now for quarters for the night," said Poirot, when at length *café noir* had completed the meal. "Shall we try our old friend, the Hôtel des Bains?"

We traced our steps there without more ado. Yes, Messieurs could be accommodated with two good rooms overlooking the sea. Then Poirot asked a question which surprised me.

"Has an English lady, Miss Robinson, arrived?"

"Yes, monsieur. She is in the little *salon*."

"Ah!"

"Poirot," I cried, keeping pace with him as he walked along the corridor, "who on earth is Miss Robinson?"

Poirot beamed kindly on me.

"It is that I have arranged you a marriage, Hastings."

"But, I say—"

"Bah!" said Poirot, giving me a friendly push over the threshold of the door. "Do you think I wish to trumpet aloud in Merlinville the name of Duveen?"

It was indeed Cinderella who rose to greet us. I took her hands in both of mine. My eyes said the rest.

Poirot cleared his throat.

"*Mes enfants*," he said, "for the moment we have no time for sentiment. There is work ahead of us. Mademoiselle, were you able to do what I asked you?"

In response, Cinderella took from her bag an object wrapped up in paper, and handed it silently to Poirot. The latter unwrapped it. I gave a start—for it was the aeroplane dagger which I understood she had cast into the sea. Strange, how reluctant women always are to destroy the most compromising of objects and documents!

"*Très bien, mon enfant*," said Poirot. "I am pleased with you. Go now and rest yourself. Hastings here and I have work to do. You shall see him tomorrow."

"Where are you going?" asked the girl, her eyes widening.

"You shall hear all about it tomorrow."

"Because wherever you're going, I'm coming too."

"But mademoiselle—"

"I'm coming too, I tell you."

Poirot realized that it was futile to argue further. He gave in.

"Come then, mademoiselle. But it will not be amusing. In all probability nothing will happen."

The girl made no reply.

Twenty minutes later we set forth. It was quite dark now, a close, oppressive evening. Poirot led the way out of the town in the direction of the Villa Geneviève. But when he reached the Villa Marguerite he paused.

"I should like to assure myself that all goes well with Jack Renauld. Come with me, Hastings. Mademoiselle will perhaps remain outside. Madame Daubreuil might say something which would wound her."

We unlatched the gate, and walked up the path. As we went round to the side of the house, I drew Poirot's attention to a window on the first floor. Thrown sharply on the blind was the profile of Marthe Daubreuil.

"Ah!" said Poirot. "I figure to myself that that is the room where we shall find Jack Renauld."

Madame Daubreuil opened the door to us. She explained that Jack was much the same, but perhaps we would like to see for ourselves. She led us upstairs and into the bedroom. Marthe Daubreuil was embroidering by a table with a lamp on it. She put her finger to her lips as we entered.

Jack Renauld was sleeping an uneasy fitful sleep, his head turning from side to side, and his face still unduly flushed.

"Is the doctor coming again?" asked Poirot in a whisper.

"Not unless we send. He is sleeping—that is the great thing. *Maman* made him a tisane."

She sat down again with her embroidery as we left the room. Madame Daubreuil accompanied us down the stairs. Since I had learned of her past history, I viewed this woman with increased interest. She stood there with her eyes cast down, the same very faint enigmatical smile that I remembered on her lips. And suddenly I felt afraid of her, as one might feel afraid of a beautiful poisonous snake.

"I hope we have not deranged you, madame," said Poirot politely as she opened the door for us to pass out.

"Not at all, monsieur."

"By the way," said Poirot, as though struck by an afterthought, "M. Stonor has not been in Merlinville today, has he?"

I could not at all fathom the point of this question which I well knew to be meaningless as far as Poirot was concerned.

Madame Daubreuil replied quite composedly:

"Not that I know of."

"He has not had an interview with Mrs. Renauld?"

"How should I know that, monsieur?"

"True," said Poirot. "I thought you might have seen him coming or going, that is all. Good night, madame."

"Why—" I began.

"No '*whys*,' Hastings. There will be time for that later."

We rejoined Cinderella and made our way rapidly in the direction of the Villa Geneviève. Poirot looked over his shoulder once at the lighted window and the profile of Marthe as she bent over her work.

"He is being guarded at all events," he muttered.

Arrived at the Villa Geneviève, Poirot took up his stand behind some bushes to the left of the drive, where, whilst enjoying a good view ourselves, we were completely hidden from sight. The Villa itself was in total darkness, everybody was without doubt in bed and asleep. We were almost immediately under the window of Mrs. Renauld's bedroom, which window, I noticed, was open. It seemed to me that it was upon this spot that Poirot's eyes were fixed.

"What are we going to do?" I whispered.

"Watch."

"But—"

"I do not expect anything to happen for at least an hour, probably two hours, but the—"

But his words were interrupted by a long thin drawn cry:

"Help!"

A light flashed up in the second floor room on the right hand side of the house. The cry came from there. And even as we watched there came a shadow on the blind as of two people struggling.

"*Mille tenerres!*" cried Poirot. "She must have changed her room!"

Dashing forward, he battered wildly on the front door. Then rushing to the tree in the flower-bed, he swarmed up it with the agility of a cat. I followed him, as with a bound he sprang in through the open window. Looking over my shoulder, I saw Dulcie reaching the branch behind me.

"Take care," I exclaimed.

"Take care of your grandmother!" retorted the girl. "This is child's play to me."

Poirot had rushed through the empty room and was pounding on the door leading into the corridor.

"Locked and bolted on the outside," he growled. "And it will take time to burst it open."

The cries for help were getting noticeably fainter. I saw despair in Poirot's eyes. He and I together put our shoulders to the door.

Cinderella's voice, calm and dispassionate, came from the window:

"You'll be too late, I guess I'm the only one who can do anything."

Before I could move a hand to stop her, she appeared to leap upward into space. I rushed and looked out. To my horror, I saw her hanging by her hands from the roof, propelling herself along by jerks in the direction of the lighted window.

"Good heavens! She'll be killed," I cried.

"You forget. She's a professional acrobat, Hastings. It was the providence of the good God that made her insist on coming with us tonight. I only pray that she may be in time. Ah!"

A cry of absolute terror floated out on to the night as the girl disappeared through the right-hand window; then in Cinderella's clear tones came the words:

"No, you don't! I've got you—and my wrists are just like steel."

At the same moment the door of our prison was opened cautiously by Françoise. Poirot brushed her aside unceremoniously and rushed down the passage to where the other maids were grouped round the further door.

"It's locked on the inside, monsieur."

There was the sound of a heavy fall within. After a moment or two the key turned and the door swung slowly open. Cinderella, very pale, beckoned us in.

"She is safe?" demanded Poirot.

"Yes, I was just in time. She was exhausted."

Mrs. Renauld was half sitting, half lying on the bed. She was gasping for breath.

"Nearly strangled me," she murmured painfully. The girl picked up something from the floor and handed it to Poirot. It was a rolled up ladder of silk rope, very fine but quite strong.

"A getaway," said Poirot. "By the window, whilst we were battering at the door. Where is—the other?"

The girl stood aside a little and pointed. On the ground lay a figure wrapped in some dark material a fold of which hid the face.

"Dead?"

She nodded.

"I think so."

"Head must have struck the marble fender."

"But who is it?" I cried.

"The murderer of M. Renauld, Hastings. And the would-be murderer of Madame Renauld."

Puzzled and uncomprehending, I knelt down, and lifting the fold of cloth, looked into the dead beautiful face of Marthe Daubreuil!

28. Journey's End

I have confused memories of the further events of that night. Poirot seemed deaf to my repeated questions. He was engaged in overwhelming Françoise with reproaches for not having told him of Mrs. Renauld's change of sleeping quarters.

I caught him by the shoulder, determined to attract his attention, and make myself heard.

"But you *must* have known," I expostulated. "You were taken up to see her this afternoon."

Poirot deigned to attend to me for a brief moment.

"She had been wheeled on a sofa into the middle room—her boudoir," he explained.

"But, monsieur," cried Françoise, "Madame changed her room almost immediately after the crime! The associations— they were too distressing!"

"Then why was I not told," vociferated Poirot, striking the table, and working himself into a first-class passion. "I demand you—why—was—I—not—told? You are an old woman completely imbecile! And Léonie and Denise are no better. All of you are triple idiots! Your stupidity has nearly caused the death of your mistress. But for this courageous child—"

He broke off, and, darting across the room to where the girl was bending over ministering to Mrs. Renauld, he embraced her with Gallic fervour—slightly to my annoyance.

I was aroused from my condition of mental fog by a sharp command from Poirot to fetch the doctor immediately on Mrs. Renauld's behalf. After that, I might summon the police. And he added, to complete my dudgeon:

"It will hardly be worth your while to return here. I shall be too busy to attend to you, and of Mademoiselle here I make a *garde-malad.*"

I retired with what dignity I could command. Having done my

errands, I returned to the hotel. I understood next to nothing of what had occurred. The events of the night seemed fantastic and impossible. Nobody would answer my questions. Nobody had seemed to hear them. Angrily, I flung myself into bed, and slept the sleep of the bewildered and utterly exhausted.

I awoke to find the sun pouring in through the open windows and Poirot, neat and smiling, sitting beside the bed.

"*Enfin* you wake! But it is that you are a famous sleeper, Hastings! Do you know that it is nearly eleven o'clock?"

I groaned and put a hand to my head.

"I must have been dreaming," I said. "Do you know, I actually dreamt that we found Marthe Daubreuil's body in Mrs. Renauld's room, and that you declared her to have murdered Mr. Renauld?"

"You were not dreaming. All that is quite true."

"But Bella Duveen killed Mr. Renauld?"

"Oh, no, Hastings, she did not! She said she did—yes—but that was to save the man she loved from the guillotine."

"What?"

"Remember Jack Renauld's story. They both arrived on the scene at the same instant, and each took the other to be the perpetrator of the crime. The girl stares at him in horror, and then with a cry rushes away. But, when she hears that the crime has been brought home to him, she cannot bear it, and comes forward to accuse herself and save him from certain death."

Poirot leaned back in his chair, and brought the tips of his fingers together in familiar style.

"The case was not quite satisfactory to me," he observed judicially. "All along I was strongly under the impression that we were dealing with a cold-blooded and premeditated crime committed by some one who had been contented (very cleverly) with using M. Renauld's own plans for throwing the police off the track. The great criminal (as you may remember my remarking to you once) is always supremely simple."

I nodded.

"Now, to support this theory, the criminal must have been fully cognizant of Mr. Renauld's plans. That leads us to Madame Renauld. But facts fail to support any theory of her guilt. Is there any one else who might have known of them? Yes. From Marthe Daubreuil's own lips we have the admission that she overheard M. Renauld's quarrel with the tramp. If she could overhear that, there is no reason why she should not have heard everything else, especially if M. and Madame Renauld were imprudent enough to discuss their plans sitting on the bench. Remember how easily you overheard Marthe's conversation with Jack Renauld from that spot."

"But what possible motive could Marthe have for murdering Mr. Renauld?" I argued.

"What motive? Money! M. Renauld was a millionaire several times over, and at his death (or so she and Jack believed) half that vast fortune would pass to his son. Let us reconstruct the scene from the standpoint of Marthe Daubreuil.

"Marthe Daubreuil overhears what passes between Renauld and his wife. So far he has been a nice little source of income to the Daubreuil mother and daughter, but now he proposes to escape from their toils. At first, possibly, her idea is to prevent that escape. But a bolder idea takes its place, and one that fails to horrify the daughter of Jeanne Beroldy! At present M. Renauld stands inexorably in the way of her marriage with Jack. If the latter defies his father, he will be a pauper—which is not at all to the mind of Mademoiselle Marthe. In fact, I doubt if she has ever cared a straw for Jack Renauld. She can simulate emotion, but in reality she is of the same cold, calculating type as her mother. I doubt, too, whether she was really very sure of her hold over the boy's affections. She had dazzled and captivated him, but separated from her, as his father could so easily manage to separate him, she might lose him. But with M. Renauld dead, and Jack the heir to half his millions, the marriage can take place at once, and at a stroke she will attain wealth—not the beggarly thousands that have been extracted from him so far. And her clever brain takes in the simplicity of the thing. It is all so easy. M. Renauld is planning all the circumstances of his death—she has only to step in at the right moment and turn the farce into a grim reality. And here comes in the second point which led me infallibly to Marthe Daubreuil— the dagger! Jack Renauld had *three* souvenirs made. One he gave to his mother, one to Bella Duveen; was it not highly probable that he had given the third one to Marthe Daubreuil?

"So then, to sum up, there were four points of note against Marthe Daubreuil:

"(1) Marthe Daubreuil could have overheard M. Renauld's plans.

"(2) Marthe Daubreuil had a direct interest in causing M. Renauld's death.

"(3) Marthe Daubreuil was the daughter of the notorious Madame Beroldy who in my opinion was morally and virtually the murderess of her husband, although it may have been Georges Conneau's hand which struck the actual blow.

"(4) Marthe Daubreuil was the only person, besides Jack Renauld, likely to have the third dagger in her possession."

Poirot paused and cleared his throat.

"Of course, when I learned of the existence of the other girl, Bella Duveen, I realized that it was quite possible that *she* might have killed M. Renauld. The solution did not commend itself to me, because, as I pointed out to you, Hastings, an expert, such as I am, likes to meet a foeman worthy of his steel. Still one must take crimes as one finds them, not as one would like them to be. It did not seem very likely that Bella Duveen would be wandering about carrying a souvenir paper-knife in her hand, but of course she might have had some idea all the time of revenging herself on Jack Renauld. When she actually came forward and confessed to the murder, it seemed that all was over. And yet—I was not satisfied, *mon ami. I was not satisfied* . . .

"I went over the case again minutely, and I came to the same conclusion as before. If it was *not* Bella Duveen, the only other person who could have committed the crime was Marthe Daubreuil. But I had not one single proof against her!

"And then you showed me that letter from Mademoiselle Dulcie, and I saw a chance of settling the matter once for all. The original dagger was stolen by Dulcie Duveen and thrown into the sea—since, as she thought, it belonged to her sister. But if, by any chance, it was *not* her sister's, but the one given by Jack to Marthe Daubreuil—why then, Bella Duveen's dagger would be still intact! I said no word to you, Hastings (it was no time for romance) but I sought out Mademoiselle Dulcie, told her as much as I deemed needful, and set her to search amongst the effects of her sister. Imagine my elation, when she sought me out (according to my instructions) as Miss Robinson with the precious souvenir in her possession!

"In the meantime I had taken steps to force Mademoiselle Marthe into the open. By my orders, Mrs. Renauld repulsed her son, and declared her intention of making a will on the morrow which should cut him off from ever enjoying even a portion of his father's fortune. It was a desperate step, but a necessary one, and Madame Renauld was fully prepared to take the risk—though unfortunately she also never thought of mentioning her change of room. I suppose she took it for granted that I knew. All happened as I thought. Marthe Daubreuil made a last bold bid for the Renauld millions—and failed!"

"What absolutely bewilders me," I said, "is how she ever got into the house without our seeing her. It seems an absolute miracle. We left her behind at the Villa Marguerite, we go straight to the Villa Geneviève—and yet she is there before us!"

"Ah, but we did not leave her behind. She was out of the Villa Marguerite by the back way whilst we were talking to her mother in the hall. That is where, as the Americans say, she 'put it over' on Hercule Poirot!"

"But the shadow on the blind? We saw it from the road."

"*Eh bien*, when we looked up, Madame Daubreuil had just had time to run upstairs and take her place."

"Madame Daubreuil?"

"Yes. One is old, and one is young, one dark, and one fair, but, for the purpose of a silhouette on a blind, their profiles are singularly alike. Even I did not suspect—triple imbecile that I was! I thought I had plenty of time before me—that she would not try to gain admission to the Villa until much later. She had brains, that beautiful Mademoiselle Marthe."

"And her object was to murder Mrs. Renauld?"

"Yes. The whole fortune would then pass to her son. But it would have been suicide, *mon ami*! On the floor by Marthe Daubreuil's body, I found a pad and a little bottle of chloroform and a hypodermic syringe containing a fatal dose of morphine. You understand? The chloroform first—then when the victim is unconscious the prick of the needle. By the morning the smell of the chloroform has quite disappeared, and the syringe lies where it has fallen from Madame Renauld's hand. What would he say, the excellent M. Hautet? 'Poor woman! What did I tell you? The shock of joy, it was too much on top of the rest! Did I not say that I should not be surprised if her brain became unhinged. Altogether a most tragic case, the Renauld Case!'

"However, Hastings, things did not go quite as Mademoiselle Marthe had planned. To begin with, Madame Renauld was awake and waiting for her. There is a struggle. But Madame Renauld is terribly weak still. There is a last chance for Marthe Daubreuil. The idea of suicide is at an end, but if she can silence Madame Renauld with her strong hands, make a getaway with her little silk ladder whilst we are still battering on the inside of the further door, and be back at the Villa Marguerite before we return there, it will be hard to prove anything against her. But she was checkmated—not by Hercule Poirot—but by *la petite acrobate* with her wrists of steel."

I mused over the whole story.

"When did you first begin to suspect Marthe Daubreuil, Poirot? When she told us she had overheard the quarrel in the garden?"

Poirot smiled.

"My friend, do you remember when we drove into Merlinville that first day? And the beautiful girl we saw standing at the gate? You asked me if I had not noticed a young goddess, and I replied to you that I had seen only a girl with anxious eyes. That is how I have thought of Marthe Daubreuil from the beginning. *The girl with the anxious eyes!* Why was she anxious? Not on Jack Renauld's behalf, for she did not know then that he had been in Merlinville the previous evening."

"By the way," I exclaimed, "how is Jack Renauld?"

"Much better. He is still at the Villa Marguerite. But Madame Daubreuil has disappeared. The police are looking for her."

"Was she in with her daughter, do you think?"

"We shall never know. Madame is a lady who can keep her secrets. And I doubt very much if the police will ever find her."

"Has Jack Renauld been—told?"

"Not yet."

"It will be a terrible shock to him."

"Naturally. And yet, do you know, Hastings, I doubt if his heart was ever seriously engaged. So far we have looked upon Bella Duveen as a siren, and Marthe Daubreuil as the girl he really loved. But I think that if we reversed the terms we should come nearer to the truth. Marthe Daubreuil was very beautiful. She set herself to fascinate Jack, and she succeeded, but remember his curious reluctance to break with the other girl. And see how he was willing to go to the guillotine rather than implicate her. I have a little idea that when he learns the truth he will be horrified—revolted, and his false love will wither away."

"What about Giraud?"

"He has a *crise* of the nerves, that one! He has been obliged to return to Paris."

We both smiled.

Poirot proved a fairly true prophet. When at length the doctor pronounced Jack Renauld strong enough to hear the truth, it was Poirot who broke it to him. The shock was indeed terrific. Yet Jack rallied better than I could have supposed possible. His mother's devotion helped him to live through those difficult days. The mother and son were inseparable now.

There was a further revelation to come. Poirot had acquainted Mrs. Renauld with the fact that he knew her secret, and had represented to her that Jack should not be left in ignorance of his father's past.

"To hide the truth, never does it avail, madame! Be brave and tell him everything."

With a heavy heart Mrs. Renauld consented, and her son learned that the father he had loved had been in actual fact a fugitive from justice. A halting question was promptly answered by Poirot.

"Reassure yourself, M. Jack. The world knows nothing. As far as I can see, there is no obligation for me to take the police into my confidence. Throughout the case I have acted, not for them, but for your father. Justice overtook him at last, but no one need ever know that he and Georges Conneau were one and the same."

There were, of course, various points in the case that remained puzzling to the police, but Poirot explained things in so plausible a fashion that all query about them was gradually stilled.

Shortly after we got back to London, I noticed a magnificent model of a foxhound adorning Poirot's mantelpiece. In answer to my inquiring glance, Poirot nodded.

"*Mais, oui*! I got my 500 francs! Is he not a splendid fellow? I call him Giraud!"

A few days later Jack Renauld came to see us with a resolute expression on his face.

"M. Poirot, I've come to say good-bye. I'm sailing for South

America almost immediately. My father had large interests over the continent, and I mean to start a new life out there."

"You go alone, M. Jack?"

"My mother comes with me—and I shall keep Stonor on as my secretary. He likes out of-the-way parts of the world."

"No one else goes with you?"

Jack flushed.

"You mean—?"

"A girl who loves you very dearly—who has been willing to lay down her life for you."

"How could I ask her?" muttered the boy. "After all that has happened, could I go to her and—oh, what sort of a lame story could I tell?"

"*Les femmes*—they have a wonderful genius for manufacturing crutches for stories like that."

"Yes, but——I've been such a damned fool!"

"So have all of us, at one time and another," observed Poirot philosophically.

But Jack's face had hardened.

"There's something else. I'm my father's son. Would any one marry me, knowing that?"

"You are your father's son, you say. Hastings here will tell you that I believe in heredity—"

"Well, then—"

"Wait. I know a woman, a woman of courage and endurance, capable of great love, of supreme self-sacrifice—"

The boy looked up. His eyes softened.

"My mother!"

"Yes. You are your mother's son as well as your father's. Go then to Mademoiselle Bella. Tell her everything. Keep nothing back—and see what she will say!"

Jack looked irresolute.

"Go to her as a boy no longer, but a man—a man bowed by the fate of the Past, and the fate of Today, but looking forward to a new and wonderful life. Ask her to share it with you. You may not realize it, but your love for each other has been tested in the fire and not found wanting. You have both been willing to lay down your lives for each other."

And what of Captain Arthur Hastings, humble chronicler of these pages?

There is some talk of his joining the Renaulds on a ranch across the seas, but for the end of this story I prefer to go back to a morning in the garden of the Villa Geneviève.

"I can't call you Bella," I said, "since it isn't your name. And Dulcie seems so unfamiliar. So it's got to be Cinderella. Cinderella married the Prince, you remember. I'm not a Prince, but—"

She interrupted me.

"Cinderella warned him, I'm sure! You see, she couldn't promise to turn into a princess. She was only a little scullion after all—"

"It's the Prince's turn to interrupt," I interpolated. "Do you know what he said?"

"No?"

"'Hell!' said the Prince—and kissed her!"

And I suited the action to the word.

The Murders in
the Rue Morgue

Edgar Allan Poe

What song the Syrens sang, or what name Achilles assumed
when he hid himself among women, although puzzling
questions, are not beyond *all* conjecture.

—*Sir Thomas Browne*

The mental features discoursed of as the analytical, are, in themselves, but little susceptible of analysis. We appreciate them only in their effects. We know of them, among other things, that they are always to their possessor, when inordinately possessed, a source of the liveliest enjoyment. As the strong man exults in his physical ability, delighting in such exercises as call his muscles into action, so glories the analyst in that moral activity which *disentangles*. He derives pleasure from even the most trivial occupations bringing his talent into play. He is fond of enigmas, of conundrums, of hieroglyphics; exhibiting in his solutions of each a degree of *acumen* which appears to the ordinary apprehension preternatural. His results, brought about by the very soul and essence of method, have, in truth, the whole air of intuition.

The faculty of resolution is possibly much invigorated by mathematical study, and especially by that highest branch of it which, unjustly, and merely on account of its retrograde operations, has been called, as if *par excellence*, analysis. Yet to calculate is not in itself to analyze. A chess-player, for example, does the one without effort at the other. It follows that the game of chess, in its effects upon mental character, is greatly misunderstood. I am not now writing a treatise, but simply prefacing a somewhat peculiar narrative by observations very much at random; I will, therefore, take occasion to assert that the higher powers of the reflective intellect are more decidedly and more usefully tasked by the unostentatious game of draughts than by all the elaborate frivolity of chess. In this latter, where the pieces have different and *bizarre* motions, with various and variable values, what is only complex is mistaken (a not unusual error) for what is profound. The *attention* is here called powerfully into play. If it flag for an instant, an oversight is committed resulting in injury or defeat. The possible moves being not only manifold but involute, the chances of such oversights are multiplied; and in nine cases out of ten it is the more concentrative rather than the more acute player who conquers. In draughts, on the contrary, where the moves are *unique* and have but little variation, the probabilities of inadvertence are diminished, and the mere attention being left comparatively unemployed, what advantages are obtained by either party are obtained by superior *acumen*. To be less abstract—Let us suppose a game of draughts where the pieces are reduced to four kings, and where, of course, no oversight is to be expected. It is obvious that here the victory can be decided (the players being at all equal) only by some *recherché* movement, the result of some strong exertion of the intellect. Deprived of ordinary resources, the analyst throws himself into the spirit of his opponent, identifies himself therewith, and not unfrequently sees thus, at a glance, the sole methods (sometime indeed absurdly simple ones) by which he may seduce into error or hurry into miscalculation.

Whist has long been noted for its influence upon what is termed the calculating power; and men of the highest order of intellect have been known to take an apparently unaccountable delight in it, while eschewing chess as frivolous. Beyond doubt there is nothing of a similar nature so greatly tasking the faculty of analysis. The best chess-player in Christendom *may* be little more than the best player of chess; but proficiency in whist implies capacity for success in all those more important undertakings where mind struggles with mind. When I say proficiency, I mean that perfection in the game which includes a comprehension of *all* the sources whence legitimate advantage may be derived. These are not only manifold but multiform, and lie frequently among recesses of thought altogether inaccessible to the ordinary understanding. To observe attentively is to remember distinctly; and, so far, the concentrative chess-player will do very well at whist; while the rules of Hoyle (themselves based upon the mere mechanism of the game) are sufficiently and generally comprehensible. Thus to have a retentive memory, and to proceed by "the book," are points commonly regarded as the sum total of good playing. But it is in matters beyond the limits of mere rule that the skill of the analyst is evinced. He makes, in silence, a host of observations and inferences. So, perhaps, do his companions; and the difference in the extent of the information obtained, lies not so much in the validity of the inference as in the quality of the observation. The necessary knowledge is that of *what* to observe. Our player confines himself not at all; nor, because the game is the object, does he reject deductions from things external to the game. He examines the countenance of his partner, comparing it carefully with that of each of his opponents. He considers the mode of assorting the cards in each hand; often counting trump by trump, and honor by honor, through the glances bestowed by their holders upon each. He notes every variation of face as the play progresses, gathering a fund of thought from the differences in the expression of certainty, of surprise, of triumph, or of chagrin. From the manner of gathering up a trick he judges whether the person taking it can make another in the suit. He recognises what is played through feint, by the air with which it is thrown upon the table. A casual or inadvertent word; the accidental dropping or turning of a card, with the accompanying anxiety or carelessness in regard to its concealment; the counting of the tricks, with the order of their arrangement; embarrassment, hesitation, eagerness or trepidation—all afford, to his apparently intuitive perception, indications of the true state of affairs. The first two or three rounds having been played, he is in full possession of the contents of each hand, and thenceforward puts down his cards with as absolute a precision of purpose as if the rest of the party had turned outward the faces of their own.

The analytical power should not be confounded with ample ingenuity; for while the analyst is necessarily ingenious, the ingenious man is often remarkably incapable of analysis. The constructive or combining power, by which ingenuity is usually manifested, and to which the phrenologists (I believe erroneously) have assigned a separate organ, supposing it a primitive faculty, has been so frequently seen in those whose intellect bordered otherwise upon idiocy, as to have attracted general observation among writers on morals. Between ingenuity and the analytic ability there exists a difference far greater, indeed, than that between the fancy and the imagination, but of a character very strictly analogous. It will be found, in fact, that the ingenious are always fanciful, and the *truly* imaginative never otherwise than analytic.

The narrative which follows will appear to the reader somewhat in the light of a commentary upon the propositions just advanced.

Residing in Paris during the spring and part of the summer of 18—, I there became acquainted with a Monsieur C. Auguste Dupin. This young gentleman was of an excellent—indeed of an illustrious family, but, by a variety of untoward events, had been reduced to such poverty that the energy of his character succumbed beneath it, and he ceased to bestir himself in the world, or to care for the retrieval of his fortunes. By courtesy of his creditors, there still remained in his possession a small remnant of his patrimony; and, upon the income arising from this, he managed, by means of a rigorous economy, to procure the necessaries of life, without troubling himself about its superfluities. Books, indeed, were his sole luxuries, and in Paris these are easily obtained.

Our first meeting was at an obscure library in the Rue Montmartre, where the accident of our both being in search of the same very rare and very remarkable volume, brought us into closer communion. We saw each other again and again. I was deeply interested in the little family history which he detailed to me with all that candor which a Frenchman indulges whenever mere self is his theme. I was astonished, too, at the vast extent of his reading; and, above all, I felt my soul enkindled within me by the wild fervor, and the vivid freshness of his imagination. Seeking in Paris the objects I then sought, I felt that the society of such a man would be to me a treasure beyond price; and this feeling I frankly confided to him. It was at length arranged that we should live together during my stay in the city; and as my worldly circumstances were somewhat less embarrassed than his own, I was permitted to be at the expense of renting, and furnishing in a style which suited the rather fantastic gloom of our common temper, a time-eaten and grotesque mansion, long deserted through superstitions into which we did not inquire, and tottering to its fall in a retired and desolate portion of the Faubourg St. Germain.

Had the routine of our life at this place been known to the world, we should have been regarded as madmen—although, perhaps, as madmen of a harmless nature. Our seclusion was perfect. We admitted no visitors. Indeed the locality of our retirement had been carefully kept a secret from my own former associates; and it had been many years since Dupin had ceased to know or be known in Paris. We existed within ourselves alone.

It was a freak of fancy in my friend (for what else shall I call it?) to be enamored of the night for her own sake; and into this *bizarrerie*, as into all his others, I quietly fell; giving myself up to his wild whims with a perfect *abandon*. The sable divinity would not herself dwell with us always; but we could counterfeit her presence. At the first dawn of the morning we closed all the messy shutters of our old building; lighting a couple of tapers which, strongly perfumed, threw out only the ghastliest and feeblest of rays. By the aid of these we then busied our souls in dreams—reading, writing, or conversing, until warned by the clock of the advent of the true Darkness. Then we sallied forth into the streets arm in arm, continuing the topics of the day, or roaming far and wide until a late hour, seeking, amid the wild lights and shadows of the populous city, that infinity of mental excitement which quiet observation can afford.

At such times I could not help remarking and admiring (although from his rich ideality I had been prepared to expect it) a peculiar analytic ability in Dupin. He seemed, too, to take an eager delight in its exercise—if not exactly in its display— and did not hesitate to confess the pleasure thus derived. He boasted to me, with a low chuckling laugh, that most men, in respect to himself, wore windows in their bosoms, and was wont to follow up such assertions by direct and very startling proofs of his intimate knowledge of my own. His manner at these moments was frigid and abstract; his eyes were vacant in expression; while his voice, usually a rich tenor, rose into a treble which would have sounded petulantly but for the deliberateness and entire distinctness of the enunciation. Observing him in these moods, I often dwelt meditatively upon the old philosophy of the Bi-Part Soul, and amused myself with the fancy of a double Dupin—the creative and the resolvent.

Let it not be supposed, from what I have just said, that I am detailing any mystery, or penning any romance. What I have described in the Frenchman, was merely the result of an excited, or perhaps of a diseased intelligence. But of the character of his remarks at the periods in question an example will best convey the idea.

We were strolling one night down a long dirty street in the vicinity of the Palais Royal. Being both, apparently, occupied with thought, neither of us had spoken a syllable for fifteen minutes at least. All at once Dupin broke forth with these words:

"He is a very little fellow, that's true, and would do better for the *Théâtre des Variétés*."

"There can be no doubt of that," I replied unwittingly, and not at first observing (so much had I been absorbed in reflection) the extraordinary manner in which the speaker had chimed in with my meditations. In an instant afterward I recollected myself, and my astonishment was profound.

"Dupin," said I, gravely, "this is beyond my comprehension. I do not hesitate to say that I am amazed, and can scarcely credit my senses. How was it possible you should know I was thinking of ———?" Here I paused, to ascertain beyond a doubt whether he really knew of whom I thought.

"Of Chantilly," said he, "why do you pause? You were remarking to yourself that his diminutive figure unfitted him for tragedy."

This was precisely what had formed the subject of my reflections. Chantilly was a quondam cobbler of the Rue St. Denis, who, becoming stage-mad, had attempted the *rôle* of Xerxes, in Crébillon's tragedy so called, and been notoriously Pasquinaded for his pains.

"Tell me, for Heaven's sake," I exclaimed, "the method—if method there is—by which you have been enabled to fathom my soul in this matter." In fact I was even more startled than I would have been willing to express.

"It was the fruiterer," replied my friend, "who brought you to the conclusion that the mender of soles was not of sufficient height for Xerxes *et id genus omne.*"

"The fruiterer!—you astonish me—I know no fruiterer whomsoever."

"The man who ran up against you as we entered the street—it may have been fifteen minutes ago."

I now remembered that, in fact, a fruiterer, carrying upon his head a large basket of apples, had nearly thrown me down, by accident, as we passed from the Rue C ——— into the thoroughfare where we stood; but what this had to do with Chantilly I could not possibly understand.

There was not a particle of *charlâtanerie* about Dupin. "I will explain," he said, "and that you may comprehend all clearly, we will first retrace the course of your meditations, from the moment in which I spoke to you until that of the *rencontre* with the fruiterer in question. The larger links of the chain run thus— Chantilly, Orion, Dr. Nichols, Epicurus, Stereotomy, the street stones, the fruiterer."

There are few persons who have not, at some period of their lives, amused themselves in retracing the steps by which particular conclusions of their own minds have been attained. The occupation is often full of interest and he who attempts it for the first time is astonished by the apparently illimitable distance and incoherence between the starting-point and the goal. What, then, must have been my amazement when I heard the Frenchman speak what he had just spoken, and when I could not help acknowledging that he had spoken the truth. He continued:

"We had been talking of horses, if I remember aright, just before leaving the Rue C ———. This was the last subject we discussed. As we crossed into this street, a fruiterer, with a large basket upon his head, brushing quickly past us, thrust you upon a pile of paving stones collected at a spot where the causeway is undergoing repair. You stepped upon one of the loose fragments, slipped, slightly strained your ankle, appeared vexed or sulky, muttered a few words, turned to look at the pile, and then proceeded in silence. I was not particularly attentive to what you did; but observation has become with me, of late, a species of necessity.

"You kept your eyes upon the ground—glancing, with a petulant expression, at the holes and ruts in the pavement, (so that I saw you were still thinking of the stones,) until we reached the little alley called Lamartine, which has been paved, by way of experiment, with the overlapping and riveted blocks. Here your countenance brightened up, and, perceiving your lips move, I could not doubt that you murmured the word 'stereotomy,' a term very affectedly applied to this species of pavement. I knew that you could not say to yourself 'stereotomy' without being brought to think of atomies, and thus of the theories of Epicurus; and since, when we discussed this subject not very long ago, I mentioned to you how singularly, yet with how little notice, the vague guesses of that noble Greek had met with confirmation in the late nebular cosmogony, I felt that you could not avoid casting your eyes upward to the great *nebula* in Orion, and I certainly expected that you would do so. You did look up; and I was now assured that I had correctly followed your steps. But in that bitter *tirade* upon Chantilly, which appeared in yesterday's *Musée*, the satirist, making some disgraceful allusions to the cobbler's change of name upon assuming the buskin, quoted a Latin line about which we have often conversed. I mean the line

Perdidit antiquum litera sonum.

"I had told you that this was in reference to Orion, formerly written Urion; and, from certain pungencies connected with this explanation, I was aware that you could not have forgotten it. It was clear, therefore, that you would not fail to combine the two ideas of Orion and Chantilly. That you did combine them I saw by the character of the smile which passed over your lips. You thought of the poor cobbler's immolation. So far, you had been stooping in your gait; but now I saw you draw yourself up to your full height. I was then sure that you reflected upon the diminutive figure of Chantilly. At this point I interrupted your meditations to remark that as, in fact, he was a very little fellow—that Chantilly—he would do better at the *Théâtre des Variétés.*"

Not long after this, we were looking over an evening edition of the *Gazette des Tribunaux*, when the following paragraphs arrested our attention.

"EXTRAORDINARY MURDERS—This morning, about three o'clock, the inhabitants of the Quartier St. Roch were aroused from sleep by a succession of terrific shrieks, issuing, apparently, from the fourth story of a house in the Rue Morgue, known to be in the sole occupancy of one Madame L'Espanaye, and her daughter Mademoiselle Camille L'Espanaye. After some delay, occasioned by a fruitless attempt to procure admission in the usual manner, the gateway was broken in with a crowbar, and eight or ten of the neighbors entered accompanied by two gendarmes. By this time the cries had ceased; but, as the party rushed up the first flight of stairs, two or more rough voices in angry contention were distinguished and seemed to proceed from the upper part of the house. As the second landing was reached, these sounds, also, had ceased and everything remained perfectly quiet. The party spread themselves and hurried from room to room. Upon arriving at a large back chamber in the fourth story (the door of which, being found locked, with the key inside, was forced open), a spectacle presented itself which struck every one present not less with horror than with astonishment.

"The apartment was in the wildest disorder—the furniture broken and thrown about in all directions. There was only one bedstead; and from this the bed had been removed, and thrown into the middle of the floor. On a chair lay a razor, besmeared with blood. On the hearth were two or three long and thick tresses of grey human hair, also dabbled in blood, and seeming to have been pulled out by the roots. Upon the floor were found four Napoleons, an earring of topaz, three large silver spoons, three smaller of *métal d'Alger*, and two bags, containing nearly four thousand francs in gold. The drawers of a bureau, which stood in one corner were open, and had been, apparently, rifled, although many articles still remained in them. A small iron safe was discovered under the *bed* (not under the bedstead). It was open, with the key still in the door. It had no contents beyond a few old letters, and other papers of little consequence.

"Of Madame L'Espanaye no traces were here seen; but an unusual quantity of soot being observed in the fire-place, a search was made in the chimney, and (horrible to relate!) the corpse of the daughter, head downward, was dragged therefrom; it having been thus forced up the narrow aperture for a considerable distance. The body was quite warm. Upon examining it, many excoriations were perceived, no doubt occasioned by the violence with which it had been thrust up and disengaged. Upon the face were many severe scratches, and, upon the throat, dark bruises, and deep indentations of finger nails, as if the deceased had been throttled to death.

"After a thorough investigation of every portion of the house, without farther discovery, the party made its way into a small paved yard in the rear of the building, where lay the corpse of the old lady, with her throat so entirely cut that, upon an attempt to raise her, the head fell off. The body, as well as the head, was fearfully mutilated—the former so much so as scarcely to retain any semblance of humanity.

"To this horrible mystery there is not as yet, we believe, the slightest clue."

The next day's paper had these additional particulars.

"*The Tragedy in the Rue Morgue.* Many individuals have been examined in relation to this most extraordinary and frightful affair. [The word '*affaire*' has not yet, in France, that levity of import which it conveys with us,] "but nothing whatever has transpired to throw light upon it. We give below all the material testimony elicited.

"*Pauline Dubourg*, laundress, deposes that she has known both the deceased for three years, having washed for them during that period. The old lady and her daughter seemed on good terms—very affectionate towards each other. They were excellent pay. Could not speak in regard to their mode or means of living. Believed that Madame L. told fortunes for a living. Was reputed to have money put by. Never met any persons in the house when she called for the clothes or took them home. Was sure that they had no servant in employ. There appeared to be no furniture in any part of the building except in the fourth story.

"*Pierre Moreau*, tobacconist, deposes that he has been in the habit of selling small quantities of tobacco and snuff to Madame L'Espanaye for nearly four years. Was born in the neighborhood, and has always resided there. The deceased and her daughter had occupied the house in which the corpses were found, for more than six years. It was formerly occupied by a jeweller, who under-let the upper rooms to various persons. The house was the property of Madame L. She became dissatisfied with the abuse of the premises by her tenant, and moved into them herself, refusing to let any portion. The old lady was childish. Witness had seen the daughter some five or six times during the six years. The two lived an exceedingly retired life—were reputed to have money. Had heard it said among the neighbors that Madame L. told fortunes—did not believe it. Had never seen any person enter the door except the old lady and her daughter, a porter once or twice, and a physician some eight or ten times.

"Many other persons, neighbors, gave evidence to the same effect. No one was spoken of as frequenting the house. It was not known whether there were any living connexions of Madame L. and her daughter. The shutters of the front windows were seldom opened. Those in the rear were always closed, with the exception of the large back room, fourth story. The house was a good house—not very old.

"*Isidore Musèt, gendarme*, deposes that he was called to the house about three o'clock in the morning, and found some twenty or thirty persons at the gateway, endeavoring to gain admittance. Forced it open, at length, with a bayonet—not with a crowbar. Had but little difficulty in getting it open, on account of its being a double or folding gate, and bolted neither at bottom not top. The shrieks were continued until the gate was forced—and then suddenly ceased. They seemed to be screams of some person (or persons) in great agony—were loud and drawn out, not short and quick. Witness led the way up stairs. Upon reaching the first landing, heard two voices in loud and angry contention—the one a gruff voice, the other much shriller—a very strange voice. Could distinguish some words of the former, which was that of a Frenchman. Was positive that it was not a woman's voice. Could distinguish the words '*sacré*' and '*diable.*' The shrill voice was that of a foreigner. Could not be sure whether it was the voice of a man or of a woman. Could not make out what was said, but believed the language to be Spanish. The state of the room and of the bodies was described by this witness as we described them yesterday.

"*Henri Duval,* a neighbor, and by trade a silversmith, deposes that he was one of the party who first entered the house. Corroborates the testimony of Musèt in general. As soon as they forced an entrance, they reclosed the door, to keep out the crowd, which collected very fast, notwithstanding the lateness of the hour. The shrill voice, this witness thinks, was that of an Italian. Was certain it was not French. Could not be sure that it was a man's voice. It might have been a woman's. Was not acquainted with the Italian language. Could not distinguish the words, but was convinced by the intonation that the speaker was an Italian. Knew Madame L. and her daughter. Had conversed with both frequently. Was sure that the shrill voice was not that of either of the deceased.

"—*Odenheimer, restaurateur.* This witness volunteered his testimony. Not speaking French, was examined through an interpreter. Is a native of Amsterdam. Was passing the house at the time of the shrieks. They lasted for several minutes—probably ten. They were long and loud—very awful and distressing. Was one of those who entered the building. Corroborated the previous evidence in every respect but one. Was sure that the shrill voice was that of a man—of a Frenchman. Could not distinguish the words uttered. They were loud and quick—unequal—spoken apparently in fear as well as in anger. The voice was harsh—not so much shrill as harsh. Could not call it a shrill voice. The gruff voice said repeatedly '*sacré*', '*diable*,' and once '*mon Dieu.*'

"*Jules Mignaud*, banker, of the firm of Mignaud et Fils, Rue Deloraine. Is the elder Mignaud. Madame L'Espanaye had some property. Had opened an account with his banking house in the spring of the year—(eight years previously). Made frequent deposits in small sums. Had checked for nothing until the third day before her death, when she took out in person the sum of 4,000 francs. This sum was paid in gold, and a clerk went home with the money.

"*Adolphe Le Bon*, clerk to Mignaud et Fils, deposes that on the day in question, about noon, he accompanied Madame L'Espanaye to her residence with the 4,000 francs, put up in two bags. Upon the door being opened, Mademoiselle L. appeared and took from his hands one of the bags, while the old lady relieved him of the other. He then bowed and departed. Did not see any person in the street at the time. It is a bye-street—very lonely.

"*William Bird*, tailor, deposes that he was one of the party who entered the house. Is an Englishman. Has lived in Paris two years. Was one of the first to ascend the stairs. Heard the voices in contention. The gruff voice was that of a Frenchman. Could make out several words, but cannot now remember all. Heard distinctly '*sacré*' and '*mon Dieu.*' There was a sound at the moment as if of several persons struggling—a scraping and scuffling sound. The shrill voice was very loud—louder than the gruff one. Is sure that it was not the voice of an Englishman. Appeared to be that of a German. Might have been a woman's voice. Does not understand German.

"Four of the above-named witnesses, being recalled, deposed that the door of the chamber in which was found the body of Mademoiselle L. was locked on the inside when the party reached it. Every thing was perfectly silent—no groans or noises of any kind. Upon forcing the door no person was seen. The windows, both of the back and front room, were down and firmly fastened from within. A door between the two rooms was closed, but not locked. The door leading from the front room into the passage was locked, with the key on the inside. A small room in the front of the house, on the fourth story, at the head of the passage was open, the door being ajar. This room was crowded with old beds, boxes, and so forth. These were carefully removed and searched. There was not an inch of any portion of the house which was not carefully searched. Sweeps were sent up and down the chimneys. The house was a four story one, with garrets (*mansardes.*) A trap-door on the roof was nailed down very securely—did not appear to have been opened for years. The time elapsing between the hearing of the voices in contention and the breaking open of the room door, was variously stated by the witnesses. Some made it as short as three minutes—some as long as five. The door was opened with difficulty.

"*Alfonzo Garcio*, undertaker, deposes that he resides in the Rue Morgue. Is a native of Spain. Was one of the party who entered the house. Did not proceed up stairs. Is nervous, and was apprehensive of the consequences of agitation. Heard the voices in contention. The gruff voice was that of a Frenchman. Could not distinguish what was said. The shrill voice was that of an Englishman—is sure of this. Does not understand the English language, but judges by the intonation.

"*Alberto Montani*, confectioner, deposes that he was among the first to ascend the stairs. Heard the voices in question. The gruff voice was that of a Frenchman. Distinguished several words. The speaker appeared to be expostulating. Could not make out the words of the shrill voice. Spoke quick and unevenly. Thinks it the voice of a Russian. Corroborates the general testimony. Is an Italian. Never conversed with a native of Russia.

"Several witnesses, recalled, here testified that the chimneys of all the rooms on the fourth story were too narrow to admit the passage of a human being. By 'sweeps' were meant cylindrical sweeping brushes, such as are employed by those who clean chimneys. These brushes were passed up and down every flue in the house. There is no back passage by which any one could have descended while the party proceeded up stairs. The body of Mademoiselle L'Espanaye was so firmly wedged in the chimney that it could not be got down until four or five of the party united their strength.

"*Paul Dumas*, physician, deposes that he was called to view the bodies about day-break. They were both then lying on the sacking of the bedstead in the chamber where Mademoiselle L. was found. The corpse of the young lady was much bruised and excoriated. The fact that it had been thrust up the chimney would sufficiently account for these appearances. The throat was greatly chafed. There were several deep scratches just below the chin, together with a series of livid spots which were evidently the impression of fingers. The face was fearfully discolored, and the eye-balls protruded. The tongue had been partially bitten through. A large bruise was discovered upon the pit of the stomach, produced, apparently, by the pressure of a knee. In the opinion of M. Dumas, Mademoiselle L'Espanaye had been throttled to death by some person or persons unknown. The corpse of the mother was horribly mutilated. All the bones of the right leg and arm were more or less shattered. The left tibia much splintered, as well as all the ribs of the left side. Whole body dreadfully bruised and discolored. It was not possible to say how the injuries had been inflicted. A heavy club of wood, or a broad bar of iron—a chair—any large, heavy, and obtuse weapon would have produced such results, if wielded by the hands of a very powerful man. No woman could have inflicted the blows with any weapon. The head of the deceased, when seen by witness, was entirely separated from the body, and was also greatly shattered. The throat had evidently been cut with some very sharp instrument—probably with a razor.

"*Alexandre Etienne*, surgeon, was called with M. Dumas to view the bodies. Corroborated the testimony, and the opinions of M. Dumas.

"Nothing farther of importance was elicited, although several other persons were examined. A murder so mysterious, and so perplexing in all its particulars, was never before committed in Paris—if indeed a murder has been committed at all. The police are entirely at fault—an unusual occurrence in affairs of this nature. There is not, however, the shadow of a clue apparent."

The evening edition of the paper stated that the greatest excitement still continued in the Quartier St. Roch—that the premises in question had been carefully re-searched, and fresh examinations of witnesses instituted, but all to no purpose. A postscript, however, mentioned that Adolphe Le Bon had been arrested and imprisoned—although nothing appeared to criminate him, beyond the facts already detailed.

Dupin seemed singularly interested in the progress of this affair—at least so I judged from his manner, for he made no comments. It was only after the announcement that Le Bon had been imprisoned, that he asked me my opinion respecting the murders.

I could merely agree with all Paris in considering them an insoluble mystery. I saw no means by which it would be possible to trace the murderer.

"We must not judge of the means," said Dupin, "by this shell of an examination. The Parisian police, so much extolled for *acumen*, are cunning, but no more. There is no method in their proceedings, beyond the method of the moment. They make a vast parade of measures; but, not unfrequently, these are so ill adapted to the objects proposed, as to put us in mind of Monsieur Jourdain's calling for his *robe-de-chambre—pour mieux entendre la musique*. The results attained by them are not unfrequently surprising, but, for the most part, are brought about by simple diligence and activity. When these qualities are unavailing, their schemes fail. Vidocq, for example, was a good guesser and a persevering man. But, without educated thought, he erred continually by the very intensity of his investigations.

He impaired his vision by holding the object too close. He might see, perhaps, one or two points with unusual clearness, but in so doing he, necessarily, lost sight of the matter as a whole. Thus there is such a thing as being too profound. Truth is not always in a well. In fact, as regards the more important knowledge, I do believe that she is invariably superficial. The depth lies in the valleys where we seek her, and not upon the mountain-tops where she is found. The modes and sources of this kind of error are well typified in the contemplation of the heavenly bodies. To look at a star by glances—to view it in a side-long way, by turning toward it the exterior portions of the *retina* (more susceptible of feeble impressions of light than the interior), is to behold the star distinctly—is to have the best appreciation of its lustre—a lustre which grows dim just in proportion as we turn our vision *fully* upon it. A greater number of rays actually fall upon the eye in the latter case, but, in the former, there is the more refined capacity for comprehension. By undue profundity we perplex and enfeeble thought; and it is possible to make even Venus herself vanish from the firmament by a scrutiny too sustained, too concentrated, or too direct.

"As for these murders, let us enter into some examinations for ourselves, before we make up an opinion respecting them. An inquiry will afford us amusement" [I thought this an odd term, so applied, but said nothing], "and, besides, Le Bon once rendered me a service for which I am not ungrateful. We will go and see the premises with our own eyes. I know G——, the Prefect of Police, and shall have no difficulty in obtaining the necessary permission."

The permission was obtained, and we proceeded at once to the Rue Morgue. This is one of those miserable thoroughfares which intervene between the Rue Richelieu and the Rue St. Roch. It was late in the afternoon when we reached it; as this quarter is at a great distance from that in which we resided. The house was readily found; for there were still many persons gazing up at the closed shutters, with an objectless curiosity, from the opposite side of the way. It was an ordinary Parisian house, with a gateway, on one side of which was a glazed watch-box, with a sliding panel in the window, indicating a *loge de concierge*. Before going in we walked up the street, turned down an alley, and then, again turning, passed in the rear of the building—Dupin, meanwhile examining the whole neighborhood, as well as the house, with a minuteness of attention for which I could see no possible object.

Retracing our steps, we came again to the front of the dwelling, rang, and, having shown our credentials, were admitted by the agents in charge. We went up stairs—into the chamber where the body of Mademoiselle L'Espanaye had been found, and where both the deceased still lay. The disorders of the room had, as usual, been suffered to exist. I saw nothing beyond what had been stated in the *Gazette des Tribunaux*. Dupin scrutinized every thing—not excepting the bodies of the victims. We then went into the other rooms, and into the yard; a *gendarme* accompanying us throughout. The examination occupied us until dark, when we took our departure. On our way home my companion stepped in for a moment at the office of one of the daily papers.

I have said that the whims of my friend were manifold, and that *Je les ménagais*:—for this phrase there is no English equivalent. It was his humor, now, to decline all conversation on the subject of the murder, until about noon the next day. He then asked me, suddenly, if I had observed any thing *peculiar* at the scene of the atrocity.

There was something in his manner of emphasizing the word "peculiar," which caused me to shudder, without knowing why.

"No, nothing *peculiar*," I said; "nothing more, at least, than we both saw stated in the paper."

"The *Gazette*," he replied, "has not entered, I fear, into the unusual horror of the thing. But dismiss the idle opinions of this print. It appears to me that this mystery is considered insoluble, for the very reason which should cause it to be regarded as easy of solution—I mean for the *outré* character of its features. The police are confounded by the seeming absence of motive—not for the murder itself—but for the atrocity of the murder. They are puzzled, too, by the seeming impossibility of reconciling the voices heard in contention, with the facts that no one was discovered up stairs but the assassinated Mademoiselle L'Espanaye, and that there were no means of egress without the notice of the party ascending. The wild disorder of the room; the corpse thrust, with the head downward, up the chimney; the frightful mutilation of the body of the old lady; these considerations, with those just mentioned, and others which I need not mention, have sufficed to paralyze the powers, by putting completely at fault the boasted *acumen*, of the government agents. They have fallen into the gross but common error of confounding the unusual with the abstruse. But it is by these deviations from the plane of the ordinary, that reason feels its way, if at all, in its search for the true. In investigations such as we are now pursuing, it should not be so much asked 'what has occurred,' as 'what has occurred that has never occurred before.' In fact, the facility with which I shall arrive, or have arrived, at the solution of this mystery, is in the direct ratio of its apparent insolubility in the eyes of the police."

I stared at the speaker in mute astonishment.

"I am now awaiting," continued he, looking toward the door of our apartment—"I am now awaiting a person who, although perhaps not the perpetrator of these butcheries, must have been in some measure implicated in their perpetration. Of the worst portion of the crimes committed, it is probable that he is innocent. I hope that I am right in this supposition; for upon it I build my expectation of reading the entire riddle. I look for the man here—in this room—every moment. It is true that he may not arrive; but the probability is that he will. Should he come, it will be necessary to detain him. Here are pistols; and we both know how to use them when occasion demands their use."

I took the pistols, scarcely knowing what I did, or believing what I heard, while Dupin went on, very much as if in a soliloquy. I have already spoken of his abstract manner at such times. His discourse was addressed to myself; but his voice, although by no means loud, had that intonation which is commonly employed in speaking to some one at a great distance. His eyes, vacant in expression, regarded only the wall.

"That the voices heard in contention," he said, "by the party upon the stairs, were not the voices of the women themselves, was fully proved by the evidence. This relieves us of all doubt upon the question whether the old lady could have first destroyed the daughter and afterward have committed suicide. I speak of this point chiefly for the sake of method; for the strength of Madame L'Espanaye would have been utterly unequal to the task of thrusting her daughter's corpse up the chimney as it was found; and the nature of the wounds upon her own person entirely preclude the idea of self-destruction. Murder, then, has been committed by some third party; and the voices of this third party were those heard in contention. Let me now advert—not to the whole testimony respecting these voices—but to what was *peculiar* in that testimony. Did you observe any thing peculiar about it?"

I remarked that, while all the witnesses agreed in supposing the gruff voice to be that of a Frenchman, there was much disagreement in regard to the shrill, or, as one individual termed it, the harsh voice.

"That was the evidence itself," said Dupin, "but it was not the peculiarity of the evidence. You have observed nothing distinctive. Yet there *was* something to be observed. The witnesses, as you remark, agreed about the gruff voice; they were here unanimous. But in regard to the shrill voice, the peculiarity is—not that they disagreed—but that, while an Italian, an Englishman, a Spaniard, a Hollander, and a Frenchman attempted to describe it, each one spoke of it as that *of a foreigner*. Each is sure that it was not the voice of one of his own countrymen. Each likens it—not to the voice of an individual of any nation with whose language he is conversant—but the converse. The Frenchman supposes it the voice of a Spaniard, and 'might have distinguished some words *had he been acquainted with the Spanish.*' The Dutchman maintains it to have been that of a Frenchman; but we find it stated that '*not understanding French this witness was examined through an interpreter.*' The Englishman thinks it the voice of a German, and '*does not understand German.*' The Spaniard 'is sure' that it was that of an Englishman, but 'judges by the intonation' altogether, '*as he has no knowledge of the English.*' The Italian believes it the voice of a Russian, but '*has never conversed with a native of Russia.*' A second Frenchman differs, moreover, with the first, and is positive that the voice was that of an Italian; but, *not being cognizant of that tongue*, is, like the Spaniard, 'convinced by the intonation.' Now, how strangely unusual must that voice have really been, about which such testimony as this *could* have been elicited!—in whose *tones*, even, denizens of the five great divisions of Europe could recognise nothing familiar! You will say that it might have been the voice of an Asiatic—of an African. Neither Asiatics nor Africans abound in Paris; but, without denying the inference, I will now merely call your attention to three points. The voice is termed by one witness 'harsh rather than shrill.' It is represented by two others to have been 'quick and *unequal.*' No words—no sounds resembling words—were by any witness mentioned as distinguishable.

"I know not," continued Dupin, "what impression I may have made, so far, upon your own understanding; but I do not hesitate to say that legitimate deductions even from this portion of the testimony—the portion respecting the gruff and shrill voices—are in themselves sufficient to engender a suspicion which should give direction to all farther progress in the investigation of the mystery. I said 'legitimate deductions;' but my meaning is not thus fully expressed. I designed to imply that the deductions are the *sole* proper ones, and that the suspicion arises *inevitably* from them as the single result. What the suspicion is, however, I will not say just yet. I merely wish you to bear in mind that, with myself, it was sufficiently forcible to give a definite form—a certain tendency—to my inquiries in the chamber.

"Let us now transport ourselves, in fancy, to this chamber. What shall we first seek here? The means of egress employed by the murderers. It is not too much to say that neither of us believe in preternatural events. Madame and Mademoiselle L'Espanaye were not destroyed by spirits. The doers of the deed were material, and escaped materially. Then how? Fortunately, there is but one mode of reasoning upon the point, and that mode *must* lead us to a definite decision. Let us examine, each by each, the possible means of egress. It is clear that the assassins were in the room where Mademoiselle L'Espanaye was found, or at least in the room adjoining, when the party ascended the stairs. It is then only from these two apartments that we have to seek issues. The police have laid bare the floors, the ceilings, and the masonry of the walls, in every direction. No *secret* issues could have escaped their vigilance. But, not trusting to *their* eyes, I examined with my own. There were, then, *no* secret issues. Both doors leading from the rooms into the passage were securely locked, with the keys inside. Let us turn to the chimneys. These, although of ordinary width for some eight or ten feet above the hearths, will not admit, throughout their extent, the body of a large cat. The impossibility of egress, by means already stated, being thus absolute, we are reduced to the windows. Through those of the front room no one could have escaped without notice from the crowd in the street. The murderers *must* have passed, then, through those of the back room. Now, brought to this conclusion in so unequivocal a manner as we are, it is not our part, as reasoners, to reject it on account of apparent impossibilities. It is only left for us to prove that these apparent 'impossibilities' are, in reality, not such.

"There are two windows in the chamber. One of them is unobstructed by furniture, and is wholly visible. The lower portion of the other is hidden from view by the head of the unwieldy bedstead which is thrust close up against it. The former was found securely fastened from within. It resisted the utmost force of those who endeavored to raise it. A large gimlet-hole had been pierced in its frame to the left, and a very stout nail was found fitted therein, nearly to the head. Upon examining the other window, a similar nail was seen similarly fitted in it; and a vigorous attempt to raise this sash, failed also. The police were now entirely satisfied that egress had not been in these directions. And, *therefore*, it was thought a matter of supererogation to withdraw the nails and open the windows.

"My own examination was somewhat more particular, and was so for the reason I have just given—because here it was, I knew, that all apparent impossibilities *must* be proved to be not such in reality.

"I proceeded to think thus—*à posteriori*. The murderers did escape from one of these windows. This being so, they could not have refastened the sashes from the inside, as they were found fastened—the consideration which put a stop, through its obviousness, to the scrutiny of the police in this quarter. Yet the sashes *were* fastened. They *must*, then, have the power of fastening themselves. There was no escape from this conclusion. I stepped to the unobstructed casement, withdrew the nail with some difficulty and attempted to raise the sash. It resisted all my efforts, as I had anticipated. A concealed spring must, I now know, exist; and this corroboration of my idea convinced me that my premises at least, were correct, however mysterious still appeared the circumstances attending the nails. A careful search soon brought to light the hidden spring. I pressed it, and, satisfied with the discovery, forbore to upraise the sash.

"I now replaced the nail and regarded it attentively. A person passing out through this window might have reclosed it, and the spring would have caught—but the nail could not have been replaced. The conclusion was plain, and again narrowed in the field of my investigations. The assassins *must* have escaped through the other window. Supposing, then, the springs upon each sash to be the same, as was probable, there *must* be found a difference between the nails, or at least between the modes of their fixture. Getting upon the sacking of the bedstead, I looked over the head-board minutely at the second casement. Passing my hand down behind the board, I readily discovered and pressed the spring, which was, as I had supposed, identical in character with its neighbor. I now looked at the nail. It was as stout as the other, and apparently fitted in the same manner— driven in nearly up to the head.

"You will say that I was puzzled; but, if you think so, you must have misunderstood the nature of the inductions. To use a sporting phrase, I had not been once 'at fault.' The scent had never for an instant been lost. There was no flaw in any link of the chain. I had traced the secret to its ultimate result— and that result was *the nail*. It had, I say, in every respect, the appearance of its fellow in the other window; but this fact was an absolute nullity (conclusive us it might seem to be) when compared with the consideration that here, at this point, terminated the clue. 'There *must* be something wrong,' I said, 'about the nail.' I touched it; and the head, with about a quarter of an inch of the shank, came off in my fingers. The rest of the shank was in the gimlet-hole where it had been broken off. The fracture was an old one (for its edges were incrusted with rust), and had apparently been accomplished by the blow of a hammer, which had partially imbedded, in the top of the bottom sash, the head portion of the nail. I now carefully replaced this head portion in the indentation whence I had taken it, and the resemblance to a perfect nail was complete— the fissure was invisible. Pressing the spring, I gently raised the sash for a few inches; the head went up with it, remaining firm in its bed. I closed the window, and the semblance of the whole nail was again perfect.

"The riddle, so far, was now unriddled. The assassin had escaped through the window which looked upon the bed. Dropping of its own accord upon his exit (or perhaps purposely closed), it had become fastened by the spring; and it was the retention of this spring which had been mistaken by the police for that of the nail—farther inquiry being thus considered unnecessary.

"The next question is that of the mode of descent. Upon this point I had been satisfied in my walk with you around the building. About five feet and a half from the casement in question there runs a lightning-rod. From this rod it would have been impossible for any one to reach the window itself, to say nothing of entering it. I observed, however, that the shutters of the fourth story were of the peculiar kind called by Parisian carpenters *ferrades*—a kind rarely employed at the present day, but frequently seen upon very old mansions at Lyons and Bourdeaux. They are in the form of an ordinary door, (a single, not a folding door) except that the lower half is latticed or worked in open trellis—thus affording an excellent hold for the hands. In the present instance these shutters are fully three feet and a half broad. When we saw them from the rear of the house, they were both about half open—that is to say, they stood off at right angles from the wall. It is probable that the police, as well as myself, examined the back of the tenement; but, if so, in looking at these *ferrades* in the line of their breadth (as they must have done), they did not perceive this great breadth itself, or, at all events, failed to take it into due consideration. In fact, having once satisfied themselves that no egress could have been made in this quarter, they would naturally bestow here a very cursory examination. It was clear to me, however, that the shutter belonging to the window at the head of the bed, would, if swung fully back to the wall, reach to within two feet of the lightning-rod. It was also evident that, by exertion of a very unusual degree of activity and courage, an entrance into the window, from the rod, might have been thus effected.—By reaching to the distance of two feet and a half (we now suppose the shutter open to its whole extent) a robber might have taken a firm grasp upon the trellis-work. Letting go, then, his hold upon the rod, placing his feet securely against the wall, and springing boldly from it, he might have swung the shutter so as to close it, and, if we imagine the window open at the time, might even have swung himself into the room.

"I wish you to bear especially in mind that I have spoken of a *very* unusual degree of activity as requisite to success in so hazardous and so difficult a feat. It is my design to show you, first, that the thing might possibly have been accomplished—but, secondly and *chiefly*, I wish to impress upon your understanding the *very extraordinary*—the almost preternatural character of that agility which could have accomplished it.

"You will say, no doubt, using the language of the law, that 'to make out my case,' I should rather undervalue, than insist upon a full estimation of the activity required in this matter. This may be the practice in law, but it is not the usage of reason. My ultimate object is only the truth. My immediate purpose is to lead you to place in juxtaposition, that *very unusual* activity of which I have just spoken with that *very peculiar* shrill (or harsh) and *unequal* voice, about whose nationality no two persons could be found to agree, and in whose utterance no syllabification could be detected."

At these words a vague and half-formed conception of the meaning of Dupin flitted over my mind. I seemed to be upon the verge of comprehension without power to comprehend—men, at times, find themselves upon the brink of remembrance without being able, in the end, to remember. My friend went on with his discourse.

"You will see," he said, "that I have shifted the question

from the mode of egress to that of ingress. It was my design to convey the idea that both were effected in the same manner, at the same point. Let us now revert to the interior of the room. Let us survey the appearances here. The drawers of the bureau, it is said, had been rifled, although many articles of apparel still remained within them. The conclusion here is absurd. It is a mere guess—a very silly one—and no more. How are we to know that the articles found in the drawers were not all these drawers had originally contained? Madame L'Espanaye and her daughter lived an exceedingly retired life—saw no company—seldom went out—had little use for numerous changes of habiliment. Those found were at least of as good quality as any likely to be possessed by these ladies. If a thief had taken any, why did he not take the best—why did he not take all? In a word, why did he abandon four thousand francs in gold to encumber himself with a bundle of linen? The gold *was* abandoned. Nearly the whole sum mentioned by Monsieur Mignaud, the banker, was discovered, in bags, upon the floor. I wish you, therefore, to discard from your thoughts the blundering idea of *motive*, engendered in the brains of the police by that portion of the evidence which speaks of money delivered at the door of the house. Coincidences ten times as remarkable as this (the delivery of the money, and murder committed within three days upon the party receiving it), happen to all of us every hour of our lives, without attracting even momentary notice. Coincidences, in general, are great stumbling blocks in the way of that class of thinkers who have been educated to know nothing of the theory of probabilities—that theory to which the most glorious objects of human research are indebted for the most glorious of illustration. In the present instance, had the gold been gone, the fact of its delivery three days before would have formed something more than a coincidence. It would have been corroborative of this idea of motive. But, under the real circumstances of the case, if we are to suppose gold the motive of this outrage, we must also imagine the perpetrator so vacillating an idiot as to have abandoned his gold and his motive together.

"Keeping now steadily in mind the points to which I have drawn your attention—that peculiar voice, that unusual agility, and that startling absence of motive in a murder so singularly atrocious as this—let us glance at the butchery itself. Here is a woman strangled to death by manual strength, and thrust up a chimney, head downward. Ordinary assassins employ no such modes of murder as this. Least of all, do they thus dispose of the murdered. In the manner of thrusting the corpse up the chimney, you will admit that there was something *excessively outré*—something altogether irreconcilable with our common notions of human action, even when we suppose the actors the most depraved of men. Think, too, how great must have been that strength which could have thrust the body *up* such an aperture so forcibly that the united vigor of several persons was found barely sufficient to drag it *down!*

"Turn, now, to other indications of the employment of a vigor most marvellous. On the hearth were thick tresses—very thick tresses—of grey human hair. These had been torn out by the roots. You are aware of the great force necessary in tearing thus from the head even twenty or thirty hairs together. You saw the locks in question as well as myself. Their roots (a hideous sight!) were clotted with fragments of the flesh of the scalp—sure token of the prodigious power which had been exerted in uprooting perhaps half a million of hairs at a time. The throat of the old lady was not merely cut, but the head absolutely severed from the body: the instrument was a mere razor. I wish you also to look at the *brutal* ferocity of these deeds. Of the bruises upon the body of Madame L'Espanaye I do not speak. Monsieur Dumas, and his worthy coadjutor Monsieur Etienne, have pronounced that they were inflicted by some obtuse instrument; and so far these gentlemen are very correct.

The obtuse instrument was clearly the stone pavement in the yard, upon which the victim had fallen from the window which looked in upon the bed. This idea, however simple it may now seem, escaped the police for the same reason that the breadth of the shutters escaped them—because, by the affair of the nails, their perceptions had been hermetically sealed against the possibility of the windows having ever been opened at all.

"If now, in addition to all these things, you have properly reflected upon the odd disorder of the chamber, we have gone so far as to combine the ideas of an agility astounding, a strength superhuman, a ferocity brutal, a butchery without motive, a *grotesquerie* in horror absolutely alien from humanity, and a voice foreign in tone to the ears of men of many nations, and devoid of all distinct or intelligible syllabification. What result, then, has ensued? What impression have I made upon your fancy?"

I felt a creeping of the flesh as Dupin asked me the question. "A madman," I said, "has done this deed—some raving maniac, escaped from a neighboring *Maison de Santé*."

"In some respects," he replied, "your idea is not irrelevant. But the voices of madmen, even in their wildest paroxysms, are never found to tally with that peculiar voice heard upon the stairs. Madmen are of some nation, and their language, however incoherent in its words, has always the coherence of syllabification. Besides, the hair of a madman is not such as I now hold in my hand. I disentangled this little tuft from the rigidly clutched fingers of Madame L'Espanaye. Tell me what you can make of it."

"Dupin!" I said, completely unnerved; "this hair is most unusual—this is no *human* hair."

"I have not asserted that it is," said he; "but, before we decide this point, I wish you to glance at the little sketch I have here traced upon this paper. It is a *facsimile* drawing of what has been described in one portion of the testimony as 'dark bruises, and deep indentations of finger nails,' upon the throat of

Mademoiselle L'Espanaye, and in another, (by Messrs. Dumas and Etienne,) as a 'series of livid spots, evidently the impression of fingers.'

"You will perceive," continued my friend, spreading out the paper upon the table before us, "that this drawing gives the idea of a firm and fixed hold. There is no *slipping* apparent. Each finger has retained—possibly until the death of the victim—the fearful grasp by which it originally imbedded itself. Attempt, now, to place all your fingers, at the same time, in the respective impressions as you see them."

I made the attempt in vain.

"We are possibly not giving this matter a fair trial," he said. "The paper is spread out upon a plane surface; but the human throat is cylindrical. Here is a billet of wood, the circumference of which is about that of the throat. Wrap the drawing around it, and try the experiment again."

I did so; but the difficulty was even more obvious than before. "This," I said, "is the mark of no human hand."

"Read now," replied Dupin, "this passage from Cuvier."

It was a minute anatomical and generally descriptive account of the large fulvous Ourang-Outang of the East Indian Islands. The gigantic stature, the prodigious strength and activity, the wild ferocity, and the imitative propensities of these mammalia are sufficiently well known to all. I understood the full horrors of the murder at once.

"The description of the digits," said I, as I made an end of reading, "is in exact accordance with this drawing. I see that no animal but an Ourang-Outang, of the species here mentioned, could have impressed the indentations as you have traced them. This tuft of tawny hair, too, is identical in character with that of the beast of Cuvier. But I cannot possibly comprehend the particulars of this frightful mystery. Besides, there were *two* voices heard in contention, and one of them was unquestionably the voice of a Frenchman."

"True; and you will remember an expression attributed almost unanimously, by the evidence, to this voice—the expression, '*mon Dieu!*' This, under the circumstances, has been justly characterized by one of the witnesses (Montani, the confectioner,) as an expression of remonstrance or expostulation. Upon these two words, therefore, I have mainly built my hopes of a full solution of the riddle. A Frenchman was cognizant of the murder. It is possible—indeed it is far more than probable—that he was innocent of all participation in the bloody transactions which took place. The Ourang-Outang may have escaped from him. He may have traced it to the chamber; but, under the agitating circumstances which ensued, he could never have recaptured it. It is still at large. I will not pursue these guesses—for I have no right to call them more—since the shades of reflection upon which they are based are scarcely of sufficient depth to be appreciable by my own intellect, and since I could not pretend to make them intelligible to the understanding of another. We will call them guesses then, and speak of them as such. If the Frenchman in question is indeed, as I suppose, innocent of this atrocity, this advertisement which I left last night, upon our return home, at the office of *Le Monde*, (a paper devoted to the shipping interest, and much sought by sailors,) will bring him to our residence."

He handed me a paper, and I read thus:

CAUGHT—*In the Bois de Boulogne, early in the morning of the—inst.,* (the morning of the murder,) *a very large, tawny Ourang-Outang of the Bornese species. The owner, (who is ascertained to be a sailor, belonging to a Maltese vessel,) may have the animal again, upon identifying it satisfactorily, and paying a few charges arising from its capture and keeping. Call at No. ——, Rue ——, Faubourg St. Germain—au troisième.*

"How was it possible," I asked, "that you should know the man to be a sailor, and belonging to a Maltese vessel?"

"I do *not* know it," said Dupin. "I am not *sure* of it. Here, however, is a small piece of ribbon, which from its form, and from its greasy appearance, has evidently been used in tying the hair in one of those long *queues* of which sailors are so fond. Moreover, this knot is one which few besides sailors can tie, and is peculiar to the Maltese. I picked the ribbon up at the foot of the lightning-rod. It could not have belonged to either of the deceased. Now if, after all, I am wrong in my induction from this ribbon, that the Frenchman was a sailor belonging to a Maltese vessel, still I can have done no harm in saying what I did in the advertisement. If I am in error, he will merely suppose that I have been misled by some circumstance into which he will not take the trouble to inquire. But if I am right, a great point is gained. Cognizant although innocent of the murder, the Frenchman will *naturally* hesitate about replying to the advertisement—about demanding the Ourang-Outang. He will reason thus:—'I am innocent; I am poor; my Ourang-Outang is of great value—to one in my circumstances a fortune of itself—why should I lose it through idle apprehensions of danger? Here it is, within my grasp. It was found in the Bois de Boulogne—at a vast distance from the scene of that butchery. How can it ever be suspected that a brute beast should have done the deed? The police are at fault—they have failed to procure the slightest clew. Should they even trace the animal, it would be impossible to prove me cognizant of the murder, or to implicate me in guilt on account of that cognizance. Above all, *I am known*. The advertiser designates me as the possessor of the beast. I am not sure to what limit his knowledge may extend. Should I avoid claiming a property of so great value, which it is known that I possess, I will render the animal at least, liable to suspicion. It is not my policy to attract attention either to myself or to the beast. I will answer the advertisement, get the Ourang-Outang, and keep it close until this matter has blown over.'"

At this moment we heard a step upon the stairs.

"Be ready," said Dupin, "with your pistols, but neither use them nor show them until at a signal from myself."

The front door of the house had been left open, and the visiter had entered, without ringing, and advanced several steps upon the staircase. Now, however, he seemed to hesitate. Presently we heard him descending. Dupin was moving quickly to the door, when we again heard him coming up. He did not turn back a second time, but stepped up with decision, and rapped at the door of our chamber.

"Come in," said Dupin, in a cheerful and hearty tone.

A man entered. He was a sailor, evidently—a tall, stout, and muscular-looking person, with a certain dare-devil expression of countenance, not altogether unprepossessing. His face, greatly sunburnt, was more than half hidden by whisker and mustachio. He had with him a huge oaken cudgel, but appeared to be otherwise unarmed. He bowed awkwardly, and bade us "good evening," in French accents, which, although somewhat Neufchatelish, were still sufficiently indicative of a Parisian origin.

"Sit down, my friend," said Dupin. "I suppose you have called about the Ourang-Outang. Upon my word, I almost envy you the possession of him; a remarkably fine, and no doubt a very valuable animal. How old do you suppose him to be?"

The sailor drew a long breath, with the air of a man relieved of some intolerable burden, and then replied, in an assured tone:

"I have no way of telling—but he can't be more than four or five years old. Have you got him here?"

"Oh no, we had no conveniences for keeping him here. He is at a livery stable in the Rue Dubourg, just by. You can get him in the morning. Of course you are prepared to identify the property?"

"To be sure I am, sir."

"I shall be sorry to part with him," said Dupin.

"I don't mean that you should be at all this trouble for nothing, sir," said the man. "Couldn't expect it. Am very willing to pay a reward for the finding of the animal—that is to say, any thing in reason."

"Well," replied my friend, "that is all very fair, to be sure. Let me think!—what should I have? Oh! I will tell you. My reward shall be this. You shall give me all the information in your power about these murders in the Rue Morgue."

Dupin said the last words in a very low tone, and very quietly. Just as quietly, too, he walked toward the door, locked it and put the key in his pocket. He then drew a pistol from his bosom and placed it, without the least flurry, upon the table.

The sailor's face flushed up as if he were struggling with suffocation. He started to his feet and grasped his cudgel, but the next moment he fell back into his seat, trembling violently, and with the countenance of death itself. He spoke not a word. I pitied him from the bottom of my heart.

"My friend," said Dupin, in a kind tone, "you are alarming yourself unnecessarily—you are indeed. We mean you no harm whatever. I pledge you the honor of a gentleman, and of a Frenchman, that we intend you no injury. I perfectly well know that you are innocent of the atrocities in the Rue Morgue. It will not do, however, to deny that you are in some measure implicated in them. From what I have already said, you must know that I have had means of information about this matter—means of which you could never have dreamed. Now the thing stands thus. You have done nothing which you could have avoided—nothing, certainly, which renders you culpable. You were not even guilty of robbery, when you might have robbed with impunity. You have nothing to conceal. You have no reason for concealment. On the other hand, you are bound by every principle of honor to confess all you know. An innocent man is now imprisoned, charged with that crime of which you can point out the perpetrator."

The sailor had recovered his presence of mind, in a great measure, while Dupin uttered these words; but his original boldness of bearing was all gone.

"So help me God," said he, after a brief pause, "I *will* tell you all I know about this affair;—but I do not expect you to believe one half I say—I would be a fool indeed if I did. Still, I am innocent, and I will make a clean breast if I die for it."

What he stated was, in substance, this. He had lately made a voyage to the Indian Archipelago. A party, of which he formed one, landed at Borneo, and passed into the interior on an excursion of pleasure. Himself and a companion had captured the Ourang-Outang. This companion dying, the animal fell into his own exclusive possession. After great trouble, occasioned by the intractable ferocity of his captive during the home voyage, he at length succeeded in lodging it safely at his own residence in Paris, where, not to attract toward himself the unpleasant curiosity of his neighbors, he kept it carefully secluded, until such time as it should recover from a wound in the foot, received from a splinter on board ship. His ultimate design was to sell it.

Returning home from some sailors' frolic the night, or rather in the morning of the murder, he found the beast occupying his own bed-room, into which it had broken from a closet adjoining, where it had been, as was thought, securely confined. Razor in hand, and fully lathered, it was sitting before a looking-glass, attempting the operation of shaving, in which it had no doubt previously watched its master through the key-hole of the closet. Terrified at the sight of so dangerous a weapon in the possession of an animal so ferocious, and so well able to use it, the man, for some moments, was at a loss what to do. He had been accustomed, however, to quiet the creature, even in its fiercest moods, by the use of a whip, and to this he now resorted. Upon sight of it, the Ourang-Outang sprang at once through the door of the chamber, down the stairs, and thence, through a window, unfortunately open, into the street.

The Frenchman followed in despair; the ape, razor still in hand, occasionally stopping to look back and gesticulate at its pursuer, until the latter had nearly come up with it. It then again made off. In this manner the chase continued for a long time. The streets were profoundly quiet, as it was nearly three o'clock in the morning. In passing down an alley in the rear of the Rue Morgue, the fugitive's attention was arrested by a light gleaming from the open window of Madame L'Espanaye's chamber, in the fourth story of her house. Rushing to the building, it perceived the lightning rod, clambered up with inconceivable agility, grasped the shutter, which was thrown fully back against the wall, and, by its means, swung itself directly upon the headboard of the bed. The whole feat did not occupy a minute. The shutter was kicked open again by the Ourang-Outang as it entered the room.

The sailor, in the meantime, was both rejoiced and perplexed. He had strong hopes of now recapturing the brute, as it could scarcely escape from the trap into which it had ventured, except by the rod, where it might be intercepted as it came down. On the other hand, there was much cause for anxiety as to what it might do in the house. This latter reflection urged the man still to follow the fugitive. A lightning rod is ascended without difficulty, especially by a sailor; but, when he had arrived as high as the window, which lay far to his left, his career was stopped; the most that he could accomplish was to reach over so as to obtain a glimpse of the interior of the room. At this glimpse he nearly fell from his hold through excess of horror. Now it was that those hideous shrieks arose upon the night, which had startled from slumber the inmates of the Rue Morgue. Madame L'Espanaye and her daughter, habited in their night clothes, had apparently been occupied in arranging some papers in the iron chest already mentioned, which had been wheeled into the middle of the room. It was open, and its contents lay beside it on the floor. The victims must have been sitting with their backs toward the window; and, from the time elapsing between the ingress of the beast and the screams, it seems probable that it was not immediately perceived. The flapping-to of the shutter would *naturally* have been attributed to the wind.

As the sailor looked in, the gigantic animal had seized Madame L'Espanaye by the hair, (which was loose, as she had been combing it,) and was flourishing the razor about her face, in imitation of the motions of a barber. The daughter lay prostrate and motionless; she had swooned. The screams and struggles of the old lady (during which the hair was torn from her head) had the effect of changing the probably pacific purposes of the Ourang-Outang into those of wrath. With one determined sweep of its muscular arm it nearly severed her head from her body. The sight of blood inflamed its anger into phrenzy. Gnashing its teeth, and flashing fire from its eyes, it flew upon the body of the girl, and imbedded its fearful talons in her throat, retaining its grasp until she expired. Its wandering and wild glances fell at this moment upon the head of the bed, over which the face of its master, rigid with horror, was just discernible. The fury of the beast, who no doubt bore still in mind the dreaded whip, was instantly converted into fear. Conscious of having deserved punishment, it seemed desirous of concealing its bloody deeds, and skipped about the chamber in an agony of nervous agitation; throwing down and breaking the furniture as it moved, and dragging the bed from the bedstead. In conclusion, it seized first the corpse of the daughter, and thrust it up the chimney, as it was found; then that of the old lady, which it immediately hurled through the window headlong.

As the ape approached the casement with its mutilated burden, the sailor shrank aghast to the rod, and, rather gliding than clambering down it, hurried at once home—dreading the consequences of the butchery, and gladly abandoning, in his terror, all solicitude about the fate of the Ourang-Outang. The words heard by the party upon the staircase were the

Frenchman's exclamations of horror and affright, commingled with the fiendish jabberings of the brute.

I have scarcely anything to add. The Ourang-Outang must have escaped from the chamber, by the rod, just before the break of the door. It must have closed the window as it passed through it. It was subsequently caught by the owner himself, who obtained for it a very large sum at the *Jardin des Plantes*. Le Don was instantly released, upon our narration of the circumstances (with some comments from Dupin) at the bureau of the Prefect of Police. This functionary, however well disposed to my friend, could not altogether conceal his chagrin at the turn which affairs had taken, and was fain to indulge in a sarcasm or two, about the propriety of every person minding his own business.

"Let him talk," said Dupin, who had not thought it necessary to reply. "Let him discourse; it will ease his conscience, I am satisfied with having defeated him in his own castle. Nevertheless, that he failed in the solution of this mystery, is by no means that matter for wonder which he supposes it; for, in truth, our friend the Prefect is somewhat too cunning to be profound. In his wisdom is no *stamen*. It is all head and no body, like the pictures of the Goddess Laverna—or, at best, all head and shoulders, like a codfish. But he is a good creature after all. I like him especially for one master stroke of cant, by which he has attained his reputation for ingenuity. I mean the way he has '*de nier ce qui est, et d'expliquer ce qui n'est pas.*'"*

---

* Rousseau—*Nouvelle Héloïse*.

Whose Body?

Dorothy Sayers

Chapter 1

O h, damn!" said Lord Peter Wimsey at Piccadilly Circus. "Hi, driver!"

The taxi man, irritated at receiving this appeal while negotiating the intricacies of turning into Lower Regent Street across the route of a 19 'bus, a 38-B and a bicycle, bent an unwilling ear.

"I've left the catalogue behind," said Lord Peter deprecatingly. "Uncommonly careless of me. D'you mind puttin' back to where we came from?"

"To the Savile Club, sir?"

"No—110 Piccadilly—just beyond—thank you."

"Thought you was in a hurry," said the man, overcome with a sense of injury.

"I'm afraid it's an awkward place to turn in," said Lord Peter, answering the thought rather than the words. His long, amiable face looked as if it had generated spontaneously from his top hat, as white maggots breed from Gorgonzola.

The taxi, under the severe eye of a policeman, revolved by slow jerks, with a noise like the grinding of teeth.

The block of new, perfect and expensive flats in which Lord Peter dwelt upon the second floor, stood directly opposite the Green Park, in a spot for many years occupied by the skeleton of a frustrate commercial enterprise. As Lord Peter let himself in he heard his man's voice in the library, uplifted in that throttled stridency peculiar to well-trained persons using the telephone.

"I believe that's his lordship just coming in again—if your Grace would kindly hold the line a moment."

"What is it, Bunter?"

"Her Grace has just called up from Denver, my lord. I was just saying your lordship had gone to the sale when I heard your lordship's latchkey."

"Thanks," said Lord Peter; "and you might find me my

catalogue, would you? I think I must have left it in my bedroom, or on the desk."

He sat down to the telephone with an air of leisurely courtesy, as though it were an acquaintance dropped in for a chat.

"Hullo, Mother—that you?"

"Oh, there you are, dear," replied the voice of the Dowager Duchess. "I was afraid I'd just missed you."

"Well, you had, as a matter of fact. I'd just started off to Brocklebury's sale to pick up a book or two, but I had to come back for the catalogue. What's up?"

"Such a quaint thing," said the Duchess. "I thought I'd tell you. You know little Mr. Thipps?"

"Thipps?" said Lord Peter. "Thipps? Oh, yes, the little architect man who's doing the church roof. Yes. What about him?"

"Mrs. Throgmorton's just been in, in quite a state of mind."

"Sorry, Mother, I can't hear. Mrs. Who?"

"Throgmorton—Throgmorton—the vicar's wife."

"Oh, Throgmorton, yes?"

"Mr. Thipps rang them up this morning. It was his day to come down, you know."

"Yes?"

"He rang them up to say he couldn't. He was so upset, poor little man. He'd found a dead body in his bath."

"Sorry, Mother, I can't hear; found what, where?"

"A dead body, dear, in his bath."

"What?—no, no, we haven't finished. Please don't cut us off. Hullo! Hullo! Is that you, Mother? Hullo!—Mother!—Oh, yes—sorry, the girl was trying to cut us off. What sort of body?"

"A dead man, dear, with nothing on but a pair of pince-nez. Mrs. Throgmorton positively blushed when she was telling me. I'm afraid people do get a little narrow-minded in country vicarages."

"Well, it sounds a bit unusual. Was it anybody he knew?"

"No, dear, I don't think so, but, of course, he couldn't give her many details. She said he sounded quite distracted. He's such a respectable little man—and having the police in the house and so on, really worried him."

"Poor little Thipps! Uncommonly awkward for him. Let's see, he lives in Battersea, doesn't he?"

"Yes, dear; 59, Queen Caroline Mansions; opposite the Park. That big block just round the corner from the Hospital. I thought perhaps you'd like to run round and see him and ask if there's anything we can do. I always thought him a nice little man."

"Oh, quite," said Lord Peter, grinning at the telephone. The Duchess was always of the greatest assistance to his hobby of criminal investigation, though she never alluded to it, and maintained a polite fiction of its non-existence.

"What time did it happen, Mother?"

"I think he found it early this morning, but, of course, he didn't think of telling the Throgmortons just at first. She came up to me just before lunch—so tiresome, I had to ask her to stay. Fortunately, I was alone. I don't mind being bored myself, but I hate having my guests bored."

"Poor old Mother! Well, thanks awfully for tellin' me. I think I'll send Bunter to the sale and toddle round to Battersea now an' try and console the poor little beast. So-long."

"Good-bye, dear."

"Bunter!"

"Yes, my lord."

"Her Grace tells me that a respectable Battersea architect has discovered a dead man in his bath."

"Indeed, my lord? That's very gratifying."

"Very, Bunter. Your choice of words is unerring. I wish Eton and Balliol had done as much for me. Have you found the catalogue?"

"Here it is, my lord."

"Thanks. I am going to Battersea at once. I want you to attend the sale for me. Don't lose time—I don't want to miss the Folio Dante* nor the de Voragine—here you are—see? 'Golden Legend'—Wynkyn de Worde, 1493—got that?—and, I say, make a special effort for the Caxton folio of the 'Four Sons of Aymon'—it's the 1489 folio and unique. Look! I've marked the lots I want, and put my outside offer against each. Do your best for me. I shall be back to dinner."

"Very good, my lord."

"Take my cab and tell him to hurry. He may for you; he doesn't like me very much. Can I," said Lord Peter, looking at himself in the eighteenth-century mirror over the mantelpiece, "can I have the heart to fluster the flustered Thipps further—that's very difficult to say quickly—by appearing in a top-hat and frock-coat? I think not. Ten to one he will overlook my trousers and mistake me for the undertaker. A grey suit, I fancy, neat but not gaudy, with a hat to tone, suits my other self better. Exit the amateur of first editions; new motive introduced by solo bassoon; enter Sherlock Holmes, disguised as a walking gentleman. There goes Bunter. Invaluable fellow—never offers to do his job when you've told him to do somethin' else. Hope he doesn't miss the 'Four Sons of Aymon.' Still, there *is* another copy of that—in the Vatican.† It might become available, you never know —if the Church of Rome went to pot or Switzerland invaded Italy— whereas a strange corpse doesn't turn up in a suburban bathroom more than once in a lifetime—at least, I should think not—at any rate, the number of times it's happened, *with* a pince-nez, might be counted on the fingers of one hand, I imagine. Dear me! it's a dreadful mistake to ride two hobbies at once."

---

* This is the first Florence edition, 1481, by Niccolo di Lorenzo. Lord Peter's collection of printed Dantes is worth inspection. It includes, besides the famous Aldine 8vo. of 1502, the Naples folio of 1477—"edizione rarissima," according to Colomb. This copy has no history, and Mr. Parker's private belief is that its present owner conveyed it away by stealth from somewhere or other. Lord Peter's own account is that he "picked it up in a little place in the hills," when making a walking-tour through Italy.

† Lord Peter's wits were wool-gathering. The book is in the possession of Earl Spencer. The Brocklebury copy is incomplete, the last five signatures being altogether missing, but is unique in possessing the colophon.

He had drifted across the passage into his bedroom, and was changing with a rapidity one might not have expected from a man of his mannerisms. He selected a dark-green tie to match his socks and tied it accurately without hesitation or the slightest compression of his lips; substituted a pair of brown shoes for his black ones, slipped a monocle into a breast pocket, and took up a beautiful Malacca walking-stick with a heavy silver knob.

"That's all, I think," he murmured to himself. "Stay—I may as well have you—you may come in useful—one never knows." He added a flat silver matchbox to his equipment, glanced at his watch, and seeing that it was already a quarter to three, ran briskly downstairs, and, hailing a taxi, was carried to Battersea Park.

* * * * *

Mr. Alfred Thipps was a small, nervous man, whose flaxen hair was beginning to abandon the unequal struggle with destiny. One might say that his only really marked feature was a large bruise over the left eyebrow, which gave him a faintly dissipated air incongruous with the rest of his appearance. Almost in the same breath with his first greeting, he made a self-conscious apology for it, murmuring something about having run against the dining-room door in the dark. He was touched almost to tears by Lord Peter's thoughtfulness and condescension in calling.

"I'm sure it's most kind of your lordship," he repeated for the dozenth time, rapidly blinking his weak little eyelids. "I appreciate it very deeply, very deeply, indeed, and so would Mother, only she's so deaf, I don't like to trouble you with making her understand. It's been very hard all day," he added, "with the policemen in the house and all this commotion. It's what Mother and me have never been used to, always living very retired, and it's most distressing to a man of regular habits, my lord, and reely, I'm almost thankful Mother doesn't understand, for I'm sure it would worry her terribly if she was to know about it. She was upset at first, but she's made up some idea of her own about it now, and I'm sure it's all for the best."

The old lady who sat knitting by the fire nodded grimly in response to a look from her son.

"I always said as you ought to complain about that bath, Alfred," she said suddenly, in the high, piping voice peculiar to the deaf, "and it's to be 'oped the landlord'll see about it now; not but what I think you might have managed without having the police in, but there! you always were one to make a fuss about a little thing, from chicken-pox up."

"There now," said Mr. Thipps apologetically, "you see how it is. Not but what it's just as well she's settled on that, because she understands we've locked up the bathroom and don't try to go in there. But it's been a terrible shock to me, sir—my lord, I should say, but there! my nerves are all to pieces. Such a thing has never 'appened—happened to me in all my born days. Such a state I was in this morning—I didn't know if I was on my head or my heels—I reely didn't, and my heart not being too strong, I hardly knew how to get out of that horrid room and telephone for the police. It's affected me, sir, it's affected me, it reely has—I couldn't touch a bit of breakfast, nor lunch neither, and what with telephoning and putting off clients and interviewing people all morning, I've hardly known what to do with myself."

"I'm sure it must have been uncommonly distressin'," said Lord Peter, sympathetically, "especially comin' like that before breakfast. Hate anything tiresome happenin' before breakfast. Takes a man at such a confounded disadvantage, what?"

"That's just it, that's just it," said Mr. Thipps, eagerly. "When I saw that dreadful thing lying there in my bath, mother-naked, too, except for a pair of eyeglasses, I assure you, my lord, it regularly turned my stomach, if you'll excuse the expression. I'm not very strong, sir, and I get that sinking feeling sometimes in the morning, and what with one thing and another I 'ad—had to send the girl for a stiff brandy, or I don't know *what* mightn't have happened. I felt so queer, though I'm anything but partial to spirits as a rule. Still, I make it a rule never to be without brandy in the house, in case of emergency, you know?"

"Very wise of you," said Lord Peter, cheerfully. "You're a very far-seein' man, Mr. Thipps. Wonderful what a little nip'll do in case of need, and the less you're used to it the more good it does you. Hope your girl is a sensible young woman, what? Nuisance to have women faintin' and shriekin' all over the place."

"Oh, Gladys is a good girl," said Mr. Thipps, "very reasonable indeed. She was shocked, of course; that's very understandable. I was shocked myself, and it wouldn't be proper in a young woman not to be shocked under the circumstances, but she is reely a helpful, energetic girl in a crisis, if you understand me. I consider myself very fortunate these days to have got a good, decent girl to do for me and Mother, even though she is a bit careless and forgetful about little things, but that's only natural. She was very sorry indeed about having left the bathroom window open, she reely was, and though I was angry at first, seeing what's come of it, it wasn't anything to speak of, not in the ordinary way, as you might say. Girls will forget things, you know, my lord, and reely she was so distressed I didn't like to say too much to her. All I said was: 'It might have been burglars,' I said, 'remember that, next time you leave a window open all night; this time it was a dead man,' I said, 'and that's unpleasant enough, but next time it might be burglars,' I said, 'and all of us murdered in our beds.' But the police-inspector—Inspector Sugg, they called him, from the Yard—he was very sharp with her, poor girl. Quite frightened her, and made her think he suspected her of something, though what good a body could be to her, poor girl, I can't imagine, and so I told the Inspector. He was quite rude to me, my lord—I may say I didn't like his manner at all. 'If you've got anything definite to accuse Gladys or me of, Inspector,' I said to him, 'bring it forward, that's what you have to do,' I said, 'but I've yet to learn that you're paid to be rude to a gentleman in his own 'ouse—house.' Reely," said Mr. Thipps, growing quite pink on the top of his head, "he regularly roused me, regularly roused me, my lord, and I'm a mild man as a rule."

"Sugg all over," said Lord Peter. "I know him. When he don't know what else to say, he's rude. Stands to reason you and the girl wouldn't go collectin' bodies. Who'd want to saddle himself with a body? Difficulty's usually to get rid of 'em. Have you got rid of this one yet, by the way?"

"It's still in the bathroom," said Mr. Thipps. "Inspector Sugg said nothing was to be touched till his men came in to move it. I'm expecting them at any time. If it would interest your lordship to have a look at it—"

"Thanks awfully," said Lord Peter. "I'd like to very much, if I'm not puttin' you out."

"Not at all," said Mr. Thipps. His manner as he led the way along the passage convinced Lord Peter of two things—first, that, gruesome as his exhibit was, he rejoiced in the importance it reflected upon himself and his flat, and secondly, that Inspector Sugg had forbidden him to exhibit it to anyone. The latter supposition was confirmed by the action of Mr. Thipps, who stopped to fetch the door-key from his bedroom, saying that the police had the other, but that he made it a rule to have two keys to every door, in case of accident.

The bathroom was in no way remarkable. It was long and narrow, the window being exactly over the head of the bath. The panes were of frosted glass; the frame wide enough to admit a man's body. Lord Peter stepped rapidly across to it, opened it and looked out.

The flat was the top one of the building and situated about the middle of the block. The bathroom window looked out upon the back-yards of the flats, which were occupied by various small outbuildings, coal-holes, garages, and the like.

Beyond these were the back gardens of a parallel line of houses. On the right rose the extensive edifice of St. Luke's Hospital, Battersea, with its grounds, and, connected with it by a covered way, the residence of the famous surgeon, Sir Julian Freke, who directed the surgical side of the great new hospital, and was, in addition, known in Harley Street as a distinguished neurologist with a highly individual point of view.

This information was poured into Lord Peter's ear at considerable length by Mr. Thipps, who seemed to feel that the neighbourhood of anybody so distinguished shed a kind of halo of glory over Queen Caroline Mansions.

"We had him round here himself this morning," he said, "about this horrid business. Inspector Sugg thought one of the young medical gentlemen at the hospital might have brought the corpse round for a joke, as you might say, they always having bodies in the dissecting-room. So Inspector Sugg went round to see Sir Julian this morning to ask if there was a body missing. He was very kind, was Sir Julian, very kind indeed, though he was at work when they got there, in the dissecting-room. He looked up the books to see that all the bodies were accounted for, and then very obligingly came round here to look at this"—he indicated the bath—"and said he was afraid he couldn't help us—there was no corpse missing from the hospital, and this one didn't answer to the description of any they'd had."

"Nor to the description of any of the patients, I hope," suggested Lord Peter casually.

At this grisly hint Mr. Thipps turned pale.

"I didn't hear Inspector Sugg inquire," he said, with some agitation. "What a very horrid thing that would be—God bless my soul, my lord, I never thought of it."

"Well, if they had missed a patient they'd probably have discovered it by now," said Lord Peter. "Let's have a look at this one."

He screwed his monocle into his eye, adding: "I see you're

troubled here with the soot blowing in. Beastly nuisance, ain't it? I get it, too—spoils all my books, you know. Here, don't you trouble, if you don't care about lookin' at it."

He took from Mr. Thipps's hesitating hand the sheet which had been flung over the bath, and turned it back.

The body which lay in the bath was that of a tall, stout man of about fifty. The hair, which was thick and black and naturally curly, had been cut and parted by a master hand, and exuded a faint violet perfume, perfectly recognisable in the close air of the bathroom. The features were thick, fleshy and strongly marked, with prominent dark eyes, and a long nose curving down to a heavy chin. The clean-shaven lips were full and sensual, and the dropped jaw showed teeth stained with tobacco. On the dead face the handsome pair of gold pince-nez mocked death with grotesque elegance; the fine gold chain curved over the naked breast. The legs lay stiffly stretched out side by side; the arms reposed close to the body; the fingers were flexed naturally. Lord Peter lifted one arm, and looked at the hand with a little frown.

"Bit of a dandy, your visitor, what?" he murmured. "Parma violet and manicure." He bent again, slipping his hand beneath the head. The absurd eyeglasses slipped off, clattering into the bath, and the noise put the last touch to Mr. Thipps's growing nervousness.

"If you'll excuse me," he murmured, "it makes me feel quite faint, it reely does."

He slipped outside, and he had no sooner done so than Lord Peter, lifting the body quickly and cautiously, turned it over and inspected it with his head on one side, bringing his monocle into play with the air of the late Joseph Chamberlain approving a rare orchid. He then laid the head over his arm, and bringing out the silver matchbox from his pocket, slipped it into the open mouth. Then making the noise usually written "Tut-tut," he laid the body down, picked up the mysterious pince-nez, looked at it, put it on his nose and looked through it, made the same noise again, readjusted the pince-nez upon the nose of the corpse, so as to leave no traces of interference for the irritation of Inspector Sugg; rearranged the body; returned to the window and, leaning out, reached upwards and sideways with his walking-stick, which he had somewhat incongruously brought along with him. Nothing appearing to come of these investigations, he withdrew his head, closed the window, and rejoined Mr. Thipps in the passage.

Mr. Thipps, touched by this sympathetic interest in the younger son of a duke, took the liberty, on their return to the sitting-room, of offering him a cup of tea. Lord Peter, who had strolled over to the window and was admiring the outlook on Battersea Park, was about to accept, when an ambulance came into view at the end of Prince of Wales Road. Its appearance reminded Lord Peter of an important engagement, and with a hurried "By Jove!" he took his leave of Mr. Thipps.

"My mother sent kind regards and all that," he said, shaking hands fervently; "hopes you'll soon be down at Denver again. Good-bye, Mrs. Thipps," he bawled kindly into the ear of the old lady. "Oh, no, my dear sir, please don't trouble to come down."

He was none too soon. As he stepped out of the door and turned towards the station, the ambulance drew up from the other direction, and Inspector Sugg emerged from it with two constables. The Inspector spoke to the officer on duty at the Mansions, and turned a suspicious gaze on Lord Peter's retreating back.

"Dear old Sugg," said that nobleman, fondly, "dear, dear old bird! How he does hate me, to be sure."

Chapter 2

Excellent, Bunter," said Lord Peter, sinking with a sigh into a luxurious armchair. "I couldn't have done better myself.

The thought of the Dante makes my mouth water—and the 'Four Sons of Aymon.' And you've saved me £60—that's glorious. What shall we spend it on, Bunter? Think of it—all ours, to do as we like with, for as Harold Skimpole so rightly observes, £60 saved is £60 gained, and I'd reckoned on spending it all. It's your saving, Bunter, and properly speaking, your £60. What do we want? Anything in your department? Would you like anything altered in the flat?"

"Well, my lord, as your lordship is so good"—the man-servant paused, about to pour an old brandy into a liqueur glass.

"Well, out with it, my Bunter, you imperturbable old hypocrite. It's no good talking as if you were announcing dinner—you're spilling the brandy. The voice is Jacob's voice, but the hands are the hands of Esau. What does that blessed darkroom of yours want now?"

"There's a Double Anastigmat with a set of supplementary lenses, my lord," said Bunter, with a note almost of religious fervour. "If it was a case of forgery now—or footprints—I could enlarge them right up on the plate. Or the wide-angled lens would be useful. It's as though the camera had eyes at the back of its head, my lord. Look—I've got it here."

He pulled a catalogue from his pocket, and submitted it, quivering, to his employer's gaze.

Lord Peter perused the description slowly, the corners of his long mouth lifted into a faint smile.

"It's Greek to me," he said, "and £50 seems a ridiculous price for a few bits of glass. I suppose, Bunter, you'd say £750 was a bit out of the way for a dirty old book in a dead language, wouldn't you?"

"It wouldn't be my place to say so, my lord."

"No, Bunter, I pay you £200 a year to keep your thoughts to yourself. Tell me, Bunter, in these democratic days, don't you think that's unfair?"

"No, my lord."

"You don't. D'you mind telling me frankly why you don't think it unfair?"

"Frankly, my lord, your lordship is paid a nobleman's income to take Lady Worthington in to dinner and refrain from exercising your lordship's undoubted powers of repartee."

Lord Peter considered this.

"That's your idea, is it, Bunter? Noblesse oblige—for a consideration. I daresay you're right. Then you're better off than I am, because I'd have to behave myself to Lady Worthington if I hadn't a penny. Bunter, if I sacked you here and now, would you tell me what you think of me?"

"No, my lord."

"You'd have a perfect right to, my Bunter, and if I sacked you on top of drinking the kind of coffee you make, I'd deserve everything you could say of me. You're a demon for coffee, Bunter—I don't want to know how you do it, because I believe it to be witchcraft, and I don't want to burn eternally. You can buy your cross-eyed lens."

"Thank you, my lord."

"Have you finished in the dining-room?"

"Not quite, my lord."

"Well, come back when you have. I have many things to tell you. Hullo! who's that?"

The doorbell had rung sharply.

"Unless it's anybody interestin' I'm not at home."

"Very good, my lord."

Lord Peter's library was one of the most delightful bachelor rooms in London. Its scheme was black and primrose; its walls were lined with rare editions, and its chairs and Chesterfield sofa suggested the embraces of the houris. In one corner stood a black baby grand, a wood fire leaped on a wide old-fashioned hearth, and the Sèvres vases on the chimneypiece were filled with ruddy and gold chrysanthemums. To the eyes of the young man who was ushered in from the raw November fog it seemed not only rare and unattainable, but friendly and familiar, like a colourful and gilded paradise in a mediaeval painting.

"Mr. Parker, my lord."

Lord Peter jumped up with genuine eagerness.

"My dear man, I'm delighted to see you. What a beastly foggy night, ain't it? Bunter, some more of that admirable coffee and another glass and the cigars. Parker, I hope you're full of crime—nothing less than arson or murder will do for us tonight. 'On such a night as this—' Bunter and I were just sitting down to carouse. I've got a Dante, and a Caxton folio that is practically unique, at Sir Ralph Brocklebury's sale. Bunter, who did the bargaining, is going to have a lens which does all kinds of wonderful things with its eyes shut, and

> *We both have got a body in a bath,*
> *We both have got a body in a bath—*
> *For in spite of all temptations*
> *To go in for cheap sensations*
> *We insist upon a body in a bath—*

"Nothing less will do for us, Parker. It's mine at present, but we're going shares in it. Property of the firm. Won't you join us? You really must put *something* in the jack-pot. Perhaps you have a body. Oh, do have a body. Every body welcome.

> *Gin a body meet a body*
> *Hauled before the beak,*
> *Gin a body jolly well knows who murdered a*
> *body and that old Sugg is on the wrong tack,*
> *Need a body speak?*

"Not a bit of it. He tips a glassy wink to yours truly and yours truly reads the truth."

"Ah," said Parker, "I knew you'd been round to Queen

Caroline Mansions. So've I, and met Sugg, and he told me he'd seen you. He was cross, too. Unwarrantable interference, he calls it."

"I knew he would," said Lord Peter. "I love taking a rise out of dear old Sugg, he's always so rude. I see by the *Star* that he has excelled himself by taking the girl, Gladys What's-her-name, into custody. Sugg of the evening, beautiful Sugg! But what were *you* doing there?"

"To tell you the truth," said Parker, "I went round to see if the Semitic-looking stranger in Mr. Thipps's bath was by any extraordinary chance Sir Reuben Levy. But he isn't."

"Sir Reuben Levy? Wait a minute, I saw something about that. I know! A headline: 'Mysterious disappearance of famous financier.' What's it all about? I didn't read it carefully."

"Well, it's a bit odd, though I daresay it's nothing really—old chap may have cleared for some reason best known to himself. It only happened this morning, and nobody would have thought anything about it, only it happened to be the day on which he had arranged to attend a most important financial meeting and do some deal involving millions—I haven't got all the details. But I know he's got enemies who'd just as soon the deal didn't come off, so when I got wind of this fellow in the bath, I buzzed round to have a look at him. It didn't seem likely, of course, but unlikelier things do happen in our profession. The funny thing is, old Sugg had got bitten with the idea it is him, and is wildly telegraphing to Lady Levy to come and identify him. But as a matter of fact, the man in the bath is no more Sir Reuben Levy than Adolf Beck, poor devil, was John Smith. Oddly enough, though, he would be really extraordinarily like Sir Reuben if he had a beard, and as Lady Levy is abroad with the family, somebody may say it's him, and Sugg will build up a lovely theory, like the Tower of Babel, and destined so to perish."

"Sugg's a beautiful, braying ass," said Lord Peter. "He's like a detective in a novel. Well, I don't know anything about Levy, but

I've seen the body, and I should say the idea was preposterous upon the face of it. What do you think of the brandy?"

"Unbelievable, Wimsey—sort of thing makes one believe in heaven. But I want your yarn."

"D'you mind if Bunter hears it, too? Invaluable man, Bunter— amazin' fellow with a camera. And the odd thing is, he's always on the spot when I want my bath or my boots. I don't know when he develops things—I believe he does 'em in his sleep. Bunter!"

"Yes, my lord."

"Stop fiddling about in there, and get yourself the proper things to drink and join the merry throng."

"Certainly, my lord."

"Mr. Parker has a new trick: The Vanishing Financier. Absolutely no deception. Hey, presto, pass! and where is he? Will some gentleman from the audience kindly step upon the platform and inspect the cabinet? Thank you, sir. The quickness of the 'and deceives the heye."

"I'm afraid mine isn't much of a story," said Parker. "It's just one of those simple things that offer no handle. Sir Reuben Levy dined last night with three friends at the Ritz. After dinner the friends went to the theatre. He refused to go with them on account of an appointment. I haven't yet been able to trace the appointment, but anyhow, he returned home to his house—9a, Park Lane—at twelve o'clock."

"Who saw him?"

"The cook, who had just gone up to bed, saw him on the doorstep, and heard him let himself in. He walked upstairs, leaving his greatcoat on the hall peg and his umbrella in the stand—you remember how it rained last night. He undressed and went to bed. Next morning he wasn't there. That's all," said Parker abruptly, with a wave of the hand.

"It isn't all, it isn't all. Daddy, go on, that's not *half* a story," pleaded Lord Peter.

"But it *is* all. When his man came to call him he wasn't there.

The bed had been slept in. His pyjamas and all his clothes were there, the only odd thing being that they were thrown rather untidily on the ottoman at the foot of the bed, instead of being neatly folded on a chair, as is Sir Reuben's custom—looking as though he had been rather agitated or unwell. No clean clothes were missing, no suit, no boots—nothing. The boots he had worn were in his dressing-room as usual. He had washed and cleaned his teeth and done all the usual things. The housemaid was down cleaning the hall at half-past six, and can swear that nobody came in or out after that. So one is forced to suppose that a respectable middle-aged Hebrew financier either went mad between twelve and six a.m. and walked quietly out of the house in his birthday suit on a November night, or else was spirited away like the lady in the 'Ingoldsby Legends,' body and bones, leaving only a heap of crumpled clothes behind him."

"Was the front door bolted?"

"That's the sort of question you *would* ask, straight off; it took me an hour to think of it. No; contrary to custom, there was only the Yale lock on the door. On the other hand, some of the maids had been given leave to go to the theatre, and Sir Reuben may quite conceivably have left the door open under the impression they had not come in. Such a thing has happened before."

"And that's really all?"

"Really all. Except for one very trifling circumstance."

"I love trifling circumstances," said Lord Peter, with childish delight; "so many men have been hanged by trifling circumstances. What was it?"

"Sir Reuben and Lady Levy, who are a most devoted couple, always share the same room. Lady Levy, as I said before, is in Mentonne at the moment for her health. In her absence, Sir Reuben sleeps in the double bed as usual, and invariably on his own side—the outside—of the bed. Last night he put the two pillows together and slept in the middle, or, if anything, rather closer to the wall than otherwise. The housemaid, who is a most intelligent girl, noticed this when she went up to make the bed, and, with really admirable detective instinct, refused to touch the bed or let anybody else touch it, though it wasn't till later that they actually sent for the police."

"Was nobody in the house but Sir Reuben and the servants?"

"No; Lady Levy was away with her daughter and her maid. The valet, cook, parlourmaid, housemaid and kitchenmaid were the only people in the house, and naturally wasted an hour or two squawking and gossiping. I got there about ten."

"What have you been doing since?"

"Trying to get on the track of Sir Reuben's appointment last night, since, with the exception of the cook, his 'appointer' was the last person who saw him before his disappearance. There may be some quite simple explanation, though I'm dashed if I can think of one for the moment. Hang it all, a man doesn't come in and go to bed and walk away again 'mid nodings on' in the middle of the night."

"He may have been disguised."

"I thought of that—in fact, it seems the only possible explanation. But it's deuced odd, Wimsey. An important city man, on the eve of an important transaction, without a word of warning to anybody, slips off in the middle of the night, disguised down to his skin, leaving behind his watch, purse, cheque-book, and—most mysterious and important of all—his spectacles, without which he can't see a step, as he is extremely short-sighted. He—"

"That *is* important," interrupted Wimsey. "You are sure he didn't take a second pair?"

"His man vouches for it that he had only two pairs, one of which was found on his dressing-table, and the other in the drawer where it is always kept."

Lord Peter whistled.

"You've got me there, Parker. Even if he'd gone out to commit suicide he'd have taken those."

"So you'd think—or the suicide would have happened the first time he started to cross the road. However, I didn't overlook the possibility. I've got particulars of all today's street accidents, and I can lay my hand on my heart and say that none of them is Sir Reuben. Besides, he took his latchkey with him, which looks as though he'd meant to come back."

"Have you seen the men he dined with?"

"I found two of them at the club. They said that he seemed in the best of health and spirits, spoke of looking forward to joining Lady Levy later on—perhaps at Christmas—and referred with great satisfaction to this morning's business transaction, in which one of them—a man called Anderson of Wyndham's—was himself concerned."

"Then up till about nine o'clock, anyhow, he had no apparent intention or expectation of disappearing."

"None—unless he was a most consummate actor. Whatever happened to change his mind must have happened either at the mysterious appointment which he kept after dinner, or while he was in bed between midnight and 5:30 a.m."

"Well, Bunter," said Lord Peter, "what do you make of it?"

"Not in my department, my lord. Except that it is odd that a gentleman who was too flurried or unwell to fold his clothes as usual should remember to clean his teeth and put his boots out. Those are two things that quite frequently get overlooked, my lord."

"If you mean anything personal, Bunter," said Lord Peter, "I can only say that I think the speech an unworthy one. It's a sweet little problem, Parker mine. Look here, I don't want to butt in, but I should dearly love to see that bedroom tomorrow. 'Tis not that I mistrust thee, dear, but I should uncommonly like to see it. Say me not nay—take another drop of brandy and a Villar Villar, but say not, say not nay!"

"Of course you can come and see it—you'll probably find lots of things I've overlooked," said the other, equably, accepting the proffered hospitality.

"Parker, acushla, you're an honour to Scotland Yard. I look at you, and Sugg appears a myth, a fable, an idiot-boy, spawned in a moonlight hour by some fantastic poet's brain. Sugg is too perfect to be possible. What does he make of the body, by the way?"

"Sugg says," replied Parker, with precision, "that the body died from a blow on the back of the neck. The doctor told him that. He says it's been dead a day or two. The doctor told him that, too. He says it's the body of a well-to-do Hebrew of about fifty. Anybody could have told him that. He says it's ridiculous to suppose it came in through the window without anybody knowing anything about it. He says it probably walked in through the front door and was murdered by the household. He's arrested the girl because she's short and frail-looking and quite unequal to downing a tall and sturdy Semite with a poker. He'd arrest Thipps, only Thipps was away in Manchester all yesterday and the day before and didn't come back till late last night—in fact, he wanted to arrest him till I reminded him that if the body had been a day or two dead, little Thipps couldn't have done him in at 10:30 last night. But he'll arrest him tomorrow as an accessory— and the old lady with the knitting, too, I shouldn't wonder."

"Well, I'm glad the little man has so much of an alibi," said Lord Peter, "though if you're only glueing your faith to cadaveric lividity, rigidity, and all the other quiddities, you must be prepared to have some sceptical beast of a prosecuting counsel walk slap-bang through the medical evidence. Remember Impey Biggs defending in that Chelsea tea-shop affair? Six bloomin' medicos contradictin' each other in the box, an' old Impey elocutin' abnormal cases from Glaister and Dixon Mann till the eyes of the jury reeled in their heads! 'Are you prepared to swear, Dr. Thingumtight, that the onset of rigor mortis indicates the hour of death without the possibility of error?' 'So far as my experience goes, in the majority of cases,' says the doctor, all stiff. 'Ah!' says Biggs, 'but this is a Court of Justice, Doctor, not a Parliamentary election. We can't get on without a minority report. The law, Dr. Thingumtight, respects the rights of the minority, alive or dead.' Some ass laughs, and old Biggs sticks his chest out and gets impressive. 'Gentlemen, this is no laughing matter. My client—an upright and honourable gentleman—is being tried for his life—for his life, gentlemen—and it is the business of the prosecution to show his guilt—if they can— without a shadow of doubt. Now, Dr. Thingumtight, I ask you again, can you solemnly swear, without the least shadow of doubt—probable, possible shadow of doubt—that this unhappy woman met her death neither sooner nor later than Thursday evening? A probable opinion? Gentlemen, we are not Jesuits, we are straightforward Englishmen. You cannot ask a British-born jury to convict any man on the authority of a probable opinion.' Hum of applause."

"Biggs's man was guilty all the same," said Parker.

"Of course he was. But he was acquitted all the same, an' what you've just said is libel." Wimsey walked over to the bookshelf and took down a volume of Medical Jurisprudence. "'Rigor mortis—can only be stated in a very general way—many factors determine the result.' Cautious brute. 'On the average, however, stiffening will have begun—neck and jaw—5 to 6 hours after death'—m'm—'in all likelihood have passed off in the bulk of cases by the end of 36 hours. Under certain circumstances, however, it may appear unusually early, or be retarded unusually long!' Helpful, ain't it, Parker? 'Brown-Séquard states . . . 3½ minutes after death . . . In certain cases not until lapse of 16 hours after death . . . present as long as 21 days thereafter.' Lord! 'Modifying factors—age—muscular state—or febrile diseases— or where temperature of environment is high'—and so on and so on—any bloomin' thing. Never mind. You can run the argument for what it's worth to Sugg. *He* won't know any better." He tossed the book away. "Come back to facts. What did *you* make of the body?"

"Well," said the detective, "not very much—I was puzzled—frankly. I should say he had been a rich man, but self-made, and that his good fortune had come to him fairly recently."

"Ah, you noticed the calluses on the hands—I thought you wouldn't miss that."

"Both his feet were badly blistered—he had been wearing tight shoes."

"Walking a long way in them, too," said Lord Peter, "to get such blisters as that. Didn't that strike you as odd, in a person evidently well off?"

"Well, I don't know. The blisters were two or three days old. He might have got stuck in the suburbs one night, perhaps—last train gone and no taxi—and had to walk home."

"Possibly."

"There were some little red marks all over his back and one leg I couldn't quite account for."

"I saw them."

"What did you make of them?"

"I'll tell you afterwards. Go on."

"He was very long-sighted—oddly long-sighted for a man in the prime of life; the glasses were like a very old man's. By the way, they had a very beautiful and remarkable chain of flat links chased with a pattern. It struck me he might be traced through it."

"I've just put an advertisement in the *Times* about it," said Lord Peter. "Go on."

"He had had the glasses some time—they had been mended twice."

"Beautiful, Parker, beautiful. Did you realize the importance of that?"

"Not specially, I'm afraid—why?"

"Never mind—go on."

"He was probably a sullen, ill-tempered man—his nails were filed down to the quick as though he habitually bit them, and his fingers were bitten as well. He smoked quantities of cigarettes without a holder. He was particular about his personal appearance."

"Did you examine the room at all? I didn't get a chance."

"I couldn't find much in the way of footprints. Sugg & Co. had tramped all over the place, to say nothing of little Thipps and the maid, but I noticed a very indefinite patch just behind the head of the bath, as though something damp might have stood there. You could hardly call it a print."

"It rained hard all last night, of course."

"Yes; did you notice that the soot on the window-sill was vaguely marked?"

"I did," said Wimsey, "and I examined it hard with this little fellow, but I could make nothing of it except that something or other had rested on the sill." He drew out his monocle and handed it to Parker.

"My word, that's a powerful lens."

"It is," said Wimsey, "and jolly useful when you want to take a good squint at somethin' and look like a bally fool all the time. Only it don't do to wear it permanently—if people see you full-face they say: 'Dear me! how weak the sight of that eye must be!' Still, it's useful."

"Sugg and I explored the ground at the back of the building," went on Parker, "but there wasn't a trace."

"That's interestin'. Did you try the roof?"

"No."

"We'll go over it tomorrow. The gutter's only a couple of feet off the top of the window. I measured it with my stick—the gentleman-scout's vade-mecum, I call it—it's marked off in inches. Uncommonly handy companion at times. There's a sword inside and a compass in the head. Got it made specially. Anything more?"

"Afraid not. Let's hear your version, Wimsey."

"Well, I think you've got most of the points. There are just one or two little contradictions. For instance, here's a man wears expensive gold-rimmed pince-nez and has had them long enough to be mended twice. Yet his teeth are not merely discoloured, but badly decayed and look as if he'd never cleaned them in his life. There are four molars missing on one side and three on the other and one front tooth broken right across. He's a man careful of his personal appearance, as witness his hair and his hands. What do you say to that?"

"Oh, these self-made men of low origin don't think much about teeth, and are terrified of dentists."

"True; but one of the molars has a broken edge so rough that it had made a sore place on the tongue. Nothing's more painful. D'you mean to tell me a man would put up with that if he could afford to get the tooth filed?"

"Well, people are queer. I've known servants endure agonies rather than step over a dentist's doormat. How did you see that, Wimsey?"

"Had a look inside; electric torch," said Lord Peter. "Handy little gadget. Looks like a matchbox. Well—I daresay it's all right, but I just draw your attention to it. Second point: Gentleman with hair smellin' of Parma violet and manicured hands and all the rest of it, never washes the inside of his ears. Full of wax. Nasty."

"You've got me there, Wimsey; I never noticed it. Still—old bad habits die hard."

"Right oh! Put it down at that. Third point: Gentleman with the manicure and the brilliantine and all the rest of it suffers from fleas."

"By Jove, you're right! Flea-bites. It never occurred to me."

"No doubt about it, old son. The marks were faint and old, but unmistakable."

"Of course, now you mention it. Still, that might happen to anybody. I loosed a whopper in the best hotel in Lincoln the week before last. I hope it bit the next occupier!"

"Oh, all these things *might* happen to anybody—separately. Fourth point: Gentleman who uses Parma violet for his hair, etc.,

etc., washes his body in strong carbolic soap—so strong that the smell hangs about twenty-four hours later."

"Carbolic to get rid of the fleas."

"I will say for you, Parker, you've an answer for everything. Fifth point: Carefully got-up gentleman, with manicured, though masticated, finger-nails, has filthy black toe-nails which look as if they hadn't been cut for years."

"All of a piece with habits as indicated."

"Yes, I know, but such habits! Now, sixth and last point: This gentleman with the intermittently gentlemanly habits arrives in the middle of a pouring wet night, and apparently through the window, when he has already been twenty-four hours dead, and lies down quietly in Mr. Thipps's bath, unseasonably dressed in a pair of pince-nez. Not a hair on his head is ruffled—the hair has been cut so recently that there are quite a number of little short hairs stuck on his neck and the sides of the bath—and he has shaved so recently that there is a line of dried soap on his cheek—"

"Wimsey!"

"Wait a minute—and *dried soap in his mouth.*"

Bunter got up and appeared suddenly at the detective's elbow, the respectful man-servant all over.

"A little more brandy, sir?" he murmured.

"Wimsey," said Parker, "you are making me feel cold all over." He emptied his glass—stared at it as though he were surprised to find it empty, set it down, got up, walked across to the bookcase, turned round, stood with his back against it and said:

"Look here, Wimsey—you've been reading detective stories; you're talking nonsense."

"No, I ain't," said Lord Peter, sleepily, "uncommon good incident for a detective story, though, what? Bunter, we'll write one, and you shall illustrate it with photographs."

"Soap in his—Rubbish!" said Parker. "It was something else—some discoloration—"

"No," said Lord Peter, "there were hairs as well. Bristly ones. He had a beard."

He took his watch from his pocket, and drew out a couple of longish, stiff hairs, which he had imprisoned between the inner and the outer case.

Parker turned them over once or twice in his fingers, looked at them close to the light, examined them with a lens, handed them to the impassible Bunter, and said:

"Do you mean to tell me, Wimsey, that any man alive would"— he laughed harshly—"shave off his beard with his mouth open, and then go and get killed with his mouth full of hairs? You're mad."

"I don't tell you so," said Wimsey. "You policemen are all alike—only one idea in your skulls. Blest if I can make out why you're ever appointed. He was shaved after he was dead. Pretty, ain't it? Uncommonly jolly little job for the barber, what? Here, sit down, man, and don't be an ass, stumpin' about the room like that. Worse things happen in war. This is only a blinkin' old shillin' shocker. But I'll tell you what, Parker, we're up against a criminal—*the* criminal—the real artist and blighter with imagination—real, artistic, finished stuff. I'm enjoyin' this, Parker."

Chapter 3

L ord Peter finished a Scarlatti sonata, and sat looking thoughtfully at his own hands. The fingers were long and muscular, with wide, flat joints and square tips. When he was playing, his rather hard grey eyes softened, and his long, indeterminate mouth hardened in compensation. At no other time had he any pretensions to good looks, and at all times he was spoilt by a long, narrow chin, and a long, receding forehead, accentuated by the brushed-back sleekness of his tow-coloured hair. Labour papers, softening down the chin, caricatured him as a typical aristocrat.

"That's a wonderful instrument," said Parker.

"It ain't so bad," said Lord Peter, "but Scarlatti wants a harpsichord. Piano's too modern—all thrills and overtones. No good for our job, Parker. Have you come to any conclusion?"

"The man in the bath," said Parker, methodically, "was *not* a well-off man careful of his personal appearance. He was a labouring man, unemployed, but who had only recently lost his employment. He had been tramping about looking for a job when he met with his end. Somebody killed him and washed him and scented him and shaved him in order to disguise him, and put him into Thipps's bath without leaving a trace. Conclusion: the murderer was a powerful man, since he killed him with a single blow on the neck, a man of cool head and masterly intellect, since he did all that ghastly business without leaving a mark, a man of wealth and refinement, since he had all the apparatus of an elegant toilet handy, and a man of bizarre, and almost perverted imagination, as is shown in the two horrible touches of putting the body in the bath and of adorning it with a pair of pince-nez."

"He is a poet of crime," said Wimsey. "By the way, your difficulty about the pince-nez is cleared up. Obviously, the pince-nez never belonged to the body."

"That only makes a fresh puzzle. One can't suppose the murderer left them in that obliging manner as a clue to his own identity."

"We can hardly suppose that; I'm afraid this man possessed what most criminals lack—a sense of humour."

"Rather macabre humour."

"True. But a man who can afford to be humorous at all in such circumstances is a terrible fellow. I wonder what he did with the body between the murder and depositing it chez Thipps. Then there are more questions. How did he get it there? And why? Was it brought in at the door, as Sugg of our heart suggests?

or through the window, as we think, on the not very adequate testimony of a smudge on the window-sill? Had the murderer accomplices? Is little Thipps really in it, or the girl? It don't do to put the notion out of court merely because Sugg inclines to it. Even idiots occasionally speak the truth accidentally. If not, why was Thipps selected for such an abominable practical joke? Has anybody got a grudge against Thipps? Who are the people in the other flats? We must find out that. Does Thipps play the piano at midnight over their heads or damage the reputation of the staircase by bringing home dubiously respectable ladies? Are there unsuccessful architects thirsting for his blood? Damn it all, Parker, there must be a motive somewhere. Can't have a crime without a motive, you know."

"A madman—" suggested Parker, doubtfully.

"With a deuced lot of method in his madness. He hasn't made a mistake—not one, unless leaving hairs in the corpse's mouth can be called a mistake. Well, anyhow, it's not Levy—you're right there. I say, old thing, neither your man nor mine has left much clue to go upon, has he? And there don't seem to be any motives knockin' about, either. And we seem to be two suits of clothes short in last night's work. Sir Reuben makes tracks without so much as a fig-leaf, and a mysterious individual turns up with a pince-nez, which is quite useless for purposes of decency. Dash it all! If only I had some good excuse for takin' up this body case officially—"

The telephone bell rang. The silent Bunter, whom the other two had almost forgotten, padded across to it.

"It's an elderly lady, my lord," he said. "I think she's deaf—I can't make her hear anything, but she's asking for your lordship."

Lord Peter seized the receiver, and yelled into it a "Hullo!" that might have cracked the vulcanite. He listened for some minutes with an incredulous smile, which gradually broadened into a grin of delight. At length he screamed: "All right! all right!" several times, and rang off.

"By Jove!" he announced, beaming, "sportin' old bird! It's

old Mrs. Thipps. Deaf as a post. Never used the 'phone before. But determined. Perfect Napoleon. The incomparable Sugg has made a discovery and arrested little Thipps. Old lady abandoned in the flat. Thipps's last shriek to her: 'Tell Lord Peter Wimsey.' Old girl undaunted. Wrestles with telephone book. Wakes up the people at the exchange. Won't take no for an answer (not bein' able to hear it), gets through, says: 'Will I do what I can?' Says she would feel safe in the hands of a real gentleman. Oh, Parker, Parker! I could kiss her, I reely could, as Thipps says. I'll write to her instead—no, hang it, Parker, we'll go round. Bunter, get your infernal machine and the magnesium. I say, we'll all go into partnership—pool the two cases and work 'em out together. You shall see my body tonight, Parker, and I'll look for your wandering Jew tomorrow. I feel so happy, I shall explode. O Sugg, Sugg, how art thou suggified! Bunter, my shoes. I say, Parker, I suppose yours are rubber-soled. Not? Tut, tut, you mustn't go out like that. We'll lend you a pair. Gloves? Here. My stick, my torch, the lampblack, the forceps, knife, pill-boxes—all complete?"

"Certainly, my lord."

"Oh, Bunter, don't look so offended. I mean no harm. I believe in you, I trust you—what money have I got? That'll do. I knew a man once, Parker, who let a world-famous poisoner slip through his fingers because the machine on the Underground took nothing but pennies. There was a queue at the booking office and the man at the barrier stopped him, and while they were arguing about accepting a five-pound-note (which was all he had) for a twopenny ride to Baker Street, the criminal had sprung into a Circle train, and was next heard of in Constantinople, disguised as an elderly Church of England clergyman touring with his niece. Are we all ready? Go!"

They stepped out, Bunter carefully switching off the lights behind them.

* * * * *

As they emerged into the gloom and gleam of Piccadilly, Wimsey stopped short with a little exclamation.

"Wait a second," he said. "I've thought of something. If Sugg's there he'll make trouble. I must short-circuit him."

He ran back, and the other two men employed the few minutes of his absence in capturing a taxi.

Inspector Sugg and a subordinate Cerberus were on guard at 59, Queen Caroline Mansions, and showed no disposition to admit unofficial inquirers. Parker, indeed, they could not easily turn away, but Lord Peter found himself confronted with a surly manner and what Lord Beaconsfield described as a masterly inactivity. It was in vain that Lord Peter pleaded that he had been retained by Mrs. Thipps on behalf of her son.

"Retained!" said Inspector Sugg, with a snort. "*She'll* be retained if she doesn't look out. Shouldn't wonder if she wasn't in it herself, only she's so deaf, she's no good for anything at all."

"Look here, Inspector," said Lord Peter, "what's the use of bein' so bally obstructive? You'd much better let me in—you know I'll get there in the end. Dash it all, it's not as if I was takin' the bread out of your children's mouths. Nobody paid me for finding Lord Attenbury's emeralds for you."

"It's my duty to keep out the public," said Inspector Sugg, morosely, "and it's going to stay out."

"I never said anything about your keeping out of the public," said Lord Peter, easily, sitting down on the staircase to thrash the matter out comfortably, "though I've no doubt pussyfoot's a good thing, on principle, if not exaggerated. The golden mean, Sugg, as Aristotle says, keeps you from bein' a golden ass. Ever been a golden ass, Sugg? I have. It would take a whole rose-garden to cure me, Sugg—

> *You are my garden of beautiful roses,*
> *My own rose, my one rose, that's you!*

"I'm not going to stay any longer talking to you," said the harassed Sugg; "it's bad enough— Hullo, drat that telephone. Here, Cawthorn, go and see what it is, if that old catamaran will let you into the room. Shutting herself up there and screaming," said the Inspector, "it's enough to make a man give up crime and take to hedging and ditching."

The constable came back:

"It's from the Yard, sir," he said, coughing apologetically; "the Chief says every facility is to be given to Lord Peter Wimsey, sir. Um!" He stood apart noncommittally, glazing his eyes.

"Five aces," said Lord Peter, cheerfully. "The Chief's a dear friend of my mother's. No go, Sugg, it's no good buckin'; you've got a full house. I'm goin' to make it a bit fuller."

He walked in with his followers.

The body had been removed a few hours previously, and when the bathroom and the whole flat had been explored by the naked eye and the camera of the competent Bunter, it became evident that the real problem of the household was old Mrs. Thipps. Her son and servant had both been removed, and it appeared that they had no friends in town, beyond a few business acquaintances of Thipps's, whose very addresses the old lady did not know. The other flats in the building were occupied respectively by a family of seven, at present departed to winter abroad, an elderly Indian colonel of ferocious manners, who lived alone with an Indian man-servant, and a highly respectable family on the third floor, whom the disturbance over their heads had outraged to the last degree. The husband, indeed, when appealed to by Lord Peter, showed a little human weakness, but Mrs. Appledore, appearing suddenly in a warm dressing-gown, extricated him from the difficulties into which he was carelessly wandering.

"I am sorry," she said, "I'm afraid we can't interfere in any way. This is a very unpleasant business, Mr.— I'm afraid I didn't catch your name, and we have always found it better not to be mixed up with the police. Of course, *if* the Thippses are innocent, and

I am sure I hope they are, it is very unfortunate for them, but I must say that the circumstances seem to me most suspicious, and to Theophilus too, and I should not like to have it said that we had assisted murderers. We might even be supposed to be accessories. Of course you are young, Mr.—"

"This is Lord Peter Wimsey, my dear," said Theophilus mildly. She was unimpressed.

"Ah, yes," she said, "I believe you are distantly related to my late cousin, the Bishop of Carisbrooke. Poor man! He was always being taken in by impostors; he died without ever learning any better. I imagine you take after him, Lord Peter."

"I doubt it," said Lord Peter. "So far as I know he is only a connection, though it's a wise child that knows its own father. I congratulate you, dear lady, on takin' after the other side of the family. You'll forgive my buttin' in upon you like this in the middle of the night, though, as you say, it's all in the family, and I'm sure I'm very much obliged to you, and for permittin' me to admire that awfully fetchin' thing you've got on. Now, don't you worry, Mr. Appledore. I'm thinkin' the best thing I can do is to trundle the old lady down to my mother and take her out of your way, otherwise you might be findin' your Christian feelin's gettin' the better of you some fine day, and there's nothin' like Christian feelin's for upsettin' a man's domestic comfort. Goodnight, sir—good-night, dear lady—it's simply rippin' of you to let me drop in like this."

"Well!" said Mrs. Appledore, as the door closed behind him.

And—

"I thank the goodness and the grace

That on my birth have smiled,"

said Lord Peter, "and taught me to be bestially impertinent when I choose. Cat!"

Two a.m. saw Lord Peter Wimsey arrive in a friend's car at the Dower House, Denver Castle, in company with a deaf and aged lady and an antique portmanteau.

* * * * *

"It's very nice to see you, dear," said the Dowager Duchess, placidly. She was a small, plump woman, with perfectly white hair and exquisite hands. In feature she was as unlike her second son as she was like him in character; her black eyes twinkled cheerfully, and her manners and movements were marked with a neat and rapid decision. She wore a charming wrap from Liberty's, and sat watching Lord Peter eat cold beef and cheese as though his arrival in such incongruous circumstances and company were the most ordinary event possible, which with him, indeed, it was.

"Have you got the old lady to bed?" asked Lord Peter.

"Oh, yes, dear. Such a striking old person, isn't she? And very courageous. She tells me she has never been in a motor-car before. But she thinks you a very nice lad, dear—that careful of her, you remind her of her own son. Poor little Mr. Thipps—whatever made your friend the inspector think he could have murdered anybody?"

"My friend the inspector—no, no more, thank you, Mother—is determined to prove that the intrusive person in Thipps's bath is Sir Reuben Levy, who disappeared mysteriously from his house last night. His line of reasoning is: We've lost a middle-aged gentleman without any clothes on in Park Lane; we've found a middle-aged gentleman without any clothes on in Battersea. Therefore they're one and the same person, Q.E.D., and put little Thipps in quod."

"You're very elliptical, dear," said the Duchess, mildly. "Why should Mr. Thipps be arrested even if they are the same?"

"Sugg must arrest somebody," said Lord Peter, "but there is one odd little bit of evidence come out which goes a long way to support Sugg's theory, only that I know it to be no go by the evidence of my own eyes. Last night at about 9:15 a young woman was strollin' up the Battersea Park Road for purposes best known to herself, when she saw a gentleman in a fur coat and top-hat saunterin' along under an umbrella, lookin' at the names of all the streets. He looked a bit out of place, so, not bein' a shy girl, you see, she walked up to him, and said: 'Good-evening.' 'Can you tell me, please,' says the mysterious stranger, 'whether this street leads into Prince of Wales Road?' She said it did, and further asked him in a jocular manner what he was doing with himself and all the rest of it, only she wasn't altogether so explicit about that part of the conversation, because she was unburdenin' her heart to Sugg, d'you see, and he's paid by a grateful country to have very pure, high-minded ideals, what? Anyway, the old boy said he couldn't attend to her just then as he had an appointment. 'I've got to go and see a man, my dear,' was how she said he put it, and he walked on up Alexandra Avenue towards Prince of Wales Road. She was starin' after him, still rather surprised, when she was joined by a friend of hers, who said: 'It's no good wasting your time with him—that's Levy—I knew him when I lived in the West End, and the girls used to call him Peagreen Incorruptible'—friend's name suppressed, owing to implications of story, but girl vouches for what was said. She thought no more about it till the milkman brought news this morning of the excitement at Queen Caroline Mansions; then she went round, though not likin' the police as a rule, and asked the man there whether the dead gentleman had a beard and glasses. Told he had glasses but no beard, she incautiously said: 'Oh, then, it isn't him,' and the man said: 'Isn't who?' and collared her. That's her story. Sugg's delighted, of course, and quodded Thipps on the strength of it."

"Dear me," said the Duchess, "I hope the poor girl won't get into trouble."

"Shouldn't think so," said Lord Peter. "Thipps is the one that's going to get it in the neck. Besides, he's done a silly thing. I got that out of Sugg, too, though he was sittin' tight on the information. Seems Thipps got into a confusion about the train he took back from Manchester. Said first he got home at 10:30. Then they pumped Gladys Horrocks, who let out he wasn't back till after 11:45. Then Thipps, bein' asked to explain the discrepancy, stammers and bungles and says, first, that he missed the train. Then Sugg makes inquiries at St. Pancras and discovers that he left a bag in the cloakroom there at ten. Thipps, again asked to explain, stammers worse an' says he walked about for a few hours—met a friend—can't say who—didn't meet a friend—can't say what he did with his time—can't explain why he didn't go back for his bag—can't say what time he *did* get in—can't explain how he got a bruise on his forehead. In fact, can't explain himself at all. Gladys Horrocks interrogated again. Says, this time, Thipps came in at 10:30. Then admits she didn't hear him come in. Can't say why she didn't hear him come in. Can't say why she said first of all that she *did* hear him. Bursts into tears. Contradicts herself. Everybody's suspicion roused. Quod 'em both."

"As you put it, dear," said the Duchess, "it all sounds very confusing, and not quite respectable. Poor little Mr. Thipps would be terribly upset by anything that wasn't respectable."

"I wonder what he did with himself," said Lord Peter thoughtfully. "I really don't think he was committing a murder. Besides, I believe the fellow has been dead a day or two, though it don't do to build too much on doctors' evidence. It's an entertainin' little problem."

"Very curious, dear. But so sad about poor Sir Reuben. I must write a few lines to Lady Levy; I used to know her quite well, you know, dear, down in Hampshire, when she was a girl. Christine Ford, she was then, and I remember so well the dreadful trouble there was about her marrying a Jew. That was before he made his money, of course, in that oil business out in America. The family wanted her to marry Julian Freke, who did so well afterwards and was connected with the family, but she fell in love with this Mr. Levy and eloped with him. He was very handsome, then, you know, dear, in a foreign-looking way, but he hadn't any means, and the Fords didn't like his religion. Of course we're all Jews nowadays, and they wouldn't have minded so much if he'd pretended to be something else, like that Mr. Simons we met at Mrs. Porchester's, who always tells everybody that he got his nose in Italy at the Renaissance, and claims to be descended somehow or other from La Bella Simonetta—so foolish, you know, dear— as if anybody believed it; and I'm sure some Jews are very good people, and personally I'd much rather they believed something, though of course it must be very inconvenient, what with not working on Saturdays and circumcising the poor little babies and everything depending on the new moon and that funny kind of meat they have with such a slang-sounding name, and never being able to have bacon for breakfast. Still, there it was, and it was much better for the girl to marry him if she was really fond of him, though I believe young Freke was really devoted to her, and they're still great friends. Not that there was ever a real engagement, only a sort of understanding with her father, but he's never married, you know, and lives all by himself in that big house next to the hospital, though he's very rich and distinguished now, and I know ever so many people have tried to get hold of him—there was Lady Mainwaring wanted him for that eldest girl of hers, though I remember saying at the time it was no use expecting a surgeon to be taken in by a figure that was all padding—they have so many opportunities of judging, you know, dear."

"Lady Levy seems to have had the knack of makin' people devoted to her," said Peter. "Look at the pea-green incorruptible Levy."

"That's quite true, dear; she was a most delightful girl, and they say her daughter is just like her. I rather lost sight of them when she married, and you know your father didn't care much about business people, but I know everybody always said they were a model couple. In fact it was a proverb that Sir Reuben was as well loved at home as he was hated abroad. I don't mean in foreign countries, you know, dear—just the proverbial way of putting things—like 'a saint abroad and a devil at home'—only the other way on, reminding one of the *Pilgrim's Progress*."

"Yes," said Peter, "I daresay the old man made one or two enemies."

"Dozens, dear—such a dreadful place, the City, isn't it? Everybody Ishmaels together—though I don't suppose Sir Reuben would like to be called that, would he? Doesn't it mean illegitimate, or not a proper Jew, anyway? I always did get confused with those Old Testament characters."

Lord Peter laughed and yawned.

"I think I'll turn in for an hour or two," he said. "I must be back in town at eight—Parker's coming to breakfast."

The Duchess looked at the clock, which marked five minutes to three.

"I'll send up your breakfast at half-past six, dear," she said. "I hope you'll find everything all right. I told them just to slip a hot-water bottle in; those linen sheets are so chilly; you can put it out if it's in your way."

Chapter 4

S o there it is, Parker," said Lord Peter, pushing his coffee-cup aside and lighting his after-breakfast pipe; "you may find it leads you to something, though it don't seem to get me any further with my bathroom problem. Did you do anything more at that after I left?"

"No; but I've been on the roof this morning."

"The deuce you have—what an energetic devil you are! I say, Parker, I think this co-operative scheme is an uncommonly good one. It's much easier to work on someone else's job than one's own—gives one that delightful feelin' of interferin' and bossin' about, combined with the glorious sensation that another fellow is takin' all one's own work off one's hands. You scratch my back and I'll scratch yours, what? Did you find anything?"

"Not very much. I looked for any footmarks of course, but naturally, with all this rain, there wasn't a sign. Of course, if this were a detective story, there'd have been a convenient shower exactly an hour before the crime and a beautiful set of marks which could only have come there between two and three in the morning, but this being real life in a London November, you might as well expect footprints in Niagara. I searched the roofs right along—and came to the jolly conclusion that any person in any blessed flat in the blessed row might have done it. All the staircases open on to the roof and the leads are quite flat; you can walk along as easy as along Shaftesbury Avenue. Still, I've got some evidence that the body did walk along there."

"What's that?"

Parker brought out his pocketbook and extracted a few shreds of material, which he laid before his friend.

"One was caught in the gutter just above Thipps's bathroom window, another in a crack of the stone parapet just over it, and the rest came from the chimney-stack behind, where they had caught in an iron stanchion. What do you make of them?"

Lord Peter scrutinized them very carefully through his lens.

"Interesting," he said, "damned interestin'. Have you developed those plates, Bunter?" he added, as that discreet assistant came in with the post.

"Yes, my lord."

"Caught anything?"

"I don't know whether to call it anything or not, my lord," said Bunter, dubiously. "I'll bring the prints in."

"Do," said Wimsey. "Hallo! here's our advertisement about the gold chain in the *Times*—very nice it looks: 'Write, 'phone or call 110, Piccadilly.' Perhaps it would have been safer to put a box number, though I always think that the franker you are with people, the more you're likely to deceive 'em; so unused is the modern world to the open hand and the guileless heart, what?"

"But you don't think the fellow who left that chain on the body is going to give himself away by coming here and inquiring about it?"

"I don't, fathead," said Lord Peter, with the easy politeness of the real aristocracy; "that's why I've tried to get hold of the jeweller who originally sold the chain. See?" He pointed to the paragraph. "It's not an old chain—hardly worn at all. Oh, thanks, Bunter. Now, see here, Parker, these are the finger-marks you noticed yesterday on the window-sash and on the far edge of the bath. I'd overlooked them; I give you full credit for the discovery, I crawl, I grovel, my name is Watson, and you need not say what you were just going to say, because I admit it all. Now we shall—Hullo, hullo, hullo!"

The three men stared at the photographs.

"The criminal," said Lord Peter, bitterly, "climbed over the roofs in the wet and not unnaturally got soot on his fingers. He arranged the body in the bath, and wiped away all traces of himself except two, which he obligingly left to show us how to do our job. We learn from a smudge on the floor that he wore india rubber boots, and from this admirable set of finger-prints on the edge of the bath that he had the usual number of fingers and wore rubber gloves. That's the kind of man he is. Take the fool away, gentlemen."

He put the prints aside, and returned to an examination of the shreds of material in his hand. Suddenly he whistled softly.

"Do you make anything of these, Parker?"

"They seemed to me to be ravellings of some coarse cotton stuff—a sheet, perhaps, or an improvised rope."

"Yes," said Lord Peter—"yes. It may be a mistake—it may be *our* mistake. I wonder. Tell me, d'you think these tiny threads are long enough and strong enough to hang a man?"

He was silent, his long eyes narrowing into slits behind the smoke of his pipe.

"What do you suggest doing this morning?" asked Parker.

"Well," said Lord Peter, "it seems to me it's about time I took a hand in your job. Let's go round to Park Lane and see what larks Sir Reuben Levy was up to in bed last night."

* * * * *

"And now, Mrs. Pemming, if you would be so kind as to give me a blanket," said Mr. Bunter, coming down into the kitchen, "and permit of me hanging a sheet across the lower part of this window, and drawing the screen across here, so—so as to shut off any reflections, if you understand me, we'll get to work."

Sir Reuben Levy's cook, with her eye upon Mr. Bunter's gentlemanly and well-tailored appearance, hastened to produce what was necessary. Her visitor placed on the table a basket, containing a water-bottle, a silver-backed hair-brush, a pair of boots, a small roll of linoleum, and the "Letters of a Self-made Merchant to His Son," bound in polished morocco. He drew an umbrella from beneath his arm and added it to the collection. He then advanced a ponderous photographic machine and set it up in the neighbourhood of the kitchen range; then, spreading a newspaper over the fair, scrubbed surface of the table, he began to roll up his sleeves and insinuate himself into a pair of surgical gloves. Sir Reuben Levy's valet, entering at the moment and finding him thus engaged, put aside the kitchenmaid, who was staring from a front-row position, and inspected the apparatus critically. Mr. Bunter nodded brightly to him, and uncorked a small bottle of grey powder.

"Odd sort of fish, your employer, isn't he?" said the valet, carelessly.

"Very singular, indeed," said Mr. Bunter. "Now, my dear," he added, ingratiatingly, to the kitchen-maid, "I wonder if you'd just pour a little of this grey powder over the edge of the bottle while I'm holding it—and the same with this boot—here, at the top—thank you, Miss—what is your name? Price? Oh, but you've got another name besides Price, haven't you? Mabel, eh? That's a name I'm uncommonly partial to—that's very nicely done, you've a steady hand, Miss Mabel—see that? That's the finger marks—three there, and two here, and smudged over in both places. No, don't you touch 'em, my dear, or you'll rub the bloom off. We'll stand 'em up here till they're ready to have their portraits taken. Now then, let's take the hair-brush next. Perhaps, Mrs. Pemming, you'd like to lift him up very carefully by the bristles."

"By the bristles, Mr. Bunter?"

"If you please, Mrs. Pemming—and lay him here. Now, Miss Mabel, another little exhibition of your skill, *if* you please. No—we'll try lamp-black this time. Perfect. Couldn't have done it better myself. Ah! there's a beautiful set. No smudges this time. That'll interest his lordship. Now the little book—no, I'll pick that up myself—with these gloves, you see, and by the edges—I'm a careful criminal, Mrs. Pemming, I don't want to leave any traces. Dust the cover all over, Miss Mabel; now this side—that's the way to do it. Lots of prints and no smudges. All according to plan. Oh, please, Mr. Graves, you mustn't touch it—it's as much as my place is worth to have it touched."

"D'you have to do much of this sort of thing?" inquired Mr. Graves, from a superior standpoint.

"Any amount," replied Mr. Bunter, with a groan calculated to appeal to Mr. Graves's heart and unlock his confidence. "If you'd kindly hold one end of this bit of linoleum, Mrs. Pemming, I'll hold up this end while Miss Mabel operates. Yes, Mr. Graves, it's a hard life, valeting by day and developing by night—morning tea at any time from 6:30 to 11, and criminal investigation at all hours. It's wonderful, the ideas these rich men with nothing to do get into their heads."

"I wonder you stand it," said Mr. Graves. "Now there's none of that here. A quiet, orderly, domestic life, Mr. Bunter, has much to be said for it. Meals at regular hours; decent, respectable families to dinner—none of your painted women—and no valeting at night, there's *much* to be said for it. I don't hold with Hebrews as a rule, Mr. Bunter, and of course I understand that you may find it to your advantage to be in a titled family, but there's less thought of that these days, and I will say, for a self-made man, no one could call Sir Reuben vulgar, and my lady at any rate is county—Miss Ford, she was, one of the Hampshire Fords, and both of them always most considerate."

"I agree with you, Mr. Graves—his lordship and me have never held with being narrow-minded—why, yes, my dear, of course it's a footmark, this is the washstand linoleum. A good Jew can be a good man, that's what I've always said. And regular hours and considerate habits have a great deal to recommend them. Very simple in his tastes, now, Sir Reuben, isn't he? for such a rich man, I mean."

"Very simple indeed," said the cook; "the meals he and her ladyship have when they're by themselves with Miss Rachel— well, there now—if it wasn't for the dinners, which is always good when there's company, I'd be wastin' my talents and education here, if you understand me, Mr. Bunter."

Mr. Bunter added the handle of the umbrella to his collection, and began to pin a sheet across the window, aided by the housemaid.

"Admirable," said he. "Now, if I might have this blanket on the table and another on a towel-horse or something of that kind by way of a background—you're very kind, Mrs. Pemming . . . Ah! I wish his lordship never wanted valeting at night. Many's the time I've sat up till three and four, and up again to call him early to go off Sherlocking at the other end of the country. And the mud he gets on his clothes and his boots!"

"I'm sure it's a shame, Mr. Bunter," said Mrs. Pemming,

warmly. "Low, I calls it. In my opinion, police-work ain't no fit occupation for a gentleman, let alone a lordship."

"Everything made so difficult, too," said Mr. Bunter nobly sacrificing his employer's character and his own feelings in a good cause; "boots chucked into a corner, clothes hung up on the floor, as they say—"

"That's often the case with these men as are born with a silver spoon in their mouths," said Mr. Graves. "Now, Sir Reuben, he's never lost his good old-fashioned habits. Clothes folded up neat, boots put out in his dressing-room, so as a man could get them in the morning, everything made easy."

"He forgot them the night before last, though."

"The clothes, not the boots. Always thoughtful for others, is Sir Reuben. Ah! I hope nothing's happened to him."

"Indeed, no, poor gentleman," chimed in the cook, "and as for what they're sayin', that he'd 'ave gone out surrepshous-like to do something he didn't ought, well, I'd never believe it of him, Mr. Bunter, not if I was to take my dying oath upon it."

"Ah!" said Mr. Bunter, adjusting his arc-lamps and connecting them with the nearest electric light, "and that's more than most of us could say of them as pays us."

* * * * *

"Five foot ten," said Lord Peter, "and not an inch more." He peered dubiously at the depression in the bed clothes, and measured it a second time with the gentleman-scout's vade-mecum. Parker entered this particular in a neat pocketbook.

"I suppose," he said, "a six-foot-two man *might* leave a five-foot-ten depression if he curled himself up."

"Have you any Scotch blood in you, Parker?" inquired his colleague, bitterly.

"Not that I know of," replied Parker. "Why?"

"Because of all the cautious, ungenerous, deliberate and cold-blooded devils I know," said Lord Peter, "you are the most cautious, ungenerous, deliberate and cold-blooded. Here am I, sweating my brains out to introduce a really sensational incident into your dull and disreputable little police investigation, and you refuse to show a single spark of enthusiasm."

"Well, it's no good jumping at conclusions."

"Jump? You don't even crawl distantly within sight of a conclusion. I believe if you caught the cat with her head in the cream-jug you'd say it was conceivable that the jug was empty when she got there."

"Well, it would be conceivable, wouldn't it?"

"Curse you," said Lord Peter. He screwed his monocle into his eye, and bent over the pillow, breathing hard and tightly through his nose. "Here, give me the tweezers," he said presently. "Good heavens, man, don't blow like that, you might be a whale." He nipped up an almost invisible object from the linen.

"What is it?" asked Parker.

"It's a hair," said Wimsey grimly, his hard eyes growing harder. "Let's go and look at Levy's hats, shall we? And you might just ring for that fellow with the churchyard name, do you mind?"

Mr. Graves, when summoned, found Lord Peter Wimsey squatting on the floor of the dressing-room before a row of hats arranged upside down before him.

"Here you are," said that nobleman cheerfully. "Now, Graves, this is a guessin' competition—a sort of three-hat trick, to mix metaphors. Here are nine hats, including three top-hats. Do you identify all these hats as belonging to Sir Reuben Levy? You do? Very good. Now I have three guesses as to which hat he wore the night he disappeared, and if I guess right, I win; if I don't, you win. See? Ready? Go. I suppose you know the answer yourself, by the way?"

"Do I understand your lordship to be asking which hat Sir Reuben wore when he went out on Monday night, your lordship?"

"No, you don't understand a bit," said Lord Peter. "I'm asking if *you* know—don't tell me, I'm going to guess."

"I do know, your lordship," said Mr. Graves, reprovingly.

"Well," said Lord Peter, "as he was dinin' at the Ritz he wore a topper. Here are three toppers. In three guesses I'd be bound to hit the right one, wouldn't I? That don't seem very sportin'. I'll take one guess. It was this one."

He indicated the hat next the window.

"Am I right, Graves—have I got the prize?"

"That *is* the hat in question, my lord," said Mr. Graves, without excitement.

"Thanks," said Lord Peter, "that's all I wanted to know. Ask Bunter to step up, would you?"

Mr. Bunter stepped up with an aggrieved air, and his usually smooth hair ruffled by the focussing cloth.

"Oh, there you are, Bunter," said Lord Peter; "look here—"

"Here I am, my lord," said Mr. Bunter, with respectful reproach, "but if you'll excuse me saying so, downstairs is where I ought to be, with all those young women about—they'll be fingering the evidence, my lord."

"I cry your mercy," said Lord Peter, "but I've quarrelled hopelessly with Mr. Parker and distracted the estimable Graves, and I want you to tell me what finger-prints you have found. I shan't be happy till I get it, so don't be harsh with me, Bunter."

"Well, my lord, your lordship understands I haven't photographed them yet, but I won't deny that their appearance is interesting, my lord. The little book off the night table, my lord, has only the marks of one set of fingers—there's a little scar on the right thumb which makes them easy recognised. The hair-brush, too, my lord, has only the same set of marks. The umbrella, the toothglass and the boots all have two sets: the hand with the scarred thumb, which I take to be Sir Reuben's, my lord, and a set of smudges superimposed upon them, if I may put it that way, my lord, which may or may not be the same hand in rubber gloves. I could tell you better when I've got the photographs made, to measure them, my lord. The linoleum in front of the washstand is very gratifying indeed, my lord, if you will excuse my mentioning it. Besides the marks of Sir Reuben's boots which your lordship pointed out, there's the print of a man's naked foot—a much smaller one, my lord, not much more than a ten-inch sock, I should say if you asked me."

Lord Peter's face became irradiated with almost a dim, religious light.

"A mistake," he breathed, "a mistake, a little one, but he can't afford it. When was the linoleum washed last, Bunter?"

"Monday morning, my lord. The housemaid did it and remembered to mention it. Only remark she's made yet, and it's to the point. The other domestics—"

His features expressed disdain.

"What did I say, Parker? Five-foot-ten and not an inch longer. And he didn't dare to use the hair-brush. Beautiful. But he *had* to risk the top-hat. Gentleman can't walk home in the rain late at night without a hat, you know, Parker. Look! what do you make of it? Two sets of finger-prints on everything but the book and the brush, two sets of feet on the linoleum, and two kinds of hair in the hat!"

He lifted the top-hat to the light, and extracted the evidence with tweezers.

"Think of it, Parker—to remember the hair-brush and forget the hat—to remember his fingers all the time, and to make that one careless step on the tell-tale linoleum. Here they are, you see, black hair and tan hair—black hair in the bowler and the panama, and black and tan in last night's topper. And then, just to make certain that we're on the right track, just one little auburn hair on the pillow, on this pillow, Parker, which isn't quite in the right place. It almost brings tears to my eyes."

"Do you mean to say—" said the detective, slowly.

"I mean to say," said Lord Peter, "that it was not Sir Reuben

Levy whom the cook saw last night on the doorstep. I say that it was another man, perhaps a couple of inches shorter, who came here in Levy's clothes and let himself in with Levy's latchkey. Oh, he was a bold, cunning devil, Parker. He had on Levy's boots, and every stitch of Levy's clothing down to the skin. He had rubber gloves on his hands which he never took off, and he did everything he could to make us think that Levy slept here last night. He took his chances, and won. He walked upstairs, he undressed, he even washed and cleaned his teeth, though he didn't use the hair-brush for fear of leaving red hairs in it. He had to guess what Levy did with boots and clothes; one guess was wrong and the other right, as it happened. The bed must look as if it had been slept in, so he gets in, and lies there in his victim's very pyjamas. Then, in the morning sometime, probably in the deadest hour between two and three, he gets up, dresses himself in his own clothes that he has brought with him in a bag, and creeps downstairs. If anybody wakes, he is lost, but he is a bold man, and he takes his chance. He knows that people do not wake as a rule—and they don't wake. He opens the street door which he left on the latch when he came in—he listens for the stray passer-by or the policeman on his beat. He slips out. He pulls the door quietly to with the latchkey. He walks briskly away in rubber-soled shoes—he's the kind of criminal who isn't complete without rubber-soled shoes. In a few minutes he is at Hyde Park Corner. After that—"

He paused, and added:

"He did all that, and unless he had nothing at stake, he had everything at stake. Either Sir Reuben Levy has been spirited away for some silly practical joke, or the man with the auburn hair has the guilt of murder upon his soul."

"Dear me!" ejaculated the detective, "you're very dramatic about it."

Lord Peter passed his hand rather wearily over his hair.

"My true friend," he murmured in a voice surcharged with

emotion, "you recall me to the nursery rhymes of my youth—
the sacred duty of flippancy:

> *There was an old man of Whitehaven*
> *Who danced a quadrille with a raven,*
> *But they said: It's absurd*
> *To encourage that bird—*
> *So they smashed that old man of Whitehaven.*

"That's the correct attitude, Parker. Here's a poor old buffer
spirited away—such a joke—and I don't believe he'd hurt a fly
himself—that makes it funnier. D'you know, Parker, I don't care
frightfully about this case after all."

"Which, this or yours?"

"Both. I say, Parker, shall we go quietly home and have lunch
and go to the Coliseum?"

"You can if you like," replied the detective; "but you forget I
do this for my bread and butter."

"And I haven't even that excuse," said Lord Peter; "well, what's
the next move? What would you do in my case?"

"I'd do some good, hard grind," said Parker. "I'd distrust
every bit of work Sugg ever did, and I'd get the family history
of every tenant of every flat in Queen Caroline Mansions. I'd
examine all their box-rooms and rooftraps, and I would inveigle
them into conversations and suddenly bring in the words 'body'
and 'pince-nez,' and see if they wriggled, like those modern
psyo-what's-his-names."

"You would, would you?" said Lord Peter with a grin. "Well,
we've exchanged cases, you know, so just you toddle off and do
it. I'm going to have a jolly time at Wyndham's."

Parker made a grimace.

"Well," he said, "I don't suppose you'd ever do it, so I'd better.
You'll never become a professional till you learn to do a little
work, Wimsey. How about lunch?"

"I'm invited out," said Lord Peter, magnificently. "I'll run around and change at the club. Can't feed with Freddy Arbuthnot in these bags; Bunter!"

"Yes, my lord."

"Pack up if you're ready, and come round and wash my face and hands for me at the club."

"Work here for another two hours, my lord. Can't do with less than thirty minutes' exposure. The current's none too strong."

"You see how I'm bullied by my own man, Parker? Well, I must bear it, I suppose. Ta-ta!"

He whistled his way downstairs.

The conscientious Mr. Parker, with a groan, settled down to a systematic search through Sir Reuben Levy's papers, with the assistance of a plate of ham sandwiches and a bottle of Bass.

* * * * *

Lord Peter and the Honourable Freddy Arbuthnot, looking together like an advertisement for gents' trouserings, strolled into the dining-room at Wyndham's.

"Haven't seen you for an age," said the Honourable Freddy. "What have you been doin' with yourself?"

"Oh, foolin' about," said Lord Peter, languidly.

"Thick or clear, sir?" inquired the waiter of the Honourable Freddy.

"Which'll you have, Wimsey?" said that gentleman, transferring the burden of selection to his guest. "They're both equally poisonous."

"Well, clear's less trouble to lick out of the spoon," said Lord Peter.

"Clear," said the Honourable Freddy.

"Consommé Polonais," agreed the waiter. "Very nice, sir."

Conversation languished until the Honourable Freddy found

a bone in the filleted sole, and sent for the head waiter to explain its presence. When this matter had been adjusted Lord Peter found energy to say:

"Sorry to hear about your gov'nor, old man."

"Yes, poor old buffer," said the Honourable Freddy; "they say he can't last long now. What? Oh! the Montrachet '08. There's nothing fit to drink in this place," he added gloomily.

After this deliberate insult to a noble vintage there was a further pause, till Lord Peter said: "How's 'Change?"

"Rotten," said the Honourable Freddy.

He helped himself gloomily to salmis of game.

"Can I do anything?" asked Lord Peter.

"Oh, no, thanks—very decent of you, but it'll pan out all right in time."

"This isn't a bad salmis," said Lord Peter.

"I've eaten worse," admitted his friend.

"What about those Argentines?" inquired Lord Peter. "Here, waiter, there's a bit of cork in my glass."

"Cork?" cried the Honourable Freddy, with something approaching animation; "you'll hear about this, waiter. It's an amazing thing a fellow who's paid to do the job can't manage to take a cork out of a bottle. What you say? Argentines? Gone all to hell. Old Levy bunkin' off like that's knocked the bottom out of the market."

"You don't say so," said Lord Peter. "What d'you suppose has happened to the old man?"

"Cursed if I know," said the Honourable Freddy; "knocked on the head by the bears, I should think."

"P'r'aps he's gone off on his own," suggested Lord Peter. "Double life, you know. Giddy old blighters, some of these City men."

"Oh, no," said the Honourable Freddy, faintly roused; "no, hang it all, Wimsey, I wouldn't care to say that. He's a decent old domestic bird, and his daughter's a charmin' girl. Besides, he's

straight enough—he'd *do* you down fast enough, but he wouldn't
let you down. Old Anderson is badly cut up about it."

"Who's Anderson?"

"Chap with property out there. He belongs here. He was goin'
to meet Levy on Tuesday. He's afraid those railway people will
get in now, and then it'll be all U. P."

"Who's runnin' the railway people over here?" inquired Lord
Peter.

"Yankee blighter, John P. Milligan. He's got an option, or says
he has. You can't trust these brutes."

"Can't Anderson hold on?"

"Anderson isn't Levy. Hasn't got the shekels. Besides, he's
only one. Levy covers the ground—he could boycott Milligan's
beastly railway if he liked. That's where he's got the pull, you
see."

"B'lieve I met the Milligan man somewhere," said Lord Peter,
thoughtfully. "Ain't he a hulking brute with black hair and a
beard?"

"You're thinkin' of somebody else," said the Honourable
Freddy. "Milligan don't stand any higher than I do, unless you
call five-feet-ten hulking—and he's bald, anyway."

Lord Peter considered this over the Gorgonzola. Then he
said: "Didn't know Levy had a charmin' daughter."

"Oh, yes," said the Honourable Freddy, with an elaborate
detachment. "Met her and Mamma last year abroad. That's how
I got to know the old man. He's been very decent. Let me into
this Argentine business on the ground floor, don't you know?"

"Well," said Lord Peter, "you might do worse. Money's money,
ain't it? And Lady Levy is quite a redeemin' point. At least, my
mother knew her people."

"Oh, *she's* all right," said the Honourable Freddy, "and the
old man's nothing to be ashamed of nowadays. He's self-made,
of course, but he don't pretend to be anything else. No side.
Toddles off to business on a 96 'bus every morning. 'Can't make

up my mind to taxis, my boy,' he says. 'I had to look at every halfpenny when I was a young man, and I can't get out of the way of it now.' Though, if he's takin' his family out, nothing's too good. Rachel—that's the girl—always laughs at the old man's little economies."

"I suppose they've sent for Lady Levy," said Lord Peter.

"I suppose so," agreed the other. "I'd better pop round and express sympathy or somethin', what? Wouldn't look well not to, d'you think? But it's deuced awkward. What am I to say?"

"I don't think it matters much what you say," said Lord Peter, helpfully. "I should ask if you can do anything."

"Thanks," said the lover, "I will. Energetic young man. Count on me. Always at your service. Ring me up any time of the day or night. That's the line to take, don't you think?"

"That's the idea," said Lord Peter.

* * * * *

Mr. John P. Milligan, the London representative of the great Milligan railroad and shipping company, was dictating code cables to his secretary in an office in Lombard Street, when a card was brought up to him, bearing the simple legend:

> LORD PETER WIMSEY
> *Marlborough Club*

Mr. Milligan was annoyed at the interruption, but, like many of his nation, if he had a weak point, it was the British aristocracy. He postponed for a few minutes the elimination from the map of a modest but promising farm, and directed that the visitor should be shown up.

"Good-afternoon," said that nobleman, ambling genially in, "it's most uncommonly good of you to let me come round wastin' your time like this. I'll try not to be too long about it, though I'm not awfully good at comin' to the point. My brother never would let me stand for the county, y'know—said I wandered on so nobody'd know what I was talkin' about."

"Pleased to meet you, Lord Wimsey," said Mr. Milligan. "Won't you take a seat?"

"Thanks," said Lord Peter, "but I'm not a peer, you know—that's my brother Denver. My name's Peter. It's a silly name, I always think, so old-world and full of homely virtue and that sort of thing, but my godfathers and godmothers in my baptism are responsible for that, I suppose, officially—which is rather hard on them, you know, as they didn't actually choose it. But we always have a Peter, after the third duke, who betrayed five kings somewhere about the Wars of the Roses, though come to think of it, it ain't anything to be proud of. Still, one has to make the best of it."

Mr. Milligan, thus ingeniously placed at that disadvantage which attends ignorance, manoeuvred for position, and offered his interrupter a Corona Corona.

"Thanks, awfully," said Lord Peter, "though you really mustn't tempt me to stay here burblin' all afternoon. By Jove, Mr. Milligan, if you offer people such comfortable chairs and cigars like these, I wonder they don't come an' live in your office." He added mentally: "I wish to goodness I could get those long-toed boots off you. How's a man to know the size of your feet? And a head like a potato. It's enough to make one swear."

"Say now, Lord Peter," said Mr. Milligan, "can I do anything for you?"

"Well, d'you know," said Lord Peter, "I'm wonderin' if you would. It's damned cheek to ask you, but fact is, it's my mother, you know. Wonderful woman, but don't realize what it means, demands on the time of a busy man like you. We don't understand hustle over here, you know, Mr. Milligan."

"Now don't you mention that," said Mr. Milligan; "I'd be surely charmed to do anything to oblige the Duchess."

He felt a momentary qualm as to whether a duke's mother were also a duchess, but breathed more freely as Lord Peter went on:

"Thanks—that's uncommonly good of you. Well, now, it's like this. My mother—most energetic, self-sacrificin' woman, don't you see, is thinkin' of gettin' up a sort of a charity bazaar down at Denver this winter, in aid of the church roof, y'know. Very sad case, Mr. Milligan—fine old antique—early English windows and decorated angel roof, and all that—all tumblin' to pieces, rain pourin' in and so on—vicar catchin' rheumatism at early service, owin' to the draught blowin' in over the altar—you know the sort of thing. They've got a man down startin' on it—little beggar called Thipps—lives with an aged mother in Battersea—vulgar little beast, but quite good on angel roofs and things, I'm told."

At this point, Lord Peter watched his interlocutor narrowly, but finding that this rigmarole produced in him no reaction more startling than polite interest tinged with faint bewilderment, he abandoned this line of investigation, and proceeded:

"I say, I beg your pardon, frightfully—I'm afraid I'm bein' beastly long-winded. Fact is, my mother is gettin' up this bazaar, and she thought it'd be an awfully interestin' side-show to have some lectures—sort of little talks, y'know—by eminent business men of all nations. 'How I Did It' kind of touch, y'know—'A Drop of Oil with a Kerosene King'—'Cash Conscience and Cocoa' and so on. It would interest people down there no end. You see, all my mother's friends will be there, and we've none of us any money—not what you'd call money, I mean—I expect our incomes wouldn't pay your telephone calls, would they?—but we like awfully to hear about the people who can make money. Gives us a sort of uplifted feelin', don't you know. Well, anyway, I mean, my mother'd be frightfully pleased and grateful to you, Mr. Milligan, if you'd come down and give us a few words as a representative American. It needn't take more than ten minutes or so, y'know, because the local people can't understand much beyond shootin' and huntin', and my mother's crowd can't keep their minds on anythin' more than ten minutes together, but we'd really appreciate it very much if you'd come and stay a day or two and just give us a little breezy word on the almighty dollar."

"Why, yes," said Mr. Milligan, "I'd like to, Lord Peter. It's kind of the Duchess to suggest it. It's a very sad thing when these fine old antiques begin to wear out. I'll come with great pleasure. And perhaps you'd be kind enough to accept a little donation to the Restoration Fund."

This unexpected development nearly brought Lord Peter up all standing. To pump, by means of an ingenious lie, a hospitable gentleman whom you are inclined to suspect of a peculiarly malicious murder, and to accept from him in the course of the proceedings a large cheque for a charitable object, has something about it unpalatable to any but the hardened Secret Service agent. Lord Peter temporized.

"That's awfully decent of you," he said. "I'm sure they'd be no end grateful. But you'd better not give it to me, you know. I might spend it, or lose it. I'm not very reliable, I'm afraid. The vicar's the right person—the Rev. Constantine Throgmorton, St. John-before-the-Latin-Gate Vicarage, Duke's Denver, if you like to send it there."

"I will," said Mr. Milligan. "Will you write it out now for a thousand pounds, Scoot, in case it slips my mind later?"

The secretary, a sandy-haired young man with a long chin and no eyebrows, silently did as he was requested. Lord Peter looked from the bald head of Mr. Milligan to the red head of the secretary, hardened his heart and tried again.

"Well, I'm no end grateful to you, Mr. Milligan, and so'll my mother be when I tell her. I'll let you know the date of the bazaar—it's not quite settled yet, and I've got to see some other business men, don't you know. I thought of askin' someone from one of the big newspaper combines to represent British advertisin' talent, what?—and a friend of mine promises me a leadin' German financier—very interestin' if there ain't too much feelin' against it down in the country, and I'll have to find somebody or other to do the Hebrew point of view. I thought of askin' Levy, y'know, only he's floated off in this inconvenient way."

"Yes," said Mr. Milligan, "that's a very curious thing, though I don't mind saying, Lord Peter, that it's a convenience to me. He had a cinch on my railroad combine, but I'd nothing against him personally, and if he turns up after I've brought off a little deal I've got on, I'll be happy to give him the right hand of welcome."

A vision passed through Lord Peter's mind of Sir Reuben kept somewhere in custody till a financial crisis was over. This was exceedingly possible, and far more agreeable than his earlier conjecture; it also agreed better with the impression he was forming of Mr. Milligan.

"Well, it's a rum go," said Lord Peter, "but I daresay he had his reasons. Much better not inquire into people's reasons, y'know, what? Specially as a police friend of mine who's connected with the case says the old johnnie dyed his hair before he went."

Out of the tail of his eye, Lord Peter saw the redheaded secretary add up five columns of figures simultaneously and jot down the answer.

"Dyed his hair, did he?" said Mr. Milligan.

"Dyed it red," said Lord Peter. The secretary looked up. "Odd thing is," continued Wimsey, "they can't lay hands on the bottle. Somethin' fishy there, don't you think, what?"

The secretary's interest seemed to have evaporated. He inserted a fresh sheet into his looseleaf ledger, and carried forward a row of digits from the preceding page.

"I daresay there's nothin' in it," said Lord Peter, rising to go. "Well, it's uncommonly good of you to be bothered with me like this, Mr. Milligan—my mother'll be no end pleased. She'll write you about the date."

"I'm charmed," said Mr. Milligan. "Very pleased to have met you."

Mr. Scoot rose silently to open the door, uncoiling as he did so a portentous length of thin leg, hitherto hidden by the desk. With a mental sigh Lord Peter estimated him at six-foot-four.

"It's a pity I can't put Scoot's head on Milligan's shoulders," said Lord Peter, emerging into the swirl of the city. "And what *will* my mother say?"

Chapter 5

Mr. Parker was a bachelor, and occupied a Georgian but inconvenient flat at No. 12A Great Ormond Street, for which he paid a pound a week. His exertions in the cause of civilization were rewarded, not by the gift of diamond rings from empresses or munificent cheques from grateful Prime Ministers, but by a modest, though sufficient, salary, drawn from the pockets of the British taxpayer. He awoke, after a long day of arduous and inconclusive labour, to the smell of burnt porridge. Through his bedroom window, hygienically open top and bottom, a raw fog was rolling slowly in, and the sight of a pair of winter pants, flung hastily over a chair the previous night, fretted him with a sense of the sordid absurdity of the human form. The telephone bell rang, and he crawled wretchedly out of bed and into the sitting-room, where Mrs. Munns, who did for him by the day, was laying the table, sneezing as she went.

Mr. Bunter was speaking.

"His lordship says he'd be very glad, sir, if you could make it convenient to step round to breakfast."

If the odour of kidneys and bacon had been wafted along the wire, Mr. Parker could not have experienced a more vivid sense of consolation.

"Tell his lordship I'll be with him in half an hour," he said, thankfully, and plunging into the bathroom, which was also the kitchen, he informed Mrs. Munns, who was just making tea from a kettle which had gone off the boil, that he should be out to breakfast.

"You can take the porridge home for the family," he added, viciously, and flung off his dressing-gown with such determination that Mrs. Munns could only scuttle away with a snort.

A 19 'bus deposited him in Piccadilly only fifteen minutes later than his rather sanguine impulse had prompted him to suggest, and Mr. Bunter served him with glorious food, incomparable coffee, and the *Daily Mail* before a blazing fire of wood and coal. A distant voice singing the "et iterum venturus est" from Bach's Mass in B minor proclaimed that for the owner of the flat cleanliness and godliness met at least once a day, and presently Lord Peter roamed in, moist and verbena-scented, in a bathrobe cheerfully patterned with unnaturally variegated peacocks.

"Mornin', old dear," said that gentleman. "Beast of a day, ain't it? Very good of you to trundle out in it, but I had a letter I wanted you to see, and I hadn't the energy to come round to your place. Bunter and I've been makin' a night of it."

"What's the letter?" asked Parker.

"Never talk business with your mouth full," said Lord Peter, reprovingly; "have some Oxford marmalade—and then I'll show you my Dante; they brought it round last night. What ought I to read this morning, Bunter?"

"Lord Erith's collection is going to be sold, my lord. There is a column about it in the *Morning Post*. I think your lordship should look at this review of Sir Julian Freke's new book on 'The Physiological Bases of the Conscience' in the *Times Literary Supplement*. Then there is a very singular little burglary in the *Chronicle*, my lord, and an attack on titled families in the *Herald*—rather ill-written, if I may say so, but not without unconscious humour which your lordship will appreciate."

"All right, give me that and the burglary," said his lordship.

"I have looked over the other papers," pursued Mr. Bunter, indicating a formidable pile, "and marked your lordship's after-breakfast reading."

"Oh, pray don't allude to it," said Lord Peter; "you take my appetite away."

There was silence, but for the crunching of toast and the crackling of paper.

"I see they adjourned the inquest," said Parker presently.

"Nothing else to do," said Lord Peter; "but Lady Levy arrived last night, and will have to go and fail to identify the body this morning for Sugg's benefit."

"Time, too," said Mr. Parker shortly.

Silence fell again.

"I don't think much of your burglary, Bunter," said Lord Peter. "Competent, of course, but no imagination. I want imagination in a criminal. Where's the *Morning Post*?"

After a further silence, Lord Peter said: "You might send for the catalogue, Bunter, that Apollonios Rhodios* might be worth looking at. No, I'm damned if I'm going to stodge through that review, but you can stick the book on the library list if you like. His book on crime was entertainin' enough as far as it went, but the fellow's got a bee in his bonnet. Thinks God's a secretion of the liver—all right once in a way, but there's no need to keep on about it. There's nothing you can't prove if your outlook is only sufficiently limited. Look at Sugg."

"I beg your pardon," said Parker; "I wasn't attending. Argentines are steadying a little, I see."

"Milligan," said Lord Peter.

"Oil's in a bad way. Levy's made a difference there. That funny little boom in Peruvians that came on just before he disappeared has died away again. I wonder if he was concerned in it. D'you know at all?"

---

* Apollonios Rhodios. Lorenzobodi Alopa. Firenze. 1496. (4to.) The excitement attendant on the solution of the Battersea Mystery did not prevent Lord Peter from securing this rare work before his departure for Corsica.

"I'll find out," said Lord Peter. "What was it?"

"Oh, an absolutely dud enterprise that hadn't been heard of for years. It suddenly took a little lease of life last week. I happened to notice it because my mother got let in for a couple of hundred shares a long time ago. It never paid a dividend. Now it's petered out again."

Wimsey pushed his plate aside and lit a pipe.

"Having finished, I don't mind doing some work," he said. "How did you get on yesterday?"

"I didn't," replied Parker. "I sleuthed up and down those flats in my own bodily shape and two different disguises. I was a gas-meter man and a collector for a Home for Lost Doggies, and I didn't get a thing to go on, except a servant in the top flat at the Battersea Bridge Road end of the row who said she thought she heard a bump on the roof one night. Asked which night, she couldn't rightly say. Asked if it was Monday night, she thought it very likely. Asked if it mightn't have been in that high wind on Saturday night that blew my chimney-pot off, she couldn't say but what it might have been. Asked if she was sure it was on the roof and not inside the flat, said to be sure they did find a picture tumbled down next morning. Very suggestive girl. I saw your friends, Mr. and Mrs. Appledore, who received me coldly, but could make no definite complaint about Thipps except that his mother dropped her h's, and that he once called on them uninvited, armed with a pamphlet about anti-vivisection. The Indian Colonel on the first floor was loud, but unexpectedly friendly. He gave me Indian curry for supper and some very good whisky, but he's a sort of hermit, and all *he* could tell me was that he couldn't stand Mrs. Appledore."

"Did you get nothing at the house?"

"Only Levy's private diary. I brought it away with me. Here it is. It doesn't tell one much, though. It's full of entries like: 'Tom and Annie to dinner'; and 'My dear wife's birthday; gave her an old opal ring'; 'Mr. Arbuthnot dropped in to tea; he wants to marry Rachel, but I should like someone steadier for my treasure.' Still, I thought it would show who came to the house and so on. He evidently wrote it up at night. There's no entry for Monday."

"I expect it'll be useful," said Lord Peter, turning over the pages. "Poor old buffer. I say, I'm not so certain now he was done away with."

He detailed to Mr. Parker his day's work.

"Arbuthnot?" said Parker. "Is that the Arbuthnot of the diary?"

"I suppose so. I hunted him up because I knew he was fond of fooling round the Stock Exchange. As for Milligan, he *looks* all right, but I believe he's pretty ruthless in business and you never can tell. Then there's the red-haired secretary—lightnin' calculator man with a face like a fish, keeps on sayin' nuthin'— got the Tarbaby in his family tree, I should think. Milligan's got a jolly good motive for, at any rate, suspendin' Levy for a few days. Then there's the new man."

"What new man?"

"Ah, that's the letter I mentioned to you. Where did I put it? Here we are. Good parchment paper, printed address of solicitor's office in Salisbury, and postmark to correspond. Very precisely written with a fine nib by an elderly business man of old-fashioned habits."

Parker took the letter and read:

CRIMPLESHAM AND WICKS,
Solicitors,
MILFORD HILL, SALISBURY,
17 November, 192—.

SIR,
With reference to your advertisement today in the personal column of *The Times*, I am disposed to

believe that the eyeglasses and chain in question may
be those I lost on the L. B. & S. C. Electric Railway
while visiting London last Monday. I left Victoria
by the 5:45 train, and did not notice my loss till I
arrived at Balham. This indication and the optician's
specification of the glasses, which I enclose, should
suffice at once as an identification and a guarantee of
my bona fides.

If the glasses should prove to be mine, I should
be greatly obliged to you if you would kindly forward
them to me by registered post, as the chain was a
present from my daughter, and is one of my dearest
possessions.

Thanking you in advance for this kindness, and
regretting the trouble to which I shall be putting you,

I am,

Yours very truly,

THOS. CRIMPLESHAM

Lord Peter Wimsey,
110, Piccadilly, W.
(Encl.)

"Dear me," said Parker, "this is what you might call
unexpected."

"Either it is some extraordinary misunderstanding," said Lord
Peter, "or Mr. Crimplesham is a very bold and cunning villain.
Or possibly, of course, they are the wrong glasses. We may as
well get a ruling on that point at once. I suppose the glasses are
at the Yard. I wish you'd just ring 'em up and ask 'em to send
round an optician's description of them at once—and you might
ask at the same time whether it's a very common prescription."

"Right you are," said Parker, and took the receiver off its hook.

"And now," said his friend, when the message was delivered,
"just come into the library for a minute."

On the library table, Lord Peter had spread out a series of bromide prints, some dry, some damp, and some but half-washed.

"These little ones are the originals of the photos we've been taking," said Lord Peter, "and these big ones are enlargements all made to precisely the same scale. This one here is the footmark on the linoleum; we'll put that by itself at present. Now these finger-prints can be divided into five lots. I've numbered 'em on the prints—see?—and made a list:

"A. The finger-prints of Levy himself, off his little bedside book and his hair-brush—this and this—you can't mistake the little scar on the thumb.

"B. The smudges made by the gloved fingers of the man who slept in Levy's room on Monday night. They show clearly on the water-bottle and on the boots—superimposed on Levy's. They are very distinct on the boots—surprisingly so for gloved hands, and I deduce that the gloves were rubber ones and had recently been in water.

"Here's another interestin' point. Levy walked in the rain on Monday night, as we know, and these dark marks are mud-splashes. You see they lie *over* Levy's finger-prints in every case. Now see: on this left boot we find the stranger's thumb-mark *over* the mud on the leather above the heel. That's a funny place to find a thumb-mark on a boot, isn't it? That is, if Levy took off his own boots. But it's the place where you'd expect to see it if somebody forcibly removed his boots for him. Again, most of the stranger's finger-marks come *over* the mud-marks, but here is one splash of mud which comes on top of them again. Which makes me infer that the stranger came back to Park Lane, wearing Levy's boots, in a cab, carriage or car, but that at some point or other he walked a little way—just enough to tread in a puddle and get a splash on the boots. What do you say?"

"Very pretty," said Parker. "A bit intricate, though, and the marks are not all that I could wish a finger-print to be."

"Well, I won't lay too much stress on it. But it fits in with our previous ideas. Now let's turn to:

"C. The prints obligingly left by my own particular villain on the further edge of Thipps's bath, where you spotted them, and I ought to be scourged for not having spotted them. The left hand, you notice, the base of the palm and the fingers, but not the tips, looking as though he had steadied himself on the edge of the bath while leaning down to adjust something at the bottom, the pince-nez perhaps. Gloved, you see, but showing no ridge or seam of any kind—I say rubber, you say rubber. That's that. Now see here:

"D and E come off a visiting-card of mine. There's this thing at the corner, marked F, but that you can disregard; in the original document it's a sticky mark left by the thumb of the youth who took it from me, after first removing a piece of chewing-gum from his teeth with his finger to tell me that Mr. Milligan might or might not be disengaged. D and E are the thumb-marks of Mr. Milligan and his red-haired secretary. I'm not clear which is which, but I saw the youth with the chewing-gum hand the card to the secretary, and when I got into the inner shrine I saw John P. Milligan standing with it in his hand, so it's one or the other, and for the moment it's immaterial to our purpose which is which. I boned the card from the table when I left.

"Well, now, Parker, here's what's been keeping Bunter and me up till the small hours. I've measured and measured every way backwards and forwards till my head's spinnin', and I've stared till I'm nearly blind, but I'm hanged if I can make my mind up. Question 1. Is C identical with B? Question 2. Is D or E identical with B? There's nothing to go on but the size and shape, of course, and the marks are so faint—what do you think?"

Parker shook his head doubtfully.

"I think E might almost be put out of the question," he said; "it seems such an excessively long and narrow thumb. But I think there is a decided resemblance between the span of B on the water-bottle and C on the bath. And I don't see any reason why D shouldn't be the same as B, only there's so little to judge from."

"Your untutored judgment and my measurements have brought us both to the same conclusion—if you can call it a conclusion," said Lord Peter, bitterly.

"Another thing," said Parker. "Why on earth should we try to connect B with C? The fact that you and I happen to be friends doesn't make it necessary to conclude that the two cases we happen to be interested in have any organic connection with one another. Why should they? The only person who thinks they have is Sugg, and he's nothing to go by. It would be different if there were any truth in the suggestion that the man in the bath was Levy, but we know for a certainty he wasn't. It's ridiculous to suppose that the same man was employed in committing two totally distinct crimes on the same night, one in Battersea and the other in Park Lane."

"I know," said Wimsey, "though of course we mustn't forget that Levy *was* in Battersea at the time, and now we know he didn't return home at twelve as was supposed, we've no reason to think he ever left Battersea at all."

"True. But there are other places in Battersea besides Thipps's bathroom. And he *wasn't* in Thipps's bathroom. In fact, come to think of it, that's the one place in the universe where we know definitely that he wasn't. So what's Thipps's bath got to do with it?"

"I don't know," said Lord Peter. "Well, perhaps we shall get something better to go on today."

He leaned back in his chair and smoked thoughtfully for some time over the papers which Bunter had marked for him.

"They've got you out in the limelight," he said. "Thank Heaven, Sugg hates me too much to give me any publicity. What a dull Agony Column! 'Darling Pipsey—Come back soon to your distracted Popsey'—and the usual young man in need of financial assistance, and the usual injunction to 'Remember thy

Creator in the days of thy youth.' Hullo! there's the bell. Oh, it's our answer from Scotland Yard."

The note from Scotland Yard enclosed an optician's specification identical with that sent by Mr. Crimplesham, and added that it was an unusual one, owing to the peculiar strength of the lenses and the marked difference between the sight of the two eyes.

"That's good enough," said Parker.

"Yes," said Wimsey. "Then Possibility No. 3 is knocked on the head. There remain Possibility No. 1: Accident or Misunderstanding, and No. 2: Deliberate Villainy, of a remarkably bold and calculating kind—of a kind, in fact, characteristic of the author or authors of our two problems. Following the methods inculcated at that University of which I have the honour to be a member, we will now examine severally the various suggestions afforded by Possibility No. 2. This Possibility may be again subdivided into two or more Hypotheses. On Hypothesis 1 (strongly advocated by my distinguished colleague Professor Snupshed), the criminal, whom we may designate as X, is not identical with Crimplesham, but is using the name of Crimplesham as his shield, or aegis. This hypothesis may be further subdivided into two alternatives. Alternative A: Crimplesham is an innocent and unconscious accomplice, and X is in his employment. X writes in Crimplesham's name on Crimplesham's office-paper and obtains that the object in question, i.e., the eyeglasses, be despatched to Crimplesham's address. He is in a position to intercept the parcel before it reaches Crimplesham. The presumption is that X is Crimplesham's charwoman, office-boy, clerk, secretary or porter. This offers a wide field of investigation. The method of inquiry will be to interview Crimplesham and discover whether he sent the letter, and if not, who has access to his correspondence. Alternative B: Crimplesham is under X's influence or in his power, and has been induced to write the letter by (*a*) bribery, (*b*) misrepresentation or (*c*) threats. X may in that case be a persuasive relation or friend, or else a creditor, blackmailer or assassin; Crimplesham, on the other hand, is obviously venal or a fool. The method of inquiry in this case, I would tentatively suggest, is again to interview Crimplesham, put the facts of the case strongly before him, and assure him in the most intimidating terms that he is liable to a prolonged term of penal servitude as an accessory after the fact in the crime of murder— Ah-hem! Trusting, gentlemen, that you have followed me thus far, we will pass to the consideration of Hypothesis No. 2, to which I personally incline, and according to which X is identical with Crimplesham.

"In this case, Crimplesham, who is, in the words of an English classic, a man of infinite resource and sagacity, correctly deduces that, of all people, the last whom we shall expect to find answering our advertisement is the criminal himself. Accordingly, he plays a bold game of bluff. He invents an occasion on which the glasses may very easily have been lost or stolen, and applies for them. If confronted, nobody will be more astonished than he to learn where they were found. He will produce witnesses to prove that he left Victoria at 5:45 and emerged from the train at Balham at the scheduled time, and sat up all Monday night playing chess with a respectable gentleman well known in Balham. In this case, the method of inquiry will be to pump the respectable gentleman in Balham, and if he should happen to be a single gentleman with a deaf housekeeper, it may be no easy matter to impugn the alibi, since, outside detective romances, few ticket-collectors and 'bus-conductors keep an exact remembrance of all the passengers passing between Balham and London on any and every evening of the week.

"Finally, gentlemen, I will frankly point out the weak point of all these hypotheses, namely: that none of them offers any explanation as to why the incriminating article was left so conspicuously on the body in the first instance."

Mr. Parker had listened with commendable patience to this academic exposition.

"Might not X," he suggested, "be an enemy of Crimplesham's, who designed to throw suspicion upon him?"

"He might. In that case he should be easy to discover, since he obviously lives in close proximity to Crimplesham and his glasses, and Crimplesham in fear of his life will then be a valuable ally for the prosecution."

"How about the first possibility of all, misunderstanding or accident?"

"Well! Well, for purposes of discussion, nothing, because it really doesn't afford any data for discussion."

"In any case," said Parker, "the obvious course appears to be to go to Salisbury."

"That seems indicated," said Lord Peter.

"Very well," said the detective, "is it to be you or me or both of us?"

"It is to be me," said Lord Peter, "and that for two reasons. First, because, if (by Possibility No. 2, Hypothesis 1, Alternative A) Crimplesham is an innocent catspaw, the person who put in the advertisement is the proper person to hand over the property. Secondly, because, if we are to adopt Hypothesis 2, we must not overlook the sinister possibility that Crimplesham-X is laying a careful trap to rid himself of the person who so unwarily advertised in the daily press his interest in the solution of the Battersea Park mystery."

"That appears to me to be an argument for our both going," objected the detective.

"Far from it," said Lord Peter. "Why play into the hands of Crimplesham-X by delivering over to him the only two men in London with the evidence, such as it is, and shall I say the wits, to connect him with the Battersea body?"

"But if we told the Yard where we were going, and we both got nobbled," said Mr. Parker, "it would afford strong presumptive evidence of Crimplesham's guilt, and anyhow, if he didn't get hanged for murdering the man in the bath he'd at least get hanged for murdering us."

"Well," said Lord Peter, "if he only murdered me you could still hang him—what's the good of wasting a sound, marriageable young male like yourself? Besides, how about old Levy? If you're incapacitated, do you think anybody else is going to find him?"

"But we could frighten Crimplesham by threatening him with the Yard."

"Well, dash it all, if it comes to that, I can frighten him by threatening him with *you*, which, seeing you hold what evidence there is, is much more to the point. And, then, suppose it's a wild-goose chase after all, you'll have wasted time when you might have been getting on with the case. There are several things that need doing."

"Well," said Parker, silenced but reluctant, "why can't I go, in that case?"

"Bosh!" said Lord Peter. "I am retained (by old Mrs. Thipps, for whom I entertain the greatest respect) to deal with this case, and it's only by courtesy I allow you to have anything to do with it."

Mr. Parker groaned.

"Will you at least take Bunter?" he said.

"In deference to your feelings," replied Lord Peter, "I will take Bunter, though he could be far more usefully employed taking photographs or overhauling my wardrobe. When is there a good train to Salisbury, Bunter?"

"There is an excellent train at 10:50, my lord."

"Kindly make arrangements to catch it," said Lord Peter, throwing off his bath-robe and trailing away with it into his bedroom. "And, Parker—if you have nothing else to do you might get hold of Levy's secretary and look into that little matter of the Peruvian oil."

* * * * *

Lord Peter took with him, for light reading in the train, Sir Reuben Levy's diary. It was a simple, and in the light of recent facts, rather a pathetic document. The terrible fighter of the Stock Exchange, who could with one nod set the surly bear dancing, or bring the savage bull to feed out of his hand, whose breath devastated whole districts with famine or swept financial potentates from their seats, was revealed in private life as kindly, domestic, innocently proud of himself and his belongings, confiding, generous and a little dull. His own small economies were duly chronicled side by side with extravagant presents to his wife and daughter. Small incidents of household routine appeared, such as: "Man came to mend the conservatory roof," or "The new butler (Simpson) has arrived, recommended by the Goldbergs. I think he will be satisfactory." All visitors and entertainments were duly entered, from a very magnificent lunch to Lord Dewsbury, the Minister for Foreign Affairs, and Dr. Jabez K. Wort, the American plenipotentiary, through a series of diplomatic dinners to eminent financiers, down to intimate family gatherings of persons designated by Christian names or nicknames. About May there came a mention of Lady Levy's nerves, and further reference was made to the subject in subsequent months. In September it was stated that "Freke came to see my dear wife and advised complete rest and change of scene. She thinks of going abroad with Rachel." The name of the famous nerve-specialist occurred as a diner or luncher about once a month, and it came into Lord Peter's mind that Freke would be a good person to consult about Levy himself. "People sometimes tell things to the doctor," he murmured to himself. "And, by Jove! if Levy was simply going round to see Freke on Monday night, that rather disposes of the Battersea incident, doesn't it?" He made a note to look up Sir Julian and turned on further. On September 18th, Lady Levy and her daughter had left for the south of France. Then suddenly, under the date October 5th, Lord Peter found what he was looking for: "Goldberg, Skriner and Milligan to dinner."

There was the evidence that Milligan had been in that house. There had been a formal entertainment—a meeting as of two duellists shaking hands before the fight. Skriner was a well-known picture-dealer; Lord Peter imagined an after-dinner excursion upstairs to see the two Corots in the drawing-room, and the portrait of the oldest Levy girl, who had died at the age of sixteen. It was by Augustus John, and hung in the bedroom. The name of the red-haired secretary was nowhere mentioned, unless the initial S., occurring in another entry, referred to him. Throughout September and October, Anderson (of Wyndham's) had been a frequent visitor.

Lord Peter shook his head over the diary, and turned to the consideration of the Battersea Park mystery. Whereas in the Levy affair it was easy enough to supply a motive for the crime, if crime it were, and the difficulty was to discover the method of its carrying out and the whereabouts of the victim, in the other case the chief obstacle to inquiry was the entire absence of any imaginable motive. It was odd that, although the papers had carried news of the affair from one end of the country to the other and a description of the body had been sent to every police station in the country, nobody had as yet come forward to identify the mysterious occupant of Mr. Thipps's bath. It was true that the description, which mentioned the clean-shaven chin, elegantly cut hair and the pince-nez, was rather misleading, but on the other hand, the police had managed to discover the number of molars missing, and the height, complexion and other data were correctly enough stated, as also the date at which death had presumably occurred. It seemed, however, as though the man had melted out of society without leaving a gap or so much as a ripple. Assigning a motive for the murder of a person without relations or antecedents or even clothes is like trying to visualize the fourth dimension—admirable exercise for the imagination, but arduous and inconclusive. Even if the day's interview should disclose black spots in the past or present of Mr. Crimplesham, how were they to be brought into connection with a person apparently without a past, and whose present was confined to the narrow limits of a bath and a police mortuary?

"Bunter," said Lord Peter, "I beg that in the future you will restrain me from starting two hares at once. These cases are gettin' to be a strain on my constitution. One hare has nowhere to run from, and the other has nowhere to run to. It's a kind of mental D.T., Bunter. When this is over I shall turn pussyfoot, forswear the police news, and take to an emollient diet of the works of the late Charles Garvice."

* * * * *

It was its comparative proximity to Milford Hill that induced Lord Peter to lunch at the Minster Hotel rather than at the White Hart or some other more picturesquely situated hostel. It was not a lunch calculated to cheer his mind; as in all Cathedral cities, the atmosphere of the Close pervades every nook and corner of Salisbury, and no food in that city but seems faintly flavoured with prayer-books. As he sat sadly consuming that impassive pale substance known to the English as "cheese" unqualified (for there are cheeses which go openly by their names, as Stilton, Camembert, Gruyère, Wensleydale or Gorgonzola, but "cheese" is cheese and everywhere the same), he inquired of the waiter the whereabouts of Mr. Crimplesham's office.

The waiter directed him to a house rather further up the street on the opposite side, adding: "But anybody'll tell you, sir; Mr. Crimplesham's very well known hereabouts."

"He's a good solicitor, I suppose?" said Lord Peter.

"Oh, yes, sir," said the waiter, "you couldn't do better than trust to Mr. Crimplesham, sir. There's folk say he's old-fashioned, but I'd rather have my little bits of business done by Mr. Crimplesham than by one of these fly-away young men. Not but what Mr. Crimplesham'll be retiring soon, sir, I don't doubt, for he must be close on eighty, sir, if he's a day, but then there's young Mr. Wicks to carry on the business, and he's a very nice, steady-like young gentleman."

"Is Mr. Crimplesham really as old as that?" said Lord Peter. "Dear me! He must be very active for his years. A friend of mine was doing business with him in town last week."

"Wonderful active, sir," agreed the waiter, "and with his game leg, too, you'd be surprised. But there, sir, I often think when a man's once past a certain age, the older he grows the tougher he gets, and women the same or more so."

"Very likely," said Lord Peter, calling up and dismissing the mental picture of a gentleman of eighty with a game leg carrying a dead body over the roof of a Battersea flat at midnight. "'He's tough, sir, tough, is old Joey Bagstock, tough and devilish sly,'" he added, thoughtlessly.

"Indeed, sir?" said the waiter. "I couldn't say, I'm sure."

"I beg your pardon," said Lord Peter; "I was quoting poetry. Very silly of me. I got the habit at my mother's knee and I can't break myself of it."

"No, sir," said the waiter, pocketing a liberal tip. "Thank you very much, sir. You'll find the house easy. Just afore you come to Penny-farthing Street, sir, about two turnings off, on the right-hand side opposite."

"Afraid that disposes of Crimplesham-X," said Lord Peter. "I'm rather sorry; he was a fine sinister figure as I had pictured him. Still, his may yet be the brain behind the hands—the aged spider sitting invisible in the centre of the vibrating web, you know, Bunter."

"Yes, my lord," said Bunter. They were walking up the street together.

"There is the office over the way," pursued Lord Peter. "I

think, Bunter, you might step into this little shop and purchase a sporting paper, and if I do not emerge from the villain's lair— say within three-quarters of an hour, you may take such steps as your perspicuity may suggest."

Mr. Bunter turned into the shop as desired, and Lord Peter walked across and rang the lawyer's bell with decision.

"The truth, the whole truth and nothing but the truth is my long suit here, I fancy," he murmured, and when the door was opened by a clerk he delivered over his card with an unflinching air.

He was ushered immediately into a confidential-looking office, obviously furnished in the early years of Queen Victoria's reign, and never altered since. A lean, frail-looking old gentleman rose briskly from his chair as he entered and limped forward to meet him.

"My dear sir," exclaimed the lawyer, "how extremely good of you to come in person! Indeed, I am ashamed to have given you so much trouble. I trust you were passing this way, and that my glasses have not put you to any great inconvenience. Pray take a seat, Lord Peter." He peered gratefully at the young man over a pince-nez obviously the fellow of that now adorning a dossier in Scotland Yard.

Lord Peter sat down. The lawyer sat down. Lord Peter picked up a glass paper-weight from the desk and weighed it thoughtfully in his hand. Subconsciously he noted what an admirable set of finger-prints he was leaving upon it. He replaced it with precision on the exact centre of a pile of letters.

"It's quite all right," said Lord Peter. "I was here on business. Very happy to be of service to you. Very awkward to lose one's glasses, Mr. Crimplesham."

"Yes," said the lawyer, "I assure you I feel quite lost without them. I have this pair, but they do not fit my nose so well— besides, that chain has a great sentimental value for me. I was terribly distressed on arriving at Balham to find that I had lost them. I made inquiries of the railway, but to no purpose. I feared they had been stolen. There were such crowds at Victoria, and the carriage was packed with people all the way to Balham. Did you come across them in the train?"

"Well, no," said Lord Peter, "I found them in rather an unexpected place. Do you mind telling me if you recognized any of your fellow-travellers on that occasion?"

The lawyer stared at him.

"Not a soul," he answered. "Why do you ask?"

"Well," said Lord Peter, "I thought perhaps the—the person with whom I found them might have taken them for a joke."

The lawyer looked puzzled.

"Did the person claim to be an acquaintance of mine?" he inquired. "I know practically nobody in London, except the friend with whom I was staying in Balham, Dr. Philpots, and I should be very greatly surprised at his practising a jest upon me. He knew very well how distressed I was at the loss of the glasses. My business was to attend a meeting of shareholders in Medlicott's Bank, but the other gentlemen present were all personally unknown to me, and I cannot think that any of them would take so great a liberty. In any case," he added, "as the glasses are here, I will not inquire too closely into the manner of their restoration. I am deeply obliged to you for your trouble."

Lord Peter hesitated.

"Pray forgive my seeming inquisitiveness," he said, "but I must ask you another question. It sounds rather melodramatic, I'm afraid, but it's this. Are you aware that you have any enemy—anyone, I mean, who would profit by your—er—-decease or disgrace?"

Mr. Crimplesham sat frozen into stony surprise and disapproval.

"May I ask the meaning of this extraordinary question?" he inquired stiffly.

"Well," said Lord Peter, "the circumstances are a little unusual. You may recollect that my advertisement was addressed to the jeweller who sold the chain."

"That surprised me at the time," said Mr. Crimplesham, "but I begin to think your advertisement and your behaviour are all of a piece."

"They are," said Lord Peter. "As a matter of fact I did not expect the owner of the glasses to answer my advertisement. Mr. Crimplesham, you have no doubt read what the papers have to say about the Battersea Park mystery. Your glasses are the pair that was found on the body, and they are now in the possession of the police at Scotland Yard, as you may see by this." He placed the specification of the glasses and the official note before Crimplesham.

"Good God!" exclaimed the lawyer. He glanced at the paper, and then looked narrowly at Lord Peter.

"Are you yourself connected with the police?" he inquired.

"Not officially," said Lord Peter. "I am investigating the matter privately, in the interests of one of the parties."

Mr. Crimplesham rose to his feet.

"My good man," he said, "this is a very impudent attempt, but blackmail is an indictable offence, and I advise you to leave my office before you commit yourself." He rang the bell.

"I was afraid you'd take it like that," said Lord Peter. "It looks as though this ought to have been my friend Detective Parker's job, after all." He laid Parker's card on the table beside the specification, and added: "If you should wish to see me again, Mr. Crimplesham, before tomorrow morning, you will find me at the Minster Hotel."

Mr. Crimplesham disdained to reply further than to direct the clerk who entered to "show this person out."

* * * * *

In the entrance Lord Peter brushed against a tall young man who was just coming in, and who stared at him with surprised recognition. His face, however, aroused no memories in Lord Peter's mind, and that baffled nobleman, calling out Bunter from the newspaper shop, departed to his hotel to get a trunk-call through to Parker.

* * * * *

Meanwhile, in the office, the meditations of the indignant Mr. Crimplesham were interrupted by the entrance of his junior partner.

"I say," said the latter gentleman, "has somebody done something really wicked at last? Whatever brings such a distinguished amateur of crime on our sober doorstep?"

"I have been the victim of a vulgar attempt at blackmail," said the lawyer; "an individual passing himself off as Lord Peter Wimsey—"

"But that *is* Lord Peter Wimsey," said Mr. Wicks, "there's no mistaking him. I saw him give evidence in the Attenbury emerald case. He's a big little pot in his way, you know, and goes fishing with the head of Scotland Yard."

"Oh, dear," said Mr. Crimplesham.

* * * * *

Fate arranged that the nerves of Mr. Crimplesham should be tried that afternoon. When, escorted by Mr. Wicks, he arrived at the Minster Hotel, he was informed by the porter that Lord Peter Wimsey had strolled out, mentioning that he thought of attending Evensong. "But his man is here, sir," he added, "if you'd like to leave a message."

Mr. Wicks thought that on the whole it would be well to leave a message. Mr. Bunter, on inquiry, was found to be sitting by the telephone, waiting for a trunk-call. As Mr. Wicks addressed him the bell rang, and Mr. Bunter, politely excusing himself, took down the receiver.

"Hullo!" he said. "Is that Mr. Parker? Oh, thanks! Exchange! Exchange! Sorry, can you put me through to Scotland Yard? Excuse me, gentlemen, keeping you waiting.—Exchange! all right—Scotland Yard—Hullo! Is that Scotland Yard?—Is Detective Parker round there?—Can I speak to him?—I shall have done in a moment, gentlemen.—Hullo! is that you, Mr. Parker? Lord Peter would be much obliged if you could find it convenient to step down to Salisbury, sir. Oh, no, sir, he's in excellent health, sir—just stepped round to hear Evensong, sir—oh, no, I think tomorrow morning would do excellently, sir, thank you, sir."

Chapter 6

It was, in fact, inconvenient for Mr. Parker to leave London. He had had to go and see Lady Levy towards the end of the morning, and subsequently his plans for the day had been thrown out of gear and his movements delayed by the discovery that the adjourned inquest of Mr. Thipps's unknown visitor was to be held that afternoon, since nothing very definite seemed forthcoming from Inspector Sugg's inquiries. Jury and witnesses had been convened accordingly for three o'clock. Mr. Parker might altogether have missed the event, had he not run against Sugg that morning at the Yard and extracted the information from him as one would a reluctant tooth. Inspector Sugg, indeed, considered Mr. Parker rather interfering; moreover, he was hand-in-glove with Lord Peter Wimsey, and Inspector Sugg had no words for the interferingness of Lord Peter. He could not, however, when directly questioned, deny that there was to be an inquest that afternoon, nor could he prevent Mr.

Parker from enjoying the inalienable right of any interested British citizen to be present. At a little before three, therefore, Mr. Parker was in his place, and amusing himself with watching the efforts of those persons who arrived after the room was packed to insinuate, bribe or bully themselves into a position of vantage. The Coroner, a medical man of precise habits and unimaginative aspect, arrived punctually, and looking peevishly round at the crowded assembly, directed all the windows to be opened, thus letting in a stream of drizzling fog upon the heads of the unfortunates on that side of the room. This caused a commotion and some expressions of disapproval, checked sternly by the Coroner, who said that with the influenza about again an unventilated room was a death-trap; that anybody who chose to object to open windows had the obvious remedy of leaving the court, and further, that if any disturbance was made he would clear the court. He then took a Formamint lozenge, and proceeded, after the usual preliminaries, to call up fourteen good and lawful persons and swear them diligently to inquire and a true presentment make of all matters touching the death of the gentleman with the pince-nez and to give a true verdict according to the evidence, so help them God. When an expostulation by a woman juror—an elderly lady in spectacles who kept a sweet-shop, and appeared to wish she was back there—had been summarily quashed by the Coroner, the jury departed to view the body. Mr. Parker gazed round again and identified the unhappy Mr. Thipps and the girl Gladys led into an adjoining room under the grim guard of the police. They were soon followed by a gaunt old lady in a bonnet and mantle. With her, in a wonderful fur coat and a motor bonnet of fascinating construction, came the Dowager Duchess of Denver, her quick, dark eyes darting hither and thither about the crowd. The next moment they had lighted on Mr. Parker, who had several times visited the Dower House, and she nodded to him, and spoke to a policeman. Before long, a way opened magically through the press, and Mr. Parker found himself accommodated with a front seat just behind the Duchess, who greeted him charmingly, and said: "What's happened to poor Peter?" Parker began to explain, and the Coroner glanced irritably in their direction. Somebody went up and whispered in his ear, at which he coughed, and took another Formamint.

"We came up by car," said the Duchess—"so tiresome—such bad roads between Denver and Gunbury St. Walters—and there were people coming to lunch—I had to put them off—I couldn't let the old lady go alone, could I? By the way, such an odd thing's happened about the Church Restoration Fund—the Vicar—oh, dear, here are these people coming back again; well, I'll tell you afterwards—do look at that woman looking shocked, and the girl in tweeds trying to look as if she sat on undraped gentlemen every day of her life—I don't mean that—corpses of course— but one finds oneself being so Elizabethan nowadays—what an awful little man the coroner is, isn't he? He's looking daggers at me—do you think he'll dare to clear me out of the court or commit me for what-you-may-call-it?"

The first part of the evidence was not of great interest to Mr. Parker. The wretched Mr. Thipps, who had caught cold in gaol, deposed in an unhappy croak to having discovered the body when he went in to take his bath at eight o'clock. He had had such a shock, he had to sit down and send the girl for brandy. He had never seen the deceased before. He had no idea how he came there.

Yes, he had been in Manchester the day before. He had arrived at St. Pancras at ten o'clock. He had cloak-roomed his bag. At this point Mr. Thipps became very red, unhappy and confused, and glanced nervously about the court.

"Now, Mr. Thipps," said the Coroner, briskly, "we must have your movements quite clear. You must appreciate the importance of the matter. You have chosen to give evidence, which you need not have done, but having done so, you will find it best to be perfectly explicit."

"Yes," said Mr. Thipps faintly.

"Have you cautioned this witness, officer?" inquired the Coroner, turning sharply to Inspector Sugg.

The Inspector replied that he had told Mr. Thipps that anything he said might be used agin' him at his trial. Mr. Thipps became ashy, and said in a bleating voice that he 'adn't—hadn't meant to do anything that wasn't right.

This remark produced a mild sensation, and the Coroner became even more acidulated in manner than before.

"Is anybody representing Mr. Thipps?" he asked, irritably. "No? Did you not explain to him that he could—that he *ought* to be represented? You did not? Really, Inspector! Did you not know, Mr. Thipps, that you had a right to be legally represented?"

Mr. Thipps clung to a chair-back for support, and said, "No," in a voice barely audible.

"It is incredible," said the Coroner, "that so-called educated people should be so ignorant of the legal procedure of their own country. This places us in a very awkward position. I doubt, Inspector, whether I should permit the prisoner—Mr. Thipps— to give evidence at all. It is a delicate position."

The perspiration stood on Mrs. Thipps's forehead.

"Save us from our friends," whispered the Duchess to Parker. "If that cough-drop-devouring creature had openly instructed those fourteen people—and what unfinished-looking faces they have—so characteristic, I always think, of the lower middle-class, rather like sheep, or calves' head (boiled, I mean), to bring in wilful murder against the poor little man, he couldn't have made himself plainer."

"He can't let him incriminate himself, you know," said Parker.

"Stuff!" said the Duchess. "How could the man incriminate himself when he never did anything in his life? You men never think of anything but your red tape."

Meanwhile Mr. Thipps, wiping his brow with a handkerchief, had summoned up courage. He stood up with a kind of weak dignity, like a small white rabbit brought to bay.

"I would rather tell you," he said, "though it's reelly very unpleasant for a man in my position. But I reelly couldn't have it thought for a moment that I'd committed this dreadful crime. I assure you, gentlemen, I *couldn't bear* that. No. I'd rather tell you the truth, though I'm afraid it places me in rather a—well, I'll tell you."

"You fully understand the gravity of making such a statement, Mr. Thipps," said the Coroner.

"Quite," said Mr. Thipps. "It's all right—I—might I have a drink of water?"

"Take your time," said the Coroner, at the same time robbing his remark of all conviction by an impatient glance at his watch.

"Thank you, sir," said Mr. Thipps. "Well, then, it's true I got to St. Pancras at ten. But there was a man in the carriage with me. He'd got in at Leicester. I didn't recognise him at first, but he turned out to be an old school-fellow of mine."

"What was this gentleman's name?" inquired the Coroner, his pencil poised.

Mr. Thipps shrank together visibly.

"I'm afraid I can't tell you that," he said. "You see—that is, you *will* see—it would get him into trouble, and I couldn't do that—no, I reelly couldn't do that, not if my life depended on it. No!" he added, as the ominous pertinence of the last phrase smote upon him, "I'm sure I couldn't do that."

"Well, well," said the Coroner.

The Duchess leaned over to Parker again. "I'm beginning quite to admire the little man," she said.

Mr. Thipps resumed.

"When we got to St. Pancras I was going home, but my friend said no. We hadn't met for a long time and we ought to—to make a night of it, was his expression. I fear I was weak, and let him overpersuade me to accompany him to one of his haunts. I use the word advisedly," said Mr. Thipps, "and I assure you, sir, that if I had known beforehand where we were going I never would have set foot in the place.

"I cloak-roomed my bag, for he did not like the notion of our being encumbered with it, and we got into a taxicab and drove to the corner of Tottenham Court Road and Oxford Street. We then walked a little way, and turned into a side street (I do not recollect which) where there was an open door, with the light shining out. There was a man at a counter, and my friend bought some tickets, and I heard the man at the counter say something to him about 'Your friend,' meaning me, and my friend said, 'Oh, yes, he's been here before, haven't you, Alf?' (which was what they called me at school), though I assure you, sir"—here Mr. Thipps grew very earnest—"I never had, and nothing in the world should induce me to go to such a place again.

"Well, we went down into a room underneath, where there were drinks, and my friend had several, and made me take one or two—though I am an abstemious man as a rule—and he talked to some other men and girls who were there—a very vulgar set of people, I thought them, though I wouldn't say but what some of the young ladies were nice-looking enough. One of them sat on my friend's knee and called him a slow old thing, and told him to come on—so we went into another room, where there were a lot of people dancing all these up-to-date dances. My friend went and danced, and I sat on a sofa. One of the young ladies came up to me and said, didn't I dance, and I said 'No,' so she said wouldn't I stand her a drink then. 'You'll stand us a drink then, darling,' that was what she said, and I said, 'Wasn't it after hours?' and she said that didn't matter. So I ordered the drink—a gin and bitters it was—for I didn't like not to, the young lady seemed to expect it of me and I felt it wouldn't be gentlemanly to refuse when she asked. But it went against my conscience—such a young girl as she was—and she put her arm round my neck afterwards and kissed me just like as if she was paying for the drink—and it reelly went to my 'eart," said Mr. Thipps, a little ambiguously, but with uncommon emphasis.

Here somebody at the back said, "Cheer-oh!" and a sound was heard as of the noisy smacking of lips.

"Remove the person who made that improper noise," said the Coroner, with great indignation. "Go on, please, Mr. Thipps."

"Well," said Mr. Thipps, "about half-past twelve, as I should reckon, things began to get a bit lively, and I was looking for my friend to say good-night, not wishing to stay longer, as you will understand, when I saw him with one of the young ladies, and they seemed to be getting on altogether too well, if you follow me, my friend pulling the ribbons off her shoulder and the young lady laughing—and so on," said Mr. Thipps, hurriedly, "so I thought I'd just slip quietly out, when I heard a scuffle and a shout—and before I knew what was happening there were half-a-dozen policemen in, and the lights went out, and everybody stampeding and shouting—quite horrid, it was. I was knocked down in the rush, and hit my head a nasty knock on a chair—that was where I got that bruise they asked me about—and I was dreadfully afraid I'd never get away and it would all come out, and perhaps my photograph in the papers, when someone caught hold of me—I think it was the young lady I'd given the gin and bitters to—and she said, 'This way,' and pushed me along a passage and out at the back somewhere. So I ran through some streets, and found myself in Goodge Street, and there I got a taxi and came home. I saw the account of the raid afterwards in the papers, and saw my friend had escaped, and so, as it wasn't the sort of thing I wanted made public, and I didn't want to get him into difficulties, I just said nothing. But that's the truth."

"Well, Mr. Thipps," said the Coroner, "we shall be able to substantiate a certain amount of this story. Your friend's name—"

"No," said Mr. Thipps, stoutly, "not on any account."

"Very good," said the Coroner. "Now, can you tell us what time you did get in?"

"About half-past one, I should think. Though reelly, I was so upset—"

"Quite so. Did you go straight to bed?"

"Yes, I took my sandwich and glass of milk first. I thought it might settle my inside, so to speak," added the witness, apologetically, "not being accustomed to alcohol so late at night and on an empty stomach, as you may say."

"Quite so. Nobody sat up for you?"

"Nobody."

"How long did you take getting to bed first and last?"

Mr. Thipps thought it might have been half-an-hour.

"Did you visit the bathroom before turning in?"

"No."

"And you heard nothing in the night?"

"No. I fell fast asleep. I was rather agitated, so I took a little dose to make me sleep, and what with being so tired and the milk and the dose, I just tumbled right off and didn't wake till Gladys called me."

Further questioning elicited little from Mr. Thipps. Yes, the bathroom window had been open when he went in in the morning, he was sure of that, and he had spoken very sharply to the girl about it. He was ready to answer any questions; he would be only too 'appy—happy to have this dreadful affair sifted to the bottom.

Gladys Horrocks stated that she had been in Mr. Thipps's employment about three months. Her previous employers would speak to her character. It was her duty to make the round of the flat at night, when she had seen Mrs. Thipps to bed at ten. Yes, she remembered doing so on Monday evening. She had looked into all the rooms. Did she recollect shutting the bathroom window that night? Well, no, she couldn't swear to it, not in particular, but when Mr. Thipps called her into the bathroom in the morning it certainly *was* open. She had not been into the bathroom before Mr. Thipps went in. Well, yes, it had happened that she had left that window open before, when anyone had been 'aving a bath in the evening and 'ad left the blind down. Mrs. Thipps 'ad 'ad a bath on Monday evening, Mondays was one of her regular bath nights. She was very much afraid she 'adn't shut the window on Monday night, though she wished her 'ead 'ad been cut off afore she'd been so forgetful.

Here the witness burst into tears and was given some water, while the Coroner refreshed himself with a third lozenge.

Recovering, witness stated that she had certainly looked into all the rooms before going to bed. No, it was quite impossible for a body to be 'idden in the flat without her seeing of it. She 'ad been in the kitchen all evening, and there wasn't 'ardly room to keep the best dinner service there, let alone a body. Old Mrs. Thipps sat in the drawing-room. Yes, she was sure she'd been into the dining-room. How? Because she put Mr. Thipps's milk and sandwiches there ready for him. There had been nothing in there—that she could swear to. Nor yet in her own bedroom, nor in the 'all. Had she searched the bedroom cupboard and the box-room? Well, no, not to say searched; she wasn't use to searchin' people's 'ouses for skelintons every night. So that a man might have concealed himself in the box-room or a wardrobe? She supposed he might.

In reply to a woman juror—well, yes, she was walking out with a young man. Williams was his name, Bill Williams—well, yes, William Williams, if they insisted. He was a glazier by profession. Well, yes, he 'ad been in the flat sometimes. Well, she supposed you might say he was acquainted with the flat. Had she ever—no, she 'adn't, and if she'd thought such a question was going to be put to a respectable girl she wouldn't 'ave offered to give evidence. The vicar of St. Mary's would speak to her character and to Mr. Williams's. Last time Mr. Williams was at the flat was a fortnight ago.

Well, no, it wasn't exactly the last time she 'ad seen Mr. Williams. Well, yes, the last time was Monday—well, yes, Monday night. Well, if she must tell the truth, she must. Yes, the officer had cautioned her, but there wasn't any 'arm in it, and it was better to lose her place than to be 'ung, though it was a cruel shame a girl couldn't 'ave a bit of fun without a nasty corpse comin' in through the window to get 'er into difficulties. After she 'ad put Mrs. Thipps to bed, she 'ad slipped out to go to the Plumbers' and Glaziers' Ball at the "Black Faced Ram." Mr. Williams 'ad met 'er and brought 'er back. 'E could testify to where she'd been and that there wasn't no 'arm in it. She'd left before the end of the ball. It might 'ave been two o'clock when she got back. She'd got the keys of the flat from Mrs. Thipps's drawer when Mrs. Thipps wasn't looking. She 'ad asked leave to go, but couldn't get it, along of Mr. Thipps bein' away that night. She was bitterly sorry she 'ad be'aved so, and she was sure she'd been punished for it. She had 'eard nothing suspicious when she came in. She had gone straight to bed without looking round the flat. She wished she were dead.

No, Mr. and Mrs. Thipps didn't 'ardly ever 'ave any visitors; they kep' themselves very retired. She had found the outside door bolted that morning as usual. She wouldn't never believe any 'arm of Mr. Thipps. Thank you, Miss Horrocks. Call Georgiana Thipps, and the Coroner thought we had better light the gas.

The examination of Mrs. Thipps provided more entertainment than enlightenment, affording as it did an excellent example of the game called "cross questions and crooked answers." After fifteen minutes' suffering, both in voice and temper, the Coroner abandoned the struggle, leaving the lady with the last word.

"You needn't try to bully me, young man," said that octogenarian with spirit, "settin' there spoilin' your stomach with them nasty jujubes."

At this point a young man arose in court and demanded to

give evidence. Having explained that he was William Williams, glazier, he was sworn, and corroborated the evidence of Gladys Horrocks in the matter of her presence at the "Black Faced Ram" on the Monday night. They had returned to the flat rather before two, he thought, but certainly later than 1:30. He was sorry that he had persuaded Miss Horrocks to come out with him when she didn't ought. He had observed nothing of a suspicious nature in Prince of Wales Road at either visit.

Inspector Sugg gave evidence of having been called in at about half-past eight on Monday morning. He had considered the girl's manner to be suspicious and had arrested her. On later information, leading him to suspect that the deceased might have been murdered that night, he had arrested Mr. Thipps. He had found no trace of breaking into the flat. There were marks on the bathroom window-sill which pointed to somebody having got in that way. There were no ladder marks or footmarks in the yard; the yard was paved with asphalt. He had examined the roof, but found nothing on the roof. In his opinion the body had been brought into the flat previously and concealed till the evening by someone who had then gone out during the night by the bathroom window, with the connivance of the girl. In that case, why should not the girl have let the person out by the door? Well, it might have been so. Had he found traces of a body or a man or both having been hidden in the flat? He found nothing to show that they might *not* have been so concealed. What was the evidence that led him to suppose that the death had occurred that night?

At this point Inspector Sugg appeared uneasy, and endeavoured to retire upon his professional dignity. On being pressed, however, he admitted that the evidence in question had come to nothing.

One of the jurors: Was it the case that any finger-marks had been left by the criminal?

Some marks had been found on the bath, but the criminal had worn gloves.

The Coroner: Do you draw any conclusion from this fact as to the experience of the criminal?

Inspector Sugg: Looks as if he was an old hand, sir.

The Juror: Is that very consistent with the charge against Alfred Thipps, Inspector?

The Inspector was silent.

The Coroner: In the light of the evidence which you have just heard, do you still press the charge against Alfred Thipps and Gladys Horrocks?

Inspector Sugg: I consider the whole set-out highly suspicious. Thipps's story isn't corroborated, and as for the girl Horrocks, how do we know this Williams ain't in it as well?

William Williams: Now, you drop that. I can bring a 'undred witnesses—

The Coroner: Silence, if you please. I am surprised, Inspector, that you should make this suggestion in that manner. It is highly improper. By the way, can you tell us whether a police raid was actually carried out on the Monday night on any Night Club in the neighbourhood of St. Giles's Circus?

Inspector Sugg (sulkily): I believe there was something of the sort.

The Coroner: You will, no doubt, inquire into the matter. I seem to recollect having seen some mention of it in the newspapers. Thank you, Inspector, that will do.

Several witnesses having appeared and testified to the characters of Mr. Thipps and Gladys Horrocks, the Coroner stated his intention of proceeding to the medical evidence.

"Sir Julian Freke."

There was considerable stir in the court as the great specialist walked up to give evidence. He was not only a distinguished man, but a striking figure, with his wide shoulders, upright carriage and leonine head. His manner as he kissed the Book presented to him with the usual deprecatory mumble by the Coroner's officer, was that of a St. Paul condescending to humour the timid mumbo-jumbo of superstitious Corinthians.

"So handsome, I always think," whispered the Duchess to Mr. Parker; "just exactly like William Morris, with that bush of hair and beard and those exciting eyes looking out of it—so splendid, these dear men always devoted to something or other—not but what I think socialism is a mistake—of course it works with all those nice people, so good and happy in art linen and the weather always perfect—Morris, I mean, you know—but so difficult in real life. Science is different—I'm sure if I had nerves I should go to Sir Julian just to look at him—eyes like that give one something to think about, and that's what most of these people want, only I never had any—nerves, I mean. Don't you think so?"

"You are Sir Julian Freke," said the Coroner, "and live at St. Luke's House, Prince of Wales Road, Battersea, where you exercise a general direction over the surgical side of St. Luke's Hospital?"

Sir Julian assented briefly to this definition of his personality.

"You were the first medical man to see the deceased?"

"I was."

"And you have since conducted an examination in collaboration with Dr. Grimbold of Scotland Yard?"

"I have."

"You are in agreement as to the cause of death?"

"Generally speaking, yes."

"Will you communicate your impressions to the Jury?"

"I was engaged in research work in the dissecting room at St. Luke's Hospital at about nine o'clock on Monday morning, when I was informed that Inspector Sugg wished to see me. He told me that the dead body of a man had been discovered under mysterious circumstances at 59 Queen Caroline Mansions. He asked me whether it could be supposed to be a joke perpetrated by any of the medical students at the hospital. I was able to assure him, by an examination of the hospital's books, that there was no subject missing from the dissecting room."

"Who would be in charge of such bodies?"

"William Watts, the dissecting-room attendant."

"Is William Watts present?" inquired the Coroner of the officer.

William Watts was present, and could be called if the Coroner thought it necessary.

"I suppose no dead body would be delivered to the hospital without your knowledge, Sir Julian?"

"Certainly not."

"Thank you. Will you proceed with your statement?"

"Inspector Sugg then asked me whether I would send a medical man round to view the body. I said that I would go myself."

"Why did you do that?"

"I confess to my share of ordinary human curiosity, Mr. Coroner."

Laughter from a medical student at the back of the room.

"On arriving at the flat I found the deceased lying on his back in the bath. I examined him, and came to the conclusion that death had been caused by a blow on the back of the neck, dislocating the fourth and fifth cervical vertebrae, bruising the spinal cord and producing internal haemorrhage and partial paralysis of the brain. I judged the deceased to have been dead at least twelve hours, possibly more. I observed no other sign of violence of any kind upon the body. Deceased was a strong, well-nourished man of about fifty to fifty-five years of age."

"In your opinion, could the blow have been self-inflicted?"

"Certainly not. It had been made with a heavy, blunt instrument from behind, with great force and considerable judgment. It is quite impossible that it was self-inflicted."

"Could it have been the result of an accident?"

"That is possible, of course."

"If, for example, the deceased had been looking out of the window, and the sash had shut violently down upon him?"

"No; in that case there would have been signs of strangulation and a bruise upon the throat as well."

"But deceased might have been killed through a heavy weight accidentally falling upon him?"

"He might."

"Was death instantaneous, in your opinion?"

"It is difficult to say. Such a blow might very well cause death instantaneously, or the patient might linger in a partially paralyzed condition for some time. In the present case I should be disposed to think that deceased might have lingered for some hours. I base my decision upon the condition of the brain revealed at the autopsy. I may say, however, that Dr. Grimbold and I are not in complete agreement on the point."

"I understand that a suggestion has been made as to the identification of the deceased. *You* are not in a position to identify him?"

"Certainly not. I never saw him before. The suggestion to which you refer is a preposterous one, and ought never to have been made. I was not aware until this morning that it had been made; had it been made to me earlier, I should have known how to deal with it, and I should like to express my strong disapproval of the unnecessary shock and distress inflicted upon a lady with whom I have the honour to be acquainted."

The Coroner: It was not my fault, Sir Julian; I had nothing to do with it; I agree with you that it was unfortunate you were not consulted.

The reporters scribbled busily, and the court asked each other what was meant, while the jury tried to look as if they knew already.

"In the matter of the eyeglasses found upon the body, Sir Julian. Do these give any indication to a medical man?"

"They are somewhat unusual lenses; an oculist would be able to speak more definitely, but I will say for myself that I should have expected them to belong to an older man than the deceased."

"Speaking as a physician, who has had many opportunities of

observing the human body, did you gather anything from the appearance of the deceased as to his personal habits?"

"I should say that he was a man in easy circumstances, but who had only recently come into money. His teeth are in a bad state, and his hands shows signs of recent manual labour."

"An Australian colonist, for instance, who had made money?"

"Something of that sort; of course, I could not say positively."

"Of course not. Thank you, Sir Julian."

Dr. Grimbold, called, corroborated his distinguished colleague in every particular, except that, in his opinion, death had not occurred for several days after the blow. It was with the greatest hesitancy that he ventured to differ from Sir Julian Freke, and he might be wrong. It was difficult to tell in any case, and when he saw the body, deceased had been dead at least twenty-four hours, in his opinion.

Inspector Sugg, recalled. Would he tell the jury what steps had been taken to identify the deceased?

A description had been sent to every police station and had been inserted in all the newspapers. In view of the suggestion made by Sir Julian Freke, had inquiries been made at all the seaports? They had. And with no results? With no results at all. No one had come forward to identify the body? Plenty of people had come forward; but nobody had succeeded in identifying it. Had any effort been made to follow up the clue afforded by the eyeglasses? Inspector Sugg submitted that, having regard to the interests of justice, he would beg to be excused from answering that question. Might the jury see the eyeglasses? The eyeglasses were handed to the jury.

William Watts, called, confirmed the evidence of Sir Julian Freke with regard to dissecting-room subjects. He explained the system by which they were entered. They usually were supplied by the workhouses and free hospitals. They were under his sole charge. The young gentlemen could not possibly get the keys. Had Sir Julian Freke, or any of the house surgeons, the keys?

No, not even Sir Julian Freke. The keys had remained in his possession on Monday night? They had. And, in any case, the inquiry was irrelevant, as there was no body missing, nor ever had been? That was the case.

The Coroner then addressed the jury, reminding them with some asperity that they were not there to gossip about who the deceased could or could not have been, but to give their opinion as to the cause of death. He reminded them that they should consider whether, according to the medical evidence, death could have been accidental or self-inflicted, or whether it was deliberate murder, or homicide. If they considered the evidence on this point insufficient, they could return an open verdict. In any case, their verdict could not prejudice any person; if they brought it in "murder," all the whole evidence would have to be gone through again before the magistrate. He then dismissed them, with the unspoken adjuration to be quick about it.

Sir Julian Freke, after giving his evidence, had caught the eye of the Duchess, and now came over and greeted her.

"I haven't seen you for an age," said that lady. "How are you?"

"Hard at work," said the specialist. "Just got my new book out. This kind of thing wastes time. Have you seen Lady Levy yet?"

"No, poor dear," said the Duchess. "I only came up this morning, for this. Mrs. Thipps is staying with me—one of Peter's eccentricities, you know. Poor Christine! I must run round and see her. This is Mr. Parker," she added, "who is investigating that case."

"Oh," said Sir Julian, and paused. "Do you know," he said in a low voice to Parker, "I am very glad to meet you. Have you seen Lady Levy yet?"

"I saw her this morning."

"Did she ask you to go on with the inquiry?"

"Yes," said Parker; "she thinks," he added, "that Sir Reuben may be detained in the hands of some financial rival or that perhaps some scoundrels are holding him to ransom."

"And is that *your* opinion?" asked Sir Julian.

"I think it very likely," said Parker, frankly.

Sir Julian hesitated again.

"I wish you would walk back with me when this is over," he said.

"I should be delighted," said Parker.

At this moment the jury returned and took their places, and there was a little rustle and hush. The Coroner addressed the foreman and inquired if they were agreed upon their verdict.

"We are agreed, Mr. Coroner, that deceased died of the effects of a blow upon the spine, but how that injury was inflicted we consider that there is not sufficient evidence to show."

* * * * *

Mr. Parker and Sir Julian Freke walked up the road together.

"I had absolutely no idea until I saw Lady Levy this morning," said the doctor, "that there was any idea of connecting this matter with the disappearance of Sir Reuben. The suggestion was perfectly monstrous, and could only have grown up in the mind of that ridiculous police officer. If I had had any idea what was in his mind I could have disabused him and avoided all this."

"I did my best to do so," said Parker, "as soon as I was called in to the Levy case—"

"Who called you in, if I may ask?" inquired Sir Julian.

"Well, the household first of all, and then Sir Reuben's uncle, Mr. Levy of Portman Square, wrote to me to go on with the investigation."

"And now Lady Levy has confirmed those instructions?"

"Certainly," said Parker in some surprise.

Sir Julian was silent for a little time.

"I'm afraid I was the first person to put the idea into Sugg's head," said Parker, rather penitently. "When Sir Reuben disappeared, my first step, almost, was to hunt up all the street accidents and suicides and so on that had turned up during the day, and I went down to see this Battersea Park body as a matter of routine. Of course, I saw that the thing was ridiculous as soon as I got there, but Sugg froze on to the idea—and it's true there was a good deal of resemblance between the dead man and the portraits I've seen of Sir Reuben."

"A strong superficial likeness," said Sir Julian. "The upper part of the face is a not uncommon type, and as Sir Reuben wore a heavy beard and there was no opportunity of comparing the mouths and chins, I can understand the idea occurring to anybody. But only to be dismissed at once. I am sorry," he added, "as the whole matter has been painful to Lady Levy. You may know, Mr. Parker, that I am an old, though I should not call myself an intimate, friend of the Levys."

"I understood something of the sort."

"Yes. When I was a young man I—in short, Mr. Parker, I hoped once to marry Lady Levy." (Mr. Parker gave the usual sympathetic groan.) "I have never married, as you know," pursued Sir Julian. "We have remained good friends. I have always done what I could to spare her pain."

"Believe me, Sir Julian," said Parker, "that I sympathize very much with you and with Lady Levy, and that I did all I could to disabuse Inspector Sugg of this notion. Unhappily, the coincidence of Sir Reuben's being seen that evening in the Battersea Park Road—"

"Ah, yes," said Sir Julian. "Dear me, here we are at home. Perhaps you would come in for a moment, Mr. Parker, and have tea or a whisky-and-soda or something."

Parker promptly accepted this invitation, feeling that there were other things to be said.

The two men stepped into a square, finely furnished hall with a fireplace on the same side as the door, and a staircase opposite. The dining-room door stood open on their right, and as Sir Julian rang the bell a man-servant appeared at the far end of the hall.

"What will you take?" asked the doctor.

"After that dreadfully cold place," said Parker, "what I really want is gallons of hot tea, if you, as a nerve specialist, can bear the thought of it."

"Provided you allow of a judicious blend of China in it," replied Sir Julian in the same tone, "I have no objection to make. Tea in the library at once," he added to the servant, and led the way upstairs.

"I don't use the downstairs rooms much, except the dining-room," he explained as he ushered his guest into a small but cheerful library on the first floor. "This room leads out of my bedroom and is more convenient. I only live part of my time here, but it's very handy for my research work at the hospital. That's what I do there, mostly. It's a fatal thing for a theorist, Mr. Parker, to let the practical work get behindhand. Dissection is the basis of all good theory and all correct diagnosis. One must keep one's hand and eye in training. This place is far more important to me than Harley Street, and some day I shall abandon my consulting practice altogether and settle down here to cut up my subjects and write my books in peace. So many things in this life are a waste of time, Mr. Parker."

Mr. Parker assented to this.

"Very often," said Sir Julian, "the only time I get for any research work—necessitating as it does the keenest observation and the faculties at their acutest—has to be at night, after a long day's work and by artificial light, which, magnificent as the lighting of the dissecting room here is, is always more trying to the eyes than daylight. Doubtless your own work has to be carried on under even more trying conditions."

"Yes, sometimes," said Parker; "but then you see," he added, "the conditions are, so to speak, part of the work."

"Quite so, quite so," said Sir Julian; "you mean that the burglar, for example, does not demonstrate his methods in the light of day, or plant the perfect footmark in the middle of a damp patch of sand for you to analyze."

"Not as a rule," said the detective, "but I have no doubt many of your diseases work quite as insidiously as any burglar."

"They do, they do," said Sir Julian, laughing, "and it is my pride, as it is yours, to track them down for the good of society. The neuroses, you know, are particularly clever criminals—they break out into as many disguises as—"

"As Leon Kestrel, the Master-Mummer," suggested Parker, who read railway-stall detective stories on the principle of the 'busman's holiday.

"No doubt," said Sir Julian, who did not, "and they cover up their tracks wonderfully. But when you can really investigate, Mr. Parker, and break up the dead, or for preference the living body with the scalpel, you always find the footmarks—the little trail of ruin or disorder left by madness or disease or drink or any other similar pest. But the difficulty is to trace them back, merely by observing the surface symptoms—the hysteria, crime, religion, fear, shyness, conscience, or whatever it may be; just as you observe a theft or a murder and look for the footsteps of the criminal, so I observe a fit of hysterics or an outburst of piety and hunt for the little mechanical irritation which has produced it."

"You regard all these things as physical?"

"Undoubtedly. I am not ignorant of the rise of another school of thought, Mr. Parker, but its exponents are mostly charlatans or self-deceivers. '*Sie haben sich so weit darin eingeheimnisst*' that, like Sludge the Medium, they are beginning to believe their own nonsense. I should like to have the exploring of some of their brains, Mr. Parker; I would show you the little faults and landslips in the cells—the misfiring and short-circuiting of the nerves, which produce these notions and these books. At least," he added, gazing sombrely at his guest, "at least, if I could not quite show you today, I shall be able to do so tomorrow—or in a year's time—or before I die."

He sat for some minutes gazing into the fire, while the red light played upon his tawny beard and struck out answering gleams from his compelling eyes.

Parker drank tea in silence, watching him. On the whole, however, he remained but little interested in the causes of nervous phenomena and his mind strayed to Lord Peter, coping with the redoubtable Crimplesham down in Salisbury. Lord Peter had wanted him to come: that meant, either that Crimplesham was proving recalcitrant or that a clue wanted following. But Bunter had said that tomorrow would do, and it was just as well. After all, the Battersea affair was not Parker's case; he had already wasted valuable time attending an inconclusive inquest, and he really ought to get on with his legitimate work. There was still Levy's secretary to see and the little matter of the Peruvian Oil to be looked into. He looked at his watch.

"I am very much afraid—if you will excuse me—" he murmured.

Sir Julian came back with a start to the consideration of actuality.

"Your work calls you?" he said, smiling. "Well, I can understand that. I won't keep you. But I wanted to say something to you in connection with your present inquiry—only I hardly know—I hardly like—"

Parker sat down again, and banished every indication of hurry from his face and attitude.

"I shall be very grateful for any help you can give me," he said.

"I'm afraid it's more in the nature of hindrance," said Sir Julian, with a short laugh. "It's a case of destroying a clue for you, and a breach of professional confidence on my side. But since—accidentally—a certain amount has come out, perhaps the whole had better do so."

Mr. Parker made the encouraging noise which, among laymen, supplies the place of the priest's insinuating, "Yes, my son?"

"Sir Reuben Levy's visit on Monday night was to me," said Sir Julian.

"Yes?" said Mr. Parker, without expression.

"He found cause for certain grave suspicions concerning his health," said Sir Julian, slowly, as though weighing how much he could in honour disclose to a stranger. "He came to me, in preference to his own medical man, as he was particularly anxious that the matter should be kept from his wife. As I told you, he knew me fairly well, and Lady Levy had consulted me about a nervous disorder in the summer."

"Did he make an appointment with you?" asked Parker.

"I beg your pardon," said the other, absently.

"Did he make an appointment?"

"An appointment? Oh, no! He turned up suddenly in the evening after dinner when I wasn't expecting him. I took him up here and examined him, and he left me somewhere about ten o'clock, I should think."

"May I ask what was the result of your examination?"

"Why do you want to know?"

"It might illuminate—well, conjecture as to his subsequent conduct," said Parker, cautiously. This story seemed to have little coherence with the rest of the business, and he wondered whether coincidence was alone responsible for Sir Reuben's disappearance on the same night that he visited the doctor.

"I see," said Sir Julian. "Yes. Well, I will tell you in confidence that I saw grave grounds of suspicion, but as yet, no absolute certainty of mischief."

"Thank you. Sir Reuben left you at ten o'clock?"

"Then or thereabouts. I did not at first mention the matter as it was so very much Sir Reuben's wish to keep his visit to me secret, and there was no question of accident in the street or anything of that kind, since he reached home safely at midnight."

"Quite so," said Parker.

"It would have been, and is, a breach of confidence," said Sir Julian, "and I only tell you now because Sir Reuben was accidentally seen, and because I would rather tell you in private than have you ferreting round here and questioning my servants, Mr. Parker. You will excuse my frankness."

"Certainly," said Parker. "I hold no brief for the pleasantness of my profession, Sir Julian. I am very much obliged to you for telling me this. I might otherwise have wasted valuable time following up a false trail."

"I am sure I need not ask you, in your turn, to respect this confidence," said the doctor. "To publish the matter abroad could only harm Sir Reuben and pain his wife, besides placing me in no favourable light with my patients."

"I promise to keep the thing to myself," said Parker, "except of course," he added hastily, "that I must inform my colleague."

"You have a colleague in the case?"

"I have."

"What sort of person is he?"

"He will be perfectly discreet, Sir Julian."

"Is he a police officer?"

"You need not be afraid of your confidence getting into the records at Scotland Yard."

"I see that you know how to be discreet, Mr. Parker."

"We also have our professional etiquette, Sir Julian."

* * * * *

On returning to Great Ormond Street, Mr. Parker found a wire awaiting him, which said: "Do not trouble to come. All well. Returning tomorrow. Wimsey."

Chapter 7

On returning to the flat just before lunch-time on the following morning, after a few confirmatory researches in Balham and the neighbourhood of Victoria Station, Lord Peter was greeted at the door by Mr. Bunter (who had gone straight home from Waterloo) with a telephone message and a severe and nursemaid-like eye.

"Lady Swaffham rang up, my lord, and said she hoped your lordship had not forgotten you were lunching with her."

"I have forgotten, Bunter, and I mean to forget. I trust you told her I had succumbed to lethargic encephalitis suddenly, no flowers by request."

"Lady Swaffham said, my lord, she was counting on you. She met the Duchess of Denver yesterday—"

"If my sister-in-law's there I won't go, that's flat," said Lord Peter.

"I beg your pardon, my lord, the Dowager Duchess."

"What's she doing in town?"

"I imagine she came up for the inquest, my lord."

"Oh, yes—we missed that, Bunter."

"Yes, my lord. Her Grace is lunching with Lady Swaffham."

"Bunter, I can't. I can't, really. Say I'm in bed with whooping cough, and ask my mother to come round after lunch."

"Very well, my lord. Mrs. Tommy Frayle will be at Lady Swaffham's, my lord, and Mr. Milligan—"

"Mr. who?"

"Mr. John P. Milligan, my lord, and—"

"Good God, Bunter, why didn't you say so before? Have I time to get there before he does? All right. I'm off. With a taxi I can just—"

"Not in those trousers, my lord," said Mr. Bunter, blocking the way to the door with deferential firmness.

"Oh, Bunter," pleaded his lordship, "do let me—just this once. You don't know how important it is."

"Not on any account, my lord. It would be as much as my place is worth."

"The trousers are all right, Bunter."

"Not for Lady Swaffham's, my lord. Besides, your lordship forgets the man that ran against you with a milk-can at Salisbury."

And Mr. Bunter laid an accusing finger on a slight stain of grease showing across the light cloth.

"I wish to God I'd never let you grow into a privileged family retainer, Bunter," said Lord Peter, bitterly, dashing his walking-stick into the umbrella-stand. "You've no conception of the mistakes my mother may be making."

Mr. Bunter smiled grimly and led his victim away.

When an immaculate Lord Peter was ushered, rather late for lunch, into Lady Swaffham's drawing-room, the Dowager Duchess of Denver was seated on a sofa, plunged in intimate conversation with Mr. John P. Milligan of Chicago.

* * * * *

"I'm vurry pleased to meet you, Duchess," had been that financier's opening remark, "to thank you for your exceedingly kind invitation. I assure you it's a compliment I deeply appreciate."

The Duchess beamed at him, while conducting a rapid rally of all her intellectual forces.

"Do come and sit down and talk to me, Mr. Milligan," she said. "I do so love talking to you great business men—let me see, is it a railway king you are or something about puss-in-the-corner—at least, I don't mean that exactly, but that game one used to play with cards, all about wheat and oats, and there was a bull and a bear, too—or was it a horse?—no, a bear, because I remember one always had to try and get rid of it and it used to get so dreadfully crumpled and torn, poor thing, always being handed about, one got to recognise it, and then one had to buy a new pack—so foolish it must seem to you, knowing the real thing, and dreadfully noisy, but really excellent for breaking the ice with rather stiff people who didn't know each other—I'm quite sorry it's gone out."

Mr. Milligan sat down.

"Wal, now," he said, "I guess it's as interesting for us business men to meet British aristocrats as it is for Britishers to meet American railway kings, Duchess. And I guess I'll make as many mistakes talking your kind of talk as you would make if you were tryin' to run a corner in wheat in Chicago. Fancy now, I called that fine lad of yours Lord Wimsey the other day, and he thought I'd mistaken him for his brother. That made me feel rather green."

This was an unhoped-for lead. The Duchess walked warily.

"Dear boy," she said, "I am so glad you met him, Mr. Milligan. *Both* my sons are a *great* comfort to me, you know, though, of course, Gerald is more conventional—just the right kind of person for the House of Lords, you know, and a splendid farmer. I can't see Peter down at Denver half so well, though he is always going to all the right things in town, and very amusing sometimes, poor boy."

"I was vurry much gratified by Lord Peter's suggestion," pursued Mr. Milligan, "for which I understand you are responsible, and I'll surely be very pleased to come any day you like, though I think you're flattering me too much."

"Ah, well," said the Duchess, "I don't know if you're the best judge of that, Mr. Milligan. Not that I know anything about business myself," she added. "I'm rather old-fashioned for these days, you know, and I can't pretend to do more than know a nice *man* when I see him; for the other things I rely on my son."

The accent of this speech was so flattering that Mr. Milligan purred almost audibly, and said:

"Wal, Duchess, I guess that's where a lady with a real, beautiful, old-fashioned soul has the advantage of these modern young blatherskites—there aren't many men who wouldn't be nice—to her, and even then, if they aren't rock-bottom she can see through them."

"But that leaves me where I was," thought the Duchess. "I believe," she said aloud, "that I ought to be thanking you in the name of the vicar of Duke's Denver for a very munificent cheque which reached him yesterday for the Church Restoration Fund. He was so delighted and astonished, poor dear man."

"Oh, that's nothing," said Mr. Milligan, "we haven't any fine old crusted buildings like yours over on our side, so it's a privilege to be allowed to drop a little kerosene into the worm-holes when we hear of one in the old country suffering from senile decay. So when your lad told me about Duke's Denver I took the liberty to subscribe without waiting for the Bazaar."

"I'm sure it was very kind of you," said the Duchess. "You are coming to the Bazaar, then?" she continued, gazing into his face appealingly.

"Sure thing," said Mr. Milligan, with great promptness. "Lord Peter said you'd let me know for sure about the date, but we can always make time for a little bit of good work anyway. Of course I'm hoping to be able to avail myself of your kind invitation to stop, but if I'm rushed, I'll manage anyhow to pop over and speak my piece and pop back again."

"I hope so very much," said the Duchess. "I must see what can be done about the date—of course, I can't promise—"

"No, no," said Mr. Milligan heartily. "I know what these things are to fix up. And then there's not only me—there's all the real big men of European eminence your son mentioned, to be consulted."

The Duchess turned pale at the thought that any one of these illustrious persons might some time turn up in somebody's drawing-room, but by this time she had dug herself in comfortably, and was even beginning to find her range.

"I can't say how grateful we are to you," she said; "it will be such a treat. Do tell me what you think of saying."

"Wal—" began Mr. Milligan.

Suddenly everybody was standing up and a penitent voice was heard to say:

"Really, most awfully sorry, y'know—hope you'll forgive me, Lady Swaffham, what? Dear lady, could I possibly forget an invitation from you? Fact is, I had to go an' see a man down in Salisbury—absolutely true, 'pon my word, and the fellow wouldn't let me get away. I'm simply grovellin' before you, Lady Swaffham. Shall I go an' eat my lunch in the corner?"

Lady Swaffham gracefully forgave the culprit.

"Your dear mother is here," she said.

"How do, Mother?" said Lord Peter, uneasily.

"How are you, dear?" replied the Duchess. "You really oughtn't to have turned up just yet. Mr. Milligan was just going to tell me what a thrilling speech he's preparing for the Bazaar, when you came and interrupted us."

Conversation at lunch turned, not unnaturally, on the Battersea inquest, the Duchess giving a vivid impersonation of Mrs. Thipps being interrogated by the Coroner.

" 'Did you hear anything unusual in the night?' says the little man, leaning forward and screaming at her, and so crimson in the face and his ears sticking out so—just like a cherubim in that poem of Tennyson's—or is a cherub blue?—perhaps it's a seraphim I mean—anyway, you know what I mean, all eyes, with little wings on its head. And dear old Mrs. Thipps saying, 'Of course I have, any time these eighty years,' and *such* a sensation in court till they found out she thought he'd said, 'Do you sleep without a light?' and everybody laughing, and then the Coroner said quite loudly, 'Damn the woman,' and she heard that, I can't think why, and said: 'Don't you get swearing, young man, sitting there in the presence of Providence, as you may say. I don't know what young people are coming to nowadays'—and he's sixty if he's a day, you know," said the Duchess.

* * * * *

By a natural transition, Mrs. Tommy Frayle referred to the man who was hanged for murdering three brides in a bath.

"I always thought that was so ingenious," she said, gazing soulfully at Lord Peter, "and do you know, as it happened, Tommy had just made me insure my life, and I got so frightened, I gave up my morning bath and took to having it in the afternoon when he was in the House—I mean, when he was *not* in the house—not at home, I mean."

"Dear lady," said Lord Peter, reproachfully, "I have a distinct recollection that all those brides were thoroughly unattractive. But it was an uncommonly ingenious plan—the first time of askin'—only he shouldn't have repeated himself."

"One demands a little originality in these days, even from murderers," said Lady Swaffham. "Like dramatists, you know—so much easier in Shakespeare's time, wasn't it? Always the same girl dressed up as a man, and even that borrowed from Boccaccio or Dante or somebody. I'm sure if I'd been a Shakespeare hero, the very minute I saw a slim-legged young page-boy I'd have said: 'Odsbodikins! There's that girl again!'"

"That's just what happened, as a matter of fact," said Lord Peter. "You see, Lady Swaffham, if ever you want to commit a murder, the thing you've got to do is to prevent people from associatin' their ideas. Most people don't associate anythin'—their ideas just roll about like so many dry peas on a tray, makin' a lot of noise and goin' nowhere, but once you begin lettin' 'em string their peas into a necklace, it's goin' to be strong enough to hang you, what?"

"Dear me!" said Mrs. Tommy Frayle, with a little scream, "what a blessing it is none of my friends have any ideas at all!"

"Y'see," said Lord Peter, balancing a piece of duck on his fork and frowning, "it's only in Sherlock Holmes and stories like that, that people think things out logically. Or'nar'ly, if somebody tells you somethin' out of the way, you just say, 'By Jove!' or 'How sad!' an' leave it at that, an' half the time you forget about it, 'nless somethin' turns up afterwards to drive it home. F'r instance, Lady Swaffham, I told you when I came in that I'd been down to Salisbury, 'n' that's true, only I don't suppose it impressed you much; 'n' I don't suppose it'd impress you much if you read in the paper tomorrow of a tragic discovery of a dead lawyer down in Salisbury, but if I went to Salisbury again next week 'n' there was a Salisbury doctor found dead the day after, you might begin to think I was a bird of ill omen for Salisbury residents; and if I went there again the week after, 'n' you heard next day that the see of Salisbury had fallen vacant suddenly, you might begin to wonder what took me to Salisbury, an' why I'd never mentioned before that I had friends down there, don't you see, an' you might think of goin' down to Salisbury yourself, an' askin' all kinds of people if they'd happened to see a young man in plum-coloured socks hangin' round the Bishop's Palace."

"I daresay I should," said Lady Swaffham.

"Quite. An' if you found that the lawyer and the doctor had once upon a time been in business at Poggleton-on-the-Marsh when the Bishop had been vicar there, you'd begin to remember you'd once heard of me payin' a visit to Poggleton-on-the-Marsh a long time ago, an' you'd begin to look up the parish registers there an' discover I'd been married under an assumed name by the vicar to the widow of a wealthy farmer, who'd died suddenly of peritonitis, as certified by the doctor, after the lawyer'd made a will leavin' me all her money, and *then* you'd begin to think I might have very good reasons for gettin' rid of such promisin' blackmailers as the lawyer, the doctor an' the bishop. Only, if I hadn't started an association in your mind by gettin' rid of 'em all in the same place, you'd never have thought of goin' to Poggleton-on-the-Marsh, 'n' you wouldn't even have remembered I'd ever been there."

"*Were* you ever there, Lord Peter?" inquired Mrs. Tommy, anxiously.

"I don't think so," said Lord Peter; "the name threads no beads in my mind. But it might, any day, you know."

"But if you were investigating a crime," said Lady Swaffham, "you'd have to begin by the usual things, I suppose—finding out what the person had been doing, and who'd been to call, and looking for a motive, wouldn't you?"

"Oh, yes," said Lord Peter, "but most of us have such dozens of motives for murderin' all sorts of inoffensive people. There's lots of people I'd like to murder, wouldn't you?"

"Heaps," said Lady Swaffham. "There's that dreadful—perhaps I'd better not say it, though, for fear you should remember it later on."

"Well, I wouldn't if I were you," said Peter, amiably. "You never know. It'd be beastly awkward if the person died suddenly tomorrow."

"The difficulty with this Battersea case, I guess," said Mr. Milligan, "is that nobody seems to have any associations with the gentleman in the bath."

"So hard on poor Inspector Sugg," said the Duchess. "I quite felt for the man, having to stand up there and answer a lot of questions when he had nothing at all to say."

Lord Peter applied himself to the duck, having got a little behindhand. Presently he heard somebody ask the Duchess if she had seen Lady Levy.

"She is in great distress," said the woman who had spoken, a Mrs. Freemantle, "though she clings to the hope that he will turn up. I suppose you knew him, Mr. Milligan—know him, I should say, for I hope he's still alive somewhere."

Mrs. Freemantle was the wife of an eminent railway director, and celebrated for her ignorance of the world of finance. Her *faux pas* in this connection enlivened the tea parties of City men's wives.

"Wal, I've dined with him," said Mr. Milligan, good-naturedly. "I think he and I've done our best to ruin each other, Mrs. Freemantle. If this were the States," he added, "I'd be much inclined to suspect myself of having put Sir Reuben in a safe place. But we can't do business that way in your old country; no, ma'am."

"It must be exciting work doing business in America," said Lord Peter.

"It is," said Mr. Milligan. "I guess my brothers are having a good time there now. I'll be joining them again before long, as soon as I've fixed up a little bit of work for them on this side."

"Well, you mustn't go till after my bazaar," said the Duchess.

Lord Peter spent the afternoon in a vain hunt for Mr. Parker. He ran him down eventually after dinner in Great Ormond Street.

Parker was sitting in an elderly but affectionate armchair, with his feet on the mantelpiece, relaxing his mind with a modern commentary on the Epistle to the Galatians. He received Lord Peter with quiet pleasure, though without rapturous enthusiasm, and mixed him a whisky-and-soda. Peter took up the book his friend had laid down and glanced over the pages.

"All these men work with a bias in their minds, one way or other," he said; "they find what they are looking for."

"Oh, they do," agreed the detective; "but one learns to discount that almost automatically, you know. When I was at college, I was all on the other side—Conybeare and Robertson and Drews and those people, you know, till I found they were all so busy looking for a burglar whom nobody had ever seen, that they couldn't recognise the footprints of the household, so to speak. Then I spent two years learning to be cautious."

"Hum," said Lord Peter, "theology must be good exercise for the brain then, for you're easily the most cautious devil I know. But I say, do go on reading—it's a shame for me to come and root you up in your off-time like this."

"It's all right, old man," said Parker.

The two men sat silent for a little, and then Lord Peter said: "D'you like your job?"

The detective considered the question, and replied:

"Yes—yes, I do. I know it to be useful, and I am fitted to it. I do it quite well—not with inspiration, perhaps, but sufficiently well to take a pride in it. It is full of variety and it forces one to keep up to the mark and not get slack. And there's a future to it. Yes, I like it. Why?"

"Oh, nothing," said Peter. "It's a hobby to me, you see. I took it up when the bottom of things was rather knocked out for me, because it was so damned exciting, and the worst of it is, I enjoy it—up to a point. If it was all on paper I'd enjoy every bit of it. I love the beginning of a job—when one doesn't know any of the people and it's just exciting and amusing. But if it comes to really running down a live person and getting him hanged, or even quodded, poor devil, there don't seem as if there was any excuse for me buttin' in, since I don't have to make my livin' by it. And I feel as if I oughtn't ever to find it amusin'. But I do."

Parker gave this speech his careful attention.

"I see what you mean," he said.

"There's old Milligan, f'r instance," said Lord Peter. "On paper, nothin' would be funnier than to catch old Milligan out. But he's rather a decent old bird to talk to. Mother likes him. He's taken a fancy to me. It's awfully entertainin' goin' and pumpin' him with stuff about a bazaar for church expenses, but when he's so jolly pleased about it and that, I feel a worm. S'pose old Milligan has cut Levy's throat and plugged him into the Thames. It ain't my business."

"It's as much yours as anybody's," said Parker; "it's no better to do it for money than to do it for nothing."

"Yes, it is," said Peter stubbornly. "Havin' to live is the only excuse there is for doin' that kind of thing."

"Well, but look here!" said Parker. "If Milligan has cut poor

367

old Levy's throat for no reason except to make himself richer, I don't see why he should buy himself off by giving £1,000 to Duke's Denver church roof, or why he should be forgiven just because he's childishly vain, or childishly snobbish."

"That's a nasty one," said Lord Peter.

"Well, if you like, even because he has taken a fancy to you."

"No, but—"

"Look here, Wimsey—do you think he *has* murdered Levy?"

"Well, he may have."

"But do you think he has?"

"I don't want to think so."

"Because he has taken a fancy to you?"

"Well, that biases me, of course—"

"I darcsay it's quite a legitimate bias. You don't think a callous murderer would be likely to take a fancy to you?"

"Well—besides, I've taken rather a fancy to him."

"I daresay that's quite legitimate, too. You've observed him and made a subconscious deduction from your observations, and the result is, you don't think he did it. Well, why not? You're entitled to take that into account."

"But perhaps I'm wrong and he did do it."

"Then why let your vainglorious conceit in your own power of estimating character stand in the way of unmasking the singularly cold-blooded murder of an innocent and lovable man?"

"I know—but I don't feel I'm playing the game somehow."

"Look here, Peter," said the other with some earnestness, "suppose you get this playing-fields-of-Eton complex out of your system once and for all. There doesn't seem to be much doubt that something unpleasant has happened to Sir Reuben Levy. Call it murder, to strengthen the argument. If Sir Reuben has been murdered, is it a game? and is it fair to treat it as a game?"

"That's what I'm ashamed of, really," said Lord Peter. "It *is* a game to me, to begin with, and I go on cheerfully, and then I suddenly see that somebody is going to be hurt, and I want to get out of it."

"Yes, yes, I know," said the detective, "but that's because you're thinking about your attitude. You want to be consistent, you want to look pretty, you want to swagger debonairly through a comedy of puppets or else to stalk magnificently through a tragedy of human sorrows and things. But that's childish. If you've any duty to society in the way of finding out the truth about murders, you must do it in any attitude that comes handy. You want to be elegant and detached? That's all right, if you find the truth out that way, but it hasn't any value in itself, you know. You want to look dignified and consistent—what's that got to do with it? You want to hunt down a murderer for the sport of the thing and then shake hands with him and say, 'Well played— hard luck—you shall have your revenge tomorrow!' Well, you can't do it like that. Life's not a football match. You want to be a sportsman. You can't be a sportsman. You're a responsible person."

"I don't think you ought to read so much theology," said Lord Peter. "It has a brutalizing influence."

He got up and paced about the room, looking idly over the bookshelves. Then he sat down again, filled and lit his pipe, and said:

"Well, I'd better tell you about the ferocious and hardened Crimplesham."

He detailed his visit to Salisbury. Once assured of his bona fides, Mr. Crimplesham had given him the fullest details of his visit to town.

"And I've substantiated it all," groaned Lord Peter, "and unless he's corrupted half Balham, there's no doubt he spent the night there. And the afternoon was really spent with the bank people. And half the residents of Salisbury seem to have seen him off on Monday before lunch. And nobody but his own family or young Wicks seems to have anything to gain by his death. And even if young Wicks wanted to make away with him, it's rather far-fetched to go and murder an unknown man in Thipps's place in order to stick Crimplesham's eyeglasses on his nose."

"Where was young Wicks on Monday?" asked Parker.

"At a dance given by the Precentor," said Lord Peter, wildly. "David—his name is David—dancing before the ark of the Lord in the face of the whole Cathedral Close."

There was a pause.

"Tell me about the inquest," said Wimsey.

Parker obliged with a summary of the evidence.

"Do you believe the body could have been concealed in the flat after all?" he asked. "I know we looked, but I suppose we might have missed something."

"We might. But Sugg looked as well."

"Sugg!"

"You do Sugg an injustice," said Lord Peter; "if there had been any signs of Thipps's complicity in the crime, Sugg would have found them."

"Why?"

"Why? Because he was looking for them. He's like your commentators on Galatians. He thinks that either Thipps, or Gladys Horrocks, or Gladys Horrocks's young man did it. Therefore he found marks on the window sill where Gladys Horrocks's young man might have come in or handed something in to Gladys Horrocks. He didn't find any signs on the roof, because he wasn't looking for them."

"But he went over the roof before me."

"Yes, but only in order to prove that there were no marks there. He reasons like this: Gladys Horrocks's young man is a glazier. Glaziers come on ladders. Glaziers have ready access to ladders. Therefore Gladys Horrocks's young man had ready access to a ladder. Therefore Gladys Horrocks's young man came on a ladder. Therefore there will be marks on the window sill and none on the roof. Therefore he finds marks on the window sill but none on the roof. He finds no marks on the ground, but he thinks he would have found them if the yard didn't happen to be paved with asphalt. Similarly, he thinks Mr. Thipps may have concealed the body in the box-room or elsewhere. Therefore you may be sure he searched the box-room and all the other places for signs of occupation. If they had been there he would have found them, because he was looking for them. Therefore, if he didn't find them it's because they weren't there."

"All right," said Parker, "stop talking. I believe you."

He went on to detail the medical evidence.

"By the way," said Lord Peter, "to skip across for a moment to the other case, has it occurred to you that perhaps Levy was going out to see Freke on Monday night?"

"He was; he did," said Parker, rather unexpectedly, and proceeded to recount his interview with the nerve-specialist.

"Humph!" said Lord Peter. "I say, Parker, these are funny cases, ain't they? Every line of inquiry seems to peter out. It's awfully exciting up to a point, you know, and then nothing comes of it. It's like rivers getting lost in the sand."

"Yes," said Parker. "And there's another one I lost this morning."

"What's that?"

"Oh, I was pumping Levy's secretary about his business. I couldn't get much that seemed important except further details about the Argentine and so on. Then I thought I'd just ask round in the City about those Peruvian Oil shares, but Levy hadn't even heard of them so far as I could make out. I routed out the brokers, and found a lot of mystery and concealment, as one always does, you know, when somebody's been rigging the market, and at last I found one name at the back of it. But it wasn't Levy's."

"No? Whose was it?"

"Oddly enough, Freke's. It seems mysterious. He bought a lot of shares last week, in a secret kind of way, a few of them in his own name, and then quietly sold 'em out on Tuesday at a small profit—a few hundreds, not worth going to all that trouble about, you wouldn't think."

"Shouldn't have thought he ever went in for that kind of gamble."

"He doesn't as a rule. That's the funny part of it."

"Well, you never know," said Lord Peter; "people do these things just to prove to themselves or somebody else that they could make a fortune that way if they liked. I've done it myself in a small way."

He knocked out his pipe and rose to go.

"I say, old man," he said suddenly, as Parker was letting him out, "does it occur to you that Freke's story doesn't fit in awfully well with what Anderson said about the old boy having been so jolly at dinner on Monday night? Would you be, if you thought you'd got anything of that sort?"

"No, I shouldn't," said Parker; "but," he added with his habitual caution, "some men will jest in the dentist's waiting-room. You, for one."

"Well, that's true," said Lord Peter, and went downstairs.

Chapter 8

Lord Peter reached home about midnight, feeling extraordinarily wakeful and alert. Something was jigging and worrying in his brain; it felt like a hive of bees, stirred up by a stick. He felt as though he were looking at a complicated riddle, of which he had once been told the answer but had forgotten it and was always on the point of remembering.

"Somewhere," said Lord Peter to himself, "somewhere I've got the key to these two things. I know I've got it, only I can't remember what it is. Somebody said it. Perhaps I said it. I can't remember where, but I know I've got it. Go to bed, Bunter, I shall sit up a little. I'll just slip on a dressing-gown."

Before the fire he sat down with his pipe in his mouth and his jazz-coloured peacocks gathered about him. He traced out this line and that line of investigation—rivers running into the sand. They ran out from the thought of Levy, last seen at ten o'clock in Prince of Wales Road. They ran back from the picture of the grotesque dead man in Mr. Thipps's bathroom—they ran over the roof, and were lost—lost in the sand. Rivers running into the sand—rivers running underground, very far down—

> *Where Alph, the sacred river, ran*
> *Through caverns measureless to man*
> *Down to a sunless sea.*

By leaning his head down, it seemed to Lord Peter that he could hear them, very faintly, lipping and gurgling somewhere in the darkness. But where? He felt quite sure that somebody had told him once, only he had forgotten.

He roused himself, threw a log on the fire, and picked up a book which the indefatigable Bunter, carrying on his daily fatigues amid the excitements of special duty, had brought from the Times Book Club. It happened to be Sir Julian Freke's "Physiological Bases of the Conscience," which he had seen reviewed two days before.

"This ought to send one to sleep," said Lord Peter; "if I can't leave these problems to my subconscious I'll be as limp as a rag tomorrow."

He opened the book slowly, and glanced carelessly through the preface.

"I wonder if that's true about Levy being ill," he thought, putting the book down; "it doesn't seem likely. And yet—Dash it all, I'll take my mind off it."

He read on resolutely for a little.

"I don't suppose Mother's kept up with the Levys much," was the next importunate train of thought. "Dad always hated self-made people and wouldn't have 'em at Denver. And old Gerald keeps up the tradition. I wonder if she knew Freke well in those days. She seems to get on with Milligan. I trust Mother's judgment a good deal. She was a brick about that bazaar business. I ought to have warned her. She said something once—"

He pursued an elusive memory for some minutes, till it vanished altogether with a mocking flicker of the tail. He returned to his reading.

Presently another thought crossed his mind aroused by a photograph of some experiment in surgery.

"If the evidence of Freke and that man Watts hadn't been so positive," he said to himself, "I should be inclined to look into the matter of those shreds of lint on the chimney."

He considered this, shook his head and read with determination.

Mind and matter were one thing, that was the theme of the physiologist. Matter could erupt, as it were, into ideas. You could carve passions in the brain with a knife. You could get rid of imagination with drugs and cure an outworn convention like a disease. "The knowledge of good and evil is an observed phenomenon, attendant upon a certain condition of the brain-cells, which is removable." That was one phrase; and again:

"Conscience in man may, in fact, be compared to the sting of a hive-bee, which, so far from conducing to the welfare of its possessor, cannot function, even in a single instance, without occasioning its death. The survival-value in each case is thus purely social; and if humanity ever passes from its present phase of social development into that of a higher individualism, as some of our philosophers have ventured to speculate, we may suppose that this interesting mental phenomenon may gradually cease to appear; just as the nerves and muscles which once controlled the movements of our ears and scalps have, in all save a few backward individuals, become atrophied and of interest only to the physiologist."

"By Jove!" thought Lord Peter, idly, "that's an ideal doctrine for the criminal. A man who believed that would never—"

And then it happened—the thing he had been half-unconsciously expecting. It happened suddenly, surely, as unmistakably, as sunrise. He remembered—not one thing, nor another thing, nor a logical succession of things, but everything—the whole thing, perfect, complete, in all its dimensions as it were and instantaneously; as if he stood outside the world and saw it suspended in infinitely dimensional space. He no longer needed to reason about it, or even to think about it. He knew it.

There is a game in which one is presented with a jumble of letters and is required to make a word out of them, as thus:

C O S S S S R I

The slow way of solving the problem is to try out all the permutations and combinations in turn, throwing away impossible conjunctions of letters, as:

S S S I R C

or

S C S R S O

Another way is to stare at the incoordinate elements until, by no logical process that the conscious mind can detect, or under some adventitious external stimulus, the combination:

S C I S S O R S

presents itself with calm certainty. After that, one does not even need to arrange the letters in order. The thing is done.

Even so, the scattered elements of two grotesque

conundrums, flung higgledy-piggledy into Lord Peter's mind, resolved themselves, unquestioned henceforward. A bump on the roof of the end house—Levy in a welter of cold rain talking to a prostitute in the Battersea Park Road—a single ruddy hair—lint bandages—Inspector Sugg calling the great surgeon from the dissecting-room of the hospital—Lady Levy with a nervous attack—the smell of carbolic soap—the Duchess's voice—"not really an engagement, only a sort of understanding with her father"—shares in Peruvian Oil—the dark skin and curved, fleshy profile of the man in the bath—Dr. Grimbold giving evidence, "In my opinion, death did not occur for several days after the blow"—india-rubber gloves—even, faintly, the voice of Mr. Appledore, "He called on me, sir, with an anti-vivisectionist pamphlet"—all these things and many others rang together and made one sound, they swung together like bells in a steeple, with the deep tenor booming through the clamour:

"The knowledge of good and evil is a phenomenon of the brain, and is removable, removable, removable. The knowledge of good and evil is removable."

Lord Peter Wimsey was not a young man who habitually took himself very seriously, but this time he was frankly appalled. "It's impossible," said his reason, feebly; "*credo quia impossibile,*" said his interior certainty with impervious self-satisfaction. "All right," said conscience, instantly allying itself with blind faith, "what are you going to do about it?"

Lord Peter got up and paced the room: "Good Lord!" he said. "Good Lord!" He took down "Who's Who" from the little shelf over the telephone and sought comfort in its pages:

FREKE, Sir Julian, Kt. *cr.* 1916; G.C.V.O. *cr.* 1919; K.C.V.O. 1917; K.C.B. 1918; M.D., F.R.C.P., F.R.C.S., Dr. en Méd. Paris; D. Sci. Cantab.; Knight of Grace of the Order of S. John of Jerusalem; Consulting

Surgeon of St. Luke's Hospital, Battersea. *b.*
Gryllingham, 16 March, 1872, *only son* of Edward
Curzon Freke, Esq., of Gryll Court, Gryllingham.
Educ. Harrow and Trinity Coll., Cambridge; Col.
A.M.S.; late Member of the Advisory Board of the
Army Medical Service. *Publications:* Some Notes on
the Pathological Aspects of Genius, 1892; Statistical
Contributions to the Study of Infantile Paralysis in
England and Wales, 1894; Functional Disturbances
of the Nervous System, 1899; Cerebro-Spinal
Diseases, 1904; The Borderland of Insanity, 1906; An
Examination into the Treatment of Pauper Lunacy in
the United Kingdom, 1906; Modern Developments in
Psycho-Therapy: A Criticism, 1910; Criminal Lunacy,
1914; The Application of Psycho-Therapy to the
Treatment of Shell-Shock, 1917; An Answer to
Professor Freud, with a Description of Some
Experiments Carried Out at the Base Hospital at
Amiens, 1919; Structural Modifications Accompanying
the More Important Neuroses, 1920. *Clubs:* White's;
Oxford and Cambridge; Alpine, etc. *Recreations:* Chess,
Mountaineering, Fishing. *Address:* 282, Harley Street
and St. Luke's House, Prince of Wales Road, Battersea
Park, S.W.11.

He flung the book away. "Confirmation!" he groaned. "As if
I needed it!"

He sat down again and buried his face in his hands. He
remembered quite suddenly how, years ago, he had stood before
the breakfast table at Denver Castle—a small, peaky boy in blue
knickers, with a thunderously beating heart. The family had not
come down; there was a great silver urn with a spirit lamp under
it, and an elaborate coffee-pot boiling in a glass dome. He had
twitched the corner of the tablecloth—twitched it harder, and

the urn moved ponderously forward and all the teaspoons rattled. He seized the tablecloth in a firm grip and pulled his hardest—he could feel now the delicate and awful thrill as the urn and the coffee machine and the whole of a Sèvres breakfast service had crashed down in one stupendous ruin—he remembered the horrified face of the butler, and the screams of a lady guest.

A log broke across and sank into a fluff of white ash. A belated motor-lorry rumbled past the window.

Mr. Bunter, sleeping the sleep of the true and faithful servant, was aroused in the small hours by a hoarse whisper, "Bunter!"

"Yes, my lord," said Bunter, sitting up and switching on the light.

"Put that light out, damn you!" said the voice. "Listen—over there—listen—can't you hear it?"

"It's nothing, my lord," said Mr. Bunter, hastily getting out of bed and catching hold of his master; "it's all right, you get to bed quick and I'll fetch you a drop of bromide. Why, you're all shivering—you've been sitting up too late."

"Hush! no, no—it's the water," said Lord Peter with chattering teeth; "it's up to their waists down there, poor devils. But listen! can't you hear it? Tap, tap, tap—they're mining us—but I don't know where—I can't hear—I can't. Listen, you! There it is again—we must find it—we must stop it . . . Listen! Oh, my God! I can't hear—I can't hear anything for the noise of the guns. Can't they stop the guns?"

"Oh, dear!" said Mr. Bunter to himself. "No, no—it's all right, Major—don't you worry."

"But I hear it," protested Peter.

"So do I," said Mr. Bunter stoutly; "very good hearing, too, my lord. That's our own sappers at work in the communication trench. Don't you fret about that, sir."

Lord Peter grasped his wrist with a feverish hand.

"Our own sappers," he said; "sure of that?"

"Certain of it," said Mr. Bunter, cheerfully.

"They'll bring down the tower," said Lord Peter.

"To be sure they will," said Mr. Bunter, "and very nice, too. You just come and lay down a bit, sir—they've come to take over this section."

"You're sure it's safe to leave it?" said Lord Peter.

"Safe as houses, sir," said Mr. Bunter, tucking his master's arm under his and walking him off to his bedroom.

Lord Peter allowed himself to be dosed and put to bed without further resistance. Mr. Bunter, looking singularly un-Bunterlike in striped pyjamas, with his stiff black hair ruffled about his head, sat grimly watching the younger man's sharp cheekbones and the purple stains under his eyes.

"Thought we'd had the last of these attacks," he said. "Been overdoin' of himself. Asleep?" He peered at him anxiously. An affectionate note crept into his voice. "Bloody little fool!" said Sergeant Bunter.

Chapter 9

Mr. Parker, summoned the next morning to 110 Piccadilly, arrived to find the Dowager Duchess in possession. She greeted him charmingly.

"I am going to take this silly boy down to Denver for the week-end," she said, indicating Peter, who was writing and only acknowledged his friend's entrance with a brief nod. "He's been doing too much—running about to Salisbury and places and up till all hours of the night—you really shouldn't encourage him, Mr. Parker, it's very naughty of you—waking poor Bunter up in the middle of the night with scares about Germans, as if that wasn't all over years ago, and he hasn't had an attack for ages, but there! Nerves are such funny things, and Peter always did have nightmares when he was quite a little boy—though very often of course it was only a little pill he wanted; but he was so dreadfully bad in 1918, you know, and I suppose we can't expect to forget all about a great war in a year or two, and, really, I ought to be very thankful with both my boys safe. Still, I think a little peace and quiet at Denver won't do him any harm."

"Sorry you've been having a bad turn, old man," said Parker, vaguely sympathetic; "you're looking a bit seedy."

"Charles," said Lord Peter, in a voice entirely void of expression, "I am going away for a couple of days because I can be no use to you in London. What has got to be done for the moment can be much better done by you than by me. I want you to take this"—he folded up his writing and placed it in an envelope—"to Scotland Yard immediately and get it sent out to all the workhouses, infirmaries, police stations, Y.M.C.A.'s and so on in London. It is a description of Thipps's corpse as he was before he was shaved and cleaned up. I want to know whether any man answering to that description has been taken in anywhere, alive or dead, during the last fortnight. You will see Sir Andrew Mackenzie personally, and get the paper sent out at once, by his authority; you will tell him that you have solved the problems of the Levy murder and the Battersea mystery"—Mr. Parker made an astonished noise to which his friend paid no attention—"and you will ask him to have men in readiness with a warrant to arrest a very dangerous and important criminal at any moment on your information. When the replies to this paper come in, you will search for any mention of St. Luke's Hospital, or of any person connected with St. Luke's Hospital, and you will send for me at once.

"Meanwhile you will scrape acquaintance—I don't care how—with one of the students at St. Luke's. Don't march in there blowing about murders and police warrants, or you may find yourself in Queer Street. I shall come up to town as soon as I hear from you, and I shall expect to find a nice ingenuous Sawbones here to meet me." He grinned faintly.

"D'you mean you've got to the bottom of this thing?" asked Parker.

"Yes. I may be wrong. I hope I am, but I know I'm not."

"You won't tell me?"

"D'you know," said Peter, "honestly I'd rather not. I say I *may* be wrong—and I'd feel as if I'd libelled the Archbishop of Canterbury."

"Well, tell me—is it one mystery or two?"

"One."

"You talked of the Levy murder. Is Levy dead?"

"God—yes!" said Peter, with a strong shudder.

The Duchess looked up from where she was reading the *Tatler*.

"Peter," she said, "is that your ague coming on again? Whatever you two are chattering about, you'd better stop it at once if it excites you. Besides, it's about time to be off."

"All right, Mother," said Peter. He turned to Bunter, standing respectfully in the door with an overcoat and suitcase. "You understand what you have to do, don't you?" he said.

"Perfectly, thank you, my lord. The car is just arriving, your Grace."

"With Mrs. Thipps inside it," said the Duchess. "She'll be delighted to see you again, Peter. You remind her so of Mr. Thipps. Good-morning, Bunter."

"Good-morning, your Grace."

Parker accompanied them downstairs.

When they had gone he looked blankly at the paper in his hand—then, remembering that it was Saturday and there was need for haste, he hailed a taxi.

"Scotland Yard!" he cried.

* * * * *

Tuesday morning saw Lord Peter and a man in a velveteen jacket swishing merrily through seven acres of turnip-tops, streaked yellow with early frosts. A little way ahead, a sinuous undercurrent of excitement among the leaves proclaimed the unseen yet ever-near presence of one of the Duke of Denver's setter pups. Presently a partridge flew up with a noise like a police rattle, and Lord Peter accounted for it very creditably for a man who, a few nights before, had been listening to imaginary German sappers. The setter bounded foolishly through the turnips, and fetched back the dead bird.

"Good dog," said Lord Peter.

Encouraged by this, the dog gave a sudden ridiculous gambol and barked, its ear tossed inside out over its head.

"Heel," said the man in velveteen, violently. The animal sidled up, ashamed.

"Fool of a dog, that," said the man in velveteen; "can't keep quiet. Too nervous, my lord. One of old Black Lass's pups."

"Dear me," said Peter, "is the old dog still going?"

"No, my lord; we had to put her away in the spring."

Peter nodded. He always proclaimed that he hated the country and was thankful to have nothing to do with the family estates, but this morning he enjoyed the crisp air and the wet leaves washing darkly over his polished boots. At Denver things moved in an orderly way; no one died sudden and violent deaths except aged setters—and partridges, to be sure. He sniffed up the autumn smell with appreciation. There was a letter in his pocket which had come by the morning post, but he did not intend to read it just yet. Parker had not wired; there was no hurry.

* * * * *

He read it in the smoking-room after lunch. His brother was there, dozing over the *Times*—a good, clean Englishman, sturdy and conventional, rather like Henry VIII in his youth; Gerald, sixteenth Duke of Denver. The Duke considered his cadet rather degenerate, and not quite good form; he disliked his taste for police-court news.

The letter was from Mr. Bunter.

110, Piccadilly,
W.1.

MY LORD:

I write (Mr. Bunter had been carefully educated and knew that nothing is more vulgar than a careful avoidance of beginning a letter with the first person singular) as your lordship directed, to inform you of the result of my investigations.

I experienced no difficulty in becoming acquainted with Sir Julian Freke's man-servant. He belongs to the same club as the Hon. Frederick Arbuthnot's man, who is a friend of mine, and was very willing to introduce me. He took me to the club yesterday (Sunday) evening, and we dined with the man, whose name is John Cummings, and afterwards I invited Cummings to drinks and a cigar in the flat. Your lordship will excuse me doing this, knowing that it is not my habit, but it has always been my experience that the best way to gain a man's confidence is to let him suppose that one takes advantage of one's employer.

("I always suspected Bunter of being a student of human nature," commented Lord Peter.)

I gave him the best old port ("The deuce you did," said Lord Peter), having heard you and Mr. Arbuthnot talk over it. ("Hum!" said Lord Peter.)

Its effects were quite equal to my expectations as regards the principal matter in hand, but I very much regret to state that the man had so little understanding of what was offered to him that he smoked a cigar with it (one of your lordship's Villar Villars). You will understand that I made no comment on this at the time, but your lordship will sympathize with my feelings. May I take this opportunity of expressing my grateful appreciation of your lordship's excellent taste in food, drink and dress? It is, if I may say so, more than a pleasure—it is an education, to valet and buttle your lordship.

Lord Peter bowed his head gravely.

"What on earth are you doing, Peter, sittin' there noddin' an' grinnin' like a what-you-may-call-it?" demanded the Duke, coming suddenly out of a snooze. "Someone writin' pretty things to you, what?"

"Charming things," said Lord Peter.

The Duke eyed him doubtfully.

"Hope to goodness you don't go and marry a chorus beauty," he muttered inwardly, and returned to the *Times*.

* * * * *

Over dinner I had set myself to discover Cummings's tastes, and found them to run in the direction of the music-hall stage. During his first glass I drew him out in this direction, your lordship having kindly given me opportunities of seeing every performance in London, and I spoke more freely than I should consider becoming in the ordinary way in order to make myself pleasant to him. I may say that his views on women and the stage were such as I should have expected from a man who would smoke with your lordship's port.

With the second glass I introduced the subject of your lordship's inquiries. In order to save time I will write our conversation in the form of a dialogue, as nearly as possible as it actually took place.

Cummings: You seem to get many opportunities of seeing a bit of life, Mr. Bunter.

Bunter: One can always make opportunities if one knows how.

Cummings: Ah, it's very easy for you to talk, Mr. Bunter. You're not married, for one thing.

Bunter: I know better than that, Mr. Cummings.

Cummings: So do I—now, when it's too late. (He sighed heavily, and I filled up his glass.)

Bunter: Does Mrs. Cummings live with you at Battersea?

Cummings: Yes, her and me we do for my governor. Such a life! Not but what there's a char comes in by the day. But what's a char? I can tell you it's dull all by ourselves in that d——d Battersea suburb.

Bunter: Not very convenient for the Halls, of course.

Cummings: I believe you. It's all right for you, here in Piccadilly, right on the spot as you might say. And I daresay your governor's often out all night, eh?

Bunter: Oh, frequently, Mr. Cummings.

Cummings: And I daresay you take the opportunity to slip off yourself every so often, eh?

Bunter: Well, what do you think, Mr. Cummings?

Cummings: That's it; there you are! But what's a man to do with a nagging fool of a wife and a blasted scientific doctor for a governor, as sits up all night cutting up dead bodies and experimenting with frogs?

Bunter: Surely he goes out sometimes.

Cummings: Not often. And always back before twelve. And the way he goes on if he rings the bell and you ain't there. I give you my word, Mr. Bunter.

Bunter: Temper?

Cummings: No-o-o—but looking through you, nasty-like, as if you was on that operating table of his and he was going to cut you up. Nothing a man could rightly complain of, you understand, Mr. Bunter, just nasty looks. Not but what I will say he's very correct. Apologizes if he's been inconsiderate. But what's the good of that when he's been and gone and lost you your night's rest?

Bunter: How does he do that? Keeps you up late, you mean?

Cummings: Not him; far from it. House locked up and household to bed at half-past ten. That's his little rule. Not but what I'm glad enough to go as a rule, it's that dreary. Still, when I *do* go to bed I like to go to sleep.

Bunter: What does he do? Walk about the house?

Cummings: Doesn't he? All night. And in and out of the private door to the hospital.

Bunter: You don't mean to say, Mr. Cummings, a great specialist like Sir Julian Freke does night work at the hospital?

Cummings: No, no; he does his own work—research work, as you may say. Cuts people up. They say he's very clever. Could take you or me to pieces like a clock, Mr. Bunter, and put us together again.

Bunter: Do you sleep in the basement, then, to hear him so plain?

Cummings: No; our bedroom's at the top. But, Lord! what's that? He'll bang the door so you can hear him all over the house.

Bunter: Ah, many's the time I've had to speak to Lord Peter about that. And talking all night. And baths.

Cummings: Baths? You may well say that, Mr. Bunter. Baths? Me and my wife sleep next to the cistern-room. Noise fit to wake the dead. All hours. When d'you think he chose to have a bath, no later than last Monday night, Mr. Bunter?

Bunter: I've known them to do it at two in the morning, Mr. Cummings.

Cummings: Have you, now? Well, this was at three. Three o'clock in the morning we was waked up. I give you *my* word.

Bunter: You don't say so, Mr. Cummings.

Cummings: He cuts up diseases, you see, Mr. Bunter, and then he don't like to go to bed till he's washed the bacilluses off, if you understand me. Very natural, too, I daresay. But what I say is, the middle of the night's no time for a gentleman to be occupying his mind with diseases.

Bunter: These great men have their own way of doing things.

Cummings: Well, all I can say is, it isn't my way.

(I could believe that, your lordship. Cummings has no signs of greatness about him, and his trousers are not what I would wish to see in a man of his profession.)

Bunter: Is he habitually as late as that, Mr. Cummings?

Cummings: Well, no, Mr. Bunter, I will say, not as a general rule. He apologized, too, in the morning, and said he would have the cistern seen to—and very necessary, in my opinion, for the air gets into the pipes, and the groaning and screeching as goes on is something awful. Just like Niagara, if you follow me, Mr. Bunter, I give you *my* word.

Bunter: Well, that's as it should be, Mr. Cummings. One can put up with a great deal from a gentleman that has the manners to apologize. And, of course, sometimes they can't help themselves. A visitor will come in unexpectedly and keep them late, perhaps.

Cummings: That's true enough, Mr. Bunter. Now I come to think of it, there *was* a gentleman come in on Monday evening. Not that he came late, but he stayed about an hour, and may have put Sir Julian behindhand.

Bunter: Very likely. Let me give you some more port, Mr. Cummings. Or a little of Lord Peter's old brandy.

Cummings: A little of the brandy, thank you, Mr. Bunter. I suppose you have the run of the cellar here. (He winked at me.)

"Trust me for that," I said, and I fetched him the Napoleon. I assure your lordship it went to my heart to pour it out for a man like that. However, seeing we had got on the right tack, I felt it wouldn't be wasted.

"I'm sure I wish it was always gentlemen that come here at night," I said. (Your lordship will excuse me, I am sure, making such a suggestion.)

("Good God," said Lord Peter, "I wish Bunter was less thorough in his methods.")

Cummings: Oh, he's that sort, his lordship, is he? (He chuckled and poked me. I suppress a portion of his conversation here, which could not fail to be as offensive to your lordship as it was to myself. He went on:) No, it's none of that with Sir Julian. Very few visitors at night, and always gentlemen. And going early as a rule, like the one I mentioned.

Bunter: Just as well. There's nothing I find more wearisome, Mr. Cummings, than sitting up to see visitors out.

Cummings: Oh, I didn't see this one out. Sir Julian let him out himself at ten o'clock or thereabouts. I heard the gentleman shout "Good-night" and off he goes.

Bunter: Does Sir Julian always do that?

Cummings: Well, that depends. If he sees visitors

downstairs, he lets them out himself: if he sees them
upstairs in the library, he rings for me.

Bunter: This was a downstairs visitor, then?

Cummings: Oh, yes. Sir Julian opened the door to
him, I remember. He happened to be working in the
hall. Though now I come to think of it, they went up
to the library afterwards. That's funny. I know they
did, because I happened to go up to the hall with coals,
and I heard them upstairs. Besides, Sir Julian rang for
me in the library a few minutes later. Still, anyway, we
heard him go at ten, or it may have been a bit before.
He hadn't only stayed about three-quarters of an hour.
However, as I was saying, there was Sir Julian banging
in and out of the private door all night, and a bath at
three in the morning, and up again for breakfast at
eight—it beats me. If I had all his money, curse me if
I'd go poking about with dead men in the middle of
the night. I'd find something better to do with my time,
eh, Mr. Bunter—

I need not repeat any more of his conversation,
as it became unpleasant and incoherent, and I could
not bring him back to the events of Monday night.
I was unable to get rid of him till three. He cried on
my neck, and said I was the bird, and you were the
governor for him. He said that Sir Julian would be
greatly annoyed with him for coming home so late, but
Sunday night was his night out and if anything was
said about it he would give notice. I think he will be
ill-advised to do so, as I feel he is not a man I could
conscientiously recommend if I were in Sir Julian
Freke's place. I noticed that his boot-heels were slightly
worn down.

I should wish to add, as a tribute to the great
merits of your lordship's cellar, that, although I was

obliged to drink a somewhat large quantity both of the Cockburn '68 and the 1800 Napoleon I feel no headache or other ill effects this morning.

Trusting that your lordship is deriving real benefit from the country air, and that the little information I have been able to obtain will prove satisfactory, I remain.

With respectful duty to all the family,

Obediently yours,

MERVYN BUNTER

"Y'know," said Lord Peter thoughtfully to himself, "I sometimes think Mervyn Bunter's pullin' my leg. What is it, Soames?"

"A telegram, my lord."

"Parker," said Lord Peter, opening it. It said:

Description recognised Chelsea Workhouse. Unknown vagrant injured street accident Wednesday week. Died workhouse Monday. Delivered St. Luke's same evening by order Freke. Much puzzled. PARKER.

"Hurray!" said Lord Peter, suddenly sparkling. "I'm glad I've puzzled Parker. Gives me confidence in myself. Makes me feel like Sherlock Holmes. 'Perfectly simple, Watson.' Dash it all, though! this is a beastly business. Still, it's puzzled Parker."

"What's the matter?" asked the Duke, getting up and yawning.

"Marching orders," said Peter, "back to town. Many thanks for your hospitality, old bird—I'm feelin' no end better. Ready to tackle Professor Moriarty or Leon Kestrel or any of 'em."

"I do wish you'd keep out of the police courts," grumbled the Duke. "It makes it so dashed awkward for me, havin' a brother makin' himself conspicuous."

"Sorry, Gerald," said the other; "I know I'm a beastly blot on the 'scutcheon."

"Why can't you marry and settle down and live quietly, doin' something useful?" said the Duke, unappeased.

"Because that was a wash-out as you perfectly well know," said Peter; "besides," he added cheerfully, "I'm bein' no end useful. You may come to want me yourself, you never know. When anybody comes blackmailin' you, Gerald, or your first deserted wife turns up unexpectedly from the West Indies, you'll realize the pull of havin' a private detective in the family. 'Delicate private business arranged with tact and discretion. Investigations undertaken. Divorce evidence a specialty. Every guarantee!' Come, now."

"Ass!" said Lord Denver, throwing the newspaper violently into his armchair. "When do you want the car?"

"Almost at once. I say, Jerry, I'm taking Mother up with me."

"Why should she be mixed up in it?"

"Well, I want her help."

"I call it most unsuitable," said the Duke.

The Dowager Duchess, however, made no objection.

"I used to know her quite well," she said, "when she was Christine Ford. Why, dear?"

"Because," said Lord Peter, "there's a terrible piece of news to be broken to her about her husband."

"Is he dead, dear?"

"Yes; and she will have to come and identify him."

"Poor Christine."

"Under very revolting circumstances, Mother."

"I'll come with you, dear."

"Thank you, Mother, you're a brick. D'you mind gettin' your things on straight away and comin' up with me? I'll tell you about it in the car."

Chapter 10

M r. Parker, a faithful though doubting Thomas, had duly secured his medical student: a large young man like an overgrown puppy, with innocent eyes and a freckled face. He sat on the Chesterfield before Lord Peter's library fire, bewildered in equal measure by his errand, his surroundings and the drink which he was absorbing. His palate, though untutored, was naturally a good one, and he realized that even to call this liquid a drink—the term ordinarily used by him to designate cheap whisky, post-war beer or a dubious glass of claret in a Soho restaurant—was a sacrilege; this was something outside normal experience: a genie in a bottle.

The man called Parker, whom he had happened to run across the evening before in the public-house at the corner of Prince of Wales Road, seemed to be a good sort. He had insisted on bringing him round to see this friend of his, who lived splendidly in Piccadilly. Parker was quite understandable; he put him down as a government servant, or perhaps something in the City. The friend was embarrassing; he was a lord, to begin with, and his clothes were a kind of rebuke to the world at large. He talked the most fatuous nonsense, certainly, but in a disconcerting way. He didn't dig into a joke and get all the fun out of it; he made it in passing, so to speak, and skipped away to something else before your retort was ready. He had a truly terrible man-servant—the sort you read about in books—who froze the marrow in your bones with silent criticism. Parker appeared to bear up under the strain, and this made you think more highly of Parker; he must be more habituated to the surroundings of the great than you would think to look at him. You wondered what the carpet had cost on which Parker was carelessly spilling cigar ash; your father was an upholsterer—Mr. Piggott, of Piggott & Piggott, Liverpool—and you knew enough about carpets to know that you couldn't even guess at the price of this one. When you moved your head on the bulging silk cushion in the corner of the sofa, it made you wish you shaved more often and more carefully. The sofa was a monster—but even so, it hardly seemed big enough to contain you. This Lord Peter was not very tall—in fact, he was rather a small man, but he didn't look undersized. He looked right; he made you feel that to be six-foot-three was rather vulgarly assertive; you felt like Mother's new drawing-room curtains—all over great big blobs. But everybody was very decent to you, and nobody said anything you couldn't understand, or sneered at you. There were some frightfully deep-looking books on the shelves all round, and you had looked into a great folio Dante which was lying on the table, but your hosts were talking quite ordinarily and rationally about the sort of books you read yourself—clinking good love stories and detective stories. You had read a lot of those, and could give an opinion, and they listened to what you had to say, though Lord Peter had a funny way of talking about books, too, as if the author had confided in him beforehand, and told him how the story was put together, and which bit was written first. It reminded you of the way old Freke took a body to pieces.

"Thing I object to in detective stories," said Mr. Piggott, "is the way fellows remember every bloomin' thing that's happened to 'em within the last six months. They're always ready with their time of day and was it rainin' or not, and what were they doin' on such an' such a day. Reel it all off like a page of poetry. But one ain't like that in real life, d'you think so, Lord Peter?" Lord Peter smiled, and young Piggott, instantly embarrassed, appealed to his earlier acquaintance. "You know what I mean, Parker. Come now. One day's so like another, I'm sure I couldn't remember—well, I might remember yesterday, p'r'aps, but I couldn't be certain about what I was doin' last week if I was to be shot for it."

"No," said Parker, "and evidence given in police statements sounds just as impossible. But they don't really get it like that, you know. I mean, a man doesn't just say, 'Last Friday I went out at 10 a.m. to buy a mutton chop. As I was turning into Mortimer Street I noticed a girl of about twenty-two with black hair and brown eyes, wearing a green jumper, check skirt, Panama hat and black shoes, riding a Royal Sunbeam Cycle at about ten miles an hour turning the corner by the Church of St. Simon and St. Jude on the wrong side of the road riding towards the market place!' It amounts to that, of course, but it's really wormed out of him by a series of questions."

"And in short stories," said Lord Peter, "it has to be put in statement form, because the real conversation would be so long and twaddly and tedious, and nobody would have the patience to read it. Writers have to consider their readers, if any, y'see."

"Yes," said Mr. Piggott, "but I bet you most people would find it jolly difficult to remember, even if you asked 'em things. I should—of course, I know I'm a bit of a fool, but then, most people are, ain't they? You know what I mean. Witnesses ain't detectives, they're just average idiots like you and me."

"Quite so," said Lord Peter, smiling as the force of the last phrase sank into its unhappy perpetrator; "you mean, if I were to ask you in a general way what you were doin'—say, a week ago today, you wouldn't be able to tell me a thing about it offhand?"

"No—I'm sure I shouldn't." He considered. "No. I was in at the Hospital as usual, I suppose, and, being Tuesday, there'd be a lecture on something or the other—dashed if I know what—and in the evening I went out with Tommy Pringle—no, that must have been Monday—or was it Wednesday? I tell you, I couldn't swear to anything."

"You do yourself an injustice," said Lord Peter gravely. "I'm sure, for instance, you recollect what work you were doing in the dissecting-room on that day, for example."

"Lord, no! not for certain. I mean, I daresay it might come back to me if I thought for a long time, but I wouldn't swear to it in a court of law."

"I'll bet you half-a-crown to sixpence," said Lord Peter, "that you'll remember within five minutes."

"I'm sure I can't."

"We'll see. Do you keep a notebook of the work you do when you dissect? Drawings or anything?"

"Oh, yes."

"Think of that. What's the last thing you did in it?"

"That's easy, because I only did it this morning. It was leg muscles."

"Yes. Who was the subject?"

"An old woman of sorts; died of pneumonia."

"Yes. Turn back the pages of your drawing book in your mind. What came before that?"

"Oh, some animals—still legs; I'm doing motor muscles at present. Yes. That was old Cunningham's demonstration on comparative anatomy. I did rather a good thing of a hare's legs and a frog's, and rudimentary legs on a snake."

"Yes. Which day does Mr. Cunningham lecture?"

"Friday."

"Friday; yes. Turn back again. What comes before that?"

Mr. Piggott shook his head.

"Do your drawings of legs begin on the right-hand page or the left-hand page? Can you see the first drawing?"

"Yes—yes—I can see the date written at the top. It's a section of a frog's hind leg, on the right-hand page."

"Yes. Think of the open book in your mind's eye. What is opposite to it?"

This demanded some mental concentration.

"Something round—coloured—oh, yes—it's a hand."

"Yes. You went on from the muscles of the hand and arm to leg- and foot-muscles?"

"Yes; that's right. I've got a set of drawings of arms."

"Yes. Did you make those on the Thursday?"

"No; I'm never in the dissecting-room on Thursday."

"On Wednesday, perhaps?"

"Yes; I must have made them on Wednesday. Yes; I did. I went in there after we'd seen those tetanus patients in the morning. I did them on Wednesday afternoon. I know I went back because I wanted to finish 'em. I worked rather hard—for me. That's why I remember."

"Yes; you went back to finish them. When had you begun them, then?"

"Why, the day before."

"The day before. That was Tuesday, wasn't it?"

"I've lost count—yes, the day before Wednesday—yes, Tuesday."

"Yes. Were they a man's arms or a woman's arms?"

"Oh, a man's arms."

"Yes; last Tuesday, a week ago today, you were dissecting a man's arms in the dissecting-room. Sixpence, please."

"By Jove!"

"Wait a moment. You know a lot more about it than that. You've no idea how much you know. You know what kind of man he was."

"Oh, I never saw him complete, you know. I got there a bit late that day, I remember. I'd asked for an arm specially, because I was rather weak in arms, and Watts—that's the attendant—had promised to save me one."

"Yes. You have arrived late and found your arm waiting for you. You are dissecting it—taking your scissors and slitting up the skin and pinning it back. Was it very young, fair skin?"

"Oh, no—no. Ordinary skin, I think—with dark hairs on it—yes, that was it."

"Yes. A lean, stringy arm, perhaps, with no extra fat anywhere?"

"Oh, no—I was rather annoyed about that. I wanted a good, muscular arm, but it was rather poorly developed and the fat got in my way."

"Yes; a sedentary man who didn't do much manual work."

"That's right."

"Yes. You dissected the hand, for instance, and made a drawing of it. You would have noticed any hard calluses."

"Oh, there was nothing of that sort."

"No. But should you say it was a young man's arm? Firm young flesh and limber joints?"

"No—no."

"No. Old and stringy, perhaps."

"No. Middle-aged—with rheumatism. I mean, there was a chalky deposit in the joints, and the fingers were a bit swollen."

"Yes. A man about fifty."

"About that."

"Yes. There were other students at work on the same body."

"Oh, yes."

"Yes. And they made all the usual sort of jokes about it."

"I expect so—oh, yes!"

"You can remember some of them. Who is your local funny man, so to speak?"

"Tommy Pringle."

"What was Tommy Pringle's doing?"

"Can't remember."

"Whereabouts was Tommy Pringle working?"

"Over by the instrument cupboard—by sink C."

"Yes. Get a picture of Tommy Pringle in your mind's eye."

Piggott began to laugh.

"I remember now. Tommy Pringle said the old Sheeny—"

"Why did he call him a Sheeny?"

"I don't know. But I know he did."

"Perhaps he looked like it. Did you see his head?"

"No."

"Who had the head?"

"I don't know—oh, yes, I do, though. Old Freke bagged the head himself, and little Bouncible Binns was very cross about it, because he'd been promised a head to do with old Scrooger."

"I see. What was Sir Julian doing with the head?"

"He called us up and gave us a jaw on spinal haemorrhage and nervous lesions."

"Yes. Well, go back to Tommy Pringle."

Tommy Pringle's joke was repeated, not without some embarrassment.

"Quite so. Was that all?"

"No. The chap who was working with Tommy said that sort of thing came from over-feeding."

"I deduce that Tommy Pringle's partner was interested in the alimentary canal."

"Yes; and Tommy said, if he'd thought they'd feed you like that he'd go to the workhouse himself."

"Then the man was a pauper from the workhouse?"

"Well, he must have been, I suppose."

"Are workhouse paupers usually fat and well-fed?"

"Well, no—come to think of it, not as a rule."

"In fact, it struck Tommy Pringle and his friend that this was something a little out of the way in a workhouse subject?"

"Yes."

"And if the alimentary canal was so entertaining to these gentlemen, I imagine the subject had come by his death shortly after a full meal."

"Yes—oh, yes—he'd have had to, wouldn't he?"

"Well, I don't know," said Lord Peter. "That's in your department, you know. That would be your inference, from what they said."

"Oh, yes. Undoubtedly."

"Yes; you wouldn't, for example, expect them to make that observation if the patient had been ill for a long time and fed on slops."

"Of course not."

"Well, you see, you really know a lot about it. On Tuesday week you were dissecting the arm muscles of a rheumatic middle-aged Jew, of sedentary habits, who had died shortly after eating a heavy meal, of some injury producing spinal haemorrhage and nervous lesions, and so forth, and who was presumed to come from the workhouse?"

"Yes."

"And you could swear to those facts, if need were?"

"Well, if you put it in that way, I suppose I could."

"Of course you could."

Mr. Piggott sat for some moments in contemplation.

"I say," he said at last, "I did know all that, didn't I?"

"Oh, yes—you knew it all right—like Socrates's slave."

"Who's he?"

"A person in a book I used to read as a boy."

"Oh—does he come in 'The Last Days of Pompeii'?"

"No—another book—I daresay you escaped it. It's rather dull."

"I never read much except Henty and Fenimore Cooper at school . . . But—have I got rather an extra good memory, then?"

"You have a better memory than you credit yourself with."

"Then why can't I remember all the medical stuff? It all goes out of my head like a sieve."

"Well, why can't you?" said Lord Peter, standing on the hearthrug and smiling down at his guest.

"Well," said the young man, "the chaps who examine one don't ask the same sort of questions you do."

"No?"

"No—they leave you to remember all by yourself. And it's beastly hard. Nothing to catch hold of, don't you know? But, I say—how did you know about Tommy Pringle being the funny man and—"

"I didn't, till you told me."

"No; I know. But how did you know he'd be there if you did ask? I mean to say—I say," said Mr. Piggott, who was becoming mellowed by influences themselves not unconnected with the alimentary canal—"I say, are you rather clever, or am I rather stupid?"

"No, no," said Lord Peter, "it's me. I'm always askin' such stupid questions, everybody thinks I must mean somethin' by 'em."

This was too involved for Mr. Piggott.

"Never mind," said Parker, soothingly, "he's always like that. You mustn't take any notice. He can't help it. It's premature senile decay, often observed in the families of hereditary legislators. Go away, Wimsey, and play us the 'Beggar's Opera,' or something."

"That's good enough, isn't it?" said Lord Peter, when the happy Mr. Piggott had been despatched home after a really delightful evening.

"I'm afraid so," said Parker. "But it seems almost incredible."

"There's nothing incredible in human nature," said Lord Peter; "at least, in educated human nature. Have you got that exhumation order?"

"I shall have it tomorrow. I thought of fixing up with the workhouse people for tomorrow afternoon. I shall have to go and see them first."

"Right you are; I'll let my mother know."

"I begin to feel like you, Wimsey, I don't like this job."

"I like it a deal better than I did."

"You are really certain we're not making a mistake?"

Lord Peter had strolled across to the window. The curtain was not perfectly drawn, and he stood gazing out through the gap into lighted Piccadilly. At this he turned round:

"If we are," he said, "we shall know tomorrow, and no harm will have been done. But I rather think you will receive a certain amount of confirmation on your way home. Look here, Parker, d'you know, if I were you I'd spend the night here. There's a spare bedroom; I can easily put you up."

Parker stared at him.

"Do you mean—I'm likely to be attacked?"

"I think it very likely indeed."

"Is there anybody in the street?"

"Not now; there was half-an-hour ago."

"When Piggott left?"

"Yes."

"I say—I hope the boy is in no danger."

"That's what I went down to see. I don't think so. Fact is, I don't suppose anybody would imagine we'd exactly made a confidant of Piggott. But I think you and I are in danger. You'll stay?"

"I'm damned if I will, Wimsey. Why should I run away?"

"Bosh!" said Peter. "You'd run away all right if you believed me, and why not? You don't believe me. In fact, you're still not certain I'm on the right tack. Go in peace, but don't say I didn't warn you."

"I won't; I'll dictate a message with my dying breath to say I was convinced."

"Well, don't walk—take a taxi."

"Very well, I'll do that."

"And don't let anybody else get into it."

"No."

It was a raw, unpleasant night. A taxi deposited a load of people returning from the theatre at the block of flats next door, and Parker secured it for himself. He was just giving the address to the driver, when a man came hastily running up from a side street. He was in evening dress and an overcoat. He rushed up, signalling frantically.

"Sir—sir!—dear me! why, it's Mr. Parker! How fortunate! If you would be so kind—summoned from the club—a sick friend—can't find a taxi—everybody going home from the theatre—if I might share your cab—you are returning to Bloomsbury? I want Russell Square—if I might presume—a matter of life and death."

He spoke in hurried gasps, as though he had been running violently and far. Parker promptly stepped out of the taxi.

"Delighted to be of service to you, Sir Julian," he said; "take my taxi. I am going down to Craven Street myself, but I'm in no hurry. Pray make use of the cab."

"It's extremely kind of you," said the surgeon. "I am ashamed—"

"That's all right," said Parker, cheerily. "I can wait." He assisted Freke into the taxi. "What number? 24 Russell Square, driver, and look sharp."

The taxi drove off. Parker remounted the stairs and rang Lord Peter's bell.

"Thanks, old man," he said. "I'll stop the night, after all."

"Come in," said Wimsey.

"Did you see that?" asked Parker.

"I saw something. What happened exactly?"

Parker told his story. "Frankly," he said, "I've been thinking you a bit mad, but now I'm not quite so sure of it."

Peter laughed.

"Blessed are they that have not seen and yet have believed. Bunter, Mr. Parker will stay the night."

"Look here, Wimsey, let's have another look at this business. Where's that letter?"

Lord Peter produced Bunter's essay in dialogue. Parker studied it for a short time in silence.

"You know, Wimsey, I'm as full of objections to this idea as an egg is of meat."

"So'm I, old son. That's why I want to dig up our Chelsea pauper. But trot out your objections."

"Well—"

"Well, look here, I don't pretend to be able to fill in all the blanks myself. But here we have two mysterious occurrences in one night, and a complete chain connecting the one with another through one particular person. It's beastly, but it's not unthinkable."

"Yes, I know all that. But there are one or two quite definite stumbling-blocks."

"Yes, I know. But, see here. On the one hand, Levy disappeared after being last seen looking for Prince of Wales Road at nine o'clock. At eight next morning a dead man, not unlike him in general outline, is discovered in a bath in Queen Caroline Mansions. Levy, by Freke's own admission, was going to see Freke. By information received from Chelsea workhouse a dead man, answering to the description of the Battersea corpse in its natural state, was delivered that same day to Freke. We have Levy with a past, and no future, as it were; an unknown vagrant with a future (in the cemetery) and no past, and Freke stands between their future and their past."

"That looks all right—"

"Yes. Now, further: Freke has a motive for getting rid of Levy—an old jealousy."

"Very old—and not much of a motive."

"People have been known to do that sort of thing.* You're thinking that people don't keep up old jealousies for twenty years or so. Perhaps not. Not just primitive, brute jealousy. That means a word and a blow. But the thing that rankles is hurt vanity. That sticks. Humiliation. And we've all got a sore spot we don't like to have touched. I've got it. You've got it. Some blighter said hell knew no fury like a woman scorned. Stickin' it on to women, poor devils. Sex is every man's loco spot—you needn't fidget, you know it's true—he'll take a disappointment, but not a humiliation. I knew a man once who'd been turned down—not too charitably—by a girl he was engaged to. He spoke quite decently about her. I asked what had become of her. 'Oh,' he said, 'she married the other fellow.' And then burst

---

* Lord Peter was not without authority for his opinion: "With respect to the alleged motive, it is of great importance to see whether there was a motive for committing such a crime, or whether there was not, or whether there is an improbability of its having been committed so strong as not to be overpowered by positive evidence. But *if there be any motive which can be assigned, I am bound to tell you that the inadequacy of that motive is of little importance.* We know, from the experience of criminal courts, that atrocious crimes of this sort have been committed from very slight motives; *not merely from malice and revenge,* but to gain a small pecuniary advantage, and to drive off for a time pressing difficulties."—L. C. J. Campbell, summing up in Reg. v. Palmer, Shorthand Report, p. 308 C. C. C., May, 1856, Sess. Pa. 5. (Italics mine. D. L. S.)

out—couldn't help himself. 'Lord, yes!' he cried. 'To think of it—jilted for a Scotchman!' I don't know why he didn't like Scots, but that was what got him on the raw. Look at Freke. I've read his books. His attacks on his antagonists are savage. And he's a scientist. Yet he can't bear opposition, even in his work, which is where any first-class man is most sane and open-minded. Do you think he's a man to take a beating from any man on a side-issue? On a man's most sensitive side-issue? People are opinionated about side-issues, you know. I see red if anybody questions my judgment about a book. And Levy—who was nobody twenty years ago—romps in and carries off Freke's girl from under his nose. It isn't the girl Freke would bother about—it's having his aristocratic nose put out of joint by a little Jewish nobody.

"There's another thing. Freke's got another side-issue. He likes crime. In that criminology book of his he gloats over a hardened murderer. I've read it, and I've seen the admiration simply glaring out between the lines whenever he writes about a callous and successful criminal. He reserves his contempt for the victims or the penitents or the men who lose their heads and get found out. His heroes are Edmond de la Pommerais, who persuaded his mistress into becoming an accessory to her own murder, and George Joseph Smith of Brides-in-a-bath fame, who could make passionate love to his wife in the night and carry out his plot to murder her in the morning. After all, he thinks conscience is a sort of vermiform appendix. Chop it out and you'll feel all the better. Freke isn't troubled by the usual conscientious deterrent. Witness his own hand in his books. Now again. The man who went to Levy's house in his place knew the house: Freke knew the house; he was a red-haired man, smaller than Levy, but not much smaller, since he could wear his clothes without appearing ludicrous: you have seen Freke—you know his height—about five-foot-eleven, I suppose, and his auburn mane; he probably wore surgical gloves: Freke is a surgeon; he was a methodical and daring man: surgeons are obliged to be both daring and methodical. Now take the other side. The man who got hold of the Battersea corpse had to have access to dead bodies. Freke obviously had access to dead bodies. He had to be cool and quick and callous about handling a dead body. Surgeons are all that. He had to be a strong man to carry the body across the roofs and dump it in at Thipps's window. Freke is a powerful man and a member of the Alpine Club. He probably wore surgical gloves and he let the body down from the roof with a surgical bandage. This points to a surgeon again. He undoubtedly lived in the neighbourhood. Freke lives next door. The girl you interviewed heard a bump on the roof of the end house. That is the house next to Freke's. Every time we look at Freke, he leads somewhere, whereas Milligan and Thipps and Crimplesham and all the other people we've honoured with our suspicion simply led nowhere."

"Yes; but it's not quite so simple as you make out. What was Levy doing in that surreptitious way at Freke's on Monday night?"

"Well, you have Freke's explanation."

"Rot, Wimsey. You said yourself it wouldn't do."

"Excellent. It won't do. Therefore Freke was lying. Why should he lie about it, unless he had some object in hiding the truth?"

"Well, but why mention it at all?"

"Because Levy, contrary to all expectation, had been seen at the corner of the road. That was a nasty accident for Freke. He thought it best to be beforehand with an explanation—of sorts. He reckoned, of course, on nobody's ever connecting Levy with Battersea Park."

"Well, then, we come back to the first question: Why did Levy go there?"

"I don't know, but he was got there somehow. Why did Freke buy all those Peruvian Oil shares?"

"I don't know," said Parker in his turn.

"Anyway," went on Wimsey, "Freke expected him, and made arrangements to let him in himself, so that Cummings shouldn't see who the caller was."

"But the caller left again at ten."

"Oh, Charles! I did not expect this of you. This is the purest Suggery! Who saw him go? Somebody said 'Good-night' and walked away down the street. And you believe it was Levy because Freke didn't go out of his way to explain that it wasn't."

"D'you mean that Freke walked cheerfully out of the house to Park Lane, and left Levy behind—dead or alive—for Cummings to find?"

"We have Cummings's word that he did nothing of the sort. A few minutes after the steps walked away from the house, Freke rang the library bell and told Cummings to shut up for the night."

"Then—"

"Well—there's a side door to the house, I suppose—in fact, you know there is—Cummings said so—through the hospital."

"Yes—well, where was Levy?"

"Levy went up into the library and never came down. You've been in Freke's library. Where would you have put him?"

"In my bedroom next door."

"Then that's where he did put him."

"But suppose the man went in to turn down the bed?"

"Beds are turned down by the housekeeper, earlier than ten o'clock."

"Yes . . . But Cummings heard Freke about the house all night."

"He heard him go in and out two or three times. He'd expect him to do that, anyway."

"Do you mean to say Freke got all that job finished before three in the morning?"

"Why not?"

"Quick work."

"Well, call it quick work. Besides, why three? Cummings never saw him again till he called him for eight o'clock breakfast."

"But he was having a bath at three."

"I don't say he didn't get back from Park Lane before three. But I don't suppose Cummings went and looked through the bathroom keyhole to see if he was in the bath."

Parker considered again.

"How about Crimplesham's pince-nez?" he asked.

"That is a bit mysterious," said Lord Peter.

"And why Thipps's bathroom?"

"Why, indeed? Pure accident, perhaps—or pure devilry."

"Do you think all this elaborate scheme could have been put together in a night, Wimsey?"

"Far from it. It was conceived as soon as that man who bore a superficial resemblance to Levy came into the workhouse. He had several days."

"I see."

"Freke gave himself away at the inquest. He and Grimbold disagreed about the length of the man's illness. If a small man (comparatively speaking) like Grimbold presumes to disagree with a man like Freke, it's because he is sure of his ground."

"Then—if your theory is sound—Freke made a mistake."

"Yes. A very slight one. He was guarding, with unnecessary caution, against starting a train of thought in the mind of anybody—say, the workhouse doctor. Up till then he'd been reckoning on the fact that people don't think a second time about anything (a body, say) that's once been accounted for."

"What made him lose his head?"

"A chain of unforeseen accidents. Levy's having been recognised—my mother's son having foolishly advertised in the *Times* his connection with the Battersea end of the mystery—Detective Parker (whose photograph has been a little prominent in the illustrated press lately) seen sitting next door to the Duchess of Denver at the inquest. His aim in life was to prevent the two ends of the problem from linking up. And there were two of the links, literally side by side. Many criminals are wrecked by over-caution."

Parker was silent.

Chapter 11

"A regular pea-souper, by Jove," said Lord Peter.

Parker grunted, and struggled irritably into an overcoat.

"It affords me, if I may say so, the greatest satisfaction," continued the noble lord, "that in a collaboration like ours all the uninteresting and disagreeable routine work is done by you."

Parker grunted again.

"Do you anticipate any difficulty about the warrant?" inquired Lord Peter.

Parker grunted a third time.

"I suppose you've seen to it that all this business is kept quiet?"

"Of course."

"You've muzzled the workhouse people?"

"Of course."

"And the police?"

"Yes."

"Because, if you haven't there'll probably be nobody to arrest."

"My dear Wimsey, do you think I'm a fool?"

"I had no such hope."

Parker grunted finally and departed.

Lord Peter settled down to a perusal of his Dante. It afforded him no solace. Lord Peter was hampered in his career as a private detective by a public-school education. Despite Parker's admonitions, he was not always able to discount it. His mind had been warped in its young growth by "Raffles" and "Sherlock Holmes," or the sentiments for which they stand. He belonged to a family which had never shot a fox.

"I am an amateur," said Lord Peter.

Nevertheless, while communing with Dante, he made up his mind.

* * * * *

In the afternoon he found himself in Harley Street. Sir Julian Freke might be consulted about one's nerves from two till four on Tuesdays and Fridays. Lord Peter rang the bell.

"Have you an appointment, sir?" inquired the man who opened the door.

"No," said Lord Peter, "but will you give Sir Julian my card? I think it possible he may see me without one."

He sat down in the beautiful room in which Sir Julian's patients awaited his healing counsel. It was full of people. Two or three fashionably dressed women were discussing shops and servants together, and teasing a toy griffon. A big, worried-looking man by himself in a corner looked at his watch twenty times a minute. Lord Peter knew him by sight. It was Wintrington, a millionaire, who had tried to kill himself a few months ago. He controlled the finances of five countries, but he could not control his nerves. The finances of five countries were in Sir Julian Freke's capable hands. By the fireplace sat a soldierly-looking young man, of about Lord Peter's own age. His face was prematurely lined and worn; he sat bolt upright, his restless eyes darting in the direction of every slightest sound. On the sofa was an elderly woman of modest appearance, with a young girl. The girl seemed listless and wretched; the woman's look showed deep affection, and anxiety tempered with a timid hope. Close beside Lord Peter was another younger woman, with a little girl, and Lord Peter noticed in both of them the broad cheekbones and beautiful grey, slanting eyes of the Slav. The child, moving restlessly about, trod on Lord Peter's patent-leather toe, and the mother admonished her in French before turning to apologize to Lord Peter.

"Mais je vous en prie, madame," said the young man, "it is nothing."

"She is nervous, pauvre petite," said the young woman.

"You are seeking advice for her?"

"Yes. He is wonderful, the doctor. Figure to yourself, monsieur, she cannot forget, poor child, the things she has seen." She leaned nearer, so that the child might not hear. "We have escaped—from starving Russia—six months ago. I dare not tell you—she has such quick ears, and then, the cries, the tremblings, the convulsions—they all begin again. We were skeletons when we arrived—mon Dieu!—but that is better now. See, she is thin, but she is not starved. She would be fatter but for the nerves that keep her from eating. We who are older, we forget—enfin, on apprend à ne pas y penser—but these children! When one is young, monsieur, tout ça impressionne trop."

Lord Peter, escaping from the thraldom of British good form, expressed himself in that language in which sympathy is not condemned to mutism.

"But she is much better, much better," said the mother, proudly; "the great doctor, he does marvels."

"C'est un homme précieux," said Lord Peter.

"Ah, monsieur, c'est un saint qui opère des miracles! Nous prions pour lui, Natasha et moi, tous les jours. N'est-ce pas, chérie? And consider, monsieur, that he does it all, ce grand homme, cet homme illustre, for nothing at all. When we come here, we have not even the clothes upon our backs—we are ruined, famished. Et avec ça que nous sommes de bonne famille—mais hélas! monsieur, en Russie, comme vous savez, ça ne vous vaut que des insultes—des atrocités. Enfin! the great Sir Julian sees us, he says—'Madame, your little girl is very interesting to me. Say no more. I cure her for nothing—pour ses beaux yeux,' a-t-il ajouté en riant. Ah, monsieur, c'est un saint, un véritable saint! and Natasha is much, much better."

"Madame, je vous en félicite."

"And you, monsieur? You are young, well, strong—you also suffer? It is still the war, perhaps?"

"A little remains of shell-shock," said Lord Peter.

"Ah, yes. So many good, brave, young men—"

"Sir Julian can spare you a few minutes, my lord, if you will come in now," said the servant.

Lord Peter bowed to his neighbour, and walked across the waiting-room. As the door of the consulting-room closed behind him, he remembered having once gone, disguised, into the staff-room of a German officer. He experienced the same feeling—the feeling of being caught in a trap, and a mingling of bravado and shame.

* * * * *

He had seen Sir Julian Freke several times from a distance, but never close. Now, while carefully and quite truthfully detailing the circumstances of his recent nervous attack, he considered the man before him. A man taller than himself, with immense breadth of shoulder, and wonderful hands. A face beautiful, impassioned and inhuman; fanatical, compelling eyes, bright blue amid the ruddy bush of hair and beard. They were not the cool and kindly eyes of the family doctor, they were the brooding eyes of the inspired scientist, and they searched one through.

"Well," thought Lord Peter, "I shan't have to be explicit, anyhow."

"Yes," said Sir Julian, "yes. You had been working too hard. Puzzling your mind. Yes. More than that, perhaps—troubling your mind, shall we say?"

"I found myself faced with a very alarming contingency."

"Yes. Unexpectedly, perhaps."

"Very unexpected indeed."

"Yes. Following on a period of mental and physical strain."

"Well—perhaps. Nothing out of the way."

"Yes. The unexpected contingency was—personal to yourself?"

"It demanded an immediate decision as to my own actions—yes, in that sense it was certainly personal."

"Quite so. You would have to assume some responsibility, no doubt."

"A very grave responsibility."

"Affecting others besides yourself?"

"Affecting one other person vitally, and a very great number indirectly."

"Yes. The time was night. You were sitting in the dark?"

"Not at first. I think I put the light out afterwards."

"Quite so—that action would naturally suggest itself to you. Were you warm?"

"I think the fire had died down. My man tells me that my teeth were chattering when I went in to him."

"Yes. You live in Piccadilly?"

"Yes."

"Heavy traffic sometimes goes past during the night, I expect."

"Oh, frequently."

"Just so. Now this decision you refer to—you had taken that decision."

"Yes."

"Your mind was made up?"

"Oh, yes."

"You had decided to take the action, whatever it was."

"Yes."

"Yes. It involved perhaps a period of inaction."

"Of comparative inaction—yes."

"Of suspense, shall we say?"

"Yes—of suspense, certainly."

"Possibly of some danger?"

"I don't know that that was in my mind at the time."

"No—it was a case in which you could not possibly consider yourself."

"If you like to put it that way."

"Quite so. Yes. You had these attacks frequently in 1918?"

"Yes—I was very ill for some months."

"Quite. Since then they have recurred less frequently?"

"Much less frequently."

"Yes—when did the last occur?"

"About nine months ago."

"Under what circumstances?"

"I was being worried by certain family matters. It was a question of deciding about some investments, and I was largely responsible."

"Yes. You were interested last year, I think, in some police case?"

"Yes—in the recovery of Lord Attenbury's emerald necklace."

"That involved some severe mental exercise?"

"I suppose so. But I enjoyed it very much."

"Yes. Was the exertion of solving the problem attended by any bad results physically?"

"None."

"No. You were interested, but not distressed."

"Exactly."

"Yes. You have been engaged in other investigations of the kind?"

"Yes. Little ones."

"With bad results for your health?"

"Not a bit of it. On the contrary. I took up these cases as a sort of distraction. I had a bad knock just after the war, which didn't make matters any better for me, don't you know."

"Ah! you are not married?"

"No."

"No. Will you allow me to make an examination? Just come a little nearer to the light. I want to see your eyes. Whose advice have you had till now?"

"Sir James Hodges'."

"Ah! yes—he was a sad loss to the medical profession. A really great man—a true scientist. Yes. Thank you. Now I should like to try you with this little invention."

"What's it do?"

"Well—it tells me about your nervous reactions. Will you sit here?"

The examination that followed was purely medical. When it was concluded, Sir Julian said:

"Now, Lord Peter, I'll tell you about yourself in quite untechnical language—"

"Thanks," said Peter, "that's kind of you. I'm an awful fool about long words."

"Yes. Are you fond of private theatricals, Lord Peter?"

"Not particularly," said Peter, genuinely surprised. "Awful bore as a rule. Why?"

"I thought you might be," said the specialist, drily. "Well, now. You know quite well that the strain you put on your nerves during the war has left its mark on you. It has left what I may call old wounds in your brain. Sensations received by your nerve-endings sent messages to your brain, and produced minute physical changes there—changes we are only beginning to be able to detect, even with our most delicate instruments. These changes in their turn set up sensations; or I should say, more accurately, that sensations are the names we give to these changes of tissue when we perceive them: we call them horror, fear, sense of responsibility and so on."

"Yes, I follow you."

"Very well. Now, if you stimulate those damaged places in your brain again, you run the risk of opening up the old wounds. I mean, that if you get nerve-sensations of any kind producing the reactions which we call horror, fear, and sense of responsibility, they may go on to make disturbance right along the old channel, and produce in their turn physical changes which you will call by the names you were accustomed to associate with them—dread of German mines, responsibility for the lives of your men, strained attention and the inability to distinguish small sounds through the overpowering noise of guns."

"I see."

"This effect would be increased by extraneous circumstances producing other familiar physical sensations—night, cold or the rattling of heavy traffic, for instance."

"Yes."

"Yes. The old wounds are nearly healed, but not quite. The ordinary exercise of your mental faculties has no bad effect. It is only when you excite the injured part of your brain."

"Yes, I see."

"Yes. You must avoid these occasions. You must learn to be irresponsible, Lord Peter."

"My friends say I'm only too irresponsible already."

"Very likely. A sensitive nervous temperament often appears so, owing to its mental nimbleness."

"Oh!"

"Yes. This particular responsibility you were speaking of still rests upon you?"

"Yes, it does."

"You have not yet completed the course of action on which you have decided?"

"Not yet."

"You feel bound to carry it through?"

"Oh, yes—I can't back out of it now."

"No. You are expecting further strain?"

"A certain amount."

"Do you expect it to last much longer?"

"Very little longer now."

"Ah! Your nerves are not all they should be."

"No?"

"No. Nothing to be alarmed about, but you must exercise care while undergoing this strain, and afterwards you should take a complete rest. How about a voyage in the Mediterranean or the South Seas or somewhere?"

"Thanks. I'll think about it."

"Meanwhile, to carry you over the immediate trouble I will give you something to strengthen your nerves. It will do you no permanent good, you understand, but it will tide you over the bad time. And I will give you a prescription."

"Thank you."

Sir Julian got up and went into a small surgery leading out of the consulting-room. Lord Peter watched him moving about—boiling something and writing. Presently he returned with a paper and a hypodermic syringe.

"Here is the prescription. And now, if you will just roll up your sleeve, I will deal with the necessity of the immediate moment."

Lord Peter obediently rolled up his sleeve. Sir Julian Freke selected a portion of his forearm and anointed it with iodine.

"What's that you're goin' to stick into me. Bugs?"

The surgeon laughed.

"Not exactly," he said. He pinched up a portion of flesh between his finger and thumb. "You've had this kind of thing before, I expect."

"Oh, yes," said Lord Peter. He watched the cool fingers, fascinated, and the steady approach of the needle. "Yes—I've had it before—and, d'you know—I don't care frightfully about it."

He had brought up his right hand, and it closed over the surgeon's wrist like a vice.

The silence was like a shock. The blue eyes did not waver; they burned down steadily upon the heavy white lids below them. Then these slowly lifted; the grey eyes met the blue—coldly, steadily—and held them.

416

When lovers embrace, there seems no sound in the world but their own breathing. So the two men breathed face to face.

"As you like, of course, Lord Peter," said Sir Julian, courteously.

"Afraid I'm rather a silly ass," said Lord Peter, "but I never could abide these little gadgets. I had one once that went wrong and gave me a rotten bad time. They make me a bit nervous."

"In that case," replied Sir Julian, "it would certainly be better not to have the injection. It might rouse up just those sensations which we are desirous of avoiding. You will take the prescription, then, and do what you can to lessen the immediate strain as far as possible."

"Oh, yes—I'll take it easy, thanks," said Lord Peter. He rolled his sleeve down neatly. "I'm much obliged to you. If I have any further trouble I'll look in again."

"Do—do—" said Sir Julian, cheerfully. "Only make an appointment another time. I'm rather rushed these days. I hope your mother is quite well. I saw her the other day at that Battersea inquest. You should have been there. It would have interested you."

Chapter 12

The vile, raw fog tore your throat and ravaged your eyes. You could not see your feet. You stumbled in your walk over poor men's graves.

The feel of Parker's old trench-coat beneath your fingers was comforting. You had felt it in worse places. You clung on now for fear you should get separated. The dim people moving in front of you were like Brocken spectres.

"Take care, gentlemen," said a toneless voice out of the yellow darkness, "there's an open grave just hereabouts."

You bore away to the right, and floundered in a mass of freshly turned clay.

"Hold up, old man," said Parker.

"Where is Lady Levy?"

"In the mortuary; the Duchess of Denver is with her. Your mother is wonderful, Peter."

"Isn't she?" said Lord Peter.

A dim blue light carried by somebody ahead wavered and stood still.

"Here you are," said a voice.

Two Dantesque shapes with pitchforks loomed up.

"Have you finished?" asked somebody.

"Nearly done, sir." The demons fell to work again with the pitchforks—no, spades.

Somebody sneezed. Parker located the sneezer and introduced him.

"Mr. Levett represents the Home Secretary. Lord Peter Wimsey. We are sorry to drag you out on such a day, Mr. Levett."

"It's all in the day's work," said Mr. Levett, hoarsely. He was muffled to the eyes.

The sound of the spades for many minutes. An iron noise of tools thrown down. Demons stooping and straining.

A black-bearded spectre at your elbow. Introduced. The Master of the Workhouse.

"A very painful matter, Lord Peter. You will forgive me for hoping you and Mr. Parker may be mistaken."

"I should like to be able to hope so too."

Something heaving, straining, coming up out of the ground.

"Steady, men. This way. Can you see? Be careful of the graves—they lie pretty thick hereabouts. Are you ready?"

"Right you are, sir. You go on with the lantern. We can follow you."

Lumbering footsteps. Catch hold of Parker's trench-coat again. "That you, old man? Oh, I beg your pardon, Mr. Levett—thought you were Parker."

"Hullo, Wimsey—here you are."

More graves. A headstone shouldered crookedly aslant. A trip and jerk over the edge of the rough grass. The squeal of gravel under your feet.

"This way, gentlemen, mind the step."

The mortuary. Raw red brick and sizzling gas-jets. Two women in black, and Dr. Grimbold. The coffin laid on the table with a heavy thump.

"''Ave you got that there screw-driver, Bill? Thank 'ee. Be keerful wi' the chisel now. Not much substance to these 'ere boards, sir."

Several long creaks. A sob. The Duchess's voice, kind but peremptory.

"Hush, Christine. You mustn't cry."

A mutter of voices. The lurching departure of the Dante demons—good, decent demons in corduroy.

Dr. Grimbold's voice—cool and detached as if in the consulting room.

"Now—have you got that lamp, Mr. Wingate? Thank you. Yes, here on the table, please. Be careful not to catch your elbow in the flex, Mr. Levett. It would be better, I think, if you came on this side. Yes—yes—thank you. That's excellent."

The sudden brilliant circle of an electric lamp over the table. Dr. Grimbold's beard and spectacles. Mr. Levett blowing his nose. Parker bending close. The Master of the Workhouse peering over him. The rest of the room in the enhanced dimness of the gas-jets and the fog.

A low murmur of voices. All heads bent over the work.

Dr. Grimbold again—beyond the circle of the lamplight.

"We don't want to distress you unnecessarily, Lady Levy. If you will just tell us what to look for—the—? Yes, yes, certainly—and—yes—stopped with gold? Yes—the lower jaw, the last but one on the right? Yes—no teeth missing—no—yes? What kind of a mole? Yes—just over the left breast? Oh, I beg your pardon, just under—yes—appendicitis? Yes—a long one—yes—in the middle? Yes, I quite understand—a scar on the arm? Yes,

I don't know if we shall be able to find that—yes—any little constitutional weakness that might—? Oh, yes—arthritis—yes—thank you, Lady Levy—that's very clear. Don't come unless I ask you to. Now, Wingate."

A pause. A murmur. "Pulled out? After death, you think—well, so do I. Where is Dr. Colegrove? You attended this man in the workhouse? Yes. Do you recollect—? No? You're quite certain about that? Yes—we mustn't make a mistake, you know. Yes, but there are reasons why Sir Julian can't be present; I'm asking *you*, Dr. Colegrove. Well, you're certain—that's all I want to know. Just bring the light closer, Mr. Wingate, if you please. These miserable shells let the damp in so quickly. Ah! what do you make of this? Yes—yes—well, that's rather unmistakable, isn't it? Who did the head? Oh, Freke—of course. I was going to say they did good work at St. Luke's. Beautiful, isn't it, Dr. Colegrove? A wonderful surgeon—I saw him when he was at Guy's. Oh, no, gave it up years ago. Nothing like keeping your hand in. Ah—yes, undoubtedly that's it. Have you a towel handy, sir? Thank you. Over the head, if you please—I think we might have another here. Now, Lady Levy—I am going to ask you to look at a scar, and see if you recognise it. I'm sure you are going to help us by being very firm. Take your time—you won't see anything more than you absolutely must."

"Lucy, don't leave me."

"No, dear."

A space cleared at the table. The lamplight on the Duchess's white hair.

"Oh, yes—oh, yes! No, no—I couldn't be mistaken. There's that funny little kink in it. I've seen it hundreds of times. Oh, Lucy—Reuben!"

"Only a moment more, Lady Levy. The mole—"

"I—I think so—oh, yes, that is the very place."

"Yes. And the scar—was it three-cornered, just above the elbow?"

"Yes, oh, yes."

"Is this it?"

"Yes—yes—"

"I must ask you definitely, Lady Levy. Do you, from these three marks identify the body as that of your husband?"

"Oh! I must, mustn't I? Nobody else could have them just the same in just those places? It is my husband. It is Reuben. Oh—"

"Thank you, Lady Levy. You have been very brave and very helpful."

"But—I don't understand yet. How did he come here? Who did this dreadful thing?"

"Hush, dear," said the Duchess; "the man is going to be punished."

"Oh, but—how cruel! Poor Reuben! Who could have wanted to hurt him? Can I see his face?"

"No, dear," said the Duchess. "That isn't possible. Come away—you mustn't distress the doctors and people."

"No—no—they've all been so kind. Oh, Lucy!"

"We'll go home, dear. You don't want us any more, Dr. Grimbold?"

"No, Duchess, thank you. We are very grateful to you and to Lady Levy for coming."

There was a pause, while the two women went out, Parker, collected and helpful, escorting them to their waiting car. Then Dr. Grimbold again:

"I think Lord Peter Wimsey ought to see—the correctness of his deductions—Lord Peter—very painful—you may wish to see—yes, I was uneasy at the inquest—yes—Lady Levy— remarkably clear evidence—yes—most shocking case—ah, here's Mr. Parker—you and Lord Peter Wimsey entirely justified—do I really understand—? Really? I can hardly believe it—so distinguished a man—as you say, when a great brain turns to crime—yes—look here! Marvellous work—marvellous—

somewhat obscured by this time, of course—but the most beautiful sections—here, you see, the left hemisphere—and here—through the corpus striatum—here again—the very track of the damage done by the blow—wonderful—guessed it—saw the effect of the blow as he struck it, you know—ah, I should like to see *his* brain, Mr. Parker—and to think that—heavens, Lord Peter, you don't know what a blow you have struck at the whole profession—the whole civilized world! Oh, my dear sir! Can you ask me? My lips are sealed of course—all our lips are sealed."

The way back through the burial ground. Fog again, and the squeal of wet gravel.

"Are your men ready, Charles?"

"They have gone. I sent them off when I saw Lady Levy to the car."

"Who is with them?"

"Sugg."

"Sugg?"

"Yes—poor devil. They've had him up on the mat at headquarters for bungling the case. All that evidence of Thipps's about the night club was corroborated, you know. That girl he gave the gin-and-bitters to was caught, and came and identified him, and they decided their case wasn't good enough, and let Thipps and the Horrocks girl go. Then they told Sugg he had overstepped his duty and ought to have been more careful. So he ought, but he can't help being a fool. I was sorry for him. It may do him some good to be in at the death. After all, Peter, you and I had special advantages."

"Yes. Well, it doesn't matter. Whoever goes won't get there in time. Sugg's as good as another."

But Sugg—an experience rare in his career—was in time.

* * * * *

Parker and Lord Peter were at 110 Piccadilly. Lord Peter was playing Bach and Parker was reading Origen when Sugg was announced.

"We've got our man, sir," said he.

"Good God!" said Peter. "Alive?"

"We were just in time, my lord. We rang the bell and marched straight up past his man to the library. He was sitting there doing some writing. When we came in, he made a grab for his hypodermic, but we were too quick for him, my lord. We didn't mean to let him slip through our hands, having got so far. We searched him thoroughly and marched him off."

"He is actually in gaol, then?"

"Oh, yes—safe enough—with two warders to see he doesn't make away with himself."

"You surprise me, Inspector. Have a drink."

"Thank you, my lord. I may say that I'm very grateful to you—this case was turning out a pretty bad egg for me. If I was rude to your lordship—"

"Oh, it's all right, Inspector," said Lord Peter, hastily. "I don't see how you could possibly have worked it out. I had the good luck to know something about it from other sources."

"That's what Freke says." Already the great surgeon was a common criminal in the inspector's eyes—a mere surname. "He was writing a full confession when we got hold of him, addressed to your lordship. The police will have to have it, of course, but seeing it's written for you, I brought it along for you to see first. Here it is."

He handed Lord Peter a bulky document.

"Thanks," said Peter. "Like to hear it, Charles?"

"Rather."

Accordingly Lord Peter read it aloud.

Chapter 13

DEAR LORD PETER—When I was a young man I used to play chess with an old friend of my father's. He was a very bad, and a very slow, player, and he could never see when a checkmate was inevitable, but insisted on playing every move out. I never had any patience with that kind of attitude, and I will freely admit now that the game is yours. I must either stay at home and be hanged or escape abroad and live in an idle and insecure obscurity. I prefer to acknowledge defeat.

If you have read my book on "Criminal Lunacy," you will remember that I wrote: "In the majority of cases, the criminal betrays himself by some abnormality attendant upon this pathological condition of the nervous tissues. His mental instability shows itself in various forms: an overweening vanity, leading him to brag of his achievement; a disproportionate sense of the importance of the offence, resulting from the hallucination of religion, and driving him to confession; egomania, producing the sense of horror or conviction of sin, and driving him to headlong flight without covering his tracks; a reckless confidence, resulting in the neglect of the most ordinary precautions, as in the case of Henry Wainwright, who left a boy in charge of the murdered woman's remains while he went to call a cab, or on the other hand, a nervous distrust of apperceptions in the past, causing him to revisit the scene of the crime to assure himself that all traces have been as safely removed as *his own judgment knows them to be*. I will not hesitate to assert that a perfectly sane man, not intimidated by religious or other delusions, could always render himself perfectly secure from detection, provided, that is, that the crime were sufficiently premeditated and that he were not pressed for time or thrown out in his calculations by purely fortuitous coincidence.

You know as well as I do, how far I have made this assertion good in practice. The two accidents which betrayed me, I could not by any possibility have foreseen. The first was the chance recognition of Levy by the girl in the Battersea Park Road, which suggested a connection between the two problems. The second was that Thipps should have arranged to go down to Denver on the Tuesday morning, thus enabling your mother to get word of the matter through to you before the body was removed by the police and to suggest a motive for the murder out of what she knew of my previous personal history. If I had been able to destroy these two accidentally forged links of circumstance, I will venture to say that you would never have so much as suspected me, still less obtained sufficient evidence to convict.

Of all human emotions, except perhaps those of hunger and fear, the sexual appetite produces the most violent, and, under some circumstances, the most persistent reactions; I think, however, I am right in saying that at the time when I wrote my book, my original sensual impulse to kill Sir Reuben Levy had already become profoundly modified by my habits of thought. To the animal lust to slay and the primitive human desire for revenge, there was added the rational intention of substantiating my own theories for the satisfaction of myself and the world. If all had turned out as I had planned, I should have deposited a sealed account of my experiment with the Bank of England, instructing my executors to publish it after my death. Now that accident has spoiled the completeness of my demonstration, I entrust the account to you, whom it cannot fail to interest, with the request that you will make it known among scientific men, in justice to my professional reputation.

The really essential factors of success in any undertaking are money and opportunity, and as a rule, the man who can make the first can make the second. During my early career, though I was fairly well-off, I had not absolute command of circumstance. Accordingly I devoted myself to my profession, and contented myself with keeping up a friendly connection with Reuben Levy and his family. This enabled me to remain in touch with his fortunes and interests, so that, when the moment for action should arrive, I might know what weapons to use.

Meanwhile, I carefully studied criminology in fiction and fact—my work on "Criminal Lunacy" was a side-product of this activity—and saw how, in every murder, the real crux of the problem was the disposal of the body. As a doctor, the means of death were always ready to my hand, and I was not likely to make any error in that connection. Nor was I likely to betray myself on account of any illusory sense of wrong-doing. The sole difficulty would be that of destroying all connection between my personality and that of the corpse. You will remember that Michael Finsbury, in Stevenson's entertaining romance, observes: "What hangs people is the unfortunate circumstance of guilt." It became clear to me that the mere leaving about of a superfluous corpse could convict nobody, provided that nobody was guilty in connection *with that particular corpse.* Thus the idea of substituting the one body for the other was early arrived at, though it was not till I obtained the practical direction of St. Luke's Hospital that I found myself perfectly unfettered in the choice and handling of dead bodies. From this period on, I kept a careful watch on all the material brought in for dissection.

My opportunity did not present itself until the week before Sir Reuben's disappearance, when the medical officer at the Chelsea workhouse sent word to me that an unknown vagrant had been injured that morning by the fall of a piece of scaffolding, and was exhibiting some very interesting nervous and cerebral reactions. I went round and saw the case, and was immediately struck by the man's strong superficial resemblance to Sir Reuben. He had been heavily struck on the back of the neck, dislocating the fourth and fifth cervical vertebrae and heavily bruising the spinal cord. It seemed highly unlikely that he could ever recover, either mentally or physically, and in any case there appeared to me to be no object in indefinitely prolonging so unprofitable an existence. He had obviously been able to support life until recently, as he was fairly well nourished, but the state of his feet and clothing showed that he was unemployed, and under present conditions he was likely to remain so. I decided that he would suit my purpose very well, and immediately put in train certain transactions in the City which I had already sketched out in my own mind. In the meantime, the reactions mentioned by the workhouse doctor were interesting, and I made careful studies of them, and arranged for the delivery of the body to the hospital when I should have completed my preparations.

On the Thursday and Friday of that week I made private arrangements with various brokers to buy the stock of certain Peruvian Oil-fields, which had gone down almost to waste-paper. This part of my experiment did not cost me very much, but I contrived to arouse considerable curiosity, and even a mild excitement. At this point I was of course careful not to let my name appear. The incidence of Saturday and Sunday gave me some anxiety lest my man should after all die before I was ready for him, but by the use of saline injections I contrived to keep him alive and, late on Sunday night, he even manifested disquieting symptoms of at any rate a partial recovery.

On Monday morning the market in Peruvians opened briskly. Rumours had evidently got about that somebody knew something, and this day I was not the only buyer in the market. I bought a couple of hundred more shares in my own name, and left the matter to take care of itself. At lunch time I made my arrangements to run into Levy accidentally at the corner of the Mansion House. He expressed (as I expected) his surprise at seeing me in that part of London. I simulated some embarrassment and suggested that we should lunch together. I dragged him to a place a bit off the usual beat, and there ordered a good wine and drank of it as much as he might suppose sufficient to induce a confidential mood. I asked him how things were going on 'Change. He said, "Oh, all right," but appeared a little doubtful, and asked me whether I did anything in that way. I said I had a little flutter occasionally, and that, as a matter of fact, I'd been put on to rather a good thing. I glanced round apprehensively at this point, and shifted my chair nearer to his.

"I suppose you don't know anything about Peruvian Oil, do you?" he said.

I started and looked round again, and leaning across to him, said, dropping my voice:

"Well, I do, as a matter of fact, but I don't want it to get about. I stand to make a good bit on it."

"But I thought the thing was hollow," he said; "it hasn't paid a dividend for umpteen years."

"No," I said, "it hasn't, but it's going to. I've got inside information." He looked a bit unconvinced, and I emptied off my glass, and edged right up to his ear.

"Look here," I said, "I'm not giving this away to everyone, but I don't mind doing you and Christine a good turn. You know, I've always kept a soft place in my heart for her, ever since the old days. You got in ahead of me that time, and now it's up to me to heap coals of fire on you both."

I was a little excited by this time, and he thought I was drunk.

"It's very kind of you, old man," he said, "but I'm a cautious bird, you know, always was. I'd like a bit of proof."

And he shrugged up his shoulders and looked like a pawnbroker.

"I'll give it to you," I said, "but it isn't safe here. Come round to my place tonight after dinner, and I'll show you the report."

"How d'you get hold of it?" said he.

"I'll tell you tonight," said I. "Come round after dinner—any time after nine, say."

"To Harley Street?" he asked, and I saw that he meant coming.

"No," I said, "to Battersea—Prince of Wales Road; I've got

some work to do at the hospital. And look here," I said, "don't you let on to a soul that you're coming. I bought a couple of hundred shares today, in my own name, and people are sure to get wind of it. If we're known to be about together, someone'll twig something. In fact, it's anything but safe talking about it in this place."

"All right," he said, "I won't say a word to anybody. I'll turn up about nine o'clock. You're sure it's a sound thing?"

"It can't go wrong," I assured him. And I meant it.

We parted after that, and I went round to the workhouse. My man had died at about eleven o'clock. I had seen him just after breakfast, and was not surprised. I completed the usual formalities with the workhouse authorities, and arranged for his delivery at the hospital at about seven o'clock.

In the afternoon, as it was not one of my days to be in Harley Street, I looked up an old friend who lives close to Hyde Park, and found that he was just off to Brighton on some business or other. I had tea with him, and saw him off by the 5:35 from Victoria. On issuing from the barrier it occurred to me to purchase an evening paper, and I thoughtlessly turned my steps to the bookstall. The usual crowds were rushing to catch suburban trains home, and on moving away I found myself involved in a contrary stream of travellers coming up out of the Underground, or bolting from all sides for the 5:45 to Battersea Park and Wandsworth Common. I disengaged myself after some buffeting and went home in a taxi; and it was not till I was safely seated there that I discovered somebody's gold-rimmed pince-nez involved in the astrakhan collar of my overcoat. The time from 6:15 to seven I spent concocting something to look like a bogus report for Sir Reuben.

At seven I went through to the hospital, and found the workhouse van just delivering my subject at the side door. I had him taken straight up to the theatre, and told the attendant, William Watts, that I intended to work there that night. I told him

I would prepare the body myself—the injection of a preservative would have been a most regrettable complication. I sent him about his business, and then went home and had dinner. I told my man that I should be working in the hospital that evening, and that he could go to bed at 10:30 as usual, as I could not tell whether I should be late or not. He is used to my erratic ways. I only keep two servants in the Battersea house—the man-servant and his wife, who cooks for me. The rougher domestic work is done by a charwoman, who sleeps out. The servants' bedroom is at the top of the house, overlooking Prince of Wales Road.

As soon as I had dined I established myself in the hall with some papers. My man had cleared dinner by a quarter past eight, and I told him to give me the syphon and tantalus; and sent him downstairs. Levy rang the bell at twenty minutes past nine, and I opened the door to him myself. My man appeared at the other end of the hall, but I called to him that it was all right, and he went away. Levy wore an overcoat with evening dress and carried an umbrella. "Why, how wet you are!" I said. "How did you come?" "By 'bus," he said, "and the fool of a conductor forgot to put me down at the end of the road. It's pouring cats and dogs and pitch-dark—I couldn't see where I was." I was glad he hadn't taken a taxi, but I had rather reckoned on his not doing so. "Your little economies will be the death of you one of these days," I said. I was right there, but I hadn't reckoned on their being the death of me as well. I say again, I could not have foreseen it.

I sat him down by the fire, and gave him a whisky. He was in high spirits about some deal in Argentines he was bringing off the next day. We talked money for about a quarter of an hour and then he said:

"Well, how about this Peruvian mare's-nest of yours?"

"It's no mare's-nest," I said; "come and have a look at it."

I took him upstairs into the library, and switched on the centre light and the reading lamp on the writing table. I gave him a chair at the table with his back to the fire, and fetched the papers I had been faking, out of the safe. He took them, and began to read them, poking over them in his short-sighted way, while I mended the fire. As soon as I saw his head in a favourable position I struck him heavily with the poker, just over the fourth cervical. It was delicate work calculating the exact force necessary to kill him without breaking the skin, but my professional experience was useful to me. He gave one loud gasp, and tumbled forward on to the table quite noiselessly. I put the poker back, and examined him. His neck was broken, and he was quite dead. I carried him into my bedroom and undressed him. It was about ten minutes to ten when I had finished. I put him away under my bed, which had been turned down for the night, and cleared up the papers in the library. Then I went downstairs, took Levy's umbrella, and let myself out at the hall door, shouting "Good-night" loudly enough to be heard in the basement if the servants should be listening. I walked briskly away down the street, went in by the hospital side door, and returned to the house noiselessly by way of the private passage. It would have been awkward if anybody had seen me then, but I leaned over the back stairs and heard the cook and her husband still talking in the kitchen. I slipped back into the hall, replaced the umbrella in the stand, cleared up my papers there, went up into the library and rang the bell. When the man appeared I told him to lock up everything except the private door to the hospital. I waited in the library until he had done so, and about 10:30 I heard both servants go up to bed. I waited a quarter of an hour longer and then went through to the dissecting-room. I wheeled one of the stretcher tables through the passage to the house door, and then went to fetch Levy. It was a nuisance having to get him downstairs, but I had not liked to make away with him in any of the ground-floor rooms, in case my servant should take a fancy to poke his head in during the few minutes that I was out of the house, or while locking up. Besides, that was a flea-bite to what I should have to do later. I put Levy on the table, wheeled him across to the hospital and substituted him for my interesting pauper. I was sorry to have to abandon the idea of getting a look at the latter's brain, but I could not afford to incur suspicion. It was still rather early, so I knocked down a few minutes getting Levy ready for dissection. Then I put my pauper on the table and trundled him over to the house. It was now five past eleven, and I thought I might conclude that the servants were in bed. I carried the body into my bedroom. He was rather heavy, but less so than Levy, and my Alpine experience had taught me how to handle bodies. It is as much a matter of knack as of strength, and I am, in any case, a powerful man for my height. I put the body into the bed—not that I expected anyone to look in during my absence, but if they should they might just as well see me apparently asleep in bed. I drew the clothes a little over his head, stripped, and put on Levy's clothes, which were fortunately a little big for me everywhere, not forgetting to take his spectacles, watch and other oddments. At a little before half-past eleven I was in the road looking for a cab. People were just beginning to come home from the theatre, and I easily secured one at the corner of Prince of Wales Road. I told the man to drive me to Hyde Park Corner. There I got out, tipped him well, and asked him to pick me up again at the same place in an hour's time. He assented with an understanding grin, and I walked on up Park Lane. I had my own clothes with me in a suitcase, and carried my own overcoat and Levy's umbrella. When I got to No. 9A there were lights in some of the top windows. I was very nearly too early, owing to the old man's having sent the servants to the theatre. I waited about for a few minutes, and heard it strike the quarter past midnight. The lights were extinguished shortly after, and I let myself in with Levy's key.

It had been my original intention, when I thought over this plan of murder, to let Levy disappear from the study or the dining-room, leaving only a heap of clothes on the hearth-rug.

The accident of my having been able to secure Lady Levy's absence from London, however, made possible a solution more misleading, though less pleasantly fantastic. I turned on the hall light, hung up Levy's wet overcoat and placed his umbrella in the stand. I walked up noisily and heavily to the bedroom and turned off the light by the duplicate switch on the landing. I knew the house well enough, of course. There was no chance of my running into the man-servant. Old Levy was a simple old man, who liked doing things for himself. He gave his valet little work, and never required any attendance at night. In the bedroom I took off Levy's gloves and put on a surgical pair, so as to leave no tell-tale finger-prints. As I wished to convey the impression that Levy had gone to bed in the usual way, I simply went to bed. The surest and simplest method of making a thing appear to have been done is to do it. A bed that has been rumpled about with one's hands, for instance, never looks like a bed that has been slept in. I dared not use Levy's brush, of course, as my hair is not of his colour, but I did everything else. I supposed that a thoughtful old man like Levy would put his boots handy for his valet, and I ought to have deduced that he would fold up his clothes. That was a mistake, but not an important one. Remembering that well-thought-out little work of Mr. Bentley's, I had examined Levy's mouth for false teeth, but he had none. I did not forget, however, to wet his tooth-brush.

At one o'clock I got up and dressed in my own clothes by the light of my own pocket torch. I dared not turn on the bedroom lights, as there were light blinds to the windows. I put on my own boots and an old pair of goloshes outside the door. There was a thick Turkey carpet on the stairs and hall-floor, and I was not afraid of leaving marks. I hesitated whether to chance the banging of the front door, but decided it would be safer to take the latchkey. (It is now in the Thames. I dropped it over Battersea Bridge the next day.) I slipped quietly down, and listened for a few minutes with my ear to the letter-box. I heard a constable tramp past. As soon as his steps had died away in the distance I stepped out and pulled the door gingerly to. It closed almost soundlessly, and I walked away to pick up my cab. I had an overcoat of much the same pattern as Levy's, and had taken the precaution to pack an opera hat in my suitcase. I hoped the man would not notice that I had no umbrella this time. Fortunately the rain had diminished for the moment to a sort of drizzle, and if he noticed anything he made no observation. I told him to stop at 50 Overstrand Mansions, and I paid him off there, and stood under the porch till he had driven away. Then I hurried round to my own side door and let myself in. It was about a quarter to two, and the harder part of my task still lay before me.

My first step was so to alter the appearance of my subject as to eliminate any immediate suggestion either of Levy or of the workhouse vagrant. A fairly superficial alteration was all I considered necessary, since there was not likely to be any hue-and-cry after the pauper. He was fairly accounted for, and his deputy was at hand to represent him. Nor, if Levy was after all traced to my house, would it be difficult to show that the body in evidence was, as a matter of fact, not his. A clean shave and a little hair-oiling and manicuring seemed sufficient to suggest a distinct personality for my silent accomplice. His hands had been well washed in hospital, and though calloused, were not grimy. I was not able to do the work as thoroughly as I should have liked, because time was getting on. I was not sure how long it would take me to dispose of him, and moreover, I feared the onset of *rigor mortis*, which would make my task more difficult. When I had him barbered to my satisfaction, I fetched a strong sheet and a couple of wide roller bandages, and fastened him up carefully, padding him with cotton wool wherever the bandages might chafe or leave a bruise.

Now came the really ticklish part of the business. I had already decided in my own mind that the only way of conveying him from the house was by the roof. To go through the garden at the back in this soft wet weather was to leave a ruinous trail behind us. To carry a dead man down a suburban street in the middle of the night seemed outside the range of practical politics. On the roof, on the other hand, the rain, which would have betrayed me on the ground, would stand my friend.

To reach the roof, it was necessary to carry my burden to the top of the house, past my servants' room, and hoist him out through the trap-door in the box-room roof. Had it merely been a question of going quietly up there myself, I should have had no fear of waking the servants, but to do so burdened by a heavy body was more difficult. It would be possible, provided that the man and his wife were soundly asleep, but if not, the lumbering tread on the narrow stair and the noise of opening the trap-door would be only too plainly audible. I tiptoed delicately up the stair and listened at their door. To my disgust I heard the man give a grunt and mutter something as he moved in his bed.

I looked at my watch. My preparations had taken nearly an hour, first and last, and I dared not be too late on the roof. I determined to take a bold step and, as it were, bluff out an alibi. I went without precaution against noise into the bathroom, turned on the hot and cold water taps to the full and pulled out the plug.

My household has often had occasion to complain of my habit of using the bath at irregular night hours. Not only does the rush of water into the cistern disturb any sleepers on the Prince of Wales Road side of the house, but my cistern is afflicted with peculiarly loud gurglings and thumpings, while frequently the pipes emit a loud groaning sound. To my delight, on this particular occasion, the cistern was in excellent form, honking, whistling and booming like a railway terminus. I gave the noise five minutes' start, and when I calculated that the sleepers would have finished cursing me and put their heads under the clothes to shut out the din, I reduced the flow of water to a small stream and left the bathroom, taking good care to leave the light burning and lock the door after me. Then I picked up my pauper and carried him upstairs as lightly as possible.

The box-room is a small attic on the side of the landing opposite to the servants' bedroom and the cistern-room. It has a trap-door, reached by a short, wooden ladder. I set this up, hoisted up my pauper and climbed up after him. The water was still racing into the cistern, which was making a noise as though it were trying to digest an iron chain, and with the reduced flow in the bathroom the groaning of the pipes had risen almost to a hoot. I was not afraid of anybody hearing other noises. I pulled the ladder through on to the roof after me.

Between my house and the last house in Queen Caroline Mansions there is a space of only a few feet. Indeed, when the Mansions were put up, I believe there was some trouble about ancient lights, but I suppose the parties compromised somehow. Anyhow, my seven-foot ladder reached well across. I tied the body firmly to the ladder, and pushed it over till the far end was resting on the parapet of the opposite house. Then I took a short run across the cistern-room and the box-room roof, and landed easily on the other side, the parapet being happily both low and narrow.

The rest was simple. I carried my pauper along the flat roofs, intending to leave him, like the hunchback in the story, on someone's staircase or down a chimney. I had got about half-way along when I suddenly thought, "Why, this must be about little Thipps's place," and I remembered his silly face, and his silly chatter about vivisection. It occurred to me pleasantly how delightful it would be to deposit my parcel with him and see what he made of it. I lay down and peered over the parapet at the back. It was pitch-dark and pouring with rain again by this time, and I risked using my torch. That was the only incautious thing I did, and the odds against being seen from the houses opposite were long enough. One second's flash showed me what I had hardly dared to hope—an open window just below me.

I knew those flats well enough to be sure it was either the bathroom or the kitchen. I made a noose in a third bandage that I had brought with me, and made it fast under the arms of the corpse. I twisted it into a double rope, and secured the end to the iron stanchion of a chimney-stack. Then I dangled our friend over. I went down after him myself with the aid of a drain-pipe and was soon hauling him in by Thipps's bathroom window.

By that time I had got a little conceited with myself, and spared a few minutes to lay him out prettily and make him shipshape. A sudden inspiration suggested that I should give him the pair of pince-nez which I had happened to pick up at Victoria. I came across them in my pocket while I was looking for a penknife to loosen a knot, and I saw what distinction they would lend his appearance, besides making it more misleading. I fixed them on him, effaced all traces of my presence as far as possible, and departed as I had come, going easily up between the drain-pipe and the rope.

I walked quietly back, re-crossed my crevasse and carried in my ladder and sheet. My discreet accomplice greeted me with a reassuring gurgle and thump. I didn't make a sound on the stairs. Seeing that I had now been having a bath for about three-quarters of an hour, I turned the water off, and enabled my deserving domestics to get a little sleep. I also felt it was time I had a little myself.

First, however, I had to go over to the hospital and make all safe there. I took off Levy's head, and started to open up the face. In twenty minutes his own wife could not have recognised him. I returned, leaving my wet goloshes and mackintosh by the garden door. My trousers I dried by the gas stove in my bedroom, and brushed away all traces of mud and brickdust. My pauper's beard I burned in the library.

I got a good two hours' sleep from five to seven, when my

man called me as usual. I apologized for having kept the water running so long and so late, and added that I thought I would have the cistern seen to.

I was interested to note that I was rather extra hungry at breakfast, showing that my night's work had caused a certain wear-and-tear of tissue. I went over afterwards to continue my dissection. During the morning a peculiarly thick-headed police inspector came to inquire whether a body had escaped from the hospital. I had him brought to me where I was, and had the pleasure of showing him the work I was doing on Sir Reuben Levy's head. Afterwards I went round with him to Thipps's and was able to satisfy myself that my pauper looked very convincing.

As soon as the Stock Exchange opened I telephoned my various brokers, and by exercising a little care, was able to sell out the greater part of my Peruvian stock on a rising market. Towards the end of the day, however, buyers became rather unsettled as a result of Levy's death, and in the end I did not make more than a few hundreds by the transaction.

Trusting I have now made clear to you any point which you may have found obscure, and with congratulations on the good fortune and perspicacity which have enabled you to defeat me, I remain, with kind remembrances to your mother,

Yours very truly,

JULIAN FREKE

Post-Scriptum: My will is made, leaving my money to St. Luke's Hospital, and bequeathing my body to the same institution for dissection. I feel sure that my brain will be of interest to the scientific world. As I shall die by my own hand, I imagine that there may be a little difficulty about this. Will you do me the favour, if you can, of seeing the persons concerned in the inquest, and obtaining that the brain is not damaged by an unskilful practitioner at the post-mortem, and that the body is disposed of according to my wish?

By the way, it may be of interest to you to know that I appreciated your motive in calling this afternoon. It conveyed a warning, and I am acting upon it in spite of the disastrous consequences to myself. I was pleased to realize that you had not underestimated my nerve and intelligence, and refused the injection. Had you submitted to it, you would, of course, never have reached home alive. No trace would have been left in your body of the injection, which consisted of a harmless preparation of strychnine, mixed with an almost unknown poison, for which there is at present no recognised test, a concentrated solution of sn—

* * * * *

At this point the manuscript broke off.

"Well, that's all clear enough," said Parker.

"Isn't it queer?" said Lord Peter. "All that coolness, all those brains—and then he couldn't resist writing a confession to show how clever he was, even to keep his head out of the noose."

"And a very good thing for us," said Inspector Sugg, "but Lord bless you, sir, these criminals are all alike."

"Freke's epitaph," said Parker, when the Inspector had departed. "What next, Peter?"

"I shall now give a dinner party," said Lord Peter, "to Mr. John P. Milligan and his secretary and to Messrs. Crimplesham and Wicks. I feel they deserve it for not having murdered Levy."

"Well, don't forget the Thippses," said Mr. Parker.

"On no account," said Lord Peter, "would I deprive myself of the pleasure of Mrs. Thipps's company. Bunter!"

"My lord?"

"The Napoleon brandy."

The Adventure of the Creeping Man

Arthur Conan Doyle

M r. Sherlock Holmes was always of opinion that I should publish the singular facts connected with Professor Presbury, if only to dispel once for all the ugly rumours which some twenty years ago agitated the university and were echoed in the learned societies of London. There were, however, certain obstacles in the way, and the true history of this curious case remained entombed in the tin box which contains so many records of my friend's adventures. Now we have at last obtained permission to ventilate the facts which formed one of the very last cases handled by Holmes before his retirement from practice. Even now a certain reticence and discretion have to be observed in laying the matter before the public.

It was one Sunday evening early in September of the year 1903 that I received one of Holmes's laconic messages:

Come at once if convenient—if inconvenient come all the same.
                                                    S. H.

The relations between us in those latter days were peculiar. He was a man of habits, narrow and concentrated habits, and I had become one of them. As an institution I was like the violin, the shag tobacco, the old black pipe, the index books, and others perhaps less excusable. When it was a case of active work and a comrade was needed upon whose nerve he could place some reliance, my role was obvious. But apart from this I had uses. I was a whetstone for his mind. I stimulated him. He liked to think aloud in my presence. His remarks could hardly be said to be made to me—many of them would have been as appropriately addressed to his bedstead—but none the less, having formed the habit, it had become in some way helpful that I should register and interject. If I irritated him by a certain methodical slowness in my mentality, that irritation served only to make his own flame-like intuitions and impressions flash up the more vividly and swiftly. Such was my humble role in our alliance.

When I arrived at Baker Street I found him huddled up in his armchair with updrawn knees, his pipe in his mouth and his brow furrowed with thought. It was clear that he was in the throes of some vexatious problem. With a wave of his hand he indicated my old armchair, but otherwise for half an hour he gave no sign that he was aware of my presence. Then with a start he seemed to come from his reverie, and with his usual whimsical smile he greeted me back to what had once been my home.

"You will excuse a certain abstraction of mind, my dear Watson," said he. "Some curious facts have been submitted to me within the last twenty-four hours, and they in turn have given rise to some speculations of a more general character. I have serious thoughts of writing a small monograph upon the uses of dogs in the work of the detective."

"But surely, Holmes, this has been explored," said I. "Bloodhounds—sleuth-hounds—"

"No, no, Watson, that side of the matter is, of course, obvious. But there is another which is far more subtle. You may recollect that in the case which you, in your sensational way, coupled with the Copper Beeches, I was able, by watching the mind of the child, to form a deduction as to the criminal habits of the very smug and respectable father."

"Yes, I remember it well."

"My line of thoughts about dogs is analogous. A dog reflects the family life. Whoever saw a frisky dog in a gloomy family, or a sad dog in a happy one? Snarling people have snarling dogs, dangerous people have dangerous ones. And their passing moods may reflect the passing moods of others."

I shook my head. "Surely, Holmes, this is a little far-fetched," said I.

He had refilled his pipe and resumed his seat, taking no notice of my comment.

"The practical application of what I have said is very close to the problem which I am investigating. It is a tangled skein, you understand. and I am looking for a loose end. One possible loose end lies in the question: Why does Professor Presbury's wolfhound, Roy, endeavour to bite him?"

I sank back in my chair in some disappointment. Was it for so trivial a question as this that I had been summoned from my work? Holmes glanced across at me.

"The same old Watson!" said he. "You never learn that the gravest issues may depend upon the smallest things. But is it not on the face of it strange that a staid, elderly philosopher— you've heard of Presbury, of course, the famous Camford physiologist?—that such a man, whose friend has been his devoted wolfhound, should now have been twice attacked by his own dog? What do you make of it?"

"The dog is ill."

"Well, that has to be considered. But he attacks no one else, nor does he apparently molest his master, save on very special occasions. Curious, Watson—very curious. But young Mr. Bennett is before his time if that is his ring. I had hoped to have a longer chat with you before he came."

There was a quick step on the stairs, a sharp tap at the door and a moment later the new client presented himself. He was a tall, handsome youth about thirty, well dressed and elegant, but with something in his bearing which suggested the shyness of the student rather than the self-possession of the man of the world. He shook hands with Holmes, and then looked with some surprise at me.

"This matter is very delicate, Mr. Holmes," he said. "Consider the relation in which I stand to Professor Presbury both privately and publicly. I really can hardly justify myself if I speak before any third person."

"Have no fear, Mr. Bennett. Dr. Watson is the very soul of discretion, and I can assure you that this is a matter in which I am very likely to need an assistant."

"As you like, Mr. Holmes. You will, I am sure, understand my having some reserves in the matter."

"You will appreciate it, Watson, when I tell you that this gentleman, Mr. Trevor Bennett, is professional assistant to the great scientist, lives under his roof, and is engaged to his only daughter. Certainly we must agree that the professor has every claim upon his loyalty and devotion. But it may best be shown by taking the necessary steps to clear up this strange mystery."

"I hope so, Mr. Holmes. That is my one object. Does Dr. Watson know the situation?"

"I have not had time to explain it."

"Then perhaps I had better go over the ground again before explaining some fresh developments."

"I will do so myself," said Holmes, "in order to show that I have the events in their due order. The professor, Watson, is a man of European reputation. His life has been academic. There has never been a breath of scandal. He is a widower with one daughter, Edith. He is, I gather, a man of very virile and positive, one might almost say combative, character. So the matter stood until a very few months ago.

"Then the current of his life was broken. He is sixty-one years of age, but he became engaged to the daughter of Professor Morphy, his colleague in the chair of comparative anatomy. It was not, as I understand, the reasoned courting of an elderly man but rather the passionate frenzy of youth, for no one could have shown himself a more devoted lover. The lady, Alice Morphy, was a very perfect girl both in mind and body, so that there was every excuse for the professor's infatuation. None the less, it did not meet with full approval in his own family."

"We thought it rather excessive," said our visitor.

"Exactly. Excessive and a little violent and unnatural. Professor Presbury was rich, however, and there was no objection upon the part of the father. The daughter, however, had other views, and there were already several candidates for her hand, who, if they were less eligible from a worldly point of view, were at least more of an age. The girl seemed to like the professor in spite of his eccentricities. It was only age which stood in the way.

"About this time a little mystery suddenly clouded the normal routine of the professor's life. He did what he had never done before. He left home and gave no indication where he was going. He was away a fortnight and returned looking rather travel-worn. He made no allusion to where he had been, although he was usually the frankest of men. It chanced, however, that our client here, Mr. Bennett, received a letter from a fellow-student in Prague, who said that he was glad to have seen Professor Presbury there, although he had not been able to talk to him. Only in this way did his own household learn where he had been.

"Now comes the point. From that time onward a curious change came over the professor. He became furtive and sly. Those around him had always the feeling that he was not the man that they had known, but that he was under some shadow which had darkened his higher qualities. His intellect was not affected. His lectures were as brilliant as ever. But always there was something new, something sinister and unexpected. His daughter, who was devoted to him, tried again and again to resume the old relations and to penetrate this mask which her father seemed to have put on. You, sir, as I understand, did the same—but all was in vain. And now, Mr. Bennett, tell in your own words the incident of the letters."

"You must understand, Dr. Watson, that the professor had no secrets from me. If I were his son or his younger brother I could not have more completely enjoyed his confidence. As his secretary I handled every paper which came to him, and I opened and subdivided his letters. Shortly after his return all this was changed. He told me that certain letters might come to him from London which would be marked by a cross under the stamp. These were to be set aside for his own eyes only. I may say that several of these did pass through my hands, that they had the E. C. mark, and were in an illiterate handwriting. If he answered them at all the answers did not pass through my hands nor into the letterbasket in which our correspondence was collected."

"And the box," said Holmes.

"Ah, yes, the box. The professor brought back a little wooden box from his travels. It was the one thing which suggested a Continental tour, for it was one of those quaint carved things which one associates with Germany. This he placed in his instrument cupboard. One day, in looking for a canula, I took up the box. To my surprise he was very angry, and reproved me in words which were quite savage for my curiosity. It was the first time such a thing had happened, and I was deeply hurt. I endeavoured to explain that it was a mere accident that I had touched the box, but all the evening I was conscious that he looked at me harshly and that the incident was rankling in his mind." Mr. Bennett drew a little diary book from his pocket. "That was on July 2d," said he.

"You are certainly an admirable witness," said Holmes. "I may need some of these dates which you have noted."

"I learned method among other things from my great teacher. From the time that I observed abnormality in his behaviour I felt that it was my duty to study his case. Thus I have it here that it was on that very day, July 2d, that Roy attacked the professor as he came from his study into the hall. Again, on July 11th, there was a scene of the same sort, and then I have a note of yet another upon July 20th. After that we had to banish Roy to the stables. He was a dear, affectionate animal—but I fear I weary you."

Mr. Bennett spoke in a tone of reproach, for it was very clear that Holmes was not listening. His face was rigid and his eyes gazed abstractedly at the ceiling. With an effort he recovered himself.

"Singular! Most singular!" he murmured. "These details were

new to me, Mr. Bennett. I think we have now fairly gone over the old ground, have we not? But you spoke of some fresh developments."

The pleasant, open face of our visitor clouded over, shadowed by some grim remembrance. "What I speak of occurred the night before last," said he. "I was lying awake about two in the morning, when I was aware of a dull muffled sound coming from the passage. I opened my door and peeped out. I should explain that the professor sleeps at the end of the passage—"

"The date being?" asked Holmes.

Our visitor was clearly annoyed at so irrelevant an interruption.

"I have said, sir, that it was the night before last—that is, September 4th."

Holmes nodded and smiled.

"Pray continue," said he.

"He sleeps at the end of the passage and would have to pass my door in order to reach the staircase. It was a really terrifying experience, Mr. Holmes. I think that I am as strong-nerved as my neighbours, but I was shaken by what I saw. The passage was dark save that one window halfway along it threw a patch of light. I could see that something was coming along the passage, something dark and crouching. Then suddenly it emerged into the light, and I saw that it was he. He was crawling, Mr. Holmes—crawling! He was not quite on his hands and knees. I should rather say on his hands and feet, with his face sunk between his hands. Yet he seemed to move with ease. I was so paralyzed by the sight that it was not until he had reached my door that I was able to step forward and ask if I could assist him. His answer was extraordinary. He sprang up, spat out some atrocious word at me, and hurried on past me, and down the staircase. I waited about for an hour, but he did not come back. It must have been daylight before he regained his room."

"Well, Watson, what make you of that?" asked Holmes with the air of the pathologist who presents a rare specimen.

"Lumbago, possibly. I have known a severe attack make a man walk in just such a way, and nothing would be more trying to the temper."

"Good, Watson! You always keep us flat-footed on the ground. But we can hardly accept lumbago, since he was able to stand erect in a moment."

"He was never better in health," said Bennett. "In fact, he is stronger than I have known him for years. But there are the facts, Mr. Holmes. It is not a case in which we can consult the police, and yet we are utterly at our wit's end as to what to do, and we feel in some strange way that we are drifting towards disaster. Edith—Miss Presbury—feels as I do, that we cannot wait passively any longer."

"It is certainly a very curious and suggestive case. What do you think, Watson?"

"Speaking as a medical man," said I, "it appears to be a case for an alienist. The old gentleman's cerebral processes were disturbed by the love affair. He made a journey abroad in the hope of breaking himself of the passion. His letters and the box may be connected with some other private transaction—a loan, perhaps, or share certificates, which are in the box."

"And the wolfhound no doubt disapproved of the financial bargain. No, no, Watson, there is more in it than this. Now, I can only suggest—"

What Sherlock Holmes was about to suggest will never be known, for at this moment the door opened and a young lady was shown into the room. As she appeared Mr. Bennett sprang up with a cry and ran forward with his hands out to meet those which she had herself outstretched.

"Edith, dear! Nothing the matter, I hope?"

"I felt I must follow you. Oh, Jack, I have been so dreadfully frightened! It is awful to be there alone."

"Mr. Holmes, this is the young lady I spoke of. This is my fiancée."

"We were gradually coming to that conclusion, were we not, Watson?" Holmes answered with a smile. "I take it, Miss Presbury, that there is some fresh development in the case, and that you thought we should know?"

Our new visitor, a bright, handsome girl of a conventional English type, smiled back at Holmes as she seated herself beside Mr. Bennett.

"When I found Mr. Bennett had left his hotel I thought I should probably find him here. Of course, he had told me that he would consult you. But, oh, Mr. Holmes, can you do nothing for my poor father?"

"I have hopes, Miss Presbury, but the case is still obscure. Perhaps what you have to say may throw some fresh light upon it."

"It was last night, Mr. Holmes. He had been very strange all day. I am sure that there are times when he has no recollection of what he does. He lives as in a strange dream. Yesterday was such a day. It was not my father with whom I lived. His outward shell was there, but it was not really he."

"Tell me what happened."

"I was awakened in the night by the dog barking most furiously. Poor Roy, he is chained now near the stable. I may say that I always sleep with my door locked; for, as Jack—as Mr. Bennett—will tell you, we all have a feeling of impending danger. My room is on the second floor. It happened that the blind was up in my window, and there was bright moonlight outside. As I lay with my eyes fixed upon the square of light, listening to the frenzied barkings of the dog, I was amazed to see my father's face looking in at me. Mr. Holmes, I nearly died of surprise and horror. There it was pressed against the windowpane, and one hand seemed to be raised as if to push up the window. If that window had opened, I think I should have gone mad. It was no delusion, Mr. Holmes. Don't deceive yourself by thinking so. I dare say it was twenty seconds or so that I lay paralyzed and watched the face. Then it vanished, but I could not—I could not spring out of bed and look out after it. I lay cold and shivering till morning. At breakfast he was sharp and fierce in manner, and made no allusion to the adventure of the night. Neither did I, but I gave an excuse for coming to town -and here I am."

Holmes looked thoroughly surprised at Miss Presbury's narrative.

"My dear young lady, you say that your room is on the second floor. Is there a long ladder in the garden?"

"No, Mr. Holmes, that is the amazing part of it. There is no possible way of reaching the window—and yet he was there."

"The date being September 5th," said Holmes. "That certainly complicates matters."

It was the young lady's turn to look surprised. "This is the second time that you have alluded to the date, Mr. Holmes," said Bennett. "Is it possible that it has any bearing upon the case?"

"It is possible—very possible—and yet I have not my full material at present."

"Possibly you are thinking of the connection between insanity and phases of the moon?"

"No, I assure you. It was quite a different line of thought. Possibly you can leave your notebook with me, and I will check the dates. Now I think, Watson, that our line of action is perfectly clear. This young lady has informed us—and I have the greatest confidence in her intuition—that her father remembers little or nothing which occurs upon certain dates. We will therefore call upon him as if he had given us an appointment upon such a date. He will put it down to his own lack of memory. Thus we will open our campaign by having a good close view of him."

"That is excellent," said Mr. Bennett. "I warn you, however, that the professor is irascible and violent at times."

Holmes smiled. "There are reasons why we should come at once—very cogent reasons if my theories hold good. To-morrow, Mr. Bennett, will certainly see us in Camford. There is, if I remember right, an inn called the Chequers where the port used to be above mediocrity and the linen was above reproach. I think, Watson, that our lot for the next few days might lie in less pleasant places."

Monday morning found us on our way to the famous university town—an easy effort on the part of Holmes, who had no roots to pull up, but one which involved frantic planning and hurrying on my part, as my practice was by this time not inconsiderable. Holmes made no allusion to the case until after we had deposited our suitcases at the ancient hostel of which he had spoken.

"I think, Watson, that we can catch the professor just before lunch. He lectures at eleven and should have an interval at home."

"What possible excuse have we for calling?"

Holmes glanced at his notebook.

"There was a period of excitement upon August 26th. We will assume that he is a little hazy as to what he does at such times. If we insist that we are there by appointment I think he will hardly venture to contradict us. Have you the effrontery necessary to put it through?"

"We can but try."

"Excellent, Watson! Compound of the Busy Bee and Excelsior. We can but try—the motto of the firm. A friendly native will surely guide us."

Such a one on the back of a smart hansom swept us past a row of ancient colleges and, finally turning into a tree-lined drive, pulled up at the door of a charming house, girt round with lawns and covered with purple wistaria. Professor Presbury was certainly surrounded with every sign not only of comfort but of luxury. Even as we pulled up, a grizzled head appeared at the front window, and we were aware of a pair of keen eyes from under shaggy brows which surveyed us through large horn glasses. A moment later we were actually in his sanctum, and the mysterious scientist, whose vagaries had brought us from

London, was standing before us. There was certainly no sign of eccentricity either in his manner or appearance, for he was a portly, large-featured man, grave, tall, and frock-coated, with the dignity of bearing which a lecturer needs. His eyes were his most remarkable feature, keen, observant, and clever to the verge of cunning.

He looked at our cards. "Pray sit down, gentlemen. What can I do for you?"

Mr. Holmes smiled amiably.

"It was the question which I was about to put to you, Professor."

"To me, sir!"

"Possibly there is some mistake. I heard through a second person that Professor Presbury of Camford had need of my services."

"Oh, indeed!" It seemed to me that there was a malicious sparkle in the intense gray eyes. "You heard that, did you? May I ask the name of your informant?"

"I am sorry, Professor, but the matter was rather confidential. If I have made a mistake there is no harm done. I can only express my regret."

"Not at all. I should wish to go funher into this matter. It interests me. Have you any scrap of writing, any letter or telegram, to bear out your assertion?"

"No, I have not."

"I presume that you do not go so far as to assert that I summoned you?"

"I would rather answer no questions," said Holmes.

"No, I dare say not," said the professor with asperity. "However, that particular one can be answered very easily without your aid."

He walked across the room to the bell. Our London friend Mr. Bennett, answered the call.

"Come in, Mr. Bennett. These two gentlemen have come from

London under the impression that they have been summoned. You handle all my correspondence. Have you a note of anything going to a person named Holmes?"

"No, sir," Bennett answered with a flush.

"That is conclusive," said the professor, glaring angrily at my companion. "Now, sir"—he leaned forward with his two hands upon the table—" it seems to me that your position is a very questionable one."

Holmes shrugged his shoulders.

"I can only repeat that I am sorry that we have made a needless intrusion."

"Hardly enough, Mr. Holmes!" the old man cried in a high screaming voice, with extraordinary malignancy upon his face. He got between us and the door as he spoke, and he shook his two hands at us with furious passion. "You can hardly get out of it so easily as that." His face was convulsed, and he grinned and gibbered at us in his senseless rage. I am convinced that we should have had to fight our way out of the room if Mr. Bennett had not intervened.

"My dear Professor," he cried, "consider your position! Consider the scandal at the university! Mr. Holmes is a well-known man. You cannot possibly treat him with such discourtesy."

Sulkily our host—if I may call him so—cleared the path to the door. We were glad to find ourselves outside the house and in the quiet of the tree-lined drive. Holmes seemed greatly amused by the episode.

"Our learned friend's nerves are somewhat out of order," said he. "Perhaps our intrusion was a little crude, and yet we have gained that personal contact which I desired. But, dear me, Watson, he is surely at our heels. The villain still pursues us."

There were the sounds of running feet behind, but it was, to my relief, not the formidable professor but his assistant who appeared round the curve of the drive. He came panting up to us.

"I am so sorry, Mr. Holmes. I wished to apologize."

"My dear sir, there is no need. It is all in the way of professional experience."

"I have never seen him in a more dangerous mood. But he grows more sinister. You can understand now why his daughter and I are alarmed. And yet his mind is perfectly clear."

"Too clear!" said Holmes. "That was my miscalculation. It is evident that his memory is much more reliable than I had thought. By the way, can we, before we go, see the window of Miss Presbury's room?"

Mr. Bennett pushed his way through some shrubs, and we had a view of the side of the house.

"It is there. The second on the left."

"Dear me, it seems hardly accessible. And yet you will observe that there is a creeper below and a water-pipe above which give some foothold."

"I could not climb it myself," said Mr. Bennett.

"Very likely. It would certainly be a dangerous exploit for any normal man."

"There was one other thing I wish to tell you, Mr. Holmes. I have the address of the man in London to whom the professor writes. He seems to have written this morning, and I got it from his blotting-paper. It is an ignoble position for a trusted secretary, but what else can I do?"

Holmes glanced at the paper and put it into his pocket.

"Dorak—a curious name. Slavonic, I imagine. Well, it is an important link in the chain. We return to London this afternoon, Mr. Bennett. I see no good purpose to be served by our remaining. We cannot arrest the professor because he has done no crime, nor can we place him under constraint, for he cannot be proved to be mad. No action is as yet possible."

"Then what on earth are we to do?"

"A little patience, Mr. Bennett. Things will soon develop. Unless I am mistaken, next Tuesday may mark a crisis. Certainly we shall be in Camford on that day. Meanwhile, the general position is undeniably unpleasant, and if Miss Presbury can prolong her visit."

"That is easy."

"Then let her stay till we can assure her that all danger is past. Meanwhile, let him have his way and do not cross him. So long as he is in a good humour all is well."

"There he is!" said Bennett in a startled whisper. Looking between the branches we saw the tall, erect figure emerge from the hall door and look around him. He stood leaning forward, his hands swinging straight before him, his head turning from side to side. The secretary with a last wave slipped off among the trees, and we saw him presently rejoin his employer, the two entering the house together in what seemed to be animated and even excited conversation.

"I expect the old gentleman has been putting two and two together," said Holmes as we walked hotelward. "He struck me as having a particularly clear and logical brain from the little I saw of him. Explosive, no doubt, but then from his point of view he has something to explode about if detectives are put on his track and he suspects his own household of doing it. I rather fancy that friend Bennett is in for an uncomfortable time."

Holmes stopped at a post-office and sent off a telegram on our way. The answer reached us in the evening, and he tossed it across to me.

Have visited the Commercial Road and seen Dorak. Suave person, Bohemian, elderly. Keeps large general store.

MERCER.

"Mercer is since your time," said Holmes. "He is my general utility man who looks up routine business. It was important to know something of the man with whom our professor was so secretly corresponding. His nationality connects up with the Prague visit."

"Thank goodness that something connects with something," said I. "At present we seem to be faced by a long series of inexplicable incidents with no bearing upon each other."For example, what possible connection can there be between an angry wolfhound and a visit to Bohemia, or either of them with a man crawling down a passage at night? As to your dates, that is the biggest mystification of all."

Holmes smiled and rubbed his hands. We were, I may say, seated in the old sitting-room of the ancient hotel, with a bottle of the famous vintage of which Holmes had spoken on the table between us.

"Well, now, let us take the dates first," said he, his fingertips together and his manner as if he were addressing a class. "This excellent young man's diary shows that there was trouble upon July 2d, and from then onward it seems to have been at nine-day intervals, with, so far as I remember, only one exception. Thus the last outbreak upon Friday was on September 3d, which also falls into the series, as did August 26th, which preceded it. The thing is beyond coincidence."

I was forced to agree.

"Let us, then, form the provisional theory that every nine days the professor takes some strong drug which has a passing but highly poisonous effect. His naturally violent nature is intensified by it. He learned to take this drug while he was in Prague, and is now supplied with it by a Bohemian intermediary in London. This all hangs together, Watson!"

"But the dog, the face at the window, the creeping man in the passage?"

"Well, well, we have made a beginning. I should not expect any fresh developments until next Tuesday. In the meantime we can only keep in touch with friend Bennett and enjoy the amenities of this charming town."

In the morning Mr. Bennett slipped round to bring us the latest report. As Holmes had imagined, times had not been easy with him. Without exactly accusing him of being responsible for our presence, the professor had been very rough and rude in his speech, and evidently felt some strong grievance. This morning he was quite himself again, however, and had delivered his usual brilliant lecture to a crowded class. "Apart from his queer fits," said Bennett, "he has actually more energy and vitality than I can ever remember, nor was his brain ever clearer. But it's not he—it's never the man whom we have known."

"I don't think you have anything to fear now for a week at least," Holmes answered. "I am a busy man, and Dr. Watson has his patients to attend to. Let us agree that we meet here at this hour next Tuesday, and I shall be surprised if before we leave you again we are not able to explain, even if we cannot perhaps put an end to, your troubles. Meanwhile, keep us posted in what occurs."

I saw nothing of my friend for the next few days, but on the following Monday evening I had a short note asking me to meet him next day at the train. From what he told me as we travelled up to Camford all was well, the peace of the professor's house had been unruffled, and his own conduct perfectly normal. This also was the report which was given us by Mr. Bennett himself when he called upon us that evening at our old quarters in the Chequers. "He heard from his London correspondent to-day. There was a letter and there was a small packet, each with the cross under the stamp which warned me not to touch them. There has been nothing else."

"That may prove quite enough," said Holmes grimly. "Now, Mr. Bennett, we shall, I think, come to some conclusion tonight. If my deductions are correct we should have an opportunity of bringing matters to a head. In order to do so it is necessary to hold the professor under observation. I would suggest, therefore, that you remain awake and on the lookout. Should you hear him pass your door, do not interrupt him, but follow him as discreetly as you can. Dr. Watson and I will not be far off. By the way, where is the key of that little box of which you spoke?"

"Upon his watch-chain."

"I fancy our researches must lie in that direction. At the worst the lock should not be very formidable. Have you any other able-bodied man on the premises?"

"There is the coachman, Macphail."

"Where does he sleep?"

"Over the stables."

"We might possibly want him. Well, we can do no more until we see how things develop, Good-bye—but I expect that we shall see you before morning."

It was nearly midnight before we took our station among some bushes immediately opposite the hall door of the professor. It was a fine night, but chilly, and we were glad of our warm overcoats. There was a breeze, and clouds were scudding across the sky, obscuring from time to time the half-moon. It would have been a dismal vigil were it not for the expectation and excitement which carried us along, and the assurance of my comrade that we had probably reached the end of the strange sequence of events which had engaged our attention.

"If the cycle of nine days holds good then we shall have the professor at his worst to-night," said Holmes. "The fact that these strange symptoms began after his visit to Prague, that he is in secret correspondence with a Bohemian dealer in London, who presumably represents someone in Prague, and that he received a packet from him this very day, all point in one direction. What he takes and why he takes it are still beyond our ken, but that it emanates in some way from Prague is clear enough. He takes it under definite directions which regulate this ninth-day system, which was the first point which attracted my attention. But his symptoms are most remarkable. Did you observe his knuckles?"

I had to confess that I did not.

"Thick and horny in a way which is quite new in my experience. Always look at the hands first, Watson. Then cuffs, trouser-knees, and boots. Very curious knuckles which can only be explained by the mode of progression observed by—" Holmes paused and suddenly clapped his hand to his forehead. "Oh, Watson, Watson, what a fool I have been! It seems incredible, and yet it must be true. All points in one direction. How could I miss seeing the connection of ideas? Those knuckles how could I have passed those knuckles? And the dog! And the ivy! It's surely time that I disappeared into that little farm of my dreams. Look out, Watson! Here he is! We shall have the chance of seeing for ourselves."

The hall door had slowly opened, and against the lamplit background we saw the tall figure of Professor Presbury. He was clad in his dressing gown. As he stood outlined in the doorway he was erect but leaning forward with dangling arms, as when we saw him last.

Now he stepped forward into the drive, and an extraordinary change came over him. He sank down into a crouching position and moved along upon his hands and feet, skipping every now and then as if he were overflowing with energy and vitality. He moved along the face of the house and then round the corner. As he disappeared Bennett slipped through the hall door and softly followed him.

"Come, Watson, come!" cried Holmes, and we stole as softly as we could through the bushes until we had gained a spot whence we could see the other side of the house, which was bathed in the light of the half-moon. The professor was clearly visible crouching at the foot of the ivy-covered wall. As we watched him he suddenly began with incredible agility to ascend it. From branch to branch he sprang, sure of foot and firm of grasp, climbing apparently in mere joy at his own powers, with no definite object in view. With his dressing-gown flapping on each side of him, he looked like some huge bat glued against the side of his own house, a great square dark patch upon the moonlit wall. Presently he tired of this amusement, and, dropping from branch to branch, he squatted down into the old attitude and moved towards the stables, creeping along in the same strange way as before. The wolfhound was out now, barking furiously, and more excited than ever when it actually caught sight of its master. It was straining on its chain and quivering with eagerness and rage. The professor squatted down very deliberately just out of reach of the hound and began to provoke it in every possible way. He took handfuls of pebbles from the drive and threw them in the dog's face, prodded him with a stick which he had picked up, flicked his hands about only a few inches from the gaping mouth, and endeavoured in every way to increase the animal's fury, which was already beyond all control. In all our adventures I do not know that I have ever seen a more strange sight than this impassive and still dignified figure crouching frog-like upon the ground and goading to a wilder exhibition of passion the maddened hound, which ramped and raged in front of him, by all manner of ingenious and calculated cruelty.

And then in a moment it happened! It was not the chain that broke, but it was the collar that slipped, for it had been made for a thick-necked Newfoundland. We heard the rattle of falling metal, and the next instant dog and man were rolling on the ground together, the one roaring in rage, the other screaming in a strange shrill falsetto of terror. It was a very narrow thing for the professor's life. The savage creature had him fairly by the throat, its fangs had bitten deep, and he was senseless before we could reach them and drag the two apart. It might have been a dangerous task for us, but Bennett's voice and presence brought the great wolfhound instantly to reason. The uproar had brought the sleepy and astonished coachman from his room above the stables. "I'm not surprised," said he, shaking his head. "I've seen him at it before. I knew the dog would get him sooner or later."

The hound was secured, and together we carried the professor up to his room, where Bennett, who had a medical degree, helped me to dress his torn throat. The sharp teeth had passed dangerously near the carotid artery, and the haemorrhage was serious. In half an hour the danger was past, I had given the patient an injection of morphia, and he had sunk into deep sleep. Then, and only then, were we able to look at each other and to take stock of the situation.

"I think a first-class surgeon should see him," said I.

"For God's sake, no!" cried Bennett. "At present the scandal is confined to our own household. It is safe with us. If it gets beyond these walls it will never stop. Consider his position at the university, his European reputation, the feelings of his daughter."

"Quite so," said Holmes. "I think it may be quite possible to keep the matter to ourselves, and also to prevent its recurrence now that we have a free hand. The key from the watch-chain, Mr. Bennett. Macphail will guard the patient and let us know if there is any change. Let us see what we can find in the professor's mysterious box."

There was not much, but there was enough—an empty phial, another nearly full, a hypodermic syringe, several letters in a crabbed, foreign hand. The marks on the envelopes showed that they were those which had disturbed the routine of the secretary, and each was dated from the Commercial Road and signed "A. Dorak." They were mere invoices to say that a fresh bottle was being sent to Professor Presbury, or receipt to acknowledge money. There was one other envelope, however, in a more educated hand and bearing the Austrian stamp with the postmark of Prague. "Here we have our material!" cried Holmes as he tore out the enclosure.

HONOURED COLLEAGUE [it ran]:
Since your esteemed visit I have thought much of your case, and though in your circumstances there are some

special reasons for the treatment, I would none the less enjoin caution, as my results have shown that it is not without danger of a kind.

It is possible that the serum of anthropoid would have been better. I have, as I explained to you, used black-faced langur because a specimen was accessible. Langur is, of course, a crawler and climber, while anthropoid walks erect and is in all ways nearer.

I beg you to take every possible precaution that there be no premature revelation of the process. I have one other client in England, and Dorak is my agent for both.

Weekly reports will oblige.

Yours with high esteem,

H. LOWENSTEIN.

Lowenstein! The name brought back to me the memory of some snippet from a newspaper which spoke of an obscure scientist who was striving in some unknown way for the secret of rejuvenescence and the elixir of life. Lowenstein of Prague! Lowenstein with the wondrous strength-giving serum, tabooed by the profession because he refused to reveal its source. In a few words I said what I remembered. Bennett had taken a manual of zoology from the shelves. "'Langur,'" he read, "'the great black-faced monkey of the Himalayan slopes, biggest and most human of climbing monkeys.' Many details are added. Well, thanks to you, Mr. Holmes, it is very clear that we have traced the evil to its source."

"The real source," said Holmes, "lies, of course, in that untimely love affair which gave our impetuous professor the idea that he could only gain his wish by turning himself into a younger man. When one tries to rise above Nature one is liable to fall below it. The highest type of man may revert to the animal if he leaves the straight road of destiny." He sat musing for a little with the phial in his hand, looking at the clear liquid within. "When I have written to this man and told him that I hold him criminally responsible for the poisons which he circulates, we will have no more trouble. But it may recur. Others may find a better way. There is danger there—a very real danger to humanity. Consider, Watson, that the material, the sensual, the worldly would all prolong their worthless lives. The spiritual would not avoid the call to something higher. It would be the survival of the least fit. What sort of cesspool may not our poor world become?" Suddenly the dreamer disappeared, and Holmes, the man of action, sprang from his chair. "I think there is nothing more to be said, Mr. Bennett. The various incidents will now fit themselves easily into the general scheme. The dog, of course, was aware of the change far more quickly than you. His smell would insure that. It was the monkey, not the professor, whom Roy attacked, just as it was the monkey who teased Roy. Climbing was a joy to the creature, and it was a mere chance, I take it, that the pastime brought him to the young lady's window. There is an early train to town, Watson, but I think we shall just have time for a cup of tea at the Chequers before we catch it."

The Blue Cross

G. K. Chesterton

B etween the silver ribbon of morning and the green glittering ribbon of sea, the boat touched Harwich and let loose a swarm of folk like flies, among whom the man we must follow was by no means conspicuous—nor wished to be. There was nothing notable about him, except a slight contrast between the holiday gaiety of his clothes and the official gravity of his face. His clothes included a slight, pale grey jacket, a white waistcoat, and a silver straw hat with a grey-blue ribbon. His lean face was dark by contrast, and ended in a curt black beard that looked Spanish and suggested an Elizabethan ruff. He was smoking a cigarette with the seriousness of an idler. There was nothing about him to indicate the fact that the grey jacket covered a loaded revolver, that the white waistcoat covered a police card, or that the straw hat covered one of the most powerful intellects in Europe. For this was Valentin himself, the head of the Paris police and the most famous investigator of the world; and he was coming from Brussels to London to make the greatest arrest of the century.

Flambeau was in England. The police of three countries had tracked the great criminal at last from Ghent to Brussels, from Brussels to the Hook of Holland; and it was conjectured that he would take some advantage of the unfamiliarity and confusion of the Eucharistic Congress, then taking place in London. Probably he would travel as some minor clerk or secretary connected with it; but, of course, Valentin could not be certain; nobody could be certain about Flambeau.

It is many years now since this colossus of crime suddenly ceased keeping the world in a turmoil; and when he ceased, as they said after the death of Roland, there was a great quiet upon the earth. But in his best days (I mean, of course, his worst) Flambeau was a figure as statuesque and international as the Kaiser. Almost every morning the daily paper announced that he had escaped the consequences of one extraordinary crime by committing another. He was a Gascon of gigantic stature and bodily daring; and the wildest tales were told of his outbursts of athletic humour; how he turned the juge d'instruction upside down and stood him on his head, "to clear his mind"; how he ran down the Rue de Rivoli with a policeman under each arm. It is due to him to say that his fantastic physical strength was generally employed in such bloodless though undignified scenes; his real crimes were chiefly those of ingenious and wholesale robbery. But each of his thefts was almost a new sin, and would make a story by itself. It was he who ran the great Tyrolean Dairy Company in London, with no dairies, no cows, no carts, no milk, but with some thousand subscribers. These he served by the simple operation of moving the little milk cans outside people's doors to the doors of his own customers. It was he who had kept up an unaccountable and close correspondence with a young lady whose whole letter-bag was intercepted, by the extraordinary trick of photographing his messages infinitesimally small upon the slides of a microscope. A sweeping simplicity, however, marked many of his experiments. It is said that he once repainted all the numbers in a street in the dead of night merely to divert one traveller into a trap. It is quite certain that he invented a portable pillar-box, which he put up at corners in quiet suburbs on the chance of strangers dropping postal orders into it. Lastly, he was known to be a startling acrobat; despite his huge figure, he could leap like a grasshopper and melt into the tree-tops like a monkey. Hence the great Valentin, when he set out to find Flambeau, was perfectly aware that his adventures would not end when he had found him.

But how was he to find him? On this the great Valentin's ideas were still in process of settlement.

There was one thing which Flambeau, with all his dexterity of disguise, could not cover, and that was his singular height. If Valentin's quick eye had caught a tall apple-woman, a tall grenadier, or even a tolerably tall duchess, he might have arrested them on the spot. But all along his train there was nobody that could be a disguised Flambeau, any more than a cat could be a disguised giraffe. About the people on the boat he had already satisfied himself; and the people picked up at Harwich or on the journey limited themselves with certainty to six. There was a short railway official travelling up to the terminus, three fairly short market gardeners picked up two stations afterwards, one very short widow lady going up from a small Essex town, and a very short Roman Catholic priest going up from a small Essex village. When it came to the last case, Valentin gave it up and almost laughed. The little priest was so much the essence of those Eastern flats; he had a face as round and dull as a Norfolk dumpling; he had eyes as empty as the North Sea; he had several brown paper parcels, which he was quite incapable of collecting. The Eucharistic Congress had doubtless sucked out of their local stagnation many such creatures, blind and helpless, like moles disinterred. Valentin was a sceptic in the severe style of France, and could have no love for priests. But he could have pity for them, and this one might have provoked pity in anybody. He had a large, shabby umbrella, which constantly fell on the floor. He did not seem to know which was the right end of his return ticket. He explained with a moon-calf simplicity to everybody in the carriage that he had to be careful, because he had something made of real silver "with blue stones" in one of his brown-paper parcels. His quaint blending of Essex flatness with saintly simplicity continuously amused the Frenchman till the priest arrived (somehow) at Tottenham with all his parcels, and came back for his umbrella. When he did the last, Valentin even had the good nature to warn him not to take care of the silver by telling everybody about it. But to whomever he talked, Valentin kept his eye open for someone else; he looked out steadily for anyone, rich or poor, male or female, who was well up to six feet; for Flambeau was four inches above it.

He alighted at Liverpool Street, however, quite conscientiously secure that he had not missed the criminal so far. He then went to Scotland Yard to regularise his position and arrange for help in case of need; he then lit another cigarette and went for a long stroll in the streets of London. As he was walking in the streets and squares beyond Victoria, he paused suddenly and stood. It was a quaint, quiet square, very typical of London, full of an accidental stillness. The tall, flat houses round looked at once prosperous and uninhabited; the square of shrubbery in the centre looked as deserted as a green Pacific islet. One of the four sides was much higher than the rest, like a dais; and the line of this side was broken by one of London's admirable accidents—a restaurant that looked as if it had strayed from Soho. It was an unreasonably attractive object, with dwarf plants in pots and long, striped blinds of lemon yellow and white. It stood specially high above the street, and in the usual patchwork way of London, a flight of steps from the street ran up to meet the front door almost as a fire-escape might run up to a first-floor window. Valentin stood and smoked in front of the yellow-white blinds and considered them long.

The most incredible thing about miracles is that they happen. A few clouds in heaven do come together into the staring shape of one human eye. A tree does stand up in the landscape of a doubtful journey in the exact and elaborate shape of a note of interrogation. I have seen both these things myself within the last few days. Nelson does die in the instant of victory; and a man named Williams does quite accidentally murder a man named Williamson; it sounds like a sort of infanticide. In short, there is in life an element of elfin coincidence which people reckoning on the prosaic may perpetually miss. As it has been well expressed in the paradox of Poe, wisdom should reckon on the unforeseen.

Aristide Valentin was unfathomably French; and the French intelligence is intelligence specially and solely. He was not "a thinking machine"; for that is a brainless phrase of modern fatalism and materialism. A machine only is a machine because it cannot think. But he was a thinking man, and a plain man at the same time. All his wonderful successes, that looked like conjuring, had been gained by plodding logic, by clear and commonplace French thought. The French electrify the world not by starting any paradox, they electrify it by carrying out a truism. They carry a truism so far—as in the French Revolution. But exactly because Valentin understood reason, he understood the limits of reason. Only a man who knows nothing of motors talks of motoring without petrol; only a man who knows nothing of reason talks of reasoning without strong, undisputed first principles. Here he had no strong first principles. Flambeau had been missed at Harwich; and if he was in London at all, he might be anything from a tall tramp on Wimbledon Common to a tall toast-master at the Hotel Metropole. In such a naked state of nescience, Valentin had a view and a method of his own.

In such cases he reckoned on the unforeseen. In such cases, when he could not follow the train of the reasonable, he coldly and carefully followed the train of the unreasonable. Instead of going to the right places—banks, police stations, rendezvous—he systematically went to the wrong places; knocked at every empty house, turned down every cul de sac, went up every lane blocked with rubbish, went round every crescent that led him uselessly out of the way. He defended this crazy course quite logically. He said that if one had a clue this was the worst way; but if one had no clue at all it was the best, because there was just the chance that any oddity that caught the eye of the pursuer might be the same that had caught the eye of the pursued. Somewhere a man must begin, and it had better be just where another man might stop. Something about that flight of steps up to the shop, something about the quietude and quaintness of the restaurant, roused all the detective's rare romantic fancy and made him resolve to strike at random. He went up the steps, and sitting down at a table by the window, asked for a cup of black coffee.

It was half-way through the morning, and he had not breakfasted; the slight litter of other breakfasts stood about on the table to remind him of his hunger; and adding a poached egg to his order, he proceeded musingly to shake some white sugar into his coffee, thinking all the time about Flambeau. He remembered how Flambeau had escaped, once by a pair of nail scissors, and once by a house on fire; once by having to pay for an unstamped letter, and once by getting people to look through a telescope at a comet that might destroy the world. He thought his detective brain as good as the criminal's, which was true. But he fully realised the disadvantage. "The criminal is the creative artist; the detective only the critic," he said with a sour smile, and lifted his coffee cup to his lips slowly, and put it down very quickly. He had put salt in it.

He looked at the vessel from which the silvery powder had come; it was certainly a sugar-basin; as unmistakably meant for sugar as a champagne-bottle for champagne. He wondered why they should keep salt in it. He looked to see if there were any more orthodox vessels. Yes; there were two salt-cellars quite full. Perhaps there was some speciality in the condiment in the salt-cellars. He tasted it; it was sugar. Then he looked round at the restaurant with a refreshed air of interest, to see if there were any other traces of that singular artistic taste which puts the sugar in the salt-cellars and the salt in the sugar-basin. Except for an odd splash of some dark fluid on one of the white-papered walls, the whole place appeared neat, cheerful and ordinary. He rang the bell for the waiter.

When that official hurried up, fuzzy-haired and somewhat blear-eyed at that early hour, the detective (who was not without an appreciation of the simpler forms of humour) asked him to taste the sugar and see if it was up to the high reputation of the hotel. The result was that the waiter yawned suddenly and woke up.

"Do you play this delicate joke on your customers every

morning?" inquired Valentin. "Does changing the salt and sugar never pall on you as a jest?"

The waiter, when this irony grew clearer, stammeringly assured him that the establishment had certainly no such intention; it must be a most curious mistake. He picked up the sugar-basin and looked at it; he picked up the salt-cellar and looked at that, his face growing more and more bewildered. At last he abruptly excused himself, and hurrying away, returned in a few seconds with the proprietor. The proprietor also examined the sugar-basin and then the salt-cellar; the proprietor also looked bewildered.

Suddenly the waiter seemed to grow inarticulate with a rush of words.

"I zink," he stuttered eagerly, "I zink it is those two clergy-men."

"What two clergymen?"

"The two clergymen," said the waiter, "that threw soup at the wall."

"Threw soup at the wall?" repeated Valentin, feeling sure this must be some singular Italian metaphor.

"Yes, yes," said the attendant excitedly, and pointed at the dark splash on the white paper; "threw it over there on the wall."

Valentin looked his query at the proprietor, who came to his rescue with fuller reports.

"Yes, sir," he said, "it's quite true, though I don't suppose it has anything to do with the sugar and salt. Two clergymen came in and drank soup here very early, as soon as the shutters were taken down. They were both very quiet, respectable people; one of them paid the bill and went out; the other, who seemed a slower coach altogether, was some minutes longer getting his things together. But he went at last. Only, the instant before he stepped into the street he deliberately picked up his cup, which he had only half emptied, and threw the soup slap on the wall. I was in the back room myself, and so was the waiter; so I could only rush out in time to find the wall splashed and the shop empty. It don't do any particular damage, but it was confounded cheek; and I tried to catch the men in the street. They were too far off though; I only noticed they went round the next corner into Carstairs Street."

The detective was on his feet, hat settled and stick in hand. He had already decided that in the universal darkness of his mind he could only follow the first odd finger that pointed; and this finger was odd enough. Paying his bill and clashing the glass doors behind him, he was soon swinging round into the other street.

It was fortunate that even in such fevered moments his eye was cool and quick. Something in a shop-front went by him like a mere flash; yet he went back to look at it. The shop was a popular greengrocer and fruiterer's, an array of goods set out in the open air and plainly ticketed with their names and prices. In the two most prominent compartments were two heaps, of oranges and of nuts respectively. On the heap of nuts lay a scrap of cardboard, on which was written in bold, blue chalk, "Best tangerine oranges, two a penny." On the oranges was the equally clear and exact description, "Finest Brazil nuts, 4d. a lb."

M. Valentin looked at these two placards and fancied he had met this highly subtle form of humour before, and that somewhat recently. He drew the attention of the red-faced fruiterer, who was looking rather sullenly up and down the street, to this inaccuracy in his advertisements. The fruiterer said nothing, but sharply put each card into its proper place. The detective, leaning elegantly on his walking-cane, continued to scrutinise the shop. At last he said, "Pray excuse my apparent irrelevance, my good sir, but I should like to ask you a question in experimental psychology and the association of ideas."

The red-faced shopman regarded him with an eye of menace; but he continued gaily, swinging his cane, "Why," he pursued, "why are two tickets wrongly placed in a greengrocer's shop like a shovel hat that has come to London for a holiday? Or, in case I do not make myself clear, what is the mystical association which connects the idea of nuts marked as oranges with the idea of two clergymen, one tall and the other short?"

The eyes of the tradesman stood out of his head like a snail's; he really seemed for an instant likely to fling himself upon the stranger. At last he stammered angrily: "I don't know what you 'ave to do with it, but if you're one of their friends, you can tell 'em from me that I'll knock their silly 'eads off, parsons or no parsons, if they upset my apples again."

"Indeed?" asked the detective, with great sympathy. "Did they upset your apples?"

"One of 'em did," said the heated shopman; "rolled 'em all over the street. I'd 'ave caught the fool but for havin' to pick 'em up."

"Which way did these parsons go?" asked Valentin.

"Up that second road on the left-hand side, and then across the square," said the other promptly.

"Thanks," replied Valentin, and vanished like a fairy. On the other side of the second square he found a policeman, and said: "This is urgent, constable; have you seen two clergymen in shovel hats?"

The policeman began to chuckle heavily. "I 'ave, sir; and if you arst me, one of 'em was drunk. He stood in the middle of the road that bewildered that—"

"Which way did they go?" snapped Valentin.

"They took one of them yellow buses over there," answered the man; "them that go to Hampstead."

Valentin produced his official card and said very rapidly: "Call up two of your men to come with me in pursuit," and crossed the road with such contagious energy that the ponderous policeman was moved to almost agile obedience. In a minute and a half the French detective was joined on the opposite pavement by an inspector and a man in plain clothes.

"Well, sir," began the former, with smiling importance, "and what may—?"

Valentin pointed suddenly with his cane. "I'll tell you on the top of that omnibus," he said, and was darting and dodging across the tangle of the traffic. When all three sank panting on the top seats of the yellow vehicle, the inspector said: "We could go four times as quick in a taxi."

"Quite true," replied their leader placidly, "if we only had an idea of where we were going."

"Well, where are you going?" asked the other, staring.

Valentin smoked frowningly for a few seconds; then, removing his cigarette, he said: "If you know what a man's doing, get in front of him; but if you want to guess what he's doing, keep behind him. Stray when he strays; stop when he stops; travel as slowly as he. Then you may see what he saw and may act as he acted. All we can do is to keep our eyes skinned for a queer thing."

"What sort of queer thing do you mean?" asked the inspector.

"Any sort of queer thing," answered Valentin, and relapsed into obstinate silence.

The yellow omnibus crawled up the northern roads for what seemed like hours on end; the great detective would not explain further, and perhaps his assistants felt a silent and growing doubt of his errand. Perhaps, also, they felt a silent and growing desire for lunch, for the hours crept long past the normal luncheon hour, and the long roads of the North London suburbs seemed to shoot out into length after length like an infernal telescope. It was one of those journeys on which a man perpetually feels that now at last he must have come to the end of the universe, and then finds he has only come to the beginning of Tufnell Park. London died away in draggled taverns and dreary scrubs, and then was unaccountably born again in blazing high streets and blatant hotels. It was like passing through thirteen separate vulgar cities all just touching each other. But though the winter twilight was already threatening the road ahead of them, the Parisian detective still sat silent and watchful, eyeing the frontage of the streets that slid by on either side. By the time they had left Camden Town behind, the policemen were nearly asleep; at least, they gave something like a jump as Valentin leapt erect, struck a hand on each man's shoulder, and shouted to the driver to stop.

They tumbled down the steps into the road without realising why they had been dislodged; when they looked round for enlightenment they found Valentin triumphantly pointing his finger towards a window on the left side of the road. It was a large window, forming part of the long facade of a gilt and palatial public-house; it was the part reserved for respectable dining, and labelled "Restaurant." This window, like all the rest along the frontage of the hotel, was of frosted and figured glass; but in the middle of it was a big, black smash, like a star in the ice.

"Our cue at last," cried Valentin, waving his stick; "the place with the broken window."

"What window? What cue?" asked his principal assistant. "Why, what proof is there that this has anything to do with them?"

Valentin almost broke his bamboo stick with rage.

"Proof!" he cried. "Good God! the man is looking for proof! Why, of course, the chances are twenty to one that it has nothing to do with them. But what else can we do? Don't you see we must either follow one wild possibility or else go home to bed?" He banged his way into the restaurant, followed by his companions, and they were soon seated at a late luncheon at a little table, and looked at the star of smashed glass from the inside. Not that it was very informative to them even then.

"Got your window broken, I see," said Valentin to the waiter as he paid the bill.

"Yes, sir," answered the attendant, bending busily over the

change, to which Valentin silently added an enormous tip. The waiter straightened himself with mild but unmistakable animation.

"Ah, yes, sir," he said. "Very odd thing, that, sir."

"Indeed?" Tell us about it," said the detective with careless curiosity.

"Well, two gents in black came in," said the waiter; "two of those foreign parsons that are running about. They had a cheap and quiet little lunch, and one of them paid for it and went out. The other was just going out to join him when I looked at my change again and found he'd paid me more than three times too much. 'Here,' I says to the chap who was nearly out of the door, 'you've paid too much.' 'Oh,' he says, very cool, 'have we?' 'Yes,' I says, and picks up the bill to show him. Well, that was a knock-out."

"What do you mean?" asked his interlocutor.

"Well, I'd have sworn on seven Bibles that I'd put 4s. on that bill. But now I saw I'd put 14s., as plain as paint."

"Well?" cried Valentin, moving slowly, but with burning eyes, "and then?"

"The parson at the door he says all serene, 'Sorry to confuse your accounts, but it'll pay for the window.' 'What window?' I says. 'The one I'm going to break,' he says, and smashed that blessed pane with his umbrella."

All three inquirers made an exclamation; and the inspector said under his breath, "Are we after escaped lunatics?" The waiter went on with some relish for the ridiculous story:

"I was so knocked silly for a second, I couldn't do anything. The man marched out of the place and joined his friend just round the corner. Then they went so quick up Bullock Street that I couldn't catch them, though I ran round the bars to do it."

"Bullock Street," said the detective, and shot up that thoroughfare as quickly as the strange couple he pursued.

Their journey now took them through bare brick ways like

tunnels; streets with few lights and even with few windows; streets that seemed built out of the blank backs of everything and everywhere. Dusk was deepening, and it was not easy even for the London policemen to guess in what exact direction they were treading. The inspector, however, was pretty certain that they would eventually strike some part of Hampstead Heath. Abruptly one bulging gas-lit window broke the blue twilight like a bull's-eye lantern; and Valentin stopped an instant before a little garish sweetstuff shop. After an instant's hesitation he went in; he stood amid the gaudy colours of the confectionery with entire gravity and bought thirteen chocolate cigars with a certain care. He was clearly preparing an opening; but he did not need one.

An angular, elderly young woman in the shop had regarded his elegant appearance with a merely automatic inquiry; but when she saw the door behind him blocked with the blue uniform of the inspector, her eyes seemed to wake up.

"Oh," she said, "if you've come about that parcel, I've sent it off already."

"Parcel?" repeated Valentin; and it was his turn to look inquiring.

"I mean the parcel the gentleman left—the clergyman gentleman."

"For goodness' sake," said Valentin, leaning forward with his first real confession of eagerness, "for Heaven's sake tell us what happened exactly."

"Well," said the woman a little doubtfully, "the clergymen came in about half an hour ago and bought some peppermints and talked a bit, and then went off towards the Heath. But a second after, one of them runs back into the shop and says, 'Have I left a parcel!' Well, I looked everywhere and couldn't see one; so he says, 'Never mind; but if it should turn up, please post it to this address,' and he left me the address and a shilling for my trouble. And sure enough, though I thought I'd looked everywhere, I found he'd left a brown paper parcel, so I posted it to the place he said. I can't remember the address now; it was somewhere in Westminster. But as the thing seemed so important, I thought perhaps the police had come about it."

"So they have," said Valentin shortly. "Is Hampstead Heath near here?"

"Straight on for fifteen minutes," said the woman, "and you'll come right out on the open." Valentin sprang out of the shop and began to run. The other detectives followed him at a reluctant trot.

The street they threaded was so narrow and shut in by shadows that when they came out unexpectedly into the void common and vast sky they were startled to find the evening still so light and clear. A perfect dome of peacock-green sank into gold amid the blackening trees and the dark violet distances. The glowing green tint was just deep enough to pick out in points of crystal one or two stars. All that was left of the daylight lay in a golden glitter across the edge of Hampstead and that popular hollow which is called the Vale of Health. The holiday makers who roam this region had not wholly dispersed; a few couples sat shapelessly on benches; and here and there a distant girl still shrieked in one of the swings. The glory of heaven deepened and darkened around the sublime vulgarity of man; and standing on the slope and looking across the valley, Valentin beheld the thing which he sought.

Among the black and breaking groups in that distance was one especially black which did not break—a group of two figures clerically clad. Though they seemed as small as insects, Valentin could see that one of them was much smaller than the other. Though the other had a student's stoop and an inconspicuous manner, he could see that the man was well over six feet high. He shut his teeth and went forward, whirling his stick impatiently. By the time he had substantially diminished the distance and magnified the two black figures as in a vast microscope, he had perceived something else; something which startled him, and yet which he had somehow expected. Whoever was the tall priest, there could be no doubt about the identity of the short one. It was his friend of the Harwich train, the stumpy little cure of Essex whom he had warned about his brown paper parcels.

Now, so far as this went, everything fitted in finally and rationally enough. Valentin had learned by his inquiries that morning that a Father Brown from Essex was bringing up a silver cross with sapphires, a relic of considerable value, to show some of the foreign priests at the congress. This undoubtedly was the "silver with blue stones"; and Father Brown undoubtedly was the little greenhorn in the train. Now there was nothing wonderful about the fact that what Valentin had found out Flambeau had also found out; Flambeau found out everything. Also there was nothing wonderful in the fact that when Flambeau heard of a sapphire cross he should try to steal it; that was the most natural thing in all natural history. And most certainly there was nothing wonderful about the fact that Flambeau should have it all his own way with such a silly sheep as the man with the umbrella and the parcels. He was the sort of man whom anybody could lead on a string to the North Pole; it was not surprising that an actor like Flambeau, dressed as another priest, could lead him to Hampstead Heath. So far the crime seemed clear enough; and while the detective pitied the priest for his helplessness, he almost despised Flambeau for condescending to so gullible a victim. But when Valentin thought of all that had happened in between, of all that had led him to his triumph, he racked his brains for the smallest rhyme or reason in it. What had the stealing of a blue-and-silver cross from a priest from Essex to do with chucking soup at wall paper? What had it to do with calling nuts oranges, or with paying for windows first and breaking them afterwards? He had come to the end of his chase; yet somehow he had missed the middle of it. When he failed (which was seldom), he had usually grasped the clue, but nevertheless missed the criminal. Here he had grasped the criminal, but still he could not grasp the clue.

The two figures that they followed were crawling like black flies across the huge green contour of a hill. They were evidently sunk in conversation, and perhaps did not notice where they were going; but they were certainly going to the wilder and more silent heights of the Heath. As their pursuers gained on them, the latter had to use the undignified attitudes of the deer-stalker, to crouch behind clumps of trees and even to crawl prostrate in deep grass. By these ungainly ingenuities the hunters even came close enough to the quarry to hear the murmur of the discussion, but no word could be distinguished except the word "reason" recurring frequently in a high and almost childish voice. Once over an abrupt dip of land and a dense tangle of thickets, the detectives actually lost the two figures they were following. They did not find the trail again for an agonising ten minutes, and then it led round the brow of a great dome of hill overlooking an amphitheatre of rich and desolate sunset scenery. Under a tree in this commanding yet neglected spot was an old ramshackle wooden seat. On this seat sat the two priests still in serious speech together. The gorgeous green and gold still clung to the darkening horizon; but the dome above was turning slowly from peacock-green to peacock-blue, and the stars detached themselves more and more like solid jewels. Mutely motioning to his followers, Valentin contrived to creep up behind the big branching tree, and, standing there in deathly silence, heard the words of the strange priests for the first time.

After he had listened for a minute and a half, he was gripped by a devilish doubt. Perhaps he had dragged the two English policemen to the wastes of a nocturnal heath on an errand no saner than seeking figs on its thistles. For the two priests were talking exactly like priests, piously, with learning and leisure, about the most aerial enigmas of theology. The little Essex priest spoke the more simply, with his round face turned to the strengthening stars; the other talked with his head bowed, as if he were not even worthy to look at them. But no more innocently clerical conversation could have been heard in any white Italian cloister or black Spanish cathedral.

The first he heard was the tail of one of Father Brown's sentences, which ended: ". . . what they really meant in the Middle Ages by the heavens being incorruptible."

The taller priest nodded his bowed head and said:

"Ah, yes, these modern infidels appeal to their reason; but who can look at those millions of worlds and not feel that there may well be wonderful universes above us where reason is utterly unreasonable?"

"No," said the other priest; "reason is always reasonable, even in the last limbo, in the lost borderland of things. I know that people charge the Church with lowering reason, but it is just the other way. Alone on earth, the Church makes reason really supreme. Alone on earth, the Church affirms that God himself is bound by reason."

The other priest raised his austere face to the spangled sky and said:

"Yet who knows if in that infinite universe—?"

"Only infinite physically," said the little priest, turning sharply in his seat, "not infinite in the sense of escaping from the laws of truth."

Valentin behind his tree was tearing his fingernails with silent fury. He seemed almost to hear the sniggers of the English detectives whom he had brought so far on a fantastic guess only to listen to the metaphysical gossip of two mild old parsons. In his impatience he lost the equally elaborate answer of the tall cleric, and when he listened again it was again Father Brown who was speaking:

"Reason and justice grip the remotest and the loneliest star. Look at those stars. Don't they look as if they were single diamonds and sapphires? Well, you can imagine any mad botany or geology you please. Think of forests of adamant with leaves of brilliants. Think the moon is a blue moon, a single elephantine sapphire. But don't fancy that all that frantic astronomy would make the smallest difference to the reason and justice of conduct. On plains of opal, under cliffs cut out of pearl, you would still find a notice-board, 'Thou shalt not steal.'"

Valentin was just in the act of rising from his rigid and crouching attitude and creeping away as softly as might be, felled by the one great folly of his life. But something in the very silence of the tall priest made him stop until the latter spoke. When at last he did speak, he said simply, his head bowed and his hands on his knees:

"Well, I think that other worlds may perhaps rise higher than our reason. The mystery of heaven is unfathomable, and I for one can only bow my head."

Then, with brow yet bent and without changing by the faintest shade his attitude or voice, he added:

"Just hand over that sapphire cross of yours, will you? We're all alone here, and I could pull you to pieces like a straw doll."

The utterly unaltered voice and attitude added a strange violence to that shocking change of speech. But the guarder of the relic only seemed to turn his head by the smallest section of the compass. He seemed still to have a somewhat foolish face turned to the stars. Perhaps he had not understood. Or, perhaps, he had understood and sat rigid with terror.

"Yes," said the tall priest, in the same low voice and in the same still posture, "yes, I am Flambeau."

Then, after a pause, he said:

"Come, will you give me that cross?"

"No," said the other, and the monosyllable had an odd sound.

Flambeau suddenly flung off all his pontifical pretensions. The great robber leaned back in his seat and laughed low but long.

"No," he cried, "you won't give it me, you proud prelate. You won't give it me, you little celibate simpleton. Shall I tell you why you won't give it me? Because I've got it already in my own breast-pocket."

The small man from Essex turned what seemed to be a dazed face in the dusk, and said, with the timid eagerness of "The Private Secretary":

"Are—are you sure?"

Flambeau yelled with delight.

"Really, you're as good as a three-act farce," he cried. "Yes, you turnip, I am quite sure. I had the sense to make a duplicate of the right parcel, and now, my friend, you've got the duplicate and I've got the jewels. An old dodge, Father Brown—a very old dodge."

"Yes," said Father Brown, and passed his hand through his hair with the same strange vagueness of manner. "Yes, I've heard of it before."

The colossus of crime leaned over to the little rustic priest with a sort of sudden interest.

"You have heard of it?" he asked. "Where have you heard of it?"

"Well, I mustn't tell you his name, of course," said the little man simply. "He was a penitent, you know. He had lived prosperously for about twenty years entirely on duplicate brown paper parcels. And so, you see, when I began to suspect you, I thought of this poor chap's way of doing it at once."

"Began to suspect me?" repeated the outlaw with increased intensity. "Did you really have the gumption to suspect me just because I brought you up to this bare part of the heath?"

"No, no," said Brown with an air of apology. "You see, I suspected you when we first met. It's that little bulge up the sleeve where you people have the spiked bracelet."

"How in Tartarus," cried Flambeau, "did you ever hear of the spiked bracelet?"

"Oh, one's little flock, you know!" said Father Brown, arching his eyebrows rather blankly. "When I was a curate in Hartlepool, there were three of them with spiked bracelets. So, as I suspected you from the first, don't you see, I made sure that the cross should go safe, anyhow. I'm afraid I watched you, you know. So at last I saw you change the parcels. Then, don't you see, I changed them back again. And then I left the right one behind."

"Left it behind?" repeated Flambeau, and for the first time there was another note in his voice beside his triumph.

"Well, it was like this," said the little priest, speaking in the same unaffected way. "I went back to that sweet-shop and asked if I'd left a parcel, and gave them a particular address if it turned up. Well, I knew I hadn't; but when I went away again I did. So, instead of running after me with that valuable parcel, they have sent it flying to a friend of mine in Westminster." Then he added rather sadly: "I learnt that, too, from a poor fellow in Hartlepool. He used to do it with handbags he stole at railway stations, but he's in a monastery now. Oh, one gets to know, you know," he added, rubbing his head again with the same sort of desperate apology. "We can't help being priests. People come and tell us these things."

Flambeau tore a brown-paper parcel out of his inner pocket and rent it in pieces. There was nothing but paper and sticks of lead inside it. He sprang to his feet with a gigantic gesture, and cried:

"I don't believe you. I don't believe a bumpkin like you could manage all that. I believe you've still got the stuff on you, and if you don't give it up—why, we're all alone, and I'll take it by force!"

"No," said Father Brown simply, and stood up also, "you won't take it by force. First, because I really haven't still got it. And, second, because we are not alone."

Flambeau stopped in his stride forward.

"Behind that tree," said Father Brown, pointing, "are two strong policemen and the greatest detective alive. How did they come here, do you ask? Why, I brought them, of course! How did I do it? Why, I'll tell you if you like! Lord bless you, we have to know twenty such things when we work among the criminal classes! Well, I wasn't sure you were a thief, and it would never do to make a scandal against one of our own clergy. So I just tested you to see if anything would make you show yourself. A man generally makes a small scene if he finds salt in his coffee; if he doesn't, he has some reason for keeping quiet. I changed the salt and sugar, and you kept quiet. A man generally objects if his bill is three times too big. If he pays it, he has some motive for passing unnoticed. I altered your bill, and you paid it."

The world seemed waiting for Flambeau to leap like a tiger. But he was held back as by a spell; he was stunned with the utmost curiosity.

"Well," went on Father Brown, with lumbering lucidity, "as you wouldn't leave any tracks for the police, of course somebody had to. At every place we went to, I took care to do something that would get us talked about for the rest of the day. I didn't do much harm—a splashed wall, spilt apples, a broken window; but I saved the cross, as the cross will always be saved. It is at Westminster by now. I rather wonder you didn't stop it with the Donkey's Whistle."

"With the what?" asked Flambeau.

"I'm glad you've never heard of it," said the priest, making a face. "It's a foul thing. I'm sure you're too good a man for a Whistler. I couldn't have countered it even with the Spots myself; I'm not strong enough in the legs."

"What on earth are you talking about?" asked the other.

"Well, I did think you'd know the Spots," said Father Brown, agreeably surprised. "Oh, you can't have gone so very wrong yet!"

"How in blazes do you know all these horrors?" cried Flambeau.

The shadow of a smile crossed the round, simple face of his clerical opponent.

"Oh, by being a celibate simpleton, I suppose," he said. "Has it never struck you that a man who does next to nothing but hear men's real sins is not likely to be wholly unaware of human evil? But, as a matter of fact, another part of my trade, too, made me sure you weren't a priest."

"What?" asked the thief, almost gaping.

"You attacked reason," said Father Brown. "It's bad theology."

And even as he turned away to collect his property, the three policemen came out from under the twilight trees. Flambeau was an artist and a sportsman. He stepped back and swept Valentin a great bow.

"Do not bow to me, mon ami," said Valentin with silver clearness. "Let us both bow to our master."

And they both stood an instant uncovered while the little Essex priest blinked about for his umbrella.

The Coin of

Dionysius

Ernest Bramah

It was eight o'clock at night and raining, scarcely a time when a business so limited in its clientele as that of a coin dealer could hope to attract any customer, but a light was still showing in the small shop that bore over its window the name of Baxter, and in the even smaller office at the back the proprietor himself sat reading the latest *Pall Mall*. His enterprise seemed to be justified, for presently the door bell gave its announcement, and throwing down his paper Mr. Baxter went forward.

As a matter of fact the dealer had been expecting someone and his manner as he passed into the shop was unmistakably suggestive of a caller of importance. But at the first glance towards his visitor the excess of deference melted out of his bearing, leaving the urbane, self-possessed shopman in the presence of the casual customer.

"Mr. Baxter, I think?" said the latter. He had laid aside his dripping umbrella and was unbuttoning overcoat and coat to reach an inner pocket. "You hardly remember me, I suppose? Mr. Carlyle—two years ago I took up a case for you—"

"To be sure. Mr. Carlyle, the private detective—"

"Inquiry agent," corrected Mr. Carlyle precisely.

"Well," smiled Mr. Baxter, "for that matter I am a coin dealer and not an antiquarian or a numismatist. Is there anything in that way that I can do for you?"

"Yes," replied his visitor; "it is my turn to consult you." He had taken a small wash-leather bag from the inner pocket and now turned something carefully out upon the counter. "What can you tell me about that?"

The dealer gave the coin a moment's scrutiny.

"There is no question about this," he replied. "It is a Sicilian tetradrachm of Dionysius."

"Yes, I know that—I have it on the label out of the cabinet. I can tell you further that it's supposed to be one that Lord Seastoke gave two hundred and fifty pounds for at the Brice sale in '94."

"It seems to me that you can tell me more about it than I can tell you," remarked Mr. Baxter. "What is it that you really want to know?"

"I want to know," replied Mr. Carlyle, "whether it is genuine or not."

"Has any doubt been cast upon it?"

"Certain circumstances raised a suspicion—that is all."

The dealer took another look at the tetradrachm through his magnifying glass, holding it by the edge with the careful touch of an expert. Then he shook his head slowly in a confession of ignorance.

"Of course I could make a guess—"

"No, don't," interrupted Mr. Carlyle hastily. "An arrest hangs on it and nothing short of certainty is any good to me."

"Is that so, Mr. Carlyle?" said Mr. Baxter, with increased interest. "Well, to be quite candid, the thing is out of my line. Now if it was a rare Saxon penny or a doubtful noble I'd stake my reputation on my opinion, but I do very little in the classical series."

Mr. Carlyle did not attempt to conceal his disappointment as he returned the coin to the bag and replaced the bag in the inner pocket.

"I had been relying on you," he grumbled reproachfully. "Where on earth am I to go now?"

"There is always the British Museum."

"Ah, to be sure, thanks. But will anyone who can tell me be there now?"

"Now? No fear!" replied Mr. Baxter. "Go round in the morning—"

"But I must know tonight," explained the visitor, reduced to despair again. "Tomorrow will be too late for the purpose."

Mr. Baxter did not hold out much encouragement in the circumstances.

"You can scarcely expect to find anyone at business now," he remarked. "I should have been gone these two hours myself only I happened to have an appointment with an American millionaire who fixed his own time." Something indistinguishable from a wink slid off Mr. Baxter's right eye. "Offmunson he's called, and a bright young pedigree-hunter has traced his descent from Offa, King of Mercia. So he—quite naturally—wants a set of Offas as a sort of collateral proof."

"Very interesting," murmured Mr. Carlyle, fidgeting with his watch. "I should love an hour's chat with you about your millionaire customers—some other time. Just now—look here, Baxter, can't you give me a line of introduction to some dealer in this sort of thing who happens to live in town? You must know dozens of experts."

"Why, bless my soul, Mr. Carlyle, I don't know a man of them away from his business," said Mr. Baxter, staring. "They may live in Park Lane or they may live in Petticoat Lane for all I know. Besides, there aren't so many experts as you seem to imagine. And the two best will very likely quarrel over it. You've had to do with 'expert witnesses,' I suppose?"

"I don't want a witness; there will be no need to give evidence. All I want is an absolutely authoritative pronouncement that I can act on. Is there no one who can really say whether the thing is genuine or not?"

Mr. Baxter's meaning silence became cynical in its implication as he continued to look at his visitor across the counter. Then he relaxed.

"Stay a bit; there is a man—an amateur—I remember hearing wonderful things about some time ago. They say he really does know."

"There you are," exclaimed Mr. Carlyle, much relieved. "There always is someone. Who is he?"

"Funny name," replied Baxter. "Something Wynn or Wynn something." He craned his neck to catch sight of an important motor car that was drawing to the kerb before his window. "Wynn Carrados! You'll excuse me now, Mr. Carlyle, won't you? This looks like Mr. Offmunson."

Mr. Carlyle hastily scribbled the name down on his cuff.

"Wynn Carrados, right. Where does he live?"

"Haven't the remotest idea," replied Baxter, referring the arrangement of his tie to the judgment of the wall mirror. "I have never seen the man myself. Now, Mr. Carlyle, I'm sorry I can't do any more for you. You won't mind, will you?"

Mr. Carlyle could not pretend to misunderstand. He enjoyed the distinction of holding open the door for the transatlantic representative of the line of Offa as he went out, and then made his way through the muddy streets back to his office. There was only one way of tracing a private individual at such short notice—through the pages of the directories, and the gentleman did not flatter himself by a very high estimate of his chances.

Fortune favoured him, however. He very soon discovered a Wynn Carrados living at Richmond, and, better still, further search failed to unearth another. There was, apparently, only one householder at all events of that name in the neighbourhood of London. He jotted down the address and set out for Richmond.

The house was some distance from the station, Mr. Carlyle learned. He took a taxicab and drove, dismissing the vehicle at the gate. He prided himself on his power of observation and the accuracy of the deductions which resulted from it—a detail of his business. "It's nothing more than using one's eyes and putting two and two together," he would modestly declare, when he wished to be deprecatory rather than impressive, and by the time he had reached the front door of "The Turrets" he had formed some opinion of the position and tastes of the man who lived there.

A man-servant admitted Mr. Carlyle and took in his card—his private card with the bare request for an interview that would not detain Mr. Carrados for ten minutes. Luck still favoured him; Mr. Carrados was at home and would see him at once. The servant, the hall through which they passed, and the room into which he was shown, all contributed something to the deductions which the quietly observant gentleman was half unconsciously recording.

"Mr. Carlyle," announced the servant.

The room was a library or study. The only occupant, a man of about Carlyle's own age, had been using a typewriter up to the moment of his visitor's entrance. He now turned and stood up with an expression of formal courtesy.

"It's very good of you to see me at this hour," apologized the caller.

The conventional expression of Mr. Carrados's face changed a little.

"Surely my man has got your name wrong?" he exclaimed. "Isn't it Louis Calling?"

The visitor stopped short and his agreeable smile gave place to a sudden flash of anger or annoyance.

"No, sir," he replied stiffly. "My name is on the card which you have before you."

"I beg your pardon," said Mr. Carrados, with perfect good-humour. "I hadn't seen it. But I used to know a Calling some years ago—at St. Michael's."

"St. Michael's!" Mr. Carlyle's features underwent another change, no less instant and sweeping than before. "St. Michael's! Wynn Carrados? Good heavens! it isn't Max Wynn—old 'Winning' Wynn?"

"A little older and a little fatter—yes," replied Carrados. "I *have* changed my name, you see."

"Extraordinary thing meeting like this," said his visitor, dropping into a chair and staring hard at Mr. Carrados. "I have changed more than my name. How did you recognize me?"

"The voice," replied Carrados. "It took me back to that little smoke-dried attic den of yours where we—"

"My God!" exclaimed Carlyle bitterly, "don't remind me of what we were going to do in those days." He looked round the well-furnished, handsome room and recalled the other signs of wealth that he had noticed. "At all events, you seem fairly comfortable, Wynn."

"I am alternately envied and pitied," replied Carrados, with a placid tolerance of circumstance that seemed characteristic of him. "Still, as you say, I am fairly comfortable."

"Envied, I can understand. But why are you pitied?"

"Because I am blind," was the tranquil reply.

"Blind!" exclaimed Mr. Carlyle, using his own eyes superlatively. "Do you mean—literally blind?"

"Literally . . . I was riding along a bridle-path through a wood about a dozen years ago with a friend. He was in front. At one point a twig sprang back—you know how easily a thing like that happens. It just flicked my eye—nothing to think twice about."

"And that blinded you?"

"Yes, ultimately. It's called amaurosis."

"I can scarcely believe it. You seem so sure and self-reliant. Your eyes are full of expression—only a little quieter than they used to be. I believe you were typing when I came . . . Aren't you having me?"

"You miss the dog and the stick?" smiled Carrados. "No; it's a fact."

"What an awful infliction for you, Max. You were always such an impulsive, reckless sort of fellow—never quiet. You must miss such a fearful lot."

"Has anyone else recognized you?" asked Carrados quietly.

"Ah, that was the voice, you said," replied Carlyle.

"Yes; but other people heard the voice as well. Only I had no blundering, self-confident eyes to be hoodwinked."

"That's a rum way of putting it," said Carlyle. "Are your ears never hoodwinked, may I ask?"

"Not now. Nor my fingers. Nor any of my other senses that have to look out for themselves."

"Well, well," murmured Mr. Carlyle, cut short in his

sympathetic emotions. "I'm glad you take it so well. Of course, if you find it an advantage to be blind, old man—" He stopped and reddened. "I beg your pardon," he concluded stiffly.

"Not an advantage perhaps," replied the other thoughtfully. "Still it has compensations that one might not think of. A new world to explore, new experiences, new powers awakening; strange new perceptions; life in the fourth dimension. But why do you beg my pardon, Louis?"

"I am an ex-solicitor, struck off in connexion with the falsifying of a trust account, Mr. Carrados," replied Carlyle, rising.

"Sit down, Louis," said Carrados suavely. His face, even his incredibly living eyes, beamed placid good-nature. "The chair on which you will sit, the roof above you, all the comfortable surroundings to which you have so amiably alluded, are the direct result of falsifying a trust account. But do I call you 'Mr. Carlyle' in consequence? Certainly not, Louis."

"I did not falsify the account," cried Carlyle hotly. He sat down, however, and added more quietly: "But why do I tell you all this? I have never spoken of it before."

"Blindness invites confidence," replied Carrados. "We are out of the running—human rivalry ceases to exist. Besides, why shouldn't you? In my case the account *was* falsified."

"Of course that's all bunkum, Max," commented Carlyle. "Still, I appreciate your motive."

"Practically everything I possess was left to me by an American cousin, on the condition that I took the name of Carrados. He made his fortune by an ingenious conspiracy of doctoring the crop reports and unloading favourably in consequence. And I need hardly remind you that the receiver is equally guilty with the thief."

"But twice as safe. I know something of that, Max . . . Have you any idea what my business is?"

"You shall tell me," replied Carrados.

"I run a private inquiry agency. When I lost my profession I had to do something for a living. This occurred. I dropped my name, changed my appearance and opened an office. I knew the legal side down to the ground and I got a retired Scotland Yard man to organize the outside work."

"Excellent!" cried Carrados. "Do you unearth many murders?"

"No," admitted Mr. Carlyle; "our business lies mostly on the conventional lines among divorce and defalcation."

"That's a pity," remarked Carrados. "Do you know, Louis, I always had a secret ambition to be a detective myself. I have even thought lately that I might still be able to do something at it if the chance came my way. That makes you smile?"

"Well, certainly, the idea—"

"Yes, the idea of a blind detective—the blind tracking the alert—"

"Of course, as you say, certain faculties are no doubt quickened," Mr. Carlyle hastened to add considerately, "but, seriously, with the exception of an artist, I don't suppose there is any man who is more utterly dependent on his eyes."

Whatever opinion Carrados might have held privately, his genial exterior did not betray a shadow of dissent. For a full minute he continued to smoke as though he derived an actual visual enjoyment from the blue sprays that travelled and dispersed across the room. He had already placed before his visitor a box containing cigars of a brand which that gentleman keenly appreciated but generally regarded as unattainable, and the matter-of-fact ease and certainty with which the blind man had brought the box and put it before him had sent a questioning flicker through Carlyle's mind.

"You used to be rather fond of art yourself, Louis," he remarked presently. "Give me your opinion of my latest purchase—the bronze lion on the cabinet there." Then, as Carlyle's gaze went about the room, he added quickly: "No, not that cabinet—the one on your left."

Carlyle shot a sharp glance at his host as he got up, but Carrados's expression was merely benignly complacent. Then he strolled across to the figure.

"Very nice," he admitted. "Late Flemish, isn't it?"

"No. It is a copy of Vidal's 'Roaring lion.'"

"Vidal?"

"A French artist." The voice became indescribably flat. "He, also, had the misfortune to be blind, by the way."

"You old humbug, Max!" shrieked Carlyle, "you've been thinking that out for the last five minutes." Then the unfortunate man bit his lip and turned his back towards his host.

"Do you remember how we used to pile it up on that obtuse ass Sanders and then roast him?" asked Carrados, ignoring the half-smothered exclamation with which the other man had recalled himself.

"Yes," replied Carlyle quietly. "This is very good," he continued, addressing himself to the bronze again. "How ever did he do it?"

"With his hands."

"Naturally. But, I mean, how did he study his model?"

"Also with his hands. He called it 'seeing near.'"

"Even with a lion—handled it?"

"In such cases he required the services of a keeper, who brought the animal to bay while Vidal exercised his own particular gifts . . . You don't feel inclined to put me on the track of a mystery, Louis?"

Unable to regard this request as anything but one of old Max's unquenchable pleasantries, Mr. Carlyle was on the point of making a suitable reply when a sudden thought caused him to smile knowingly. Up to that point he had, indeed, completely forgotten the object of his visit. Now that he remembered the doubtful Dionysius and Mr. Baxter's recommendation he immediately assumed that some mistake had been made. Either Max was not the Wynn Carrados he had been seeking or else the dealer had been misinformed; for although his host was wonderfully expert in the face of his misfortune, it was inconceivable that he could decide the genuineness of a coin without seeing it. The opportunity seemed a good one of getting even with Carrados by taking him at his word.

"Yes," he accordingly replied, with crisp deliberation, as he recrossed the room; "yes, I will, Max. Here is the clue to what seems to be a rather remarkable fraud." He put the tetradrachm into his host's hand. "What do you make of it?"

For a few seconds Carrados handled the piece with the delicate manipulation of his finger-tips while Carlyle looked on with a self-appreciative grin. Then with equal gravity the blind man weighed the coin in the balance of his hand. Finally he touched it with his tongue.

"Well?" demanded the other.

"Of course I have not much to go on, and if I was more fully in your confidence I might come to another conclusion—"

"Yes, yes," interposed Carlyle, with amused encouragement.

"Then I should advise you to arrest the parlourmaid, Nina Brun, communicate with the police authorities of Padua for particulars of the career of Helene Brunesi, and suggest to Lord Seastoke that he should return to London to see what further depredations have been made in his cabinet."

Mr. Carlyle's groping hand sought and found a chair, on to which he dropped blankly. His eyes were unable to detach themselves for a single moment from the very ordinary spectacle of Mr. Carrados's mildly benevolent face, while the sterilized ghost of his now forgotten amusement still lingered about his features.

"Good heavens!" he managed to articulate, "how do you know?"

"Isn't that what you wanted of me?" asked Carrados suavely.

"Don't humbug, Max," said Carlyle severely. "This is no joke." An undefined mistrust of his own powers suddenly possessed him in the presence of this mystery. "How do you come to know of Nina Brun and Lord Seastoke?"

"You are a detective, Louis," replied Carrados. "How does one know these things? By using one's eyes and putting two and two together."

Carlyle groaned and flung out an arm petulantly.

"Is it all bunkum, Max? Do you really see all the time— though that doesn't go very far towards explaining it."

"Like Vidal, I see very well—at close quarters," replied Carrados, lightly running a forefinger along the inscription on the tetradrachm. "For longer range I keep another pair of eyes. Would you like to test them?"

Mr. Carlyle's assent was not very gracious; it was, in fact, faintly sulky. He was suffering the annoyance of feeling distinctly unimpressive in his own department; but he was also curious.

"The bell is just behind you, if you don't mind," said his host. "Parkinson will appear. You might take note of him while he is in."

The man who had admitted Mr. Carlyle proved to be Parkinson.

"This gentleman is Mr. Carlyle, Parkinson," explained Carrados the moment the man entered. "You will remember him for the future?"

Parkinson's apologetic eye swept the visitor from head to foot, but so lightly and swiftly that it conveyed to that gentleman the comparison of being very deftly dusted.

"I will endeavour to do so, sir," replied Parkinson, turning again to his master.

"I shall be at home to Mr. Carlyle whenever he calls. That is all."

"Very well, sir."

"Now, Louis," remarked Mr. Carrados briskly, when the door had closed again, "you have had a good opportunity of studying Parkinson. What is he like?"

"In what way?"

"I mean as a matter of description. I am a blind man—I haven't seen my servant for twelve years—what idea can you give me of him? I asked you to notice."

"I know you did, but your Parkinson is the sort of man who has very little about him to describe. He is the embodiment of the ordinary. His height is about average—"

"Five feet nine," murmured Carrados. "Slightly above the mean."

"Scarcely noticeably so. Clean-shaven. Medium brown hair. No particularly marked features. Dark eyes. Good teeth."

"False," interposed Carrados. "The teeth—not the statement."

"Possibly," admitted Mr. Carlyle. "I am not a dental expert and I had no opportunity of examining Mr. Parkinson's mouth in detail. But what is the drift of all this?"

"His clothes?"

"Oh, just the ordinary evening dress of a valet. There is not much room for variety in that."

"You noticed, in fact, nothing special by which Parkinson could be identified?"

"Well, he wore an unusually broad gold ring on the little finger of the left hand."

"But that is removable. And yet Parkinson has an ineradicable mole—a small one, I admit—on his chin. And you a human sleuth-hound. Oh, Louis!"

"At all events," retorted Carlyle, writhing a little under this good-humoured satire, although it was easy enough to see in it Carrados's affectionate intention—"at all events, I dare say I can give as good a description of Parkinson as he can give of me."

"That is what we are going to test. Ring the bell again."

"Seriously?"

"Quite. I am trying my eyes against yours. If I can't give you fifty out of a hundred I'll renounce my private detectorial ambition for ever."

"It isn't quite the same," objected Carlyle, but he rang the bell.

"Come in and close the door, Parkinson," said Carrados when the man appeared. "Don't look at Mr. Carlyle again—in fact, you had better stand with your back towards him, he won't mind. Now describe to me his appearance as you observed it."

Parkinson tendered his respectful apologies to Mr. Carlyle for the liberty he was compelled to take, by the deferential quality of his voice.

"Mr. Carlyle, sir, wears patent leather boots of about size seven and very little used. There are five buttons, but on the left boot one button—the third up—is missing, leaving loose threads and not the more usual metal fastener. Mr. Carlyle's trousers, sir, are of a dark material, a dark grey line of about a quarter of an inch width on a darker ground. The bottoms are turned permanently up and are, just now, a little muddy, if I may say so."

"Very muddy," interposed Mr. Carlyle generously. "It is a wet night, Parkinson."

"Yes, sir; very unpleasant weather. If you will allow me, sir, I will brush you in the hall. The mud is dry now, I notice. Then, sir," continued Parkinson, reverting to the business in hand, "there are dark green cashmere hose. A curb-pattern key-chain passes into the left-hand trouser pocket."

From the visitor's nether garments the photographic-eyed Parkinson proceeded to higher ground, and with increasing wonder Mr. Carlyle listened to the faithful catalogue of his possessions. His fetter-and-link albert of gold and platinum was minutely described. His spotted blue ascot, with its gentlemanly pearl scarfpin, was set forth, and the fact that the buttonhole in the left lapel of his morning coat showed signs of use was duly noted. What Parkinson saw he recorded but he made no deductions. A handkerchief carried in the cuff of the right sleeve was simply that to him and not an indication that Mr. Carlyle was, indeed, left-handed.

But a more delicate part of Parkinson's undertaking remained. He approached it with a double cough.

"As regards Mr. Carlyle's personal appearance; sir—"

"No, enough!" cried the gentleman concerned hastily. "I am more than satisfied. You are a keen observer, Parkinson."

"I have trained myself to suit my master's requirements, sir," replied the man. He looked towards Mr. Carrados, received a nod and withdrew.

Mr. Carlyle was the first to speak.

"That man of yours would be worth five pounds a week to me, Max," he remarked thoughtfully. "But, of course—"

"I don't think that he would take it," replied Carrados, in a voice of equally detached speculation. "He suits me very well. But you have the chance of using his services—indirectly."

"You still mean that—seriously?"

"I notice in you a chronic disinclination to take me seriously, Louis. It is really—to an Englishman—almost painful. Is there something inherently comic about me or the atmosphere of The Turrets?"

"No, my friend," replied Mr. Carlyle, "but there is something essentially prosperous. That is what points to the improbable. Now what is it?"

"It might be merely a whim, but it is more than that," replied Carrados. "It is, well, partly vanity, partly *ennui*, partly"—certainly there was something more nearly tragic in his voice than comic now—"partly hope."

Mr. Carlyle was too tactful to pursue the subject.

"Those are three tolerable motives," he acquiesced. "I'll do anything you want, Max, on one condition."

"Agreed. And it is?"

"That you tell me how you knew so much of this affair." He tapped the silver coin which lay on the table near them. "I am not easily flabbergasted," he added.

"You won't believe that there is nothing to explain—that it was purely second-sight?"

"No," replied Carlyle tersely; "I won't."

"You are quite right. And yet the thing is very simple."

"They always are—when you know," soliloquized the other. "That's what makes them so confoundedly difficult when you don't."

"Here is this one then. In Padua, which seems to be regaining its old reputation as the birthplace of spurious antiques, by the way, there lives an ingenious craftsman named Pietro Stelli. This simple soul, who possesses a talent not inferior to that of Cavino at his best, has for many years turned his hand to the not unprofitable occupation of forging rare Greek and Roman coins. As a collector and student of certain Greek colonials and a specialist in forgeries I have been familiar with Stelli's workmanship for years. Latterly he seems to have come under the influence of an international crook called—at the moment—Dompierre, who soon saw a way of utilizing Stelli's genius on a royal scale. Helene Brunesi, who in private life is—and really is, I believe—Madame Dompierre, readily lent her services to the enterprise."

"Quite so," nodded Mr. Carlyle, as his host paused.

"You see the whole sequence, of course?"

"Not exactly—not in detail," confessed Mr. Carlyle.

"Dompierre's idea was to gain access to some of the most celebrated cabinets of Europe and substitute Stelli's fabrications for the genuine coins. The princely collection of rarities that he would thus amass might be difficult to dispose of safely but I have no doubt that he had matured his plans. Helene, in the person of Nina Bran, an Anglicised French parlourmaid—a part which she fills to perfection—was to obtain wax impressions of the most valuable pieces and to make the exchange when the counterfeits reached her. In this way it was obviously hoped that the fraud would not come to light until long after the real coins had been sold, and I gather that she has already done her work successfully in several houses. Then, impressed by her excellent references and capable manner, my housekeeper engaged her, and for a few weeks she went about her duties here. It was fatal to this detail of the scheme, however, that I have the misfortune to be blind. I am told that Helene has so innocently angelic a face as to disarm suspicion, but I was incapable of being impressed and that good material was thrown away. But one morning my material fingers—which, of course, knew nothing of Helene's angelic face—discovered an unfamiliar touch about the surface of my favourite Euclideas, and, although there was doubtless nothing to be seen, my critical sense of smell reported that wax had been recently pressed against it. I began to make discreet inquiries and in the meantime my cabinets went to the local bank for safety. Helene countered by receiving a telegram from Angiers, calling her to the death-bed of her aged mother. The aged mother succumbed; duty compelled Helene to remain at the side of her stricken patriarchal father, and doubtless The Turrets was written off the syndicate's operations as a bad debt."

"Very interesting," admitted Mr. Carlyle; "but at the risk of seeming obtuse"—his manner had become delicately chastened—"I must say that I fail to trace the inevitable connexion between Nina Brun and this particular forgery—assuming that it is a forgery."

"Set your mind at rest about that, Louis," replied Carrados. "It is a forgery, and it is a forgery that none but Pietro Stelli could have achieved. That is the essential connexion. Of course, there are accessories. A private detective coming urgently to see me with a notable tetradrachm in his pocket, which he announces to be the clue to a remarkable fraud—well, really, Louis, one scarcely needs to be blind to see through that."

"And Lord Seastoke? I suppose you happened to discover that Nina Brun had gone there?"

"No, I cannot claim to have discovered that, or I should certainly have warned him at once when I found out—only recently—about the gang. As a matter of fact, the last information I had of Lord Seastoke was a line in yesterday's

Morning Post to the effect that he was still at Cairo. But many of these pieces—" He brushed his finger almost lovingly across the vivid chariot race that embellished the reverse of the coin, and broke off to remark: "You really ought to take up the subject, Louis. You have no idea how useful it might prove to you some day."

"I really think I must," replied Carlyle grimly. "Two hundred and fifty pounds the original of this cost, I believe."

"Cheap, too; it would make five hundred pounds in New York today. As I was saying, many are literally unique. This gem by Kimon is—here is his signature, you see; Peter is particularly good at lettering—and as I handled the genuine tetradrachm about two years ago, when Lord Seastoke exhibited it at a meeting of our society in Albemarle Street, there is nothing at all wonderful in my being able to fix the locale of your mystery. Indeed, I feel that I ought to apologize for it all being so simple."

"I think," remarked Mr. Carlyle, critically examining the loose threads on his left boot, "that the apology on that head would be more appropriate from me."

The Anthropologist

at Large

R. Austin Freeman

Thorndyke was not a newspaper reader. He viewed with extreme disfavour all scrappy and miscellaneous forms of literature, which, by presenting a disorderly series of unrelated items of information, tended, as he considered, to destroy the habit of consecutive mental effort.

"It is most important," he once remarked to me, "habitually to pursue a definite train of thought, and to pursue it to a finish, instead of flitting indolently from one uncompleted topic to another, as the newspaper reader is so apt to do. Still, there is no harm in a daily paper—so long as you don't read it."

Accordingly, he patronized a morning paper, and his method of dealing with it was characteristic. The paper was laid on the table after breakfast, together with a blue pencil and a pair of office shears. A preliminary glance through the sheets enabled him to mark with the pencil those paragraphs that were to be read, and these were presently cut out and looked through, after which they were either thrown away or set aside to be pasted in an indexed book.

The whole proceeding occupied, on an average, a quarter of an hour.

On the morning of which I am now speaking he was thus engaged. The pencil had done its work, and the snick of the shears announced the final stage. Presently he paused with a newly-excised cutting between his fingers, and, after glancing at it for a moment, he handed it to me.

"Another art robbery," he remarked. "Mysterious affairs, these—as to motive, I mean. You can't melt down a picture or an ivory carving, and you can't put them on the market as they stand. The very qualities that give them their value make them totally unnegotiable."

"Yet I suppose," said I, "the really inveterate collector— the pottery or stamp maniac, for instance—will buy these contraband goods even though he dare not show them."

"Probably. No doubt the *cupiditas habendi*, the mere desire to possess, is the motive force rather than any intelligent purpose—"

The discussion was at this point interrupted by a knock at the door, and a moment later my colleague admitted two gentlemen. One of these I recognized as a Mr. Marchmont, a solicitor, for whom we had occasionally acted; the other was a stranger—a typical Hebrew of the blonde type—good-looking, faultlessly dressed, carrying a bandbox, and obviously in a state of the most extreme agitation.

"Good-morning to you, gentlemen," said Mr. Marchmont, shaking hands cordially. "I have brought a client of mine to see you, and when I tell you that his name is Solomon Löwe, it will be unnecessary for me to say what our business is."

"Oddly enough," replied Thorndyke, "we were, at the very moment when you knocked, discussing the bearings of his case."

"It is a horrible affair!" burst in Mr. Löwe. "I am distracted! I am ruined! I am in despair!"

He banged the bandbox down on the table, and flinging himself into a chair, buried his face in his hands.

"Come, come," remonstrated Marchmont, "we must be brave, we must be composed. Tell Dr. Thorndyke your story, and let us hear what he thinks of it."

He leaned back in his chair, and looked at his client with that air of patient fortitude that comes to us all so easily when we contemplate the misfortunes of other people.

"You must help us, sir," exclaimed Löwe, starting up again—"you must, indeed, or I shall go mad. But I shall tell you what has happened, and then you must act at once. Spare no effort and no expense. Money is no object—at least, not in reason," he added, with native caution. He sat down once more, and in perfect English, though with a slight German accent, proceeded volubly: "My brother Isaac is probably known to you by name."

Thorndyke nodded.

"He is a great collector, and to some extent a dealer—that is to say, he makes his hobby a profitable hobby."

"What does he collect?" asked Thorndyke.

"Everything," replied our visitor, flinging his hands apart with a comprehensive gesture—"everything that is precious and beautiful—pictures, ivories, jewels, watches, objects of art and *vertu*—everything. He is a Jew, and he has that passion for things that are rich and costly that has distinguished our race from the time of my namesake Solomon onwards. His house in Howard Street, Piccadilly, is at once a museum and an art gallery. The rooms are filled with cases of gems, of antique jewellery, of coins and historic relics—some of priceless value—and the walls are covered with paintings, every one of which is a masterpiece. There is a fine collection of ancient weapons and armour, both European and Oriental; rare books, manuscripts, papyri, and valuable antiquities from Egypt, Assyria, Cyprus, and elsewhere. You see, his taste is quite catholic, and his knowledge of rare and curious things is probably greater than that of any other living man. He is never mistaken. No forgery deceives him, and hence the great prices that he obtains; for a work of art purchased from Isaac Löwe is a work certified as genuine beyond all cavil."

He paused to mop his face with a silk handkerchief, and then, with the same plaintive volubility, continued:

"My brother is unmarried. He lives for his collection, and he lives with it. The house is not a very large one, and the collection takes up most of it; but he keeps a suite of rooms for his own occupation, and has two servants—a man and wife—to look after him. The man, who is a retired police sergeant, acts as caretaker and watchman; the woman as housekeeper and cook, if required, but my brother lives largely at his club. And now I come to this present catastrophe."

He ran his fingers through his hair, took a deep breath, and continued:

"Yesterday morning Isaac started for Florence by way of

Paris, but his route was not certain, and he intended to break his journey at various points as circumstances determined. Before leaving, he put his collection in my charge, and it was arranged that I should occupy his rooms in his absence. Accordingly, I sent my things round and took possession.

"Now, Dr. Thorndyke, I am closely connected with the drama, and it is my custom to spend my evenings at my club, of which most of the members are actors. Consequently, I am rather late in my habits; but last night I was earlier than usual in leaving my club, for I started for my brother's house before half-past twelve. I felt, as you may suppose, the responsibility of the great charge I had undertaken; and you may, therefore, imagine my horror, my consternation, my despair, when, on letting myself in with my latchkey, I found a police-inspector, a sergeant, and a constable in the hall. There had been a robbery, sir, in my brief absence, and the account that the inspector gave of the affair was briefly this:

"While taking the round of his district, he had noticed an empty hansom proceeding in leisurely fashion along Howard Street. There was nothing remarkable in this, but when, about ten minutes later, he was returning, and met a hansom, which he believed to be the same, proceeding along the same street in the same direction, and at the same easy pace, the circumstance struck him as odd, and he made a note of the number of the cab in his pocket-book. It was 72,863, and the time was 11:35.

"At 11:45 a constable coming up Howard Street noticed a hansom standing opposite the door of my brother's house, and, while he was looking at it, a man came out of the house carrying something, which he put in the cab. On this the constable quickened his pace, and when the man returned to the house and reappeared carrying what looked like a portmanteau, and closing the door softly behind him, the policeman's suspicions were aroused, and he hurried forward, hailing the cabman to stop.

"The man put his burden into the cab, and sprang in himself. The cabman lashed his horse, which started off at a gallop, and the policeman broke into a run, blowing his whistle and flashing his lantern on to the cab. He followed it round the two turnings into Albemarle Street, and was just in time to see it turn into Piccadilly, where, of course, it was lost. However, he managed to note the number of the cab, which was 72,863, and he describes the man as short and thick-set, and thinks he was not wearing any hat.

"As he was returning, he met the inspector and the sergeant, who had heard the whistle, and on his report the three officers hurried to the house, where they knocked and rang for some minutes without any result. Being now more than suspicious, they went to the back of the house, through the mews, where, with great difficulty, they managed to force a window and effect an entrance into the house.

"Here their suspicions were soon changed to certainty, for, on reaching the first-floor, they heard strange muffled groans proceeding from one of the rooms, the door of which was locked, though the key had not been removed. They opened the door, and found the caretaker and his wife sitting on the floor, with their backs against the wall. Both were bound hand and foot, and the head of each was enveloped in a green-baize bag; and when the bags were taken off, each was found to be lightly but effectively gagged.

"Each told the same story. The caretaker, fancying he heard a noise, armed himself with a truncheon, and came downstairs to the first-floor, where he found the door of one of the rooms open, and a light burning inside. He stepped on tiptoe to the open door, and was peering in, when he was seized from behind, half suffocated by a pad held over his mouth, pinioned, gagged, and blindfolded with the bag.

"His assailant—whom he never saw—was amazingly strong and skilful, and handled him with perfect ease, although he—the caretaker—is a powerful man, and a good boxer and wrestler. The same thing happened to the wife, who had come down to look for her husband. She walked into the same trap, and was gagged, pinioned, and blindfolded without ever having seen the robber. So the only description that we have of this villain is that furnished by the constable."

"And the caretaker had no chance of using his truncheon?" said Thorndyke.

"Well, he got in one backhanded blow over his right shoulder, which he thinks caught the burglar in the face; but the fellow caught him by the elbow, and gave his arm such a twist that he dropped the truncheon on the floor."

"Is the robbery a very extensive one?"

"Ah!" exclaimed Mr. Löwe, "that is just what we cannot say. But I fear it is. It seems that my brother had quite recently drawn out of his bank four thousand pounds in notes and gold. These little transactions are often carried out in cash rather than by cheque"—here I caught a twinkle in Thorndyke's eye—"and the caretaker says that a few days ago Isaac brought home several parcels, which were put away temporarily in a strong cupboard. He seemed to be very pleased with his new acquisitions, and gave the caretaker to understand that they were of extraordinary rarity and value.

"Now, this cupboard has been cleared out. Not a vestige is left in it but the wrappings of the parcels, so, although nothing else has been touched, it is pretty clear that goods to the value of four thousand pounds have been taken; but when we consider what an excellent buyer my brother is, it becomes highly probable that the actual value of those things is two or three times that amount, or even more. It is a dreadful, dreadful business, and Isaac will hold me responsible for it all."

"Is there no further clue?" asked Thorndyke. "What about the cab, for instance?"

"Oh, the cab," groaned Löwe—"that clue failed. The police

must have mistaken the number. They telephoned immediately to all the police stations, and a watch was set, with the result that number 72,863 was stopped as it was going home for the night. But it then turned out that the cab had not been off the rank since eleven o'clock, and the driver had been in the shelter all the time with several other men. But there is a clue; I have it here."

Mr. Löwe's face brightened for once as he reached out for the bandbox.

"The houses in Howard Street," he explained, as he untied the fastening, "have small balconies to the first-floor windows at the back. Now, the thief entered by one of these windows, having climbed up a rain-water pipe to the balcony. It was a gusty night, as you will remember, and this morning, as I was leaving the house, the butler next door called to me and gave me this; he had found it lying in the balcony of his house."

He opened the bandbox with a flourish, and brought forth a rather shabby billycock hat.

"I understand," said he, "that by examining a hat it is possible to deduce from it, not only the bodily characteristics of the wearer, but also his mental and moral qualities, his state of health, his pecuniary position, his past history, and even his domestic relations and the peculiarities of his place of abode. Am I right in this supposition?"

The ghost of a smile flitted across Thorndyke's face as he laid the hat upon the remains of the newspaper. "We must not expect too much," he observed. "Hats, as you know, have a way of changing owners. Your own hat, for instance" (a very spruce, hard felt), "is a new one, I think."

"Got it last week," said Mr. Löwe.

"Exactly. It is an expensive hat, by Lincoln and Bennett, and I see you have judiciously written your name in indelible marking-ink on the lining. Now, a new hat suggests a discarded predecessor. What do you do with your old hats?"

"My man has them, but they don't fit him. I suppose he sells them or gives them away."

"Very well. Now, a good hat like yours has a long life, and remains serviceable long after it has become shabby; and the probability is that many of your hats pass from owner to owner; from you to the shabby-genteel, and from them to the shabby ungenteel. And it is a fair assumption that there are, at this moment, an appreciable number of tramps and casuals wearing hats by Lincoln and Bennett, marked in indelible ink with the name S. Löwe; and anyone who should examine those hats, as you suggest, might draw some very misleading deductions as to the personal habits of S. Löwe."

Mr. Marchmont chuckled audibly, and then, remembering the gravity of the occasion, suddenly became portentously solemn.

"So you think that the hat is of no use, after all?" said Mr. Löwe, in a tone of deep disappointment.

"I won't say that," replied Thorndyke. "We may learn something from it. Leave it with me, at any rate; but you must let the police know that I have it. They will want to see it, of course."

"And you will try to get those things, won't you?" pleaded Löwe.

"I will think over the case. But you understand, or Mr. Marchmont does, that this is hardly in my province. I am a medical jurist, and this is not a medico-legal case."

"Just what I told him," said Marchmont. "But you will do me a great kindness if you will look into the matter. Make it a medico-legal case," he added persuasively.

Thorndyke repeated his promise, and the two men took their departure.

For some time after they had left, my colleague remained silent, regarding the hat with a quizzical smile. "It is like a game of forfeits," he remarked at length, "and we have to find the owner of 'this very pretty thing.'" He lifted it with a pair of forceps into a better light, and began to look at it more closely.

"Perhaps," said he, "we have done Mr. Löwe an injustice, after all. This is certainly a very remarkable hat."

"It is as round as a basin," I exclaimed. "Why, the fellow's head must have been turned in a lathe!"

Thorndyke laughed. "The point," said he, "is this. This is a hard hat, and so must have fitted fairly, or it could not have been worn; and it was a cheap hat, and so was not made to measure. But a man with a head that shape has got to come to a clear understanding with his hat. No ordinary hat would go on at all.

"Now, you see what he has done—no doubt on the advice of some friendly hatter. He has bought a hat of a suitable size, and he has made it hot—probably steamed it. Then he has jammed it, while still hot and soft, on to his head, and allowed it to cool and set before removing it. That is evident from the distortion of the brim. The important corollary is, that this hat fits his head exactly—is, in fact, a perfect mould of it; and this fact, together with the cheap quality of the hat, furnishes the further corollary that it has probably only had a single owner.

"And now let us turn it over and look at the outside. You notice at once the absence of old dust. Allowing for the circumstance that it had been out all night, it is decidedly clean. Its owner has been in the habit of brushing it, and is therefore presumably a decent, orderly man. But if you look at it in a good light, you see a kind of bloom on the felt, and through this lens you can make out particles of a fine white powder which has worked into the surface."

He handed me his lens, through which I could distinctly see the particles to which he referred.

"Then," he continued, "under the curl of the brim and in the folds of the hatband, where the brush has not been able to reach it, the powder has collected quite thickly, and we can see that it is a very fine powder, and very white, like flour. What do you make of that?"

"I should say that it is connected with some industry. He may be engaged in some factory or works, or, at any rate, may live near a factory, and have to pass it frequently."

"Yes; and I think we can distinguish between the two possibilities. For, if he only passes the factory, the dust will be on the outside of the hat only; the inside will be protected by his head. But if he is engaged in the works, the dust will be inside, too, as the hat will hang on a peg in the dust-laden atmosphere, and his head will also be powdered, and so convey the dust to the inside."

He turned the hat over once more, and as I brought the powerful lens to bear upon the dark lining, I could clearly distinguish a number of white particles in the interstices of the fabric.

"The powder is on the inside, too," I said.

He took the lens from me, and, having verified my statement, proceeded with the examination. "You notice," he said, "that the leather head-lining is stained with grease, and this staining is more pronounced at the sides and back. His hair, therefore, is naturally greasy, or he greases it artificially; for if the staining were caused by perspiration, it would be most marked opposite the forehead."

He peered anxiously into the interior of the hat, and eventually turned down the head-lining; and immediately there broke out upon his face a gleam of satisfaction.

"Ha!" he exclaimed. "This is a stroke of luck. I was afraid our neat and orderly friend had defeated us with his brush. Pass me the small dissecting forceps, Jervis."

I handed him the instrument, and he proceeded to pick out daintily from the space behind the head-lining some half a dozen short pieces of hair, which he laid, with infinite tenderness, on a sheet of white paper.

"There are several more on the other side," I said, pointing them out to him.

"Yes, but we must leave some for the police," he answered,

with a smile. "They must have the same chance as ourselves, you know."

"But surely," I said, as I bent down over the paper, "these are pieces of horsehair!"

"I think not," he replied; "but the microscope will show. At any rate, this is the kind of hair I should expect to find with a head of that shape."

"Well, it is extraordinarily coarse," said I, "and two of the hairs are nearly white."

"Yes; black hairs beginning to turn grey. And now, as our preliminary survey has given such encouraging results, we will proceed to more exact methods; and we must waste no time, for we shall have the police here presently to rob us of our treasure."

He folded up carefully the paper containing the hairs, and taking the hat in both hands, as though it were some sacred vessel, ascended with me to the laboratory on the next floor.

"Now, Polton," he said to his laboratory assistant, "we have here a specimen for examination, and time is precious. First of all, we want your patent dust-extractor."

The little man bustled to a cupboard and brought forth a singular appliance, of his own manufacture, somewhat like a miniature vacuum cleaner. It had been made from a bicycle foot-pump, by reversing the piston-valve, and was fitted with a glass nozzle and a small detachable glass receiver for collecting the dust, at the end of a flexible metal tube.

"We will sample the dust from the outside first," said Thorndyke, laying the hat upon the work-bench. "Are you ready, Polton?"

The assistant slipped his foot into the stirrup of the pump and worked the handle vigorously, while Thorndyke drew the glass nozzle slowly along the hat-brim under the curled edge. And as the nozzle passed along, the white coating vanished as if by magic, leaving the felt absolutely clean and black, and simultaneously the glass receiver became clouded over with a white deposit.

"We will leave the other side for the police," said Thorndyke, and as Polton ceased pumping he detached the receiver, and laid it on a sheet of paper, on which he wrote in pencil, "Outside," and covered it with a small bell-glass. A fresh receiver having been fitted on, the nozzle was now drawn over the silk lining of the hat, and then through the space behind the leather head-lining on one side; and now the dust that collected in the receiver was much of the usual grey colour and fluffy texture, and included two more hairs.

"And now," said Thorndyke, when the second receiver had been detached and set aside, "we want a mould of the inside of the hat, and we must make it by the quickest method; there is no time to make a paper mould. It is a most astonishing head," he added, reaching down from a nail a pair of large callipers, which he applied to the inside of the hat; "six inches and nine-tenths long by six and six-tenths broad, which gives us"—he made a rapid calculation on a scrap of paper—"the extraordinarily high cephalic index of 95•6."

Polton now took possession of the hat, and, having stuck a band of wet tissue-paper round the inside, mixed a small bowl of plaster-of-Paris, and very dexterously ran a stream of the thick liquid on to the tissue-paper, where it quickly solidified. A second and third application resulted in a broad ring of solid plaster an inch thick, forming a perfect mould of the inside of the hat, and in a few minutes the slight contraction of the plaster in setting rendered the mould sufficiently loose to allow of its being slipped out on to a board to dry.

We were none too soon, for even as Polton was removing the mould, the electric bell, which I had switched on to the laboratory, announced a visitor, and when I went down I found a police-sergeant waiting with a note from Superintendent Miller, requesting the immediate transfer of the hat.

"The next thing to be done," said Thorndyke, when the sergeant had departed with the bandbox, "is to measure the thickness of the hairs, and make a transverse section of one, and examine the dust. The section we will leave to Polton—as time is an object, Polton, you had better imbed the hair in thick gum and freeze it hard on the microtome, and be very careful to cut the section at right angles to the length of the hair—meanwhile, we will get to work with the microscope."

The hairs proved on measurement to have the surprisingly large diameter of 1/135 of an inch—fully double that of ordinary hairs, although they were unquestionably human. As to the white dust, it presented a problem that even Thorndyke was unable to solve. The application of reagents showed it to be carbonate of lime, but its source for a time remained a mystery.

"The larger particles," said Thorndyke, with his eye applied to the microscope, "appear to be transparent, crystalline, and distinctly laminated in structure. It is not chalk, it is not whiting, it is not any kind of cement. What can it be?"

"Could it be any kind of shell?" I suggested. "For instance—"

"Of course!" he exclaimed, starting up; "you have hit it, Jervis, as you always do. It must be mother-of-pearl. Polton, give me a pearl shirt-button out of your oddments box."

The button was duly produced by the thrifty Polton, dropped into an agate mortar, and speedily reduced to powder, a tiny pinch of which Thorndyke placed under the microscope.

"This powder," said he, "is, naturally, much coarser than our specimen, but the identity of character is unmistakable. Jervis, you are a treasure. Just look at it."

I glanced down the microscope, and then pulled out my watch. "Yes," I said, "there is no doubt about it, I think; but I must be off. Anstey urged me to be in court by 11:30 at the latest."

With infinite reluctance I collected my notes and papers and departed, leaving Thorndyke diligently copying addresses out of the Post Office Directory.

My business at the court detained me the whole of the day, and it was near upon dinner-time when I reached our chambers. Thorndyke had not yet come in, but he arrived half an hour later, tired and hungry, and not very communicative.

"What have I done?" he repeated, in answer to my inquiries. "I have walked miles of dirty pavement, and I have visited every pearl-shell cutter's in London, with one exception, and I have not found what I was looking for. The one mother-of-pearl factory that remains, however, is the most likely, and I propose to look in there to-morrow morning. Meanwhile, we have completed our data, with Polton's assistance. Here is a tracing of our friend's skull taken from the mould; you see it is an extreme type of brachycephalic skull, and markedly unsymmetrical. Here is a transverse section of his hair, which is quite circular—unlike yours or mine, which would be oval. We have the mother-of-pearl dust from the outside of the hat, and from the inside similar dust mixed with various fibres and a few granules of rice starch. Those are our data."

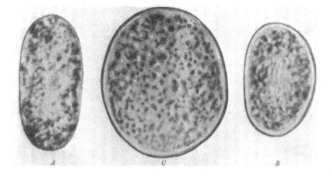

Transverse sections of human hair: *A*, of a Negro; *B*, of an Englishman; *C*, of the Burglar. All magnified 600 diameters.

"Supposing the hat should not be that of the burglar after all?" I suggested.

"That would be annoying. But I think it is his, and I think I can guess at the nature of the art treasures that were stolen."

"And you don't intend to enlighten me?"

"My dear fellow," he replied, "you have all the data. Enlighten yourself by the exercise of your own brilliant faculties. Don't give way to mental indolence."

I endeavoured, from the facts in my possession, to construct the personality of the mysterious burglar, and failed utterly; nor was I more successful in my endeavour to guess at the nature of the stolen property; and it was not until the following morning, when we had set out on our quest and were approaching Limehouse, that Thorndyke would revert to the subject.

"We are now," he said, "going to the factory of Badcomb and Martin, shell importers and cutters, in the West India Dock Road. If I don't find my man there, I shall hand the facts over to the police, and waste no more time over the case."

"What is your man like?" I asked.

"I am looking for an elderly Japanese, wearing a new hat or, more probably, a cap, and having a bruise on his right cheek or temple. I am also looking for a cab-yard; but here we are at the works, and as it is now close on the dinner-hour, we will wait and see the hands come out before making any inquiries."

We walked slowly past the tall, blank-faced building, and were just turning to re-pass it when a steam whistle sounded, a wicket opened in the main gate, and a stream of workmen—each powdered with white, like a miller—emerged into the street. We halted to watch the men as they came out, one by one, through the wicket, and turned to the right or left towards their homes or some adjacent coffee-shop; but none of them answered to the description that my friend had given.

The outcoming stream grew thinner, and at length ceased;

the wicket was shut with a bang, and once more Thorndyke's quest appeared to have failed.

"Is that all of them, I wonder?" he said, with a shade of disappointment in his tone; but even as he spoke the wicket opened again, and a leg protruded. The leg was followed by a back and a curious globular head, covered with iron-grey hair, and surmounted by a cloth cap, the whole appertaining to a short, very thick-set man, who remained thus, evidently talking to someone inside.

Suddenly he turned his head to look across the street; and immediately I recognized, by the pallid yellow complexion and narrow eye-slits, the physiognomy of a typical Japanese. The man remained talking for nearly another minute; then, drawing out his other leg, he turned towards us; and now I perceived that the right side of his face, over the prominent cheekbone, was discoloured as though by a severe bruise.

"Ha!" said Thorndyke, turning round sharply as the man approached, "either this is our man or it is an incredible coincidence." He walked away at a moderate pace, allowing the Japanese to overtake us slowly, and when the man had at length passed us, he increased his speed somewhat, so as to maintain the distance.

Our friend stepped along briskly, and presently turned up a side street, whither we followed at a respectful distance, Thorndyke holding open his pocket-book, and appearing to engage me in an earnest discussion, but keeping a sharp eye on his quarry.

"There he goes!" said my colleague, as the man suddenly disappeared—"the house with the green window-sashes. That will be number thirteen."

It was; and, having verified the fact, we passed on, and took the next turning that would lead us back to the main road.

Some twenty minutes later, as we were strolling past the door of a coffee-shop, a man came out, and began to fill his pipe with an air of leisurely satisfaction. His hat and clothes were powdered with white like those of the workmen whom we had seen come out of the factory. Thorndyke accosted him.

"Is that a flour-mill up the road there?"

"No, sir; pearl-shell. I work there myself."

"Pearl-shell, eh?" said Thorndyke. "I suppose that will be an industry that will tend to attract the aliens. Do you find it so?"

"No, sir; not at all. The work's too hard. We've only got one foreigner in the place, and he ain't an alien—he's a Jap."

"A Jap!" exclaimed Thorndyke. "Really. Now, I wonder if that would chance to be our old friend Kotei—you remember Kotei?" he added, turning to me.

"No, sir; this man's name is Futashima. There was another Jap in the works, a chap named Itu, a pal of Futashima's, but he's left."

"Ah! I don't know either of them. By the way, usen't there to be a cab-yard just about here?"

"There's a yard up Rankin Street where they keep vans and one or two cabs. That chap Itu works there now. Taken to horseflesh. Drives a van sometimes. Queer start for a Jap."

"Very." Thorndyke thanked the man for his information, and we sauntered on towards Rankin Street. The yard was at this time nearly deserted, being occupied only by an ancient and crazy four-wheeler and a very shabby hansom.

"Curious old houses, these that back on to the yard," said Thorndyke, strolling into the enclosure. "That timber gable, now," pointing to a house, from a window of which a man was watching us suspiciously, "is quite an interesting survival."

"What's your business, mister?" demanded the man in a gruff tone.

"We are just having a look at these quaint old houses," replied Thorndyke, edging towards the back of the hansom, and opening his pocket-book, as though to make a sketch.

"Well, you can see 'em from outside," said the man.

Thorndyke's strategy.

"So we can," said Thorndyke suavely, "but not so well, you know."

At this moment the pocket-book slipped from his hand and fell, scattering a number of loose papers about the ground under the hansom, and our friend at the window laughed joyously.

"No hurry," murmured Thorndyke, as I stooped to help him to gather up the papers—which he did in the most surprisingly slow and clumsy manner. "It is fortunate that the ground is dry." He stood up with the rescued papers in his hand, and, having scribbled down a brief note, slipped the book in his pocket.

"Now you'd better mizzle," observed the man at the window.

"Thank you," replied Thorndyke, "I think we had;" and, with a pleasant nod at the custodian, he proceeded to adopt the hospitable suggestion.

* * * * *

"Mr. Marchmont has been here, sir, with Inspector Badger and another gentleman," said Polton, as we entered our chambers. "They said they would call again about five."

"Then," replied Thorndyke, "as it is now a quarter to five, there is just time for us to have a wash while you get the tea ready. The particles that float in the atmosphere of Limehouse are not all mother-of-pearl."

Our visitors arrived punctually, the third gentleman being, as we had supposed, Mr. Solomon Löwe. Inspector Badger I had not seen before, and he now impressed me as showing a tendency to invert the significance of his own name by endeavouring to "draw" Thorndyke; in which, however, he was not brilliantly successful.

"I hope you are not going to disappoint Mr. Löwe, sir," he commenced facetiously. "You have had a good look at that hat—we saw your marks on it—and he expects that you will be able to point us out the man, name and address all complete."

He grinned patronizingly at our unfortunate client, who was looking even more haggard and worn than he had been on the previous morning.

"Have you—have you made any—discovery?" Mr Löwe asked with pathetic eagerness.

"We examined the hat very carefully, and I think we have established a few facts of some interest."

"Did your examination of the hat furnish any information as to the nature of the stolen property, sir?" inquired the humorous inspector.

Thorndyke turned to the officer with a face as expressionless as a wooden mask.

"We thought it possible," said he, "that it might consist of works of Japanese art, such as netsukes, paintings, and such like."

Mr. Löwe uttered an exclamation of delighted astonishment, and the facetiousness faded rather suddenly from the inspector's countenance.

"I don't know how you can have found out," said he. "We have only known it half an hour ourselves, and the wire came direct from Florence to Scotland Yard."

"Perhaps you can describe the thief to us," said Mr. Löwe, in the same eager tone.

"I dare say the inspector can do that," replied Thorndyke.

"Yes, I think so," replied the officer. "He is a short strong man, with a dark complexion and hair turning grey. He has a very round head, and he is probably a workman engaged at some whiting or cement works. That is all we know; if you can tell us any more, sir, we shall be very glad to hear it."

"I can only offer a few suggestions," said Thorndyke, "but perhaps you may find them useful. For instance, at 13, Birket Street, Limehouse, there is living a Japanese gentleman named Futashima, who works at Badcomb and Martin's mother-of-pearl factory. I think that if you were to call on him, and let him try on the hat that you have, it would probably fit him."

The inspector scribbled ravenously in his notebook, and Mr. Marchmont—an old admirer of Thorndyke's—leaned back in his chair, chuckling softly and rubbing his hands.

"Then," continued my colleague, "there is in Rankin Street, Limehouse, a cab-yard, where another Japanese gentleman named Itu is employed. You might find out where Itu was the night before last; and if you should chance to see a hansom cab there—number 22,481—have a good look at it. In the frame of the number-plate you will find six small holes. Those holes may have held brads, and the brads may have held a false number card. At any rate, you might ascertain where that cab was at 11:30 the night before last. That is all I have to suggest."

Mr. Löwe leaped from his chair. "Let us go—now—at once—there is no time to be lost. A thousand thanks to you, doctor—a thousand million thanks. Come!"

He seized the inspector by the arm and forcibly dragged him towards the door, and a few moments later we heard the footsteps of our visitors clattering down the stairs.

"It was not worth while to enter into explanations with them," said Thorndyke, as the footsteps died away—"nor perhaps with you?"

"On the contrary," I replied, "I am waiting to be fully enlightened."

"Well, then, my inferences in this case were perfectly simple ones, drawn from well-known anthropological facts. The human race, as you know, is roughly divided into three groups—the black, the white, and the yellow races. But apart from the variable quality of colour, these races have certain fixed characteristics associated especially with the shape of the skull, of the eye-sockets, and the hair.

"Thus in the black races the skull is long and narrow, the eye-sockets are long and narrow, and the hair is flat and ribbon-like, and usually coiled up like a watch-spring. In the white races the skull is oval, the eye-sockets are oval, and the hair is slightly flattened or oval in section, and tends to be wavy; while in the yellow or Mongol races, the skull is short and round, the eye-sockets are short and round, and the hair is straight and circular in section. So that we have, in the black races, long skull, long orbits, flat hair; in the white races, oval skull, oval orbits, oval hair; and in the yellow races, round skull, round orbits, round hair.

"Now, in this case we had to deal with a very short round skull. But you cannot argue from races to individuals; there are many short-skulled Englishmen. But when I found, associated with that skull, hairs which were circular in section, it became practically certain that the individual was a Mongol of some kind. The mother-of-pearl dust and the granules of rice starch from the inside of the hat favoured this view, for the pearl-shell industry is specially connected with China and Japan, while starch granules from the hat of an Englishman would probably be wheat starch.

"Then as to the hair: it was, as I mentioned to you, circular in section, and of very large diameter. Now, I have examined many thousands of hairs, and the thickest that I have ever seen came from the heads of Japanese; but the hairs from this hat were as thick as any of them. But the hypothesis that the burglar was a Japanese received confirmation in various ways. Thus, he was short, though strong and active, and the Japanese are the shortest of the Mongol races, and very strong and active.

"Then his remarkable skill in handling the powerful caretaker—a retired police-sergeant—suggested the Japanese art of ju-jitsu, while the nature of the robbery was consistent with the value set by the Japanese on works of art. Finally, the fact that only a particular collection was taken, suggested a special, and probably national, character in the things stolen, while their portability—you will remember that goods of the value of from eight to twelve thousand pounds were taken away in two hand-packages—was much more consistent with Japanese than

Chinese works, of which the latter tend rather to be bulky and ponderous. Still, it was nothing but a bare hypothesis until we had seen Futashima—and, indeed, is no more now. I may, after all, be entirely mistaken."

He was not, however; and at this moment there reposes in my drawing-room an ancient netsuke, which came as a thank-offering from Mr. Isaac Löwe on the recovery of the booty from a back room in No. 13, Birket Street, Limehouse. The treasure, of course, was given in the first place to Thorndyke, but transferred by him to my wife on the pretence that but for my suggestion of shell-dust the robber would never have been traced. Which is, on the face of it, preposterous.

The Thirty-nine Steps

Steps

John Buchan

1. The Man Who Died

I returned from the City about three o'clock on that May afternoon pretty well disgusted with life. I had been three months in the Old Country, and was fed up with it. If anyone had told me a year ago that I would have been feeling like that I should have laughed at him; but there was the fact. The weather made me liverish, the talk of the ordinary Englishman made me sick. I couldn't get enough exercise, and the amusements of London seemed as flat as soda-water that has been standing in the sun. "Richard Hannay," I kept telling myself, "you have got into the wrong ditch, my friend, and you had better climb out."

It made me bite my lips to think of the plans I had been building up those last years in Buluwayo. I had got my pile—not one of the big ones, but good enough for me; and I had figured out all kinds of ways of enjoying myself. My father had brought me out from Scotland at the age of six, and I had never been home since; so England was a sort of Arabian Nights to me, and I counted on stopping there for the rest of my days.

But from the first I was disappointed with it. In about a week I was tired of seeing sights, and in less than a month I had had enough of restaurants and theatres and race-meetings. I had no real pal to go about with, which probably explains things. Plenty of people invited me to their houses, but they didn't seem much interested in me. They would fling me a question or two about South Africa, and then get on to their own affairs. A lot of Imperialist ladies asked me to tea to meet schoolmasters from New Zealand and editors from Vancouver, and that was the dismalest business of all. Here was I, thirty-seven years old, sound in wind and limb, with enough money to have a good time, yawning my head off all day. I had just about settled to clear out and get back to the veld, for I was the best bored man in the United Kingdom.

That afternoon I had been worrying my brokers about investments to give my mind something to work on, and on my way home I turned into my club—rather a pot-house, which took in Colonial members. I had a long drink, and read the evening papers. They were full of the row in the Near East, and there was an article about Karolides, the Greek Premier. I rather fancied the chap. From all accounts he seemed the one big man in the show; and he played a straight game too, which was more than could be said for most of them. I gathered that they hated him pretty blackly in Berlin and Vienna, but that we were going to stick by him, and one paper said that he was the only barrier between Europe and Armageddon. I remember wondering if I could get a job in those parts. It struck me that Albania was the sort of place that might keep a man from yawning.

About six o'clock I went home, dressed, dined at the Café Royal, and turned into a music-hall. It was a silly show, all capering women and monkey-faced men, and I did not stay long. The night was fine and clear as I walked back to the flat I had hired near Portland Place. The crowd surged past me on the pavements, busy and chattering, and I envied the people for having something to do. These shop-girls and clerks and dandies and policemen had some interest in life that kept them going. I gave half-a-crown to a beggar because I saw him yawn; he was a fellow-sufferer. At Oxford Circus I looked up into the spring sky and I made a vow. I would give the Old Country another day to fit me into something; if nothing happened, I would take the next boat for the Cape.

My flat was the first floor in a new block behind Langham Place. There was a common staircase, with a porter and a liftman at the entrance, but there was no restaurant or anything of that sort, and each flat was quite shut off from the others. I hate servants on the premises, so I had a fellow to look after me who came in by the day. He arrived before eight o'clock every morning and used to depart at seven, for I never dined at home.

I was just fitting my key into the door when I noticed a man at my elbow. I had not seen him approach, and the sudden appearance made me start. He was a slim man, with a short brown beard and small, gimlety blue eyes. I recognized him as the occupant of a flat on the top floor, with whom I had passed the time of day on the stairs.

"Can I speak to you?" he said. "May I come in for a minute?" He was steadying his voice with an effort, and his hand was pawing my arm.

I got my door open and motioned him in. No sooner was he over the threshold than he made a dash for my back room, where I used to smoke and write my letters. Then he bolted back.

"Is the door locked?" he asked feverishly, and he fastened the chain with his own hand.

"I'm very sorry," he said humbly. "It's a mighty liberty, but you looked the kind of man who would understand. I've had you in my mind all this week when things got troublesome. Say, will you do me a good turn?"

"I'll listen to you," I said. "That's all I'll promise." I was getting worried by the antics of this nervous little chap.

There was a tray of drinks on a table beside him, from which he filled himself a stiff whisky-and-soda. He drank it off in three gulps, and cracked the glass as he set it down.

"Pardon," he said, "I'm a bit rattled tonight. You see, I happen at this moment to be dead."

I sat down in an armchair and lit my pipe.

"What does it feel like?" I asked. I was pretty certain that I had to deal with a madman.

A smile flickered over his drawn face. "I'm not mad—yet. Say, sir, I've been watching you, and I reckon you're a cool customer. I reckon, too, you're an honest man, and not afraid of playing a bold hand. I'm going to confide in you. I need help worse than any man ever needed it, and I want to know if I can count you in."

"Get on with your yarn," I said, "and I'll tell you."

He seemed to brace himself for a great effort, and then started on the queerest rigmarole. I didn't get hold of it at first, and I had to stop and ask him questions. But here is the gist of it:

He was an American, from Kentucky, and after college, being pretty well off, he had started out to see the world. He wrote a bit, and acted as war correspondent for a Chicago paper, and spent a year or two in South-Eastern Europe. I gathered that he was a fine linguist, and had got to know pretty well the society in those parts. He spoke familiarly of many names that I remembered to have seen in the newspapers.

He had played about with politics, he told me, at first for the interest of them, and then because he couldn't help himself. I read him as a sharp, restless fellow, who always wanted to get down to the roots of things. He got a little further down than he wanted.

I am giving you what he told me as well as I could make it out. Away behind all the Governments and the armies there was a big subterranean movement going on, engineered by very dangerous people. He had come on it by accident; it fascinated him; he went further, and then he got caught. I gathered that most of the people in it were the sort of educated anarchists that make revolutions, but that beside them there were financiers who were playing for money. A clever man can make big profits on a falling market, and it suited the book of both classes to set Europe by the ears.

He told me some queer things that explained a lot that had puzzled me—things that happened in the Balkan War, how one state suddenly came out on top, why alliances were made and broken, why certain men disappeared, and where the sinews of war came from. The aim of the whole conspiracy was to get Russia and Germany at loggerheads.

When I asked why, he said that the anarchist lot thought it would give them their chance. Everything would be in the melting-pot, and they looked to see a new world emerge. The capitalists would rake in the shekels, and make fortunes by buying up wreckage. Capital, he said, had no conscience and no fatherland. Besides, the Jew was behind it, and the Jew hated Russia worse than hell.

"Do you wonder?" he cried. "For three hundred years they have been persecuted, and this is the return match for the pogroms. The Jew is everywhere, but you have to go far down the backstairs to find him. Take any big Teutonic business concern. If you have dealings with it the first man you meet is Prince von und zuSomething, an elegant young man who talks Eton-and-Harrow English. But he cuts no ice. If your business is big, you get behind him and find a prognathous Westphalian with a retreating brow and the manners of a hog. He is the German business man that gives your English papers the shakes. But if you're on the biggest kind of job and are bound to get to the real boss, ten to one you are brought up against a little white-faced Jew in a bath-chair with an eye like a rattlesnake. Yes, sir, he is the man who is ruling the world just now, and he has his knife in the Empire of the Tsar, because his aunt was outraged and his father flogged in some one-horse location on the Volga."

I could not help saying that his Jew-anarchists seemed to have got left behind a little.

"Yes and no," he said. "They won up to a point, but they struck a bigger thing than money, a thing that couldn't be bought, the old elemental fighting instincts of man. If you're going to be killed you invent some kind of flag and country to fight for, and if you survive you get to love the thing. Those foolish devils of soldiers have found something they care for, and that has upset the pretty plan laid in Berlin and Vienna. But my friends haven't played their last card by a long sight. They've gotten the ace up their sleeves, and unless I can keep alive for a month they are going to play it and win."

"But I thought you were dead," I put in.

"*Mors janua vitae*," he smiled. (I recognized the quotation: it was about all the Latin I knew.) "I'm coming to that, but I've got to put you wise about a lot of things first. If you read your newspaper, I guess you know the name of Constantine Karolides?"

I sat up at that, for I had been reading about him that very afternoon.

"He is the man that has wrecked all their games. He is the one big brain in the whole show, and he happens also to be an honest man. Therefore he has been marked down these twelve months past. I found that out—not that it was difficult, for any fool could guess as much. But I found out the way they were going to get him, and that knowledge was deadly. That's why I have had to decease."

He had another drink, and I mixed it for him myself, for I was getting interested in the beggar.

"They can't get him in his own land, for he has a bodyguard of Epirotes that would skin their grandmothers. But on the 15th day of June he is coming to this city. The British Foreign Office has taken to having international tea-parties, and the biggest of them is due on that date. Now Karolides is reckoned the principal guest, and if my friends have their way he will never return to his admiring countrymen."

"That's simple enough, anyhow," I said. "You can warn him and keep him at home."

"And play their game?" he asked sharply. "If he does not come they win, for he's the only man that can straighten out the tangle. And if his Government are warned he won't come, for he does not know how big the stakes will be on June the 15th."

"What about the British Government?" I said. "They're not going to let their guests be murdered. Tip them the wink, and they'll take extra precautions."

"No good. They might stuff your city with plain-clothes detectives and double the police and Constantine would still be a doomed man. My friends are not playing this game for candy. They want a big occasion for the taking off, with the eyes of all Europe on it. He'll be murdered by an Austrian, and there'll be plenty of evidence to show the connivance of the big folk in Vienna and Berlin. It will all be an infernal lie, of course, but the case will look black enough to the world. I'm not talking hot air, my friend. I happen to know every detail of the hellish contrivance, and I can tell you it will be the most finished piece of blackguardism since the Borgias. But it's not going to come off if there's a certain man who knows the wheels of the business alive right here in London on the 15th day of June. And that man is going to be your servant, Franklin P. Scudder."

I was getting to like the little chap. His jaw had shut like a rat-trap, and there was the fire of battle in his gimlety eyes. If he was spinning me a yarn he could act up to it.

"Where did you find out this story?" I asked.

"I got the first hint in an inn on the Achensee in Tyrol. That set me inquiring, and I collected my other clues in a fur-shop in the Galician quarter of Buda, in a Strangers' Club in Vienna, and in a little bookshop off the Racknitzstrasse in Leipsig. I completed my evidence ten days ago in Paris. I can't tell you the details now, for it's something of a history. When I was quite sure in my own mind I judged it my business to disappear, and I reached this city by a mighty queer circuit. I left Paris a dandified young French-American, and I sailed from Hamburg a Jew diamond merchant. In Norway I was an English student of Ibsen collecting materials for lectures, but when I left Bergen I was a cinema-man with special ski films. And I came here from Leith with a lot of pulp-wood propositions in my pocket to put before the London newspapers. Till yesterday I thought I had muddied my trail some, and was feeling pretty happy. Then . . ."

The recollection seemed to upset him, and he gulped down some more whisky.

"Then I saw a man standing in the street outside this block. I used to stay close in my room all day, and only slip out after dark for an hour or two. I watched him for a bit from my window, and I thought I recognized him . . . He came in and spoke to the porter . . . When I came back from my walk last night I found a card in my letter-box. It bore the name of the man I want least to meet on God's earth."

I think that the look in my companion's eyes, the sheer naked scare on his face, completed my conviction of his honesty. My own voice sharpened a bit as I asked him what he did next.

"I realized that I was bottled as sure as a pickled herring, and that there was only one way out. I had to die. If my pursuers knew I was dead they would go to sleep again."

"How did you manage it?"

"I told the man that valets me that I was feeling pretty bad, and I got myself up to look like death. That wasn't difficult, for I'm no slouch at disguises. Then I got a corpse—you can always get a body in London if you know where to go for it. I fetched it back in a trunk on the top of a four-wheeler, and I had to be assisted upstairs to my room. You see I had to pile up some evidence for the inquest. I went to bed and got my man to mix me a sleeping-draught, and then told him to clear out. He wanted to fetch a doctor, but I swore some and said I couldn't abide leeches. When I was left alone I started in to fake up that corpse. He was my size, and I judged had perished from too much alcohol, so I put some spirits handy about the place. The jaw was the weak point in the likeness, so I blew it away with a revolver. I daresay there will be somebody tomorrow to swear to having heard a shot, but there are no neighbours on my floor, and I guessed I could risk it. So I left the body in bed dressed up in my pyjamas, with a revolver lying on the bed-clothes and a considerable mess around. Then I got into a suit of clothes I had kept waiting for emergencies. I didn't dare to shave for fear of leaving tracks, and besides, it wasn't any kind of use my trying to get into the streets. I had had you in my mind all day, and there seemed nothing to do but to make an appeal to you. I watched from my window till I saw you come home, and then slipped down the stair to meet you . . . There, sir, I guess you know about as much as me of this business."

He sat blinking like an owl, fluttering with nerves and yet desperately determined. By this time I was pretty well convinced that he was going straight with me. It was the wildest sort of narrative, but I had heard in my time many steep tales which had turned out to be true, and I had made a practice of judging the man rather than the story. If he had wanted to get a location in my flat, and then cut my throat, he would have pitched a milder yarn.

"Hand me your key," I said, "and I'll take a look at the corpse. Excuse my caution, but I'm bound to verify a bit if I can."

He shook his head mournfully. "I reckoned you'd ask for that, but I haven't got it. It's on my chain on the dressing-table. I had to leave it behind, for I couldn't leave any clues to breed suspicions. The gentry who are after me are pretty bright-eyed citizens. You'll have to take me on trust for the night, and tomorrow you'll get proof of the corpse business right enough."

I thought for an instant or two. "Right. I'll trust you for the night. I'll lock you into this room and keep the key. Just one word, Mr. Scudder. I believe you're straight, but if so be you are not I should warn you that I'm a handy man with a gun."

"Sure," he said, jumping up with some briskness. "I haven't the privilege of your name, sir, but let me tell you that you're a white man. I'll thank you to lend me a razor."

I took him into my bedroom and turned him loose. In half an hour's time a figure came out that I scarcely recognized. Only his gimlety, hungry eyes were the same. He was shaved clean, his hair was parted in the middle, and he had cut his eyebrows. Further, he carried himself as if he had been drilled, and was the very model, even to the brown complexion, of some British officer who had had a long spell in India. He had a monocle, too, which he stuck in his eye, and every trace of the American had gone out of his speech.

"My hat! Mr.. Scudder—" I stammered.

"Not Mr. Scudder," he corrected; "Captain Theophilus Digby, of the 40th Gurkhas, presently home on leave. I'll thank you to remember that, sir."

I made him up a bed in my smoking-room and sought my own couch, more cheerful than I had been for the past month. Things did happen occasionally, even in this God-forgotten metropolis.

I woke next morning to hear my man, Paddock, making the deuce of a row at the smoking-room door. Paddock was a fellow I had done a good turn to out on the Selakwe, and I had inspanned him as my servant as soon as I got to England. He had about as much gift of the gab as a hippopotamus, and was not a great hand at valeting, but I knew I could count on his loyalty.

"Stop that row, Paddock," I said. "There's a friend of mine, Captain—Captain" (I couldn't remember the name) "dossing down in there. Get breakfast for two and then come and speak to me."

I told Paddock a fine story about how my friend was a great swell, with his nerves pretty bad from overwork, who wanted absolute rest and stillness. Nobody had got to know he was here, or he would be besieged by communications from the India Office and the Prime Minister and his cure would be ruined. I am bound to say Scudder played up splendidly when he came to breakfast. He fixed Paddock with his eyeglass, just like a British officer, asked him about the Boer War, and slung out at me a lot of stuff about imaginary pals. Paddock couldn't learn to call me "sir," but he "sirred" Scudder as if his life depended on it.

I left him with the newspaper and a box of cigars, and went down to the City till luncheon. When I got back the liftman had an important face.

"Nawsty business 'ere this morning, sir. Gent in No. 15 been and shot 'isself. They've just took 'im to the mortiary. The police are up there now."

I ascended to No. 15, and found a couple of bobbies and an inspector busy making an examination. I asked a few idiotic questions, and they soon kicked me out. Then I found the man that had valeted Scudder, and pumped him, but I could see he suspected nothing. He was a whining fellow with a churchyard face, and half-a-crown went far to console him.

I attended the inquest next day. A partner of some publishing firm gave evidence that the deceased had brought him wood-pulp propositions, and had been, he believed, an agent of an American business. The jury found it a case of suicide while of unsound mind, and the few effects were handed over to the American Consul to deal with. I gave Scudder a full account of the affair, and it interested him greatly. He said he wished he could have attended the inquest, for he reckoned it would be about as spicy as to read one's own obituary notice.

The first two days he stayed with me in that back room he was very peaceful. He read and smoked a bit, and made a heap of jottings in a note-book, and every night we had a game of chess, at which he beat me hollow. I think he was nursing his nerves back to health, for he had had a pretty trying time. But on the third day I could see he was beginning to get restless. He fixed up a list of the days till June 15th, and ticked each off with a red pencil, making remarks in shorthand against them. I would find him sunk in a brown study, with his sharp eyes abstracted, and after those spells of meditation he was apt to be very despondent.

Then I could see that he began to get edgy again. He listened for little noises, and was always asking me if Paddock could be trusted. Once or twice he got very peevish, and apologized for it. I didn't blame him. I made every allowance, for he had taken on a fairly stiff job.

It was not the safety of his own skin that troubled him, but the success of the scheme he had planned. That little man was clean grit all through, without a soft spot in him. One night he was very solemn.

"Say, Hannay," he said, "I judge I should let you a bit deeper into this business. I should hate to go out without leaving somebody else to put up a fight." And he began to tell me in detail what I had only heard from him vaguely.

I did not give him very close attention. The fact is, I was more interested in his own adventures than in his high politics. I reckoned that Karolides and his affairs were not my business, leaving all that to him. So a lot that he said slipped clean out of my memory. I remember that he was very clear that the danger to Karolides would not begin till he had got to London, and would come from the very highest quarters, where there would be no thought of suspicion. He mentioned the name of a woman—Julia Czechenyi—as having something to do with the danger. She would be the decoy, I gathered, to get Karolides out of the care of his guards. He talked, too, about a Black Stone and a man that lisped in his speech, and he described very particularly somebody that he never referred to without a shudder—an old man with a young voice who could hood his eyes like a hawk.

He spoke a good deal about death, too. He was mortally anxious about winning through with his job, but he didn't care a rush for his life.

"I reckon it's like going to sleep when you are pretty well tired out, and waking to find a summer day with the scent of hay coming in at the window. I used to thank God for such mornings way back in the Blue-Grass country, and I guess I'll thank Him when I wake up on the other side of Jordan."

Next day he was much more cheerful, and read the life of Stonewall Jackson much of the time. I went out to dinner with a mining engineer I had got to see on business, and came back about half-past ten in time for our game of chess before turning in.

I had a cigar in my mouth, I remember, as I pushed open the smoking-room door. The lights were not lit, which struck me as odd. I wondered if Scudder had turned in already.

I snapped the switch, but there was nobody there. Then I saw something in the far corner which made me drop my cigar and fall into a cold sweat.

My guest was lying sprawled on his back. There was a long knife through his heart which skewered him to the floor.

2. The Milkman Sets Out on His Travels

I sat down in an armchair and felt very sick. That lasted for maybe five minutes, and was succeeded by a fit of the horrors. The poor staring white face on the floor was more than I could bear, and I managed to get a table-cloth and cover it. Then I staggered to a cupboard, found the brandy and swallowed several mouthfuls. I had seen men die violently before; indeed I had killed a few myself in the Matabele War; but this cold-blooded indoor business was different. Still I managed to pull myself together. I looked at my watch, and saw that it was half-past ten.

An idea seized me, and I went over the flat with a small-tooth comb. There was nobody there, nor any trace of anybody, but I shuttered and bolted all the windows and put the chain on the door. By this time my wits were coming back to me, and I could think again. It took me about an hour to figure the thing out, and I did not hurry, for, unless the murderer came back, I had till about six o'clock in the morning for my cogitations.

I was in the soup—that was pretty clear. Any shadow of a doubt I might have had about the truth of Scudder's tale was now gone. The proof of it was lying under the table-cloth. The men who knew that he knew what he knew had found him, and had taken the best way to make certain of his silence. Yes; but he had been in my rooms four days, and his enemies must have reckoned that he had confided in me. So I would be the next to go. It might be that very night, or next day, or the day after, but my number was up all right.

Then suddenly I thought of another probability. Supposing I went out now and called in the police, or went to bed and let Paddock find the body and call them in the morning. What kind of a story was I to tell about Scudder? I had lied to Paddock about him, and the whole thing looked desperately fishy. If I made a clean breast of it and told the police everything he had told me, they would simply laugh at me. The odds were a thousand to one that I would be charged with the murder, and the circumstantial evidence was strong enough to hang me. Few people knew me in England; I had no real pal who could come forward and swear to my character. Perhaps that was what those secret enemies were playing for. They were clever enough for anything, and an English prison was as good a way of getting rid of me till after June 15th as a knife in my chest.

Besides, if I told the whole story, and by any miracle was believed, I would be playing their game. Karolides would stay at home, which was what they wanted. Somehow or other the sight of Scudder's dead face had made me a passionate believer in his scheme. He was gone, but he had taken me into his confidence, and I was pretty well bound to carry on his work.

You may think this ridiculous for a man in danger of his life, but that was the way I looked at it. I am an ordinary sort of fellow, not braver than other people, but I hate to see a good man downed, and that long knife would not be the end of Scudder if I could play the game in his place.

It took me an hour or two to think this out, and by that time I had come to a decision. I must vanish somehow, and keep vanished till the end of the second week in June. Then I must somehow find a way to get in touch with the Government people and tell them what Scudder had told me. I wished to Heaven he had told me more, and that I had listened more carefully to the little he had told me. I knew nothing but the barest facts. There was a big risk that, even if I weathered the other dangers, I would not be believed in the end. I must take my chance of that, and hope that something might happen which would confirm my tale in the eyes of the Government.

My first job was to keep going for the next three weeks. It was now the 24th day of May, and that meant twenty days of hiding before I could venture to approach the powers that be. I reckoned that two sets of people would be looking for me— Scudder's enemies to put me out of existence, and the police, who would want me for Scudder's murder. It was going to be a giddy hunt, and it was queer how the prospect comforted me. I had been slack so long that almost any chance of activity was welcome. When I had to sit alone with that corpse and wait on Fortune I was no better than a crushed worm, but if my neck's safety was to hang on my own wits I was prepared to be cheerful about it.

My next thought was whether Scudder had any papers about him to give me a better clue to the business. I drew back the table-cloth and searched his pockets, for I had no longer any shrinking from the body. The face was wonderfully calm for a man who had been struck down in a moment. There was nothing in the breast-pocket, and only a few loose coins and a cigar-holder in the waistcoat. The trousers held a little penknife and some silver, and the side pocket of his jacket contained an old crocodile-skin cigar-case. There was no sign of the little black book in which I had seen him making notes. That had no doubt been taken by his murderer.

But as I looked up from my task I saw that some drawers had been pulled out in the writing-table. Scudder would never have left them in that state, for he was the tidiest of mortals.

Someone must have been searching for something—perhaps for the pocket-book.

I went round the flat and found that everything had been ransacked—the inside of books, drawers, cupboards, boxes, even the pockets of the clothes in my wardrobe, and the sideboard in the dining-room. There was no trace of the book. Most likely the enemy had found it, but they had not found it on Scudder's body.

Then I got out an atlas and looked at a big map of the British Isles. My notion was to get off to some wild district, where my veldcraft would be of some use to me, for I would be like a trapped rat in a city. I considered that Scotland would be best, for my people were Scotch and I could pass anywhere as an ordinary Scotsman. I had half an idea at first to be a German tourist, for my father had had German partners, and I had been brought up to speak the tongue pretty fluently, not to mention having put in three years prospecting for copper in German Damaraland. But I calculated that it would be less conspicuous to be a Scot, and less in a line with what the police might know of my past. I fixed on Galloway as the best place to go. It was the nearest wild part of Scotland, so far as I could figure it out, and from the look of the map was not over thick with population.

A search in Bradshaw informed me that a train left St. Pancras at 7:10, which would land me at any Galloway station in the late afternoon. That was well enough, but a more important matter was how I was to make my way to St. Pancras, for I was pretty certain that Scudder's friends would be watching outside. This puzzled me for a bit; then I had an inspiration, on which I went to bed and slept for two troubled hours.

I got up at four and opened my bedroom shutters. The faint light of a fine summer morning was flooding the skies, and the sparrows had begun to chatter. I had a great revulsion of feeling, and felt a God-forgotten fool. My inclination was to let things slide, and trust to the British police taking a reasonable view of my case. But as I reviewed the situation I could find no arguments to bring against my decision of the previous night, so with a wry mouth I resolved to go on with my plan. I was not feeling in any particular funk; only disinclined to go looking for trouble, if you understand me.

I hunted out a well-used tweed suit, a pair of strong nailed boots, and a flannel shirt with a collar. Into my pockets I stuffed a spare shirt, a cloth cap, some handkerchiefs, and a tooth-brush. I had drawn a good sum in gold from the bank two days before, in case Scudder should want money, and I took fifty pounds of it in sovereigns in a belt which I had brought back from Rhodesia. That was about all I wanted. Then I had a bath, and cut my moustache, which was long and drooping, into a short stubbly fringe.

Now came the next step. Paddock used to arrive punctually at 7:30 and let himself in with a latch-key. But about twenty minutes to seven, as I knew from bitter experience, the milkman turned up with a great clatter of cans, and deposited my share outside my door. I had seen that milkman sometimes when I had gone out for an early ride. He was a young man about my own height, with an ill-nourished moustache, and he wore a white overall. On him I staked all my chances.

I went into the darkened smoking-room where the rays of morning light were beginning to creep through the shutters. There I breakfasted off a whisky-and-soda and some biscuits from the cupboard. By this time it was getting on for six o'clock. I put a pipe in my pocket and filled my pouch from the tobacco jar on the table by the fireplace.

As I poked into the tobacco my fingers touched something hard, and I drew out Scudder's little black pocket-book . . .

That seemed to me a good omen. I lifted the cloth from the body and was amazed at the peace and dignity of the dead face. "Goodbye, old chap," I said; "I am going to do my best for you. Wish me well, wherever you are."

Then I hung about in the hall waiting for the milkman. That was the worst part of the business, for I was fairly choking to get out of doors. Six-thirty passed, then six-forty, but still he did not come. The fool had chosen this day of all days to be late.

At one minute after the quarter to seven I heard the rattle of the cans outside. I opened the front door, and there was my man, singling out my cans from a bunch he carried and whistling through his teeth. He jumped a bit at the sight of me.

"Come in here a moment," I said. "I want a word with you." And I led him into the dining-room.

"I reckon you're a bit of a sportsman," I said, "and I want you to do me a service. Lend me your cap and overall for ten minutes, and here's a sovereign for you."

His eyes opened at the sight of the gold, and he grinned broadly. "Wot's the gyme?" he asked.

"A bet," I said. "I haven't time to explain, but to win it I've got to be a milkman for the next ten minutes. All you've got to do is to stay here till I come back. You'll be a bit late, but nobody will complain, and you'll have that quid for yourself."

"Right-o!" he said cheerily. "I ain't the man to spoil a bit of sport. 'Ere's the rig, guv'nor."

I stuck on his flat blue hat and his white overall, picked up the cans, banged my door, and went whistling downstairs. The porter at the foot told me to shut my jaw, which sounded as if my make-up was adequate.

At first I thought there was nobody in the street. Then I caught sight of a policeman a hundred yards down, and a loafer shuffling past on the other side. Some impulse made me raise my eyes to the house opposite, and there at a first-floor window was a face. As the loafer passed he looked up, and I fancied a signal was exchanged.

I crossed the street, whistling gaily and imitating the jaunty swing of the milkman. Then I took the first side street, and went up a left-hand turning which led past a bit of vacant ground. There was no one in the little street, so I dropped the milk-cans inside the hoarding and sent the cap and overall after them. I had only just put on my cloth cap when a postman came round the corner. I gave him good morning and he answered me unsuspiciously. At the moment the clock of a neighbouring church struck the hour of seven.

There was not a second to spare. As soon as I got to Euston Road I took to my heels and ran. The clock at Euston Station showed five minutes past the hour. At St. Pancras I had no time to take a ticket, let alone that I had not settled upon my destination. A porter told me the platform, and as I entered it I saw the train already in motion. Two station officials blocked the way, but I dodged them and clambered into the last carriage.

Three minutes later, as we were roaring through the northern tunnels, an irate guard interviewed me. He wrote out for me a ticket to Newton-Stewart, a name which had suddenly come back to my memory, and he conducted me from the first-class compartment where I had ensconced myself to a third-class smoker, occupied by a sailor and a stout woman with a child. He went off grumbling, and as I mopped my brow I observed to my companions in my broadest Scots that it was a sore job catching trains. I had already entered upon my part.

"The impidence o' that gyaird!" said the lady bitterly. "He needit a Scotch tongue to pit him in his place. He was complainin' o' this wean no haein' a ticket and her no fower till August twalmonth, and he was objectin' to this gentleman spittin'."

The sailor morosely agreed, and I started my new life in an atmosphere of protest against authority. I reminded myself that a week ago I had been finding the world dull.

3. The Adventure of the Literary Innkeeper

I had a solemn time travelling north that day. It was fine May weather, with the hawthorn flowering on every hedge, and I asked myself why, when I was still a free man, I had stayed on in London and not got the good of this heavenly country. I didn't dare face the restaurant car, but I got a luncheon-basket at Leeds and shared it with the fat woman. Also I got the morning's papers, with news about starters for the Derby and the beginning of the cricket season, and some paragraphs about how Balkan affairs were settling down and a British squadron was going to Kiel.

When I had done with them I got out Scudder's little black pocket-book and studied it. It was pretty well filled with jottings, chiefly figures, though now and then a name was printed in. For example, I found the words "Hofgaard," "Luneville," and "Avocado" pretty often, and especially the word "Pavia."

Now I was certain that Scudder never did anything without a reason, and I was pretty sure that there was a cypher in all this. That is a subject which has always interested me, and I did a bit at it myself once as intelligence officer at Delagoa Bay during the Boer War. I have a head for things like chess and puzzles, and I used to reckon myself pretty good at finding out cyphers. This one looked like the numerical kind where sets of figures correspond to the letters of the alphabet, but any fairly shrewd man can find the clue to that sort after an hour or two's work, and I didn't think Scudder would have been content with anything so easy. So I fastened on the printed words, for you can make a pretty good numerical cypher if you have a key word which gives you the sequence of the letters.

I tried for hours, but none of the words answered. Then I fell asleep and woke at Dumfries just in time to bundle out and get into the slow Galloway train. There was a man on the platform whose looks I didn't like, but he never glanced at me, and when I caught sight of myself in the mirror of an automatic machine I didn't wonder. With my brown face, my old tweeds, and my slouch, I was the very model of one of the hill farmers who were crowding into the third-class carriages.

I travelled with half a dozen in an atmosphere of shag and clay pipes. They had come from the weekly market, and their mouths were full of prices. I heard accounts of how the lambing had gone up the Cairn and the Deuch and a dozen other mysterious waters. Above half the men had lunched heavily and were highly flavoured with whisky, so they took no notice of me. We rumbled slowly into a land of little wooded glens and then to a great wide moorland place, gleaming with lochs, with high blue hills showing northwards.

About five o'clock the carriage had emptied, and I was left alone as I had hoped. I got out at the next station, a little place whose name I scarcely noted, set right in the heart of a bog. It reminded me of one of those forgotten little stations in the Karroo. An old station-master was digging in his garden, and with his spade over his shoulder sauntered to the train, took charge of a parcel, and went back to his potatoes. A child of ten received my ticket, and I emerged on a white road that straggled over the brown moor.

It was a gorgeous spring evening, with every hill showing as clear as a cut amethyst. The air had the queer, rooty smell of bogs, but it was as fresh as mid-ocean, and it had the strangest effect on my spirits. I actually felt light-hearted. I might have been a boy out for a spring holiday tramp, instead of a man of thirty-seven very much wanted by the police. I felt just as I used to feel when I was starting for a big trek on a frosty morning on the high veld. If you believe me, I swung along that road whistling. There was no plan of campaign in my head, only just to go on and on in this blessed, honest-smelling hill country, for every mile put me in better humour with myself.

In a roadside planting I cut a walking-stick of hazel, and presently struck off the highway up a by-path which followed the glen of a brawling stream. I reckoned that I was still far ahead of any pursuit, and for that night might please myself. It was some hours since I had tasted food, and I was getting very hungry when I came to a herd's cottage set in a nook beside a waterfall. A brown-faced woman was standing by the door, and greeted me with the kindly shyness of moorland places. When I asked for a night's lodging she said I was welcome to the "bed in the loft," and very soon she set before me a hearty meal of ham and eggs, scones, and thick sweet milk.

At the darkening her man came in from the hills, a lean giant, who in one step covered as much ground as three paces of ordinary mortals. They asked me no questions, for they had the perfect breeding of all dwellers in the wilds, but I could see they set me down as a kind of dealer, and I took some trouble to confirm their view. I spoke a lot about cattle, of which my host knew little, and I picked up from him a good deal about the local Galloway markets, which I tucked away in my memory for future use. At ten I was nodding in my chair, and the "bed in the loft" received a weary man who never opened his eyes till five o'clock set the little homestead a-going once more.

They refused any payment, and by six I had breakfasted and was striding southwards again. My notion was to return to the railway line a station or two farther on than the place where I had alighted yesterday and to double back. I reckoned that that was the safest way, for the police would naturally assume that I was always making farther from London in the direction of some western port. I thought I had still a good bit of a start, for, as I reasoned, it would take some hours to fix the blame on me, and several more to identify the fellow who got on board the train at St. Pancras.

It was the same jolly, clear spring weather, and I simply could not contrive to feel careworn. Indeed I was in better spirits than

I had been for months. Over a long ridge of moorland I took my road, skirting the side of a high hill which the herd had called Cairnsmore of Fleet. Nesting curlews and plovers were crying everywhere, and the links of green pasture by the streams were dotted with young lambs. All the slackness of the past months was slipping from my bones, and I stepped out like a four-year-old. By-and-by I came to a swell of moorland which dipped to the vale of a little river, and a mile away in the heather I saw the smoke of a train.

The station, when I reached it, proved to be ideal for my purpose. The moor surged up around it and left room only for the single line, the slender siding, a waiting-room, an office, the station-master's cottage, and a tiny yard of gooseberries and sweet-william. There seemed no road to it from anywhere, and to increase the desolation the waves of a tarn lapped on their grey granite beach half a mile away. I waited in the deep heather till I saw the smoke of an east-going train on the horizon. Then I approached the tiny booking-office and took a ticket for Dumfries.

The only occupants of the carriage were an old shepherd and his dog—a wall-eyed brute that I mistrusted. The man was asleep, and on the cushions beside him was that morning's Scotsman. Eagerly I seized on it, for I fancied it would tell me something.

There were two columns about the Portland Place Murder, as it was called. My man Paddock had given the alarm and had the milkman arrested. Poor devil, it looked as if the latter had earned his sovereign hardly; but for me he had been cheap at the price, for he seemed to have occupied the police for the better part of the day. In the latest news I found a further instalment of the story. The milkman had been released, I read, and the true criminal, about whose identity the police were reticent, was believed to have got away from London by one of the northern lines. There was a short note about me as the owner of the flat. I guessed the police had stuck that in, as a clumsy contrivance to persuade me that I was unsuspected.

There was nothing else in the paper, nothing about foreign politics or Karolides, or the things that had interested Scudder. I laid it down, and found that we were approaching the station at which I had got out yesterday. The potato-digging station-master had been gingered up into some activity, for the west-going train was waiting to let us pass, and from it had descended three men who were asking him questions. I supposed that they were the local police, who had been stirred up by Scotland Yard, and had traced me as far as this one-horse siding. Sitting well back in the shadow I watched them carefully. One of them had a book, and took down notes. The old potato-digger seemed to have turned peevish, but the child who had collected my ticket was talking volubly. All the party looked out across the moor where the white road departed. I hoped they were going to take up my tracks there.

As we moved away from that station my companion woke up. He fixed me with a wandering glance, kicked his dog viciously, and inquired where he was. Clearly he was very drunk.

"That's what comes o' bein' a teetotaller," he observed in bitter regret.

I expressed my surprise that in him I should have met a blue-ribbon stalwart.

"Ay, but I'm a strong teetotaller," he said pugnaciously. "I took the pledge last Martinmas, and I havena touched a drop o' whisky sinsyne. Not even at Hogmanay, though I was sair temptit."

He swung his heels up on the seat, and burrowed a frowsy head into the cushions.

"And that's a' I get," he moaned. "A heid better than hell fire, and twae een lookin' different ways for the Sabbath."

"What did it?" I asked.

"A drink they ca' brandy. Bein' a teetotaller I keepit off the whisky, but I was nip-nippin' a' day at this brandy, and I doubt I'll no be weel for a fortnicht." His voice died away into a splutter, and sleep once more laid its heavy hand on him.

My plan had been to get out at some station down the line, but the train suddenly gave me a better chance, for it came to a standstill at the end of a culvert which spanned a brawling porter-coloured river. I looked out and saw that every carriage window was closed and no human figure appeared in the landscape. So I opened the door, and dropped quickly into the tangle of hazels which edged the line.

It would have been all right but for that infernal dog. Under the impression that I was decamping with its master's belongings, it started to bark, and all but got me by the trousers. This woke up the herd, who stood bawling at the carriage door in the belief that I had committed suicide. I crawled through the thicket, reached the edge of the stream, and in cover of the bushes put a hundred yards or so behind me. Then from my shelter I peered back, and saw the guard and several passengers gathered round the open carriage door and staring in my direction. I could not have made a more public departure if I had left with a bugler and a brass band.

Happily the drunken herd provided a diversion. He and his dog, which was attached by a rope to his waist, suddenly cascaded out of the carriage, landed on their heads on the track, and rolled some way down the bank towards the water. In the rescue which followed the dog bit somebody, for I could hear the sound of hard swearing. Presently they had forgotten me, and when after a quarter of a mile's crawl I ventured to look back, the train had started again and was vanishing in the cutting.

I was in a wide semicircle of moorland, with the brown river as radius, and the high hills forming the northern circumference. There was not a sign or sound of a human being, only the plashing water and the interminable crying of curlews. Yet, oddly enough, for the first time I felt the terror of the hunted on me. It was not the police that I thought of, but the other folk, who knew that I knew Scudder's secret and dared not let me live. I was certain that they would pursue me with a keenness and vigilance unknown to the British law, and that once their grip closed on me I should find no mercy.

I looked back, but there was nothing in the landscape. The sun glinted on the metals of the line and the wet stones in the stream, and you could not have found a more peaceful sight in the world. Nevertheless I started to run. Crouching low in the runnels of the bog, I ran till the sweat blinded my eyes. The mood did not leave me till I had reached the rim of mountain and flung myself panting on a ridge high above the young waters of the brown river.

From my vantage-ground I could scan the whole moor right away to the railway line and to the south of it where green fields took the place of heather. I have eyes like a hawk, but I could see nothing moving in the whole countryside. Then I looked east beyond the ridge and saw a new kind of landscape—shallow green valleys with plentiful fir plantations and the faint lines of dust which spoke of highroads. Last of all I looked into the blue May sky, and there I saw that which set my pulses racing . . .

Low down in the south a monoplane was climbing into the heavens. I was as certain as if I had been told that that aeroplane was looking for me, and that it did not belong to the police. For an hour or two I watched it from a pit of heather. It flew low along the hill-tops, and then in narrow circles over the valley up which I had come. Then it seemed to change its mind, rose to a great height, and flew away back to the south.

I did not like this espionage from the air, and I began to think less well of the countryside I had chosen for a refuge. These heather hills were no sort of cover if my enemies were in the sky, and I must find a different kind of sanctuary. I looked with more satisfaction to the green country beyond the ridge, for there I should find woods and stone houses.

About six in the evening I came out of the moorland to a white ribbon of road which wound up the narrow vale of a lowland stream. As I followed it, fields gave place to bent, the glen became a plateau, and presently I had reached a kind of pass where a solitary house smoked in the twilight. The road swung over a bridge, and leaning on the parapet was a young man.

He was smoking a long clay pipe and studying the water with spectacled eyes. In his left hand was a small book with a finger marking the place. Slowly he repeated—

> *As when a Gryphon through the wilderness*
> *With wingèd step, o'er hill and moory dale*
> *Pursues the Arimaspian.*

He jumped round as my step rung on the keystone, and I saw a pleasant sunburnt boyish face.

"Good evening to you," he said gravely. "It's a fine night for the road."

The smell of peat smoke and of some savoury roast floated to me from the house.

"Is that place an inn?" I asked.

"At your service," he said politely. "I am the landlord, sir, and I hope you will stay the night, for to tell you the truth I have had no company for a week."

I pulled myself up on the parapet of the bridge and filled my pipe. I began to detect an ally.

"You're young to be an innkeeper," I said.

"My father died a year ago and left me the business. I live there with my grandmother. It's a slow job for a young man, and it wasn't my choice of profession."

"Which was?"

He actually blushed. "I want to write books," he said.

"And what better chance could you ask?" I cried. "Man, I've often thought that an innkeeper would make the best story-teller in the world."

"Not now," he said eagerly. "Maybe in the old days when

you had pilgrims and ballad-makers and highwaymen and mail-coaches on the road. But not now. Nothing comes here but motor-cars full of fat women, who stop for lunch, and a fisherman or two in the spring, and the shooting tenants in August. There is not much material to be got out of that. I want to see life, to travel the world, and write things like Kipling and Conrad. But the most I've done yet is to get some verses printed in Chambers's Journal."

I looked at the inn standing golden in the sunset against the brown hills.

"I've knocked a bit about the world, and I wouldn't despise such a hermitage. D'you think that adventure is found only in the tropics or among gentry in red shirts? Maybe you're rubbing shoulders with it at this moment."

"That's what Kipling says," he said, his eyes brightening, and he quoted some verse about "Romance brings up the 9:15."

"Here's a true tale for you then," I cried, "and a month from now you can make a novel out of it."

Sitting on the bridge in the soft May gloaming I pitched him a lovely yarn. It was true in essentials, too, though I altered the minor details. I made out that I was a mining magnate from Kimberley, who had had a lot of trouble with I.D.B. and had shown up a gang. They had pursued me across the ocean, and had killed my best friend, and were now on my tracks.

I told the story well, though I say it who shouldn't. I pictured a flight across the Kalahari to German Africa, the crackling, parching days, the wonderful blue-velvet nights. I described an attack on my life on the voyage home, and I made a really horrid affair of the Portland Place murder. "You're looking for adventure," I cried; "well, you've found it here. The devils are after me, and the police are after them. It's a race that I mean to win."

"By God!" he whispered, drawing his breath in sharply, "it is all pure Rider Haggard and Conan Doyle."

"You believe me," I said gratefully.

"Of course I do," and he held out his hand. "I believe everything out of the common. The only thing to distrust is the normal."

He was very young, but he was the man for my money.

"I think they're off my track for the moment, but I must lie close for a couple of days. Can you take me in?"

He caught my elbow in his eagerness and drew me towards the house. "You can lie as snug here as if you were in a moss-hole. I'll see that nobody blabs, either. And you'll give me some more material about your adventures?"

As I entered the inn porch I heard from far off the beat of an engine. There silhouetted against the dusky West was my friend, the monoplane.

He gave me a room at the back of the house, with a fine outlook over the plateau, and he made me free of his own study, which was stacked with cheap editions of his favourite authors. I never saw the grandmother, so I guessed she was bedridden. An old woman called Margit brought me my meals, and the innkeeper was around me at all hours. I wanted some time to myself, so I invented a job for him. He had a motor bicycle, and I sent him off next morning for the daily paper, which usually arrived with the post in the late afternoon. I told him to keep his eyes skinned, and make note of any strange figures he saw, keeping a special sharp look-out for motors and aeroplanes. Then I sat down in real earnest to Scudder's note-book.

He came back at midday with the Scotsman. There was nothing in it, except some further evidence of Paddock and the milkman, and a repetition of yesterday's statement that the murderer had gone North. But there was a long article, reprinted from the Times, about Karolides and the state of affairs in the Balkans, though there was no mention of any visit to England. I got rid of the innkeeper for the afternoon, for I was getting very warm in my search for the cypher.

As I told you, it was a numerical cypher, and by an elaborate system of experiments I had pretty well discovered what were the nulls and stops. The trouble was the key word, and when I thought of the odd million words he might have used I felt pretty hopeless. But about three o'clock I had a sudden inspiration.

The name Julia Czechenyi flashed across my memory. Scudder had said it was the key to the Karolides business, and it occurred to me to try it on his cypher.

It worked. The five letters of "Julia" gave me the position of the vowels. A was J, the tenth letter of the alphabet, and so represented by X in the cypher. E was U=XXI, and so on. "Czechenyi" gave me the numerals for the principal consonants. I scribbled that scheme on a bit of paper and sat down to read Scudder's pages.

In half an hour I was reading with a whitish face and fingers that drummed on the table.

I glanced out of the window and saw a big touring-car coming up the glen towards the inn. It drew up at the door, and there was the sound of people alighting. There seemed to be two of them, men in aquascutums and tweed caps.

Ten minutes later the innkeeper slipped into the room, his eyes bright with excitement.

"There's two chaps below looking for you," he whispered. "They're in the dining-room having whiskies-and-sodas. They asked about you and said they had hoped to meet you here. Oh! and they described you jolly well, down to your boots and shirt. I told them you had been here last night and had gone off on a motor bicycle this morning, and one of the chaps swore like a navvy."

I made him tell me what they looked like. One was a dark-eyed thin fellow with bushy eyebrows, the other was always smiling and lisped in his talk. Neither was any kind of foreigner; on this my young friend was positive.

I took a bit of paper and wrote these words in German as if they were part of a letter—

". . . Black Stone. Scudder had got on to this, but he could not act for a fortnight. I doubt if I can do any good now, especially as Karolides is uncertain about his plans. But if Mr. T. advises I will do the best I . . ."

I manufactured it rather neatly, so that it looked like a loose page of a private letter.

"Take this down and say it was found in my bedroom, and ask them to return it to me if they overtake me."

Three minutes later I heard the car begin to move, and peeping from behind the curtain caught sight of the two figures. One was slim, the other was sleek; that was the most I could make of my reconnaissance.

The innkeeper appeared in great excitement. "Your paper woke them up," he said gleefully. "The dark fellow went as white as death and cursed like blazes, and the fat one whistled and looked ugly. They paid for their drinks with half-a-sovereign and wouldn't wait for change."

"Now I'll tell you what I want you to do," I said. "Get on your bicycle and go off to Newton-Stewart to the Chief Constable. Describe the two men, and say you suspect them of having had something to do with the London murder. You can invent reasons. The two will come back, never fear. Not tonight, for they'll follow me forty miles along the road, but first thing tomorrow morning. Tell the police to be here bright and early."

He set off like a docile child, while I worked at Scudder's notes. When he came back we dined together, and in common decency I had to let him pump me. I gave him a lot of stuff about lion hunts and the Matabele War, thinking all the while what tame businesses these were compared to this I was now engaged in! When he went to bed I sat up and finished Scudder. I smoked in a chair till daylight, for I could not sleep.

About eight next morning I witnessed the arrival of two

constables and a sergeant. They put their car in a coach-house under the innkeeper's instructions, and entered the house. Twenty minutes later I saw from my window a second car come across the plateau from the opposite direction. It did not come up to the inn, but stopped two hundred yards off in the shelter of a patch of wood. I noticed that its occupants carefully reversed it before leaving it. A minute or two later I heard their steps on the gravel outside the window.

My plan had been to lie hid in my bedroom, and see what happened. I had a notion that, if I could bring the police and my other more dangerous pursuers together, something might work out of it to my advantage. But now I had a better idea. I scribbled a line of thanks to my host, opened the window, and dropped quietly into a gooseberry bush. Unobserved I crossed the dyke, crawled down the side of a tributary burn, and won the highroad on the far side of the patch of trees. There stood the car, very spick and span in the morning sunlight, but with the dust on her which told of a long journey. I started her, jumped into the chauffeur's seat, and stole gently out on to the plateau.

Almost at once the road dipped so that I lost sight of the inn, but the wind seemed to bring me the sound of angry voices.

4. *The Adventure of the Radical Candidate*

You may picture me driving that 40 h.p. car for all she was worth over the crisp moor roads on that shining May morning; glancing back at first over my shoulder, and looking anxiously to the next turning; then driving with a vague eye, just wide enough awake to keep on the highway. For I was thinking desperately of what I had found in Scudder's pocket-book.

The little man had told me a pack of lies. All his yarns about the Balkans and the Jew-Anarchists and the Foreign Office Conference were eyewash, and so was Karolides. And yet not quite, as you shall hear. I had staked everything on my belief in his story, and had been let down; here was his book telling me a different tale, and instead of being once-bitten-twice-shy, I believed it absolutely.

Why, I don't know. It rang desperately true, and the first yarn, if you understand me, had been in a queer way true also in spirit. The fifteenth day of June was going to be a day of destiny, a bigger destiny than the killing of a Dago. It was so big that I didn't blame Scudder for keeping me out of the game and wanting to play a lone hand. That, I was pretty clear, was his intention. He had told me something which sounded big enough, but the real thing was so immortally big that he, the man who had found it out, wanted it all for himself. I didn't blame him. It was risks after all that he was chiefly greedy about.

The whole story was in the notes—with gaps, you understand, which he would have filled up from his memory. He stuck down his authorities, too, and had an odd trick of giving them all a numerical value and then striking a balance, which stood for the reliability of each stage in the yarn. The four names he had printed were authorities, and there was a man, Ducrosne, who got five out of a possible five; and another fellow, Ammersfoort, who got three. The bare bones of the tale were all that was in the book—these, and one queer phrase which occurred half a dozen times inside brackets. ("Thirty-nine steps") was the phrase; and at its last time of use it ran—("Thirty-nine steps, I counted them—high tide 10:17 p.m."). I could make nothing of that.

The first thing I learned was that it was no question of preventing a war. That was coming, as sure as Christmas: had been arranged, said Scudder, ever since February 1912. Karolides was going to be the occasion. He was booked all right, and was to hand in his checks on June 14th, two weeks and four days from that May morning. I gathered from Scudder's notes that nothing on earth could prevent that. His talk of Epirote guards that would skin their own grandmothers was all billy-o.

The second thing was that this war was going to come as a mighty surprise to Britain. Karolides' death would set the Balkans by the ears, and then Vienna would chip in with an ultimatum. Russia wouldn't like that, and there would be high words. But Berlin would play the peacemaker, and pour oil on the waters, till suddenly she would find a good cause for a quarrel, pick it up, and in five hours let fly at us. That was the idea, and a pretty good one too. Honey and fair speeches, and then a stroke in the dark. While we were talking about the goodwill and good intentions of Germany our coast would be silently ringed with mines, and submarines would be waiting for every battleship.

But all this depended upon the third thing, which was due to happen on June 15th. I would never have grasped this if I hadn't once happened to meet a French staff officer, coming back from West Africa, who had told me a lot of things. One was that, in spite of all the nonsense talked in Parliament, there was a real working alliance between France and Britain, and that the two General Staffs met every now and then, and made plans for joint action in case of war. Well, in June a very great swell was coming over from Paris, and he was going to get nothing less than a statement of the disposition of the British Home Fleet on mobilization. At least I gathered it was something like that; anyhow, it was something uncommonly important.

But on the 15th day of June there were to be others in London—others, at whom I could only guess. Scudder was content to call them collectively the "Black Stone." They represented not our Allies, but our deadly foes; and the information, destined for France, was to be diverted to their pockets. And it was to be used, remember—used a week or two later, with great guns and swift torpedoes, suddenly in the darkness of a summer night.

This was the story I had been deciphering in a back room of a country inn, overlooking a cabbage garden. This was the story that hummed in my brain as I swung in the big touring-car from glen to glen.

My first impulse had been to write a letter to the Prime Minister, but a little reflection convinced me that that would be useless. Who would believe my tale? I must show a sign, some token in proof, and Heaven knew what that could be. Above all, I must keep going myself, ready to act when things got riper, and that was going to be no light job with the police of the British Isles in full cry after me and the watchers of the Black Stone running silently and swiftly on my trail.

I had no very clear purpose in my journey, but I steered east by the sun, for I remembered from the map that if I went north I would come into a region of coalpits and industrial towns. Presently I was down from the moorlands and traversing the broad haugh of a river. For miles I ran alongside a park wall, and in a break of the trees I saw a great castle. I swung through little old thatched villages, and over peaceful lowland streams, and past gardens blazing with hawthorn and yellow laburnum. The land was so deep in peace that I could scarcely believe that somewhere behind me were those who sought my life; ay, and that in a month's time, unless I had the almightiest of luck, these round country faces would be pinched and staring, and men would be lying dead in English fields.

About midday I entered a long straggling village, and had a mind to stop and eat. Half-way down was the Post Office, and on the steps of it stood the postmistress and a policeman hard at work conning a telegram. When they saw me they wakened up, and the policeman advanced with raised hand, and cried on me to stop.

I nearly was fool enough to obey. Then it flashed upon me that the wire had to do with me; that my friends at the inn had come to an understanding, and were united in desiring to see more of me, and that it had been easy enough for them to wire the description of me and the car to thirty villages through which I might pass. I released the brakes just in time. As it was, the policeman made a claw at the hood, and only dropped off when he got my left in his eye.

I saw that main roads were no place for me, and turned into the byways. It wasn't an easy job without a map, for there was the risk of getting on to a farm road and ending in a duck-pond or a stable-yard, and I couldn't afford that kind of delay. I began to see what an ass I had been to steal the car. The big green brute would be the safest kind of clue to me over the breadth of Scotland. If I left it and took to my feet, it would be discovered in an hour or two and I would get no start in the race.

The immediate thing to do was to get to the loneliest roads. These I soon found when I struck up a tributary of the big river, and got into a glen with steep hills all about me, and a corkscrew road at the end which climbed over a pass. Here I met nobody, but it was taking me too far north, so I slewed east along a bad track and finally struck a big double-line railway. Away below me I saw another broadish valley, and it occurred to me that if I crossed it I might find some remote inn to pass the night. The evening was now drawing in, and I was furiously hungry, for I had eaten nothing since breakfast except a couple of buns I had bought from a baker's cart.

Just then I heard a noise in the sky, and lo and behold there was that infernal aeroplane, flying low, about a dozen miles to the south and rapidly coming towards me.

I had the sense to remember that on a bare moor I was at the aeroplane's mercy, and that my only chance was to get to the leafy cover of the valley. Down the hill I went like blue lightning, screwing my head round, whenever I dared, to watch that damned flying machine. Soon I was on a road between hedges, and dipping to the deep-cut glen of a stream. Then came a bit of thick wood where I slackened speed.

Suddenly on my left I heard the hoot of another car, and realized to my horror that I was almost up on a couple of gateposts through which a private road debouched on the highway. My horn gave an agonized roar, but it was too late. I clapped on my brakes, but my impetus was too great, and there before me a car was sliding athwart my course. In a second there would have been the deuce of a wreck. I did the only thing possible, and ran slap into the hedge on the right, trusting to find something soft beyond.

But there I was mistaken. My car slithered through the hedge like butter, and then gave a sickening plunge forward. I saw what was coming, leapt on the seat and would have jumped out. But a branch of hawthorn got me in the chest, lifted me up and held me, while a ton or two of expensive metal slipped below me, bucked and pitched, and then dropped with an almighty smash fifty feet to the bed of the stream.

Slowly that thorn let me go. I subsided first on the hedge, and then very gently on a bower of nettles. As I scrambled to my feet a hand took me by the arm, and a sympathetic and badly scared voice asked me if I were hurt.

I found myself looking at a tall young man in goggles and a leather ulster, who kept on blessing his soul and whinnying apologies. For myself, once I got my wind back, I was rather glad than otherwise. This was one way of getting rid of the car.

"My blame, sir," I answered him. "It's lucky that I did not add homicide to my follies. That's the end of my Scotch motor tour, but it might have been the end of my life."

He plucked out a watch and studied it. "You're the right sort of fellow," he said. "I can spare a quarter of an hour, and my house is two minutes off. I'll see you clothed and fed and snug in bed. Where's your kit, by the way? Is it in the burn along with the car?"

"It's in my pocket," I said, brandishing a toothbrush. "I'm a colonial and travel light."

"A colonial," he cried. "By Gad, you're the very man I've been praying for. Are you by any blessed chance a Free Trader?"

"I am," said I, without the foggiest notion of what he meant.

He patted my shoulder and hurried me into his car. Three minutes later we drew up before a comfortable-looking shooting-box set among pine trees, and he ushered me indoors. He took me first to a bedroom and flung half a dozen of his suits before me, for my own had been pretty well reduced to rags. I selected a loose blue serge, which differed most conspicuously from my former garments, and borrowed a linen collar. Then he haled me to the dining-room, where the remnants of a meal stood on the table, and announced that I had just five minutes to feed. "You can take a snack in your pocket, and we'll have supper when we get back. I've got to be at the Masonic Hall at eight o'clock, or my agent will comb my hair."

I had a cup of coffee and some cold ham, while he yarned away on the hearthrug.

"You find me in the deuce of a mess, Mr. ——; by-the-by, you haven't told me your name. Twisdon? Any relation of old Tommy Twisdon of the Sixtieth? No? Well, you see I'm Liberal Candidate for this part of the world, and I had a meeting on tonight at Brattleburn—that's my chief town, and an infernal Tory stronghold. I had got the Colonial ex-Premier fellow, Crumpleton, coming to speak for me tonight, and had the thing tremendously billed and the whole place ground-baited. This afternoon I had a wire from the ruffian saying he had got influenza at Blackpool, and here am I left to do the whole thing myself. I had meant to speak for ten minutes and must now go on for forty, and, though I've been racking my brains for three hours to think of something, I simply cannot last the course. Now you've got to be a good chap and help me. You're a Free Trader and can tell our people what a wash-out Protection is in the Colonies. All you fellows have the gift of the gab—I wish to Heaven I had it. I'll be for evermore in your debt."

I had very few notions about Free Trade one way or the other, but I saw no other chance to get what I wanted. My young gentleman was far too absorbed in his own difficulties to think how odd it was to ask a stranger who had just missed death by an ace and had lost a 1,000-guinea car to address a meeting for him on the spur of the moment. But my necessities did not allow me to contemplate oddnesses or to pick and choose my supports.

"All right," I said. "I'm not much good as a speaker, but I'll tell them a bit about Australia."

At my words the cares of the ages slipped from his shoulders, and he was rapturous in his thanks. He lent me a big driving coat—and never troubled to ask why I had started on a motor tour without possessing an ulster—and, as we slipped down the dusty roads, poured into my ears the simple facts of his history. He was an orphan, and his uncle had brought him up—I've forgotten the uncle's name, but he was in the Cabinet, and you can read his speeches in the papers. He had gone round the world after leaving Cambridge, and then, being short of a job, his uncle had advised politics. I gathered that he had no preference in parties. "Good chaps in both," he said cheerfully, "and plenty of blighters, too. I'm Liberal, because my family have always been Whigs." But if he was lukewarm politically he had strong views on other things. He found out I knew a bit about horses, and jawed away about the Derby entries; and he was full of plans for improving his shooting. Altogether, a very clean, decent, callow young man.

As we passed through a little town two policemen signalled us to stop, and flashed their lanterns on us.

"Beg pardon, Sir Harry," said one. "We've got instructions to look out for a car, and the description's no unlike yours."

"Right-o," said my host, while I thanked Providence for the devious ways I had been brought to safety. After that he spoke no more, for his mind began to labour heavily with his coming speech. His lips kept muttering, his eye wandered, and I began to prepare myself for a second catastrophe. I tried to think of something to say myself, but my mind was dry as a stone. The next thing I knew we had drawn up outside a door in a street, and were being welcomed by some noisy gentlemen with rosettes.

The hall had about five hundred in it, women mostly, a lot of bald heads, and a dozen or two young men. The chairman, a weaselly minister with a reddish nose, lamented Crumpleton's absence, soliloquized on his influenza, and gave me a certificate as a "trusted leader of Australian thought." There were two policemen at the door, and I hoped they took note of that testimonial. Then Sir Harry started.

I never heard anything like it. He didn't begin to know how to talk. He had about a bushel of notes from which he read, and when he let go of them he fell into one prolonged stutter. Every now and then he remembered a phrase he had learned by heart, straightened his back, and gave it off like Henry Irving, and the next moment he was bent double and crooning over his papers. It was the most appalling rot, too. He talked about the "German menace," and said it was all a Tory invention to cheat the poor of their rights and keep back the great flood of social reform, but that "organized labour" realized this and laughed the Tories to scorn. He was all for reducing our Navy as a proof of our good faith, and then sending Germany an ultimatum telling her to do the same or we would knock her into a cocked hat. He said that, but for the Tories, Germany and Britain would be fellow-workers in peace and reform. I thought of the little black book in my pocket! A giddy lot Scudder's friends cared for peace and reform.

Yet in a queer way I liked the speech. You could see the niceness of the chap shining out behind the muck with which he had been spoon-fed. Also it took a load off my mind. I mightn't be much of an orator, but I was a thousand per cent better than Sir Harry.

I didn't get on so badly when it came to my turn. I simply told them all I could remember about Australia, praying there should be no Australian there—all about its labour party and emigration and universal service. I doubt if I remembered to mention Free Trade, but I said there were no Tories in Australia, only Labour and Liberals. That fetched a cheer, and I woke them up a bit when I started in to tell them the kind of glorious business I thought could be made out of the Empire if we really put our backs into it.

Altogether I fancy I was rather a success. The minister didn't like me, though, and when he proposed a vote of thanks, spoke of Sir Harry's speech as "statesmanlike" and mine as having "the eloquence of an emigration agent."

When we were in the car again my host was in wild spirits at having got his job over. "A ripping speech, Twisdon," he said. "Now, you're coming home with me. I'm all alone, and if you'll stop a day or two I'll show you some very decent fishing."

We had a hot supper—and I wanted it pretty badly—and then drank grog in a big cheery smoking-room with a crackling wood fire. I thought the time had come for me to put my cards on the table. I saw by this man's eye that he was the kind you can trust.

"Listen, Sir Harry," I said. "I've something pretty important to say to you. You're a good fellow, and I'm going to be frank. Where on earth did you get that poisonous rubbish you talked tonight?"

His face fell. "Was it as bad as that?" he asked ruefully. "It did sound rather thin. I got most of it out of the Progressive Magazine and pamphlets that agent chap of mine keeps sending me. But you surely don't think Germany would ever go to war with us?"

"Ask that question in six weeks and it won't need an answer," I said. "If you'll give me your attention for half an hour I am going to tell you a story."

I can see yet that bright room with the deers' heads and the old prints on the walls, Sir Harry standing restlessly on the stone curb of the hearth, and myself lying back in an armchair, speaking. I seemed to be another person, standing aside and listening to my own voice, and judging carefully the reliability of my tale. It was the first time I had ever told anyone the exact truth, so far as I understood it, and it did me no end of good, for it straightened out the thing in my own mind. I blinked no detail. He heard all about Scudder, and the milkman, and the note-book, and my doings in Galloway. Presently he got very excited and walked up and down the hearthrug.

"So you see," I concluded, "you have got here in your house the man that is wanted for the Portland Place murder. Your duty is to send your car for the police and give me up. I don't think I'll get very far. There'll be an accident, and I'll have a knife in my ribs an hour or so after arrest. Nevertheless, it's your duty, as a law-abiding citizen. Perhaps in a month's time you'll be sorry, but you have no cause to think of that."

He was looking at me with bright steady eyes. "What was your job in Rhodesia, Mr. Hannay?" he asked.

"Mining engineer," I said. "I've made my pile cleanly and I've had a good time in the making of it."

"Not a profession that weakens the nerves, is it?"

I laughed. "Oh, as to that, my nerves are good enough." I took down a hunting-knife from a stand on the wall, and did the old Mashona trick of tossing it and catching it in my lips. That wants a pretty steady heart.

He watched me with a smile. "I don't want proofs. I may be an ass on the platform, but I can size up a man. You're no murderer and you're no fool, and I believe you are speaking the truth. I'm going to back you up. Now, what can I do?"

"First, I want you to write a letter to your uncle. I've got to get in touch with the Government people sometime before the 15th of June."

He pulled his moustache. "That won't help you. This is Foreign Office business, and my uncle would have nothing to do with it. Besides, you'd never convince him. No, I'll go one better. I'll write to the Permanent Secretary at the Foreign Office. He's my godfather, and one of the best going. What do you want?"

He sat down at a table and wrote to my dictation. The gist of it was that if a man called Twisdon (I thought I had better stick to that name) turned up before June 15th he was to entreat him kindly. He said Twisdon would prove his bona fides by passing the word "Black Stone" and whistling "Annie Laurie."

"Good," said Sir Harry. "That's the proper style. By the way, you'll find my godfather—his name's Sir Walter Bullivant—down at his country cottage for Whitsuntide. It's close to Artinswell on the Kennet. That's done. Now, what's the next thing?"

"You're about my height. Lend me the oldest tweed suit you've got. Anything will do, so long as the colour is the opposite of the clothes I destroyed this afternoon. Then show me a map of the neighbourhood and explain to me the lie of the land. Lastly, if the police come seeking me, just show them the car in the glen. If the other lot turn up, tell them I caught the south express after your meeting."

He did, or promised to do, all these things. I shaved off the remnants of my moustache, and got inside an ancient suit of what I believe is called heather mixture. The map gave me some notion of my whereabouts, and told me the two things I wanted to know—where the main railway to the south could be joined, and what were the wildest districts near at hand.

At two o'clock he wakened me from my slumbers in the smoking-room armchair, and led me blinking into the dark starry night. An old bicycle was found in a tool-shed and handed over to me.

"First turn to the right up by the long fir-wood," he enjoined. "By daybreak you'll be well into the hills. Then I should pitch the machine into a bog and take to the moors on foot. You can put in a week among the shepherds, and be as safe as if you were in New Guinea."

I pedalled diligently up steep roads of hill gravel till the skies grew pale with morning. As the mists cleared before the sun, I found myself in a wide green world with glens falling on every side and a far-away blue horizon. Here, at any rate, I could get early news of my enemies.

5. The Adventure of the Spectacled Roadman

I sat down on the very crest of the pass and took stock of my position.

Behind me was the road climbing through a long cleft in the hills, which was the upper glen of some notable river. In front was a flat space of maybe a mile, all pitted with bog-holes and rough with tussocks, and then beyond it the road fell steeply down another glen to a plain whose blue dimness melted into the distance. To left and right were round-shouldered green hills as smooth as pancakes, but to the south—that is, the left hand—there was a glimpse of high heathery mountains, which I remembered from the map as the big knot of hill which I had chosen for my sanctuary. I was on the central boss of a huge upland country, and could see everything moving for miles. In the meadows below the road half a mile back a cottage smoked, but it was the only sign of human life. Otherwise there was only the calling of plovers and the tinkling of little streams.

It was now about seven o'clock, and as I waited I heard once again that ominous beat in the air. Then I realized that my vantage-ground might be in reality a trap. There was no cover for a tomtit in those bald green places.

I sat quite still and hopeless while the beat grew louder. Then I saw an aeroplane coming up from the east. It was flying high, but as I looked it dropped several hundred feet and began to circle round the knot of hill in narrowing circles, just as a hawk wheels before it pounces. Now it was flying very low, and now the observer on board caught sight of me. I could see one of the two occupants examining me through glasses.

Suddenly it began to rise in swift whorls, and the next I knew it was speeding eastward again till it became a speck in the blue morning.

That made me do some savage thinking. My enemies had located me, and the next thing would be a cordon round me. I didn't know what force they could command, but I was certain it would be sufficient. The aeroplane had seen my bicycle, and would conclude that I would try to escape by the road. In that case there might be a chance on the moors to the right or left. I wheeled the machine a hundred yards from the highway, and plunged it into a moss-hole, where it sank among pond-weed and water-buttercups. Then I climbed to a knoll which gave me a view of the two valleys. Nothing was stirring on the long white ribbon that threaded them.

I have said there was not cover in the whole place to hide a rat. As the day advanced it was flooded with soft fresh light till it had the fragrant sunniness of the South African veld. At other times I would have liked the place, but now it seemed to suffocate me. The free moorlands were prison walls, and the keen hill air was the breath of a dungeon.

I tossed a coin—heads right, tails left—and it fell heads, so I turned to the north. In a little I came to the brow of the ridge which was the containing wall of the pass. I saw the highroad for maybe ten miles, and far down it something that was moving, and that I took to be a motor-car. Beyond the ridge I looked on a rolling green moor, which fell away into wooded glens.

Now my life on the veld has given me the eyes of a kite, and I can see things for which most men need a telescope . . . Away down the slope, a couple of miles away, several men were advancing, like a row of beaters at a shoot.

I dropped out of sight behind the sky-line. That way was shut to me, and I must try the bigger hills to the south beyond the highway. The car I had noticed was getting nearer, but it was still a long way off with some very steep gradients before it. I ran hard, crouching low except in the hollows, and as I ran I kept scanning the brow of the hill before me. Was it imagination, or did I see figures—one, two, perhaps more—moving in a glen beyond the stream?

If you are hemmed in on all sides in a patch of land there is only one chance of escape. You must stay in the patch, and let your enemies search it and not find you. That was good sense, but how on earth was I to escape notice in that table-cloth of a place? I would have buried myself to the neck in mud or lain below water or climbed the tallest tree. But there was not a stick of wood, the bog-holes were little puddles, the stream was a slender trickle. There was nothing but short heather, and bare hill bent, and the white highway.

Then in a tiny bight of road, beside a heap of stones, I found the roadman.

He had just arrived, and was wearily flinging down his hammer. He looked at me with a fishy eye and yawned.

"Confoond the day I ever left the herdin'!" he said, as if to the world at large. "There I was my ain maister. Now I'm a slave to the Goavernment, tethered to the roadside, wi' sair een, and a back like a suckle."

He took up the hammer, struck a stone, dropped the implement with an oath, and put both hands to his ears. "Mercy on me! My heid's burstin'!" he cried.

He was a wild figure, about my own size but much bent, with a week's beard on his chin, and a pair of big horn spectacles.

"I canna dae't," he cried again. "The Surveyor maun just report me. I'm for my bed."

I asked him what was the trouble, though indeed that was clear enough.

"The trouble is that I'm no sober. Last nicht my dochter Merran was waddit, and they danced till fower in the byre. Me and some ither chiels sat down to the drinkin', and here I am. Peety that I ever lookit on the wine when it was red!"

I agreed with him about bed.

"It's easy speakin'," he moaned. "But I got a postcard yestreen sayin' that the new Road Surveyor would be round the day. He'll come and he'll no find me, or else he'll find me fou, and either way I'm a done man. I'll awa' back to my bed and say I'm no weel, but I doot that'll no help me, for they ken my kind o' no-weel-ness."

Then I had an inspiration. "Does the new Surveyor know you?" I asked.

"No him. He's just been a week at the job. He rins about in a wee motor-cawr, and wad speir the inside oot o' a whelk."

"Where's your house?" I asked, and was directed by a wavering finger to the cottage by the stream.

"Well, back to your bed," I said, "and sleep in peace. I'll take on your job for a bit and see the Surveyor."

He stared at me blankly; then, as the notion dawned on his fuddled brain, his face broke into the vacant drunkard's smile.

"You're the billy," he cried. "It'll be easy eneuch managed. I've finished that bing o' stanes, so you needna chap ony mair this forenoon. Just take the barry, and wheel eneuch metal frae yon quarry doon the road to mak anither bing the morn. My name's Alexander Trummle, and I've been seeven year at the trade, and twenty afore that herdin' on Leithen Water. My freens ca' me Ecky, and whiles Specky, for I wear glesses, being waik i' the sicht. Just you speak the Surveyor fair, and ca' him Sir, and he'll be fell pleased. I'll be back or midday."

I borrowed his spectacles and filthy old hat; stripped off coat, waistcoat, and collar, and gave him them to carry home; borrowed, too, the foul stump of a clay pipe as an extra property. He indicated my simple tasks, and without more ado set off at an amble bedwards. Bed may have been his chief object, but I think there was also something left in the foot of a bottle.

I prayed that he might be safe under cover before my friends arrived on the scene.

Then I set to work to dress for the part. I opened the collar of my shirt—it was a vulgar blue-and-white check such as ploughmen wear—and revealed a neck as brown as any tinker's. I rolled up my sleeves, and there was a forearm which might have been a blacksmith's, sunburnt and rough with old scars. I got my boots and trouser-legs all white from the dust of the road, and hitched up my trousers, tying them with string below the knee. Then I set to work on my face. With a handful of dust I made a water-mark round my neck, the place where Mr. Turnbull's Sunday ablutions might be expected to stop. I rubbed a good deal of dirt also into the sunburn of my cheeks. A roadman's eyes would no doubt be a little inflamed, so I contrived to get some dust in both of mine, and by dint of vigorous rubbing produced a bleary effect.

The sandwiches Sir Harry had given me had gone off with my coat, but the roadman's lunch, tied up in a red handkerchief, was at my disposal. I ate with great relish several of the thick slabs of scone and cheese and drank a little of the cold tea. In the handkerchief was a local paper tied with string and addressed to Mr. Turnbull—obviously meant to solace his midday leisure. I did up the bundle again, and put the paper conspicuously beside it.

My boots did not satisfy me, but by dint of kicking among the stones I reduced them to the granite-like surface which marks a roadman's footgear. Then I bit and scraped my finger-nails till the edges were all cracked and uneven. The men I was matched against would miss no detail. I broke one of the bootlaces and retied it in a clumsy knot, and loosed the other so that my thick grey socks bulged over the uppers. Still no sign of anything on the road. The motor I had observed half an hour ago must have gone home.

My toilet complete, I took up the barrow and began my journeys to and from the quarry a hundred yards off.

I remember an old scout in Rhodesia, who had done many queer things in his day, once telling me that the secret of playing a part was to think yourself into it. You could never keep it up, he said, unless you could manage to convince yourself that you were it. So I shut off all other thoughts and switched them on to the road-mending. I thought of the little white cottage as my home, I recalled the years I had spent herding on Leithen Water, I made my mind dwell lovingly on sleep in a box-bed and a bottle of cheap whisky. Still nothing appeared on that long white road.

Now and then a sheep wandered off the heather to stare at me. A heron flopped down to a pool in the stream and started to fish, taking no more notice of me than if I had been a milestone. On I went, trundling my loads of stone, with the heavy step of the professional. Soon I grew warm, and the dust on my face changed into solid and abiding grit. I was already counting the hours till evening should put a limit to Mr. Turnbull's monotonous toil.

Suddenly a crisp voice spoke from the road, and looking up I saw a little Ford two-seater, and a round-faced young man in a bowler hat.

"Are you Alexander Turnbull?" he asked. "I am the new County Road Surveyor. You live at Blackhopefoot, and have charge of the section from Laidlawbyres to the Riggs? Good! A fair bit of road, Turnbull, and not badly engineered. A little soft about a mile off, and the edges want cleaning. See you look after that. Good morning. You'll know me the next time you see me."

Clearly my get-up was good enough for the dreaded Surveyor. I went on with my work, and as the morning grew towards noon I was cheered by a little traffic. A baker's van breasted the hill, and sold me a bag of ginger biscuits which I stowed in my trouser-pockets against emergencies. Then a herd passed with sheep, and disturbed me somewhat by asking loudly, "What had become o' Specky?"

"In bed wi' the colic," I replied, and the herd passed on . . .

Just about midday a big car stole down the hill, glided past and drew up a hundred yards beyond. Its three occupants descended as if to stretch their legs, and sauntered towards me.

Two of the men I had seen before from the window of the Galloway inn—one lean, sharp, and dark, the other comfortable and smiling. The third had the look of a countryman—a vet, perhaps, or a small farmer. He was dressed in ill-cut knickerbockers, and the eye in his head was as bright and wary as a hen's.

"Morning," said the last. "That's a fine easy job o' yours."

I had not looked up on their approach, and now, when accosted, I slowly and painfully straightened my back, after the manner of roadmen; spat vigorously, after the manner of the low Scot; and regarded them steadily before replying. I confronted three pairs of eyes that missed nothing.

"There's waur jobs and there's better," I said sententiously. "I wad rather hae yours, sittin' a' day on your hinderlands on thae cushions. It's you and your muckle cawrs that wreck my roads! If we a' had oor richts, ye sud be made to mend what ye break."

The bright-eyed man was looking at the newspaper lying beside Turnbull's bundle.

"I see you get your papers in good time," he said.

I glanced at it casually. "Aye, in gude time. Seein' that that paper cam' out last Setterday I'm just sax days late."

He picked it up, glanced at the superscription, and laid it down again. One of the others had been looking at my boots, and a word in German called the speaker's attention to them.

"You've a fine taste in boots," he said. "These were never made by a country shoemaker."

"They were not," I said readily. "They were made in London. I got them frae the gentleman that was here last year for the shootin'. What was his name now?" And I scratched a forgetful head. Again the sleek one spoke in German. "Let us get on," he said. "This fellow is all right."

They asked one last question.

"Did you see anyone pass early this morning? He might be on a bicycle or he might be on foot."

I very nearly fell into the trap and told a story of a bicyclist hurrying past in the grey dawn. But I had the sense to see my danger. I pretended to consider very deeply.

"I wasna up very early," I said. "Ye see, my dochter was merrit last nicht, and we keepit it up late. I opened the house door about seeven and there was naebody on the road then. Since I cam up here there has just been the baker and the Ruchill herd, besides you gentlemen."

One of them gave me a cigar, which I smelt gingerly and stuck in Turnbull's bundle. They got into their car and were out of sight in three minutes.

My heart leaped with an enormous relief, but I went on wheeling my stones. It was as well, for ten minutes later the car returned, one of the occupants waving a hand to me. Those gentry left nothing to chance.

I finished Turnbull's bread and cheese, and pretty soon I had finished the stones. The next step was what puzzled me. I could not keep up this roadmaking business for long. A merciful Providence had kept Mr. Turnbull indoors, but if he appeared on the scene there would be trouble. I had a notion that the cordon was still tight round the glen, and that if I walked in any direction I should meet with questioners. But get out I must. No man's nerve could stand more than a day of being spied on.

I stayed at my post till five o'clock. By that time I had resolved to go down to Turnbull's cottage at nightfall and take my chance of getting over the hills in the darkness. But suddenly a new car came up the road, and slowed down a yard or two from me. A fresh wind had risen, and the occupant wanted to light a cigarette.

It was a touring car, with the tonneau full of an assortment of baggage. One man sat in it, and by an amazing chance I knew him. His name was Marmaduke Jopley, and he was an offence to creation. He was a sort of blood stockbroker, who did his business by toadying eldest sons and rich young peers and foolish old ladies. "Marmie" was a familiar figure, I understood, at balls and polo-weeks and country houses. He was an adroit scandal-monger, and would crawl a mile on his belly to anything that had a title or a million. I had a business introduction to his firm when I came to London, and he was good enough to ask me to dinner at his club. There he showed off at a great rate, and pattered about his duchesses till the snobbery of the creature turned me sick. I asked a man afterwards why nobody kicked him, and was told that Englishmen reverenced the weaker sex.

Anyhow there he was now, nattily dressed, in a fine new car, obviously on his way to visit some of his smart friends. A sudden daftness took me, and in a second I had jumped into the tonneau and had him by the shoulder.

"Hullo, Jopley," I sang out. "Well met, my lad!" He got a horrid fright. His chin dropped as he stared at me. "Who the devil are you?" he gasped.

"My name's Hannay," I said. "From Rhodesia, you remember."

"Good God, the murderer!" he choked.

"Just so. And there'll be a second murder, my dear, if you don't do as I tell you. Give me that coat of yours. That cap, too."

He did as he was bid, for he was blind with terror. Over my dirty trousers and vulgar shirt I put on his smart driving-coat, which buttoned high at the top and thereby hid the deficiencies of my collar. I stuck the cap on my head, and added his gloves to my get-up. The dusty roadman in a minute was transformed into one of the neatest motorists in Scotland. On Mr. Jopley's head I clapped Turnbull's unspeakable hat, and told him to keep it there.

Then with some difficulty I turned the car. My plan was to go back the road he had come, for the watchers, having seen it before, would probably let it pass unremarked, and Marmie's figure was in no way like mine.

"Now, my child," I said, "sit quite still and be a good boy. I mean you no harm. I'm only borrowing your car for an hour or two. But if you play me any tricks, and above all if you open your mouth, as sure as there's a God above me I'll wring your neck. Savez?"

I enjoyed that evening's ride. We ran eight miles down the valley, through a village or two, and I could not help noticing several strange-looking folk lounging by the roadside. These were the watchers who would have had much to say to me if I had come in other garb or company. As it was, they looked incuriously on. One touched his cap in salute, and I responded graciously.

As the dark fell I turned up a side glen which, as I remember from the map, led into an unfrequented corner of the hills. Soon the villages were left behind, then the farms, and then even the wayside cottage. Presently we came to a lonely moor where the night was blackening the sunset gleam in the bog pools. Here we stopped, and I obligingly reversed the car and restored to Mr. Jopley his belongings.

"A thousand thanks," I said. "There's more use in you than I thought. Now be off and find the police."

As I sat on the hillside, watching the tail-light dwindle, I reflected on the various kinds of crime I had now sampled. Contrary to general belief, I was not a murderer, but I had become an unholy liar, a shameless impostor, and a highwayman with a marked taste for expensive motor-cars.

6. The Adventure of the Bald Archaeologist

I spent the night on a shelf of the hillside, in the lee of a boulder where the heather grew long and soft. It was a cold business, for I had neither coat nor waistcoat. These were in Mr. Turnbull's keeping, as was Scudder's little book, my watch and—

worst of all—my pipe and tobacco pouch. Only my money accompanied me in my belt, and about half a pound of ginger biscuits in my trousers pocket.

I supped off half those biscuits, and by worming myself deep into the heather got some kind of warmth. My spirits had risen, and I was beginning to enjoy this crazy game of hide-and-seek. So far I had been miraculously lucky. The milkman, the literary innkeeper, Sir Harry, the roadman, and the idiotic Marmie, were all pieces of undeserved good fortune. Somehow the first success gave me a feeling that I was going to pull the thing through.

My chief trouble was that I was desperately hungry. When a Jew shoots himself in the City and there is an inquest, the newspapers usually report that the deceased was "well-nourished." I remember thinking that they would not call me well-nourished if I broke my neck in a bog-hole. I lay and tortured myself—for the ginger biscuits merely emphasized the aching void—with the memory of all the good food I had thought so little of in London. There were Paddock's crisp sausages and fragrant shavings of bacon, and shapely poached eggs—how often I had turned up my nose at them! There were the cutlets they did at the club, and a particular ham that stood on the cold table, for which my soul lusted. My thoughts hovered over all varieties of mortal edible, and finally settled on a porterhouse steak and a quart of bitter with a welsh rabbit to follow. In longing hopelessly for these dainties I fell asleep.

I woke very cold and stiff about an hour after dawn. It took me a little while to remember where I was, for I had been very weary and had slept heavily. I saw first the pale blue sky through a net of heather, then a big shoulder of hill, and then my own boots placed neatly in a blaeberry bush. I raised myself on my arms and looked down into the valley, and that one look set me lacing up my boots in mad haste.

For there were men below, not more than a quarter of a mile

off, spaced out on the hillside like a fan, and beating the heather. Marmie had not been slow in looking for his revenge.

I crawled out of my shelf into the cover of a boulder, and from it gained a shallow trench which slanted up the mountain face. This led me presently into the narrow gully of a burn, by way of which I scrambled to the top of the ridge. From there I looked back, and saw that I was still undiscovered. My pursuers were patiently quartering the hillside and moving upwards.

Keeping behind the skyline I ran for maybe half a mile, till I judged I was above the uppermost end of the glen. Then I showed myself, and was instantly noted by one of the flankers, who passed the word to the others. I heard cries coming up from below, and saw that the line of search had changed its direction. I pretended to retreat over the skyline, but instead went back the way I had come, and in twenty minutes was behind the ridge overlooking my sleeping place. From that viewpoint I had the satisfaction of seeing the pursuit streaming up the hill at the top of the glen on a hopelessly false scent.

I had before me a choice of routes, and I chose a ridge which made an angle with the one I was on, and so would soon put a deep glen between me and my enemies. The exercise had warmed my blood, and I was beginning to enjoy myself amazingly. As I went I breakfasted on the dusty remnants of the ginger biscuits.

I knew very little about the country, and I hadn't a notion what I was going to do. I trusted to the strength of my legs, but I was well aware that those behind me would be familiar with the lie of the land, and that my ignorance would be a heavy handicap. I saw in front of me a sea of hills, rising very high towards the south, but northwards breaking down into broad ridges which separated wide and shallow dales. The ridge I had chosen seemed to sink after a mile or two to a moor which lay like a pocket in the uplands. That seemed as good a direction to take as any other.

My stratagem had given me a fair start—call it twenty

minutes—and I had the width of a glen behind me before I saw the first heads of the pursuers. The police had evidently called in local talent to their aid, and the men I could see had the appearance of herds or gamekeepers. They hallooed at the sight of me, and I waved my hand. Two dived into the glen and began to climb my ridge, while the others kept their own side of the hill. I felt as if I were taking part in a schoolboy game of hare and hounds.

But very soon it began to seem less of a game. Those fellows behind were hefty men on their native heath. Looking back I saw that only three were following direct, and I guessed that the others had fetched a circuit to cut me off. My lack of local knowledge might very well be my undoing, and I resolved to get out of this tangle of glens to the pocket of moor I had seen from the tops. I must so increase my distance as to get clear away from them, and I believed I could do this if I could find the right ground for it. If there had been cover I would have tried a bit of stalking, but on these bare slopes you could see a fly a mile off. My hope must be in the length of my legs and the soundness of my wind, but I needed easier ground for that, for I was not bred a mountaineer. How I longed for a good Afrikander pony!

I put on a great spurt and got off my ridge and down into the moor before any figures appeared on the skyline behind me. I crossed a burn, and came out on a highroad which made a pass between two glens. All in front of me was a big field of heather sloping up to a crest which was crowned with an odd feather of trees. In the dyke by the roadside was a gate, from which a grass-grown track led over the first wave of the moor.

I jumped the dyke and followed it, and after a few hundred yards—as soon as it was out of sight of the highway—the grass stopped and it became a very respectable road, which was evidently kept with some care. Clearly it ran to a house, and I began to think of doing the same. Hitherto my luck had held, and it might be that my best chance would be found in this remote dwelling. Anyhow there were trees there, and that meant cover.

I did not follow the road, but the burnside which flanked it on the right, where the bracken grew deep and the high banks made a tolerable screen. It was well I did so, for no sooner had I gained the hollow than, looking back, I saw the pursuit topping the ridge from which I had descended.

After that I did not look back; I had no time. I ran up the burnside, crawling over the open places, and for a large part wading in the shallow stream. I found a deserted cottage with a row of phantom peat-stacks and an overgrown garden. Then I was among young hay, and very soon had come to the edge of a plantation of wind-blown firs. From there I saw the chimneys of the house smoking a few hundred yards to my left. I forsook the burnside, crossed another dyke, and almost before I knew was on a rough lawn. A glance back told me that I was well out of sight of the pursuit, which had not yet passed the first lift of the moor.

The lawn was a very rough place, cut with a scythe instead of a mower, and planted with beds of scrubby rhododendrons. A brace of black-game, which are not usually garden birds, rose at my approach. The house before me was the ordinary moorland farm, with a more pretentious whitewashed wing added. Attached to this wing was a glass veranda, and through the glass I saw the face of an elderly gentleman meekly watching me.

I stalked over the border of coarse hill gravel and entered the open veranda door. Within was a pleasant room, glass on one side, and on the other a mass of books. More books showed in an inner room. On the floor, instead of tables, stood cases such as you see in a museum, filled with coins and queer stone implements.

There was a knee-hole desk in the middle, and seated at it, with some papers and open volumes before him, was the benevolent old gentleman. His face was round and shiny, like

Mr. Pickwick's, big glasses were stuck on the end of his nose, and the top of his head was as bright and bare as a glass bottle. He never moved when I entered, but raised his placid eyebrows and waited on me to speak.

It was not an easy job, with about five minutes to spare, to tell a stranger who I was and what I wanted, and to win his aid. I did not attempt it. There was something about the eye of the man before me, something so keen and knowledgeable, that I could not find a word. I simply stared at him and stuttered.

"You seem in a hurry, my friend," he said slowly.

I nodded towards the window. It gave a prospect across the moor through a gap in the plantation, and revealed certain figures half a mile off straggling through the heather.

"Ah, I see," he said, and took up a pair of field-glasses through which he patiently scrutinized the figures.

"A fugitive from justice, eh? Well, we'll go into the matter at our leisure. Meantime I object to my privacy being broken in upon by the clumsy rural policeman. Go into my study, and you will see two doors facing you. Take the one on the left and close it behind you. You will be perfectly safe."

And this extraordinary man took up his pen again.

I did as I was bid, and found myself in a little dark chamber which smelt of chemicals, and was lit only by a tiny window high up in the wall. The door had swung behind me with a click like the door of a safe. Once again I had found an unexpected sanctuary.

All the same I was not comfortable. There was something about the old gentleman which puzzled and rather terrified me. He had been too easy and ready, almost as if he had expected me. And his eyes had been horribly intelligent.

No sound came to me in that dark place. For all I knew the police might be searching the house, and if they did they would want to know what was behind this door. I tried to possess my soul in patience, and to forget how hungry I was.

Then I took a more cheerful view. The old gentleman could scarcely refuse me a meal, and I fell to reconstructing my breakfast. Bacon and eggs would content me, but I wanted the better part of a flitch of bacon and half a hundred eggs. And then, while my mouth was watering in anticipation, there was a click and the door stood open.

I emerged into the sunlight to find the master of the house sitting in a deep armchair in the room he called his study, and regarding me with curious eyes.

"Have they gone?" I asked.

"They have gone. I convinced them that you had crossed the hill. I do not choose that the police should come between me and one whom I am delighted to honour. This is a lucky morning for you, Mr. Richard Hannay."

As he spoke his eyelids seemed to tremble and to fall a little over his keen grey eyes. In a flash the phrase of Scudder's came back to me, when he had described the man he most dreaded in the world. He had said that he "could hood his eyes like a hawk." Then I saw that I had walked straight into the enemy's headquarters.

My first impulse was to throttle the old ruffian and make for the open air. He seemed to anticipate my intention, for he smiled gently, and nodded to the door behind me. I turned, and saw two men-servants who had me covered with pistols.

He knew my name, but he had never seen me before. And as the reflection darted across my mind I saw a slender chance.

"I don't know what you mean," I said roughly. "And who are you calling Richard Hannay? My name's Ainslie."

"So?" he said, still smiling. "But of course you have others. We won't quarrel about a name."

I was pulling myself together now, and I reflected that my garb, lacking coat and waistcoat and collar, would at any rate not betray me. I put on my surliest face and shrugged my shoulders.

"I suppose you're going to give me up after all, and I call it a damned dirty trick. My God, I wish I had never seen that cursed motor-car! Here's the money and be damned to you," and I flung four sovereigns on the table.

He opened his eyes a little. "Oh no, I shall not give you up. My friends and I will have a little private settlement with you, that is all. You know a little too much, Mr. Hannay. You are a clever actor, but not quite clever enough."

He spoke with assurance, but I could see the dawning of a doubt in his mind.

"Oh, for God's sake stop jawing," I cried. "Everything's against me. I haven't had a bit of luck since I came on shore at Leith. What's the harm in a poor devil with an empty stomach picking up some money he finds in a bust-up motor-car? That's all I done, and for that I've been chivvied for two days by those blasted bobbies over those blasted hills. I tell you I'm fair sick of it. You can do what you like, old boy! Ned Ainslie's got no fight left in him."

I could see that the doubt was gaining.

"Will you oblige me with the story of your recent doings?" he asked.

"I can't, guv'nor," I said in a real beggar's whine. "I've not had a bite to eat for two days. Give me a mouthful of food, and then you'll hear God's truth."

I must have showed my hunger in my face, for he signalled to one of the men in the doorway. A bit of cold pie was brought and a glass of beer, and I wolfed them down like a pig—or rather, like Ned Ainslie, for I was keeping up my character. In the middle of my meal he spoke suddenly to me in German, but I turned on him a face as blank as a stone wall.

Then I told him my story—how I had come off an Archangel ship at Leith a week ago, and was making my way overland to my brother at Wigtown. I had run short of cash—I hinted vaguely at a spree—and I was pretty well on my uppers when I had come on a hole in a hedge, and, looking through, had seen a big motor-car lying in the burn. I had poked about to see what had happened, and had found three sovereigns lying on the seat and one on the floor. There was nobody there or any sign of an owner, so I had pocketed the cash. But somehow the law had got after me. When I had tried to change a sovereign in a baker's shop, the woman had cried on the police, and a little later, when I was washing my face in a burn, I had been nearly gripped, and had only got away by leaving my coat and waistcoat behind me.

"They can have the money back," I cried, "for a fat lot of good it's done me. Those perishers are all down on a poor man. Now, if it had been you, guv'nor, that had found the quids, nobody would have troubled you."

"You're a good liar, Hannay," he said.

I flew into a rage. "Stop fooling, damn you! I tell you my name's Ainslie, and I never heard of anyone called Hannay in my born days. I'd sooner have the police than you with your Hannays and your monkey-faced pistol tricks . . . No, guv'nor, I beg pardon, I don't mean that. I'm much obliged to you for the grub, and I'll thank you to let me go now the coast's clear."

It was obvious that he was badly puzzled. You see he had never seen me, and my appearance must have altered considerably from my photographs, if he had got one of them. I was pretty smart and well dressed in London, and now I was a regular tramp.

"I do not propose to let you go. If you are what you say you are, you will soon have a chance of clearing yourself. If you are what I believe you are, I do not think you will see the light much longer."

He rang a bell, and a third servant appeared from the veranda.

"I want the Lanchester in five minutes," he said. "There will be three to luncheon."

Then he looked steadily at me, and that was the hardest ordeal of all.

There was something weird and devilish in those eyes, cold, malignant, unearthly, and most hellishly clever. They fascinated me like the bright eyes of a snake. I had a strong impulse to throw myself on his mercy and offer to join his side, and if you consider the way I felt about the whole thing you will see that that impulse must have been purely physical, the weakness of a brain mesmerized and mastered by a stronger spirit. But I managed to stick it out and even to grin.

"You'll know me next time, guv'nor," I said.

"Karl," he spoke in German to one of the men in the doorway, "you will put this fellow in the storeroom till I return, and you will be answerable to me for his keeping."

I was marched out of the room with a pistol at each ear.

The storeroom was a damp chamber in what had been the old farmhouse. There was no carpet on the uneven floor, and nothing to sit down on but a school form. It was black as pitch, for the windows were heavily shuttered. I made out by groping that the walls were lined with boxes and barrels and sacks of some heavy stuff. The whole place smelt of mould and disuse. My gaolers turned the key in the door, and I could hear them shifting their feet as they stood on guard outside.

I sat down in that chilly darkness in a very miserable frame of mind. The old boy had gone off in a motor to collect the two ruffians who had interviewed me yesterday. Now, they had seen me as the roadman, and they would remember me, for I was in the same rig. What was a roadman doing twenty miles from his beat, pursued by the police? A question or two would put them on the track. Probably they had seen Mr. Turnbull, probably Marmie too; most likely they could link me up with Sir Harry, and then the whole thing would be crystal clear. What chance had I in this moorland house with three desperadoes and their armed servants?

I began to think wistfully of the police, now plodding over the hills after my wraith. They at any rate were fellow-countrymen and honest men, and their tender mercies would be kinder than these ghoulish aliens. But they wouldn't have listened to me. That old devil with the eyelids had not taken long to get rid of them. I thought he probably had some kind of graft with the constabulary. Most likely he had letters from Cabinet Ministers saying he was to be given every facility for plotting against Britain. That's the sort of owlish way we run our politics in this jolly old country.

The three would be back for lunch, so I hadn't more than a couple of hours to wait. It was simply waiting on destruction, for I could see no way out of this mess. I wished that I had Scudder's courage, for I am free to confess I didn't feel any great fortitude. The only thing that kept me going was that I was pretty furious. It made me boil with rage to think of those three spies getting the pull on me like this. I hoped that at any rate I might be able to twist one of their necks before they downed me.

The more I thought of it the angrier I grew, and I had to get up and move about the room. I tried the shutters, but they were the kind that lock with a key, and I couldn't move them. From the outside came the faint clucking of hens in the warm sun. Then I groped among the sacks and boxes. I couldn't open the latter, and the sacks seemed to be full of things like dog-biscuits that smelt of cinnamon. But, as I circumnavigated the room, I found a handle in the wall which seemed worth investigating.

It was the door of a wall cupboard—what they call a "press" in Scotland—and it was locked. I shook it, and it seemed rather flimsy. For want of something better to do I put out my strength on that door, getting some purchase on the handle by looping my braces round it. Presently the thing gave with a crash which I thought would bring in my warders to inquire. I waited for a bit, and then started to explore the cupboard shelves.

There was a multitude of queer things there. I found an odd vesta or two in my trouser pockets and struck a light. It was out in a second, but it showed me one thing. There was a little stock of electric torches on one shelf. I picked up one, and found it was in working order.

With the torch to help me I investigated further. There were bottles and cases of queer-smelling stuffs, chemicals no doubt for experiments, and there were coils of fine copper wire and yanks and yanks of thin oiled silk. There was a box of detonators, and a lot of cord for fuses. Then away at the back of the shelf I found a stout brown cardboard box, and inside it a wooden case. I managed to wrench it open, and within lay half a dozen little grey bricks, each a couple of inches square.

I took up one, and found that it crumbled easily in my hand. Then I smelt it and put my tongue to it. After that I sat down to think. I hadn't been a mining engineer for nothing, and I knew lentonite when I saw it.

With one of these bricks I could blow the house to smithereens. I had used the stuff in Rhodesia and knew its power. But the trouble was that my knowledge wasn't exact. I had forgotten the proper charge and the right way of preparing it, and I wasn't sure about the timing. I had only a vague notion, too, as to its power, for though I had used it I had not handled it with my own fingers.

But it was a chance, the only possible chance. It was a mighty risk, but against it was an absolute black certainty. If I used it the odds were, as I reckoned, about five to one in favour of my blowing myself into the tree-tops; but if I didn't I should very likely be occupying a six-foot hole in the garden by the evening. That was the way I had to look at it. The prospect was pretty dark either way, but anyhow there was a chance, both for myself and for my country.

The remembrance of little Scudder decided me. It was about the beastliest moment of my life, for I'm no good at these cold-blooded resolutions. Still I managed to rake up the pluck to set my teeth and choke back the horrid doubts that flooded in on me. I simply shut off my mind and pretended I was doing an experiment as simple as Guy Fawkes fireworks.

I got a detonator, and fixed it to a couple of feet of fuse. Then I took a quarter of a lentonite brick, and buried it near the door below one of the sacks in a crack of the floor, fixing the detonator in it. For all I knew half those boxes might be dynamite. If the cupboard held such deadly explosives, why not the boxes? In that case there would be a glorious skyward journey for me and the German servants and about an acre of surrounding country. There was also the risk that the detonation might set off the other bricks in the cupboard, for I had forgotten most that I knew about lentonite. But it didn't do to begin thinking about the possibilities. The odds were horrible, but I had to take them.

I ensconced myself just below the sill of the window, and lit the fuse. Then I waited for a moment or two. There was dead silence—only a shuffle of heavy boots in the passage, and the peaceful cluck of hens from the warm out-of-doors. I commended my soul to my Maker, and wondered where I would be in five seconds . . .

A great wave of heat seemed to surge upwards from the floor, and hang for a blistering instant in the air. Then the wall opposite me flashed into a golden yellow and dissolved with a rending thunder that hammered my brain into a pulp. Something dropped on me, catching the point of my left shoulder.

And then I think I became unconscious.

My stupor can scarcely have lasted beyond a few seconds. I felt myself being choked by thick yellow fumes, and struggled out of the debris to my feet. Somewhere behind me I felt fresh air. The jambs of the window had fallen, and through the ragged rent the smoke was pouring out to the summer noon. I stepped over the broken lintel, and found myself standing in a yard in a dense and acrid fog. I felt very sick and ill, but I could move my limbs, and I staggered blindly forward away from the house.

A small mill-lade ran in a wooden aqueduct at the other side of the yard, and into this I fell. The cool water revived me, and

I had just enough wits left to think of escape. I squirmed up the lade among the slippery green slime till I reached the mill-wheel. Then I wriggled through the axle hole into the old mill and tumbled on to a bed of chaff. A nail caught the seat of my trousers, and I left a wisp of heather-mixture behind me.

The mill had been long out of use. The ladders were rotten with age, and in the loft the rats had gnawed great holes in the floor. Nausea shook me, and a wheel in my head kept turning, while my left shoulder and arm seemed to be stricken with the palsy. I looked out of the window and saw a fog still hanging over the house and smoke escaping from an upper window. Please God I had set the place on fire, for I could hear confused cries coming from the other side.

But I had no time to linger, since this mill was obviously a bad hiding-place. Anyone looking for me would naturally follow the lade, and I made certain the search would begin as soon as they found that my body was not in the storeroom. From another window I saw that on the far side of the mill stood an old stone dovecot. If I could get there without leaving tracks I might find a hiding-place, for I argued that my enemies, if they thought I could move, would conclude I had made for open country, and would go seeking me on the moor.

I crawled down the broken ladder, scattering chaff behind me to cover my footsteps. I did the same on the mill floor, and on the threshold where the door hung on broken hinges. Peeping out, I saw that between me and the dovecot was a piece of bare cobbled ground, where no footmarks would show. Also it was mercifully hid by the mill buildings from any view from the house. I slipped across the space, got to the back of the dovecot and prospected a way of ascent.

That was one of the hardest jobs I ever took on. My shoulder and arm ached like hell, and I was so sick and giddy that I was always on the verge of falling. But I managed it somehow. By the use of out-jutting stones and gaps in the masonry and a tough ivy root I got to the top in the end. There was a little parapet behind which I found space to lie down. Then I proceeded to go off into an old-fashioned swoon.

I woke with a burning head and the sun glaring in my face. For a long time I lay motionless, for those horrible fumes seemed to have loosened my joints and dulled my brain. Sounds came to me from the house—men speaking throatily and the throbbing of a stationary car. There was a little gap in the parapet to which I wriggled, and from which I had some sort of prospect of the yard. I saw figures come out—a servant with his head bound up, and then a younger man in knickerbockers. They were looking for something, and moved towards the mill. Then one of them caught sight of the wisp of cloth on the nail, and cried out to the other. They both went back to the house, and brought two more to look at it. I saw the rotund figure of my late captor, and I thought I made out the man with the lisp. I noticed that all had pistols.

For half an hour they ransacked the mill. I could hear them kicking over the barrels and pulling up the rotten planking. Then they came outside, and stood just below the dovecot arguing fiercely. The servant with the bandage was being soundly rated. I heard them fiddling with the door of the dovecote and for one horrid moment I fancied they were coming up. Then they thought better of it, and went back to the house.

All that long blistering afternoon I lay baking on the rooftop. Thirst was my chief torment. My tongue was like a stick, and to make it worse I could hear the cool drip of water from the mill-lade. I watched the course of the little stream as it came in from the moor, and my fancy followed it to the top of the glen, where it must issue from an icy fountain fringed with cool ferns and mosses. I would have given a thousand pounds to plunge my face into that.

I had a fine prospect of the whole ring of moorland. I saw the car speed away with two occupants, and a man on a hill pony riding east. I judged they were looking for me, and I wished them joy of their quest.

But I saw something else more interesting. The house stood almost on the summit of a swell of moorland which crowned a sort of plateau, and there was no higher point nearer than the big hills six miles off. The actual summit, as I have mentioned, was a biggish clump of trees—firs mostly, with a few ashes and beeches. On the dovecot I was almost on a level with the tree-tops, and could see what lay beyond. The wood was not solid, but only a ring, and inside was an oval of green turf, for all the world like a big cricket-field.

I didn't take long to guess what it was. It was an aerodrome, and a secret one. The place had been most cunningly chosen. For suppose anyone were watching an aeroplane descending here, he would think it had gone over the hill beyond the trees. As the place was on the top of a rise in the midst of a big amphitheatre, any observer from any direction would conclude it had passed out of view behind the hill. Only a man very close at hand would realize that the aeroplane had not gone over but had descended in the midst of the wood. An observer with a telescope on one of the higher hills might have discovered the truth, but only herds went there, and herds do not carry spy-glasses. When I looked from the dovecot I could see far away a blue line which I knew was the sea, and I grew furious to think that our enemies had this secret conning-tower to rake our waterways.

Then I reflected that if that aeroplane came back the chances were ten to one that I would be discovered. So through the afternoon I lay and prayed for the coming of darkness, and glad I was when the sun went down over the big western hills and the twilight haze crept over the moor. The aeroplane was late. The gloaming was far advanced when I heard the beat of wings and saw it volplaning downward to its home in the wood. Lights twinkled for a bit and there was much coming and going from the house. Then the dark fell, and silence.

Thank God it was a black night. The moon was well on its last quarter and would not rise till late. My thirst was too great to allow me to tarry, so about nine o'clock, so far as I could judge, I started to descend. It wasn't easy, and half-way down I heard the back door of the house open, and saw the gleam of a lantern against the mill wall. For some agonizing minutes I hung by the ivy and prayed that whoever it was would not come round by the dovecot. Then the light disappeared, and I dropped as softly as I could on to the hard soil of the yard.

I crawled on my belly in the lee of a stone dyke till I reached the fringe of trees which surrounded the house. If I had known how to do it I would have tried to put that aeroplane out of action, but I realized that any attempt would probably be futile. I was pretty certain that there would be some kind of defence round the house, so I went through the wood on hands and knees, feeling carefully every inch before me. It was as well, for presently I came on a wire about two feet from the ground. If I had tripped over that, it would doubtless have rung some bell in the house and I would have been captured.

A hundred yards farther on I found another wire cunningly placed on the edge of a small stream. Beyond that lay the moor, and in five minutes I was deep in bracken and heather. Soon I was round the shoulder of the rise, in the little glen from which the mill-lade flowed. Ten minutes later my face was in the spring, and I was soaking down pints of the blessed water.

But I did not stop till I had put half a dozen miles between me and that accursed dwelling.

7. The Dry-Fly Fisherman

I sat down on a hill-top and took stock of my position. I wasn't feeling very happy, for my natural thankfulness at my escape was clouded by my severe bodily discomfort. Those lentonite fumes had fairly poisoned me, and the baking hours on the dovecot hadn't helped matters. I had a crushing headache, and felt as sick as a cat. Also my shoulder was in a bad way. At first I thought it was only a bruise, but it seemed to be swelling, and I had no use of my left arm.

My plan was to seek Mr. Turnbull's cottage, recover my garments, and especially Scudder's note-book, and then make for the main line and get back to the south. It seemed to me that the sooner I got in touch with the Foreign Office man, Sir Walter Bullivant, the better. I didn't see how I could get more proof than I had got already. He must just take or leave my story, and anyway, with him I would be in better hands than those devilish Germans. I had begun to feel quite kindly towards the British police.

It was a wonderful starry night, and I had not much difficulty about the road. Sir Harry's map had given me the lie of the land, and all I had to do was to steer a point or two west of south-west to come to the stream where I had met the roadman. In all these travels I never knew the names of the places, but I believe this stream was no less than the upper waters of the river Tweed. I calculated I must be about eighteen miles distant, and that meant I could not get there before morning. So I must lie up a day somewhere, for I was too outrageous a figure to be seen in the sunlight. I had neither coat, waistcoat, collar, nor hat, my trousers were badly torn, and my face and hands were black with the explosion. I daresay I had other beauties, for my eyes felt as if they were furiously bloodshot. Altogether I was no spectacle for God-fearing citizens to see on a highroad.

Very soon after daybreak I made an attempt to clean myself in a hill burn, and then approached a herd's cottage, for I was feeling the need of food. The herd was away from home, and his wife was alone, with no neighbour for five miles. She was a decent old body, and a plucky one, for though she got a fright when she saw me, she had an axe handy, and would have used it on any evil-doer. I told her that I had had a fall—I didn't say how—and she saw by my looks that I was pretty sick. Like a true Samaritan she asked no questions, but gave me a bowl of milk with a dash of whisky in it, and let me sit for a little by her kitchen fire. She would have bathed my shoulder, but it ached so badly that I would not let her touch it.

I don't know what she took me for—a repentant burglar, perhaps; for when I wanted to pay her for the milk and tendered a sovereign which was the smallest coin I had, she shook her head and said something about "giving it to them that had a right to it." At this I protested so strongly that I think she believed me honest, for she took the money and gave me a warm new plaid for it, and an old hat of her man's. She showed me how to wrap the plaid around my shoulders, and when I left that cottage I was the living image of the kind of Scotsman you see in the illustrations to Burns's poems. But at any rate I was more or less clad.

It was as well, for the weather changed before midday to a thick drizzle of rain. I found shelter below an overhanging rock in the crook of a burn, where a drift of dead brackens made a tolerable bed. There I managed to sleep till nightfall, waking very cramped and wretched, with my shoulder gnawing like a toothache. I ate the oatcake and cheese the old wife had given me and set out again just before the darkening.

I pass over the miseries of that night among the wet hills. There were no stars to steer by, and I had to do the best I could from my memory of the map. Twice I lost my way, and I had some nasty falls into peat-bogs. I had only about ten miles to go as the crow flies, but my mistakes made it nearer twenty. The last bit was completed with set teeth and a very light and dizzy head. But I managed it, and in the early dawn I was knocking at Mr. Turnbull's door. The mist lay close and thick, and from the cottage I could not see the highroad.

Mr. Turnbull himself opened to me—sober and something more than sober. He was primly dressed in an ancient but well-tended suit of black; he had been shaved not later than the night before; he wore a linen collar; and in his left hand he carried a pocket Bible. At first he did not recognize me.

"Whae are ye that comes stravaigin' here on the Sabbath mornin'?" he asked.

I had lost all count of the days. So the Sabbath was the reason for this strange decorum.

My head was swimming so wildly that I could not frame a coherent answer. But he recognized me, and he saw that I was ill.

"Hae ye got my specs?" he asked.

I fetched them out of my trouser pocket and gave him them.

"Ye'll hae come for your jaicket and westcoat," he said. "Come in-bye. Losh, man, ye're terrible dune i' the legs. Haud up till I get ye to a chair."

I perceived I was in for a bout of malaria. I had a good deal of fever in my bones, and the wet night had brought it out, while my shoulder and the effects of the fumes combined to make me feel pretty bad. Before I knew, Mr. Turnbull was helping me off with my clothes, and putting me to bed in one of the two cupboards that lined the kitchen walls.

He was a true friend in need, that old roadman. His wife was dead years ago, and since his daughter's marriage he lived alone.

For the better part of ten days he did all the rough nursing I needed. I simply wanted to be left in peace while the fever took its course, and when my skin was cool again I found that the bout had more or less cured my shoulder. But it was a baddish go, and though I was out of bed in five days, it took me some time to get my legs again.

He went out each morning, leaving me milk for the day, and locking the door behind him; and came in in the evening to sit silent in the chimney corner. Not a soul came near the place. When I was getting better, he never bothered me with a question. Several times he fetched me a two days' old Scotsman, and I noticed that the interest in the Portland Place murder seemed to have died down. There was no mention of it, and I could find very little about anything except a thing called the General Assembly—some ecclesiastical spree, I gathered.

One day he produced my belt from a lockfast drawer. "There's a terrible heap o' siller in't," he said. "Ye'd better coont it to see it's a' there."

He never even sought my name. I asked him if anybody had been around making inquiries subsequent to my spell at the road-making.

"Ay, there was a man in a motor-cawr. He speired whae had ta'en my place that day, and I let on I thocht him daft. But he keepit on at me, and syne I said he maun be thinkin' o' my gude-brither frae the Cleuch that whiles lent me a haun'. He was a wersh-lookin' sowl, and I couldna understand the half o' his English tongue."

I was getting restless those last days, and as soon as I felt myself fit I decided to be off. That was not till the twelfth day of June, and as luck would have it a drover went past that morning taking some cattle to Moffat. He was a man named Hislop, a friend of Turnbull's, and he came in to his breakfast with us and offered to take me with him.

I made Turnbull accept five pounds for my lodging, and a hard job I had of it. There never was a more independent being. He grew positively rude when I pressed him, and shy and red, and took the money at last without a thank you. When I told him how much I owed him, he grunted something about "ae guid turn deservin' anitherv" You would have thought from our leave-taking that we had parted in disgust.

Hislop was a cheery soul, who chattered all the way over the pass and down the sunny vale of Annan. I talked of Galloway markets and sheep prices, and he made up his mind I was a "pack-shepherd" from those parts—whatever that may be. My plaid and my old hat, as I have said, gave me a fine theatrical Scots look. But driving cattle is a mortally slow job, and we took the better part of the day to cover a dozen miles.

If I had not had such an anxious heart I would have enjoyed that time. It was shining blue weather, with a constantly changing prospect of brown hills and far green meadows, and a continual sound of larks and curlews and falling streams. But I had no mind for the summer, and little for Hislop's conversation, for as the fateful fifteenth of June drew near I was overweighed with the hopeless difficulties of my enterprise.

I got some dinner in a humble Moffat public-house, and walked the two miles to the junction on the main line. The night express for the south was not due till near midnight, and to fill up the time I went up on the hillside and fell asleep, for the walk had tired me. I all but slept too long, and had to run to the station and catch the train with two minutes to spare. The feel of the hard third-class cushions and the smell of stale tobacco cheered me up wonderfully. At any rate, I felt now that I was getting to grips with my job.

I was decanted at Crewe in the small hours and had to wait till six to get a train for Birmingham. In the afternoon I got to Reading, and changed into a local train which journeyed into the deeps of Berkshire. Presently I was in a land of lush water-meadows and slow reedy streams. About eight o'clock in the evening, a weary and travel-stained being—a cross between a farm-labourer and a vet—with a checked black-and-white plaid over his arm (for I did not dare to wear it south of the Border), descended at the little station of Artinswell. There were several people on the platform, and I thought I had better wait to ask my way till I was clear of the place.

The road led through a wood of great beeches and then into a shallow valley, with the green backs of downs peeping over the distant trees. After Scotland the air smelt heavy and flat, but infinitely sweet, for the limes and chestnuts and lilac bushes were domes of blossom. Presently I came to a bridge, below which a clear slow stream flowed between snowy beds of water-buttercups. A little above it was a mill; and the lasher made a pleasant cool sound in the scented dusk. Somehow the place soothed me and put me at my ease. I fell to whistling as I looked into the green depths, and the tune which came to my lips was "Annie Laurie."

A fisherman came up from the waterside, and as he neared me he too began to whistle. The tune was infectious, for he followed my suit. He was a huge man in untidy old flannels and a wide-brimmed hat, with a canvas bag slung on his shoulder. He nodded to me, and I thought I had never seen a shrewder or better-tempered face. He leaned his delicate ten-foot split-cane rod against the bridge, and looked with me at the water.

"Clear, isn't it?" he said pleasantly. "I back our Kennet any day against the Test. Look at that big fellow. Four pounds if he's an ounce. But the evening rise is over and you can't tempt 'em."

"I don't see him," said I.

"Look! There! A yard from the reeds just above that stickle."

"I've got him now. You might swear he was a black stone."

"So," he said, and whistled another bar of "Annie Laurie."

"Twisdon's the name, isn't it?" he said over his shoulder, his eyes still fixed on the stream.

"No," I said. "I mean to say, Yes." I had forgotten all about my alias.

"It's a wise conspirator that knows his own name," he observed, grinning broadly at a moor-hen that emerged from the bridge's shadow.

I stood up and looked at him, at the square, cleft jaw and broad, lined brow and the firm folds of cheek, and began to think that here at last was an ally worth having. His whimsical blue eyes seemed to go very deep.

Suddenly he frowned. "I call it disgraceful," he said, raising his voice. "Disgraceful that an able-bodied man like you should dare to beg. You can get a meal from my kitchen, but you'll get no money from me."

A dog-cart was passing, driven by a young man who raised

his whip to salute the fisherman. When he had gone, he picked up his rod.

"That's my house," he said, pointing to a white gate a hundred yards on. "Wait five minutes and then go round to the back door." And with that he left me.

I did as I was bidden. I found a pretty cottage with a lawn running down to the stream, and a perfect jungle of guelder-rose and lilac flanking the path. The back door stood open, and a grave butler was awaiting me.

"Come this way, sir," he said, and he led me along a passage and up a back staircase to a pleasant bedroom looking towards the river. There I found a complete outfit laid out for me—dress clothes with all the fixings, a brown flannel suit, shirts, collars, ties, shaving things and hair-brushes, even a pair of patent shoes. "Sir Walter thought as how Mr. Reggie's things would fit you, sir," said the butler. "He keeps some clothes 'ere, for he comes regular on the week-ends. There's a bathroom next door, and I've prepared a 'ot bath. Dinner in 'alf an hour, sir. You'll 'ear the gong."

The grave being withdrew, and I sat down in a chintz-covered easy-chair and gaped. It was like a pantomime, to come suddenly out of beggardom into this orderly comfort. Obviously Sir Walter believed in me, though why he did I could not guess. I looked at myself in the mirror and saw a wild, haggard brown fellow, with a fortnight's ragged beard, and dust in ears and eyes, collarless, vulgarly shirted, with shapeless old tweed clothes and boots that had not been cleaned for the better part of a month. I made a fine tramp and a fair drover; and here I was ushered by a prim butler into this temple of gracious ease. And the best of it was that they did not even know my name.

I resolved not to puzzle my head but to take the gifts the gods had provided. I shaved and bathed luxuriously, and got into the dress clothes and clean crackling shirt, which fitted me not so badly. By the time I had finished the looking-glass showed a not unpersonable young man.

Sir Walter awaited me in a dusky dining-room where a little round table was lit with silver candles. The sight of him—so respectable and established and secure, the embodiment of law and government and all the conventions—took me aback and made me feel an interloper. He couldn't know the truth about me, or he wouldn't treat me like this. I simply could not accept his hospitality on false pretences.

"I'm more obliged to you than I can say, but I'm bound to make things clear," I said. "I'm an innocent man, but I'm wanted by the police. I've got to tell you this, and I won't be surprised if you kick me out."

He smiled. "That's all right. Don't let that interfere with your appetite. We can talk about these things after dinner." I never ate a meal with greater relish, for I had had nothing all day but railway sandwiches. Sir Walter did me proud, for we drank a good champagne and had some uncommon fine port afterwards. It made me almost hysterical to be sitting there, waited on by a footman and a sleek butler, and remember that I had been living for three weeks like a brigand, with every man's hand against me. I told Sir Walter about tiger-fish in the Zambesi that bite off your fingers if you give them a chance, and we discussed sport up and down the globe, for he had hunted a bit in his day.

We went to his study for coffee, a jolly room full of books and trophies and untidiness and comfort. I made up my mind that if ever I got rid of this business and had a house of my own, I would create just such a room. Then when the coffee-cups were cleared away, and we had got our cigars alight, my host swung his long legs over the side of his chair and bade me get started with my yarn.

"I've obeyed Harry's instructions," he said, "and the bribe he offered me was that you would tell me something to wake me up. I'm ready, Mr. Hannay."

I noticed with a start that he called me by my proper name.

I began at the very beginning. I told of my boredom in

London, and the night I had come back to find Scudder gibbering on my doorstep. I told him all Scudder had told me about Karolides and the Foreign Office conference, and that made him purse his lips and grin.

Then I got to the murder, and he grew solemn again. He heard all about the milkman and my time in Galloway, and my deciphering Scudder's notes at the inn.

"You've got them here?" he asked sharply, and drew a long breath when I whipped the little book from my pocket.

I said nothing of the contents. Then I described my meeting with Sir Harry, and the speeches at the hall. At that he laughed uproariously.

"Harry talked dashed nonsense, did he? I quite believe it. He's as good a chap as ever breathed, but his idiot of an uncle has stuffed his head with maggots. Go on, Mr. Hannay."

My day as roadman excited him a bit. He made me describe the two fellows in the car very closely, and seemed to be raking back in his memory. He grew merry again when he heard of the fate of that ass Jopley.

But the old man in the moorland house solemnized him. Again I had to describe every detail of his appearance.

"Bland and bald-headed and hooded his eyes like a bird . . . He sounds a sinister wild-fowl! And you dynamited his hermitage, after he had saved you from the police. Spirited piece of work, that!" Presently I reached the end of my wanderings. He got up slowly, and looked down at me from the hearthrug.

"You may dismiss the police from your mind," he said. "You're in no danger from the law of this land."

"Great Scot!" I cried. "Have they got the murderer?"

"No. But for the last fortnight they have dropped you from the list of possibles."

"Why?" I asked in amazement.

"Principally because I received a letter from Scudder. I knew something of the man, and he did several jobs for me. He was half crank, half genius, but he was wholly honest. The trouble about him was his partiality for playing a lone hand. That made him pretty well useless in any Secret Service—a pity, for he had uncommon gifts. I think he was the bravest man in the world, for he was always shivering with fright, and yet nothing would choke him off. I had a letter from him on the 31st of May."

"But he had been dead a week by then."

"The letter was written and posted on the 23rd. He evidently did not anticipate an immediate decease. His communications usually took a week to reach me, for they were sent under cover to Spain and then to Newcastle. He had a mania, you know, for concealing his tracks."

"What did he say?" I stammered.

"Nothing. Merely that he was in danger, but had found shelter with a good friend, and that I would hear from him before the 15th of June. He gave me no address, but said he was living near Portland Place. I think his object was to clear you if anything happened. When I got it I went to Scotland Yard, went over the details of the inquest, and concluded that you were the friend. We made inquiries about you, Mr. Hannay, and found you were respectable. I thought I knew the motives for your disappearance—not only the police, the other one too— and when I got Harry's scrawl I guessed at the rest. I have been expecting you any time this past week."

You can imagine what a load this took off my mind. I felt a free man once more, for I was now up against my country's enemies only, and not my country's law.

"Now let us have the little note-book," said Sir Walter.

It took us a good hour to work through it. I explained the cypher, and he was jolly quick at picking it up. He emended my reading of it on several points, but I had been fairly correct, on the whole. His face was very grave before he had finished, and he sat silent for a while.

"I don't know what to make of it," he said at last. "He is

right about one thing—what is going to happen the day after tomorrow. How the devil can it have got known? That is ugly enough in itself. But all this about war and the Black Stone—it reads like some wild melodrama. If only I had more confidence in Scudder's judgement. The trouble about him was that he was too romantic. He had the artistic temperament, and wanted a story to be better than God meant it to be. He had a lot of odd biases, too. Jews, for example, made him see red. Jews and the high finance.

"The Black Stone," he repeated. "Der Schwarze Stein. It's like a penny novelette. And all this stuff about Karolides. That is the weak part of the tale, for I happen to know that the virtuous Karolides is likely to outlast us both. There is no State in Europe that wants him gone. Besides, he has just been playing up to Berlin and Vienna and giving my Chief some uneasy moments. No! Scudder has gone off the track there. Frankly, Hannay, I don't believe that part of his story. There's some nasty business afoot, and he found out too much and lost his life over it. But I am ready to take my oath that it is ordinary spy work. A certain great European Power makes a hobby of her spy system, and her methods are not too particular. Since she pays by piecework her blackguards are not likely to stick at a murder or two. They want our naval dispositions for their collection at the Marina; but they will be pigeon-holed—nothing more."

Just then the butler entered the room.

"There's a trunk-call from London, Sir Walter. It's Mr. 'Eath, and he wants to speak to you personally."

My host went off to the telephone.

He returned in five minutes with a whitish face. "I apologize to the shade of Scudder," he said. "Karolides was shot dead this evening at a few minutes after seven."

8. The Coming of the Black Stone

I came down to breakfast next morning, after eight hours of blessed dreamless sleep, to find Sir Walter decoding a telegram in the midst of muffins and marmalade. His fresh rosiness of yesterday seemed a thought tarnished.

"I had a busy hour on the telephone after you went to bed," he said. "I got my Chief to speak to the First Lord and the Secretary for War, and they are bringing Royer over a day sooner. This wire clinches it. He will be in London at five. Odd that the code word for a Sous-chef d'État Major-General should be 'Porker.'"

He directed me to the hot dishes and went on.

"Not that I think it will do much good. If your friends were clever enough to find out the first arrangement they are clever enough to discover the change. I would give my head to know where the leak is. We believed there were only five men in England who knew about Royer's visit, and you may be certain there were fewer in France, for they manage these things better there."

While I ate he continued to talk, making me to my surprise a present of his full confidence.

"Can the dispositions not be changed?" I asked.

"They could," he said. "But we want to avoid that if possible. They are the result of immense thought, and no alteration would be as good. Besides, on one or two points change is simply impossible. Still, something could be done, I suppose, if it were absolutely necessary. But you see the difficulty, Hannay. Our enemies are not going to be such fools as to pick Royer's pocket or any childish game like that. They know that would mean a row and put us on our guard. Their aim is to get the details without any one of us knowing, so that Royer will go back to Paris in the belief that the whole business is still deadly secret. If they can't do that they fail, for, once we suspect, they know that the whole thing must be altered."

"Then we must stick by the Frenchman's side till he is home again," I said. "If they thought they could get the information in Paris they would try there. It means that they have some deep scheme on foot in London which they reckon is going to win out."

"Royer dines with my Chief, and then comes to my house where four people will see him—Whittaker from the Admiralty, myself, Sir Arthur Drew, and General Winstanley. The First Lord is ill, and has gone to Sheringham. At my house he will get a certain document from Whittaker, and after that he will be motored to Portsmouth where a destroyer will take him to Havre. His journey is too important for the ordinary boat-train. He will never be left unattended for a moment till he is safe on French soil. The same with Whittaker till he meets Royer. That is the best we can do, and it's hard to see how there can be any miscarriage. But I don't mind admitting that I'm horribly nervous. This murder of Karolides will play the deuce in the chancelleries of Europe."

After breakfast he asked me if I could drive a car. "Well, you'll be my chauffeur today and wear Hudson's rig. You're about his size. You have a hand in this business and we are taking no risks. There are desperate men against us, who will not respect the country retreat of an overworked official."

When I first came to London I had bought a car and amused myself with running about the south of England, so I knew something of the geography. I took Sir Walter to town by the Bath Road and made good going. It was a soft breathless June morning, with a promise of sultriness later, but it was delicious enough swinging through the little towns with their freshly watered streets, and past the summer gardens of the Thames valley. I landed Sir Walter at his house in Queen Anne's Gate punctually by half-past eleven. The butler was coming up by train with the luggage.

The first thing he did was to take me round to Scotland Yard. There we saw a prim gentleman, with a clean-shaven, lawyer's face.

"I've brought you the Portland Place murderer," was Sir Walter's introduction.

The reply was a wry smile. "It would have been a welcome present, Bullivant. This, I presume, is Mr. Richard Hannay, who for some days greatly interested my department."

"Mr. Hannay will interest it again. He has much to tell you, but not today. For certain grave reasons his tale must wait for four hours. Then, I can promise you, you will be entertained and possibly edified. I want you to assure Mr. Hannay that he will suffer no further inconvenience."

This assurance was promptly given. "You can take up your life where you left off," I was told. "Your flat, which probably you no longer wish to occupy, is waiting for you, and your man is still there. As you were never publicly accused, we considered that there was no need of a public exculpation. But on that, of course, you must please yourself."

"We may want your assistance later on, MacGillivray," Sir Walter said as we left.

Then he turned me loose.

"Come and see me tomorrow, Hannay. I needn't tell you to keep deadly quiet. If I were you I would go to bed, for you must have considerable arrears of sleep to overtake. You had better lie low, for if one of your Black Stone friends saw you there might be trouble."

I felt curiously at a loose end. At first it was very pleasant to be a free man, able to go where I wanted without fearing anything. I had only been a month under the ban of the law, and it was quite enough for me. I went to the Savoy and ordered very carefully a very good luncheon, and then smoked the best cigar the house could provide. But I was still feeling nervous. When I saw anybody look at me in the lounge, I grew shy, and wondered if they were thinking about the murder.

After that I took a taxi and drove miles away up into North London. I walked back through fields and lines of villas and terraces and then slums and mean streets, and it took me pretty nearly two hours. All the while my restlessness was growing worse. I felt that great things, tremendous things, were happening or about to happen, and I, who was the cog-wheel of the whole business, was out of it. Royer would be landing at Dover, Sir Walter would be making plans with the few people in England who were in the secret, and somewhere in the darkness the Black Stone would be working. I felt the sense of danger and impending calamity, and I had the curious feeling, too, that I alone could avert it, alone could grapple with it. But I was out of the game now. How could it be otherwise? It was not likely that Cabinet Ministers and Admiralty Lords and Generals would admit me to their councils.

I actually began to wish that I could run up against one of my three enemies. That would lead to developments. I felt that I wanted enormously to have a vulgar scrap with those gentry, where I could hit out and flatten something. I was rapidly getting into a very bad temper.

I didn't feel like going back to my flat. That had to be faced some time, but as I still had sufficient money I thought I would put it off till next morning, and go to a hotel for the night.

My irritation lasted through dinner, which I had at a restaurant in Jermyn Street. I was no longer hungry, and let several courses pass untasted. I drank the best part of a bottle of Burgundy, but it did nothing to cheer me. An abominable restlessness had taken possession of me. Here was I, a very ordinary fellow, with no particular brains, and yet I was convinced that somehow I was needed to help this business through—that without me it would all go to blazes. I told myself it was sheer silly conceit, that four or five of the cleverest people living, with all the might of the British Empire at their back, had the job in hand. Yet I couldn't be convinced. It seemed as if a voice kept speaking in my ear, telling me to be up and doing, or I would never sleep again.

The upshot was that about half-past nine I made up my mind to go to Queen Anne's Gate. Very likely I would not be admitted, but it would ease my conscience to try.

I walked down Jermyn Street, and at the corner of Duke Street passed a group of young men. They were in evening dress, had been dining somewhere, and were going on to a music-hall. One of them was Mr. Marmaduke Jopley.

He saw me and stopped short.

"By God, the murderer!" he cried. "Here, you fellows, hold him! That's Hannay, the man who did the Portland Place murder!" He gripped me by the arm, and the others crowded round. I wasn't looking for any trouble, but my ill-temper made me play the fool. A policeman came up, and I should have told him the truth, and, if he didn't believe it, demanded to be taken to Scotland Yard, or for that matter to the nearest police station. But a delay at that moment seemed to me unendurable, and the sight of Marmie's imbecile face was more than I could bear. I let out with my left, and had the satisfaction of seeing him measure his length in the gutter.

Then began an unholy row. They were all on me at once, and the policeman took me in the rear. I got in one or two good blows, for I think, with fair play, I could have licked the lot of them, but the policeman pinned me behind, and one of them got his fingers on my throat.

Through a black cloud of rage I heard the officer of the law asking what was the matter, and Marmie, between his broken teeth, declaring that I was Hannay the murderer.

"Oh, damn it all," I cried, "make the fellow shut up. I advise you to leave me alone, constable. Scotland Yard knows all about me, and you'll get a proper wigging if you interfere with me."

"You've got to come along of me, young man," said the policeman. "I saw you strike that gentleman crool 'ard. You began it too, for he wasn't doing nothing. I seen you. Best go quietly or I'll have to fix you up."

Exasperation and an overwhelming sense that at no cost must I delay gave me the strength of a bull elephant. I fairly wrenched the constable off his feet, floored the man who was gripping my collar, and set off at my best pace down Duke Street. I heard a whistle being blown, and the rush of men behind me.

I have a very fair turn of speed, and that night I had wings. In a jiffy I was in Pall Mall and had turned down towards St. James's Park. I dodged the policeman at the Palace gates, dived through a press of carriages at the entrance to the Mall, and was making for the bridge before my pursuers had crossed the roadway. In the open ways of the Park I put on a spurt. Happily there were few people about and no one tried to stop me. I was staking all on getting to Queen Anne's Gate.

When I entered that quiet thoroughfare it seemed deserted. Sir Walter's house was in the narrow part, and outside it three or four motor-cars were drawn up. I slackened speed some yards off and walked briskly up to the door. If the butler refused me admission, or if he even delayed to open the door, I was done.

He didn't delay. I had scarcely rung before the door opened.

"I must see Sir Walter," I panted. "My business is desperately important."

That butler was a great man. Without moving a muscle he held the door open, and then shut it behind me. "Sir Walter is engaged, sir, and I have orders to admit no one. Perhaps you will wait."

The house was of the old-fashioned kind, with a wide hall and rooms on both sides of it. At the far end was an alcove with a telephone and a couple of chairs, and there the butler offered me a seat.

"See here," I whispered. "There's trouble about and I'm in it. But Sir Walter knows, and I'm working for him. If anyone comes and asks if I am here, tell him a lie."

He nodded, and presently there was a noise of voices in the

street, and a furious ringing at the bell. I never admired a man more than that butler. He opened the door, and with a face like a graven image waited to be questioned. Then he gave them it. He told them whose house it was, and what his orders were, and simply froze them off the doorstep. I could see it all from my alcove, and it was better than any play.

I hadn't waited long till there came another ring at the bell. The butler made no bones about admitting this new visitor.

While he was taking off his coat I saw who it was. You couldn't open a newspaper or a magazine without seeing that face—the grey beard cut like a spade, the firm fighting mouth, the blunt square nose, and the keen blue eyes. I recognized the First Sea Lord, the man, they say, that made the new British Navy.

He passed my alcove and was ushered into a room at the back of the hall. As the door opened I could hear the sound of low voices. It shut, and I was left alone again.

For twenty minutes I sat there, wondering what I was to do next. I was still perfectly convinced that I was wanted, but when or how I had no notion. I kept looking at my watch, and as the time crept on to half-past ten I began to think that the conference must soon end. In a quarter of an hour Royer should be speeding along the road to Portsmouth . . .

Then I heard a bell ring, and the butler appeared. The door of the back room opened, and the First Sea Lord came out. He walked past me, and in passing he glanced in my direction, and for a second we looked each other in the face.

Only for a second, but it was enough to make my heart jump. I had never seen the great man before, and he had never seen me. But in that fraction of time something sprang into his eyes, and that something was recognition. You can't mistake it. It is a flicker, a spark of light, a minute shade of difference which means one thing and one thing only. It came involuntarily, for in a moment it died, and he passed on. In a maze of wild fancies I heard the street door close behind him.

I picked up the telephone book and looked up the number of his house. We were connected at once, and I heard a servant's voice.

"Is his Lordship at home?" I asked.

"His Lordship returned half an hour ago," said the voice, "and has gone to bed. He is not very well tonight. Will you leave a message, sir?"

I rang off and almost tumbled into a chair. My part in this business was not yet ended. It had been a close shave, but I had been in time.

Not a moment could be lost, so I marched boldly to the door of that back room and entered without knocking.

Five surprised faces looked up from a round table. There was Sir Walter, and Drew the War Minister, whom I knew from his photographs. There was a slim elderly man, who was probably Whittaker, the Admiralty official, and there was General Winstanley, conspicuous from the long scar on his forehead. Lastly, there was a short stout man with an iron-grey moustache and bushy eyebrows, who had been arrested in the middle of a sentence.

Sir Walter's face showed surprise and annoyance.

"This is Mr. Hannay, of whom I have spoken to you," he said apologetically to the company. "I'm afraid, Hannay, this visit is ill-timed."

I was getting back my coolness. "That remains to be seen, sir," I said; "but I think it may be in the nick of time. For God's sake, gentlemen, tell me who went out a minute ago?"

"Lord Alloa," Sir Walter said, reddening with anger.

"It was not," I cried; "it was his living image, but it was not Lord Alloa. It was someone who recognized me, someone I have seen in the last month. He had scarcely left the doorstep when I rang up Lord Alloa's house and was told he had come in half an hour before and had gone to bed."

"Who—who—" someone stammered.

"The Black Stone," I cried, and I sat down in the chair so recently vacated and looked round at five badly scared gentlemen.

9. The Thirty-nine Steps

N onsense!" said the official from the Admiralty.

Sir Walter got up and left the room while we looked blankly at the table. He came back in ten minutes with a long face. "I have spoken to Alloa," he said. "Had him out of bed—very grumpy. He went straight home after Mulross's dinner."

"But it's madness," broke in General Winstanley. "Do you mean to tell me that that man came here and sat beside me for the best part of half an hour and that I didn't detect the imposture? Alloa must be out of his mind."

"Don't you see the cleverness of it?" I said. "You were too interested in other things to have any eyes. You took Lord Alloa for granted. If it had been anybody else you might have looked more closely, but it was natural for him to be here, and that put you all to sleep."

Then the Frenchman spoke, very slowly and in good English.

"The young man is right. His psychology is good. Our enemies have not been foolish!"

He bent his wise brows on the assembly.

"I will tell you a tale," he said. "It happened many years ago in Senegal. I was quartered in a remote station, and to pass the time used to go fishing for big barbel in the river. A little Arab mare used to carry my luncheon basket—one of the salted dun breed you got at Timbuctoo in the old days. Well, one morning I had good sport, and the mare was unaccountably restless. I could hear her whinnying and squealing and stamping her feet, and I kept soothing her with my voice while my mind was intent on fish. I could see her all the time, as I thought, out of a corner of my eye, tethered to a tree twenty yards away. After a couple of hours I began to think of food. I collected my fish in a tarpaulin bag, and moved down the stream towards the mare, trolling my line. When I got up to her I flung the tarpaulin on her back—"

He paused and looked round.

"It was the smell that gave me warning. I turned my head and found myself looking at a lion three feet off . . . An old man-eater, that was the terror of the village . . . What was left of the mare, a mass of blood and bones and hide, was behind him."

"What happened?" I asked. I was enough of a hunter to know a true yarn when I heard it.

"I stuffed my fishing-rod into his jaws, and I had a pistol. Also my servants came presently with rifles. But he left his mark on me." He held up a hand which lacked three fingers.

"Consider," he said. "The mare had been dead more than an hour, and the brute had been patiently watching me ever since. I never saw the kill, for I was accustomed to the mare's fretting, and I never marked her absence, for my consciousness of her was only of something tawny, and the lion filled that part. If I could blunder thus, gentlemen, in a land where men's senses are keen, why should we busy preoccupied urban folk not err also?"

Sir Walter nodded. No one was ready to gainsay him.

"But I don't see," went on Winstanley. "Their object was to get these dispositions without our knowing it. Now it only required one of us to mention to Alloa our meeting tonight for the whole fraud to be exposed."

Sir Walter laughed dryly. "The selection of Alloa shows their acumen. Which of us was likely to speak to him about tonight? Or was he likely to open the subject?"

I remembered the First Sea Lord's reputation for taciturnity and shortness of temper.

"The one thing that puzzles me," said the General, "is what good his visit here would do that spy fellow? He could not carry away several pages of figures and strange names in his head."

"That is not difficult," the Frenchman replied. "A good spy is trained to have a photographic memory. Like your own Macaulay. You noticed he said nothing, but went through these papers again and again. I think we may assume that he has every detail stamped on his mind. When I was younger I could do the same trick."

"Well, I suppose there is nothing for it but to change the plans," said Sir Walter ruefully.

Whittaker was looking very glum. "Did you tell Lord Alloa what has happened?" he asked. "No? Well, I can't speak with absolute assurance, but I'm nearly certain we can't make any serious change unless we alter the geography of England."

"Another thing must be said," it was Royer who spoke. "I talked freely when that man was here. I told something of the military plans of my Government. I was permitted to say so much. But that information would be worth many millions to our enemies. No, my friends, I see no other way. The man who came here and his confederates must be taken, and taken at once."

"Good God," I cried, "and we have not a rag of a clue."

"Besides," said Whittaker, "there is the post. By this time the news will be on its way."

"No," said the Frenchman. "You do not understand the habits of the spy. He receives personally his reward, and he delivers personally his intelligence. We in France know something of the breed. There is still a chance, mes amis. These men must cross the sea, and there are ships to be searched and ports to be watched. Believe me, the need is desperate for both France and Britain."

Royer's grave good sense seemed to pull us together. He was the man of action among fumblers. But I saw no hope in any face, and I felt none. Where among the fifty millions of these islands and within a dozen hours were we to lay hands on the three cleverest rogues in Europe?

Then suddenly I had an inspiration.

"Where is Scudder's book?" I cried to Sir Walter. "Quick, man, I remember something in it."

He unlocked the door of a bureau and gave it to me.

I found the place. "Thirty-nine steps," I read, and again, "Thirty-nine steps—I counted them—High tide, 10:17 p.m."

The Admiralty man was looking at me as if he thought I had gone mad.

"Don't you see it's a clue," I shouted. "Scudder knew where these fellows laired—he knew where they were going to leave the country, though he kept the name to himself. Tomorrow was the day, and it was some place where high tide was at 10:17."

"They may have gone tonight," someone said.

"Not they. They have their own snug secret way, and they won't be hurried. I know Germans, and they are mad about working to a plan. Where the devil can I get a book of Tide Tables?"

Whittaker brightened up. "It's a chance," he said. "Let's go over to the Admiralty."

We got into two of the waiting motor-cars—all but Sir Walter, who went off to Scotland Yard—to "mobilize MacGillivray," so he said.

We marched through empty corridors and big bare chambers where the charwomen were busy, till we reached a little room lined with books and maps. A resident clerk was unearthed, who presently fetched from the library the Admiralty Tide Tables. I sat at the desk and the others stood round, for somehow or other I had got charge of this expedition.

It was no good. There were hundreds of entries, and so far as I could see 10:17 might cover fifty places. We had to find some way of narrowing the possibilities.

I took my head in my hands and thought. There must be some way of reading this riddle. What did Scudder mean by steps? I thought of dock steps, but if he had meant that I didn't think he would have mentioned the number. It must be some place where there were several staircases, and one marked out from the others by having thirty-nine steps.

Then I had a sudden thought, and hunted up all the steamer sailings. There was no boat which left for the Continent at 10:17 p.m.

Why was high tide so important? If it was a harbour it must be some little place where the tide mattered, or else it was a heavy-draught boat. But there was no regular steamer sailing at that hour, and somehow I didn't think they would travel by a big boat from a regular harbour. So it must be some little harbour where the tide was important, or perhaps no harbour at all.

But if it was a little port I couldn't see what the steps signified. There were no sets of staircases on any harbour that I had ever seen. It must be some place which a particular staircase identified, and where the tide was full at 10:17. On the whole it seemed to me that the place must be a bit of open coast. But the staircases kept puzzling me.

Then I went back to wider considerations. Whereabouts would a man be likely to leave for Germany, a man in a hurry, who wanted a speedy and a secret passage? Not from any of the big harbours. And not from the Channel or the West Coast or Scotland, for, remember, he was starting from London. I measured the distance on the map, and tried to put myself in the enemy's shoes. I should try for Ostend or Antwerp or Rotterdam, and I should sail from somewhere on the East Coast between Cromer and Dover.

All this was very loose guessing, and I don't pretend it was ingenious or scientific. I wasn't any kind of Sherlock Holmes. But I have always fancied I had a kind of instinct about questions like this. I don't know if I can explain myself, but I used to use my brains as far as they went, and after they came to a blank wall I guessed, and I usually found my guesses pretty right.

So I set out all my conclusions on a bit of Admiralty paper. They ran like this:

Fairly Certain

(1) Place where there are several sets of stairs; one that matters distinguished by having thirty-nine steps.

(2) Full tide at 10:17 p.m. Leaving shore only possible at full tide.

(3) Steps not dock steps, and so place probably not harbour.

(4) No regular night steamer at 10:17. Means of transport must be tramp (unlikely), yacht, or fishing-boat.

There my reasoning stopped. I made another list, which I headed "Guessed," but I was just as sure of the one as the other.

Guessed

(1) Place not harbour but open coast.

(2) Boat small—trawler, yacht, or launch.

(3) Place somewhere on East Coast between Cromer and Dover.

It struck me as odd that I should be sitting at that desk with a Cabinet Minister, a Field-Marshal, two high Government officials, and a French General watching me, while from the scribble of a dead man I was trying to drag a secret which meant life or death for us.

Sir Walter had joined us, and presently MacGillivray arrived. He had sent out instructions to watch the ports and railway stations for the three men whom I had described to Sir Walter. Not that he or anybody else thought that that would do much good.

"Here's the most I can make of it," I said. "We have got to find a place where there are several staircases down to the beach, one of which has thirty-nine steps. I think it's a piece of open coast with biggish cliffs, somewhere between the Wash and the

Channel. Also it's a place where full tide is at 10:17 tomorrow night."

Then an idea struck me. "Is there no Inspector of Coastguards or some fellow like that who knows the East Coast?"

Whittaker said there was, and that he lived in Clapham. He went off in a car to fetch him, and the rest of us sat about the little room and talked of anything that came into our heads. I lit a pipe and went over the whole thing again till my brain grew weary.

About one in the morning the coastguard man arrived. He was a fine old fellow, with the look of a naval officer, and was desperately respectful to the company. I left the War Minister to cross-examine him, for I felt he would think it cheek in me to talk.

"We want you to tell us the places you know on the East Coast where there are cliffs, and where several sets of steps run down to the beach."

He thought for a bit. "What kind of steps do you mean, sir? There are plenty of places with roads cut down through the cliffs, and most roads have a step or two in them. Or do you mean regular staircases—all steps, so to speak?"

Sir Arthur looked towards me. "We mean regular staircases," I said.

He reflected a minute or two. "I don't know that I can think of any. Wait a second. There's a place in Norfolk—Brattlesham— beside a golf-course, where there are a couple of staircases, to let the gentlemen get a lost ball."

"That's not it," I said.

"Then there are plenty of Marine Parades, if that's what you mean. Every seaside resort has them."

I shook my head. "It's got to be more retired than that," I said.

"Well, gentlemen, I can't think of anywhere else. Of course, there's the Ruff—"

"What's that?" I asked.

"The big chalk headland in Kent, close to Bradgate. It's got a lot of villas on the top, and some of the houses have staircases down to a private beach. It's a very high-toned sort of place, and the residents there like to keep by themselves."

I tore open the Tide Tables and found Bradgate. High tide there was at 10:27 p.m. on the 15th of June.

"We're on the scent at last," I cried excitedly. "How can I find out what is the tide at the Ruff?"

"I can tell you that, sir," said the coastguard man. "I once was lent a house there in this very month, and I used to go out at night to the deep-sea fishing. The tide's ten minutes before Bradgate."

I closed the book and looked round at the company.

"If one of those staircases has thirty-nine steps we have solved the mystery, gentlemen," I said. "I want the loan of your car, Sir Walter, and a map of the roads. If Mr. MacGillivray will spare me ten minutes, I think we can prepare something for tomorrow."

It was ridiculous in me to take charge of the business like this, but they didn't seem to mind, and after all I had been in the show from the start. Besides, I was used to rough jobs, and these eminent gentlemen were too clever not to see it. It was General Royer who gave me my commission. "I for one," he said, "am content to leave the matter in Mr. Hannay's hands."

By half-past three I was tearing past the moonlit hedgerows of Kent, with MacGillivray's best man on the seat beside me.

10. Various Parties Converging on the Sea

A pink and blue June morning found me at Bradgate looking from the Griffin Hotel over a smooth sea to the lightship on the Cock sands which seemed the size of a bell-buoy. A couple of miles farther south and much nearer the shore a small destroyer was anchored. Scaife, MacGillivray's man, who had been in the Navy, knew the boat, and told me her name and her commander's, so I sent off a wire to Sir Walter.

After breakfast Scaife got from a house-agent a key for the gates of the staircases on the Ruff. I walked with him along the sands, and sat down in a nook of the cliffs while he investigated the half-dozen of them. I didn't want to be seen, but the place at this hour was quite deserted, and all the time I was on that beach I saw nothing but the seagulls.

It took him more than an hour to do the job, and when I saw him coming towards me, conning a bit of paper, I can tell you my heart was in my mouth. Everything depended, you see, on my guess proving right.

He read aloud the number of steps in the different stairs. "Thirty-four, thirty-five, thirty-nine, forty-two, forty-seven," and "twenty-one" where the cliffs grew lower. I almost got up and shouted.

We hurried back to the town and sent a wire to MacGillivray. I wanted half a dozen men, and I directed them to divide themselves among different specified hotels. Then Scaife set out to prospect the house at the head of the thirty-nine steps.

He came back with news that both puzzled and reassured me. The house was called Trafalgar Lodge, and belonged to an old gentleman called Appleton—a retired stockbroker, the house-agent said. Mr. Appleton was there a good deal in the summer time, and was in residence now—had been for the better part of a week. Scaife could pick up very little information about him, except that he was a decent old fellow, who paid his bills regularly, and was always good for a fiver for a local charity. Then Scaife seemed to have penetrated to the back door of the house, pretending he was an agent for sewing-machines. Only three servants were kept, a cook, a parlour-maid, and a housemaid, and they were just the sort that you would find in a respectable middle-class household. The cook was not the gossiping kind, and had pretty soon shut the door in his face, but Scaife said he was positive she knew nothing. Next door there was a new house building which would give good cover for observation, and the villa on the other side was to let, and its garden was rough and shrubby.

I borrowed Scaife's telescope, and before lunch went for a walk along the Ruff. I kept well behind the rows of villas, and found a good observation point on the edge of the golf-course. There I had a view of the line of turf along the cliff top, with seats placed at intervals, and the little square plots, railed in and planted with bushes, whence the staircases descended to the beach. I saw Trafalgar Lodge very plainly, a red-brick villa with a veranda, a tennis lawn behind, and in front the ordinary seaside flower-garden full of marguerites and scraggy geraniums. There was a flagstaff from which an enormous Union Jack hung limply in the still air.

Presently I observed someone leave the house and saunter along the cliff. When I got my glasses on him I saw it was an old man, wearing white flannel trousers, a blue serge jacket, and a straw hat. He carried field-glasses and a newspaper, and sat down on one of the iron seats and began to read. Sometimes he would lay down the paper and turn his glasses on the sea. He looked for a long time at the destroyer. I watched him for half an hour, till he got up and went back to the house for his luncheon, when I returned to the hotel for mine.

I wasn't feeling very confident. This decent common-place dwelling was not what I had expected. The man might be the bald archaeologist of that horrible moorland farm, or he might not. He was exactly the kind of satisfied old bird you will find in every suburb and every holiday place. If you wanted a type of the perfectly harmless person you would probably pitch on that.

But after lunch, as I sat in the hotel porch, I perked up, for I saw the thing I had hoped for and had dreaded to miss. A yacht came up from the south and dropped anchor pretty well opposite the Ruff. She seemed about a hundred and fifty tons, and I saw she belonged to the Squadron from the white ensign. So Scaife and I went down to the harbour and hired a boatman for an afternoon's fishing.

I spent a warm and peaceful afternoon. We caught between us about twenty pounds of cod and lythe, and out in that dancing blue sea I took a cheerier view of things. Above the white cliffs of the Ruff I saw the green and red of the villas, and especially the great flagstaff of Trafalgar Lodge. About four o'clock, when we had fished enough, I made the boatman row us round the yacht, which lay like a delicate white bird, ready at a moment to flee. Scaife said she must be a fast boat for her build, and that she was pretty heavily engined.

Her name was the Ariadne, as I discovered from the cap of one of the men who was polishing brasswork. I spoke to him, and got an answer in the soft dialect of Essex. Another hand that came along passed me the time of day in an unmistakable English tongue. Our boatman had an argument with one of them about the weather, and for a few minutes we lay on our oars close to the starboard bow.

Then the men suddenly disregarded us and bent their heads to their work as an officer came along the deck. He was a pleasant, clean-looking young fellow, and he put a question to us about our fishing in very good English. But there could be no doubt about him. His close-cropped head and the cut of his collar and tie never came out of England.

That did something to reassure me, but as we rowed back to Bradgate my obstinate doubts would not be dismissed. The thing that worried me was the reflection that my enemies knew that I had got my knowledge from Scudder, and it was Scudder who had given me the clue to this place. If they knew that Scudder had this clue, would they not be certain to change their plans? Too much depended on their success for them to take any risks. The whole question was how much they understood about Scudder's knowledge. I had talked confidently last night about Germans always sticking to a scheme, but if they had any suspicions that I was on their track they would be fools not to cover it. I wondered if the man last night had seen that I recognized him. Somehow I did not think he had, and to that I had clung. But the whole business had never seemed so difficult as that afternoon when by all calculations I should have been rejoicing in assured success.

In the hotel I met the commander of the destroyer, to whom Scaife introduced me, and with whom I had a few words. Then I thought I would put in an hour or two watching Trafalgar Lodge.

I found a place farther up the hill, in the garden of an empty house. From there I had a full view of the court, on which two figures were having a game of tennis. One was the old man, whom I had already seen; the other was a younger fellow, wearing some club colours in the scarf round his middle. They played with tremendous zest, like two city gents who wanted hard exercise to open their pores. You couldn't conceive a more innocent spectacle. They shouted and laughed and stopped for drinks, when a maid brought out two tankards on a salver. I rubbed my eyes and asked myself if I was not the most immortal fool on earth. Mystery and darkness had hung about the men who hunted me over the Scotch moor in aeroplane and motor-car, and notably about that infernal antiquarian. It was easy enough to connect those folk with the knife that pinned Scudder to the floor, and with fell designs on the world's peace. But here were two guileless citizens taking their innocuous exercise, and soon about to go indoors to a humdrum dinner, where they would talk of market prices and the last cricket scores and the gossip of their native Surbiton. I had been making a net to catch vultures and falcons, and lo and behold! two plump thrushes had blundered into it.

Presently a third figure arrived, a young man on a bicycle, with a bag of golf-clubs slung on his back. He strolled round to the tennis lawn and was welcomed riotously by the players. Evidently they were chaffing him, and their chaff sounded horribly English. Then the plump man, mopping his brow with a silk handkerchief, announced that he must have a tub. I heard his very words—"I've got into a proper lather," he said. "This will bring down my weight and my handicap, Bob. I'll take you on tomorrow and give you a stroke a hole." You couldn't find anything much more English than that.

They all went into the house, and left me feeling a precious idiot. I had been barking up the wrong tree this time. These men might be acting; but if they were, where was their audience? They didn't know I was sitting thirty yards off in a rhododendron. It was simply impossible to believe that these three hearty fellows were anything but what they seemed—three ordinary, game-playing, suburban Englishmen, wearisome, if you like, but sordidly innocent.

And yet there were three of them; and one was old, and one was plump, and one was lean and dark; and their house chimed in with Scudder's notes; and half a mile off was lying a steam yacht with at least one German officer. I thought of Karolides lying dead and all Europe trembling on the edge of earthquake, and the men I had left behind me in London who were waiting anxiously for the events of the next hours. There was no doubt that hell was afoot somewhere. The Black Stone had won, and if it survived this June night would bank its winnings.

There seemed only one thing to do—go forward as if I had no doubts, and if I was going to make a fool of myself to do it handsomely. Never in my life have I faced a job with greater disinclination. I would rather in my then mind have walked into a den of anarchists, each with his Browning handy, or faced a charging lion with a popgun, than enter that happy home of three cheerful Englishmen and tell them that their game was up. How they would laugh at me!

But suddenly I remembered a thing I once heard in Rhodesia

from old Peter Pienaar. I have quoted Peter already in this narrative. He was the best scout I ever knew, and before he had turned respectable he had been pretty often on the windy side of the law, when he had been wanted badly by the authorities. Peter once discussed with me the question of disguises, and he had a theory which struck me at the time. He said, barring absolute certainties like fingerprints, mere physical traits were very little use for identification if the fugitive really knew his business. He laughed at things like dyed hair and false beards and such childish follies. The only thing that mattered was what Peter called "atmosphere."

If a man could get into perfectly different surroundings from those in which he had been first observed, and—this is the important part—really play up to these surroundings and behave as if he had never been out of them, he would puzzle the cleverest detectives on earth. And he used to tell a story of how he once borrowed a black coat and went to church and shared the same hymn-book with the man that was looking for him. If that man had seen him in decent company before he would have recognized him; but he had only seen him snuffing the lights in a public-house with a revolver.

The recollection of Peter's talk gave me the first real comfort that I had had that day. Peter had been a wise old bird, and these fellows I was after were about the pick of the aviary. What if they were playing Peter's game? A fool tries to look different: a clever man looks the same and is different.

Again, there was that other maxim of Peter's which had helped me when I had been a roadman. "If you are playing a part, you will never keep it up unless you convince yourself that you are it." That would explain the game of tennis. Those chaps didn't need to act, they just turned a handle and passed into another life, which came as naturally to them as the first. It sounds a platitude, but Peter used to say that it was the big secret of all the famous criminals.

It was now getting on for eight o'clock, and I went back and saw Scaife to give him his instructions. I arranged with him how to place his men, and then I went for a walk, for I didn't feel up to any dinner. I went round the deserted golf-course, and then to a point on the cliffs farther north beyond the line of the villas.

On the little trim newly-made roads I met people in flannels coming back from tennis and the beach, and a coastguard from the wireless station, and donkeys and pierrots padding homewards. Out at sea in the blue dusk I saw lights appear on the Ariadne and on the destroyer away to the south, and beyond the Cock sands the bigger lights of steamers making for the Thames. The whole scene was so peaceful and ordinary that I got more dashed in spirits every second. It took all my resolution to stroll towards Trafalgar Lodge about half-past nine.

On the way I got a piece of solid comfort from the sight of a greyhound that was swinging along at a nursemaid's heels. He reminded me of a dog I used to have in Rhodesia, and of the time when I took him hunting with me in the Pali hills. We were after rhebok, the dun kind, and I recollected how we had followed one beast, and both he and I had clean lost it. A greyhound works by sight, and my eyes are good enough, but that buck simply leaked out of the landscape. Afterwards I found out how it managed it. Against the grey rock of the kopjes it showed no more than a crow against a thundercloud. It didn't need to run away; all it had to do was to stand still and melt into the background.

Suddenly as these memories chased across my brain I thought of my present case and applied the moral. The Black Stone didn't need to bolt. They were quietly absorbed into the landscape. I was on the right track, and I jammed that down in my mind and vowed never to forget it. The last word was with Peter Pienaar.

Scaife's men would be posted now, but there was no sign of a soul. The house stood as open as a market-place for anybody to observe. A three-foot railing separated it from the cliff road; the windows on the ground-floor were all open, and shaded lights and the low sound of voices revealed where the occupants were finishing dinner. Everything was as public and above-board as a charity bazaar. Feeling the greatest fool on earth, I opened the gate and rang the bell.

A man of my sort, who has travelled about the world in rough places, gets on perfectly well with two classes, what you may call the upper and the lower. He understands them and they understand him. I was at home with herds and tramps and roadmen, and I was sufficiently at my ease with people like Sir Walter and the men I had met the night before. I can't explain why, but it is a fact. But what fellows like me don't understand is the great comfortable, satisfied middle-class world, the folk that live in villas and suburbs. He doesn't know how they look at things, he doesn't understand their conventions, and he is as shy of them as of a black mamba. When a trim parlour-maid opened the door, I could hardly find my voice.

I asked for Mr. Appleton, and was ushered in. My plan had been to walk straight into the dining-room, and by a sudden appearance wake in the men that start of recognition which would confirm my theory. But when I found myself in that neat hall the place mastered me. There were the golf-clubs and tennis-rackets, the straw hats and caps, the rows of gloves, the sheaf of walking-sticks, which you will find in ten thousand British homes. A stack of neatly folded coats and waterproofs covered the top of an old oak chest; there was a grandfather clock ticking; and some polished brass warming-pans on the walls, and a barometer, and a print of Chiltern winning the St. Leger. The place was as orthodox as an Anglican church. When the maid asked me for my name I gave it automatically, and was shown into the smoking-room, on the right side of the hall.

That room was even worse. I hadn't time to examine it, but I could see some framed group photographs above the mantelpiece, and I could have sworn they were English public school or college.

I had only one glance, for I managed to pull myself together and go after the maid. But I was too late. She had already entered the dining-room and given my name to her master, and I had missed the chance of seeing how the three took it.

When I walked into the room the old man at the head of the table had risen and turned round to meet me. He was in evening dress—a short coat and black tie, as was the other, whom I called in my own mind the plump one. The third, the dark fellow, wore a blue serge suit and a soft white collar, and the colours of some club or school.

The old man's manner was perfect. "Mr. Hannay?" he said hesitatingly. "Did you wish to see me? One moment, you fellows, and I'll rejoin you. We had better go to the smoking-room."

Though I hadn't an ounce of confidence in me, I forced myself to play the game. I pulled up a chair and sat down on it.

"I think we have met before," I said, "and I guess you know my business."

The light in the room was dim, but so far as I could see their faces, they played the part of mystification very well.

"Maybe, maybe," said the old man. "I haven't a very good memory, but I'm afraid you must tell me your errand, sir, for I really don't know it."

"Well, then," I said, and all the time I seemed to myself to be talking pure foolishness—"I have come to tell you that the game's up. I have a warrant for the arrest of you three gentlemen."

"Arrest," said the old man, and he looked really shocked. "Arrest! Good God, what for?"

"For the murder of Franklin Scudder in London on the 23rd day of last month."

"I never heard the name before," said the old man in a dazed voice.

One of the others spoke up. "That was the Portland Place murder. I read about it. Good heavens, you must be mad, sir! Where do you come from?"

"Scotland Yard," I said.

After that for a minute there was utter silence. The old man was staring at his plate and fumbling with a nut, the very model of innocent bewilderment.

Then the plump one spoke up. He stammered a little, like a man picking his words.

"Don't get flustered, uncle," he said. "It is all a ridiculous mistake; but these things happen sometimes, and we can easily set it right. It won't be hard to prove our innocence. I can show that I was out of the country on the 23rd of May, and Bob was in a nursing home. You were in London, but you can explain what you were doing."

"Right, Percy! Of course that's easy enough. The 23rd! That was the day after Agatha's wedding. Let me see. What was I doing? I came up in the morning from Woking, and lunched at the club with Charlie Symons. Then—oh yes, I dined with the Fishmongers. I remember, for the punch didn't agree with me, and I was seedy next morning. Hang it all, there's the cigar-box I brought back from the dinner." He pointed to an object on the table, and laughed nervously.

"I think, sir," said the young man, addressing me respectfully, "you will see you are mistaken. We want to assist the law like all Englishmen, and we don't want Scotland Yard to be making fools of themselves. That's so, uncle?"

"Certainly, Bob." The old fellow seemed to be recovering his voice. "Certainly, we'll do anything in our power to assist the authorities. But—but this is a bit too much. I can't get over it."

"How Nellie will chuckle," said the plump man. "She always said that you would die of boredom because nothing ever happened to you. And now you've got it thick and strong," and he began to laugh very pleasantly.

"By Jove, yes. Just think of it! What a story to tell at the club. Really, Mr. Hannay, I suppose I should be angry, to show my innocence, but it's too funny! I almost forgive you the fright you gave me! You looked so glum, I thought I might have been walking in my sleep and killing people."

It couldn't be acting, it was too confoundedly genuine. My heart went into my boots, and my first impulse was to apologize and clear out. But I told myself I must see it through, even though I was to be the laughing-stock of Britain. The light from the dinner-table candlesticks was not very good, and to cover my confusion I got up, walked to the door and switched on the electric light. The sudden glare made them blink, and I stood scanning the three faces.

Well, I made nothing of it. One was old and bald, one was stout, one was dark and thin. There was nothing in their appearance to prevent them being the three who had hunted me in Scotland, but there was nothing to identify them. I simply can't explain why I who, as a roadman, had looked into two pairs of eyes, and as Ned Ainslie into another pair, why I, who have a good memory and reasonable powers of observation, could find no satisfaction. They seemed exactly what they professed to be, and I could not have sworn to one of them.

There in that pleasant dining-room, with etchings on the walls, and a picture of an old lady in a bib above the mantelpiece, I could see nothing to connect them with the moorland desperadoes. There was a silver cigarette-box beside me, and I saw that it had been won by Percival Appleton, Esq., of the St. Bede's Club, in a golf tournament. I had to keep a firm hold of Peter Pienaar to prevent myself bolting out of that house.

"Well," said the old man politely, "are you reassured by your scrutiny, sir?"

I couldn't find a word.

"I hope you'll find it consistent with your duty to drop this ridiculous business. I make no complaint, but you'll see how annoying it must be to respectable people."

I shook my head.

"O Lord," said the young man. "This is a bit too thick!"

"Do you propose to march us off to the police station?" asked the plump one. "That might be the best way out of it, but I suppose you won't be content with the local branch. I have the right to ask to see your warrant, but I don't wish to cast any aspersions upon you. You are only doing your duty. But you'll admit it's horribly awkward. What do you propose to do?"

There was nothing to do except to call in my men and have them arrested, or to confess my blunder and clear out. I felt mesmerized by the whole place, by the air of obvious innocence—not innocence merely, but frank honest bewilderment and concern in the three faces.

"Oh, Peter Pienaar," I groaned inwardly, and for a moment I was very near damning myself for a fool and asking their pardon.

"Meantime I vote we have a game of bridge," said the plump one. "It will give Mr. Hannay time to think over things, and you know we have been wanting a fourth player. Do you play, sir?"

I accepted as if it had been an ordinary invitation at the club. The whole business had mesmerized me. We went into the smoking-room where a card-table was set out, and I was offered things to smoke and drink. I took my place at the table in a kind of dream. The window was open and the moon was flooding the cliffs and sea with a great tide of yellow light. There was moonshine, too, in my head. The three had recovered their composure, and were talking easily—just the kind of slangy talk you will hear in any golf club-house. I must have cut a rum figure, sitting there knitting my brows with my eyes wandering.

My partner was the young dark one. I play a fair hand at bridge, but I must have been rank bad that night. They saw that they had got me puzzled, and that put them more than ever at their ease. I kept looking at their faces, but they conveyed nothing to me. It was not that they looked different; they were different. I clung desperately to the words of Peter Pienaar.

Then something awoke me.

The old man laid down his hand to light a cigar. He didn't pick it up at once, but sat back for a moment in his chair, with his fingers tapping on his knees.

It was the movement I remembered when I had stood before him in the moorland farm, with the pistols of his servants behind me.

A little thing, lasting only a second, and the odds were a thousand to one that I might have had my eyes on my cards at the time and missed it. But I didn't, and, in a flash, the air seemed to clear. Some shadow lifted from my brain, and I was looking at the three men with full and absolute recognition.

The clock on the mantelpiece struck ten o'clock.

The three faces seemed to change before my eyes and reveal their secrets. The young one was the murderer. Now I saw cruelty and ruthlessness, where before I had only seen good-humour. His knife, I made certain, had skewered Scudder to the floor. His kind had put the bullet in Karolides.

The plump man's features seemed to dislimn, and form again, as I looked at them. He hadn't a face, only a hundred masks that he could assume when he pleased. That chap must have been a superb actor. Perhaps he had been Lord Alloa of the night before; perhaps not; it didn't matter. I wondered if he was the fellow who had first tracked Scudder, and left his card on him. Scudder had said he lisped, and I could imagine how the adoption of a lisp might add terror.

But the old man was the pick of the lot. He was sheer brain, icy, cool, calculating, as ruthless as a steam hammer. Now that my eyes were opened I wondered where I had seen the benevolence. His jaw was like chilled steel, and his eyes had the inhuman luminosity of a bird's. I went on playing, and every second a greater hate welled up in my heart. It almost choked me, and I couldn't answer when my partner spoke. Only a little longer could I endure their company.

"Whew! Bob! Look at the time," said the old man. "You'd

better think about catching your train. Bob's got to go to town tonight," he added, turning to me. The voice rang now as false as hell. I looked at the clock, and it was nearly half-past ten.

"I am afraid he must put off his journey," I said.

"Oh, damn," said the young man. "I thought you had dropped that rot. I've simply got to go. You can have my address, and I'll give any security you like."

"No," I said, "you must stay."

At that I think they must have realized that the game was desperate. Their only chance had been to convince me that I was playing the fool, and that had failed. But the old man spoke again.

"I'll go bail for my nephew. That ought to content you, Mr. Hannay." Was it fancy, or did I detect some halt in the smoothness of that voice?

There must have been, for as I glanced at him, his eyelids fell in that hawk-like hood which fear had stamped on my memory.

I blew my whistle.

In an instant the lights were out. A pair of strong arms gripped me round the waist, covering the pockets in which a man might be expected to carry a pistol.

"Schnell, Franz,' cried a voice, "das Boot, das Boot!" As it spoke I saw two of my fellows emerge on the moonlit lawn.

The young dark man leapt for the window, was through it, and over the low fence before a hand could touch him. I grappled the old chap, and the room seemed to fill with figures. I saw the plump one collared, but my eyes were all for the out-of-doors, where Franz sped on over the road towards the railed entrance to the beach stairs. One man followed him, but he had no chance. The gate of the stairs locked behind the fugitive, and I stood staring, with my hands on the old boy's throat, for such a time as a man might take to descend those steps to the sea.

Suddenly my prisoner broke from me and flung himself on the wall. There was a click as if a lever had been pulled. Then came a low rumbling far, far below the ground, and through the window I saw a cloud of chalky dust pouring out of the shaft of the stairway.

Someone switched on the light.

The old man was looking at me with blazing eyes.

"He is safe," he cried. "You cannot follow in time . . . He is gone . . . He has triumphed . . . *Der Schwarze Stein ist in der Siegeskrone.*"

There was more in those eyes than any common triumph. They had been hooded like a bird of prey, and now they flamed with a hawk's pride. A white fanatic heat burned in them, and I realized for the first time the terrible thing I had been up against. This man was more than a spy; in his foul way he had been a patriot.

As the handcuffs clinked on his wrists I said my last word to him.

"I hope Franz will bear his triumph well. I ought to tell you that the Ariadne for the last hour has been in our hands."

* * * * *

Three weeks later, as all the world knows, we went to war. I joined the New Army the first week, and owing to my Matabele experience got a captain's commission straight off. But I had done my best service, I think, before I put on khaki.

Word Cloud Classics

For more titles, please visit our website:
www.canterburyclassicsbooks.com